Robert U. Johnson, Clarence C. Buel

Battles and Leaders of the Civil War

being for the most part contributions by Union and Confederate officers - Vol. 22,

Part 2

Robert U. Johnson, Clarence C. Buel

Battles and Leaders of the Civil War
being for the most part contributions by Union and Confederate officers - Vol. 22, Part 2

ISBN/EAN: 9783337221294

Printed in Europe, USA, Canada, Australia, Japan

Cover: Foto ©Andreas Hilbeck / pixelio.de

More available books at **www.hansebooks.com**

BATTLES AND LEADERS OF THE CIVIL WAR

Grant-Lee Edition

VOLUME II

PART II

BEING FOR THE MOST PART CONTRIBUTIONS BY UNION AND CONFEDERATE OFFICERS. BASED UPON "THE CENTURY WAR SERIES." EDITED BY ROBERT UNDERWOOD JOHNSON AND CLARENCE CLOUGH BUEL, OF THE EDITORIAL STAFF OF "THE CENTURY MAGAZINE."

NEW-YORK

The Century Co.

McCLELLAN'S CHANGE OF BASE AND MALVERN HILL.

BY DANIEL H. HILL, LIEUTENANT-GENERAL, C. S. A.

FIVE of the six Confederate divisions north of the Chickahominy at the close of the battle of Gaines's Mill remained in bivouac all the next day (June 28th), it being deemed too hazardous to force the passage of the river. Ewell was sent with his division to Dispatch Station on the York River Railroad. He found the station and the railroad-bridge burnt. J. E. B. Stuart, who followed the retreating Federal cavalry to White House on the Pamunkey, found ruins of stations and stores all along the line. These things proved that General McClellan did not intend to retreat by the short line of the York River Railroad; but it was possible he might take the Williamsburg road. General Lee, therefore, kept his troops on the north side of the river, that he might be ready to move on the Federal flank, should that route be attempted. New Bridge was repaired on Saturday (the 28th), and our troops were then ready to move in either direction. The burnings and explosions in the Federal camp Saturday afternoon and night showed that General McClellan had determined to abandon his strong fortifications around Richmond. Ewell, who was watching him at Bottom's Bridge, and the cavalry, holding the crossings lower down, both reported that there was no attempt at the Williamsburg route. Longstreet and A. P. Hill were sent across the river at New Bridge early on Sunday morning to move down the Darbytown road to the Long Bridge road to intercept the retreat to the James River. This movement began before it was known that General

REGION OF THE SEVEN DAYS' FIGHTING.

A SAMPLE OF THE CHICKAHOMINY SWAMP. FROM A PHOTOGRAPH OF 1862.

McClellan had evacuated his stronghold. Lee gave here the first illustration of a quality for which he became noted — the remarkable discernment of his adversary's plans through the study of his character. McClellan could have retreated to Yorktown with as little loss as Johnston sustained on his retreat from it. The roads from Richmond to Yorktown lead through a wooded and swampy country, on which strong rear-guards could have afforded perfect protection to a retreating column without bringing on a general engagement. General Johnston, on his retreat from Yorktown, did fight at Williamsburg, but it was a battle of his own choosing, and not forced upon him by the vigor of pursuit. Lee had but little idea that McClellan would return to Yorktown, judging rightly that the military pride of his distinguished opponent would not permit him to march back a defeated column to the point from which he had started, a few months before, for the capture of the Confederate capital, with his splendid army and magnificent outfit. ⏀ It is a proof of Lee's sagacity that he predicated his orders for an advance upon the belief that General McClellan was too proud a man to fall back by the same route by which the triumphal advance had been made. A great commander must study the mental and moral characteristics of the opposing leader, and Lee was specially endowed with an aptitude in that direction. At the battle of Salzbach, Montecuculi, the Austrian commander, noticed the French troops making a movement so different from the cautious style of his famous rival that he exclaimed, "Either Turenne is dead or mortally wounded." So it proved to be; the French marshal had been killed by a cannon-ball before the movement began.

In pursuance of General Lee's plan, Huger was directed (on the 29th) to take the Charles City road to strike the retreating column below White Oak Swamp. Holmes was to take possession of Malvern Hill, and Magruder to follow the line of retreat, as soon as the works were abandoned. The abandonment became known about sunrise on Sunday morning, but Grapevine Bridge was not completed till sunset. Jackson then crossed his corps at that point, my division leading. We bivouacked that night near Savage's Station, where McLaws's division had had a severe fight a few hours before. Just at dawn on Monday, the 30th, we were in motion, when I discovered what appeared to be a line of battle drawn up at the station, but which proved to be a line of sick and of hospital attendants, 2500 in number. About half a mile from the station we saw what seemed to be an entire regiment of Federals cold in death, and learned that a Vermont regiment [the 5th] had been in the desperate charge upon the division of McLaws, and had suffered great loss [killed, 31 ; wounded, 143]. From the time of crossing the river, we had evidence everywhere of the precipitate nature of the Federal retreat.⏀ Dabney, in his life of Jackson, says :

"The whole country was full of deserted plunder, army wagons, and pontoon-trains partially burned or crippled; mounds of grain and rice and hillocks of mess beef smoldering; tens of thousands of axes, picks, and shovels; camp kettles gashed with hatchets; medicine chests with their drugs stirred into a foul medley, and all the apparatus of a vast and lavish host; while the mire under foot was mixed with blankets lately new, and with overcoats torn from the waist up. For weeks afterward agents of our army were busy in gathering in the spoils. Great stores of fixed ammunition were saved, while more were destroyed."

In our march from Savage's Station my division picked up a thousand prisoners, stragglers from the retreating army, and gathered a large number of abandoned rifles. I detached two regiments (the Fourth and Fifth North

⏀ The capture of Petersburg would have been almost as disastrous to the South as the capture of Richmond, and for many days Petersburg was at the mercy of the Federal army. There were no troops and no fortifications there when McClellan reached the James. Some two weeks after the battle of Malvern Hill the first earth-works were begun at Petersburg, by my order.— D. H. H.

⏀ The Union reports do not indicate precipitancy. The greater part of McClellan's army was within three miles of the original lines at the close of the second day after the battle of Gaines's Mill, that is, on the evening of June 29th. The third day after that battle, the Army of the Potomac fought on three separate fields (White Oak Bridge, Charles City road, and Glendale), at distances of from 7 to 10 miles from the old positions in front of Richmond. General Wm. B. Franklin was with the rear columns of the army during the movement to the James River. [See p. 366.]— EDITORS.

UNION FIELD-HOSPITAL AT SAVAGE'S STATION, AFTER THE BATTLE OF GAINES'S MILL.
FROM A PHOTOGRAPH TAKEN BEFORE THE ARMY WITHDREW, EARLY ON THE MORNING OF JUNE 30TH.

Carolina) to take the prisoners and arms to Richmond. We reached White Oak Swamp about noon, and there found another hospital camp, with about five hundred sick in it. Truly, the Chickahominy swamps were fatal to the Federal forces. A high bluff was on our side of the little stream called White Oak, and a large uncultivated field on the other side. In this field could be seen a battery of artillery, supported by a brigade of infantry — artillerists and infantry lying down and apparently asleep. Under cover of Thomas T. Munford's 2d Virginia cavalry, thirty-one field-pieces were placed upon the bluff, and were ordered to open fire as soon as the cavalry mask was removed. The battery fired its loaded guns in reply, and then galloped off, followed by its infantry supports and the long lines of infantry farther back in the field. Munford crossed his regiment over the ford, and Jackson and myself went with him to see what had become of the enemy. We soon found out. The battery had taken up a position behind a point of woods, where it was perfectly sheltered from our guns, but could play upon the broken bridge and ford, and upon every part of the uncultivated field. It opened with grape and canister upon us, and we retired rapidly. Fast riding in the wrong direction is not military, but it is sometimes healthy. We had taken one prisoner, a drunken Irishman, but he declined the honor of going back with us, and made fight with his naked fists. A soldier asked me naïvely whether he should shoot the Irishman or let him go. I am glad that I told him to let the man go, to be a comfort to his family. That Irishman must have had a charmed life. He was under the shelter of his gum-cloth coat hung on a stick, near the ford, when a citizen fired at him four times, from a distance of about fifty paces; and the only recognition that I could see the man make was to raise his hand as if to brush off a fly.↓ One of the shells set the farm-house on fire. We learned from the owner that Franklin's corps was in front of us.

Our cavalry returned by the lower ford, and pronounced it perfectly practicable for infantry. But Jackson did not advance. Why was this? It was the critical day for both commanders, but especially for McClellan. With consummate skill he had crossed his vast train of five thousand wagons and his immense parks of artillery safely over White Oak Swamp, but he was more exposed now than at any time in his flank march. Three columns of attack were converging upon him, and a strong corps was pressing upon his rear. Escape seemed impossible for him, but he *did* escape, at the same time inflicting heavy damage upon his pursuers. General Lee, through no fault in his plans, was to see his splendid prize slip through his hands. Longstreet and A. P. Hill struck the enemy at Frayser's farm (or Glendale) at 3 P. M. on the 30th, and, both being always ready for a fight, immediately attacked. Magruder, who followed them down the Darbytown road, was ordered to the assistance of General Holmes on the New Market road, who was not then engaged, and their two divisions took no part in the action. Huger, on the Charles City road, came upon Franklin's left flank, but made no attack. I sent my engineer officer, Captain W. F. Lee, to him through the swamp, to ask him whether he could not engage Franklin. He replied that the road was obstructed by fallen timber. So there were five divisions within sound of the firing, and within supporting distance, but not one of them moved. Longstreet and A. P. Hill made a desperate fight, contending against Sumner's corps, and the divisions of McCall, Kearny, and Hooker; but they failed to gain possession of the Quaker road, upon which McClellan was retreating. That night Franklin glided silently by them. He had to pass within easy range of the artillery of Longstreet and Hill, but they did not know he was there. It had been a gallant fight on their part. General Lee reported: "Many prisoners, including a general of division, McCall, were captured, and several batteries, with some thousands of small-arms, were taken." But as an obstruction to the Federal retreat, the fight amounted to nothing.

↓ After the appearance of this article in "The Century" magazine, E. McLaughlin, of East Saginaw, Michigan, wrote me that he was a member of Co. C of the 7th Maine Volunteers, General W. F. Smith's division, and said: "The statement in regard to the drunken Irishman is true. That man belonged to my company and told us, when he came to the company at Malvern Hill, that he had been inside your lines and had been repeatedly shot at. He further said that if he had had one more canteen of whisky he could have held the position all day."—D. H. H.

THE ARTILLERY ENGAGEMENT AT WHITE OAK BRIDGE. FROM A SKETCH MADE AT THE TIME.

The view is from Franklin's position south of the bridge, Jackson's and D. H. Hill's troops being seen in the distance.

Major Dabney, in his life of Jackson, thus comments on the inaction of that officer: "On this occasion it would appear, if the vast interests dependent upon General Jackson's coöperation with the proposed attack upon the center were considered, that he came short of the efficiency in action for which he was everywhere else noted." After showing how the crossing of White Oak might have been effected, Dabney adds: "The list of casualties would have been larger than that presented on the 30th, of one cannoneer wounded; but how much shorter would have been the bloody list filled up the next day at Malvern Hill! This temporary eclipse of Jackson's genius was probably to be explained by physical causes. The labor of the previous days, the sleeplessness, the wear of gigantic cares, with the drenching of the comfortless night, had sunk the elasticity of his will and the quickness of his invention for the nonce below their wonted tension. And which of the sons of man is so great as never to experience this?"

I think that an important factor in this inaction was Jackson's pity for his own corps, worn out by long and exhausting marches, and reduced in numbers by its numerous sanguinary battles. He thought that the garrison of Richmond ought now to bear the brunt of the fighting. None of us knew that the veterans of Longstreet and A. P. Hill were unsupported; nor did we even know that the firing that we heard was theirs. Had all our troops been at Frayser's farm, there would have been no Malvern Hill.

Jackson's genius never shone when he was under the command of another. It seemed then to be shrouded or paralyzed. Compare his inertness on this occasion with the wonderful vigor shown a few weeks later at Slaughter's [Cedar] Mountain in the stealthy march to Pope's rear, and later still in the capture of Harper's Ferry. MacGregor on his native heath was not more different from MacGregor in prison than was Jackson his own master from Jackson in a subordinate position. He wrote once to Richmond requesting that he might have "fewer orders and more men." That was the keynote to his whole character. The hooded falcon cannot strike the quarry.

The gentleman who tried his "splendid rifle" on the drunken Irishman was the Rev. L. W. Allen. Mr. Allen had been raised in that neighborhood, and knew Malvern Hill well. He spoke of its commanding height, the difficulties of approach to it, its amphitheatrical form and ample area, which would enable McClellan to arrange his 350 field-guns tier above tier and sweep the plain in every direction. I became satisfied that an attack upon the concentrated Federal army so splendidly posted, and with such vast superiority in artillery, could only be fatal to us. The anxious thought then was, Have Holmes and Magruder been able to keep McClellan from Malvern Hill? General Holmes arrived at Malvern at 10:30 A. M. on the 30th, with 5170 infantry, 4 batteries of artillery, and 130 improvised or irregular cavalry. He did not attempt to occupy the hill, although only 1500 Federals had yet reached it. Our cavalry had passed over it on the afternoon of the 29th, and had had a sharp skirmish with the Federal cavalry on the Quaker road.

As General Holmes marched down the river, his troops became visible to the gun-boats, which opened fire upon them, throwing those awe-inspiring shells familiarly called by our men "lamp-posts," on account of their size and appearance. Their explosion was very much like that of a small volcano, and had a very demoralizing effect upon new troops, one of whom expressed the general sentiment by saying: "The Yankees throwed them lamp-posts about too careless like." The roaring, howling gun-boat shells were usually harmless to flesh, blood, and bones, but they had a wonderful effect upon the nervous system. General Junius Daniel, a most gallant and accomplished officer, who had a brigade under General Holmes, gave me an incident connected with the affair on the 30th, known as the "Battle of Malvern Cliff." General Holmes, who was very deaf, had gone into a little house concealed from the boats by some intervening woods, and was engaged in some business when the bellowing of the "lamp-posts" began. The irregular cavalry stampeded and made a brilliant charge to the rear. The artillerists of two guns of Graham's Petersburg battery were also panic-struck, and cutting their horses loose mounted them, and, with dangling traces, tried to catch up with the fleet-footed cavaliers. The infantry troops were inexperienced in the wicked ways of war, having never been under fire before. The fright of the fleeing cavalry would have pervaded their ranks also with the same mischievous result but for the strenuous efforts of their officers, part of whom were veterans. Some of the raw levies crouched behind little saplings to get protection from the shrieking, blustering shells. At this juncture General Holmes, who from his deafness, was totally unaware of the rumpus, came out of the hut, put his hand behind his right ear, and said: "I thought I heard firing." Some of the pale-faced infantry thought that they also had heard firing.

Part of Wise's brigade joined Holmes on the 30th, with two batteries of artillery and two regiments of cavalry. His entire force then consisted of 5820 infantry, 6 batteries of artillery, and 2 regiments of cavalry. He remained inactive until 4 P. M., when he was told that the Federal army was passing over Malvern Hill in a demoralized condition. He then opened upon the supposed fugitives with six rifled guns, and was speedily undeceived in regard to the disorganization in the Army of the Potomac by a reply from thirty guns, which in a brief time silenced his own. The audacity of the Federals and the large number of their guns (which had gone in advance of the main body of Porter's corps) made General Holmes believe that he was about to be attacked, and he called for assistance, and, by Longstreet's order, Magruder was sent to him. After a weary march, Magruder was recalled to aid Longstreet; but the day was spent in fruitless marching and countermarching, so that his fine body of troops took no part in what might have been a decisive battle at Frayser's farm. General Holmes was a veteran soldier of well-known personal courage, but he was deceived as to the strength and intentions of the enemy. General Porter says that the force opposed to General Holmes consisted of Warren's brigade and the Eleventh U. S. Infantry; in all, 1500 infantry and 30 pieces of artillery. Here was afforded an example of the proneness to overestimate the number of troops opposed to us. The Federals reported Holmes to have 25,000 men, and he thought himself confronted by a large part of McClellan's army. That night he fell back to a stronger position,✩ thinking apparently that there would be an "on to Richmond" movement by the River road. He lost 2 killed, 49 wounded, 2 pieces of artillery, and 6 caissons. The guns and caissons, General Porter states, were afterward abandoned by the Federals. General Holmes occupied the extreme Confederate right the next day, July 1st, but he took no part in the attack upon Malvern Hill, believing, as he says in his official report, "that it was out of the question to attack the strong position of Malvern Hill from that side with my inadequate force."

Mahone's brigade had some skirmishing with Slocum's Federal division on the 30th, but nothing else was done on that day by Huger's division. Thus it happened that Longstreet and A. P. Hill, with the fragments of their divisions which had been engaged at Gaines's Mill, were struggling alone, while Jackson's whole corps and the divisions of Huger, Magruder, Holmes, McLaws, and my own were near by.

Jackson moved over the swamp early on the first of July, Whiting's division leading. Our march was much delayed by the crossing of troops and trains. At Willis's Church I met General Lee. He bore grandly his terrible disappointment of the day before, and made no allusion to it. I gave him Mr. Allen's description of Malvern Hill, and presumed to say, "If General McClellan is there in force, we had better let him alone." Longstreet laughed and said, "Don't get scared, now that we have got him whipped." It was this belief in the demoralization of the Federal army that made our leader risk the attack. It was near noon when Jackson reached the immediate neighbor-

✩ Half a mile below the upper gate at Curl's Neck. (See "Official Records," Vol. XI., Part II., p. 908.)—D. H. H.

SKETCH MAP OF THE VICINITY OF MALVERN HILL.
(JULY 1, 1862).

The Union troops reached the field by the so-called Quaker road (more properly the Church road); the Confederates chiefly by this and the Long Bridge road. The general lines were approximately as indicated above. The Confederates on the River road are the troops of General Holmes, who had been repulsed at Turkey Island Bridge the day before by Warren's brigade, with the aid of the gun-boats. The main fighting was in the space between the words "Confederate" and "Union," together with one or two assaults upon the west side of the Crew Hill from the meadow. Morell's and Couch's divisions formed the first Union line, and General Porter's batteries extended from the Crew house to the West house.

hood of Malvern Hill. Some time was spent in reconnoitering, and in making tentative efforts with our few batteries to ascertain the strength and position of the enemy. I saw Jackson helping with his own hands to push Reilly's North Carolina battery farther forward. It was soon disabled, the woods around us being filled with shrieking and exploding shells. I noticed an artilleryman seated comfortably behind a very large tree, and apparently feeling very secure. A moment later a shell passed through the huge tree and took off the man's head. This gives an idea of the great power of the Federal rifled artillery. Whiting's division was ordered to the left of the Quaker road, and mine to the right; Ewell's was in reserve. Jackson's own division had been halted at Willis's Church. The divisions of Magruder, Huger, and McLaws were still farther over to my right. Those of Longstreet and A. P. Hill were in reserve on the right and were not engaged.

At length we were ordered to advance. The brigade of General George B. Anderson first encountered the enemy, and its commander was wounded and borne from the field. His troops, however, crossed the creek and took position in the woods, commanded by Colonel C. C. Tew, a skillful and gallant man. Rodes being sick, his brigade was commanded by that peerless soldier, Colonel J. B. Gordon. Ripley, Garland, and Colquitt also got over without serious loss. My five brigade commanders and myself now made an examination of the enemy's position. He was found to be strongly posted on a commanding hill, all the approaches to which could be swept by his artillery and were guarded by swarms of infantry, securely sheltered by fences, ditches, and ravines. Armistead was immediately on my right. We remained a long while awaiting orders, when I received the following:

"July 1st, 1862.

"GENERAL D. H. HILL: Batteries have been established to act upon the enemy's line. If it is broken, as is probable, Armistead, who can witness the effect of the fire, has been ordered to charge with a yell. Do the same. R. H. CHILTON, A. A. G."

A similar order was sent to each division commander. However, only one battery of our artillery came up at a time, and each successive one, as it took position, had fifty pieces turned upon it, and was crushed in a minute. Not knowing what to do under the circumstances, I wrote to General Jackson that the condition upon which the order was predicated was not fulfilled, and that I wanted instructions. He replied to advance when I heard the shouting. We did advance at the signal, and after an unassisted struggle for an hour and a half, and after meeting with some success, we were compelled to fall back under cover of the woods. Magruder advanced at the same signal, having portions of the divisions of Huger and McLaws, comprising the brigades of Mahone, Wright, Barksdale, Ransom, Cobb, Semmes, Kershaw, Armistead, and G. T. Anderson; but he met with some delay, and did not get in motion till he received a second order from General Lee, and we were then beaten.

The Comte de Paris, who was on McClellan's staff, gives this account of the charge of my gallant division :

"Hill advanced alone against the Federal positions. . . . He had therefore before him Morell's right, Couch's division, reënforced by Caldwell's brigade, . . . and finally the left of Kearny. The woods skirting the foot of Malvern Hill had hitherto protected the Confed-

WILLIS'S CHURCH, ON THE QUAKER ROAD, NEAR GLEN-DALE. USED AS A CONFEDERATE HOSPITAL AFTER THE BATTLE OF MALVERN HILL.

erates, but as soon as they passed beyond the edge of the forest, they were received by a fire from all the batteries at once, some posted on the hill, others ranged midway, close to the Federal infantry. The latter joined its musketry fire to the cannonade when Hill's first line had come within range, and threw it back in disorder on the reserves. While it was re-forming, new [Confederate] battalions marched up to the assault in their turn. The remembrance of Cold Harbor doubles the energy of Hill's soldiers. They try to pierce the line, sometimes at one point, sometimes at another, charging Kearny's left first, and Couch's right, . . . and afterward throwing themselves upon the left of Couch's division. But, here also, after nearly reaching the Federal positions, they are repulsed. The conflict is carried on with great fierceness on both sides, and, for a moment, it seems as if the Confederates are at last about to penetrate the very center of their adversaries and of the formidable artillery, which but now was dealing destruction in their ranks. But Sumner, who commands on the right, detaches Sickles's and Meagher's brigades successively to Couch's assistance. During this time, Whiting on the left, and Huger on the right, suffer Hill's soldiers to become exhausted without supporting them. Neither Lee nor Jackson has sent the slightest order, and the din of the battle which is going on in their immediate vicinity has not sufficed to make them march against the enemy. . . . At seven o'clock Hill reorganized the débris of his troops in the woods; . . . his tenacity and the courage of his soldiers have only had the effect of causing him to sustain heavy losses." (Pp. 141, 142, Vol. II.)

Truly, the courage of the soldiers was sublime ! Battery after battery was in their hands for a few moments, only to be wrested away by fresh troops of the enemy. If one division could effect this much, what might have been done had the other nine coöperated with it! General Lee says:

" D. H. Hill pressed forward across the open field and engaged the enemy gallantly, breaking and driving back his first line; but a simultaneous advance of the other troops not taking place, he found himself unable to maintain the ground he had gained against the overwhelming numbers and the numerous batteries of the enemy. Jackson sent to his support his own division, and that part of Ewell's which was in reserve; but owing to the increasing darkness, and the intricacy of the forest and swamp, they did not arrive in time to render the desired assistance. Hill was therefore compelled to abandon part of the ground that he had gained, after suffering severe loss and inflicting heavy damage upon the enemy."

I never saw anything more grandly heroic than the advance after sunset of the nine brigades under Magruder's orders. ☩ Unfortunately, they did not move together, and were beaten in detail. As each brigade emerged from the woods, from fifty to one hundred guns opened upon it, tearing great gaps in its ranks; but the heroes reeled on and were shot down by the reserves at the guns, which a few squads reached. Most of them had an open field half a mile wide to cross, under the fire of field-artillery in front, and the fire of the heavy ordnance of the gun-boats in their rear. It was not war—it was murder.

Our loss was double that of the Federals at Malvern Hill. Not only did the fourteen brigades which were engaged suffer, but also the inactive troops and those brought up as reserves too late to be of any use met many casualties from the fearful artillery fire which reached all parts of the woods. Hence, more than half the casualties were from field-pieces—an unprecedented thing in warfare. The artillery practice was kept up till nine o'clock at night, and the darkness added to the glory of the pyrotechnics. It was quite late when I had posted for the night the last of the reënforcements that had come up when the battle was over. A half-hour before, an incident occurred which is thus related by General Trimble:

"I proposed to General D. H. Hill to ride forward and reconnoiter the enemy's position. We approached within one hundred steps of the enemy's batteries, and could hear plainly the ordinary tone of conversation. The guns were then firing on the woods to our left, where the last attack had been made, at right angles to that part of the field we were then in. I suggested to General Hill the advantage of making an attack on this battery, and that it must be successful, as the enemy would not expect one from our position, and under cover of the darkness we could approach them undiscovered. General Hill did not seem inclined to make the movement."

The chivalrous Trimble proposed to make the attack with his own brigade, but there were many troops now in the woods, and I thought that the attack would but expose them to a more intense artillery fire. We saw men going about with lanterns, looking up and carrying off the dead and wounded. There were no pickets out, and the rumbling of wheels in the distance seemed to indicate that the retreat had begun. The morning revealed the bare plateau stripped of its terrible batteries. The battle of Malvern Hill was a disaster to the Confederates, and the fourteen brigades that had been so badly repulsed were much demoralized. But there were six divisons intact, and they could have made a formidable fight on the 2d.

☩ Toombs's brigade belonged to Magruder, but had moved to my assistance by my order when we were hard pressed. It was not, therefore, in the final attack made by Magruder.—D. H. H.

Possibly owing to the belief that Longstreet and A. P. Hill were making a march between Malvern and Harrison's Landing, the retreat was the most disorderly that took place. Wagons and ambulances were abandoned; knapsacks, cartridge-boxes, clothing, and rifles by the thousand were thrown away by the Federals. Colonel James D. Nance, of the 3d South Carolina regiment, gathered 925 rifles in fine condition that had been thrown away in the wheat-field at Shirley, a farm between Malvern and Haxall's. The fruits of the Seven Days' Fighting were the relief of Richmond, the capture of 9000 prisoners [including 3000 in hospitals], 52 pieces of artillery, and 35,000 stand of arms, and the destruction or capture of many military stores.

I crossed the Chickahominy with 10,000 effective men. Of these 3907 were killed or wounded and 48 were reported missing, either captives or fugitives from the field. With the infantry and artillery detached, and the losses before Malvern Hill, I estimate that my division in that battle was 6500 strong, and that the loss was 2000. Magruder puts his force at between 26,000 and 28,000 (I think a high estimate), and states his loss as 2900.

Throughout this campaign we attacked just when and where the enemy wished us to attack. This was owing to our ignorance of the country and

GEORGE W. RANDOLPH, SECRETARY OF WAR OF THE CONFEDERACY FROM MARCH 17, 1862, UNTIL NOVEMBER 17, 1862. FROM A PHOTOGRAPH.

lack of reconnoissance of the successive battle-fields. Porter's weak point at Gaines's Mill was his right flank. A thorough examination of the ground would have disclosed that; and had Jackson's command gone in on the left of the road running by the McGehee house, Porter's whole position would have been turned and the line of retreat cut off. An armed reconnoissance at Malvern would have shown the immense preponderance of the Federal artillery, and that a contest with it must be hopeless. The battle, with all its melancholy results, proved, however, that the Confederate infantry and Federal artillery, side by side on the same field, need fear no foe on earth.

Both commanders had shown great ability. McClellan, if not always great in the advance, was masterly in retreat, and was unquestionably the greatest of Americans as an organizer of an army. Lee's plans were perfect; and had not his dispositions for a decisive battle at Frayser's farm miscarried, through no fault of his own, he would have won a most complete victory. It was not the least part of his greatness that he did not complain of his disappointment, and that he at no time sought a scape-goat upon which to lay a failure. As reunited Americans, we have reason to be proud of both commanders.

"THE SEVEN DAYS," INCLUDING FRAYSER'S FARM. |

BY JAMES LONGSTREET, LIEUTENANT-GENERAL, C. S. A.

WHEN General Joseph E. Johnston was wounded at the battle of Seven Pines, and General Lee assumed his new duties as commander of the Army of Northern Virginia, General Stonewall Jackson was in the Shenandoah Valley, and the rest of the Confederate troops were east and north of Richmond in front of General George B. McClellan's army, then encamped about the Chickahominy River, 100,000 strong, and preparing for a regular siege of the Confederate capital. The situation required prompt and successful action by General Lee. Very early in June he called about him, on the noted Nine-mile road near Richmond, all his commanders, and asked each in turn his opinion of the military situation. I had my own views, but did not express them, believing that if they were important it was equally important that they should be unfolded privately to the commanding general. The next day I called on General Lee, and suggested my plan for driving the Federal forces away from the Chickahominy. McClellan had a small force at Mechanicsville, and farther back, at Beaver Dam Creek, a considerable portion of his army in a stronghold that was simply unassailable from the front. The banks of Beaver Dam Creek were so steep as to be impassable except on bridges. I proposed an echelon movement, and suggested that Jackson be called down from the Valley, and passed to the rear of the Federal right, in order to turn the position behind Beaver Dam, while the rest of the Confederate forces who were to engage in the attack could cross the Chickahominy at points suitable for the succession in the move, and be ready to attack the Federals as soon as they were thrown from their position. After hearing me, General Lee sent General J. E. B. Stuart on his famous ride around McClellan. The dashing horseman, with a strong reconnoitering force of cavalry, made a forced reconnoissance, passing above and around the Federal forces, recrossing the Chickahominy below them, and returning safe to Confederate headquarters. He made a favorable report of the situation and the practicability of the proposed plan. On the 23d of June General Jackson was summoned to General Lee's headquarters, and was there met by General A. P. Hill, General D. H. Hill, and myself. A conference resulted in the selection of the 26th as the day on which we should move against the Federal position at Beaver Dam. General Jackson was ordered down from the Valley. General A. P. Hill was to pass the Chickahominy with part of his division, and hold the rest in readiness to cross at Meadow Bridge, following

| The usual spelling is Frazier or Frazer. The authority for the form here adopted is Captain R. E. Frayser, of Richmond.—EDITORS.

Jackson's swoop along the dividing ridge betewen the Pamunkey and the Chickahominy. D. H. Hill and I were ordered to be in position on the Mechanicsville pike early on the 26th, ready to cross the river at Mechanicsville Bridge as soon as it was cleared by the advance of Jackson and A. P. Hill.

Thus matters stood when the morning of the 26th arrived. The weather was clear, and the roads were in fine condition. Everything seemed favorable to the move. But the morning passed and we received no tidings from Jackson. As noon approached, General Hill, who was to move behind Jackson, grew impatient at the delay and begged permission to hurry him up by a fusillade. General Lee consented, and General Hill opened his batteries on Mechanicsville, driving the Federals off. When D. H. Hill and I crossed at the Mechanicsville Bridge we found A. P. Hill severely engaged, trying to drive the Federals from their strong position behind Beaver Dam Creek. Without Jackson to turn the Federal right, the battle could not be ours. Although the contest lasted until some time after night, the Confederates made no progress. The next day the fight was renewed, and the position was hotly contested by the Federals until 7 o'clock in the morning, when the advance of Jackson speedily caused the Federals to abandon their position, thus ending the battle.‡

‡ According to General Fitz John Porter, it was not Jackson's approach, but information of that event, that caused the withdrawal of the Union troops, who, with the exception of "some batteries and infantry skirmishers," were withdrawn before sunrise on the 27th.

EDITORS.

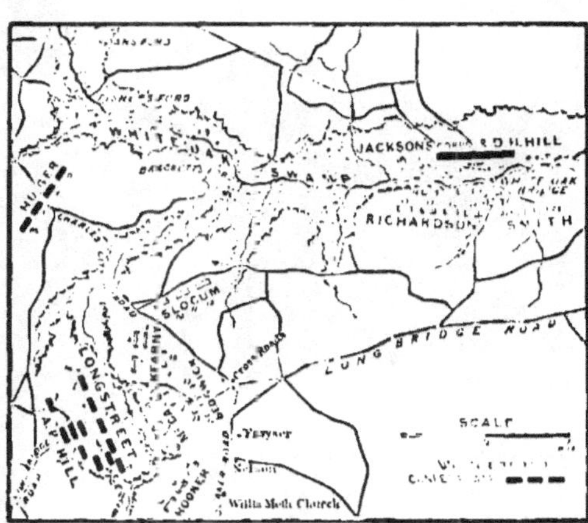

MAP OF THE BATTLE OF FRAYSER'S FARM (CHARLES CITY CROSSROADS OR GLENDALE), JUNE 30, 1862, SHOWING APPROXIMATE POSITIONS OF UNION AND CONFEDERATE TROOPS. ALSO DISPOSITION OF TROOPS DURING THE ARTILLERY ENGAGEMENT AT WHITE OAK BRIDGE.

Union brigades: 1, Sickles; 2, Carr; 3, Grover; 4, Seymour; 5, Reynolds (Simmons); 6, Meade (this brigade should be represented as north of the road); 7, Robinson; 8, Birney; 9, Berry; 10, Newton; 11, Bartlett; 12, 12, Taylor; 13, Burns; 14, 14, Dana; 15, 15, Sully; 16, 16, Caldwell; 17, French; 18, Meagher; 19, Naglee (of Keyes's corps); 20, Davidson; 21, Brooks; 22, Hancock. Randol's battery was on the right of the road, Kerns's and Cooper's on the left, and Diederichs's and Knieriem's yet farther to the left. Thompson's battery of Kearny's division was with General Robinson's brigade (7).

Confederate brigades: a, Kemper; b, Pickett (Hunton); c, R. H. Anderson (Jenkins); d, Wilcox; e, Featherston; f, Pryor; g, Branch; h, Archer; i, Field; j, J. R. Anderson; k, Pender; l, Gregg; m, n, o, p, Armistead, Wright, Mahone, and Ransom. Of the Confederate batteries, Rogers's, Dearing's, the Thomas artillery, Pegram's, Davidson's, and others were engaged.

The action at White Oak Bridge, about 11 A. M., and that between Huger and Slocum to the left, beginning about 3 P. M., were of artillery only, and were successful from the Union point of view, in that they prevented the Confederate forces at these points from reënforcing Longstreet, while they enabled four Union brigades (12, 14, 15, and 16) to reënforce his opponents. The battle of Frayser's farm, beginning about 4 P. M., resulted in the accomplishment of General McClellan's object, the protection of his trains from rear and flank attack as they were passing down the Long Bridge and Quaker roads to the James River. General Kearny's report characterized this battle as "one of the most desperate of the war, tho one the most fatal if lost." The fighting began in force on the left of Seymour's brigade (4), and the brunt of the attack fell upon McCall and the left of Kearny. "Of the four divisions that day engaged," says General McCall's report, "each manœuvred and fought independently." McCall's division, being flanked on the left by Longstreet's right, was driven from its position after a stubborn resistance; its place was taken by Burns's brigade, reënforced by Dana's and Sully's, and these troops recovered part of the ground lost by McCall. The fury of the battle now shifted to the front of Kearny, who was reënforced by Taylor's and Caldwell's brigades. The Confederates gained some ground, but no substantial advantage, and the Union troops withdrew during the night to Malvern Hill.— EDITORS.

FRAYSER'S FARM-HOUSE, FROM THE QUAKER OR CHURCH ROAD, LOOKING SOUTH. FROM A PHOTOGRAPH TAKEN IN 1885.

This house was used as General Sumner's headquarters and as a hospital during the battle. The fighting took place from half to three-quarters of a mile to the right, or westward. The National Cemetery is shown in the middle distance.

It is easy to see that the battle of the previous day would have been a quick and bloodless Confederate victory if Jackson could have reached his position at the time appointed. In my judgment the evacuation of Beaver Dam Creek was very unwise on the part of the Federal commanders. We had attacked at Beaver Dam, and had failed to make an impression at that point, losing several thousand men and officers. This demonstrated that the position was safe. If the Federal commanders knew of Jackson's approach on the 26th, they had ample time to reënforce Porter's right before Friday morning (27th) with men and field defenses, to such extent as to make the remainder of the line to the right secure against assault. So that the Federals in withdrawing not only abandoned a strong position, but gave up the *morale* of their success, and transferred it to our somewhat disheartened forces; for, next to Malvern Hill, the sacrifice at Beaver Dam was unequaled in demoralization during the entire summer.

From Beaver Dam we followed the Federals closely, encountering them again under Porter beyond Powhite Creek, where the battle of Gaines's Mill occurred. General A. P. Hill, being in advance, deployed his men and opened the attack without consulting me. A very severe battle followed. I came up with my reserve forces and was preparing to support Hill, who was suffering very severely, when I received an order from General Lee to make a demonstration against the Federal left, as the battle was not progressing to suit him. I threw in three brigades opposite the Federal left and engaged them in a severe skirmish with infantry and artillery. The battle then raged with great fierceness. General Jackson was again missing, and General Lee grew fearful of the result. Soon I received another message from General Lee, saying that unless I could do something the day seemed to be lost. I then determined to make the heaviest attack I could. The position in front of me was very strong. An open field led down to a difficult ravine a short distance beyond the Powhite Creek. From there the ground made a steep ascent, and was covered with trees and slashed timber and hastily made rifle-trenches. General Whiting came to me with two brigades of Jackson's men and asked me to put him in. I told him I was just organizing an attack and would give him position. My column of attack then was R. H. Anderson's and Pickett's brigades, with Law's and Hood's of Whiting's division. We attacked and defeated the Federals on their left, capturing many thousand stand of arms, fifty-two pieces of artillery, a large quantity of supplies, and many prisoners,— among them General Reynolds, who afterward fell at Gettysburg. The Federals made some effort to reënforce and recover their lost ground, but failed, and during the afternoon and night withdrew their entire forces from that side of the Chickahominy, going in the direction of James River. On the 29th General Lee ascertained that McClellan was marching toward the James. He determined to make a vigorous move and strike the enemy a severe blow. He decided to intercept them in the neighborhood of Charles City cross-roads, and with that end in view planned a pursuit as follows: I was to march to a point below Frayser's farm with General A. P. Hill. General Holmes was to take up position below me on the New Market or River road, to be in readiness to coöperate with me and to attack such Federals as would come within his reach. Jackson was to pursue closely the Federal

rear, crossing at the Grapevine Bridge, and coming in on the north of the cross-roads. Huger was to attend to the Federal right flank, and take position on the Charles City road west of the cross-roads. Thus we were to envelop the Federal rear and make the destruction of that part of McClellan's army sure. To reach my position south of the cross-roads, I had about sixteen miles to march. I marched 14 miles on the 29th, crossing over into the Darbytown road and moving down to its intersection, with the New Market road, where I camped for the night, about 3 miles south-west of Frayser's farm. On the morning of the 30th I moved two miles nearer up and made preparation to intercept the Federals as they retreated toward James River. General McCall, with a division of ten thousand Federals, was at the cross-roads and about Frayser's farm. My division, being in advance, was deployed in front of the enemy. I placed such of my batteries as I could find position for, and kept Hill's troops in my rear. As I had twice as far to march as the other commanders, I considered it certain that Jackson and

OPENING OF THE BATTLE OF FRAYSER'S FARM: SLOCUM'S ARTILLERY ENGAGED WITH THAT OF HUGER,
AT BRACKETT'S, ON THE CHARLES CITY ROAD.   FROM A SKETCH MADE AT THE TIME.

Huger would be in position when I was ready. After getting my troops in position I called upon General A. P. Hill to throw one of his brigades to cover my right and to hold the rest of his troops in readiness to give pursuit when the enemy had been dislodged. My line extended from near the Quaker road across the New Market road to the Federal right. The ground upon which I approached was much lower than that occupied by General McCall, and was greatly cut up by ravines and covered with heavy timber and tangled undergrowth. On account of these obstructions we were not disturbed while getting into position, except by the firing of a few shots that did no damage. Holmes got into position below me on the New Market road, and was afterward joined by Magruder, who had previously made an unsuccessful attack on the Federal rear-guard at Savage's Station.

By 11 o'clock our troops were in position, and we waited for the signal from Jackson and Huger. Everything was quiet on my part of the line, except occasional firing between my pickets and McCall's. I was in momentary expectation of the signal. About half-past 2 o'clock artillery firing was heard on my left, evidently at the point near White Oak Swamp where Huger was to attack. I very naturally supposed this firing to be the expected signal, and ordered some of my batteries to reply, as a signal that I was ready to coöperate. While the order to open was going around to the batteries, President Davis and General Lee, with their staff and followers, were with me in a little open field near the rear of my right. We were in pleasant conversation, anticipating fruitful results from the fight, when our batteries opened. Instantly the Federal batteries responded most spitefully. It was impossible for the enemy to see us as we sat on our horses in the little field, surrounded by tall, heavy timber and thick undergrowth; yet a battery by chance had our range and exact distance, and poured upon us a terrific fire. The second or third shell burst in the midst of us, killing two or three horses and wounding one or two men. Our little party speedily retired to safer quarters. The Federals doubtless had no idea that the Confederate President, commanding general, and division commanders were receiving point-blank shot from their batteries. Colonel Micah Jenkins was in front of us, and I sent him an order to silence the Federal battery, supposing that he could do so with his long-range rifles. He became engaged, and finally determined to charge the battery. That brought on a general fight between my division and the troops in front of us. Kemper on my right advanced his brigade over difficult ground and captured a battery. Jenkins moved his brigade forward and made a bold fight. He was followed by the other four brigades successively.

The enemy's line was broken, and he was partly dislodged from his position. The batteries were taken, but our line was very much broken up by the rough ground we had to move over, and we were not in sufficiently solid form to maintain a proper battle. The battle was continued, however, until we encountered succor from the corps of Generals Sumner and Heintzelman, when we were obliged to halt and hold the position the enemy had left. This line was held throughout the day, though at times, when vigorous combinations were made against me, McCall regained points along his line. Our counter-movements, however, finally pushed him back again, and more formidable efforts from our adversary were required. Other advances were made, and reënforcements came to the support of the Federals, who contested the line with varying fortune, sometimes recovering batteries we had taken, and again losing them. Finally McCall's division was driven off, and fresh troops seemed to come in to their relief. Ten thousand men of A. P. Hill's division had been held in reserve, in the hope that Jackson and Huger would come up on our left, enabling us to dislodge the Federals, after which Hill's troops could be put in fresh to give pursuit, and follow them down to Harrison's Landing. Jackson found Grapevine Bridge destroyed and could not reach his position; while for some unaccountable reason Huger failed to take part, though near enough to do so.‡ As neither Jackson nor Huger came up, and as night drew on, I put Hill in to relieve my troops. When he came into the fight the Federal line had been broken at every point except one. He formed his line and followed up in the position occupied by my troops. By night we succeeded in getting the entire field, though all of it was not actually occupied until we advanced in pursuit next day. As the enemy moved off they continued the fire of their artillery upon us from various points, and it was after 9 o'clock when the shells ceased to fall. Just before dark General McCall, while looking up a fragment of his division, found us where he supposed his troops were, and was taken prisoner. At the time he was brought in General Lee happened to be with us. As I had known General McCall pleasantly in our

‡ General Huger says, in his official report, that the road was very effectively obstructed.— EDITORS.

CHARGE OF CONFEDERATES UPON RANDOL'S BATTERY AT FRAYSER'S FARM.

The contest for this battery was one of the most severe encounters of the day. The Confederates (the 55th and 60th Virginia Regiments) advanced out of formation, in wedge shape, and with trailing arms, and began a hand-to-hand conflict over the guns, which were finally yielded to them [see p. 413].

service together in the 4th Infantry, I moved to offer my hand as he dismounted. At the first motion, however, I saw he did not regard the occasion as one for renewing the old friendship, and I merely offered him some of my staff as an escort to Richmond.] But for the succoring forces, which should have been engaged by Jackson, Huger, Holmes, and Magruder, McCall would have been entirely dislodged by the first attack. All of our other forces were within a radius of 3 miles, and in easy hearing of the battle, yet of the 50,000 none came in to coöperate. (Jackson should have done more for me than he did. When he wanted me at the Second Manassas, I marched two columns by night to clear the way at Thoroughfare Gap, and joined

] Major W. Roy Mason, who served on the staff of General C. W. Field, C. S. A., gives this account of the capture of General McCall at Glendale, on the evening of June 30th:

"We occupied as headquarters [at the close of the battle] the center of an old road that ran through a dense pine-wood which the enemy had occupied only two hours before, and the dead and wounded were lying about us. General Field asked me to remain with the other members of the staff, and volunteered to go down to a water-course, where he had seen water trickling, to fill the canteens and make some coffee for me, for I was much exhausted, having been thrown violently by a wounded horse during the battle. While General Field was absent we saw, in the shadows, three or four men riding toward us, one of them being in advance and having a cloak thrown around him. I recognized the figure at once as that of a Federal officer. 'What command is this?' he asked. 'General Field's, sir,' was my answer. 'General Field! I don't know him.' 'Perhaps not, as you are evidently in the wrong place.'

"He at once turned to retreat, spurring his horse, and I gave the alarm. A soldier of the 47th Virginia (S. Brooke Rollins) now came forward and seized the bridle of the horse, saying to the rider, 'Not so fast.' The captured officer proved to be General McCall, of the Pennsylvania Reserves."

The staff-officers were fired upon while attempting to ride back, and Captain H. J. Biddle, McCall's adjutant-general, was instantly killed. Owing to the darkness the others escaped.— EDITORS.

him in due season.) Hooker claimed at Glendale to have rolled me up and hurriedly thrown me over on Kearny,—tennis-like, I suppose; but McCall showed in his supplementary report that Hooker could as well claim, with a little tension of the hyperbole, that he had thrown me over the moon. On leaving Frayser's farm the Federals withdrew to Malvern Hill, and Lee concentrated his forces and followed them.

On the morning of July 1st, the day after the battle at Frayser's farm, we encountered the enemy at Malvern Hill, and General Lee asked me to make a reconnoissance and see if I could find a good position for the artillery. I found position offering good play for batteries across the Federal left over to the right, and suggested that sixty pieces should be put in while Jackson engaged the Federal front. I suggested that a heavy play of this cross-fire on the Federals would so discomfit them as to warrant an assault by infantry. General Lee issued his orders accordingly, and designated the advance of Armistead's brigade as the signal for the grand assault. Later it was found that the ground over which our batteries were to pass into position on our right was so rough and obstructed that of the artillery ordered for use there only one or two batteries could go in at a time. As our guns in front did not engage, the result was the enemy concentrated the fire of fifty or sixty guns upon our isolated batteries, and tore them into fragments in a few minutes after they opened, piling horses upon each other and guns upon horses. Before night, the fire from our batteries failing of execution, General Lee seemed to abandon the idea of an attack. He proposed to me to move around to the left with my own and A. P. Hill's division, turning the Federal right. I issued my orders accordingly for the two divisions to go around and turn the Federal right, when in some way unknown to me the battle was drawn on. We were repulsed at all points with fearful slaughter, losing six thousand men and accomplishing nothing.

The Federals withdrew after the battle, and the next day I moved on around by the route which it was proposed we should take the day before. I followed the enemy to Harrison's Landing, and Jackson went down by another route in advance of Lee. As soon as we reached the front of the Federal position we put out our skirmish-lines, and I ordered an advance, intending to make another attack, but revoked it on Jackson urging me to wait until the arrival of General Lee. Very soon General Lee came, and, after carefully considering the position of the enemy and of their gun-boats on the James, decided that it would be better to forego any further operations. Our skirmish-lines were withdrawn, we ordered our troops back to their old lines around Richmond, and a month later McClellan's army was withdrawn to the North.

The Seven Days' Fighting, although a decided Confederate victory, was a succession of mishaps. If Jackson had arrived on the 26th,—the day of his own selection,—the Federals would have been driven back from Mechanicsville without a battle. His delay there, caused by obstructions placed in his road by the enemy, was the first mishap. He was too late in entering the fight at Gaines's Mill, and the destruction of Grapevine Bridge kept him from

GENERAL GEORGE A. McCALL. FROM A PHOTOGRAPH.

reaching Frayser's farm until the day after that battle. If he had been there, we might have destroyed or captured McClellan's army. Huger was in position for the battle of Frayser's farm, and after his batteries had misled me into opening the fight he subsided. Holmes and Magruder, who were on the New Market road to attack the Federals as they passed that way, failed to do so.

General McClellan's retreat was successfully managed; therefore we must give it credit for being well managed. He had 100,000 men, and insisted to the authorities at Washington that Lee had 200,000. In fact, Lee had only 90,000. General McClellan's plan to take Richmond by a siege was wise enough, and it would have been a success if the Confederates had consented to such a programme. In spite of McClellan's excellent plans, General Lee, with a force inferior in numbers, completely routed him, and while suffering less than McClellan, captured over six thousand of his men.\ General Lee's

\ In this estimate General Longstreet follows General Lee's unspecific report. The Union returns state the "Captured or missing" of McClellan's army at 6053, and the total loss at 15,849. The Confederate loss was 20,135.— EDITORS.

plans in the Seven Days' Fight were excellent, but were poorly executed. General McClellan was a very accomplished soldier and a very able engineer, but hardly equal to the position of field-marshal as a military chieftain. He organized the Army of the Potomac cleverly, but did not handle it skillfully when in actual battle. Still I doubt if his retreat could have been better handled, though the rear of his army should have been more positively either in his own hands or in the hands of Sumner. Heintzelman crossed the White Oak Swamp prematurely and left the rear of McClellan's army exposed, which would have been fatal had Jackson come up and taken part in Magruder's affair of the 29th near Savage's Station.

I cannot close this sketch without referring to the Confederate commander when he came upon the scene for the first time. General Lee was an unusually handsome man, even in his advanced life. He seemed fresh from West Point, so trim was his figure and so elastic his step. Out of battle he was as gentle as a woman, but when the clash of arms came he loved fight, and urged his battle with wonderful determination. As a usual thing he was remarkably well-balanced — always so, except on one or two occasions of severe trial when he failed to maintain his exact equipoise. Lee's orders were always well considered and well chosen. He depended almost too much on his officers for their execution. Jackson was a very skillful man against such men as Shields, Banks, and Frémont, but when pitted against the best of the Federal commanders he did not appear so well. Without doubt the greatest man of rebellion times, the one matchless among forty millions for the peculiar difficulties of the period, was Abraham Lincoln.

GENERAL HEINTZELMAN'S HEADQUARTERS AT NELSON'S HOUSE, JUNE 30, DURING THE BATTLE OF GLENDALE.
FROM A SKETCH MADE AT THE TIME.

THE BATTLE OF MALVERN HILL.

BY FITZ JOHN PORTER, MAJOR-GENERAL, U. S. V.

BEFORE the battle of Gaines's Mill (already described by me in these pages), a change of base from the York to the James River had been anticipated and prepared for by General McClellan. After the battle this change became a necessity, in presence of a strong and aggressive foe, who had already turned our right, cut our connection with the York River, and was also in large force behind the intrenchments between us and Richmond. The transfer was begun the moment our position became perilous. It now involved a series of battles by day and marches by night which brought into relief the able talents, active foresight, and tenacity of purpose of our commander, the unity of action on the part of his subordinates, and the great bravery, firmness, and confidence in their superiors on the part of the rank and file.

These conflicts from the beginning of the Seven Days' fighting were the engagement at Oak Grove, the battles of Beaver Dam Creek and Gaines's Mill, the engagements at Golding's and Garnett's farms, and at Allen's farm or Peach Orchard; the battle of Savage's Station; the artillery duel at White Oak Swamp; the battle of Glendale (or Charles City cross-roads); the action of Turkey Creek, and the battle of Malvern Hill. Each was a success to our army, the engagement of Malvern Hill being the most decisive. The result of the movement was that on the 2d of July our army was safely established at Harrison's Landing, on the James, in accordance with General McClellan's design. The present narrative will be confined to events coming under my own observation, and connected with my command, the Fifth Army Corps.

Saturday, June 28th, 1862, the day after the battle of Gaines's Mill, my corps spent in bivouac at the Trent farm on the south bank of the Chickahominy. Artillery and infantry detachments guarded the crossings at the sites of the destroyed bridges. Our antagonists of the 27th were still north of the river, but did not molest us. We rested and recuperated as best we could, amid the noise of battle close by, at Garnett's and Golding's farms, in which part of Franklin's corps was engaged, refilling the empty cartridge-boxes and haversacks, so as to be in readiness for immediate duty.

Our antagonists on the north bank of the river were apparently almost inactive. They seemed puzzled as to our intentions, or paralyzed by the effect of their own labors and losses, and, like ourselves, were recuperating for a renewal of the contest in the early future; though to them, as well as to us, it was difficult to conjecture where that renewal would be made. The only evidence of activity on their part was the dust rising on the road down the river, which we attributed, with the utmost unconcern, to the movements of troops seeking to interrupt our already abandoned communications with York River. The absence of any indication of our intention to maintain those communications, together with the rumble of our artillery, which that night was moving southward, opened the eyes of our opponents to the fact that we had accomplished the desired and perhaps necessary object of withdrawing to the south bank of the Chickahominy, and for the first time had aroused their suspicion that we were either intending to attack Richmond or temporarily abandon the siege, during a change of base to the James River. But the active spurts on the 27th and 28th of June made by the defenders of that city against our left created the false impression that they designed to attack the Second, Third, and Fourth Corps, and thereby succeeded in preventing an attack upon them. So, in order to thwart our plans, whatever they might be, promptly on the 29th our opponents renewed their activity by advancing from Richmond, and by recrossing to the south bank of the river all their forces lately employed at Gaines's Mill. But at that time the main body of our army was beyond their immediate reach, taking positions to cover the passage of our trains to the new base and to be ready again to welcome our eager and earnest antagonists.

Between 2 and 9 P. M. on the 28th, my corps was in motion and marched by the way of Savage Station to the south side of White Oak Swamp; and at the junction of the roads from Richmond (Glendale) to be prepared to repel attacks from the direction of that city. General Morell, leading the advance, aided General Woodbury, of the engineer corps, to build the causeways and bridges necessary for the easy passage of the trains and troops over the swamps and streams. Sykes and McCall followed at 5 and 9 o'clock, respectively, McCall being accompanied by Hunt's Artillery Reserve. We expected to reach our destination, which was only ten miles distant, early on the 29th; but, in consequence of the dark night and of the narrow and muddy roads, cut up and blocked by numerous trains and herds of cattle, the head of the column did not arrive till 10 A. M., the rear not until midnight. McCall arrived latest, and all were greatly fatigued.

The enemy not having appeared at Glendale on the afternoon of the 29th, and other troops arriving to take the place of mine, General McClellan ordered me to move that night by the direct road to the elevated and cleared lands (Malvern Hill) on the north bank of Turkey Creek, there to select and hold a position behind which the army and all its trains could be withdrawn with safety. General Keyes was to move by a different road and form to my right and rear.

Again the dangers and difficulties of night marches attended us, followed by the consequent delay, which, though fortunately it was counterbalanced by the slowness of our opponents in moving to the same point, endangered the safety of our whole army. Although we started before dark, and were led by an intelligent cavalry officer who had passed over the route and professed to know it, my command did not reach Turkey Creek, which was only five miles distant, until 9 A. M. on the 30th. In fact, we were misled up the

THE PARSONAGE, NEAR MALVERN HILL.

This house was in the rear of the Confederate line, which was formed in the woods shown in the background. It was used as a Confederate hospital after the fight. The road is the Church road (known also as the Quaker road), and the view is from near C. W. Smith's, which was for a short time the headquarters of General Lee. The trees of this neighborhood were riddled with bullets and torn with shell, and in 1885, when this view was photographed, the corn was growing out of many a soldier's grave.—EDITORS.

Long Bridge road toward Richmond until we came in contact with the enemy's pickets. Then we returned and started anew. Fortunately I was at the head of the column to give the necessary orders, so that no delay occurred in retracing our steps.

Our new field of battle embraced Malvern Hill, just north of Turkey Creek and Crew's Hill, about one mile farther north. Both hills have given name to the interesting and eventful battle which took place on July 1st, and which I shall now attempt to describe.

The forces which on this occasion came under my control, and were engaged in or held ready to enter the contest, were my own corps, consisting of Morell's, Sykes's and McCall's divisions, Colonel H. J. Hunt's Artillery Reserve of one hundred pieces, including Colonel R. O. Tyler's Connecticut siege artillery, Couch's division of Keyes's corps, the brigades of John C. Caldwell and Thomas F. Meagher of Sumner's corps, and the brigade of D. E. Sickles of Heintzelman's corps. Though Couch was placed under my command, he was left uncontrolled by me, as will be seen hereafter. The other brigades were sent to me by their respective division commanders, in anticipation of my needs or at my request.

This new position, with its elements of great strength, was better adapted for a defensive battle than any with which we had been favored. It was elevated, and was more or less protected on each flank by small streams or by swamps, while the woods in front through which the enemy had to pass to attack us were in places marshy, and the timber so thick that artillery could not be brought up, and even troops were moved in it with difficulty. Slightly in rear of our line of battle on Crew's Hill the reserve artillery and infantry were held for immediate service. The hill concealed them from the view of the enemy and sheltered them to some extent from his fire. These hills, both to the east and west, were connected with the adjacent valleys by gradually sloping plains except at the Crew house, where for a little distance the slope was quite abrupt, and was easily protected by a small force. With the exception of the River road, all the roads from Richmond, along which the enemy would be obliged to approach, meet in front of Crew's Hill. This hill was flanked with ravines, enfiladed by our fire. The ground in front was sloping, and over it our artillery and infantry, themselves protected by the crest and ridges, had clear sweep for their fire. In all directions, for sev-

eral hundred yards, the land over which an attacking force must advance was almost entirely cleared of forest and was generally cultivated.

I reached Malvern Hill some two hours before my command on Monday, June 30th; each division, as it came upon the field, was assigned to a position covering the approaches from Richmond along the River road and the debouches from the New Market, Charles City, and Williamsburg roads. Warren, with his brigade of about six hundred men, took position on the lowlands to the left, to guard against the approach of the enemy along the River road, or over the low, extensive, and cultivated plateau beyond and extending north along Crew's Hill. Warren's men were greatly in need of rest. The brigade had suffered greatly at Gaines's Mill, and was not expected to perform much more than picket duty, and it was large enough for the purpose designed, as it was not probable that any large force would be so reckless as to advance on that road. Warren was supported by the 11th U. S. Infantry, under Major Floyd-Jones, and late in the afternoon was strengthened by Martin's battery of 12-pounders and a detachment of the 3d Pennsylvania cavalry under Lieutenant Frank W. Hess.

On the west side of Malvern Hill, overlooking Warren, were some thirty-six guns, some of long range, having full sweep up the valley and over the cleared lands north of the River road. These batteries comprised Captain S. H. Weed's Battery I, 5th U. S. Artillery, Captain John Edwards's Batteries L and M, 3d U. S. Artillery, J. H. Carlisle's Battery E, 2d U. S. Artillery, John R. Smead's Battery K, 5th U. S. Artillery, and Adolph Voegelee's, Battery B, 1st N. Y. Artillery Battalion, with others in reserve. To these, later in the day, were added the siege-guns of the 1st Connecticut Artillery, under Colonel Robert O. Tyler, which were placed on elevated

THE CREW HOUSE. THE UPPER PICTURE SHOWS THE OLD HOUSE, AND IS FROM A COLOR-SKETCH TAKEN SOON AFTER THE WAR; THE NEW HOUSE SHOWN IN THE LOWER PICTURE IS FROM A PHOTOGRAPH TAKEN EARLY IN 1885.

The old building, sometimes called Dr. Mellert's, was the headquarters of General Morell; during the battle members of the Signal Corps were at work on the roof. It was burned after the war and rebuilt on the old foundations. The view in each case is from the east.

The lane, in the lower picture, leads to the Quaker road and was the line of Griffin's guns. McQuade's repulse of the attack on the hill took place behind the cabin on the left of the picture. The Crew farm is said to be one of the most fertile on the Peninsula.— EDITORS.

ground immediately to the left of the Malvern house, so as to fire over our front line at any attacking force, and to sweep the low meadow on the left.

To General (then Colonel) Hunt, the accomplished and energetic chief of artillery, was due the excellent posting of these batteries on June 30th, and the rearrangement of all the artillery along the whole line on Tuesday (July 1st), together with the management of the reserve artillery on that day.

Major Charles S. Lovell, commanding Colonel William Chapman's brigade of Sykes's division, supported some of these batteries, and, with the brigade of Buchanan on his right, in a clump of pines, extended the line northward, near the Crew (sometimes called the Mellert) house.

Morell, prolonging Sykes's line on Crew's Hill, with headquarters at Crew's house, occupied the right of the line extending to the Quaker road. To his left front, facing west, was the 14th New York Volunteers, under Colonel

McQuade, with a section of Captain W. B. Weeden's Battery C, 1st Rhode Island Artillery, both watching the Richmond road and the valley and protecting our left. On their right, under cover of a narrow strip of woods, skirting the Quaker road, were the brigades of Martindale and Butterfield, while in front of these, facing north, was Griffin's brigade. All were supporting batteries of Morell's division, commanded by Captain Weeden and others, under the general supervision of Griffin, a brave and skilled artillery officer. ǀ

About 3 o'clock on Monday the enemy was seen approaching along the River road, and Warren and Hunt made all necessary dispositions to receive them. About 4 o'clock the enemy advanced and opened fire from their artillery upon Warren and Sykes and on the extreme left of Morell, causing a few casualties in Morell's division. In return for this intrusion the concentrated rapid fire of the artillery was opened upon them, soon smashing one battery to pieces, silencing another, and driving back their infantry and cavalry in rapid retreat, much to the satisfaction of thousands of men watching the result. The enemy left behind in possession of Warren a few prisoners, two guns and six caissons, the horses of which had been killed. The battery which had disturbed Morell was also silenced by this fire of our artillery. On this occasion the gun-boats in the James [see p. 268] made apparent their welcome presence and gave good support by bringing their heavy guns to bear upon the enemy. Though their fire caused a few casualties among our men, and inflicted but little, if any, injury upon the enemy, their large shells, bursting amid the enemy's troops far beyond the attacking force, carried great moral influence with them, and naturally tended, in addition to the effect of our artillery, to prevent any renewed attempt to cross the open valley on our left. This attacking force formed a small part of Wise's brigade of Holmes's division. They were all raw troops, which accounts for their apparently demoralized retreat. This affair is known as the action of Turkey Bridge or Malvern Cliff. ‡

Our forces lay on their arms during the night, in substantially the positions I have described, patiently awaiting the attack expected on the following day.

ǀ These batteries as located on Tuesday, the day of the battle, were those of Edwards, Livingston, Kingsbury, Ames, part of Weeden's under Waterman, part of Allen's under Hyde, and Bramhall's. Other batteries as they arrived were posted in reserve south of Crew's Hill, and were used to replace batteries whose ammunition was exhausted, or were thrown forward into action to strengthen the line.

The different commands as soon as they were posted prepared to pass the night [June 30th] in securing the rest greatly needed both by man and beast. Later on June 30th Couch's division of Keyes's corps came up and took its place, extending Morell's line to the right of the Quaker road. The greater part of the supply trains of the army and of the reserve artillery passed safely beyond Turkey Creek through the commands thus posted, the movement only ceasing about 4 o'clock in the afternoon.—F. J. P.

‡ Some idea may be formed from the following incident of how indifferent to noises or unconscious of sudden alarms one may become when asleep, under the sense of perfect security or from the effect of fatigue. For several days I had been able to secure but little sleep, other than such as I could catch on horseback, or while resting for a few minutes. During this heavy artillery firing I was asleep in the Malvern house. Although the guns were within one hundred yards of me, and the windows and doors were wide open, I was greatly surprised some two hours afterward to learn that the engagement had taken place. For weeks I had slept with senses awake to the sound of distant cannon, and even of a musket-shot, and would be instantly aroused by either. But on this occasion I had gone to sleep free from care, feeling confident that however strong an attack might be made, the result would be the repulse of the enemy without much damage to us. My staff, as much in need of rest as myself, sympathized with me and let me sleep.—F. J. P.

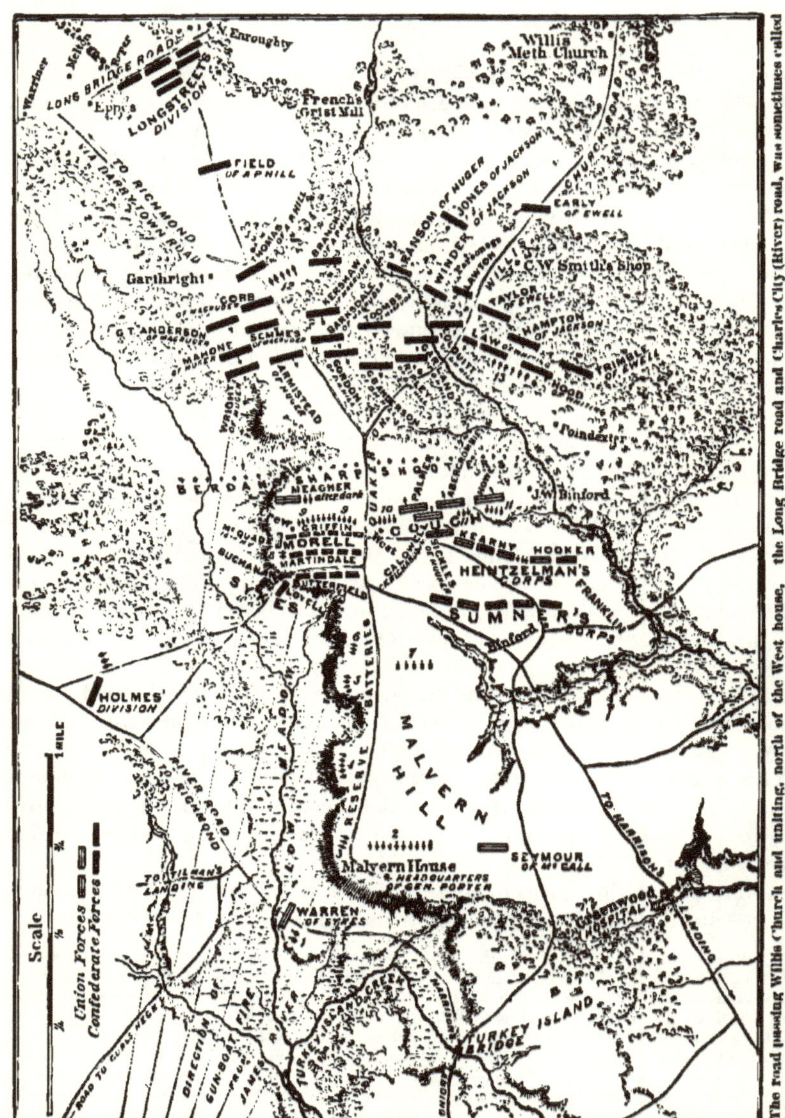

MAP OF THE BATTLE OF MALVERN HILL, SHOWING, APPROXIMATELY, POSITIONS OF BRIGADES AND BATTERIES.

The Union batteries, as indicated on the map, were: 1, Martin's; 2, Tyler's; 3, 4, 5, 6, batteries in reserve; 7, Hunt's reserve artillery; 8 and 11, first and second positions of Waterman's (Weeden's); 9—9, Edwards's, Livingston's, Ames's, Kingsbury's, and Hyde's; 10, Snow's, Frank's, and Hyde's; 11, Kingsbury's and Seeley's.

On the Union side the chief variations from these positions were the advance of a part of Butterfield's brigade, between Griffin and Couch, and the transfer of batteries from Morell to Couch. During the afternoon Sickles's brigade took the place of Caldwell's, which had come up to Couch's aid and had suffered severely. Meagher advanced about 5 o'clock, accompanied by 32-pounders under Colonel H. J. Hunt, which did terrible execution.

The Confederate brigades are placed in the order of their attack; those marked with an arrow were in the charges or in the front line after dark. It is difficult to fix the positions of the Confederate artillery. In general, 12 indicates Moorman's, Grimes's, and Pegram's; and 13 denotes the position of Balthis's, Poague's, and Carpenter's. In other positions, the batteries of Wooding (one section under Lieutenant Jones), Carrington, Hardaway, Bondurant, Hart, McCarthy, and the Baltimore Light Artillery were engaged to some extent.—EDITORS.

McCall's division of Pennsylvania Reserves, now under General Truman Seymour, arrived during the night and was posted just in front of the Malvern house, and was held in reserve, to be called upon for service only in case of absolute necessity. ↓

Early on Tuesday our lines were re-formed and slightly advanced to take full advantage of the formation of the ground, the artillery of the front line being re-posted in commanding positions, and placed under General Griffin's command, but under Captain Weeden's care, just behind the crest of the hill. The infantry was arranged between the artillery to protect and be protected by its

BERDAN'S SHARP-SHOOTERS (OF MORELL'S DIVISION) SKIRMISHING IN THE MEADOW WHEAT-FIELD.

neighbors, and prepared to be thrown forward, if at any time advisable, so as not to interfere with the artillery fire.

↓ This division had reached me at New Market cross-roads, at midnight of the 29th, greatly in need of rest. This fact, and the necessity that a reliable force should hold that point until the whole army had crossed the White Oak Swamp and the trains had passed to the rear, compelled the assignment of McCall to the performance of that duty. During the afternoon of the 30th he was attacked by large forces of the enemy, which he several times repulsed; but he failed to enjoy the advantages of his success through the recklessness and irrepressible impetuosity of his men or the forgetfulness of orders by infantry subordinates. They were strictly cautioned, unless unusual fortune favored them, not to pass through a battery for the purpose of pursuing a repulsed enemy, and under no circumstances to return in face of one, so as to check its fire. In the excitement of presumed success at repulsing a heavy attack, a brigade pushed after a rapidly fleeing foe, and was impulsively joined by its neighbors, who wished not to be excelled in dash or were perhaps encouraged by injudicious orders. Passing through their own batteries as they advanced, they lost the benefit of their fire, as they did also when returning after being repulsed and pursued by the enemy's reserves. Disregard of these principles at this time caused heavy losses of men, and led to the demoralization at a critical moment of one good volunteer battery and the capture, through no fault of its commander, of one of the best batteries of the regular army [see p. 402]. This battery was commanded by Lieutenant A. M. Randol, a brave and accomplished artillery officer of the regular army. This division had otherwise suffered heavily. At Gaines's Mill it had lost, by capture, one of the ablest generals, John F. Reynolds, with other gallant and efficient officers and men, captured, killed, or wounded. Its misfortunes culminated in the capture at New Market cross-roads of McCall, the wounding of General George G. Meade, his able assistant, and the loss of many excellent subordinates. Fortunately the brave and experienced soldier, General Seymour, with his worthy officers, escaped to lead the survivors of the division to our camp, where they were welcomed by their sympathizing comrades.—F. J. P.

THE WEST HOUSE, LOOKING TOWARD THE CREW HOUSE. FROM A PHOTOGRAPH TAKEN EARLY IN 1885.

This house was the dividing point between Couch's division and Morell's line, the artillery fronting the fence and being nearly on the line indicated by it. The West house was occupied as headquarters by General Couch.— EDITORS.

The corps of Heintzelman and Sumner had arrived during the night and taken position in the order named to the right and rear of Couch's division, protecting that flank effectively toward Western Run.⸗ They did not expect to be seriously engaged, but were ready to resist attack and to give assistance to the center and left, if circumstances should require it. At an early hour in the day Sumner kindly sent me Caldwell's brigade, as he thought I might need help. This brigade I placed near Butterfield, who was directed to send it forward wherever it should be needed or called for. He sent it to Couch at an opportune moment early in the day.

General McClellan, accompanied by his staff, visited our lines at an early hour, and approved my measures and those of General Couch, or changed them where it was deemed advisable. Though he left me in charge of that part of the field occupied by Couch, I at no time undertook to control that general, or even indicated a desire to do so, but with full confidence in his ability, which was justified by the result of his action, left him free to act in accordance with his own judgment. I coöperated with him fully, however, having Morell's batteries, under Weeden, posted so as to protect his front, and sending him help when I saw he needed it. The division of Couch, though

⸗ Franklin's corps, and French's brigade of Sumner's corps, arrived at Malvern Hill on the morning of July 1st. During the day Franklin's columns were in line of battle on the right of Sumner.— EDITORS.

it suffered severely in the battle of Fair Oaks, had seen less service and met with fewer losses in these "Seven Days' battles" than any one of my three, and was prepared with full ranks to receive an attack, seeming impatient and eager for the fight. Its conduct soon confirmed this impression. Batteries of Hunt's Artillery Reserve were sent to him when needed — and also Caldwell's brigade, voluntarily sent to me early in the day by Sumner, and Sickles's brigade, borrowed of Heintzelman for the purpose.

About 10 A. M. the enemy's skirmishers and artillery began feeling for us along our line; they kept up a desultory fire until about 12 o'clock, with no severe injury to our infantry, who were well masked, and who revealed but little of our strength or position by retaliatory firing or exposure.

Up to this time and until nearly 1 o'clock our infantry were resting upon their arms and waiting the moment, certain to come, when the column of the enemy rashly advancing would render it necessary to expose themselves. Our desire was to hold the enemy where our artillery would be most destructive, and to reserve our infantry ammunition for close quarters to repel the more determined assaults of our obstinate and untiring foe. Attacks by brigade were made upon Morell, both on his left front and on his right, and also upon Couch; but our artillery, admirably handled, without exception, was generally sufficient to repel all such efforts and to drive back the assailants in confusion, and with great loss.

VIEW FROM THE MEADOW WEST OF THE CREW HOUSE. FROM A PHOTOGRAPH TAKEN EARLY IN 1885.

The Crew house is in the extreme right of the picture. The hill to the left is the high ground shown on p. 419. The ravine between the two is the ravine shown in the right of the picture on p. 418. At the time of the battle the low ground was in wheat, partly shocked, affording protection for the Union sharpshooters under Berdan. Farther to the left, up this valley, and in the rear of the hill, was the right of the Confederate line, which late in the evening made several assaults upon the Crew Hill, by way of the ravine and meadow.— EDITORS.

SCENE OF THE CONFEDERATE ATTACK ON THE WEST SIDE OF CREW'S HILL, LOOKING FROM THE CREW
HOUSE SOUTH-WEST TOWARD THE JAMES RIVER. FROM A PHOTOGRAPH TAKEN EARLY IN 1885.

The Confederates came down the valley or meadow from the right, and advanced up this slope toward the two
guns of Weeden, which were supported by the Fourteenth New York Volunteers. The road
across the meadow leads to Holmes's position on the River road.— EDITORS.

While the enemy's artillery was firing upon us General Sumner withdrew part of his corps to the slope of Malvern Hill, to the right of the Malvern house, which descended into the valley of Western Run. Then, deeming it advisable to withdraw all our troops to that line, he ordered me to fall back to the Malvern house; but I protested that such a movement would be disastrous, and declined to obey the order until I could confer with General McClellan, who had approved of the disposition of our troops. Fortunately Sumner did not insist upon my complying with the order, and, as we were soon vigorously attacked, he advanced his troops to a point where he was but little disturbed by the enemy, but from which he could quickly render aid in response to calls for help or where need for help was apparent.\

The spasmodic, though sometimes formidable attacks of our antagonists, at different points along our whole front, up to about 4 o'clock, were presumably demonstrations or feelers, to ascertain our strength, preparatory to their engaging in more serious work. An ominous silence, similar to that which had preceded the attack in force along our whole line at Gaines's Mill, now intervened, until, at about 5:30 o'clock, the enemy opened upon both Morell

\ On one occasion, when I sent an urgent request for two brigades, Sumner read my note aloud, and, fearing he could not stand another draft on his forces, was hesitating to respond, when Heintzelman, ever prompt and generous, sprang to his feet and exclaimed: "By Jove! if Porter asks for help, I know he needs it and I will send it." The immediate result was the sending of Meagher by Sumner and Sickles by Heintzelman. This was the second time that Sumner had selected and sent me Meagher's gallant Irish brigade, and each time it rendered invaluable service. I had served under General Heintzelman up to the capture of Yorktown, and I ever appreciated his act as the prompting of a thoughtful, generous, and chivalrous nature.— F. J. P.

and Couch with artillery from nearly the whole of his front, and soon afterward pressed forward his columns of infantry, first on one and then on the other, or on both. As if moved by a reckless disregard of life, equal to that displayed at Gaines's Mill, with a determination to capture our army, or destroy it by driving us into the river, regiment after regiment, and brigade after brigade, rushed at our batteries; but the artillery of both Morell and Couch mowed them down with shrapnel, grape, and canister; while our infantry, withholding their fire until the enemy were within short range, scattered the remnants of their columns, sometimes following them up and capturing prisoners and colors. ☆

As column after column advanced, only to meet the same disastrous repulse, the sight became one of the most interesting imaginable. The havoc made by the rapidly bursting shells from guns arranged so as to sweep any position

REPULSE OF THE CONFEDERATES ON THE SLOPE OF CREW'S HILL [SEE P. 416].

☆ Captain William B. Weeden, in a letter dated May 24th, 1885, says of the battle:

"It was a fine afternoon, hot but tempered by a cooling breeze. The soldiers waited; patience, not courage, kept them steady. The ranks were full now; each knew that in himself he might be a possible victor or a possible victim at nightfall. Crew's deserted house, more hospitable than its owner, had furnished a luxury seldom enjoyed on the field. Water, not warm in the canteen, but iced in a delf pitcher, with glasses, was literally 'handed round.' Pickets and skirmishers had kept us informed of the opposing formations and of batteries going into position. The sharp-shooters' bullets began to thicken. Action might begin at any moment, and between 2 and 3 o'clock it did begin. Out of the woods, puffs of smoke from guns and nearer light wreaths from their shells lent new colors to the green of woods and fields and the deep blue sky. The musketry cracked before it loudened into a roar, and whizzing bullets mingled with ragged exploding shells. The woods swarmed with butternut coats and gray. These colors were worn by a lively race of men and they stepped forward briskly, firing as they moved. The regimental formations were plainly visible, with the colors flying. It was the onset of battle with the good order of a review. In this first heavy skirmish — the prelude of the main action — Magruder's right made a determined attack by way of the meadow to pierce Griffin's line to turn Ames's Battery and to break the solid advantages of position held by the Union forces.

"The brunt of the blow fell upon Colonel McQuade's 14th New York. This was a gallant regiment which had suffered much in the rough work at Gaines's Mill. The Confederate charge was sudden and heavy. The New Yorkers began to give ground, and it looked for a moment as if the disasters of Gaines's Mill might be repeated. But only for a moment. The men stiffened up to the color line, charged forward with a cheer, and drove back the enemy. Weeden's Rhode Island Battery of three-inch rifled ordnance guns had lost three pieces at Gaines's Mill. The remaining guns, under command of Lieutenant Waterman, were stationed south and west of Crew's fronting left and rearward. It was the angle of our position, and so far west that Tyler's heavy guns mistook it for the enemy and fired 4½-inch shells into it. One caused severe casualties. The battery was withdrawn from this dangerous range, and later in the afternoon, when the main action was raging, Waterman's three guns, with two of the same type under Lieutenant Phillips of Massachusetts, relieved Kingsbury and Hazlitt's regular batteries of Parrotts on Couch's right. The service here was admirable. Waterman with only half a battery had a whole company of experienced gunners. When the ammunition gave out they were in turn relieved by a fresh battery."　EDITORS.

THE MAIN BATTLE-FIELD.—VIEW OF THE UNION POSITION FROM THE WOODED KNOLL SHOWN IN THE FOLLOWING PAGE. FROM A PHOTOGRAPH TAKEN IN 1885.

—ded from the Crew house on the right to the West house in the extreme left of the picture. Crew's Creek extended the line a third of a mile to the left of the West house. The ravine, to the right of the barn and buildings in the middle-ground, descends to the meadow; it was by this ravine and the shelter of the out-buildings that the Confederates effected a lodgment on the hill, at dusk, compelling Griffin to shift his guns to avoid capture. General A. R. Wright, who commanded a brigade in Huger's division, in his official report describes as follows the aspect of the Federal position, as seen from the wooded knoll shown on the following page: "I suggested to General Armistead that we go forward to the edge of the field, and, under protection of a strong force of skirmishers, ascend a high knoll or hill which abruptly sprung from the meadow below and on our right, from the summit of which we would be able to observe the enemy's movements. Having reached this position, we were enabled to get a very complete view of McClellan's army. Immediately in our front, and extending our rifle, stretched a field, at the farther extremity of which was situated the dwelling and farm-buildings of Mr. Crew (formerly Dr. Mellert). In front and to our left the land rose gently from the edge of the woods up to the farm-yard, when it became high and rolling. Upon the right the field was broken by a series of ridges and valleys, which ran out at right angles to a line drawn from our position to that of the enemy, and all of which terminated upon our extreme right in a precipitous bluff, which dropped suddenly down upon a low, flat meadow, covered with wheat and intersected with a number of ditches, which run from the bluff across the meadow to a swamp or dense woods about five hundred yards farther to our right. This low, flat meadow stretched up to, and swinging around, Crew's house, extended as far as Turkey Bend, on James River. The enemy had drawn up his artillery (as well as could be ascertained about fifty pieces) in a crescent-shaped line, the convex line being next to our position, with its right (on our left) resting upon a road which passed three hundred yards to the left of Crew's house on to Malvern Hill, the left of their advanced line of batteries resting upon the high bluff which overlooked the meadow to the right (our right) and rear of Crew's house." Their infantry, a little in the rear of the artillery, and protected by the crest of the ridge upon which the batteries were placed, extended from the woods on our left along the crest of the hill and through a lane in the meadow on our right to the dense woods there. In rear of this and beyond a narrow ravine, the sides of which were covered with timber, and which ran parallel to their line of battle and but a few rods in the rear of Crew's house, was another line of infantry, its right resting upon a heavy, dense woods, which covered the Malvern Hill farm on the east. The left of this line rested upon the precipitous bluff which overlooking the low meadow on the west of the farm. At this point the high bluff stretched out to the west for two hundred yards, in a long ridge or ledge nearly separating the meadow from the lowlands of the river), upon the extreme western terminus of which was planted a battery of heavy guns. This latter battery commanded the whole meadow in front of it, and by a direct fire was able to dispute the maneuvering of troops over any portion of the meadow. Just behind the ravine which ran in rear of Crew's house, and under cover of the timber, was planted a heavy battery in a small redoubt, whose fire swept across the meadow. These two batteries completely controlled the meadow from one extremity of it to the other, and effectually prevented the movement of troops in large masses upon it. The whole number of guns in these several batteries could not have fallen far short of one hundred. The infantry force of the enemy I estimated at least 25,000 or 30,000 from what I saw. Large numbers, as I ascertained afterward, were posted in the woods on our extreme right and left, and the line of ditches across the meadow were lined with sharp-shooters."—Editor.

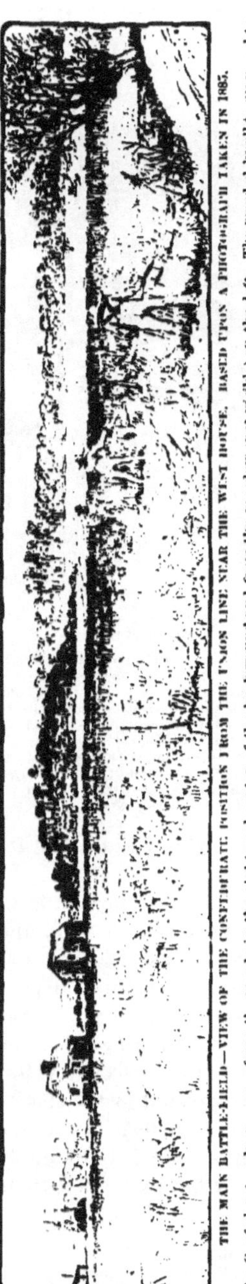

THE MAIN BATTLE-FIELD—VIEW OF THE CONFEDERATE POSITIONS FROM THE UNION LINE NEAR THE WEST HOUSE. BASED UPON A PHOTOGRAPH TAKEN IN 1885.

The Confederate advance was from the woods in the right and center of the background and from the meadow (not visible) on the left. The wooded knoll is supposed to be the point from which Generals Wright and Armistead reconnoitered the Federal position, as described by General Wright in his report. [See p. 418.]—EDITORS.

far and near, and in any direction, was fearful to behold. Pressed to the extreme as they were, the courage of our men was fully tried. The safety of our army—the life of the Union—was felt to be at stake. In one case the brigades of Howe, Abercrombie, and Palmer, of Couch's division, under impulse, gallantly pushed after the retreating foe, captured colors, and advantageously advanced the right of the line, but at considerable loss and great risk. The brigades of Morell, cool, well-disciplined, and easily controlled, let the enemy return after each repulse, but permitted few to escape their fire. Colonel McQuade, on Morell's left, with the 14th New York, against orders and at the risk of defeat and disaster, yielding to impulse, gallantly dashed forward and repulsed an attacking party. Assisted by Buchanan of Sykes's division, Colonel Rice, with the 44th New York Volunteers, likewise drove a portion of the enemy from the field, taking a flag bearing the inscription "Seven Pines." Colonel Hunt, directing the artillery, was twice dismounted by having his horse shot under him, but though constantly exposed continued his labors until after dark. General Couch, who was also dismounted in like manner, took advantage of every opportunity to make his opponents feel his blows.

It is not to be supposed that our men, though concealed by the irregularities of the ground, were not sufferers from the enemy's fire. The fact is that before they exposed themselves by pursuing the enemy, the ground was literally covered with the killed and wounded from dropping bullets and bursting shells and their contents; but they bravely bore the severe trial of having to remain inactive under a damaging fire.

As Morell's front ranks became thinned out and the ammunition was exhausted, other regiments eagerly advanced; all were stimulated by the hope of a brilliant and permanent success, and nerved by the approving shouts of their comrades and the cry of "Revenge, boys!" "Remember McLane!" "Remember Black!" "Remember Gove!" or "Remember Cass!" Black and McLane and Gove had been killed at Gaines's Mill;

MALVERN HILL, FROM THE DIRECTION OF TURKEY ISLAND BRIDGE, FROM A SKETCH MADE SOON AFTER THE WAR.

VIEW FROM MALVERN HILL, LOOKING TOWARD THE JAMES, FROM A PHOTOGRAPH TAKEN IN 1885.

This view is taken from near the position of Tyler's siege-guns (see map). The engagement of Malvern Cliff, or Turkey Island bridge, on the 30th of June, between Generals Warren and Holmes, took place on the road at the foot of the hill which passes near the house in the middle-ground. The bridge is to the left on this road. The winding stream is Turkey Creek. In the middle distance is the position of the three gun-boats which shelled the woods at the right both on the 30th of June and the 1st of July.— EDITORS.

Woodbury and Cass were then lying before them.‡ Colonel McQuade was the only regimental commander of Griffin's brigade who escaped death during the Seven Days, and he was constantly exposed.

During that ominous silence of which I have spoken, I determined that our opponents should reap no advantage, even if our lines yielded to attack, and therefore posted batteries, as at Gaines's Mill, to secure against the disaster of a break in our lines, should such a misfortune be ours. For this purpose I sent Weed, Carlisle, and Smead, with their batteries, to the gorge of the roads on Crew's Hill, from which the enemy must emerge in pursuit if he should break our lines; instructing them to join in the fight if necessary, but not to permit the advance of the foe, even if it must be arrested at the risk of firing upon friends. To these Colonel Hunt added three batteries of horse artillery. Though they were all thus posted and their guns loaded with double canister, "they were," as Captain Smead reported, "very happy to find their services not needed on that occasion."

‡ Colonel Samuel W. Black, of the 62d Pennsylvania, Colonel John W. McLane, of the 83d Pennsylvania, Colonel Jesse A. Gove, of the 22d Massachusetts, Colonel Dwight A. Woodbury, of the 4th Michigan, and Colonel Thomas Cass, of the 9th Massachusetts.— EDITORS.

It was at this time, in answer to my call for aid, that Sumner sent me Meagher, and Heintzelman sent Sickles, both of whom reached me in the height of battle, when, if ever, fresh troops would renew our confidence and insure our success. While riding rapidly forward to meet Meagher, who was approaching at a "double-quick" step, my horse fell, throwing me over his head, much to my discomfort both of body and mind. On rising and remounting I was greeted with hearty cheers, which alleviated my chagrin. This incident gave rise to the report, spread through the country, that I was wounded. Fearing that I might fall into the hands of the enemy, and if so that my diary and dispatch-book of the campaign, then on my person, would meet with the same fate and reveal information to the injury of our cause, I tore it up, scattering the pieces to the winds, as I rode rapidly forward, leading Meagher into action. I have always regretted my act as destroying interesting and valuable memoranda of our campaign.

Advancing with Meagher's brigade, accompanied by my staff, I soon found that our forces had successfully driven back their assailants. Determined, if possible, satisfactorily to finish the contest, regardless of the risk of being fired upon by our artillery in case of defeat, I pushed on beyond our lines into the woods held by the enemy. About fifty yards in front of us, a large force of the enemy suddenly rose and opened with fearful volleys upon our advancing line. I turned to the brigade, which thus far had kept pace with my horse, and found it standing "like a stone-wall," and returning a fire more destruc-

BREVET BRIGADIER GENERAL JAMES M. QUADE, (DIED 1885.) AT MALVERN HILL, COLONEL OF THE 14TH NEW YORK, FROM A PHOTOGRAPH.

tive than it received and from which the enemy fled. The brigade was planted. My presence was no longer needed, and I sought General Sickles, whom I found giving aid to Couch. I had the satisfaction of learning that night that a Confederate detachment, undertaking to turn Meagher's left, was met by a portion of the 69th New York Regiment, which, advancing, repelled the attack and captured many prisoners.

After seeing that General Sickles was in a proper position, I returned to my own corps, where I was joined by Colonel Hunt with some 32-pounder howitzers. Taking those howitzers, we rode forward beyond our lines, and, in parting salutation to our opponents, Colonel Hunt sent a few shells, as a warning of what would be ready to welcome them on the morrow if they undertook to disturb us.

THE MALVERN HOUSE, FROM A PHOTOGRAPH TAKEN IN 1885.

During the engagement at Turkey bridge and the battle of Malvern Hill, this house was the headquarters of General Porter, and was a signal-station in communication with the gun-boats in the James River, toward which it fronts. It was built of imported English brick, of a dark but vivid red. The main battle-field is in the direction of the trees on the right, and Tyler's siege-guns were near the small trees in the left distance.— EDITORS.

Almost at the crisis of the battle—just before the advance of Meagher and Sickles—the gun-boats on the James River opened their fire with the good intent of aiding us, but either mistook our batteries at the Malvern house for those of the enemy, or were unable to throw their projectiles beyond us. If the former was the case, their range was well estimated, for all their shot landed in or close by Tyler's battery, killing and wounding a few of his men. Fortunately members of our excellent signal-service corps were present as usual on such occasions, and the message signaled to the boats, "For God's sake, stop firing," promptly relieved us from further damage and the demoralization of a "fire in the rear." Reference is occasionally seen in Confederate accounts of this battle to the fearful sounds of the projectiles from those gun-boats. But that afternoon not one of their projectiles passed beyond my headquarters; and I have always believed and said, as has General Hunt, that the enemy mistook the explosions of shells from Tyler's siege-guns and Kusserow's 32-pounder howitzers, which Hunt had carried forward, for shells from the gun-boats.

While Colonel Hunt and I were returning from the front, about 9 o'clock, we were joined by Colonel A. V. Colburn, of McClellan's staff. We all rejoiced over the day's success. By these officers I sent messages to the commanding general, expressing the hope that our withdrawal had ended and that we should hold the ground we now occupied, even if we did not assume the offensive. From my standpoint I thought we could maintain our position, and perhaps in a few days could improve it by advancing. But I knew only the circumstances before me, and these were limited by controlling influences. It was now after 9 o'clock at night. Within an hour of the time that Colonels Hunt and Colburn left me, and before they could have reached the commanding general, I received orders from him to withdraw, and to direct Generals Sumner and Heintzelman to move at specified hours to Harrison's Landing and General Couch to rejoin his corps, which was then under way to the same point.⚓

These orders were immediately sent to the proper officers, and by daybreak, July 2d, our troops, preceded by their trains, were well on their way to their destination, which they reached that day, greatly wearied after a hard march over muddy roads, in the midst of a heavy rain. That night, freed from care and oblivions of danger, all slept a long sleep; and they awoke the next morning with the clear sun, a happier, brighter, and stronger body of men than that which all the day before, depressed and fatigued, had shivered in the rain.

The conduct of the rear-guard was intrusted to Colonel Averell, commander of the 3d Pennsylvania Cavalry, sustained by Colonel Buchanan, with his brigade of regulars, and the 67th New York Regiment. No trying trust was ever better bestowed or more satisfactorily fulfilled. At daybreak Colonel Averell found himself accidentally without artillery to protect his command in its difficult task of preventing an attack before our rear was well out of range. He at once arranged his cavalry in bodies to represent horse-batteries, and, manœuvring them to create the impression that they were artillery ready for action, he secured himself from attack until the rest of the army and trains had passed sufficiently to the rear to permit him to retire rapidly without molestation. His stratagem was successful, and without loss he rejoined the main body of the army that night. Thus ended the memorable "Seven Days' battles," which, for severity and for stubborn resistance and endurance of hardships by the contestants, were not surpassed during the war. Each antagonist accomplished the result for which he aimed: one insuring the temporary relief of Richmond; the other gaining security on the north bank of the James, where the Union army, if our civil and military authorities were disposed, could be promptly reënforced, and from whence only, as subsequent events proved, it could renew the contest successfully. Preparations were commenced and dispositions were at once made under

---

⚓ The order referred to read as follows:

"HEADQUARTERS ARMY OF THE POTOMAC, 9 P. M., JULY 1ST, 1862; BRIGADIER-GENERAL F. J. PORTER, COMMANDING FIFTH PROVISIONAL CORPS.— GENERAL: The General Commanding desires you to move your command at once, the artillery reserve moving first to Harrison's Bar. In case you should find it impossible to move your heavy artillery, you are to spike the guns and destroy the carriages. Couch's command will move under your orders. Communicate these instructions to him at once. The corps of Heintzelman and Sumner will move next. Please communicate to General Heintzelman the time of your moving. Additional gun-boats, supplies, and reïnforcements will be met at Harrison's Bar. Stimulate your men by informing them that reïnforcements, etc., have arrived at our new base. By command of MAJOR-GENERAL McCLELLAN, JAMES A. HARDIE, LIEUTENANT-COLONEL, A. D. C., A. A. A. G."

I.—HEADQUARTERS OF GENERAL HEINTZELMAN ON THE RIVER SIDE OF MALVERN HILL.
II.—TURKEY BRIDGE, UNDER MALVERN HILL. FROM WAR-TIME SKETCHES.

every prospect, if not direct promise, of large reënforcements for a renewal of the struggle on the south side of the James, and in the same manner as subsequently brought a successful termination of the war.

In the Fifth Corps, however, mourning was mingled with rejoicing. Greatly injured by the mishap of a cavalry blunder at Gaines's Mill, it had at Malvern, with the brave and gallant help of Couch and the generous and chivalric assistance of Heintzelman and Sumner, successfully repulsed the foe in every quarter, and was ready to renew the contest at an opportune moment. Our killed and wounded were numbered by thousands; the loss of the Confederates may be imagined. ↓

While taking Meagher's brigade to the front, I crossed a portion of the ground over which a large column had advanced to attack us, and had a fair opportunity of judging of the effect of our fire upon the ranks of the enemy.

↓ It is impossible to estimate the casualties of each of these battles, so quickly did one follow another. Our total loss in these battles is recorded as 15,849, while that of the Confederates sums up to 20,135. The loss in the Fifth Corps was 7601. This does not include the losses of Slocum's division and Cooke's cavalry engaged with us at Gaines's Mill, nor of Couch's division and the brigades of Caldwell, Meagher, and Sickles serving with it at Malvern. [See pp. 314-318.]—F. J. P.

GENERAL FITZ JOHN PORTER'S HEADQUARTERS IN THE WESTOVER MANSION, CAMP AT HARRISON'S LANDING, JULY, 1862, FROM A WAR TIME SKETCH.

It was something fearful and sad to contemplate; few steps could be taken without trampling upon the body of a dead or wounded soldier, or without hearing a piteous cry, begging our party to be careful. In some places the bodies were in continuous lines and in heaps. In Mexico I had seen fields of battle on which our armies had been victorious, and had listened to pitiful appeals; but the pleaders were not of my countrymen then, and did not, as now, cause me to deplore the effects of a fratricidal war.

Sadder still were the trying scenes I met in and around the Malvern house, which at an early hour that day had been given up to the wounded, and was soon filled with our unfortunate men, suffering from all kinds of wounds. At night, after issuing orders for the withdrawal of our troops, I passed through the building and the adjoining hospitals with my senior medical officer, Colonel George H. Lyman. Our object was to inspect the actual condition of the men, to arrange for their care and comfort, and to cheer them as best we could. Here, as usual, were found men mortally wounded, by necessity left unattended by the surgeons, so that prompt and proper care might be given to those in whom there was hope of recovery.

While passing through this improvised hospital I heard of many sad cases. One was that of the major of the 12th New York Volunteers, a brave and gallant officer, highly esteemed, who was believed to be mortally wounded. While breathing his last, as was supposed, a friend asked him if he had any message to leave. He replied, "Tell my wife that in my last thoughts were blended herself, my boy, and my flag." Then he asked how the battle had gone, and when told that we had been successful he said, "God bless the old fla——" and fell back apparently dead. For a long time he was mourned as dead, and it was believed that he had expired with the prayer left unfinished on his closing lips. Though still an invalid, suffering from the wound then received, that officer recovered to renew his career in the war.]

On the occasion of this visit we frequently witnessed scenes which would melt the stoutest heart: bearded men piteously begging to be sent home; others requesting that a widowed mother or orphan sisters might be cared for; more sending messages to wife or children, or to others near and dear to them. We saw the amputated limbs and the bodies of the dead hurried out of the room for burial. On every side we heard the appeals of the unattended, the moans of the dying, and the shrieks of those under the knife of the surgeon. We gave what cheer we could, and left with heavy hearts.

At noon on the 4th of July the usual national salute was fired, and the different corps were reviewed. General McClellan, as opportunity offered, made a few remarks full of hope and encouragement, thanking the men in most feeling terms for their uniform bravery, fortitude, and good conduct, but intimating that this was not the last of the campaign.

Contrary, however, to his expectations, the Peninsular campaign of the Army of the Potomac for 1862 virtually ended on the 4th of July. From that date to August 14th, when the army at sundown took up its march for Fort Monroe, its commander was engaged in the struggle to retain it on the James, as against the determination of the Secretary of War to withdraw it to the line of the Rappahannock, there to act in conjunction with the Army of Virginia.

Although General McClellan was assured, in writing, that he was to have command of both armies after their junction, he preferred, as a speedy and the only practicable mode of taking Richmond, to remain on the James, and

] Afterward Brevet Major-General Henry A. Barnum. — EDITORS.

SUPPLYING THE HUNGRY ARMY AT HARRISON'S LANDING. FROM A WAR-TIME SKETCH.

BERKELEY, HARRISON'S LANDING, AS SEEN FROM McCLELLAN'S HEADQUARTERS TENTS.   FROM A WAR-TIME SKETCH.

This house was the birthplace of General (afterward President) William Henry Harrison.
During the month of July, 1862, it was used as a hospital and signal station.

renew the contest from the south bank, for which he had commenced operations.] During this period he omitted nothing which would insure the removal of the army without loss of men and material. The withdrawal of the army changed the issue from the capture of Richmond to the security of Washington, transferred to the Federals the anxiety of the Confederates for their capital, and sounded an alarm throughout the Northern States.

[It was publicly announced that Halleck would assume command and take the field. Pope had reason to believe that "he would eventually supersede McClellan," and McDowell had been so satisfied of his future supremacy that he confided to a friend that "he would be at the highest round of the ladder."— F. J. P.

THE ARMY OF THE POTOMAC AT HARRISON'S LANDING.

BY GEORGE L. KILMER, CO. D, 27TH NEW YORK VOLUNTEERS.

THE withdrawal of General McClellan's army from Malvern Hill, a position that seemed to be impregnable, was a surprise to the men in the ranks, and for the first time in the campaign they became discouraged. During July 2d rain fell copiously, and when the columns arrived at Harrison's Landing the fields were soaked and the soil was quickly reduced to paste by the men and trains. The infantry and the division wagons and batteries were drawn up in an immense field of standing wheat near the Harrison mansion, also called Berkeley. The grain was trampled into the soil, or laid down so as to serve under the tents as protection from the wet ground. Neither wood nor boards were to be had, and the army was exceedingly uncomfortable. Transports in the James landed rations, which proved a great blessing, since many of the men had not had food in forty-eight hours. The rain continued all night, and the flimsy wheat floors were soon floating in pools of water; besides,

the soil would not hold the tent-pins, and in the morning the tents were nearly all down, exposing men whose beds were sinking deeper and deeper into the mud to the pelting rain. About 8 o'clock, while some of the men were yet asleep and others were attempting to get breakfast, the camp was startled by a sudden outburst of artillery fire, and shells came whistling over the plain. The shots were scattering, and seemed to be directed principally at the shipping. The troops were summoned to arms, but, as very little damage was done by the shells, the affair was soon turned to account as a joke. General J. E. B. Stuart for some days had been operating in the center of the Peninsula, and learning of the exposed position of McClellan's army on the James had hastened there and stationed his battery near Westover Church, across Herring Creek, north of the landing. A few shells from our gun-boats caused his guns to speedily shift their position, and General Nathan Kimball, of Shields's division (just arrived from the Shenandoah), advanced and cleared the field after some lively skirmishing.

The army immediately took position on the high ground about Harrison's Landing, and went into camp on an intrenched line several miles in extent. The air was filled with rumors about future operations. To the soldiers McClellan was less a hero now, perhaps, than before, but he was more a martial leader than ever. The unusual strain imposed upon the men, the malarial character of the region around Richmond, the lack of proper nourishment, the want of rest, combined with the excitement of the change of base, and the midsummer heat prostrated great numbers. In my notes written at the time, it is stated that 50 of the regiment, about 15 per cent. of the duty men, were sick in the camp hospital July 24th. This was in addition to the casualties of 162 sustained in the "Seven Days." According to the report of Surgeon Jonathan Letterman, Medical Director (Vol. XI., Part I., "Official Records," pp. 210-220), about 6000 sick were sent away soon after the army reached Harrison's Landing, over 12,000 remaining in camp. On July 30th, the report says, there were 12,000 sick with the army, and of these only 2000 were able to take the field. Fortunately the Sanitary Commission hastened to our relief with tents, food, medical supplies, and competent nurses.

‡ A Confederate force under General S. G. French had been sent out from the command of D. H. Hill, at Petersburg. General W. N. Pendleton reported that

After the departure of Stuart from Westover, July 4th, the army did not see or hear the enemy, with a slight exception, until search was made for him toward Richmond early in August. The exception was on the night of Thursday, July 31st. About midnight the whole army was startled by a lively cannonade and by shells flying over the lines, some bursting within them. The troops turned out under arms, and it was soon discovered that a mild fusillade from across the James was being directed on the shipping and on the supply depots near the camps.‡ Comparatively little damage was done. The next day a Union force was thrown across the river to seize Coggins's Point, where the elevated ground favored that style of attack on our camps. The army soon became restless for want of work, and there was great rejoicing at the prospect of a forward movement. On the 2d of August, Hooker marched a portion of his division to Malvern Hill, and on the 4th extended his advance to Charles City Cross-roads, near Glendale. But orders came to withdraw from the Peninsula, so we marched to Williamsburg, Yorktown, Newport News, and Fort Monroe. The Fifth and Third Corps embarked, on August 20th and 21st, for Aquia Creek and Alexandria; also for Alexandria the Sixth (Aug. 23d and 24th), the Second (Aug. 26th), and the Fourth (except Peck's division, which remained at Yorktown), Aug. 29th.

1000 rounds were fired. The casualties in the Union camps, as reported by General McClellan, were 10 killed and 15 wounded.—G. L. K.

DUMMIES AND QUAKER GUNS LEFT IN THE WORKS AT HARRISON'S LANDING ON THE EVACUATION BY THE ARMY OF THE POTOMAC. FROM A SKETCH MADE AT THE TIME.

WITH THE CAVALRY ON THE PENINSULA.

BY WILLIAM W. AVERELL, BREVET MAJOR-GENERAL, U. S. A.

A PART OF THE FORTIFIED CAMP AT HARRISON'S LANDING. AFTER A SKETCH MADE AT THE TIME.

IN the Peninsular campaign of 1862 there were employed fourteen regiments of cavalry, entire or in parts, and two independent squadrons [see p. 314]. Considerably over half this force was composed of volunteers, and had been in existence about six months. In the regular cavalry three years had been regarded as necessary to transform a recruit into a good cavalryman. The amount of patient and persistent hard work required to convert 1200 untrained citizens, unaccustomed to the care of a horse or to his use under the saddle, and wholly inexperienced in the use of arms, into the semblance of a cavalry regiment in six months is known only to those who have done it.

The topography and soil of the peninsula presented a most difficult field for cavalry operations. From Fort Monroe to Hanover Court House there was hardly a field with sufficient scope for the manœuvres of a single regiment of cavalry. After a rain the deep alluvium became, under the tread of horses, a bed of mortar knee-deep. The forests between the York and the James rivers were filled with tangled thickets and unapproachable morasses. The tributaries of the rivers, mostly deep, crooked, and sluggish, became more tortuous as they approach their confluence, and the expanse of floods is converted by evaporation into stagnant swamps. A heavy rain in a few hours rendered these streams formidable obstacles. Above this dismal landscape the fierce rays of the sun were interrupted only at night, or by deluges of rains, so that men and animals were alternately scorched and drenched. These conditions made cavalry operations in this region affairs of squadrons.

The cavalry had been organized into a division under General George Stoneman, chief of cavalry, and distributed by assignment to the corps of the army, excepting the cavalry reserve under General P. St. George Cooke and that portion which was attached to general headquarters. During the month of the siege of Yorktown not an hour was lost which could be applied to cavalry instruction. Alertness and steadiness soon characterized our cavalrymen. No incident was fruitless. When grindstones were procured and the sabers of my regiment were sharpened at Hampton, it produced a similar effect upon the men.

Few but cavalry names reached the ears of the army on the day of the evacuation and pursuit. Stoneman and Cooke, on the right, with the 1st and 6th Regulars, struck cavalry, infantry, batteries, redoubts, and ravines, and pushed their attack with audacity. Cavalrymen galloped around field-works. We soon heard of the gallantry of Colonel Grier, Major Lawrence Williams, Captains Sanders, Davis, Baker, and others in cavalry charges, and that the French Princes were among the first in the advance. Lieutenant-Colonel Grier, commanding the 1st ("Old Billy Grier, the *bueno commandante*"), had led a charge and engaged two of the enemy in personal combat, wounding one and himself receiving a wound. Then came tidings of the dash of Chambliss and McLean leading Hancock's column and crowding the left-center of the enemy's line, and soon the 3d Pennsylvania cavalry met the enemy in the woods and drove him out with skirmishers and canister, and cleared our left toward the James of the enemy's cavalry under Stuart. During the following day, the cavalry were spectators of the battle at Williamsburg (except the 3d Pennsylvania actively engaged on our left) and were only occupied with the rather serious business of procuring food for the horses.

Although pursuit was again undertaken on the morning of the 6th by squadrons of the 3d Pennsylvania and 8th Illinois Cavalry and was continued for four miles, and five pieces of artillery were recovered and some prisoners were captured, it came to a dead halt from necessity. During the succeeding twenty days the cavalry swept the country in advance of our marching army by day and hovered around its bivouacs by night.

When the army was in line about seven miles from Richmond, on the 25th of May, I was directed to communicate with the gun-boats on the James River at City Point. Lieutenant Davis, of the 3d Pennsylvania, with ten men, was selected for the duty, and he made his way along various roads infested with the pickets and patrols of the enemy to the bank of the James, where, taking a skiff, with two negroes, he went on board the *Galena* and communicated to Captain Rodgers the position of the army, and received from the captain a statement of the position of the gun-boats.

On the 27th, not satisfied with the picnic appearance of our front on our left, south of the Chickahominy, I reported its perilous condition to McClellan, who at once sent Colonel N. B. Sweitzer, of his staff, to me, and together we rode to the front. As a result, orders were given at once for slashing the forest, and positions for batteries and outposts were determined,—precautions which, three days later, disclosed their value in the battle of Fair Oaks.

On the same day (27th) we were scratching the ground away up to our right at Hanover Court House, in invitation to McDowell to come down from Fredericksburg. Almost within his sight, and quite within his hearing, the principal northern gate to Richmond was set ajar, the Virginia Central and the Richmond and Fredericksburg railroads were destroyed. In the resultant mêlée about Hanover Court House, the cavalry, under Emory, Royall, Lawrence Williams, Chambliss, Whiting, Harrison, and Arnold, and Rush's 6th Pennsylvania, aggressively attacked infantry, captured whole companies with arms, swept right, left, and rear, and generally filled the ideal of cavalry activities in such a battle.

General Lee assumed command June 1st. On the 13th he announced himself, through his cavalry, in Stuart's raid around our army. This expedition was appointed with excellent judgment, and was conducted with superb address. Stuart pursued the line of least resistance, which was the unexpected. His subordinate commanders were Colonels Fitz Lee, W. H. F. Lee, and W. T. Martin, all intrepid cavalrymen. It was an easy thing to do, but being his first raid, Stuart was nervous, and, imagining perils which did not exist, neglected one great opportunity — the destruction of our base of supplies at the White House. Had he, at Garlick's, exchanged purposes with his detachment, sending it on the road home while he with the main body bent all his energies to the destruction of our base of supplies, we might have had something to lament even had we captured his command. On our side were developed many things to remember with pride, and one thing to regret with mortification. The memories are glorious that not a single vedette or picket was surprised, and that never was outpost duty more honorably and correctly performed than by Captain W. B. Royall and Lieutenant McLean of the 5th United States Cavalry. They met the enemy repeatedly, and the lieutenant gave his life and the captain was prostrated with saber wounds in resisting Stuart's column. The killing of the dashing Confederate Captain Latané and several men with the saber, and the checking of the invading forces for an hour attest the courage and devotion of Royall and his picket. We had to regret that there was no reserve to the outpost within supporting distance, and that when the reserve was alarmed in its camp precious time was lost by indirections. This raid of Stuart's added a new feature to cavalry history. A similar expedition, however, had been projected previously. Just before the Army of the Potomac advanced on Manassas, in March, '62, in a conference with General McClellan, it was suggested that I

should take my brigade, consisting of the 3d and 8th Pennsylvania Cavalry, the first brigade of cavalry formed in the war, and go around the enemy, then at Manassas, destroying the bridge at Rappahannock Station, and that at Fredericksburg; but the immediate movement of the enemy from Manassas prevented its being carried out.

Our general's plans were not disturbed by Stuart's raid, and two days after it was over the 3d Pennsylvania Cavalry crossed the Pamunkey River on our right and rear, ascended to King William Court House and Ellett's Mills, burned the bridge and ferry-boat, and a schooner and other boats, and a storehouse containing 30,000 bushels of grain. Scouts were pushed out many miles in quest of news of Jackson's coming. This was the last extension of our hands toward McDowell, for Jackson came sooner than he was expected, on the 26th, the day upon which a general advance had been determined and the battle of Gaines's Mill was opened.

McClellan met and mastered the occasion. Alert, radiant, and cheerful, he stood out in front of his tent in his shirt-sleeves nearly all day of the 26th listening to his army. To the north, across the Chickahominy, his clipped right wing, environed with our cavalry, was sullenly retracting its lines to the position at Gaines's Mill. Stoneman, with infirmities that would have kept a man of less fortitude in hospital, was in the saddle confronting Stuart's cavalry and covering the White House Landing.

The ensuing night was without rest for the cavalry. The strain of the following day to help the Fifth Corps to hold its ground until dark will never be forgotten, and it was not devoid of heroic cavalry effort. Fragments of the reserve under General Cooke stood massed in the valley of the Chickahominy, on its left bank. About 5 P. M., when it was evident that we were being pressed on the right and left of our line by all the force the enemy could bring into action against Porter, and that we were not likely to be able to resist his attack, the cavalry was moved from its masked position to the edge of the hill and placed in a formation to charge, should a charge seem likely to do good. It was there exposed to the enemy's fire, and must either retire, advance, or be destroyed. In a few minutes the order to charge was given to the 5th Regulars, not 300 strong. Chambliss, leading, rode as straight as man ever rode, into the face of Longstreet's corps, and the 5th Cavalry was destroyed and dispersed. Six out of the seven officers present and fifty men were struck down. Chambliss, hit by seven balls, lost consciousness, and when he recovered found himself in the midst of the enemy. The charge at Balaklava had not this desperation and was not better ridden. Chambliss lay on the field ten days, and was finally taken to Richmond, where he was rescued from death by the kind care of Generals Hood and Field. In this battle there were two and a half squadrons of the 5th and two squadrons of the 1st U. S. Cavalry, three squadrons Rush's Lancers (6th Pennsylvania Cavalry), and one squadron 4th Pennsylvania (Col. Childs).

Two or three weeks before this several officers of the 3d Pennsylvania Cavalry, Newhall, Treichel, W. E. Miller, and others, penetrated the region between the Chickahominy and the James, taking bearings and making notes. Their fragmentary sketches, when put together, made a map which exhibited all the roadways, fields, forests, bridges, the streams, and houses, so that our commander knew the country to be traversed through the seven days far better than any Confederate commander.

On the evening of June 27th, my pickets from Tunstall's Station and other points were called in, and at 6:30 A. M., on the 28th, the regiment crossed White Oak Swamp, leading Keyes's corps, and advanced to the Charles City road. Lieutenant Davis was again sent to communicate with the gun-boats on the James.

At daylight, on the 29th, Captain White's squadron, with 200 infantry and 2 guns, was sent to picket and hold Jones's Bridge on the Chickahominy. About 9 A. M. my scouts reported a regiment of the enemy's cavalry advancing in column about a mile away. Some woodland intervened. Between this and my position was an open field a quarter of a mile across. A picket was quickly posted at the hither edge of the wood, with orders to fire upon the enemy when he should come within range and then turn and run away, thus inviting pursuit. On my position two guns were already placed to enfilade the road, and a few squadrons held in readiness to charge. The enemy came, was fired upon, and the picket fled, followed by the enemy in hot pursuit. Upon arriving within two hundred yards of our position, the picket quitted the road through the gaps in the fences made for that purpose, thus unmasking the enemy's column; the two guns of Major West fired two rounds, and two squadrons, led by Captains Walsh and Russell, of the 3d Pennsylvania, were let loose upon the enemy, and over 60 of his officers and men were left on the ground, whilst the survivors fled in great disorder toward Richmond. The command was the 1st North Carolina and 3d Virginia Cavalry, led by Colonel Lawrence Baker, a comrade of mine in the old army. The 3d Pennsylvania lost 1 man killed and 5 wounded.

After this affair I galloped back to see General McClellan, and found him near a house south of White Oak Swamp Bridge. Near him were groups of a hundred officers eagerly but quietly discussing our progress and situation. So soon as McClellan descried me, he came with the Prince de Joinville to the fence, where I dismounted. After telling him all I knew and had learned from prisoners and scouts, I ventured to suggest that the roads were tolerably clear toward Richmond, and that we might go there. The Prince seemed to exhibit a favorable interest in my suggestion, but the general, recognizing its weakness, said promptly: "The roads will be full enough to-morrow"; and then earnestly, "Averell, if any army can save this country, it will be the Army of the Potomac, and it must be saved for that purpose." The general rode to the front with me, and reconnoitered the ground in all directions. In the afternoon, with Hays's regiment of infantry and Benson's

battery, I established our outposts and pickets within one mile of New Market, where we were first touched with some of the enemy's infantry during the night. On the 30th, there were battles on our center and right, and having joined the Fifth Corps, I proceeded to Malvern Hill in the evening and rode over the field with Captain Colburn, my classmate and the favorite aide of McClellan, and made a topographical sketch of the position, which was of some use afterward in posting the infantry and artillery as they arrived.

During the night of the 30th, the general commanding asked me for two officers for hazardous service. Lieutenants Newhall and Treichel, because of their intimate knowledge of the country, were sent to communicate with our right and center, and a second time that night made their way for a mile and a half through the enemy's camps.

During the battle of July 1st (Malvern Hill), my cavalry was deployed as a close line of skirmishers with drawn sabers in rear of our lines, with orders to permit no one to pass to the rear who could not show blood. The line of battle was ready and reserves of infantry and artillery in position some time before the enemy came in force and developed his attack. There were some preliminary bursts of artillery, but the great crash of all arms did not begin before 6 P. M. It lasted about two hours. The commanding general, with his mounted staff, was standing on the plateau in front of the farm-house at the rear verge of the hill, a conspicuous group, when a round shot from the enemy struck the ground a few yards directly in front of him and threw dirt and gravel over the little group around him. General Porter, with whom I was riding, had just started toward the front when he turned and said to McClellan: "General, everything is all right here and you are not needed; if you will look after our center and right that would help us here more than you can by remaining." Then we separated from them and rode toward our left, at Crew's house. The wounded were already coming away from the lines.

When the battle was over and the field had become quiet, the cavalry bivouacked half a mile in rear of the line of battle. Men and horses were too tired to do aught but sleep for hours. At midnight I found myself in the saddle with a cup of hot coffee held to my lips, a portion of its contents having scalded its way down my throat. When awakened I was informed by the Duc de Chartres that General McClellan desired to see me. We found him near by, in a little orchard by a campfire, giving orders rapidly to his generals and staff-officers. When my turn came, McClellan said: "Averell I want you to take command of the rear-guard at daylight in the morning, and hold this position until our trains are out of the way. What force do you want?" I asked for just enough to cover the front with a strong skirmish line. The orders were given for Buchanan's brigade of Sykes's division, Fifth Corps, to report to me at daylight, and also a battery.

At daylight the cavalry advanced toward the front. There was a fog so dense that we could not see a man at fifty paces distance. Colonel

Buchanan was met with his staff returning from the front on foot, their horses being led. He informed me that the enemy was threatening his pickets, and advancing on both flanks. I asked him to halt his command until further orders, and galloped to the front, where our line of battle had been the night before. I could see nothing, but could hear shrieks, and groans, and the murmur of a multitude, but no sounds of wheels nor trampling horses. I ordered the line reëstablished, with skirmishers and a squadron of cavalry on either flank. Colonel Hall, with the 2d Regiment Excelsior Brigade, also reported for duty, and took position in the line. The battery not having reported, some cavalry was organized into squads, resembling sections of artillery, at proper intervals behind the crest. By this time the level rays of the morning sun from our right were just penetrating the fog, and slowly lifting its clinging shreds and yellow masses. Our ears had been filled with agonizing cries from thousands before the fog was lifted, but now our eyes saw an appalling spectacle upon the slopes down to the woodlands half a mile away. Over five thousand dead and wounded men were on the ground, in every attitude of distress. A third of them were dead or dying, but enough were alive and moving to give to the field a singular crawling effect. The different stages of the ebbing tide are often marked by the lines of flotsam and jetsam left along the sea-shore. So here could be seen three distinct lines of dead and wounded marking the last front of three Confederate charges of the night before. Groups of men, some mounted, were groping about the field.

As soon as the woodland beyond, which masked the enemy, could be clearly seen, I offered battle by directing the infantry lines to show on the crest, the sham sections of artillery to execute the movements of going "into battery, action front," and the flank squadrons to move toward the enemy until fired upon. All these details were executed simultaneously at the sound of the trumpet. The squadrons had not proceeded three hundred yards when they were fired upon and halted. At the same time, a horseman from among those on the field approached our line with a white flag. An aide was sent to meet and halt him. The Confederate horseman, who was an officer, requested a truce of two hours in which to succor their wounded. I was about to send a demand that his request be put in writing, when I reflected that it would be embarrassing for me to reply in writing, so word was sent to him to dismount and wait until his request had been submitted to the commanding general. In the meantime the scattered parties of the enemy withdrew hastily from the field to the woods, and there was some threatening desultory firing on my flanks, killing one man and wounding another. After waiting thirty minutes, word was sent to the officer with the flag that the truce was granted, and that their men could come out without arms, and succor their wounded. I had no idea that the flag was properly authorized, else there would have been no firing on my flanks, but time was the precious thing I wished to gain for our trains which crowded the bottom-lands below Malvern. My squadrons were withdrawn to the line, the infantry lay down, while officers took position in front of the line to prevent conversation with the enemy. In a few minutes thousands of men swarmed from the woods and scattered over the field. I kept myself informed by couriers of the movements of our army and trains, and had already sent officers to reassure our rear of its security, and also to bring me back a battery of artillery. Captain Frank with his battery responded. I sent a request to General Wessells, commanding Keyes's rear brigade, to select a good position about two miles in my rear in case I should need a checking force when the time for withdrawal should come. That excellent soldier had already chosen such a position and established his brigade in line of battle.

When the quasi-truce had expired, at the sound of the trumpet, the line resumed its attitude of attack, and the officer with the flag again appeared with a request that the truce be extended two hours. After a reasonable wait, answer was returned that the time was extended but that no further extension would be granted. I had come on the line at 4 A. M., and these manœuvres and truces had consumed the time until after 9 o'clock. The Army of the Potomac was then at its new base on the James, and all its trains were safely on the way there, with Keyes's corps some miles below in my rear awaiting the enemy. So when the extended truce had expired, my command, with the exception of the cavalry, had left the field. Our dead and wounded, about 2500 in number, had been cared for during the night. Not above a dozen bodies could be found on our field during the truce, and these were buried. Twelve stalled and abandoned wagons were destroyed, and two captured guns which could not be removed were spiked and their carriages were broken. The 3d Pennsylvania Cavalry, which had led the Army of the Potomac across White Oak Swamp, now saw its last serviceable man safe beyond Malvern Hill, before it left that glorious field, about 10 A. M., July 2d. A heavy rainstorm was prevailing. When everything movable was across Turkey Bridge it was destroyed by my rear squadron. My command passed through Wessells's lines about noon, and the lines of General Naglee a little later. Everything was now quiet and in good order, and the 3d Pennsylvania proceeded to camp at Westover after dark.

The 8th Pennsylvania Cavalry, under Colonel D. McM. Gregg, had scoured the left bank of the Chickahominy, on the 28th, and had swum the river to the right bank, rafting its arms across at Long Bridge. He subsequently picketed the front of our center and right on the 30th, and on July 1st and 2d — an extremely important service. The 4th Pennsylvania Cavalry, after its efficient service, at and about Gaines's Mill, during the day and night of the 27th of June, performed similar duties with General McCall at Charles City road on the 30th. The 11th Pennsylvania, Colonel Harlan, which, on the 13th, had covered the White House Landing during Stuart's raid, on the 28th, joined Stoneman on similar duty, and retired with him.

Colonel Farnsworth, 8th Illinois, after his active

participation in covering our right wing on the 26th, and guiding trains and maintaining steadiness of lines on the 27th, guided Keyes's corps to the James River below Malvern, on the 29th, and assisted the 8th Pennsylvania in covering that corps on the 30th and 1st of July. The 2d U. S. Cavalry and McClellan Dragoons, under Major Pleasonton, escorted Colonel B. S. Alexander, of the Corps of Engineers, on the 29th, to Carter's Landing, on the James. Captains Norris and Green, of the 2d, performed scouting service in the direction of the Chickahominy and Charles City Court House, after the arrival of the regiment on the James. And so ended the first lesson of the cavalry service of the Army of the Potomac. ☆

Near the White House, on the morning of the 29th of June (at the very time that the 3d Pennsylvania Cavalry was repelling the 1st North Carolina and 3d Virginia Cavalry at Willis Church, south of the Chickahominy), Stuart received a note from General Lee asking for his impressions in regard to the designs of the Union Army. He replied that there was no evidence of a retreat down the Williamsburg road, and that he had no doubt that it was endeavoring to reach the James. On the 30th, while we were establishing our advance on Malvern Hill, Stuart, north of the Chickahominy, was directing his cavalry columns toward the bridges of that river behind us. Had the disposition of his forces been reversed at the outset, and had he, with his main body, gone to Charles City road and obstructed and defended the crossings of White Oak Swamp, he could have annoyed and perhaps embarrassed our movements. Finally, had his cavalry ascertained on July 1st, any time before 3 P. M., that the center

and right of our lines were more vulnerable and favorable to attack than the left, the enemy need not have delivered the unsuccessful and disastrous assault on Malvern Hill, but, while maintaining a strong demonstration at that point, might have thrown two or three corps upon our center below Malvern with hopes of dividing the Union Army. Undoubtedly Gregg and Farnsworth, with the 8th Pennsylvania and 8th Illinois cavalry, would have successfully prevented the reconnoissance of our center and right, but that it was not attempted was a discredit to Stuart's cavalry.

At Harrison's Landing, General Stoneman having taken sick-leave and General Cooke having been relieved, on the 5th of July I was appointed acting Brigadier-General and placed in command of all the cavalry of the Army of the Potomac, and at once issued orders organizing it into a cavalry corps, and the history of cavalry brigades was begun. Stoneman, returning the same day, resumed command, and I took the First Brigade, composed of the 5th United States, the 3d and 4th Pennsylvania, and the 1st New York Cavalry.

Active scouting followed in the direction of Richmond and up the Chickahominy. On the 3d of August I crossed the James, with the 5th United States and 3d Pennsylvania Cavalry, to explore the ways to Petersburg, encountering the 13th Virginia Cavalry in a charge led by Lieutenant McIntosh, of the 5th United States, supported by Captain Miller, of the 3d Pennsylvania. The enemy was driven over seven miles, and his camp and supplies destroyed.

All the successes and sacrifices of the army were now to be worse than lost — they were to be thrown away by the withdrawal of the army from the Peninsula, instead of reënforcing it.

☆ The total losses of our cavalry reported in the Seven Days' battles was 284; that of the Confederates 71, of which number 61 were credited to the 3d Pennsylvania Cavalry, at Willis Church, on the 29th of June.—W. W. A.

ROLL-BOOK OF CO. D, 27TH NEW YORK REGIMENT. FROM THE "HISTORY OF THE 27TH NEW YORK VOLUNTEERS."

The scars show where a bullet passed through the roll-book and entered the heart of Lieutenant (formerly Orderly-Sergeant) John L. Bailey, who carried the roll-book in his breast-pocket. Lieutenant Bailey was shot by a Confederate picket named W. Hartley, of the 4th Alabama, the night of May 6th, 1862, at West Point on the York River. Hartley was shot and instantly killed by Corporal H. M. Crocker, whose name, the eighth in the list of corporals, was obliterated by the tear and the blood-stains.— EDITORS.

THE REAR-GUARD AT MALVERN HILL.

I.—BY HENRY E. SMITH, BREVET MAJOR, U. S. A.

REFERRING to the retreat from Malvern Hill, July 2d, General McClellan gives Keyes's corps the credit of furnishing the entire rear-guard. According to the report of Colonel Averell, of the 3d Pennsylvania Cavalry, the rear-guard was made his command and consisted of his regiment of Heintzelman's corps, First Brigade of Regular Infantry, consisting of the 3d, 4th, 12th, and 14th Infantry, of Porter's corps, and the New York Chasseurs, of Keyes's corps. The "Official Records," Vol. XI., Part II., p. 235, confirm this statement. In the same volume, p. 193, will be found Keyes's official report, but no mention of Averell. In fact, Averell was the rear-guard to Turkey Bridge and a mile beyond that point, where he found General Wessells of Keyes's corps. The official reports of Fitz John Porter, Sykes, and Buchanan all speak of Averell as having covered this retreat. The writer was a first lieutenant in the 12th Infantry, and in command of Company D, First Battalion, at Malvern Hill, and remembers distinctly that the First Brigade of Regulars slept on the field on the night of July 1st in line of battle. We were surprised the next morning to find that the entire army had retreated during the night, leaving Averell with his small command as a rear-guard to cover the retreat, which was done in the masterly manner stated by General McClellan, but by Averell, and not by Keyes.

UNITED SERVICE CLUB, PHILADELPHIA, May 25th, 1885.

II.—BY ERASMUS D. KEYES, MAJOR-GENERAL, U. S. V.

A FEW days ago, in Switzerland, my attention was called to a communication in the August [1885] number of "The Century," p. 642, which falsifies history. It is under the heading, "The Rear-Guard after Malvern Hill," and is signed Henry E. Smith. Mr. Smith asserts that it was General Averell who commanded the rear-guard, and that to Averell, and not to Keyes, belongs the credit which General McClellan gives the latter in his article. Mr. Smith cites authorities for his statements, and refers to the "Official Records of the Rebellion," Vol. XI., Part II., p. 235, and to my report, p. 193, same volume, in which he says there is "no mention of Averell." It is not unreasonable to suppose that Mr. Smith had read General McClellan's and my reports, since he refers to them, but it is certain that he discredits both, and that he rejects my claim to approval unceremoniously [see p. 435]. General McClellan says, in his book, "Report . . . of the Army of the Potomac," etc., p. 273:

"The greater portion of the transportation of the army having been started for Harrison's Landing during the night of the 30th of June and the 1st of July, the order for the movement of the troops was at once issued upon the final repulse of the enemy at Malvern Hill. The order prescribed a movement by the left and rear, General Keyes's corps to cover the manœuvre. It was not carried out in detail as regards the divisions on the left, the roads being somewhat blocked by the rear of our trains. Porter and Couch were not able to move out as early as had been anticipated, and Porter found it necessary to place a rear-guard between his command and the enemy. Colonel Averell, of the 3d Pennsylvania Cavalry, was intrusted with this delicate duty. He had under his command his own regiment and Lieutenant-Colonel Buchanan's brigade of regular infantry and one battery. By a judicious use of the resources at his command, he deceived the enemy so as to cover the withdrawal of the left wing without being attacked, remaining himself on the previous day's battle-field until about 7 o'clock of the 2d of July. Meantime General Keyes, having received his orders, commenced vigorous preparations for covering the movement of the entire army, and protecting the trains. It being evident that the immense number of wagons and artillery pertaining to the army could not move with celerity along a single road, General Keyes took advantage of every accident of the ground to open new avenues, and to facilitate the movement. He made preparations for obstructing the roads after the army had passed, so as to prevent any rapid pursuit, destroying effectually Turkey Bridge, on the main road, and rendering other roads and approaches temporarily impassable, by felling trees across them. He kept the trains well closed up, and directed the march so that the troops could move on each side of the road, not obstructing the passage, but being in good position to repel an attack from any quarter. His dispositions were so successful that, to use his own words, 'I do not think that more vehicles or more public property were abandoned on the march from Turkey Bridge than would have been left, in the same state of the roads, if the army had been moving toward the enemy, instead of away from him'—and when it is understood that the carriages and teams belonging to this army, stretched out in one line, would extend not far from forty miles, the energy and caution necessary for their safe withdrawal from the presence of an enemy vastly superior in numbers, will be appreciated. . . . Great credit must be awarded to General Keyes for the skill and energy which characterized his performance of the important and delicate duties intrusted to his charge."

The above extract defines General Averell's duties on the field of Malvern, and gives him credit, and it is equally distinct in reference to me, but General McClellan's article is vague in its expressions regarding the same subjects. As Mr. Smith's article is historically erroneous, I trust you will consider it just to give place to this explanation, and to the following short account of "The Rear-Guard after Malvern Hill."

After the battle of Malvern Hill, which was fought on the 1st of July, 1862, the army retired to Harrison's Landing. Late in the evening of that day I received orders from Adjutant-General Seth Williams to command the rear-guard. I spent nearly the whole night making preparatory arrangements; dispatched a party to destroy Turkey Bridge; selected twenty-five expert axe-men under Captain Clarke, 8th Illinois Cavalry, with orders to chop nearly through all the large trees that lined the road below the bridge. All my orders were well executed, and within fifteen minutes after the tail of the column passed, the bridge was destroyed without blowing up, and the road blocked beyond the possibility of passage by wheels and cavalry, and made difficult for infantry for several hours.

The force composing the rear-guard consisted of Peck's division of infantry and four batteries of artillery of my own corps, Gregg's 8th Pennsylvania Cavalry and Farnsworth's 8th Illinois Cavalry. Averell's regiment of cavalry was also designated in a dispatch sent me by Adjutant-General Williams, and he may have taken part below the bridge, but I do not remember to have seen him during the day.

The danger to the trains arose from the fact that the narrow country roads were insufficient in number, and their composition was mostly clay, which was soon converted into mud by the torrents of rain which fell nearly the whole day, and from the liability to attack on the flank. The main road was skirted with woods on the left the entire distance, which is about seven miles from Turkey Bridge to Harrison's Landing. The opposite side of the main road was open, and the columns of troops could move parallel with the wagons. When General W. F. Smith came along at the head of his division, I was opposite an opening in the woods at the highest point of the road. Smith exclaimed to me: "Here's a good place for a battle!" "Would you like to have a fight?" said I. "Yes; just here, and now!" While the columns of troops were moving alongside the trains I felt no apprehension, but after they had all passed there still remained in rear not less than five hundred wagons struggling in the mud, and it was not above ten minutes after the last vehicle had entered the large field bordering the intended camp when the enemy appeared and commenced a cannonade upon us. Fortunately I had in position Miller's and Mc-Carthy's batteries, and they replied with such effect that the attack was discontinued.

The anxiety at headquarters was such that I was authorized, in case of necessity, to cut the traces and drive the animals forward without their loads. Nothing of that kind was done, and we saved all the wagons except a small number that broke down and were as necessarily abandoned as a vessel in a convoy would be after it had sunk in the ocean.

About the middle of the day I received a note from headquarters at Harrison's Landing, of which the following is a copy:

"GENERAL: I have ordered back to your assistance all the cavalry that can be raised here. It is of the utmost importance that we should save all our artillery, and as many of our wagons as possible; and the commanding general feels the utmost confidence that you will do all that can be done to accomplish this. Permit me to say that if you bring in everything you will accomplish a most signal and meritorious exploit, which the commanding general will not fail to represent in its proper light to the Department. Very respectfully,

R. B. MARCY,
"*Chief of Staff.*

July 2d.
"BRIGADIER-GENERAL KEYES."

General McClellan came out half a mile and met me. I was engaged sending forward sheaves of wheat to fill the ruts in the road near camp, which were so deep that in spite of all efforts to fill them, about 1200 wagons were parked for the night under guard outside. The general appeared well satisfied with what had been done by the rear-guard, and after all the proofs cited above, it is scarcely probable that he made a mistake in the name of its commander.

BLANGY, SEINE-INFÉRIEURE, FRANCE, August 20, 1885.

THE ADMINISTRATION IN THE PENINSULAR CAMPAIGN.

BY RICHARD B. IRWIN, LIEUTENANT-COLONEL AND ASSISTANT ADJUTANT-GENERAL, U. S. V.

THE views entertained by General McClellan as to the manner and extent to which his plans and operations on the Peninsula were interfered with or supported by the Government having been fully set forth by him in these pages, it is now proper to show, as far as this can be done from the official reports, how the case must have presented itself to the President and the Secretary of War.

Appointed on the 25th of July, 1861, immediately after Bull Run, to the command of the shattered and reduced forces then gathered about Washington, at one time not exceeding 42,000 all told, General McClellan was rapidly reënforced, until on the 15th of March, 1862, he had under his command within the division or department of the Potomac 203,213 men present for duty. The field-artillery was increased from 30 guns to 520; to these had been added a siege train of nearly 100 heavy guns. From these materials he organized the Army of the Potomac.

In the last days of October General McClellan presented to the Secretary of War a written statement of his views as to the conduct of operations, in which, after representing the Confederate forces in his front at not less than 150,000, his own movable force as 76,285, with 228 guns, and the force required for active operations as 150,000 men, with 400 guns, he recommended that all operations in other quarters be confined to the defensive, and that all surplus troops be sent to reënforce the Army of the Potomac.

"A vigorous employment of these means [he proceeds] will, in my opinion, enable the Army of the Potomac to assume successfully this season the offensive operations which, ever since entering upon the command, it has been my anxious desire and diligent effort to prepare for and prosecute. The advance should not be postponed beyond the 25th of November, if possible to avoid it.

"Unity in councils, the utmost vigor and energy in action are indispensable. The entire military field should be grasped as a whole, and not in detached parts. One plan should be agreed upon and pursued: a single will should direct and carry out these plans. The great object to be accomplished, the crushing defeat of the rebel army (now) at Manassas, should never for one instant be lost sight of, but all the intellect and means and men of the Government poured upon that point."

On the 1st of November, 1861, the President, "with the concurrence of the entire Cabinet," designated General McClellan "to command the whole army" of the United States. No trust approaching this in magnitude had ever before been confided to any officer of the United States.

Everywhere the armies remained inactive. For seven months the Army of the Potomac was held within the defenses of Washington. Its only important movement had resulted in the disheartening disaster of Ball's Bluff. The Confederates, with headquarters at Manassas, confronted them with an army, represented by General McClellan, on the faith of his secret-service department, as numbering at least 115,500, probably 150,000, but now known to have at no time exceeded 63,000. ⌡ The Potomac was closed to navigation by Confederate batteries established on its banks within twenty-three miles of the capital. Norfolk, with its navy-yard, was left untouched and unmenaced. The loyal States had furnished three-quarters of a million of soldiers, and the country had rolled up a daily increasing war debt of $600,000,000. There is no indication that General McClellan appreciated, or even perceived, the consequences that must inevitably follow the loss of confidence on the part of the people, as month after month passed without action and without success in any quarter, or the position in which, under these circumstances, he placed the President, with respect to the continued support of the people and and their representatives, by withholding full information of his plans. In his "Own Story" he tells how he refused to give this information when called upon by the President in the presence of his Cabinet.

The President having, on the 31st of January, ordered the movement of all the disposable force of the Army of the Potomac, for the purpose of seizing a point on the railroad beyond Manassas Junction, General McClellan on the same day submitted his own plan for moving on Richmond by way of Urbana, on the lower Rappahannock. On the 8th of March, yielding to General McClellan's views, supported by the majority of his division commanders, the President approved the Urbana movement, with certain conditions; but on the 9th the Confederates evacuated Manassas, and thus rendered the whole plan inoperative. On the 13th, upon General McClellan's recommendation, supported by the commanders of all four of the newly constituted army corps, the President authorized the movement by Fort Monroe, as it was finally made.

McClellan expected to take with him to the Peninsula 146,000 men of all arms, to be increased to 156,000 by a division to be drawn from Fort Monroe. On the 31st of March, the President informed him that he had been obliged to order Blenker's division of about 10,000 men, ⚓ with 18 guns, to Frémont. "I did this with great pain," he says, "knowing that you would wish it otherwise. If you could know the full pressure of the case, I am confident you would approve."

The council of corps commanders had annexed to their approval, among other conditions, the following: "Fourth, that the force to be left to cover Washington shall be such as to give an entire feeling of security for its safety from menace. . . . NOTE.—That with the forts on the right bank of the Potomac fully garrisoned and those on the left bank occupied, a covering force in front of the Virginia line of 25,000 men would suffice (Keyes, Heintzelman, and McDowell). A total of 40,000 men for the defense of the city would suffice. (Sumner.)" Upon this point the President's orders were: "1st. Leave such a force at Manassas Junction as shall make it entirely certain that the enemy shall not repossess himself of that position and line of communication. 2d. Leave Washington secure."

On the 1st of April, as he was on the point of sailing, General McClellan reported from his headquarters on board the steamer *Commodore*, the arrangements he had made to carry out these provisions, and at once set out for Fort Monroe without knowing whether they were satisfactory to the Government or not. They were not. General McClellan had arranged to leave 7780 men at Warrenton, 10,859 at Manassas, 1350 on the Lower Potomac, and 18,000 men for the garrisons and the front of Washington, to be augmented by about 4000 new troops from New York. The President, deeming this provision wholly insufficient for the defense of the capital, ordered McDowell with his corps of 33,510 men and 68 guns to remain, and charged him with the duty of covering and defending Washington.

This led to a telegraphic correspondence, thus characterized in the President's letter to General McClellan, dated April 9th: "Your dispatches complaining that you are not properly sustained, while they do not offend me, pain me very much." Then, after again explaining the detachment of Blenker and the retention of McDowell, Mr. Lincoln concludes with these noteworthy admonitions: "I suppose the whole force which has gone forward to you is with you by this time; and if so, I think it is the precise time for you to strike a blow. By delay, the enemy will steadily gain on you — that is, he will gain faster by fortifications and reënforcements than you can by reënforcements alone.

"And once more, let me tell you, it is indispensable to *you* ↓ that you strike a blow! I am powerless to help this. You will do me the justice to remember I always insisted that going down the bay in search of a field instead of fighting at or near Manassas, was only shifting and not surmounting a difficulty; that we would find the same enemy and the same or equal intrenchments at either place. The country will not fail to note — is noting now — that the present hesitation to move upon an intrenched enemy is but the story of Manassas repeated.

"I beg to assure you that I have never written or spoken to you in greater kindness of feeling than now, nor with a fuller purpose to sustain you, so far as in my most anxious judgment I consistently can. *But you must act.*" ↓

On the 11th of April, Franklin's division was

⌡ Of which only 44,563 were at Manassas.

↓ Original italicized.

⚓ General McClellan's figures. The latest return, Feb. 28th, showed 8396 for duty. — R. B. I.

ordered to the Peninsula, in response to General McClellan's earnest renewal of his request.

General McClellan estimates his force before Franklin's arrival at 85,000, apparently meaning fighting men, since the returns show 105,235 present for duty on the 13th of April. On the 30th, including Franklin, this number was increased to 112,392. General McClellan also estimated the Confederate forces at "probably not less than 100,000 men, and possibly more,"["probably greater a good deal than my own."] We now know that their total effective strength on the 30th of April was 55,633 of all arms. When the Army of the Potomac halted before the lines of the Warwick, Magruder's whole force was but 11,000. General McClellan estimated it at only 15,000, and his own, confronting it, at the same period, at 53,000.

The plan of a rapid movement up the Peninsula having resolved itself into an endeavor to take Yorktown by regular approaches in front, leaving its rear necessarily open, General McClellan thus describes the result:

"Our batteries would have been ready to open on the morning of the 6th of May at latest; but on the morning of the 4th it was discovered that the enemy had already been compelled to evacuate his position during the night."

The effect of these delays on Mr. Lincoln's mind is curiously indicated by his telegram of May 1st:

"Your call for Parrott guns from Washington alarms me, chiefly because it argues indefinite procrastination. Is anything to be done?"

Then followed the confused and unduly discouraging battle of Williamsburg; the attempt to cut off the Confederate retreat by a landing at West Point came to nothing; and on the 20th of May, the Army of the Potomac, having moved forward 52 miles in 16 days, reached the banks of the Chickahominy. There it lay, astride of that sluggish stream, imbedded in its pestilential swamps, for thirty-nine days.

On the 31st of May, at Fair Oaks, Johnston failed, though narrowly missing success, in a well-meant attempt to crush McClellan's forces on the right bank of the swollen stream before they could be reënforced. On the 1st of June the Confederate forces were driven back in disorder upon the defenses of Richmond, but the damage suffered by the Union forces on the first day being over-estimated, and their success on the second day insufficiently appreciated, or inadequately represented, and no apparent advantage being taken of them, the general effect was to add to the discouragement already prevailing.

Reënforcements continuing to be urgently called for, Fort Monroe, with its dependencies, reporting 9277 for duty, was placed under General McClellan's orders; McCall's division, with 22 guns, was detached from McDowell, and arrived by water 9514 strong on the 12th and 13th of June; while McDowell, with the rest of his command, was ordered to march to join McClellan by land: this movement was, however, promptly brought to

naught by Jackson's sudden incursion against Banks in the Shenandoah.

Meanwhile, the flow of telegrams indicated an ever-increasing tension, the Executive urging to action, the General promising to act soon, not acting, yet criticising and objecting to the President's orders to him and to others. On the 25th of May the President said: "I think the time is near when you must either attack Richmond or give up the job and come to the defense of Washington." McClellan replied: "The time is very near when I shall attack Richmond." Then, June 10th, he says: "I shall be in perfect readiness to move forward to take Richmond the moment that McCall reaches here and the ground will admit the passage of artillery." June 14th: "If I cannot control all his (McDowell's) troops I want none of them, but would prefer to fight the battle with what I have, and let others be responsible for the results." On the 18th: "After to-morrow we shall fight the rebel army as soon as Providence will permit. We shall await only a favorable condition of the earth and sky and the completion of some necessary preliminaries." While appealing to the President when some of his telegrams to the Secretary remained for a time unanswered, General McClellan allowed Mr. Stanton's cordial assurances of friendship and support to pass unnoticed.

At last, on the 25th, General McClellan advanced his picket lines on the left to within four miles of Richmond, and was apparently preparing for a further movement, though none was ordered, and the next day, as at Manassas and Yorktown and Fair Oaks, his adversary once more took the initiative out of his hands. Jackson had come from the Valley.

As soon as this was known, on the evening of the 25th, General McClellan reported it to Mr. Stanton, added that he thought Jackson would attack his right and rear, that the Confederate force was stated at 200,000, that he regretted his great inferiority in numbers, but was in no way responsible for it, and concluded:

"I will do all that a general can do with the splendid army I have the honor to command, and if it is destroyed by overwhelming numbers can at least die with it and share its fate. But if the result of the action, which will probably occur to-morrow, or within a short time, is a disaster, the responsibility cannot be thrown on my shoulders; it must rest where it belongs."

The battle of Gaines's Mill followed, where, on the 27th, one-fifth of the Union forces contended against the whole Confederate army, save Magruder's corps and Huger's division; then the retreat, or "change of base," to the James, crowned by the splendid yet unfruitful victory of Malvern; then a month of inaction and discussion at Harrison's Landing.

At 12:20 A.M., on the 28th of June, General McClellan sent a long telegram, of which these sentences strike the key-note:

"Our men [at Gaines's Mill] did all that men could do . . . but they were overwhelmed by vastly superior numbers, even after I brought my last reserves into action. . . . I have lost this battle because my force is too small. . . . The Government must not and cannot hold me responsible for the result. I feel too earnestly to-night. I have seen too many dead and wounded comrades to feel otherwise than that the Government has not sustained this army. . . . *If I save this army now, I tell you plainly that I owe no thanks to you or to any other persons in Washington. You have done your best to sacrifice this army.* ☆

On reaching the James River, General McClellan reported that he had saved his army, but it was completely exhausted and would require reënforcements to the extent of 50,000 men. On the 3d of July, he wrote more fully from Harrison's Landing, then saying that "reënforcements should be sent to me rather much over, than much less, than 100,000 men." He referred to his memorandum of the 20th of August, 1861. That memorandum called for 273,000 men. General Marcy, his chief-of-staff, who bore this dispatch to Washington, telegraphed back:

"I have seen the President and Secretary of War. 10,000 men from Hunter, 10,000 from Burnside, and 11,000 from here have been ordered to reënforce you as soon as possible. Halleck [who had been originally called on for 25,000 men which he had reported he could not spare] has been urged by the President to send you at once 10,000 men from Corinth. The President and Secretary speak very kindly of you and find no fault."

The dispatches of the President and Secretary breathe the same spirit.

"Allow me to reason with you a moment [wrote Mr. Lincoln on the 2d of July, adding that he had not fifty thousand men who could be sent promptly]. If, in your frequent mention of responsibility, you have the impression that I blame you for not doing more than you can, please be relieved of such impression. I only beg that in like manner you will not ask impossibilities of me. If you think you are not strong enough to take Richmond just now, I do not ask you to try just now. Save the army, material and personal, and I will strengthen it for the offensive again as fast as I can. The governors of 18 States offer me a new levy of 300,000, which I accept."

On the 5th, Mr. Stanton wrote that he had nominated all the corps commanders for promotion.

"The gallantry of every officer and man in your noble army shall be suitably acknowledged. General Marcy will take you cheering news. Be assured that you shall have the support of this Department and the Government as cordially and faithfully as ever was rendered by man to man, and if we should ever live to see each other face to face, you will be satisfied that you have never had from me anything but the most confiding integrity."

The next day Mr. Stanton followed this by a personal letter, couched in still warmer terms.

"No man [he wrote] had ever a truer friend than I have been to you, and shall continue to be. You are seldom absent from my thoughts, and I am ready to make any sacrifice to aid you. Time allows me to say no more than that I pray Almighty God to deliver you and your army from all perils and lead you on to victory."

General McClellan's reply was long, cold, and formal. He reviewed their past relations, and alluded to the Secretary's official conduct toward him as "marked by repeated acts done in such manner as to be deeply offensive to my feelings, and calculated to affect me injuriously in public estimation."

"After commencing the present campaign [he continued], your concurrence in the withholding of a large portion of my force, so essential to the success of my plans, led me to believe that your mind was warped by a bitter personal prejudice against me. Your letter compels me to believe that I have been mistaken in regard to your real feelings and opinions, and that your conduct, so unaccountable to my own fallible judgment, must have proceeded from views and motives which I did not understand."

The campaign had failed. The President visited Harrison's Landing to see for himself what was to be done next. Then General McClellan handed him his well-known letter "upon a civil and military policy covering the whole ground of our national trouble." He called Mr. Stanton's attention to this letter, in the reply we have just cited, and told him that for no other policy would our armies continue to fight. This must have been the last straw. ∫ On one point, however, he was in accord with the President. He wound up by recommending the appointment of a commander-in-chief of the army who should possess the President's confidence. On the 11th General Halleck was appointed.

On the 26th General Halleck arrived at General McClellan's camp. He reports that McClellan "expressed the opinion that with 30,000 reënforcements he could attack Richmond, with 'a good chance of success.' I replied that I was authorized by the President to promise only 20,000, and that if he could not take Richmond with that number we must devise some plan for withdrawing his troops from their present position to some point where they could unite with those of General Pope without exposing Washington. . . . He . . . the next morning informed me he would attack Richmond with the reënforcements promised. He would not say that he thought the probabilities of success were in his favor, but that there was 'a chance,' and he was 'willing to try it.'

"With regard to the force of the enemy he expressed the opinion that it was not less than 200,000."

The orders for the removal followed. "There was, to my mind," General Halleck says, "no alternative." "I have taken the responsibility of doing so and am to risk my reputation on it."

Upon whatever side, if upon either, of these many-sided controversies, history shall at last adjudge the right to be, upon whatever shoulders and in whatever degree the burden of blame shall finally rest, certain it is that no fair account of these operations can ever be written without taking note of these delays, whereby the initiative was transferred to the adversary; of these disasters, these unproductive victories, this ceaseless flow of telegrams, surcharged with the varying words of controversy, criticism, objection, reproach; and of the inevitable effect of all these causes combined, in weakening the confidence of the President and in undermining his authority and influence, which, however, to the last were exerted to uphold the general of his first choice at the head of his greatest army.

☆ Original not italicized. These words are omitted in the dispatch as printed in the report of the Committee on the Conduct of the War.— R. B. I.   ∫ Confirmed by Chase and Welles.— R. B. I.

RICHMOND SCENES IN '62.

BY CONSTANCE CARY HARRISON.

THE first winter of the war was spent by our family in Richmond, where we found lodgings in a dismal rookery familiarly dubbed by its new occupants "The Castle of Otranto." It was the old-time Clifton Hotel, honeycombed by subterranean passages, and crowded to its limits with refugees like ourselves from country homes within or near the enemy's lines — or "'fugees," as we were all called. For want of any common sitting-room, we took possession of what had been a doctor's office, a few steps distant down the hilly street, fitting it up to the best of our ability; and there we received our friends, passing many merry hours. In rainy weather we reached it by an underground passage-way from the hotel, an alley through the catacombs; and many a dignitary of camp or state will recall those "Clifton" evenings. Already the pinch of war was felt in the commissariat; and we had recourse occasionally to a contribution supper, or "Dutch treat," when the guests brought brandied peaches, boxes of sardines, French prunes, and bags of biscuit, while the hosts contributed only a roast turkey or a ham, with knives and forks. Democratic feasts those were, where major-generals and "high privates" met on an equal footing. The hospitable old town was crowded with the families of officers and members of the Government. One house was made to do the work of several, many of the wealthy citizens generously giving up their superfluous space to receive the new-comers. The only public event of note was the inauguration of Mr. Davis as President of the "Permanent Government" of the Confederate States, which we viewed by the courtesy of Mr. John R. Thompson, the State Librarian, from one of the windows of the Capitol, where, while waiting for the exercises to begin, we read "Harper's Weekly" and other Northern papers, the latest per underground express. That 22d of February was a day of pouring rain, and the concourse of umbrellas in the square beneath us had the effect of an immense mushroom-bed. As the bishop and

THE OLD CLIFTON HOTEL.

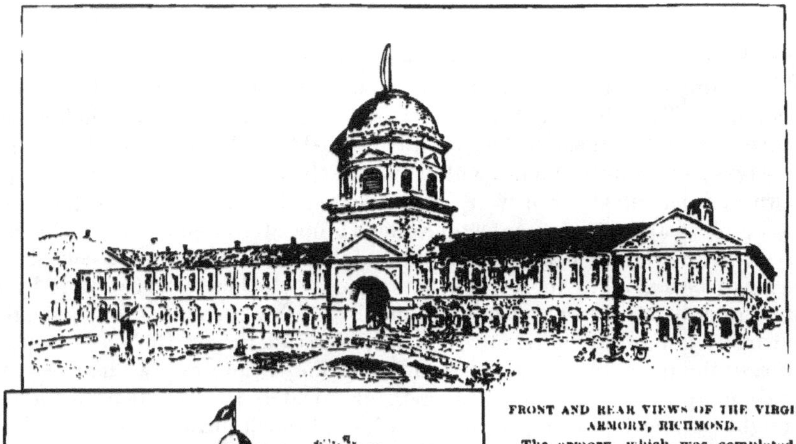

FRONT AND REAR VIEWS OF THE VIRGINIA ARMORY, RICHMOND.

The armory, which was completed in 1805, was garrisoned during the war by a company known as the State Guard. The building was destroyed in the fire that followed the evacuation in April, 1865.

the president-elect came upon the stand, there was an almost painful hush in the crowd. All seemed to feel the gravity of the trust our chosen leader was assuming. When he kissed the book a shout went up; but there was no elation visible as the people slowly dispersed. And it was thought ominous afterward, when the story was repeated, that, as Mrs. Davis, who had a Virginia negro for coachman, was driven to the inauguration, she observed the carriage went at a snail's pace and was escorted by four negro men in black clothes, wearing white cotton gloves and walking solemnly, two on either side of the equipage; she asked the coachman what such a spectacle could mean, and was answered, " Well, ma'am, you tole me to arrange everything as it should be; and this is the way we do in Richmon' at funerals and sich-like." Mrs. Davis promptly ordered the outwalkers away, and with them departed all the pomp and circumstance the occasion admitted of. In the mind of a negro, everything of dignified ceremonial is always associated with a funeral.

About March 1st martial law was proclaimed in Richmond, and a fresh influx of refugees from Norfolk claimed shelter there. When the spring opened, as the spring does open in Richmond, with a sudden glory of green leaves, magnolia blooms, and flowers among the grass, our spirits rose after the depression of the latter months. If only to shake off the atmosphere of doubts and fears engendered by the long winter of disaster and uncertainty, the coming activity of arms was welcome! Personally speaking, there was vast improvement in our situation, since we had been fortunate enough to find a real home in a pleasant brown-walled house on Franklin street, divided from the pavement by a garden full of bounteous greenery, where it was easy to forget the discomforts of our previous mode of life. I shall not attempt to describe the rapidity with which thrilling excitements succeeded each other in our experiences in this house. The gathering of many troops around the town filled the streets with a continually moving panorama of war, and we spent our time in greeting, cheering, choking with sudden emotion, and quivering in anticipation of what was yet to follow. We had now finished other battle-flags [see "Virginia Scenes in '61," Vol. I., p. 160], and one of them was bestowed upon the "Washington Artillery" of New Orleans, a body of admirable soldiers who had wakened to enthusiasm the daughters of Virginia in proportion, I dare say, to the woe they had created among the daughters of Louisiana in bidding them good-bye. One morning an orderly arrived to request that the ladies would be out upon the veranda at a given hour; and, punctual to the time fixed, the travel-stained battalion filed past our house. These were no holiday soldiers. Their gold was tarnished and their scarlet faded by sun and wind and gallant service — they were veterans now on their way to the front, where the call of duty never failed to find the flower of Louisiana. As they came in line with us, the officers saluted with their swords, the band struck up "My Maryland," the tired soldiers sitting upon the caissons that dragged heavily through the muddy street set up a rousing cheer. And there in the midst of them, taking the April wind with daring color, was our flag, dipping low until it passed us! One must grow old and cold indeed before such things are forgotten.

A few days later, on coming out of church — it is a curious fact that most of our exciting news spread over Richmond on Sunday, and just at that hour — we heard of the crushing blow of the fall of New Orleans and the destruction of our iron-clads. My brother had just reported aboard one of those splendid ships, as yet unfinished. As the news came directly from our kinsman, General Randolph, the Secretary of War, there was no doubting it; and while the rest of us broke into lamentation, Mr. Jules de St. Martin, the brother-in-law of Mr. Judah P. Benjamin, merely shrugged his shoulders, with a thoroughly characteristic gesture, making no remark.

"This must affect your interests," some one said to him inquiringly.

"I am ruined, *voilà tout!*" was the rejoinder — and this was soon confirmed.

This debonair little gentleman was one of the greatest favorites of our war society in Richmond. His cheerfulness, his wit, his exquisite courtesy, made him friends everywhere; and although his nicety of dress, after the pattern of the *boulevardier fini* of Paris, was the subject of much wonderment to the populace when he first appeared upon the streets, it did not prevent him from joining the volunteers before Richmond when occasion called, and roughing it in the trenches like a veteran. His cheerful endurance of hardship during a freezing winter of camp life became a proverb in the army later in the siege.

For a time nothing was talked of but the capture of New Orleans. Of the midshipman, my brother, we heard that on the day previous to the taking of the forts, after several days' bombardment by the United States fleet under

RICHMOND FROM THE MANCHESTER SIDE OF THE JAMES.

Flag-Officer Farragut, he had been sent in charge of ordnance and deserters to a Confederate vessel in the river; that Lieutenant R——, a friend of his, on the way to report at Fort Jackson during the hot shelling, had invited the lad to accompany him by way of a pleasure trip; that while they were crossing the moat around Fort Jackson, in a canoe, and under heavy fire, a thirteen-inch mortar-shell had struck the water near, half filling their craft; and that, after watching the fire from this point for an hour, C—— had pulled back again alone, against the Mississippi current, under fire for a mile and a half of the way—passing an astonished alligator who had been hit on the head by a piece of shell and was dying under protest. Thus ended a trip alluded to by C—— twenty years later as an example of juvenile foolhardiness.

Aboard the steamship *Star of the West*, ☆ next day, he and other midshipmen in charge of gold and silver coin from the mint and banks of New Orleans, and millions more of paper money, over which they were ordered to keep guard with drawn swords, hurried away from the doomed city, where the enemy's arrival was momentarily expected, and where the burning ships and steamers and bales of cotton along the levee made a huge crescent of fire. Keeping just ahead of the enemy's fleet, they reached Vicksburg, and thence went overland to Mobile, where their charge was given up in safety.

And now we come to the 31st of May, 1862, when the eyes of the whole continent turned to Richmond. On that day Johnston assaulted the Federals who had been advanced to Seven Pines [see pp. 203, 220]. In face of recent reverses, we in Richmond had begun to feel like the prisoner of the Inquisition in Poe's story, cast into a dungeon of slowly contracting walls. With the sound of guns, therefore, in the direction of Seven Pines, every heart leaped as if deliverance were at hand. And yet there was no joy in the wild pulsation, since those to whom we looked for succor were our own flesh and blood, barring the way to a foe of superior numbers, abundantly provided, as we

☆ The same vessel that drew the opening shots of the war at Charleston; seized at Indianola, Tex., in April, 1861; later, sunk by the Confederates in the Yazoo, near Fort Pemberton.—EDITORS.

were not, with all the equipments of modern warfare, and backed by a mighty nation as determined as ourselves to win. Hardly a family in the town whose father, son, or brother was not part and parcel of the defending army.

When on the afternoon of the 31st it became known that the engagement had begun, the women of Richmond were still going about their daily vocations quietly, giving no sign of the inward anguish of apprehension. There was enough to do now in preparation for the wounded; yet, as events proved, all that was done was not enough by half. Night brought a lull in the cannonading. People lay down dressed upon beds, but not to sleep, while the weary soldiers slept upon their arms. Early next morning the whole town was on the street. Ambulances, litters, carts, every vehicle that the city could produce, went and came with a ghastly burden; those who could walk limped painfully home, in some cases so black with gunpowder they passed unrecognized. Women with pallid faces flitted bareheaded through the streets searching for their dead or wounded. The churches were thrown open, many people visiting them for a sad communion-service or brief time of prayer; the lecture-rooms of various places of worship were crowded with ladies volun-

FOOD FOR THE CONFEDERATE WOUNDED.

teering to sew, as fast as fingers could fly, the rough beds called for by the surgeons. Men too old or infirm to fight went on horseback or afoot to meet the returning ambulances, and in some cases served as escort to their own dying sons. By afternoon of the day following the battle, the streets were one vast hospital. To find shelter for the sufferers a number of unused buildings were thrown open. I remember, especially, the St. Charles Hotel, a gloomy place, where two young girls went to look for a member of their family, reported wounded. We had tramped in vain over pavements burning with the intensity of the sun, from one scene of horror to another, until our feet and brains alike seemed about to serve us no further. The cool of those vast dreary rooms of the St. Charles was refreshing; but such a spectacle! Men in every stage of mutilation lying on the bare boards, with perhaps a haversack or an army blanket beneath their

IN THE STREETS OF RICHMOND - WOUNDED FROM THE BATTLE OF SEVEN PINES.

heads,—some dying, all suffering keenly, while waiting their turn to be attended to. To be there empty-handed and impotent nearly broke our hearts. We passed from one to the other, making such slight additions to their comfort as were possible, while looking in every upturned face in dread to find the object of our search. This sorrow, I may add, was spared, the youth arriving at home later with a slight flesh-wound. The condition of things at this and other improvised hospitals was improved next day by the offerings from many churches of pew-cushions, which, sewn together, served as comfortable beds; and for the remainder of the war their owners thanked God upon bare benches for every "misery missed" that was "mercy gained." To supply food for the hospitals the contents of larders all over town were emptied into baskets; while cellars long sealed and cobwebbed, belonging to the old Virginia gentry who knew good Port and Madeira, were opened by the Ithuriel's spear of universal sympathy. There was not much going to bed that night, either; and I remember spending the greater part of it leaning from my window to seek the cool night air, while wondering as to the fate of those near to me. There was a summons to my mother about midnight. Two soldiers came to tell her of the wounding of one close of kin; but she was already on duty elsewhere, tireless and watchful as ever. Up to that time the younger girls had been regarded as superfluities in hospital service; but on Monday two of us found a couple of rooms where fifteen wounded men lay upon pallets around the floor, and, on offering our services to the surgeons in charge, were proud to have them accepted and to be installed as responsible nurses, under direction of an older and more experienced woman. The constant activity our work entailed was a relief from the strained excitement of life after the battle of Seven Pines. When the first flurry of distress was over, the residents of those pretty houses standing back in gardens full of roses set their cooks to work, or, better still, went themselves into the kitchen, to compound delicious messes for the wounded, after the appetizing old Virginia recipes. Flitting about the streets in the direction of the hospitals were smiling, white-jacketed negroes, carrying silver trays with dishes of fine porcelain under napkins of thick white damask, containing soups, creams, jellies, thin biscuit, eggs *à la crème*, boiled chicken, etc., surmounted by clusters of freshly gathered flowers. A year later we had cause to pine after these culinary glories when it came to measuring out, with sinking hearts, the meager portions of milk and food we could afford to give our charges.

As an instance, however, that quality in food was not always appreciated by the patients, my mother urged upon one of her sufferers (a gaunt and soft-voiced Carolinian from the "piney woods district") a delicately served trifle from some neighboring kitchen.

"Jes ez you say, old miss," was the weary answer; "I ain't a-contradictin' you. It mont be good for me, but my stomick's kinder sot agin

VIEW OF WASHINGTON MONUMENT, IN CAPITOL SQUARE, RICHMOND.

it. There ain't but one thing I'm sorter yarnin' arter, an' that's a dish o' greens en bacon fat, with a few molarses poured onto it."

From our patients, when they could syllable the tale, we had accounts of the fury of the fight, which were made none the less horrible by such assistance as imagination could give to the facts. I remember they told us of shot thrown from the enemy's batteries, that plowed their way through lines of flesh and blood before exploding in showers of musket-balls to do still further havoc. Before these awful missiles, it was said, our men had fallen in swaths, the living closing over them to press forward in the charge.

It was at the end of one of these narrations that a piping voice came from a pallet in the corner: "They fit right smart, them Yanks did, I tell *you!*" and not to laugh was as much of an effort as it had just been not to cry.

From one scene of death and suffering to another we passed during those days of June. Under a withering heat that made the hours preceding dawn the only ones of the twenty-four endurable in point of temperature, and a shower-bath the only form of diversion we had time or thought to indulge in, to go out-of-doors was sometimes worse than remaining in our wards. But one night after several of us had been walking about town in a state of panting exhaustion, palm-leaf fans in hand, a friend persuaded us to ascend to the small platform on the summit of the Capitol, in search of fresher air. To reach it was like going through a vapor-bath, but an hour amid the cool breezes above the tree-tops of the square was a thing of joy unspeakable.

Day by day we were called to our windows by the wailing dirge of a military band preceding a soldier's funeral. One could not number those sad pageants: the coffin crowned with cap and sword and gloves, the riderless horse following with empty boots fixed in the stirrups of an army saddle; such soldiers as could be spared from the front marching after with arms reversed and crape-enfolded banners; the passers-by standing with bare, bent heads. Funerals less honored outwardly were continually occurring. Then and thereafter the green hillsides of lovely Hollywood were frequently upturned to find resting-places for the heroic dead. So much taxed for time and for attendants were those who officiated that it was not unusual to perform the last rites for the departed at night. A solemn scene was that in the July moonlight, when, in the presence of the few who valued him most, we laid to rest one of my own nearest kinsmen, of whom in the old service of the United States, as in that of the Confederacy, it was said, "He was a spotless knight."

Spite of its melancholy uses, there was no more favorite walk in Richmond than Hollywood, a picturesquely beautiful spot, where high hills sink into velvet undulations, profusely shaded with holly, pine, and cedar, as well as by trees of deciduous foliage. In spring the banks of the stream that runs through the valley were enameled with wild flowers, and the thickets were full of May-blossom and dogwood. Mounting to the summit of the bluff, one may sit under the shade of some ample oak, to view the spires and roofs of the town, with the white colonnade of the distant Capitol. Richmond, thus seen beneath her verdant foliage "upon hills, girdled by hills," confirms what an old writer felt called to exclaim about it, "Verily, this city hath a pleasant seat." On the right, below this point, flows the rushing yellow river, making ceaseless turmoil around islets of rock whose rifts are full of birch and willow, or leaping impetuously over the bowlders of granite that strew its bed. Old-time Richmond folk used to say that the sound of their favorite James (or, to be exact, "Jeems") went with them into foreign countries, during no matter how many years of absence, haunting them like a strain of sweetest music; nor would they permit a suggestion of superiority in the flavor of any other fluid to that of a draught of its amber waters. So blent with my own memories of war is the voice of that tireless river, that I seem to hear it yet, over the tramp of rusty battalions, the short imperious stroke of the alarm-bell, the clash of passing bands, the gallop of eager horsemen, the roar of battle, the moan of hospitals, the stifled note of sorrow!

During all this time President Davis was a familiar and picturesque figure on the streets, walking through the Capitol square from his residence to the executive office in the morning, not to return until late in the afternoon, or riding just before nightfall to visit one or another of the encampments near the city.   He was tall, erect, slender, and of a dignified and soldierly bearing, with clear-cut and high-bred features, and of a demeanor of stately courtesy to all.   He was clad always in Confederate gray cloth, and wore a soft felt hat with wide brim.   Afoot, his step was brisk and firm; in the saddle he rode admirably and with a martial aspect.   His early life had been spent in the Military Academy at West Point and upon the then north-western frontier in the Black Hawk War, and he afterward greatly distinguished himself at Monterey and Buena Vista in Mexico; at the time when we knew him, everything in his appearance and manner was suggestive of such a training.   He was reported to feel quite out of place in the office of President, with executive and administrative duties, in the midst of such a war; General Lee always spoke of him as the best of military advisers; his own inclination was to be with the army, and at the first tidings of sound of a gun, anywhere within reach of Richmond, he was in the saddle and off for the spot — to the dismay of his staff-officers, who were expected to act as an escort on such occasions, and who never knew at what hour of the night or of the next day they should get back to bed or to a meal.   The stories we were told of his adventures on such excursions were many, and sometimes amusing.   For instance, when General Lee had crossed the Chickahominy, President Davis, with several staff-officers, overtook the column, and, with the Secretary of War and a few other non-combatants, forded the river just as the battle at Mechanicsville began.   General Lee, surrounded by members of his own staff and other officers, was found a few hundred yards north of the bridge, in the middle of the broad road, mounted and busily engaged in directing the attack then about to be made by a brigade sweeping in line over the fields to the east of the road and toward Ellerson's Mill, where in a few minutes a hot engagement commenced.   Shot, from the enemy's guns out of sight, went whizzing overhead in quick succession, striking every moment nearer the group of horsemen in the road as the gunners improved their range.   General Lee observed the President's approach, and was evidently annoyed at what he considered a foolhardy expedition of needless exposure of the head of the Government, whose duties were elsewhere.   He turned his back for a moment, until Colonel Chilton had been dispatched at a gallop with the last direction to the commander of the attacking brigade; then, facing the cavalcade and looking like the god of war indignant, he exchanged with the President a salute, with the most frigid reserve of anything like welcome or cordiality.   In an instant, and without allowance of opportunity for a word from the President, the general, looking not at him but at the assemblage at large, asked in a tone of irritation:

"Who are all this army of people, and what are they doing here?"

No one moved or spoke, but all eyes were upon the President; everybody perfectly understood that this was only an order for him to retire to a place of safety, and the roar of the guns, the rattling fire of musketry, and the bustle of a battle in progress, with troops continually arriving across the bridge to go into action, went on. The President twisted in his saddle, quite taken aback at such a greeting—the general regarding him now with glances of growing severity. After a painful pause the President said, deprecatingly: " It is not my army, General." " It certainly is not *my* army, Mr. President," was the prompt reply, "and this is no place for it "—in an accent of command. Such a rebuff was a stunner to Mr. Davis, who, however, soon regained his serenity and answered:

" Well, General, if I withdraw, perhaps they will follow," and, raising his hat in another cold salute, he turned his horse's head to ride slowly toward the bridge—seeing, as he turned, a man killed immediately before him by a shot from a gun which at that moment got the range of the road. The President's own staff-officers followed him, as did various others; but he presently drew rein in a stream, where the high bank and the bushes concealed him from General Lee's repelling observation, and there remained while the battle raged. The Secretary of War had also made a show of withdrawing, but improved the opportunity afforded by rather a deep ditch on the roadside to attempt to conceal himself and his horse there for a time from General Lee, who at that moment was more to be dreaded than the enemy's guns.

When on the 27th of June the Seven Days' strife began, there was none of the excitement that had attended the battle of Seven Pines. People had shaken themselves down, as it were, to the grim reality of a fight that must be fought. " Let the war bleed, and let the mighty fall," was the spirit of their cry.

It is not my purpose to deal with the history of those awful Seven Days. Mine only to speak of the other side of that canvas in which heroes of two armies were passing and repassing, as on some huge Homeric frieze, in the manœuvres of a strife that hung our land in mourning. The scars of war are healed when this is written, and the vast "pity of it" fills the heart that wakes the retrospect.

What I have said of Richmond before these battles will suffice for a picture of the summer's experience. When the tide of battle receded, what wrecked hopes it left to tell the tale of the Battle Summer! Victory was ours, but in how many homes was heard the voice of lamentation to drown the shouts of triumph! Many families, rich and poor alike, were bereaved of their dearest; and for many of the dead there was mourning by all the town. No incident of the war, for instance, made a deeper impression than the fall in battle of Colonel Munford's beautiful and brave young son, Ellis, whose body, laid across his own caisson, was carried that summer to his father's house at nightfall, where the family, unconscious of their loss, were sitting in cheerful talk around the portal. Another son of Richmond, whose death was keenly felt by everybody, received his mortal wound at the front of the first charge to break the enemy's line at Gaines's Mill. This was Lieutenant-Colonel Bradfute Warwick, a young hero who had won his spurs in service with Garibaldi. Losses like these are irreparable in any community; and so, with lamentations in nearly every household, while the spirit along the lines continued unabated, it was a chastened "Thank God" that went up among us when we knew the siege of Richmond was over.

THE SECOND BATTLE OF BULL RUN.[J]

BY JOHN POPE, MAJOR-GENERAL, U. S. A.

PICKETING THE RAPIDAN.

EARLY in June, 1862, I was in command of the army corps known as the "Army of the Mississippi," which formed the left wing of the army engaged in operations against Corinth, Miss., commanded by General Halleck. A few days after Corinth was evacuated I went to St. Louis on a short leave of absence from my command, and while there I received a telegram from Mr. Stanton, Secretary of War, requesting me to come to Washington immediately. I at once communicated the fact to General Halleck by telegraph, and received a reply from him strongly objecting to my leaving the army which was under his command. I quite concurred with him both as to his objections to my going to Washington for public reasons and as to the unadvisability of such a step on personal considerations. I was obliged, however, to go, and I went accordingly, but with great reluctance and against the urgent protests of my friends in St. Louis, and subsequently of many friends in the Army of the West.

When I reached Washington the President was absent at West Point, but I reported in person to Secretary Stanton. I had never seen him before, and his peculiar appearance and manners made a vivid impression on me. He was short and stout. His long beard, which hung over his breast, was slightly tinged with gray even at that time, and he had the appearance of a man who had lost much sleep and was tired both in body and mind. Certainly, with his large eye-glasses and rather disheveled appearance, his presence was not imposing. Although he was very kind and civil to me, his manner was abrupt and his speech short and rather dictatorial. He entered at once on the business in hand, seemingly without the least idea that any one should object to, or be reluctant to agree to, his views and purposes. He was surprised, and, it seemed to me, not well pleased, that I did not assent to his plans with effusion; but went on to unfold them in the seeming certainty that they must be submitted to. He informed me that the purpose was to unite the armies under McDowell, Frémont, and Banks, all three of whom were my seniors in rank, and to place me in general command. These armies were scattered over the northern part of Virginia, with little or no communication or concert of action with one another; Frémont and Banks being at Middletown, in the Shenandoah Valley, and McDowell's corps widely separated, King's division at Fredericksburg, and Ricketts's at and beyond Manassas Junction.

The general purpose at that time was to demonstrate with the army toward Gordonsville and Charlottesville and draw off as much as possible of the force

[J] Accompanying General Beauregard's paper on the First Battle of Bull Run Vol. I., pp. 196–227) are maps and many pictures of interest with reference to the second battle.— EDITORS.

in front of General McClellan, who then occupied the line of the Chickahominy, and to distract the attention of the enemy in his front so as to reduce as far as practicable the resistance opposed to his advance on Richmond.

It became apparent to me at once that the duty to be assigned to me was in the nature of a forlorn-hope, and my position was still further embarrassed by the fact that I was called from another army and a different field of duty to command an army of which the corps commanders were all my seniors in rank. I therefore strongly urged that I be not placed in such a position, but be permitted to return to my command in the West, to which I was greatly attached and with which I had been closely identified in several successful operations on the Mississippi. It was not difficult to forecast the delicate and embarrassing position in which I should be placed, nor the almost certainly disagreeable, if not unfortunate, issue of such organization for such a purpose.

It would be tedious to relate the conversations between the President, the Secretary of War, and myself on this subject. Sufficient to say that I was finally informed that the public interests required my assignment to this command, and that it was my duty to submit cheerfully. An order from the War Department was accordingly issued organizing the Army of Virginia, to consist of the army corps of McDowell, Banks, and Frémont, and placing me in command.

One result of this order was the very natural protest of General Frémont against being placed under the command of his junior in rank, and his request to be relieved from the command of his corps.⚹

⚹ This request was complied with, and on the 29th of June, 1862, General Franz Sigel assumed command of the First Corps.—EDITORS.

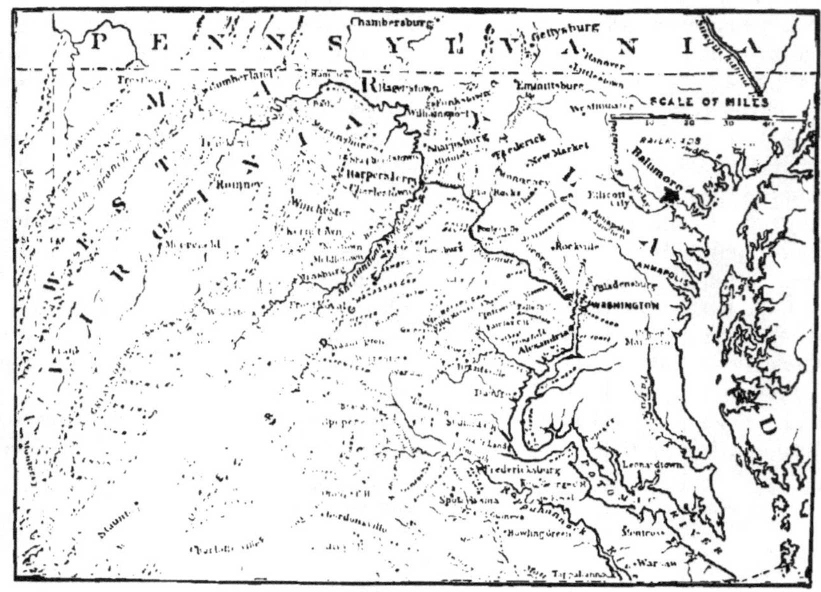

OUTLINE MAP OF THE CAMPAIGN.

It was equally natural that the subordinate officers and the enlisted men of those corps should have been ill-pleased at the seeming affront to their own officers, involved in calling an officer strange to them and to the country in which they were operating, and to the character of the service in which they were engaged, to super-

VIEW IN CULPEPER DURING THE OCCUPATION BY POPE. FROM A PHOTOGRAPH.

The building with the ball and vane is the Court House, in which
Confederate prisoners were confined.

sede well-known and trusted officers who had been with them from the beginning, and whose reputation was so closely identified with their own. How far this feeling prevailed among them, and how it influenced their actions, if it did so at all, I am not able to tell; but it is only proper for me to say (and it is a pleasure as well as a duty to say it) that Generals McDowell and Banks never exhibited to me the slightest feeling on the subject either in their conversation or acts. Indeed, I think it would be hard to find officers more faithful to their duty or more deeply interested in the success of the army. To General McDowell especially is due my gratitude for his zeal and fidelity in what was and ought to have been considered a common cause, the success of the Union Army.

Knowing very well the difficulties and embarrassments certain to arise from all these sources, and the almost hopeless character of the service demanded of me, I, nevertheless, felt obliged, in deference to the wish of the President and Secretary of War, to submit; but I entered on this command with great reluctance and serious forebodings.

On the 27th of June, accordingly, I assumed command of the Army of Virginia, which consisted of the three corps above named, which numbered as follows: Frémont's corps, 11,500; Banks's corps, 8000, and McDowell's corps, 18,500,—in all, 38,000 men.‡ The cavalry numbered about 5000, but most of it was badly organized and armed, and in poor condition for service. These forces were scattered over a wide district of country, not within supporting

‡ On the 27th of June, according to the "Official Records," the strength of the Army of Virginia appears to have been about as follows: Headquarters, 200; Sigel's corps (Frémont's), 13,200; Banks's, 12,100; McDowell's, 19,300; cavalry, 5800. Total of the three army corps, 44,600, or 6600 more than General Pope's estimate: Aggregate, 50,600, or 7600 more than General Pope's estimate. On the 31st of July the consolidated report showed 46,858 "effectives." An error in the report of Banks's corps reduced this aggregate to 40,358. After the battle of Cedar Mountain, and when he had been reënforced by Reno (7000), Pope estimated his force at barely 40,000. With this force were 27 field-batteries numbering about 150 guns.— EDITORS.

distance of one another, and some of the brigades and divisions were badly organized and in a more or less demoralized condition. This was especially the case in the army corps of General Frémont, as shown in the report of General Sigel which was sent me when he had assumed command of it.

My first object was, therefore, to bring the three corps of the army together, or near enough together to be within supporting distance of one another, and to put them in as efficient a condition for active service as was possible with the time and means at my disposal. When I assumed this command, the troops under General Stonewall Jackson had retired from the valley of the Shenandoah to Richmond, so there was not at that time any force of the enemy of any consequence within several days' march of my command. I accordingly sent orders to General Sigel to move forward, cross the Shenandoah at Front Royal, and, pursuing the west side of the Blue Ridge to Luray, and then crossing it at Thornton's Gap, take post at Sperryville. At the same time I directed General Banks to cross the Shenandoah at Front Royal and proceed by way of Chester Gap to Little Washington. Ricketts's division of McDowell's corps, then at and beyond Manassas Junction, was ordered to move forward to Waterloo Bridge, where the turnpike from Warrenton to Sperryville crosses the Rappahannock, there known as Hedgman's River. In deference to the wishes of the Government, and much against my opinion, King's division of the same corps was kept at Fredericksburg. The wide separation of this division from the main body of the army not only deprived me of its use when, as became plain afterward, it was much needed, but left us exposed to the constant danger that the enemy might interpose between us.

The partial concentration of the corps so near to the Blue Ridge and with open communications with the Shenandoah Valley seemed to me best to fulfill the object of covering that valley from any movements from the direction of Richmond with any force less than the army under my command. The position was one also which gave most favorable facilities for the intended operations toward Gordonsville and Charlottesville.

At the date of my orders for this concentration of the army under my command,‡ the Army of the Potomac under General McClellan occupied both banks of the Chickahominy, and it was hoped that his advance against Richmond, so long delayed, might be facilitated by vigorous use of the Army of Virginia.

During the preparation for the march of the corps of Banks and Sigel toward Sperryville and Little Washington, began the series of battles which preceded and attended the retreat of General McClellan from the Chickahominy toward Harrison's Landing.

When first General McClellan began to intimate by his dispatches that he designed making this retreat toward the James River, I suggested to the President the impolicy of such a movement, and the serious consequences

‡ The President's order constituting the Army of Virginia is dated June 26th. On that day the second of the Seven Days' battles referred to in the next paragraph began with Lee's attack on McClellan's right near Mechanicsville. General Pope took command on the 27th; on that day was fought the battle of Gaines's Mill, and the march to the James began that night.— EDITORS.

FROM A PHOTOGRAPH TAKEN SINCE THE WAR.

Jno. Pope

that would be likely to result from it; I urged upon him that he send orders to General McClellan, if he were unable to maintain his position on the Chickahominy, and were pushed by superior forces of the enemy, to mass his whole force on the north side of that stream, even at the risk of losing some of his material of war, and endeavor to retire in the direction of Hanover Court House, but in no event to retreat farther south than the White House on the Pamunkey River. I told the President that by the movement to the James River the whole army of the enemy would be interposed between General McClellan and myself, and that they would then be able to strike in either direction as might seem most advantageous to them; that this movement would leave entirely unprotected, except so far as the small force under my command could protect it, the whole region in front of Washington, and that it would therefore be impossible to send him any of my troops without putting it in the power of the enemy to exchange Richmond for Washington; that to them the loss of Richmond would be comparatively a small loss, while to us the loss of Washington would be almost a fatal blow. I was so impressed with these opinions that I several times urged them upon the attention of the President and the Secretary of War.

The soundness of these views can be easily tested by subsequent facts. The enemy actually did choose between the danger of losing Richmond and the chance of capturing Washington.[Stonewall Jackson's corps was detached from Lee's army confronting McClellan at Harrison's Landing early in July, and on the 19th of that month was concentrated at Gordonsville in my front; while Stuart's cavalry division, detached from Lee's army about the same time, was at or near Fredericksburg watching our movements from that direction. On the 13th of August Longstreet's whole corps was dispatched to join Jackson at Gordonsville, to which place he had fallen back from Cedar Mountain, and the head of Longstreet's corps had joined Jackson at that place on August 15th. These forces were commanded by Lee in person, who was at Gordonsville on that day. The first troops of the Army of the Potomac which left Harrison's Landing moved out from that place on August 14th,\ at which date there was nothing of Lee's army, except D. H. Hill's corps, left in front

[General Lee says in his report dated April 18th, 1863:

"To meet the advance of the latter [Pope] . . . General Jackson, with his own and Ewell's divisions, was ordered to proceed toward Gordonsville on July 13th. Upon reaching that vicinity he ascertained that the force under General Pope was superior to his own, but the uncertainty that then surrounded the designs of McClellan rendered it inexpedient to reënforce him from the army at Richmond. . . . Assistance was promised should the progress of General Pope put it in our power to strike an effectual blow without withdrawing the troops too long from the defense of the capital. The army at Westover [Harrison's Landing], continuing to manifest no intention of resuming active operations, and General Pope's advance having reached the Rapidan, General A. P. Hill, with his division, was ordered on July 27th to join General Jackson. At the same time, in order to keep McClellan stationary, or, if possible, to cause him to withdraw, General D. H. Hill, commanding south of James River, was directed to threaten his communications."

And in his report, dated June 8th, 1863:

"The victory at Cedar Run [August 9th] effectually checked the progress of the enemy for the time, but it soon became apparent that his army was being largely increased. The corps of Major-General Burnside from North Carolina, which had reached Fredericksburg [August 4th and 5th], was reported to have moved up the Rappahannock a few days after the battle, to unite with General Pope, and a part of General McClellan's army was believed to have left Westover for the same purpose. It therefore seemed that active operations on the James were no longer contemplated, and that the most effectual way to relieve Richmond from any danger of attack from that quarter would be to reënforce General Jackson and advance upon General Pope."   EDITORS.

\ On the 30th of July General Halleck ordered General McClellan to send away his sick as rapidly as possible. On the 3d of August General Halleck telegraphed: "It is determined to withdraw your army from the Peninsula to Aquia Creek. You will take immediate measures to effect this. . . . Your material and transportation should be removed first." General McClellan protested against the movement, as did Generals Dix, Burnside, and Sumner. General Halleck replied to General McClellan that he saw no alternative. "There is no change of plans." "I . . . have taken the responsibility . . . and am to risk my reputation on it."

The movement of the sick began at once. Between the 1st of August, when the order was received, and the 16th, when the evacuation of Harrison's Landing was completed, 14,159 were sent away, many of them necessarily to the North. The first troops arrived at Aquia within seven days, and the last of the infantry within 26 days, after the receipt of the order.

(The original movement of the Army of the Potomac, from Alexandria to Fort Monroe, had taken 37 days, and Mr. Tucker, who had superintended its transport, said of it: "I confidently submit that for economy and celerity this expedition is without a parallel on record.")

In the terms of General Halleck's order of August 3d, there were to be transported first the 14,159 sick; next all the material of the army, and the transportation, embracing 3100 wagons, 350 ambulances, 13,000 horses and mules; then 89,407 officers and men, 360 guns, and 13,000 artillery and cavalry horses, together with the baggage and stores in use; but in order to hasten the movement this routine was not rigidly observed, and the movement of Peck's division (ordered to move last) of 7581 men and 10 guns was countermanded by General Halleck.— EDITORS.

of McClellan or near to him. Hill's corps could have opposed but little effective resistance to the advance of the Army of the Potomac upon Richmond.

It seems clear, then, that the views expressed to the President and Secretary of War, as heretofore set forth, were sound, and that the enemy

RETREAT OF THE UNION TROOPS ACROSS THE RAPPAHANNOCK AT RAPPAHANNOCK STATION, AFTER A SKETCH MADE AT THE TIME.

had left McClellan to work his will on Richmond, while they pushed forward against the small army under my command and to the capture of Washington. This movement of Lee was, in my opinion, in accordance with true military principle, and was the natural result of McClellan's retreat to Harrison's Landing, which completely separated the Army of the Potomac from the Army of Virginia and left the entire force of the enemy interposed between them.

The retreat of General McClellan to Harrison's Landing was, however, continued to the end. During these six days of anxiety and apprehension Mr. Lincoln spent much of his time in the office of the Secretary of War, most of that time reclining on a sofa or lounge. The Secretary of War was always with him, and from time to time his Cabinet officers came in. Mr. Lincoln himself appeared much depressed and wearied, though occasionally, while waiting for telegrams, he would break into some humorous remark, which seemed rather a protest against his despondent manner than any genuine expression of enjoyment. He spoke no unkind word of any one, and appeared to be anxious himself to bear all the burden of the situation; and when the final result was reported he rose with a sorrowful face and left the War Department.

A day or two after General McClellan reached the James River I was called before the President and his Cabinet to consult upon means and movements to relieve him. I do not know that it would be proper even at this day for me to state what occurred or what was said during this consultation, except so far as I was myself directly concerned. General McClellan was calling for reënforcements, and stating that "much over rather than under one hundred thousand men" were necessary before he could resume operations against Richmond. I had not under my command one-half that force.

I stated to the President and Cabinet that I stood ready to undertake any movement, however hazardous, to relieve the Army of the Potomac. Some suggestions which seemed to me impracticable were made, and much was said which under the circumstances will not bear repetition.

I stated that only on one condition would I be willing to involve the army

THE BATTLE OF CEDAR MOUNTAIN — VIEW FROM THE UNION LINES. FROM A SKETCH MADE AT THE TIME.
The picture shows the artillery duel and deployment of troops before the main attack toward
the right, in the middle distance.

under my command in direct operations against the enemy to relieve the Army of the Potomac. That condition was, that such peremptory orders be given to General McClellan, and in addition such measures taken in advance as would render it certain that he would make a vigorous attack on the enemy with his whole force the moment he heard that I was engaged.

In face of the extraordinary difficulties which existed and the terrible responsibility about to be thrown on me, I considered it my duty to state plainly to the President that I could not risk the destruction of my army in such a movement as was suggested if it were left to the discretion of General McClellan or any one else to withhold the vigorous use of his whole force when my attack was made.

The whole plan of campaign for the army under my command was necessarily changed by the movement of the Army of the Potomac to Harrison's Landing. A day or two after General McClellan had reached his position on James River I addressed him a letter stating to him my position, the disposition of the troops under my command, and what was required of them, and requesting him in all good faith and earnestness to write me freely and fully his views, and to suggest to me any measures which he thought desirable to enable me to coöperate with him, and offering to render any assistance in my power to the operations of the army under his command. I stated to him that I was very anxious to assist him in his operations, and that I would undertake any labor or run any risk for that purpose. I therefore requested him to feel no hesitation in communicating freely with me, as he might rest assured that any suggestions he made would meet all respect and consideration from me, and that, so far as was within my power, I would carry out his wishes with all energy and all the means at my command. In reply to this communication I received a letter from General McClellan very general in its terms and proposing nothing toward the accomplishment of the purpose I suggested to him.

It became very apparent, therefore, considering the situation in which the Army of the Potomac and the Army of Virginia were placed in relation to each other and the absolute necessity of harmonious and prompt coöperation between them, that some military superior both of General McClellan and myself should be placed in general command of all the operations in Virginia, with power to enforce joint action between the two armies within that field of operations. General Halleck was accordingly called to Washington and assigned to the command-in-chief of the army,☆ though Mr. Stanton was opposed to it and used some pretty strong language to me concerning General Halleck and my action in the matter. They, however, established friendly relations soon after General Halleck assumed command.

The reasons which induced me, in the first instance, to ask to be relieved from the command of the

BRIGADIER-GENERAL CHARLES S. WINDER, C. S. A., KILLED AT CEDAR MOUNTAIN.—FROM A PHOTOGRAPH.

Army of Virginia, as heretofore set forth, were greatly intensified by the retreat of General McClellan to James River and the bitter feelings and controversies which it occasioned, and I again requested the President to relieve me from the command and permit me to return to the West. The utter impossibility of sending General McClellan anything like the reënforcements he asked for, the extreme danger to Washington involved in sending him even a fraction of the small force under my command, and the glaring necessity of concentrating these two armies in some judicious manner and as rapidly as possible, resulted in a determination to withdraw the Army of the Potomac from the James River and unite it with the Army of Virginia. The question of the command of these armies when united was never discussed in my presence, if at all, and I left Washington with the natural impression that when this junction was accomplished General Halleck would himself assume the command in the field. Under the changed condition of things brought about by General McClellan's retreat to James River, and

---

☆ The first step toward calling General Halleck to Washington appears in the President's telegram of July 2d asking if he could not come "for a flying visit." On the 6th Governor Sprague was sent to him at Corinth, on a confidential mission, arriving there on the 10th. Meanwhile the President had visited General McClellan and received from his hands the Harrison's Bar letter. On the 11th, General Halleck was appointed General-in-chief. Mr. Chase says in his diary (see "Life and Public Services of S. P. Chase," by J. W. Schuckers, p.

447) that he and Mr. Stanton "proposed to the President to send Pope to the James and give [Ormsby M.] Mitchel the command of the front of Washington. . . . The President was not prepared for anything so decisive, and sent for Halleck and made him Commander-in-chief." Secretary Welles says ("Lincoln and Seward," p. 191): "Pope also . . . uniting with Stanton and General Scott in advising that McClellan should be superseded and Halleck placed in charge of military affairs at Washington."— EDITORS.

the purpose to withdraw his army and unite it with that under my command, the campaign of the Army of Virginia was limited to the following objects:

1. To cover the approaches to Washington from any enemy advancing from the direction of Richmond, and to oppose and delay its advance to the last extremity, so as to give all the time possible for the withdrawal of the Army of the Potomac from the James River.

2. If no heavy forces of the enemy moved north, to operate on their lines of communication with Gordonsville and Charlottesville, so as to force Lee to make heavy detachments from his force at Richmond and facilitate to that extent the withdrawal of the Army of the Potomac.

Halleck was of the opinion that the junction of the two armies could be made on the line of the Rappahannock, and my orders to hold fast to my communications with Fredericksburg, through which place McClellan's army was to make its junction with the Army of Virginia, were repeated positively.

The decision of the enemy to move north with the bulk of his army was promptly made and vigorously carried out, so that it became apparent, even before General McClellan began to embark his army, that the line of the Rappahannock was too far to the front. That fact, however, was not realized by Halleck until too late for any change which could be effectively executed.

Such was the organization of the Army of Virginia, and such its objects and the difficulties with which it was embarrassed from the very beginning. This rather long preface appears to me to be essential to any sufficient understanding of the second battle of Bull Run, and why and how it was fought. It is also necessary as a reply to a statement industriously circulated at the time and repeated again and again for obvious purposes, until no doubt it is generally believed, that I had set out to capture Richmond with a force sufficient for the purpose, and that the falling back from the Rapidan was unexpected by the Government, and a great disappointment to it. The whole campaign was, and perhaps

HOUSE ON THE BATTLE-FIELD OF CEDAR MOUNTAIN WHERE GENERAL C. S. WINDER DIED. FROM A PHOTOGRAPH.

General Winder, who was in command of Stonewall Jackson's old division, was struck by a shell while directing the movements of the batteries of his division.—EDITORS.

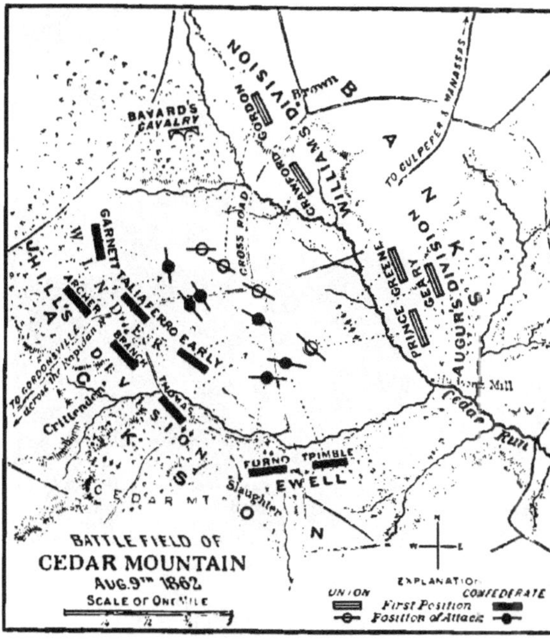

Banks's line was formed in the valley of Cedar Run, and overlapped the Confederate left. Geary and Prince, advancing, encountered Early and Taliaferro on the broad cultivated plateau south of the Culpeper road, while Crawford closed in from the north on the enemy's left. The advantage was with Banks. At 6 o'clock the battle was at its height; Garnett struck the flank of Crawford, and the fresh brigades of Hill's division were led against Prince and Geary. The extreme right of Banks's line, the brigade of General G. H. Gordon (Williams's division), now charged up to the point where Crawford had gone in, and General G. S. Greene's brigade (Augur's division) moved to the aid of Prince and Geary. Meanwhile, Banks's artillery having been forced back by the guns on the mountain-sides, Ewell threw forward his brigades on the right, Thomas (Hill's division) came forward into the gap between Early and Forno, and the battle was decided by the repulse everywhere of Banks's troops. The last charge was made by Bayard's cavalry on the extreme Union right. The advance of Branch brought fresh muskets against Bayard, and the successes of Jackson all along the line closed the day. After dark Banks withdrew to his first position north of Cedar Creek and was there met by Ricketts's division and by General Pope in person.

The journal of General L. O'B. Branch, written August 14th, contains the following description of the battle: "General Jackson came to me and told me his left was beaten and broken, and the enemy was turning him and he wished me to advance. I was already in line of battle and instantly gave the order, 'Forward, march.' I had not gone 100 yards through the woods before we met the celebrated Stonewall Brigade, utterly routed and fleeing as fast as they could run. After proceeding a short distance farther we met the enemy pursuing. My brigade opened upon them and quickly drove the enemy back from the woods into a large field. Following up to the edge of the field, I came in view of large bodies of the enemy, and having a very fine position, I opened upon them with great effect. The enemy's cavalry attempted to charge us in two columns, but the fire soon broke them and sent them fleeing across the field in every direction. The infantry then retreated also. Advancing into the field, I halted near the middle of it, in doubt which direction to take. Just at that moment General Jackson came riding up from my rear alone. I reported my brigade as being solid, and asked for orders. My men recognized him and raised a terrific shout as he rode along the line with his hat off. He evidently knew how to appreciate a brigade that had gone through a hot battle and was then following the retreating enemy without having broken its line of battle, and remained with me . . . until the pursuit ceased."

General S. W. Crawford gives this account of the flank movement attempted by his brigade: "Onward these regiments charged, driving the enemy's infantry back through the wood beyond. . . . But the reserves of the enemy were at once brought up and thrown upon the broken ranks. The field-officers had all been killed, wounded, or taken prisoners; the support I looked for did not arrive, and my gallant men, broken, decimated by that fearful fire, that unequal contest, fell back again across the space, leaving most of their number upon the field." Crawford's brigade lost 494 killed or wounded, and 373 missing, out of a total of 1767 engaged.— EDITORS.

NOTE ON THE BATTLE OF CEDAR MOUNTAIN: On the 13th of July, the regular command of Jackson, consisting of the divisions of Ewell and Winder, marched from Mechanicsville, on the Chickahominy, under orders to dispute the advance of Pope's army south of the Rapidan. The column reached Gordonsville on the 19th, and Jackson, on learning that Pope's forces outnumbered his own, remained inactive until reinforced early in August by the division of A. P. Hill. Pope was now on the Upper Rappahannock, with the corps of Banks and Sigel, the former at Culpeper, the latter at Sperryville. The outposts of infantry and cavalry under Generals S. W. Crawford and George D. Bayard were along the Rapidan, covering the approaches to Culpeper and Sperryville [see map, p. 459]. On the 8th Bayard's pickets discovered the enemy crossing at Barnett's Ford in large force, and retired along the Orange Court House road toward Culpeper.

Jackson's object was to strike Banks at Culpeper before the latter could be reinforced. On Jackson's approach, Pope ordered Banks's corps forward to Cedar Mountain, about eight miles beyond Culpeper, where it arrived in detachments, being in hand by noon of the 9th, in two divisions, numbering about 8000 men, under Generals C. C. Augur and A. S. Williams. General J. B. Ricketts's division, of McDowell's corps, was coming up as support. The Confederate divisions of Generals C. S. Winder and R. S. Ewell were now disposed along the northern base of the mountain, the brigades of General I. R. Trimble, Colonel H. Forno, and General J. A. Early, of Ewell's division, on the right, with those of General W. B. Taliaferro and Lieutenant-Colonel T. S. Garnett, of Winder's division, on the left, and Winder's "Stonewall" brigade, under Colonel C. A. Ronald, in reserve. The brigades of Generals L. O'B. Branch, J. J. Archer, and E. L. Thomas, of A. P. Hill's division, were within call, the entire command under Jackson on the field, numbering at least 20,000. The Confederates opened the battle, sending forward Early and Taliaferro at 3 o'clock, but moving with caution. [See p. 498.]

CHARGE OF UNION CAVALRY UPON THE CONFEDERATE ADVANCE NEAR BRANDY STATION, AUGUST 20, 1862.
FROM A SKETCH MADE AT THE TIME.

is yet, misunderstood because of the false impressions created by this statement.

Under the orders heretofore referred to, the concentration of the three corps of the Army of Virginia (except King's division of McDowell's corps) was completed, Sigel's corps being at Sperryville, Banks's at Little Washington, and Ricketts's division of McDowell's corps at Waterloo Bridge. I assumed the command in person July 29th, 1862.

As this paper is mainly concerned with the second battle of Bull Run, I shall not recount any of the military operations beyond the Rappahannock, nor give any account of the battle of Cedar Mountain [see p. 459] and the skirmishes which followed.

It is only necessary to say that the course of these operations made it plain enough that the Rappahannock was too far to the front, and that the movements of Lee were too rapid and those of McClellan too slow to make it possible, with the small force I had, to hold that line, or to keep open communication with Fredericksburg without being turned on my right flank by Lee's whole army and cut off altogether from Washington.

On the 21st of August, being then at Rappahannock Station, my little army confronted by nearly the whole force under General Lee, which had compelled the retreat of McClellan to Harrison's Landing, I was positively assured that two days more would see me largely enough reënforced by the Army of the Potomac to be not only secure, but to assume the offensive against Lee, and I was instructed to hold on "and fight like the devil."

I accordingly held on till the 26th of August, when, finding myself to be outflanked on my right by the main body of Lee's army, while Jackson's corps having passed Salem and Rectortown the day before were in rapid march in the direction of Gainesville and Manassas Junction, and seeing that none of the reënforcements promised me were likely to arrive, I determined to abandon the line of the Rappahannock and communications with Fredericksburg, and concentrate my whole force in the direction of Warrenton and Gainesville, to cover the Warrenton pike, and still to confront the enemy rapidly marching to my right.]

Stonewall Jackson's movement on Manassas Junction was plainly seen and promptly reported, and I notified General Halleck of it. He informed me on the 23d of August that heavy reënforcements would begin to arrive at Warrenton Junction on the next day (24th), and as my orders still held me to the Rappahannock I naturally supposed that these troops would be hurried forward to me with all speed. Franklin's corps especially, I asked, should be sent rapidly to Gainesville. I also telegraphed Colonel Herman Haupt, chief of railway transportation, to direct one of the strongest divisions coming forward, and to be at Warrenton Junction on the 24th, to be put in the works at Manassas Junction. A cavalry force had been sent forward to observe the Thoroughfare Gap early on the morning of the 26th, but nothing was heard from it.‡

On the night of August 26th Jackson's advance, having passed Thoroughfare Gap, struck the Orange and Alexandria railroad at Manassas Junction, and made it plain to me that all of the reënforcements and movements of the troops promised me had altogether failed.↓ Had Franklin been even at Centreville, or had Cox's and Sturgis's divisions been as far west as Bull Run on that day, the movement of Jackson on Manassas Junction would not have been practicable.

As Jackson's movement on Manassas Junction marks the beginning of the second battle of Bull Run, it is essential to a clear understanding of subsequent operations to give the positions of the army under my command on the night of August 26th, as also the movements and operations of the enemy as far as we knew them.

] Reynolds's division of Porter's corps, having arrived at Aquia on August 13th and 20th, joined General Pope on the 22d, and was assigned to McDowell's corps. General Porter reported to General Burnside (who had arrived at Aquia on August 5th with about 12,000 men from North Carolina) for orders on the 21st. Being pushed out toward the Upper Rappahannock to connect with Reno, his advance under Morell, on the 24th, found Reno and Reynolds gone; no troops of General Pope's were to be seen or heard of (except one company of cavalry, afterward discovered, which had been left to guard Kelly's ford), nor were any orders from General Pope or any information as to his whereabouts received by General Porter or General Burnside until the 26th. So far as appears, no information of this movement was communicated to General Halleck. On the 24th, in reply to General McClellan's inquiry from Falmouth, 9:40 P. M., "Please inform me exactly where General Pope's troops are. . . .

Up to what point is the Orange and Alexandria railroad now available? Where are the enemy in force?" General Halleck telegraphed: "You ask me for information which I cannot give. I do not know either where General Pope is or where the enemy in force is. These are matters which I have all day been most anxious to ascertain."— EDITORS.

‡ General Pope's orders of the 25th disposed his troops on the line of the Rappahannock, from Waterloo to Kelly's Ford, as for an advance toward the Rapidan. Reno was ordered back to Kelly's Ford to resume communication with the forces under Burnside at Falmouth.— EDITORS.

↓ The first information appears to have been received in a communication between the telegraph operators at Pope's headquarters and at Manassas Junction, dated 8:20 P. M., on August 26th. From this time until the 30th all direct communication between General Pope and Washington remained cut off, and nothing was heard of him except via Falmouth.— EDITORS.

From the 18th until the night of the 26th of August the troops had been marching and fighting almost continuously. As was to be expected under such circumstances, the effective force had been greatly diminished by death, by wounds, by sickness, and by fatigue.‖

Heintzelman's corps, which had come up from Alexandria, was at Warrenton Junction, and numbered, as he reported to me, less than eight thousand men,‖ but it was without wagons, without artillery, without horses even for the field-officers, and with only forty rounds of ammunition to the man. The corps of General F. J. Porter consisted of about ten thousand men, and was by far the freshest if not the best in the army. He had made very short and deliberate marches from Fredericksburg, and his advance division, mainly troops of the regular army under Sykes, had arrived at Warrenton Junction by eleven o'clock on the morning of the 27th, Morell's division of the same corps arriving later in the same day.

I saw General F. J. Porter at Warrenton Junction about 11 o'clock on the morning of the 27th. Sykes's division of his corps was encamped near; Morell's was expected in a few hours. I had seen General Porter at West Point while we were both cadets, but I think I never had an acquaintance with him there,

BREVET MAJOR-GENERAL JOHN W. GEARY.
FROM A PHOTOGRAPH MADE IN 1866.

nor do I think I ever met him afterward in the service except for about five minutes in Philadelphia in 1861, when I called at his office for a pass, which was then required to go to Washington *via* Annapolis. This, I think, was the first and only time I ever met him previous to the meeting at Warrenton Junction. He had so high a reputation in the army and for services since the outbreak of the war, that I was not only curious to see him, but was exceedingly glad that he had joined the army under my command with a corps which I knew to be one of the most effective in the service. This feeling was so strong that I expressed it warmly and on several occasions. He appeared to me a most gentlemanlike man, of a soldierly and striking appearance. I had but little

‖ August 18th, skirmishes at Rapidan Station and on Clark's Mountain, near Orange Court House; 20th, skirmishes at Raccoon Ford, Stevensburg, Brandy Station, Rappahannock Station, and near Kelly's Ford; 21st, skirmishes along the Rappahannock, at Kelly's, Beverly (or Cunningham's), and Freeman's Fords; 22d, actions at Freeman's Ford and Hazel River, and skirmishes along the Rappahannock; 23d, engagement at Rappahannock Station, action at Beverly Ford, and skirmish at Fant's Ford. 23d and 24th, actions at Sulphur (or Warrenton) Springs; 24th and 25th, actions at Waterloo Bridge; 25th, skirmish at Sulphur Springs; 26th, skirmishes at Bristoe Station, Bull Run Bridge, Gainesville, Haymarket, Manassas Junction, and Sulphur Springs.— EDITORS.

‖ Heintzelman's infantry (effectives) numbered 15,011 on the 10th of August, and the full corps, replenished by six new regiments, reported 16,000 for duty September 10th. There are no intermediate reports.— EDITORS.

conversation with him, as I was engaged, as he was, in writing telegrams. He seemed to me to exhibit a listlessness and indifference not quite natural under the circumstances, which, however, it is not unusual for men to assume in the midst of dangers and difficulties, merely to impress one with their superior coolness.

The troops were disposed as follows: McDowell's corps and Sigel's corps were at Warrenton under general command of General McDowell, with Banks's corps at Fayetteville as a reserve. Reno's corps was directed upon the Warrenton turnpike to take post three miles east of Warrenton. Porter's corps was near Bealeton Station moving slowly toward Warrenton Junction; Heintzelman at Warrenton Junction, with very small means to move in any direction.

Up to this time I had been placed by the positive orders of General Halleck much in the position of a man tied by one leg and fighting with a person much his physical superior and free to move in any direction. The following telegrams will explain exactly the situation as heretofore indicated:

"August 25th, 1862.

"MAJOR-GENERAL HALLECK: Your dispatch just received. Of course I shall be ready to recross the Rappahannock at a moment's notice. You will see from the positions taken that each army corps is on the best roads across the river. You wished forty-eight hours to assemble the forces from the Peninsula behind the Rappahannock, and four days have passed without the enemy yet being permitted to cross. I don't think he is yet ready to do so. In ordinarily dry weather the Rappahannock can be crossed almost anywhere, and these crossing-places are best protected by concentrating at central positions to strike at any force which attempts to cross. I had clearly understood that you wished to unite our whole forces before a forward movement was begun, and that I must take care to keep united with Burnside on my left, so that no movement to separate us could be made. This withdrew me lower down the Rappahannock than I wished to come. I am not acquainted with your views, as you seem to suppose, and would be glad to know them so far as my own position and operations are concerned. I understood you clearly that, at all hazards. I was to prevent the enemy from passing the Rappahannock. This I have done, and shall do. I don't like to be on the defensive if I can help it, but must be so as long as I am tied to Burnside's forces, not yet wholly arrived at Fredericksburg. Please let me know, if it can be done, what is to be my own command, and if I am to act independently against the enemy. I certainly understood that, as soon as the whole of our forces were concentrated, you designed to take command in person, and that, when everything was ready, we were to move forward in concert. I judge from the tone of your dispatch that you are dissatisfied with something. Unless I know what it is, of course I can't correct it. The troops arriving here come in fragments. Am I to assign them to brigades and corps? I would suppose not, as several of the new regiments coming have been assigned to army corps directly from your office. In case I commence offensive operations I must know what forces I am to take and what you wish left, and what connection must be kept up with Burnside. It has been my purpose to conform my operations to your plans, yet I was not informed when McClellan evacuated Harrison's Landing, so that I might know what to expect in that direction; and when I say these things in no complaining spirit I think that you know well that I am anxious to do everything to advance your plans of campaign. I understood that this army was to maintain the line of the Rappahannock until all the forces from the Peninsula had united behind that river. I have done so. I understood distinctly that I was not to hazard anything except for this purpose, as delay was what was wanted.

"The enemy this morning has pushed a considerable infantry force up opposite Waterloo Bridge, and is planting batteries, and long lines of his infantry are moving up from Jeffersonville toward Sulphur Springs. His whole force, as far as can be ascertained, is massed in front of me, from railroad crossing of Rappahannock around to Waterloo Bridge, their main body being opposite Sulphur Springs. "JOHN POPE. Major-General."

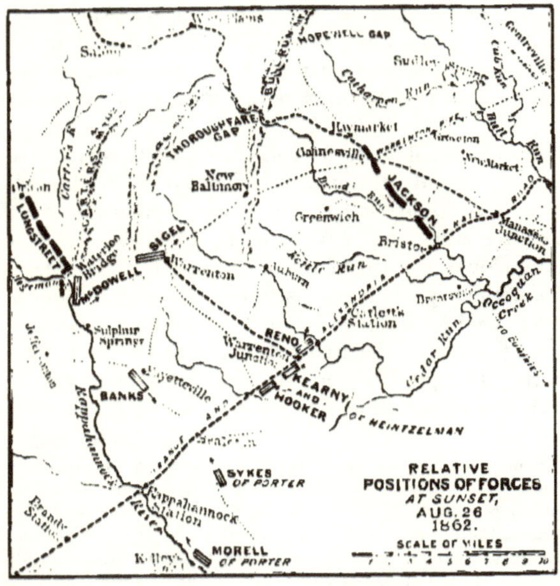

"U. S. MILITARY TELEGRAPH. (Received Aug. 26th, 1862, from War Dep't, 11:45 A. M.) "MAJOR-GENERAL POPE:— Not the slightest dissatisfaction has been felt in regard to your operations on the Rappahannock. The main object has been accomplished in getting up troops from the Peninsula, although they have been greatly delayed by storms. Moreover, the telegraph has been interrupted, leaving us for a time ignorant of the progress of the evacuation. . . . If possible to attack the enemy in flank, do so, but the main object now is to ascertain his position. Make cavalry excursions for that purpose, especially toward Front Royal. If possible to get in his rear, pursue with vigor.   H. W. HALLECK, "General-in-Chief."

The movements of the enemy toward my right forced me either to abandon the line of the Rappahannock and the communications with Fredericksburg, or to risk the loss of my army and the almost certain loss of Washington. Of course between these two alternatives I could not hesitate in a choice. I considered it my duty, at whatever sacrifice to my army and myself, to retard, as far as I could, the movement of the enemy toward Washington, until I was certain that the Army of the Potomac had reached Alexandria.

The movement of Jackson presented the only opportunity which had offered to gain any success over the superior forces of the enemy. I determined, therefore, on the morning of the 27th of August to abandon the line of the Rappahannock and throw my whole force in the direction of Gainesville and Manassas Junction, to crush any force of the enemy that had passed through Thoroughfare Gap, and to interpose between Lee's army and Bull Run. Having the interior line of operations, and the enemy at Manassas being inferior in force, it appeared to me, and still so appears, that with even ordinary promptness and energy we might feel sure of success.

In the meantime heavy forces of the enemy still confronted us at Waterloo Bridge, \ while his main body continued its march toward our right, following the course of Hedgman's River (the Upper Rappahannock). I accordingly sent orders, early on the 27th of August, to General McDowell to move rapidly on Gainesville by the Warrenton pike with his own corps, reënforced by Reynolds's division and Sigel's corps. I directed Reno, followed by Kearny's division of Heintzelman's corps, to move on Greenwich, so as to reach there

\ On the afternoon of August 26th, Longstreet's corps moved to Hinson's Mill Ford, six miles above, leaving R. H. Anderson's division (about 6000 effectives) at Waterloo Bridge.— EDITORS.

THE REAR OF THE COLUMN. FROM A WAR-TIME SKETCH.

that night, to report thence at once to General McDowell, and to support him in operations against the enemy which were expected near Gainesville. With Hooker's division of Heintzelman's corps I moved along the railroad toward Manassas Junction, to reopen our communications and to be in position to coöperate with the forces along the Warrenton pike.

On the afternoon of that day a severe engagement took place between Hooker's division and Ewell's division of Jackson's corps, near Bristoe Station, on the railroad. Ewell was driven back along the railroad, but at dark still confronted Hooker along the banks of Broad Run. The loss in this action was about three hundred killed and wounded on each side. Ewell left his dead, many of his wounded, and some of his baggage on the field. ‡

I had not seen Hooker for many years, and I remembered him as a very handsome young man, with florid complexion and fair hair, and with a figure agile and graceful. As I saw him that afternoon on his white horse riding in rear of his line of battle, and close up to it, with the excitement of battle in his eyes, and that gallant and chivalric appearance which he always presented under fire, I was struck with admiration. As a corps commander, with his whole force operating under his own eye, it is much to be doubted whether Hooker had a superior in the army.

The railroad had been torn up and the bridges burned in several places just west of Bristoe Station. I therefore directed General Banks, who had reached Warrenton Junction, to cover the railroad trains at that place until General Porter marched, and then to run back the trains toward Manassas as

‡ This engagement is known as Kettle Run (see map, p. 467). The Confederate force consisted of Early's brigade, with two regiments of Forno's, two of Lawton's, and Brown's and Johnson's batteries. After disputing Hooker's advance for some hours, Ewell withdrew under fire.—EDITORS.

far as he could and rebuild the railroad bridges. Captain Merrill of the Engineers was also directed to repair the railroad track and bridges toward Bristoe. This work was done by that accomplished officer as far east as Kettle Run on the 27th, and the trains were run back to that point next morning.

At dark on the 27th Hooker informed me that his ammunition was nearly exhausted, only five rounds to the man being on hand. Before this time it had become apparent that Jackson, with his whole force, was south of the Warrenton pike and in the immediate neighborhood of Manassas Junction.

McDowell reached his position at Gainesville during the night of the 27th, and Kearny and Reno theirs at Greenwich. It was clear on that night that we had completely interposed between Jackson and the enemy's main body, which was still west of the Bull Run range, and in the vicinity of White Plains.

In consequence of Hooker's report, and the weakness of the small division which he commanded, and to strengthen my right wing moving in the direction of Manassas, I sent orders to Porter at dark, which reached him at 9 P. M., to move forward from Warrenton Junction at 1 A. M. night, and to report to me at Bristoe Station by daylight next morning (August 28th).

There were but two courses left to Jackson by this sudden movement of the army. He could not retrace his steps through Gainesville, as that place was occupied by McDowell with a force equal if not superior to his own. To retreat through Centreville would carry him still farther away from the main body of Lee's army. It was possible, however, to mass his whole force at Manassas Junction and assail our right (Hooker's division), which had fought a severe battle that afternoon, and was almost out of ammunition. Jackson, with A. P. Hill's division, retired through Centreville. Thinking it altogether within the probabilities that he might adopt the other alternative, I sent the orders above mentioned to General Porter. He neither obeyed them nor attempted to obey them, ☆ but afterward gave as a reason for not doing so that his men were tired, the night was too dark to march, and that there was a wagon train on the road toward Bristoe. The distance was nine miles along the railroad track, with a wagon road on each side of it most of the way; but his corps did not reach Bristoe Station until 10:30 o'clock next morning, six hours after daylight; and the moment he found that the enemy had left our front he asked to halt and rest his corps. Of his first reason for not complying with my orders, it is only necessary to say that Sykes's division had reached Warrenton Junction at 11 o'clock on the morning of the 27th, and had been in camp all day. Morell's division arrived later in the day at Warrenton Junction, and would have been in camp for at least eight hours before the time it was ordered to march. The marches of these two divisions from Fredericksburg had been extremely deliberate, and involved but little more exercise than is needed for good health. The diaries of these marches make

<hr>

☆ Porter marched about 3 A. M., instead of at 1, as ordered. The leading brigade lit candles to look for the road. On the Confederate side Colonel Henry Forno, 5th Louisiana, reports: "After 12 o'clock at night of the 27th, the brigade was put in motion with orders to follow General Early, but owing to the darkness I was unable to find him." Two orders addressed by Pope at Bristoe to McDowell at Gainesville fell into the hands of A. P. Hill, at Centreville. Some of the Confederates (Jackson, Trimble, and Stuart) mention the darkness of the night of the 26th; and General McDowell lost his way from this cause on the night of the 28th.—EDITORS.

Porter's claim of fatigue ridiculous. To compare the condition of this corps and its marches with those of any of the troops of the Army of Virginia is a sufficient answer to such a pretext. The impossibility of marching on account of the darkness of that night finds its best

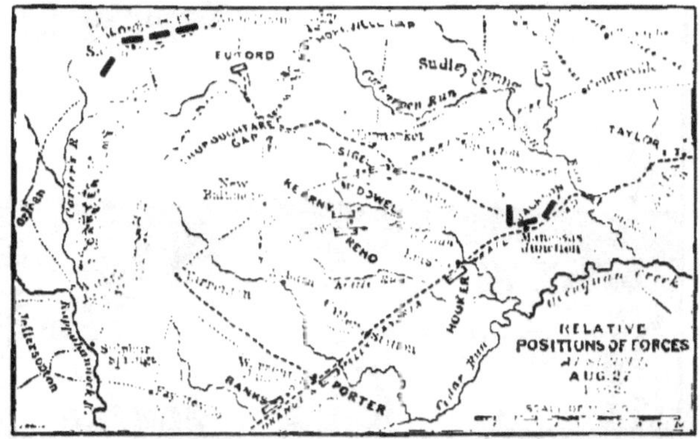

answer in the fact that nearly every other division of the army, and the whole of Jackson's corps, marched during the greater part of the night in the immediate vicinity of Porter's corps, and from nearly every point of the compass. The plea of darkness and of the obstruction of a wagon train along the road will strike our armies with some surprise in the light of their subsequent experience of night marches. The railroad track itself was clear and entirely practicable for the march of infantry.

According to the testimony of Colonel Myers, quartermaster in charge of the train, the train was drawn off the roads and parked after dark that night; and even if this had not been the case, it is not necessary to tell any officer who served in the war that the infantry advance could easily have pushed the wagons off the road to make way for the artillery. Colonel Myers also testified that he could have gone on with his train that night, and that he drew off the road and parked his train for rest and because of the action of Hooker's division in his front, and not because he was prevented from continuing his march by darkness or other obstacles.

At 9 o'clock on the night of the 27th, satisfied of Jackson's position, I sent orders to General McDowell at Gainesville to push forward at the earliest dawn of day upon Manassas Junction, resting his right on the Manassas Gap Railroad and extending his left to the east. I directed General Reno at the same time to march from Greenwich, also direct on Manassas Junction, and Kearny to move from the same place upon Bristoe Station. This move of Kearny was to strengthen my right at Bristoe and unite the two divisions of Heintzelman's corps.∫

Jackson began to evacuate Manassas Junction during the night (the 27th) and marched toward Centreville and other points of the Warrenton pike west of that place, and by 11 o'clock next morning was at and beyond Centreville and north of the Warrenton pike.⚓ I arrived at Manassas Junction shortly after the last of Jackson's force had moved off, and immediately pushed for-

<hr>

∫ General Pope's orders of the 27th for the movements of the 28th directed his whole army upon Manassas. Full information of these dispositions reached General A. P. Hill early the next morning, through the captured orders.— EDITORS.

⚓ At this time Jackson's command was concen-

COLLISION ON THURSDAY, AUGUST 28, BETWEEN REYNOLDS'S DIVISION AND JACKSON'S RIGHT WING.

The view is from the north side of the turnpike (from a war-time sketch), east of Gainesville, and looking toward Groveton. The smoke along the woods indicates the position of the Confederates, who fell back toward Groveton, while Reynolds turned off to the right toward Manassas. During the battles of Friday and Saturday (the 29th and 30th), the lines were nearly reversed. Jackson was then to the left, looking south toward Manassas, and Longstreet's lines, facing like Reynolds's in the above picture, but extending farther to the right, and confronting McDowell and Porter (see maps, pp. 473 and 482).— EDITORS.

ward Hooker, Kearny, and Reno upon Centreville,‡ and sent orders to Porter to come forward to Manassas Junction. I also wrote McDowell the situation and directed him to call back to Gainesville any part of his force which had moved in the direction of Manassas Junction, and march upon Centreville along the Warrenton pike with the whole force under his command to intercept the retreat of Jackson toward Thoroughfare Gap. With King's division in advance, McDowell, marching toward Centreville, encountered late in the afternoon the advance of Jackson's corps retreating toward Thoroughfare Gap.‡ Late in the afternoon, also, Kearny drove the rear-guard of Jackson

trated near Groveton. General Pope says in his report: "I reached Manassas Junction . . . about 12 o'clock . . . less than an hour after Jackson, in person, had retired." Jackson was, however, on the old "battle-field of Manassas" at 8 A. M., as appears from the order of that date to A. P. Hill, and about noon when he sent orders to Taliaferro to attack the Federal troops (evidently Reynolds), supposed to be marching on Centreville, but actually moving from Gainesville to Manassas under Pope's first orders. Jackson says: "My command had hardly concentrated north of the turnpike before the enemy's advance reached the vicinity of Groveton from the direction of Warrenton." In the above sketch, Meade's brigade and Cooper's battery are seen deploying for action.— EDITORS.

‡ At 1:20 or 2 P. M. Pope repeated his orders sent "a few minutes ago" to McDowell to march toward Gum Springs, distant 20 miles in the direction of Aldie Gap. The note sent "a few minutes ago," reached McDowell at 3:15 P. M. The orders to march on Centreville were dated 4:15 P. M., and McDowell appears to have received the second while preparing to execute the first.— EDITORS.

‡ Jackson says: "Dispositions were promptly made to attack the enemy, based upon the idea that he would continue to press forward upon the turnpike toward Alexandria; but as he did not appear to advance in force, and there was reason to believe that his main body was leaving the road and inclining toward Manassas Junction, my command was advanced through the woods, leaving Groveton on the left, until it reached a commanding position near Brawner's house. By this time it was sunset; but as his column appeared to be moving by, with its flank exposed, I determined to attack at once, which was vigorously done by the divisions of Taliaferro and Ewell."— EDITORS.

out of Centreville and occupied that place with his advance beyond it toward Gainesville. A very severe engagement occurred between King's division and Jackson's forces near the village of Groveton on the Warrenton pike, which was terminated by the darkness, both parties maintaining their ground.\ The conduct of this division in this severe engagement was admirable, and reflects the utmost credit both upon its commanders and the men under their command. That this division was not reënforced by Reynolds☆ and Sigel ǀ seems unaccountable. The reason given, though it is not satisfactory, was the fact that General McDowell had left the command just before it encountered the enemy, and had gone toward Manassas Junction, where he

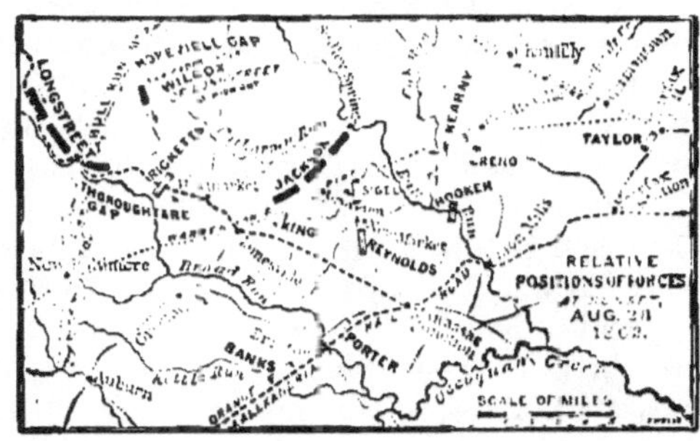

supposed me to be, in order to give me some information about the immediate country in which we were operating, and with which, of course, he was much more familiar from former experience than I could be. ‡ I had

\ King's division (which had not been at Gainesville on the night of the 27th, but near Buckland Mills, and was consequently near the Warrenton pike instead of at Manassas, when, by General Pope's 4:15 P. M. order, the army was directed upon Centreville instead of upon Manassas) encountered Jackson's forces in position as stated in the preceding note about 5:30 P. M. Gibbon's brigade, with two regiments of Doubleday's (the 56th Pennsylvania and 76th New York), contended against Taliaferro's division and two brigades (Lawton's and Trimble's) of Ewell's division. General Jackson says:

"The batteries of Wooding, Poague, and Carpenter were placed in position in front of Starke's brigade, and above the village of Groveton, and, firing over the heads of our skirmishers, poured a heavy fire of shot and shell upon the enemy. This was responded to by a very heavy fire from the enemy, forcing our batteries to select another position. By this time Taliaferro's command, with Lawton's and Trimble's brigades on his left, was advanced from the woods to the open field, and was now moving in gallant style until it reached an orchard on the right of our line and was less than 100 yards from a large force of the enemy. The conflict here was fierce and sanguinary. Although largely reënforced, the Federals did not attempt to advance, but maintained their ground with obstinate determination. Both lines stood exposed to the discharges of musketry and artillery until about 9 o'clock, when the enemy slowly fell back, yielding the field to our troops. The loss on both sides was heavy, and among our wounded were Major-General Ewell and Brigadier-General Taliaferro."

Gibbon's brigade lost 133 killed, 539 wounded, 79 missing, total, 751, "or considerably over one-third of the command." King held his ground until 1 A. M. on the 29th, when, being without support, without communication with either of the generals in command over him, and without orders since those of 4:15 P. M., he marched to Manassas Junction.—Editors.

☆ Reynolds, ordered to march *en échelon* on King's right, was moving toward Manassas (see note to picture, p. 468), when, at 5 P. M., he received McDowell's order, based on Pope's of 4:15, to march on Centreville. He turned off at Bethlehem Church and took the Sudley Springs road toward the Warrenton pike. General Reynolds says:

"About this time heavy cannonading was heard both to our front and left, the former supposed to be from Sigel's corps, and the latter from King's division, which had taken the Warrenton pike from Gainesville. I sent word to the column to hasten its march, and proceeded to the left at once myself in the direction of the firing, arriving on the field just before dark, and found that Gibbon's brigade, of King's division, was engaged with the enemy, with Doubleday's and Patrick's brigades in the vicinity. After the firing ceased I saw General King, who, determining to maintain his position, I left about 9 o'clock P. M. to return to my division, promising to bring it up early in the morning to his support. Before leaving, however, I heard the division moving off, and I learned from General Hatch that it was moving by Gainesville toward Manassas. I then returned to my own division, which I reached at daylight."

Editors.

ǀ Sigel was ordered to move at 2:45 A. M. and to march *en échelon* on Reynolds's right. His advance appears to have reached Manassas about noon. He states that during the afternoon he was ordered by General Pope to march by New Market on Centreville, and arrived on the field of the First Bull Run, near the Henry house (see p. 473), too late to take part in King's engagement.—Editors.

‡ According to General McDowell, this was "after putting these divisions in motion (under the 4:15 P. M. order) and going with Reynolds's

left Manassas Junction, however, for Centreville. Hearing the sound of the guns indicating King's engagement with the enemy, McDowell set off to rejoin his command, but lost his way, and I first heard of him next morning at Manassas Junction. As his troops did not know of his absence, there was no one to give orders to Sigel and Reynolds.

The engagement of King's division was reported to me about 10 o'clock at night near Centreville. I felt sure then, and so stated, that there was no escape for Jackson. On the west of him were McDowell's corps (I did not then know that he had detached Ricketts\), Sigel's corps, and Reynolds's division, all under command of McDowell. On the east of him, and with the advance of Kearny nearly in contact with him on the Warrenton pike, were the corps of Reno and Heintzelman. Porter was supposed to be at Manassas Junction, where he ought to have been on that afternoon.

I sent orders to McDowell (supposing him to be with his command), and also direct to General King, ⸸ several times during that night and once by his own staff-officer, to hold his ground at all hazards, to prevent the retreat of Jackson toward Lee, and that at daylight our whole force from Centreville and Manassas would assail him from the east, and he would be crushed between us. I sent orders also to General Kearny at Centreville to move forward cautiously that night along the Warrenton pike; to drive in the pickets of the enemy, and to keep as closely as possible in contact with him during the night, resting his left on the Warrenton pike and throwing his right to the north, if practicable, as far as the Little River pike, and at daylight next morning to assault vigorously with his right advance, and that Hooker and Reno would certainly be with him shortly after daylight. I sent orders to General Porter, who I supposed was at Manassas Junction, to move upon Centreville at dawn, stating to him the position of our forces, and that a severe battle would be fought that morning (the 29th).

With Jackson at and near Groveton, with McDowell on the west, and the rest of the army on the east of him, while Lee, with the mass of his army, was still west of Thoroughfare Gap, the situation for us was certainly as favorable as the most sanguine person could desire, and the prospect of crushing Jackson, sandwiched between such forces, were certainly excellent. There is no doubt, had General McDowell been with his command when King's division of his corps became engaged with the enemy, he would have brought forward to its support both Sigel and Reynolds, and the result would have been to hold the ground west of Jackson at least until morning brought against him also the forces moving from the direction of Centreville.

division to near Manassas"; and in compliance with General Pope's request of 1:20 or 2 P. M., viz., "Give me your views fully: you know the country much better than I do." General Mc-Dowell found Reynolds at daybreak on the 29th.— Editors.

⸸ In the exercise of his discretion McDowell, then commanding two corps, sent Ricketts to Thoroughfare Gap on the morning of the 28th, to delay Longstreet's advance, notwithstanding

General Pope's orders to move on Manassas with his whole command. But for this, the movement on Manassas as ordered in the morning, as well as the movement on Centreville as ordered in the afternoon, would have left no troops except Buford's broken down cavalry between Longstreet and Jackson, or between Longstreet and Pope's left.—Editors.

† But see Captain Charles King's denial on page 495.—Editors.

To my great disappointment and surprise, however, I learned toward daylight the next morning (the 29th) that King's division had fallen back toward Manassas Junction, and that neither Sigel nor Reynolds had been engaged or had gone to the support of King. The route toward Thoroughfare Gap had thus been left open by the wholly unexpected retreat of King's division, due to the fact that he was not supported by Sigel and Reynolds, and an immediate change was necessary in the disposition of the troops under my command. Sigel and Reynolds were near Groveton, almost in contact with Jackson; Ricketts had fallen back toward Bristoe from Thoroughfare Gap, after offering (as might have been expected) ineffectual resistance to the passage of the Bull Run range by very superior forces; King had fallen back to Manassas Junction; Porter was at Manassas Junction or near there; Reno [and Hooker near Centreville; Kearny at Centreville and beyond toward Groveton; Jackson near Groveton with his whole corps; Lee with the main army of the enemy, except three brigades of Longstreet which had passed Hopewell Gap, north of Thoroughfare Gap.

The field of battle was practically limited to the space between the old railroad grade from Sudley to Gainesville if prolonged across the Warrenton pike and the Sudley Springs road east of it. The railroad grade indicates almost exactly the line occupied by Jackson's force, our own line confronting it from left to right.

The ridge which bounded the valley of Dawkins's Branch on the west, and on which were the Hampton Cole and Monroe houses, offered from the Monroe house a full view of the field of battle from right to left, and the Monroe house being on the crest of the ridge overlooked and completely commanded the approach to Jackson's right by the Warrenton turnpike. To the result of the battle this ridge was of the last importance, and, if seized and held by noon, would absolutely have prevented any reënforcement of Jackson's right from the direction of Gainesville. The northern slope of this ridge was held by our troops near the Douglass house, near which, also, the right of Jackson's line rested. The advance of Porter's corps at Dawkins's Branch was less than a mile and a half from the Monroe house, and the road in his front was one of several which converged on that point.

The whole field was free from obstacles to movement of troops and nearly so to manœuvres, with only a few eminences, and these of a nature to have been seized and easily held by our troops even against very superior numbers. The ground was gently undulating and the water-courses insignificant, while the intersecting system of roads and lanes afforded easy communication with all parts of the field. It would be difficult to find anywhere in Virginia a more perfect field of battle than that on which the second battle of Bull Run was fought.

About daylight, therefore, on the 29th of August, almost immediately after I received information of the withdrawal of King's division toward Manassas Junction, I sent orders to General Sigel, in the vicinity of Groveton, to attack

[Reno appears not to have been at Centreville at this time, since General Pope's headquarters "near Bull Run" were between him and Centreville at 3 A. M. on the 30th.— EDITORS.

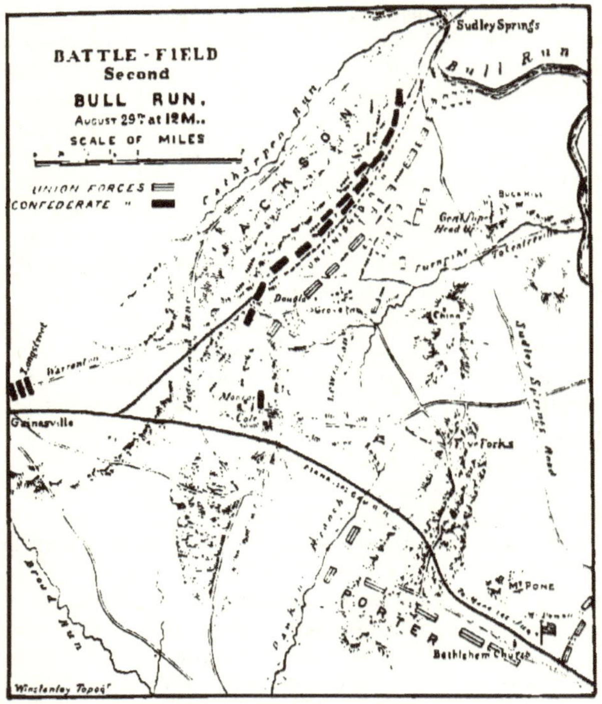

RELATIVE POSITIONS AT NOON, FRIDAY, AUGUST 29TH.

This map represents General Pope's view of the situation at noon, August 29th, with Longstreet placed at Gainesville; but, according to General Longstreet (see p. 510) and others (see p. 525), Longstreet was at that hour on Jackson's right and capable of resisting an advance on the part of Porter.— EDITORS.

the enemy vigorously at daylight and bring him to a stand if possible. ☆ He was to be supported by Reynolds's division. I instructed Heintzelman ♪ to push forward from Centreville toward Gainesville on the Warrenton pike at the earliest dawn with the divisions of Kearny and Hooker, and gave orders also to Reno with his corps to follow closely in their rear. They were directed to use all speed, and as soon as they came up with the enemy to establish communication with Sigel, and to attack vigorously and promptly. I also sent orders to General Porter ♱ at Manassas Junction to move forward rapidly with his own corps and King's division of McDowell's corps, which was there also, upon Gainesville by the direct route from Manassas Junction to that place. I urged him to make all possible speed, with the purpose that he should come up with the enemy or connect himself with the left of our line near where the Warrenton pike is crossed by the road from Manassas Junction to Gainesville.

Shortly after sending this order I received a note from General McDowell, whom I had not been able to find during the night of the 28th, dated Manassas

☆ These orders to Sigel are not found in the "Official Records," but they correspond with the orders given to Kearny and Heintzelman at 9:50 and 10 P. M., on the 28th. General Sigel says he received them during the night, made his preparations at night, and "formed in order of battle at daybreak." Such of the subordinate reports as mention the time, as well as the reports of Generals McDowell and Reynolds, tend to confirm General Sigel's statement.— EDITORS.

♪ These orders to Heintzelman are dated 10 P. M..

August 28th; similar orders to Kearny direct are dated 9:50 P. M.— EDITORS.

♱ At 3 A. M. on the 29th, General Pope ordered Porter, then at Bristoe, to "move upon Centreville at the first dawn of day." In the order of the 29th to Porter, "Push forward with your corps and King's division, which you will take with you upon Gainesville," the hour is not noted, but General Pope testified on the Porter court-martial that he sent it between 8 and 9 A. M. Porter appears to have received it about 9:30.— EDITORS.

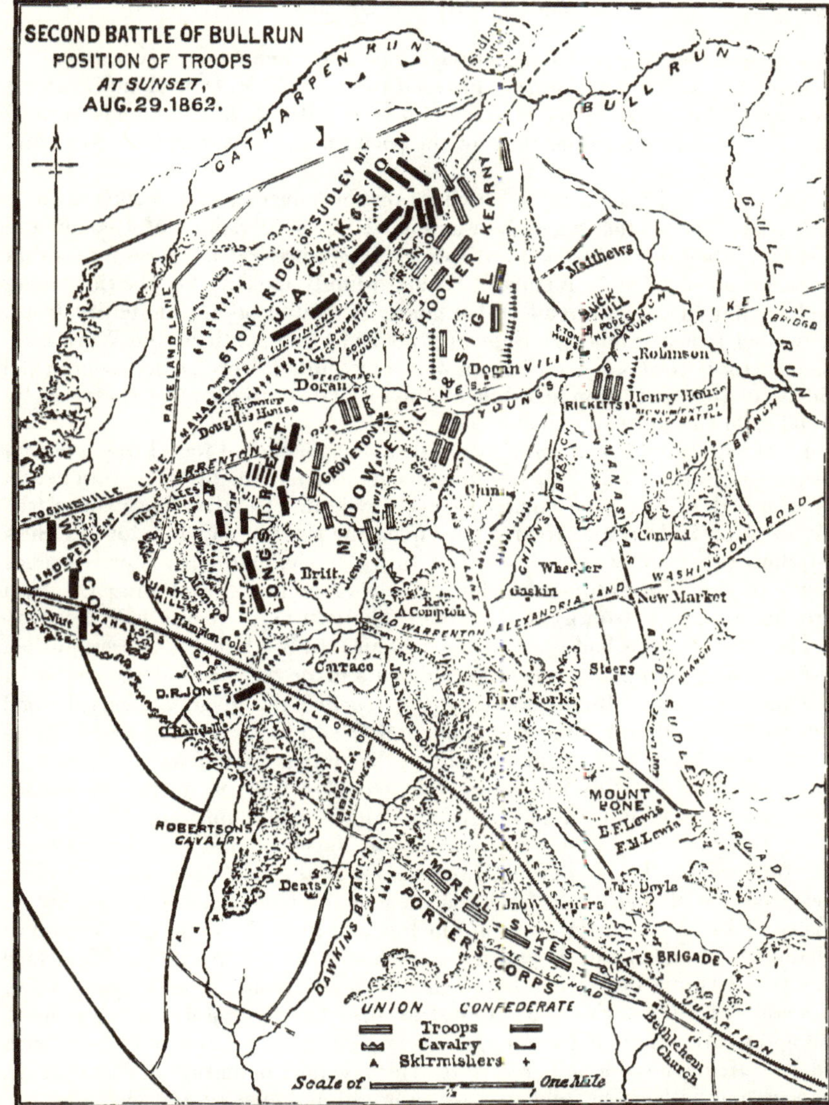

RELATIVE POSITIONS AT SUNSET, FRIDAY, AUGUST 29TH.

At noon of that day Porter's corps was in much the same position as at sunset. According to General Pope, at noon Porter, with very little resistance to overcome, might have occupied the hill of the Monroe and Hampton Cole houses, a position of great importance. But, according to other authorities (see p. 527), Longstreet was in position between Jackson and Porter by noon. At that hour the right of the Union army was arrayed in continuous line in front of Jackson from a point on the turnpike three-quarters of a mile west of Groveton to the point where the Sudley Springs road crosses the unfinished railroad which was Jackson's stronghold. The map above illustrates the situation at the time of the greatest success on the right, when Jackson's left had been turned upon itself by Kearny's, Reno's, and Hooker's divisions.— EDITORS.

Junction, requesting that King's division be not taken from his command. I immediately sent a joint order, addressed to Generals McDowell and Porter, ‡ repeating the instructions to move forward with their commands toward Gainesville, and informing them of the position and movements of Sigel and Heintzelman.

Sigel attacked the enemy at daylight on the morning of the 29th about a mile east of Groveton, where he was joined by the divisions of Hooker and Kearny. Jackson fell back, ‖ but was so closely pressed by these forces that he was obliged to make a stand. He accordingly took up his position along and behind the old railroad embankment extending along his entire front, with his left near Sudley Springs and his right just south of the Warrenton pike. His batteries, some of them of heavy caliber, were posted behind the ridges in the open ground, while the mass of his troops were sheltered by woods and the railroad embankment.

I arrived on the field from Centreville about noon, and found the opposing forces confronting each other, both considerably cut up by the severe action in which they had been engaged since daylight. Heintzelman's corps (the divisions of Hooker and Kearny) occupied the right of our line toward Sudley Springs. Sigel was on his left, with his line extending a short distance south of the Warrenton pike, the division of Schenck occupying the high ground to the left (south) of the pike. The extreme left was held by Reynolds. Reno's corps had reached the field and the most of it had been pushed forward into action, leaving four regiments in reserve behind the center of the line of battle. Immediately after I reached the ground, General Sigel reported to me that his line was weak, that the divisions of Schurz and Steinwehr were much cut up and ought to be drawn back from the front. I informed him that this was impossible, as there were no troops to replace them, and that he must hold his ground; that I would not immediately push his troops again into action, as the corps of McDowell and Porter were moving forward on the road from Manassas Junction to Gainesville, and must very soon be in position to fall upon the enemy's right flank and possibly on his rear. I rode along the front of our line and gave the same information to Heintzelman and Reno. I shall not soon forget the bright and confident face and the alert and hearty manner of that most accomplished and loyal soldier, General J. L. Reno. From first to last in this campaign he was always cheerful and ready; anxious to anticipate if possible, and prompt to execute with all his might, the orders he received. He was short in stature and upright in person, and with a face and manner so bright and engaging at all times, but most especially noticeable in the fury of battle, that it was both a pleasure

‡ This joint order refers to the one just cited as having been sent "an hour and a half ago," under which Porter was marching toward Gainesville when McDowell joined him near Manassas Junction. After receiving the joint order, General McDowell again joined Porter, at the front, and showed him a dispatch just received from Buford, dated 9:30 A. M., and addressed to Ricketts. It appears to have escaped notice that this dispatch was forwarded by Ricketts to McDowell at 11:30 A. M., which fixes the time of the meeting between Generals McDowell and Porter at the front as *after* 11:30.—Editors.

‖ Not mentioned by Jackson or any of the subordinate commanders of either army. Jackson appears to have received the attack in position as stated by General Pope in the next sentence.—Editors.

and a comfort to see him. In his death, two weeks afterward, during the battle of South Mountain, when he led his troops with his usual gallantry and daring, the Government lost one of its best and most promising officers. Had he lived to see the end of the war, he would undoubtedly have attained one of the highest, if not the very highest position in the army. His superior abilities were unquestioned, and if he lacked one single element that goes to make a perfect soldier, certainly it was not discovered before his death.

The troops were permitted to rest for a time, and to resupply themselves with ammunition. From 1:30 to 4 o'clock P. M. very severe conflicts occurred repeatedly all along the line, and there was a continuous roar of artillery and small-arms, with scarcely an intermission. About two o'clock in the afternoon three discharges of artillery were heard on the extreme left of our line or right of the enemy's, and I for the moment, and naturally, believed that Porter and McDowell had reached their positions and were engaged with the enemy. I heard only three shots, and as nothing followed I was at a loss to know what had become of these corps, or what was delaying them, as before this hour they should have been, even with ordinary marching, well up on our left. Shortly afterward I received information that McDowell's corps was advancing to join the left of our line by the Sudley Springs road, and would probably be up within two hours [about 4 P. M.—EDITORS]. At 4:30 o'clock I sent a peremptory order to General Porter, who was at or near Dawkins's Branch, about four or five miles distant from my headquarters, to push forward at once into action on the enemy's right, and if possible on his rear, stating to him generally the condition of things on the field in front of me. At 5:30 o'clock, when General Porter should have been going into action in compliance with this order, I directed Heintzelman and Reno to attack the enemy's left. The attack was made promptly and with vigor and persistence, and the left of the enemy was doubled back toward his center. After a severe and bloody action of an hour Kearny forced the position on the left of the enemy and occupied the field of battle there.

By this time General McDowell had arrived on the field, and I pushed his corps, supported by Reynolds, forward at once into action along the Warrenton pike toward the enemy's right, then said to be falling back. This attack along the pike was made by King's division near sunset; but, as Porter made no movement whatever toward the field, Longstreet, who was pushing to the front, was able to extend his lines beyond King's left with impunity, and King's attack did not accomplish what was expected, in view of the anticipated attack which Porter was ordered to make, and should have been making at the same time.

From 5 o'clock in the day until some time after dark the fighting all along our lines was severe and bloody, and our losses were very heavy. To show clearly the character of the battle on the 29th, I embody extracts from the official reports of General Lee, of General T. J. Jackson, and of Longstreet and Hill, who commanded the enemy's forces on that day. I choose the reports of the officers commanding against us for several reasons, but especially to show Longstreet's movements and operations on the afternoon of the 29th of August, when, it is alleged, he was held in check by Porter. General Lee says:

THE BATTLE OF GROVETON, AUGUST 29TH, AS SEEN FROM CENTREVILLE. FROM A SKETCH MADE AT THE TIME.

. . . "Generals Jones and Wilcox bivouacked that night [28th] east of the mountain; and on the morning of the 29th the whole command resumed the march, the sound of cannon at Manassas announcing that Jackson was already engaged. Longstreet entered the turnpike near Gainesville, and, moving down toward Groveton, the head of his column came upon the field in rear of the enemy's left, which had already opened with artillery upon Jackson's right, as previously described. He immediately placed some of his batteries in position, but before he could complete his dispositions to attack, the enemy withdrew; not, however, without loss from our artillery. Longstreet took position on the right of Jackson, Hood's two brigades, supported by Evans, being deployed across the turnpike, at right angles to it. These troops were supported on the left by three brigades under General Wilcox, and by a light force on the right under General Kemper. D. R. Jones's division formed the extreme right of the line, resting on the Manassas Gap railroad. The cavalry guarded our right and left flanks; that on the right being under General Stuart in person. After the arrival of Longstreet the enemy changed his position and began to concentrate opposite Jackson's left, opening a brisk artillery fire, which was responded to with effect by some of General A. P. Hill's batteries. Colonel Walton placed a part of his artillery upon a commanding position between the lines of Generals Jackson and Longstreet, by order of the latter, and engaged the enemy vigorously for several hours. Soon afterward General Stuart reported the approach of a large force from the direction of Bristoe Station, threatening Longstreet's right. The brigades under General Wilcox were sent to reënforce General Jones, but no serious attack was made, and after firing a few shots the enemy withdrew. While this demonstration was being made on our right, a large force advanced to assail the left of Jackson's position, occupied by the division of General A. P. Hill. The attack was received by his troops with their accustomed steadiness, and the battle raged with great fury. The enemy was repeatedly repulsed, but again pressed on to the attack with fresh troops. Once he succeeded in penetrating an interval between General Gregg's brigade, on the extreme left, and that of General Thomas, but was quickly driven back with great slaughter by the 14th South Carolina regiment, then in reserve, and the 49th Georgia, of Thomas's brigade. The contest was close and obstinate; the combatants sometimes delivering their fire at ten paces. General Gregg, who was most exposed, was reënforced by Hays's brigade under Colonel Forno, and successfully and gallantly resisted the attacks of the enemy, until, the ammunition of his brigade being exhausted, and all his field-officers but two killed or wounded, it was relieved, after several hours of severe fighting, by Early's brigade and the 8th Louisiana regiment. General Early drove the enemy back, with heavy loss, and pursued about two hundred yards beyond the line of battle, when he was recalled to the position of the railroad where Thomas, Pender, and Archer had firmly held their ground against every attack. While the battle was raging on Jackson's left, General Longstreet ordered Hood and Evans to advance, but before the order could be obeyed Hood was himself attacked, and his command at once became warmly engaged. General Wilcox was recalled from the right and ordered to advance on Hood's left, and one of Kemper's brigades, under Colonel Hunton, moved forward on his right. The enemy was repulsed by Hood after a severe contest, and fell back, closely followed by our troops. The battle continued until 9 P. M., the enemy retreating until he reached a strong position, which he held with a large force. The darkness of the night put a stop to the engagement, and our troops remained in their advanced position until early next morning, when they were withdrawn to their first line. One piece of artillery, several stands of colors, and a number of prisoners were captured. Our loss was severe in this engagement; Brigadier-Generals Field and Trimble, and Colonel Forno, commanding Hays's brigade, were severely wounded, and several other valuable officers killed or disabled whose names are mentioned in the accompanying reports."

General Jackson in his report, dated April 27th, 1863, says:

. . . "My troops on this day were distributed along and in the vicinity of the cut of an unfinished railroad (intended as a part of the track to connect the Manassas road directly with Alexandria), stretching from the Warrenton turnpike in the direction of Sudley's Mill. It was mainly along the excavation of this unfinished road that my line of battle was formed on the 29th: Jackson's division, under Brigadier-General Starke, on the right; Ewell's division, under Brigadier-General Lawton, in the center; and Hill's division on the left. In the morning, about 10 o'clock, the Federal artillery opened with spirit and animation upon our right, which was soon replied to by

BREVET MAJOR-GENERAL CUVIER GROVER.
FROM A PHOTOGRAPH.

the batteries of Poague, Carpenter, Dement, Brockenbrough, and Latimer, under Major [L. M.] Shumaker. This lasted for some time, when the enemy moved around more to our left, to another point of attack. His next effort was directed against our left. This was vigorously

¶ Both on Friday and Saturday afternoons there was desperate fighting about the railroad cut and embankment opposite, and to the right of the site of the battle monument (see map, p. 473). On Friday afternoon Grover's brigade, of Hooker's division, here charged Jackson's center before Kearny's successful and bloody charge on Jackson's left. Grover led 5 regiments, altogether about 1500 men, and in 20 minutes lost 486, or nearly one-third of his command. In his report, General Grover says:

"I rode over the field in front as far as the position of the enemy would admit. After rising the hill under which my command lay, an open field was entered, and from one edge of it gradually fell off in a slope to a valley, through which ran a railroad embankment. Beyond this embankment the forest continued, and the corresponding heights beyond were held by the enemy in force, supported by artillery. At 3 P. M. I received an order to advance in line of battle over this ground, pass the embankment, cut over the edge of the woods beyond, and hold it. Dispositions for carrying out such orders were immediately made. Pieces were loaded, bayonets fixed, and instructions given for the line to move slowly upon the enemy until it felt his fire, then close upon him rapidly, fire one well-directed volley, and rely upon the bayonet to secure the position on the other side. We rapidly and firmly pressed upon the embankment, and here occurred a short, sharp, and obstinate hand-to-hand conflict with bayonets and clubbed muskets. Many of the enemy were bayoneted in their tracks, others struck down with the butts of pieces, and onward pressed our line. In a few yards more it met a terrible fire from a second line, which, in its turn, broke. The enemy's third line now bore down upon our thinned ranks in close order, and swept back the right center and a portion of our left. With the gallant 16th Massachusetts on our left I tried to turn his flank, but the breaking of our right and center and the weight of the enemy's lines caused the necessity of falling back, first to the embankment, and then to our first position, behind which we rallied to our colors."

EDITORS.

THE HALT ON THE LINE OF BATTLE. FROM A WAR-TIME SKETCH.

repulsed by the batteries of Braxton, Crenshaw, and Pegram. About 2 o'clock P. M. the Federal infantry, in large force, advanced to the attack of our left, occupied by the division of General Hill. It pressed forward in defiance of our fatal and destructive fire with great determination, a portion of it crossing a deep cut in the railroad track, and penetrating in heavy force an interval of nearly 175 yards, which separated the right of Gregg's from the left of Thomas's brigade. For a short time Gregg's brigade, on the extreme left, was isolated from the main body of the command. But the 14th South Carolina regiment, then in reserve, with the 49th Georgia, left of Colonel Thomas, attacked the exultant enemy with vigor and drove them back across the railroad track with great slaughter." . . .

General Longstreet says in his report, dated October 10th, 1862:

. . . "Early on the 29th [August] the columns [that had passed Thoroughfare and Hopewell Gaps] were united, and the advance to join General Jackson was resumed. The noise of battle was heard before we reached Gainesville. The march was quickened to the extent of our capacity. The excitement of battle seemed to give new life and strength to our jaded men, and the head of my column soon reached a position in rear of the enemy's left flank, and within easy cannon-shot.

"On approaching the field some of Brigadier-General Hood's batteries were ordered into position, and his division was deployed on the right and left of the turnpike, at right angles with it, and supported by Brigadier-General Evans's brigade. Before these batteries could open, the enemy discovered our movements and withdrew his left. Another battery (Captain Stribling's) was placed upon a commanding position to my right, which played upon the rear of the enemy's left and drove him entirely from that part of the field. · He changed his front rapidly, so as to meet the advance of Hood and Evans.

"Three brigades, under General Wilcox, were thrown forward to the support of the left; and three others, under General Kemper, to the support of the right of these commands. General D. R. Jones's division was placed upon the Manassas Gap railroad to the right, and *en échelon* with regard to the last three brigades. Colonel Walton placed his batteries in a commanding position between my line and that of General Jackson, and engaged the enemy for several hours in a severe and successful artillery duel. At a late hour in the day Major-General Stuart reported the approach of the enemy in heavy columns against my extreme right. I withdrew General

Wilcox, with his three brigades, from the left, and placed his command in position to support Jones in case of an attack against my right. After some few shots the enemy withdrew his forces, moving them around toward his front, and about 4 o'clock in the afternoon began to press forward against General Jackson's position. Wilcox's brigades were moved back to their former position, and Hood's two brigades, supported by Evans, were quickly pressed forward to the attack. At the same time Wilcox's three brigades made a like advance, as also Hunton's brigade, of Kemper's command.

"These movements were executed with commendable zeal and ability. Hood, supported by Evans, made a gallant attack, driving the enemy back till 9 o'clock at night. One piece of artillery, several regimental standards, and a number of prisoners were taken. The enemy's entire force was found to be massed directly in my front, and in so strong a position that it was not deemed advisable to move on against his immediate front; so the troops were quietly withdrawn at 1 o'clock the following morning. The wheels of the captured piece were cut down, and it was left on the ground. The enemy seized that opportunity to claim a victory, and the Federal commander was so imprudent as to dispatch his Government, by telegraph, tidings to that effect. After withdrawing from the attack, my troops were placed in the line first occupied, and in the original order."

General A. P. Hill says in his report, dated February 25th, 1863:

. . . "Friday morning, in accordance with orders from General Jackson, I occupied the line of the unfinished railroad, my extreme left resting near Sudley Ford, my right near the point where the road strikes the open field, Gregg, Field, and Thomas in the front line; Gregg on the left and Field on the right; with Branch, Pender, and Archer as supports. . . .

"The evident intention of the enemy this day was to turn our left and overwhelm Jackson's corps before Longstreet came up, and to accomplish this the most persistent and furious onsets were made, by column after column of infantry, accompanied by numerous batteries of artillery. Soon my reserves were all in, and up to 6 o'clock my division, assisted by the Louisiana brigade of General Hays, commanded by Colonel Forno, with a heroic courage and obstinacy almost beyond parallel, had met and repulsed six distinct and separate assaults, a portion of the time the majority of the men being without a cartridge. . . .

"The enemy prepared for a last and determined attempt. Their serried masses, overwhelming superiority of numbers, and bold bearing made the chances of victory to tremble in the balance; my own division exhausted by seven hours' unremitted fighting, hardly one round per man remaining, and weakened in all things save its unconquerable spirit. Casting about for help, fortunately it was here reported to me that the brigades of Generals Lawton and Early were near by, and, sending to them, they promptly moved to my front at the most opportune moment, and this last charge met the same disastrous fate that had befallen those preceding. Having received an order from General Jackson to endeavor to avoid a general engagement, my commanders of brigades contented themselves with repulsing the enemy and following them up but a few hundred yards."

General J. E. B. Stuart says in his report, dated February 28th, 1863:

. . . "I met with the head of General Longstreet's column between Hay Market and Gainesville, and there communicated to the commanding general General Jackson's position and the enemy's. I then passed the cavalry through the column so as to place it on Longstreet's right flank, and advanced directly toward Manassas, while the column kept directly down the pike to join General Jackson's right. I selected a fine position for a battery on the right, and one having been sent to me, I fired a few shots at the enemy's supposed position, which induced him to shift his position. General Robertson, who, with his command, was sent to reconnoiter farther down the road toward Manassas, reported the enemy in his front. Upon repairing to that front, I found that Rosser's regiment was engaged with the enemy to the left of the road, and Robertson's vedettes had found the enemy approaching from the direction of Bristoe Station toward Sudley. The prolongation of his line of march would have passed through my position, which was a very fine one for artillery as well as observation, and struck Longstreet in flank. I waited his approach long enough to ascertain that there was at least an army corps, at the same

COLLECTING THE WOUNDED.

In his "Recollections of a Private" [see "The Century" magazine for January, 1886] Warren Lee Goss says: "At the end of the first day's battle, August 29th, so soon as the fighting ceased, many sought without orders to rescue comrades lying wounded between the opposing lines. There seemed to be an understanding between the men of both armies that such parties were not to be disturbed in their mission of mercy. After the failure of the attempt of Grover and Kearny to carry the railroad embankment, the Confederates followed their troops back and formed a line in the edge of the woods. When the fire had died away along the darkling woods, little groups of men from the Union lines went stealthily about, bringing in the wounded from the exposed positions. Blankets attached to poles or muskets often served as stretchers to bear the wounded to the ambulances and surgeons. There was a great lack here of organized effort to care for our wounded. Vehicles of various kinds were pressed into service. The removal went on during the entire night, and tired soldiers were roused from their slumbers by the plaintive cries of comrades passing in the comfortless vehicles. In one instance a Confederate and a Union soldier were found cheering each other on the field. They were put into the same Virginia farm-cart and sent to the rear, talking and groaning in fraternal sympathy."

time keeping detachments of cavalry dragging brush down the road from the direction of Gainesville, so as to deceive the enemy, — a ruse which Porter's report shows was successful, — and notified the commanding general, then opposite me on the turnpike, that Longstreet's flank and rear were seriously threatened, and of the importance to us of the ridge I then held. Immediately upon the receipt of that intelligence, Jenkins's, Kemper's, and D. R. Jones's brigades, and several pieces of artillery were ordered to me by General Longstreet, and, being placed in position fronting Bristoe, awaited the enemy's advance. After exchanging a few shots with rifle-pieces this corps withdrew toward Manassas, leaving artillery and supports to hold the position until night. Brigadier-General Fitz Lee returned to the vicinity of Sudley, after a very successful expedition, of which his official report has not been received, and was instructed to cooperate with Jackson's left. Late in the afternoon the artillery on this commanding ridge was, to an important degree, auxiliary to the attack upon the enemy, and Jenkins's brigade repulsed the enemy in handsome style at one volley, as they advanced across a corn-field. Thus the day ended, our lines having considerably advanced."

What would have been the effect of the application on the enemy's right at, or any time after, 4 o'clock that afternoon of ten or twelve thousand effective men who had not been in battle at all, I do not myself consider doubtful.

In this battle the Fifth Corps, under General F. J. Porter, took no part whatever, but remained all day in column, without even deploying into line of battle or making any effort in force to find out what was in their front. ☆ That General Porter knew of the progress of the battle on his right, and that he believed the Union army was being defeated, is shown by his own dispatches to McDowell, several times repeated during the day. That subjoined will be sufficient:

"GENERALS McDOWELL AND KING :—I found it impossible to communicate by crossing the woods to Groveton. The enemy are in great force on this road, and as they appear to have driven our forces back, the fire of the enemy having advanced and ours retired, I have determined to withdraw to Manassas. I have attempted to communicate with McDowell and Sigel, but my messengers have run into the enemy. They have gathered artillery and cavalry and infantry, and the advancing masses of dust show the enemy coming in force. I am now going to the head of the column to see what is passing and how affairs are going, and I will communicate with you. Had you not better send your train back ?

"F. J. PORTER, Major-General."

Not the artillery only, but the volleys of musketry in this battle were also plainly heard on their right and front by the advance of Porter's troops much of the day. In consequence of his belief that the army on his right was being defeated, as stated in more than one of these dispatches, he informed General McDowell that he intended to retire to Manassas, and advised McDowell to send back his trains in the same direction.

For this action, or non-action, he has been on the one hand likened to Benedict Arnold, and on the other favorably compared with George Washington. I presume he would not accept the first position, and probably would hardly lay claim to the second. Certainly I have not the inclination, even had I the power, to assign him to either or to any position between the two; and if he were alone concerned in the question, I should make no comment at all on the subject at this day. Many others than himself and the result of a battle, however, are involved in it, and they do not permit silence when the second battle of Bull Run is discussed. Without going into the merits of the case, which has been obscured and confused by so many and such varied controversies, I shall confine myself to a bare statement of the facts as they are known to me personally, or communicated officially by officers of rank and standing, and by the official reports of both armies engaged in the battle. General Porter was tried by court-martial a few months after the battle and was cashiered. The reasons given by him at the time for his failure to go into action, or take any part in the battle, were: first, that he considered himself under General McDowell's orders, who told him that they were too far to

☆ For another account of Porter's action see "The Fitz John Porter Case," to follow.—EDITORS.

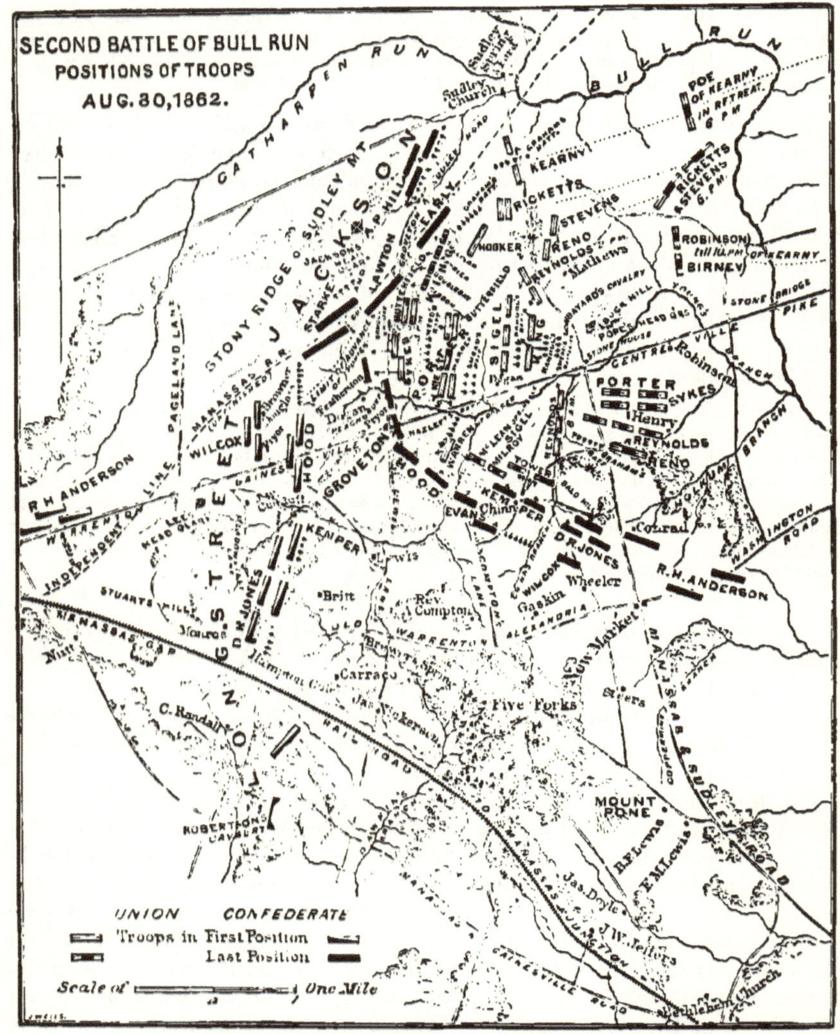

FIRST AND LAST POSITIONS IN THE FIGHTING OF AUGUST 30TH.

During the assault by Porter's corps and King's division, Jackson's forces were behind the unfinished railway. When that assault failed, the Unionists north of the turnpike were attacked by the brigades of Featherston and Pryor (of Wilcox), which were acting with some of Jackson's troops and with one brigade of Hood. Wilcox, with his own proper brigade, passed far to the right and fought his way to an advanced position, after Evans and D. R. Jones had compelled Sigel and McDowell to loosen their hold on and west of Bald Hill. [NOTE.—Tower, Milroy, and McLean, on the map, should be placed more to the east on and near Bald Hill.] At dark the Confederates were somewhat in advance of the positions indicated on the map.—EDITORS.

the front for a battle; and, second, that the enemy was in such heavy force in his front that he would have been defeated had he attacked. General McDowell stated before the court-martial that, so far from saying that they were too far to the front for battle, he directed General Porter before leaving him to put his corps into the action where he was, and that he (McDowell) would move farther to the right and go into the battle there. Upon Porter remarking that he could not go in there without getting into a fight, McDowell replied, "I thought that was what we came here for."

General J. E. B. Stuart, who commanded the cavalry in Lee's army, tells in his official report above quoted precisely what was in General Porter's front, and what means he took to produce upon General Porter the impression that there were heavy forces in front of him and advancing toward him. General Porter certainly made no reconnoissance in force to ascertain whether or not there was a heavy force in his front; and Stuart's report makes it quite certain that, at the time referred to by him, Porter could easily have moved forward from Dawkins's Branch and seized the ridge on which are the Hampton Cole and Monroe houses, from which he would have had a complete view of the field from right to left. Not only this, but his occupation of that ridge would have connected him closely with our left and absolutely prevented Longstreet from forming on Jackson's right until he had dislodged Porter, which would have occupied him too long to have permitted the effective use of his troops for any other purpose, and certainly for the advance which he subsequently made against our left. Longstreet now asserts that he was in front of Porter with part of his corps at some indefinite hour of the day,

MAJOR-GENERAL GEORGE SYKES.
FROM A PHOTOGRAPH.

variously fixed, but according to him by 11 o'clock in the morning, about the time that Porter's corps reached Dawkins's Branch. He further asserts, somewhat extravagantly, that if Porter had attacked he (Longstreet) would have annihilated him. He seems to have thought it a simple matter to annihilate an army corps of ten or twelve thousand men, much of which was composed of regular troops, but perhaps his statement to that effect would hardly be accepted by military men. If such an assertion made by a corps commander of one army is sufficient reason for a corps commander of the opposing army not to attack, even under orders to do so, it is hard to see how any general commanding an army could direct a battle at all; and certainly if such assertions as Longstreet's are considered reliable, there would have been no battle fought in our civil war, since they could easily have been had from either side in advance of any battle that was fought.

It seems pertinent to ask why General Longstreet did not annihilate Porter's corps during the day if it were so easily in his power to do so. It is also proper to suggest that it would have required a long time and all of his force to do this annihilating business on such a corps as Porter's; and in that case, what would have become of Jackson's right deprived of Longstreet's active support, which barely enabled Jackson to hold the ground that afternoon, Longstreet himself falling back at least a mile from our front at 1 o'clock that night after several hours of severe fighting?

I shall not discuss the various statements concerning the time of Longstreet's arrival on the field. That he may have been there in person at the hour he mentions is of course possible; but that his corps was with him, that it was in line of battle at any such hour, or was in any such condition to fight as Porter was, can neither be truthfully asserted nor successfully maintained. Whatever Porter supposed to be Longstreet's position, however, in no respect touches his obligation to move forward under the circumstances and force Longstreet to develop what he really had, which he (Porter) certainly did not know and had taken no measures to know. The severe fighting on his right, which he heard and interpreted into a defeat for the Union army, did not permit him to rest idle on the field with his troops in column and with no sufficient effort even to find out anything of the field in front of him.

If a mere impression that the enemy is in heavy force and that an attack or further advance might be hazardous is a sufficient reason for a corps commander to keep out of a battle, raging in his hearing, especially when he thinks that his friends are being defeated, it is extremely difficult to see how any army commander would venture to engage in battle at all, unless he could ascertain in advance and keep himself acquainted during the day with the impressions of his corps commanders about the propriety of going into the battle. Certainly Porter did not know at that time that Longstreet was in his front, and his non-action was based on fancy, and not on any fact that he knew.

But wherever Longstreet was in the morning, it is certain that at 4 o'clock that day, or about 4 o'clock, according to his own official report, he withdrew the larger part of his force and advanced to Jackson's right flank to resist the last attack of the Union army on Jackson's line, and that for several hours he was engaged in a severe battle on our left, utterly ignoring Porter and presenting his right flank to Porter's attack during that whole time. He seems also to have entirely forgotten that he was "held in check," as he was good-natured enough to say he was years afterward. During these long hours General Porter still remained idle with his corps in column, and many of them lying on the ground, for ease of position probably, as they were not under fire.

Taking the enemy's own account of the battle that afternoon, which lasted several hours, and its result, it is not unreasonable to say that, if General Porter had attacked Longstreet's right with ten or twelve thousand men while the latter was thus engaged, the effect would have been conclusive. Porter's case is the first I have ever known, or that I find recorded in military history, in which the theory has been seriously put forth that the hero of a battle is the man who keeps out of it. With this theory in successful operation, war will be stripped of most of its terrors, and a pitched battle need not be much more dangerous to human life than a militia muster.

When the battle ceased on the 29th of August, we were in possession of the field on our right, and occupied on our left the position held early in the day, and had every right to claim a decided success. What that success might have been, if a corps of twelve thousand men who had not been in battle that day had been thrown against Longstreet's right while engaged in the severe fight that afternoon, I need not indicate. To say that General Porter's non-action during that whole day was wholly unexpected and disappointing, and that it provoked severe comment on all hands, is to state the facts mildly.

Every indication during the night of the 29th and up to 10 o'clock on the morning of the 30th pointed to the retreat of the enemy from our front. Paroled prisoners of our own army, taken on the evening of the 29th, who came into our lines on the morning of the 30th, reported the enemy retreating during the whole night in the direction of and along the Warrenton pike (a fact since confirmed by Longstreet's report).☆ Generals McDowell and Heintzelman, who reconnoitered the position held by the enemy's left on the evening of the 29th, also confirmed this statement. They reported to me the evacuation of these positions by the enemy, and that there was every indication of their retreat in the direction of Gainesville. On the morning of the 30th, as may be easily believed, our troops, who had been marching and fighting almost continuously for many days, were greatly exhausted. They had had little to eat for two days, and artillery and cavalry horses had been in harness and under the saddle for ten days, and had been almost out of forage for the last two days. It may be readily imagined how little these troops, after such severe labors and hardships, were in condition for further active marching and fighting. On the 28th I had telegraphed General Halleck our condition, and had begged of him to have rations and forage sent forward to us from Alexandria with all speed; but about daylight on the 30th I received a note from

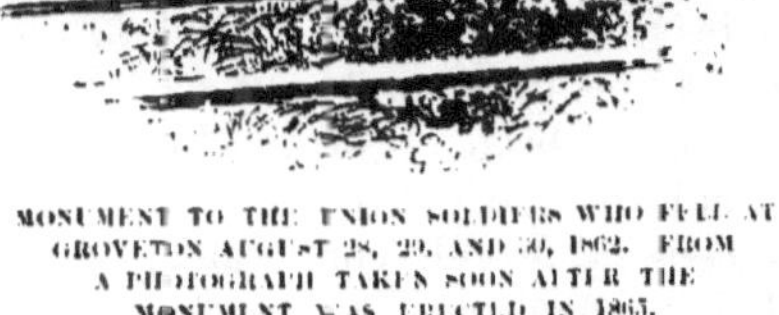

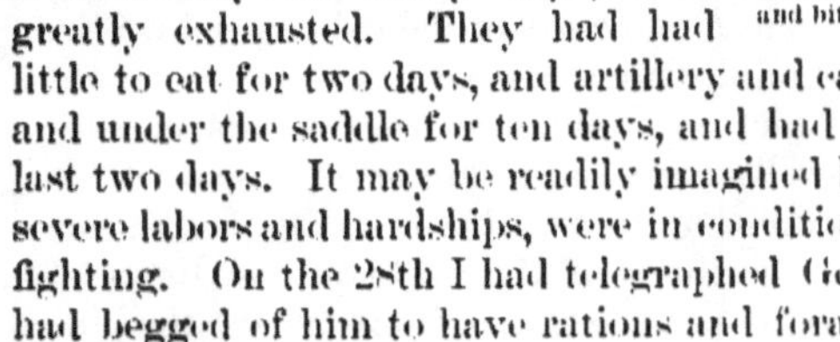

MONUMENT TO THE UNION SOLDIERS WHO FELL AT GROVETON AUGUST 28, 29, AND 30, 1862. FROM A PHOTOGRAPH TAKEN SOON AFTER THE MONUMENT WAS ERECTED IN 1865.

This view is taken from the edge of the railway cut, looking toward the Union lines. The shaft is of brown sandstone, and in design and material is like the monument erected on the Henry hill at the same time. The shot and shell that were fixed with mortar to the base and to the top of the shaft, and every vestige of the inclosing fence, have been carried off by relic-hunters. In May, 1884, the monument was partly hidden by the four evergreens which were planted at the corners. The field behind the railway cut and behind the embankment, east of the cut, was even then strewn with the tins of cartridge-boxes, rusty camp-utensils, and bits of broken accouterments.— EDITORS.

☆ According to General Longstreet's and other Confederate reports, their troops withdrew at night to their line of battle of the day, occupying the same positions and in the same order. General Pope's orders for the 30th directed that the corps of McDowell, Heintzelman, and Porter, with the necessary cavalry, should move "forward in pursuit of the enemy," and "press him vigorously all day." The command of the pursuit was assigned to General McDowell.— EDITORS.

General Franklin, written by direction of General McClellan, informing me that rations and forage would be loaded into the available wagons and cars at Alexandria as soon as I should send back a cavalry escort to guard the trains. Such a letter, when we were fighting the enemy and when Alexandria was full of troops, needs no comment. Our cavalry was well-nigh broken down completely, and certainly we were in no condition to spare troops from the front, nor could they have gone to Alexandria and returned within the time by which we must have had provisions and forage or have fallen back toward supplies; nor am I able to understand of what use cavalry could be to guard railroad trains. It was not until I received this letter that I began to be hopeless of any successful issue to our operations; but I felt it to be my duty, notwithstanding the broken-down condition of the forces under my command, to hold my position. I had received no sort of information of any troops coming forward to reënforce me since the 24th, and did not expect on the morning of the 30th that any assistance would reach me from the direction of Washington, but I determined again to give battle to the enemy and delay as long as possible his farther advance toward Washington. I accordingly prepared to renew the engagement.

General Porter, with whose non-action of the day before I was naturally dissatisfied, had been peremptorily ordered that night to report to me in person with his corps, and arrived on the field early in the morning. His corps had been reënforced by Piatt's brigade of Sturgis's division, and was estimated to be about twelve thousand strong; but in some hitherto unexplained manner one brigade ǀ of his (Porter's) corps had straggled off from the corps and appeared at Centreville during the day. With this straggling brigade was General Morell, commander of the division to which it belonged.

This brigade remained at Centreville all day, in sight and sound of the battle in which the corps to which it belonged was engaged, but made no move to join it or to approach the field of battle. On the contrary, the brigade commander made requisition for ten thousand pairs of shoes on one of my aides-de-camp who was at Centreville in charge of the headquarters train. The troops under General Sturgis and General A. Sanders Piatt had followed this brigade by a misunderstanding of the situation; but the moment they found themselves away from the battle these two officers, with true soldierly spirit, passed Morell and brought their commands to the field and into the battle, where they rendered gallant and distinguished services.

Between 12 and 2 o'clock during the day I advanced Porter's corps, supported by King's division of McDowell's corps, and supported also on their left by Sigel's corps and Reynolds's division, to attack the enemy along the Warrenton pike. At the same time the corps of Heintzelman and Reno on our right were directed to push forward to the left and front toward the pike and attack the enemy's left flank. For a time Ricketts's division of McDowell's corps was placed in support of this movement. I was obliged to assume the

---

ǀ Griffin's brigade. Griffin testified that he was ordered by General Morell to follow Sykes, who was supposed to have gone to Centreville. Griffin moved thence toward the battle-field about 5 P. M. He found the road blocked, and the bridge over Cub Run broken.—EDITORS.

aggressive or to fall back, as from want of provisions I was not able to await an attack from the enemy or the result of any other movement he might make.

Every moment of delay increased the odds against us, and I therefore pushed forward the attack as rapidly as possible. Soon after Porter advanced to attack along the Warrenton pike and the assault was made by Heintzelman and Reno on the right, it became apparent that the enemy was massing his forces as fast as they arrived on the right of Jackson, and was moving forward to force our left. General McDowell was therefore directed to recall Ricketts's division from our right, and put it so as to strengthen our left thus threatened.

Porter's corps was repulsed after some severe fighting, and began to retire, and the enemy advancing to the assault, our whole line was soon furiously engaged. The main attack of the enemy was made against our left, but was met with stubborn resistance by the divisions of Schenck and Reynolds, and the brigade of Milroy, who were soon reënforced on the left by Ricketts's division. The action was severe for several hours, the enemy bringing up heavy reserves and pouring mass after mass of his troops on our left. He was able also to present at least an equal force all along our line of battle. Porter's corps was halted and re-formed, and as soon as it was in condition it was pushed forward to the support of our left, where it rendered distinguished service, especially the brigade of regulars under Colonel (then Lieutenant-Colonel) Buchanan.

McLean's brigade of Schenck's division, which was posted in observation on our left flank, and in support of Reynolds, became exposed to the attack of the enemy on our left when Reynolds's division was drawn back to form line to support Porter's corps, then retiring from their attack, and it was fiercely assailed by Hood and Evans, in greatly superior force. This brigade was commanded in person by General Schenck, the division commander, and fought with supreme gallantry and tenacity. The enemy's attack was repulsed several times with severe loss, but he returned again and again to the assault.

It is needless for me to describe the appearance of a man so well known to the country as General R. C. Schenck. I have only to say that a more gallant and devoted soldier never lived, and to his presence and the fearless exposure of his person during these attacks is largely due the protracted resistance made by this brigade. He fell, badly wounded, in the front of his command, and his loss was deeply felt and had a marked effect on the final result in that part of the field.

Tower's brigade of Ricketts's division was pushed forward to his support, and the brigade was led by General Tower in person with conspicuous gallantry. The conduct of these two brigades and their commanders in plain view of our whole left was especially distinguished, and called forth hearty and enthusiastic cheers. Their example was of great service, and seemed to infuse new spirit into the troops that witnessed their intrepid conduct.

I have always considered it a misfortune to the country that in this action General Tower received a severe wound which disabled him from active

THE RETREAT OVER THE STONE BRIDGE, SATURDAY EVENING, AUGUST 30TH. ☆

service. He is a man of very superior abilities, zealous, and full of spirit and *élan*, and might easily have expected to serve his country in a much higher position than the one that he held on that field.

Reno's corps was withdrawn from our right center late in the afternoon and thrown into action on our left, where the assaults of the enemy were persistent and unintermitting. Notwithstanding the disadvantages under which we labored, our troops held their ground with the utmost firmness and obstinacy. The loss on both sides was heavy. By dark our left had been forced back half or three-fourths of a mile, but still remained firm and unbroken and still held the Warrenton pike on our rear, while our right was also driven back equally far, but in good order and without confusion. At dark the enemy took possession of the Sudley Springs road, and was in position to threaten our line of communication *via* stone bridge. After 6 o'clock in the evening I learned, accidentally, that Franklin's corps had arrived at a point about 4 miles east of Centreville, or 12 miles in our rear, and that it was only about 8000 strong. [But see General Franklin's statement, p. 539.]

The result of the battle of the 30th convinced me that we were no longer able to hold our position so far to the front, and so far away from the absolute necessaries of life, suffering, as were men and horses, from fatigue and hunger, and weakened by the heavy losses in battle. About 8 o'clock in the evening, therefore, I sent written orders to the corps commanders to withdraw leisurely to Centreville, and stated to them what route each should pursue and where they should take position at and near Centreville. General Reno, with his corps, was ordered to take post to cover this movement. The withdrawal was made slowly, quietly, and in good order, no attempt whatever being made by the enemy to obstruct our movement. A division of infantry, with its batteries, was posted to cover the crossing of Cub Run.

☆ Captain William H. Powell, of the 4th Regular Infantry, in a letter to "The Century," dated Fort Omaha, Nebraska, March 12th, 1885, thus describes the retreat upon Washington and McClellan's reception by his old army:

"The last volley had been fired, and as night fell upon us the division of regulars of Porter's corps was ordered to retire to Centreville. It had fought hard on the extreme left to preserve the line of retreat by the turnpike and the stone bridge. We were gloomy, despondent, and about 'tired out'; we had not had a change of clothing from the 14th to the 31st of August, and had been living, in the words of the men, on 'salt horse,' 'hard-tack,' and 'chicory juice.' As we filed from the battle-field into the turnpike leading over the stone bridge, we came upon a group of mounted officers, one of whom wore a peculiar style of hat which had been seen on the field that day, and which had been the occasion of a great deal of comment in the ranks. As we passed these officers, the one with the peculiar hat called out in a loud voice:

"'What troops are these?'

"'The regulars,' answered somebody.

"'Second Division, Fifth Corps,' replied another.

"'God bless them! they saved the army,' added the officer, solemnly. We learned that he was General Irvin McDowell.

"As we neared the bridge we came upon confusion. Men singly and in detachments were mingled with sutlers' wagons, artillery, caissons, supply wagons, and ambulances, each striving to get ahead of the other. Vehicles rushed through organized bodies, and broke the columns into fragments. Little detachments gathered by the roadside, after crossing the bridge, crying out the numbers of their regiments as a guide to scattered comrades.

"And what a night it was! Dark, gloomy, and beclouded by the volumes of smoke which had risen from the battle-field. To our disgust with the situation was added the discomfort of a steady rain setting in after nightfall. With many threats to reckless drivers, and through the untiring efforts of our officers,—not knowing how, when, or where we should meet the enemy again,—we managed to preserve our organization intact, keeping out of the road as much as possible, in order to avoid mingling with others. In this way we arrived at Centreville some time before midnight, and on the morning of the 31st of August we were placed in the old Confederate earth-works surrounding that village to await developments.

"It was Sunday. The morning was cold and rainy; everything bore a look of sadness in unison with our feelings. All about were the *disjecta membra* of a shattered army; here were stragglers plodding through the mud, inquiring for their regiments; little squads, just issuing from their shelterless bivouac on the wet ground; wagons wrecked and forlorn; half-formed regiments, part of the men with guns and part without; wanderers driven in by the patrols; while every one you met had an unwashed, sleepy, downcast aspect, and looked as if he would like to hide his head somewhere from all the world.

"During the afternoon of Sept. 1st, a council of war was held in the bivouac of the regular division, at which

The exact losses in this battle I am unable to give, as the reports from corps commanders only indicated the aggregate losses since August 22d, but they were very heavy. [See "Opposing Forces," p. 497.—EDITORS.]

Before leaving the field I sent orders to General Banks, at Bristoe Station, where the railroad was broken, to destroy the cars and such of the stores as he could not take off in the wagon trains, and join me at Centreville. I had previously sent him instructions to bring off from Warrenton Junction and Bristoe Station all of the ammunition and all of the sick and wounded who could bear transportation, throwing personal baggage and property out of the regimental trains, if necessary, for the purpose.

At no time during the 29th, 30th, or 31st of August was the road between Bristoe and Centreville interrupted by the enemy. The orders will show conclusively that every arrangement was made in the minutest detail for the security of our wagon train and supplies; and General Banks's subsequent report to me is positive that none of the wagons or mules were lost. I mention this matter merely to answer the wholly unfounded statements made at the time, and repeated often since, of our loss of wagons, mules, and supplies.

I arrived personally at Centreville about 9 or 10 o'clock that night [the 30th]. The next morning the various corps were posted in the old intrenchments in and around Centreville, and ammunition trains and some supplies were brought up during the day and distributed. We spent that whole day resting the men and resupplying them with ammunition and provisions as far as our means permitted.

Franklin's corps arrived at Centreville late on the afternoon of the 30th; Sumner's the next day. What was then thought by the Government of our operations up to this time is shown in the subjoined dispatch:

I noticed all the prominent generals of that army. It was a long one, and apparently not over-pleasant, if one might judge of it by the expressions on the faces of the officers when they separated. The information it developed, however, was that the enemy was between the Army of the Potomac and Washington; that Kearny was then engaged with him at Chantilly, and that we must fall back toward the defenses of the city. Dejection disappeared, activity took the place of immobility, and we were ready again to renew the contest. But who was to be our leader? and where were we to fight? Those were the questions that sprang to our lips. We had been ordered to keep our camp-fires burning brightly until 'tattoo'; and then, after the rolls had been called, we stole away—out into a gloomy night, made more desolate by the glare of dying embers. Nothing occurred to disturb our march; we arrived at Fairfax Court House early on the morning of the 2d of September. At this point we were turned off on the road to Washington, and went into bivouac. Here all sorts of rumors reached us; but, tired out from the weary night march, our blankets were soon spread on the ground, and we enjoyed an afternoon and night of comparative repose.

"About 4 o'clock on the next afternoon, from a prominent point, we descried in the distance the dome of the Capitol. We would be there at least in time to defend it! Darkness came upon us and still we marched. As the night wore on, we found at each halt that it was more and more difficult to arouse the men from the sleep into which they would fall apparently as soon as they touched the ground. During one of these halts, while Colonel Buchanan, the brigade commander, was resting a little off the road, some distance in advance of the head of the column, it being starlight, two horsemen came down the road toward us. I thought I observed a familiar form, and, turning to Colonel Buchanan, said:

"'Colonel, if I did not know that General McClellan had been relieved of all command, I should say that he was one of that party,' adding immediately, 'I do really believe it is he!'

"'Nonsense,' said the colonel; 'what would General McClellan be doing out in this lonely place, at this time of night, without an escort?'

"The two horsemen passed on to where the men of the column were lying, standing, or sitting, and were soon lost in the shadowy gloom. But a few moments had elapsed, however, when Captain John D. Wilkins, of the 3d Infantry (now colonel of the 5th) came running toward Colonel Buchanan, crying out:

"'Colonel! Colonel! General McClellan is here!'

"The enlisted men caught the sound! Whoever was awake aroused his neighbor. Eyes were rubbed, and those tired fellows, as the news passed down the column, jumped to their feet, and sent up such a hurrah as the Army of the Potomac had never heard before. Shout upon shout went out into the stillness of the night; and as it was taken up along the road and repeated by regiment, brigade, division, and corps, we could hear the roar dying away in the distance. The effect of this man's presence upon the Army of the Potomac—in sunshine or rain, in darkness or in daylight, in victory or defeat—was electrical, and too wonderful to make it worth while attempting to give a reason for it. Just two weeks from this time this defeated army, under the leadership of McClellan, won the battles of South Mountain and Antietam, having marched ten days out of the two weeks in order to do it."

WASHINGTON, August 31st, 1862. 11 A. M.

MY DEAR GENERAL: You have done nobly. Don't yield another inch if you can avoid it. All reserves are being sent forward. . . . I am doing all I can for you and your noble army. God bless you and it. . . .

H. W. HALLECK, General-in-chief.

The enemy's cavalry appeared in front of Cub Run that morning, but made no attempt to attack. Our cavalry, under Buford and Bayard, was completely broken down, and both of these officers reported to me that not five horses to the company could be forced into a trot. No horses whatever had reached us for remounts since the beginning of operations. It was impracticable, therefore, to use the cavalry as cavalry to cover our front with pickets or to make reconnoissances of the enemy's front.

MAJOR-GENERAL ROBERT C. SCHENCK.
FROM A PHOTOGRAPH.

This paper would be incomplete indeed did it fail to contain some short, if entirely insufficient, tribute to that most gallant and loyal soldier, John Buford. I remember very well how surprised I was when I was first placed in command of the Army of Virginia that General Buford, then only a major in the inspector-general's department, reported to me for duty as inspector.

I asked him how he could possibly remain in such a position while a great war was going on, and what objections he could have (if he had any) to being placed in a command in the field. He seemed hurt to think I could have even a doubt of his wish to take the field, and told me that he had tried to get a command, but was without influence enough to accomplish it. I went at once to the Secretary of War and begged him to have Major Buford appointed a brigadier-general of volunteers and ordered to report to me for service. The President was good enough to make the appointment, and certainly a better one was never made. Buford's coolness, his fine judgment, and his splendid courage were known of all men who had to do with him; but besides, and in addition to these high qualities, he acquired in a few months, through his presence and manner, an influence over men as remarkable as it was useful. His quiet dignity, covering a fiery spirit and a military sagacity as far-reaching as it was accurate, made him in the short period of his active service one of the most respected and trusted officers in the service. His death, brought about by disease contracted during the months of active service and constant exposure, was widely lamented in the army.

On the morning of the 1st of September I directed General Sumner to push forward a reconnoissance toward Little River pike, which enters the

Warrenton pike at Fairfax, with two brigades, to ascertain if the enemy was making any movement toward our right by that road. The enemy was found moving again slowly toward the right, heavy columns moving along the Little River pike in the direction of Fairfax. This movement had become so developed by the afternoon of that day, and was so evidently directed to turn our right, that I made the necessary disposition of troops to fight a

battle between the Little River pike and the road from Fairfax to Centreville. General Hooker was sent early in the afternoon to Fairfax Court House, and directed to concentrate all the troops in that vicinity and to push forward to Germantown with his advance. I instructed McDowell to move along the road from Centreville toward Fairfax Court House, as far as Difficult Creek, and to connect on his right with Hooker. Reno was directed to push forward north of the road to Centreville, and in the direction of Chantilly, toward the flank of the enemy's advance; Heintzelman's corps to support Reno. Just before sunset the enemy attacked us toward our right, but was met by Hooker, McDowell, and Reno, and by Kearny's division of Heintzelman's corps. A very severe action was fought in the midst of a terrific thunder-storm, and was only ended by the darkness. The enemy was driven back entirely from our front, and did not again renew his attack upon us.

In this short but severe action the army lost two officers of the highest capacity and distinction, whose death caused general lamentation in the army and country. The first was Major-General Philip Kearny, killed in advance of his division and while commanding it. There have been few such officers as Kearny in our own or any other army. In war he was an enthusiast, and he never seemed so much at home and so cheerful and confident as in battle. Tall and lithe in figure, with a most expressive and mobile countenance, and a manner which inspired confidence and zeal in all under his command, no one could fail to admire his chivalric bearing and his supreme courage. He seemed to think that it was his mission to make up the shortcomings of others, and in proportion as these shortcomings were made plain, his exertions and exposure were multiplied. He was a great and most accomplished soldier, and died as he would himself have wished to die, and as became his heroic character, at the head of his troops and in the front of the battle.

General Isaac I. Stevens, who was killed at the same time and nearly on the same ground, was an officer in many respects contrasted to Kearny. He was short and rather stout, with a swarthy complexion and very bright dark eyes. He was a man of very superior abilities and of marked skill and courage. His extreme political opinions before the war, ardently asserted, as was his habit in all matters which interested him, made it somewhat difficult for him to secure such a position in the army as one of his capacity might well have expected. The prejudice against him on this account was soon shown to be utterly groundless, for a more zealous and faithful officer never lived. His conduct in the battle in which he lost his life, and in every other operation of the campaign, was marked by high intelligence and the coolest courage, and his death in the front of battle ended too soon a career which would have placed him among the foremost officers of the war. As an officer of engineers before the war, and as Governor of, and delegate to Congress from Washington Territory, he was always a man of note, and possessed the abilities and the force to have commanded in time any position to which he might have aspired. The loss of these two officers was a heavy blow to the army, not so much perhaps because of their soldierly capacity as because of their well-known and unshakable fidelity to duty, and their entire loyalty to their comrades in arms.

On the morning of the 2d of September the army was posted behind Difficult Creek from Flint Hill to the Alexandria pike. The enemy disappeared from our front, moving toward the Upper Potomac with no attempt to force our position. And here the second battle of Bull Run may be said to terminate. On that day I received orders from General Halleck to take position in the intrenchments in front of Washington, with a view to reorganizing the army and eliminating such of the discordant elements in it as had largely caused the misfortunes of the latter part of that campaign.

The transactions at Alexandria and Washington City during these eventful days, as also at Centreville during part of them, are as closely connected with these battles, and had nearly as much to do with their results, as any part of the operations in the field; but they demand more space than is accorded to this article. The materials to write a complete account of these matters are at hand, and it is quite probable that the course of events may yet make their publication necessary.

There are other matters which, although not important, seem not out of

MAJOR-GENERAL ISAAC I. STEVENS.
FROM A PHOTOGRAPH.

place in this paper. A good deal of cheap wit has been expended upon a fanciful story that I published an order or wrote a letter or made a remark that my "headquarters would be in the saddle." It is an expression harmless and innocent enough, but it is even stated that it furnished General Lee with the basis for the only joke of his life. I think it due to army tradition, and to the comfort of those who have so often repeated this ancient joke in the days long before the civil war, that these later wits should not be allowed with impunity to poach on this well-tilled manor. This venerable joke I first heard when a cadet at West Point, and it was then told of that gallant soldier and gentleman, General W. J. Worth, and I presume it could be easily traced back to the Crusades and beyond. Certainly I never used this expression or wrote or dictated it, nor does any such expression occur in any order of mine; and as it has perhaps served its time and effected its purpose, it ought to be retired.

I thus conclude for the present this account of the second battle of Bull Run. The battle treated of, as well as the campaign which preceded it, have been, and no doubt still are, greatly misunderstood. Probably they will remain during this generation a matter of controversy, into which personal feeling and prejudice so largely enter that dispassionate judgment cannot now be looked for.

I submit this article to the public judgment with all confidence that it will be fairly considered, and as just a judgment passed upon it as is possible at this time. I well understood, as does every military man, how difficult and how thankless was the task imposed on me, and I do not hesitate to say that I would gladly have avoided it if I could have done so consistent with duty.

To confront with a small army greatly superior forces, to fight battles without the hope of victory, but only to gain time by delaying the forward movement of the enemy, is a duty the most hazardous and the most difficult that can be imposed upon any general or any army. While such operations require the highest courage and endurance on the part of the troops, they are unlikely to be understood or appreciated, and the results, however successful in view of the object aimed at, have little in them to attract public commendation or applause.

At no time could I have hoped to fight a successful battle with the superior forces of the enemy which confronted me, and which were able at any time to outflank and bear my small army to the dust. It was only by constant movement, incessant watchfulness, and hazardous skirmishes and battles, that the forces under my command were saved from destruction, and that the enemy was embarrassed and delayed in his advance until the army of General McClellan was at length assembled for the defense of Washington.

I did hope that in the course of these operations the enemy might commit some imprudence, or leave some opening of which I could take such advantage as to gain at least a partial success. This opportunity was presented by the advance of Jackson on Manassas Junction; but although the best dispositions possible in my view were made, the object was frustrated by causes which could not have been foreseen, and which perhaps are not yet completely known to the country.

IN VINDICATION OF GENERAL RUFUS KING.

BY CHARLES KING, CAPTAIN, U. S. A.

IN writing for "The Century" magazine his recollections of "The Second Battle of Bull Run," General Pope has, perhaps inadvertently, used the exact language which, in 1863, and long after, so bitterly hurt one of his most loyal subordinates. In the course of his article appear these words [see p. 470]:

"I sent orders to McDowell (supposing him to be with his command), and also direct to General King, several times during that night and once by his own staff-officer, to hold his ground at all hazards."

Now the casual reader, ignoring the commas before and after the words "and also direct to General King," would say that orders were sent to King several times that night and once by his own staff-officer. Indeed, these words have been used as authority in the army, in histories, even in Congressional debate, for the statement that General King received repeated orders to hold his ground on the evening of August 28th, 1862, and abandoned it in spite of them.

No order or message of any kind, sort, or description reached General King that night from General Pope or any other superior officer; no staff-officer of General King saw or heard of General Pope that night; and, in point of fact, no matter how many he may have sent to McDowell, Pope has since admitted that he sent none to King.

Early in 1863, when those words first met General King's eyes, he wrote at once to his late commander to have the error rectified. General Pope claimed that the construction of the sentence proved that McDowell was meant as the one to whom the repeated orders were sent, but at that time he thought he *had* sent *one* message to King by a staff-officer. I quote from his letter now in my possession, the italics being mine:

"It was far from my intention to imply even that any blame attached to you in the matter. . . . The officer came into my camp about 10 o'clock looking for McDowell, to report the result of your action. I told him I had no idea where McDowell was, but to return at once to you with the message to hold your ground. He got something to eat, I think with Ruggles, and went off. . . . Whether he was on your staff or not I really do not know, though I thought he was your staff-officer.

"Several officers of McDowell's staff came to me during the night looking for him, and to more than one of them I gave the same message *for McDowell*. If McDowell had been with his command, as I supposed he was, Sigel and Reynolds could have been brought to your support. I was disappointed, of course, but did not for a moment attach any sort of blame to you. I

never knew whether the aide-de-camp reached you that night or not, but I felt always perfectly satisfied that whether he did or not you had done the very best you could have done under the circumstances."

Now the aide-de-camp in question was Major D. C. Houston, Chief of Engineers, of General McDowell's staff. He had witnessed the severe engagement of King's division, west of Groveton, and some time after dark had ridden off through the woods in search of his general, who had not been seen by King or his officers since 2 o'clock in the afternoon. McDowell, in hunting for Pope, got lost in the woods, and Houston, hunting for McDowell, stumbled in on Pope's camp late at night, told there of King's battle, got refreshment, he says, of Ruggles, and went off; but he remembered no message from Pope to King, and if there was one, which he doubts, he did not deliver it, for he never attempted to return to King, but went on in search of McDowell until he found him late the following day. No other officer from King got within range of Pope that night, so far as rigid investigation has ever disclosed, and that none at all came from Pope to King is beyond peradventure. Indeed, in 1878 General Pope declared it was to McDowell that all the orders were sent. ☆

As to King's falling back to Manassas Junction, that was the result of the conference between him and his four brigade commanders, and was vehemently urged upon him as the only practicable way to save what was left of the command after the fierce conflict that raged at sunset. King's orders were to march to Centreville, which was objected to strenuously by Stonewall Jackson's corps, and they were in the majority. The brigade commanders voted for a deflection to the right toward Manassas, General John Gibbon being most urgent, and the following extract from a letter from him to King, dated Baltimore, March 7th, 1863, gives his views:

"I deem it not out of place to say that that retreat was suggested and urged by myself as a necessary military measure . . . I do not hesitate to say, and if is susceptible of proof, that of the two courses which I considered open to you, of obeying your orders to march to Centreville or retreat on Manassas on your own responsibility, the one you adopted was the proper one.

"Having first suggested the movement and urged it on military grounds, I am perfectly willing to bear my full share of the responsibility, and you are at liberty to make any use of this communication you may deem proper. I am, General, very respectfully, your obedient servant, JOHN GIBBON, Brig.-Gen. Vols."

☆ General Pope also repeated this statement in a conversation with me in July, 1887, and expressed his regret that this phraseology had not been corrected in his article which appeared in "The Century" magazine for January, 1886.— C. K.

THE OPPOSING FORCES AT CEDAR MOUNTAIN, VA.
August 9th, 1862.

The composition, losses, and strength of each army as here stated give the gist of all the data obtainable in the Official Records. K stands for killed; w for wounded; m w for mortally wounded; m for captured or missing; c for captured.

THE UNION ARMY.

ARMY OF VIRGINIA. — Major-General John Pope.

Escort: A and C, 1st Ohio Cavalry, Capt. Nathan D. Menken. Loss: m, 2.

SECOND ARMY CORPS, Maj.-Gen. N. P. Banks.
Escort: L, 1st Mich. Cav., Capt. Melvin Brewer; M, 5th N. Y. Cav., Lieut. Eugene Dimmick; H, 1st W. Va. Cav., Capt. Isaac P. Kerr. Escort loss: k, 5; w, 5; m, 6 = 16.

FIRST DIVISION, Brig.-Gen. A. S. Williams. Staff loss: m, 1.
Escort: M, 1st Mich. Cav., Capt. R. C. Dennison.
First Brigade, Brig.-Gen. Samuel W. Crawford: 5th Conn., Col. George B. Chapman (w and c); 10th Me.,

Col. George L. Beal; 28th N. Y., Col. Dudley Donnelly (m w), Lieut.-Col. Edwin F. Brown (w); 46th Pa., Col. Joseph F. Knipe (w), Lieut.-Col. James L. Selfridge. Brigade loss: k, 97; w, 397; m, 373 = 867. *Third Brigade*, Brig.-Gen. George H. Gordon; 27th Ind., Col. Silas Colgrove; 2d Mass., Col. George L. Andrews; Pa. Zouaves d'Afrique, Lieut. S. A. Barthoulot; 3d Wis., Col. Thomas H. Ruger. Brigade loss: k, 74; w, 191; m, 79 = 344.

SECOND DIVISION, Brig.-Gen. Christopher C. Augur (w), Brig.-Gen. Henry Prince (c), Brig.-Gen. George S. Greene. Staff loss: w, 1; m, 2 = 3.

First Brigade, Brig.-Gen. John W. Geary (w), Col. Charles Candy; 5th Ohio, Lieut.-Col. John H. Patrick; 7th Ohio, Col. William R. Creighton; 29th Ohio, Capt. Wilbur F. Stevens; 66th Ohio, Col. Charles Candy; 28th Pa. (on a reconnoissance and not in the action), Lieut.-Col. Hector Tyndale. Brigade loss: k, 61; w, 385; m, 19 = 465. *Second Brigade*, Brig.-Gen. Henry Prince, Col. David P. De Witt; 3d Md., Col. David P. De Witt; 102d N. Y., Maj. Joseph C. Lane; 109th Pa., Col. Henry J. Stainrook; 111th Pa., Maj. Thomas M. Walker; 8th and 12th U. S. (Battalion), Capt. Thomas G. Pitcher (w), Capt. Thomas M. Anderson. Brigade loss: k, 58; w, 311; m, 83 = 452. *Third Brigade*, Brig.-Gen. George S. Greene; 1st D. C., Col. James A. Tait; 78th N. Y., Lieut.-Col. Jonathan Austin. Brigade loss: w, 3; m, 23 = 26. *Artillery*, Capt. Clermont L. Best; 4th Me., Capt. O'Neil W. Robinson; 6th Me., Capt. Freeman McGilvery; K, 1st N. Y., Capt. Lorenzo Crounse; L, 1st N. Y., Capt. John A. Reynolds; M, 1st N. Y., Capt. George W. Cothran; L, 2d N. Y., Capt. Jacob Roemer; 10th N. Y., Capt. John T. Bruen; E, Pa., Capt. Joseph M. Knap; F, 4th U. S., Lieut. E. D. Muhlenberg. Artillery loss: k, 7; w, 27; m, 6 = 40.

THIRD ARMY CORPS, Maj.-Gen. Irvin McDowell. SECOND DIVISION, Brig.-Gen. James B. Ricketts.

First Brigade, Brig.-Gen. Abram Duryée; 97th N. Y., Lieut.-Col. John P. Spofford; 104th N. Y., Maj. Lewis C. Skinner; 105th N. Y., Col. James M. Fuller; 107th Pa., Lieut.-Col. Robert W. McAllen. Brigade loss: w, 12; m, 1 = 13. *Second Brigade*, Brig.-Gen. Zealous B. Tower; 26th N. Y., Col. William H. Christian; 94th N. Y., Col. Adrian R. Root; 88th Pa., Col. George P. McLean; 90th Pa., Col. Peter Lyle. Brigade loss: w, 1. *Third Brigade*, Brig.-Gen. George L. Hartsuff; 12th Mass., Col. Fletcher Webster; 13th Mass., Col. Samuel H. Leonard; 83d N. Y. (9th Militia), Col. John W. Stiles; 11th Pa., Col. Richard Coulter. Brigade loss: k, 2; w, 11; m, 4 = 17. *Fourth Brigade*, Col. Samuel S. Carroll; 7th Ind., Lieut.-Col. John F. Cheek; 84th Pa., Col. Samuel M. Bowman; 110th Pa., Col. William D. Lewis, Jr.; 1st W. Va., Col. Joseph Thoburn. Brigade loss: w, 54; m, 15 = 69. *Artillery*, Maj. Davis Tillson; 2d Me., Capt. James A. Hall; 5th Me., Capt. George F. Leppien; F, 1st Pa., Capt. Ezra W. Matthews; C, Pa., Capt. James Thompson. Artillery loss: w, 2. *Unattached:* 16th Ind. Battery, Capt. Charles A. Naylor; 13th Pa. Reserve or 1st Rifles (Battalion), Capt. Hugh McDonald.

CAVALRY, Brig.-Gen. George D. Bayard; 1st Me., Col. Samuel H. Allen; 1st N. J., Lieut.-Col. Joseph Kargé; 1st Pa., Col. Owen Jones; 1st R. I., Col. Alfred N. Duffié. Cavalry loss: k, 10; w, 45; m, 6 = 61.

Total Union loss: killed, 314; wounded, 1445; captured or missing, 622 = 2381.

The number engaged on the Union side is not specifically stated, but it is estimated that Pope's effective force in Banks's and McDowell's commands and the cavalry, on the field from first to last, aggregated about 17,000.

THE CONFEDERATE ARMY.

Major-General Thomas J. Jackson.

FIRST DIVISION, Brig.-Gen. Charles S. Winder (k), Brig.-Gen. W. B. Taliaferro. Staff loss: k, 1; w, 1 = 2.

First Brigade, Col. Charles A. Ronald; 2d Va., Lieut.-Col. Lawson Botts; 4th Va., Lieut.-Col. R. D. Gardner; 5th Va., Maj. H. J. Williams; 27th Va., Capt. Charles L. Haynes; 33d Va., Lieut., Col. Edwin G. Lee. Brigade loss: k, 10; w, 48 = 58. *Second Brigade*, Lieut.-Col. Thomas S. Garnett; 21st Va., Lieut.-Col. R. H. Cunningham (k), Capt. W. A. Witcher; 42d Va., Maj. Henry Lane (m w), Capt. Abner Dobyns; 48th Va., Capt. William Y. C. Hannum; 1st Va. (Irish) Battalion, Maj. John Seddon. Brigade loss: k, 91; w, 210 = 301. *Third Brigade*, Brig.-Gen. William B. Taliaferro, Col. Alexander G. Taliaferro; 10th Va., Maj. Joshua Stover; 23d Va., Col. Alexander G. Taliaferro, Lieut.-Col. George W. Curtis (m w), Maj. Simon T. Walton; 37th Va., Col. T. V. Williams (w), Maj. H. C. Wood; 47th Ala., Lieut.-Col. James W. Jackson; 48th Ala., Col. James L. Sheffield (w), Lieut.-Col. Abner A. Hughes. Brigade loss: k, 51; w, 271 = 322. *Fourth Brigade*, Col. Leroy A. Stafford; 2d La., ——; 9th La., ——; 10th La., ——; 15th La., ——. Brigade loss: k, 4; w, 20 = 24. *Cavalry*, Brig.-Gen. Beverly H. Robertson; 7th Va., Col. William E. Jones; 17th Va. Battalion, Maj. W. Patrick. Cavalry loss: k, 1; w, 18 = 19. *Artillery*, Maj. R. Snowden Andrews; Va. Battery (Alleghany Art'y), Capt. Joseph Carpenter (w), Lieut. John C. Carpenter; Va. Battery (Rockbridge Art'y), Capt. William T. Poague; Va. Battery (Hampden Art'y), Capt. William H. Caskie. Artillery loss: w, 6. LIGHT DIVISION, Maj.-Gen. A. P. Hill. Staff loss: w, 2.

Branch's Brigade, Brig.-Gen. L. O'B. Branch; 7th N. C., Col. Edward G. Haywood; 18th N. C., Lieut.-Col. T. J. Purdie; 28th N. C., Col. James H. Lane; 33d N. C., Col. Robert F. Hoke; 37th N. C., ——. Brigade loss: k, 2; w, 88 = 100. *Archer's Brigade*, Brig.-Gen. James J. Archer; 5th Ala. Battalion, ——; 19th Ga., ——; 1st Tenn. (Prov. Army), Col. Peter Turney; 7th Tenn., ——;

14th Tenn., Col. W. A. Forbes. Brigade loss: k, 19; w, 116 = 135. *Thomas's Brigade*, Col. Edward L. Thomas; 14th Ga., Col. R. W. Folsom; 35th Ga., ——; 45th Ga., ——; 49th Ga., ——. Brigade loss: k, 24; w, 133 = 157. *Field's Brigade*, Brig.-Gen. Charles W. Field; 22d Va. Battalion, ——; 40th Va., ——; 55th Va., ——. Brigade loss: k, 7; w, 6 = 13. *Pender's Brigade*, Brig.-Gen. William D. Pender; 16th N. C., ——; 22d N. C., Lieut.-Col. Robert H. Gray; 34th N. C., Col. Richard H. Riddick; 38th N. C., Capt. John Ashford. Brigade loss: k, 2; w, 11; m, 2 = 15. *Artillery*, Lieut.-Col. R. L. Walker; Va. Battery (Purcell Art'y), Capt. W. J. Pegram; Va. Battery (Middlesex Art'y), Lieut. W. B. Hardy; Va. Battery (Fredericksburg Art'y), Capt. Carter M. Braxton; N. C. Battery (Branch Art'y), Capt. A. C. Latham. Artillery loss: k, 2; w, 12 = 14. THIRD DIVISION, Maj.-Gen. Richard S. Ewell.

Fourth Brigade, Brig.-Gen. Jubal A. Early; 12th Ga., Capt. William F. Brown; 13th Va., Col. James A. Walker; 25th Va., Maj. John C. Higginbotham; 31st Va., Lieut.-Col. Alfred H. Jackson (w); 44th Va., ——; 52d Va., Lieut.-Col. James H. Skinner; 58th Va., Maj. John G. Kasey. Brigade loss: k, 16; w, 145; m, 2 = 163. *Seventh Brigade*, Brig.-Gen. Isaac R. Trimble; 15th Ala., Maj. A. A. Lowther; 21st Ga., ——; 21st N. C., ——. Brigade loss: k, 1; w, 17 = 18. *Eighth Brigade*, Col. Henry Forno; 5th La., ——; 6th La., ——; 7th La., ——; 8th La., ——; 14th La., ——. Brigade loss: w, 8. *Artillery*, Maj. A. R. Courtney; 1st Md., Battery, Capt. William F. Dement; 4th Md. Battery (Chesapeake Art'y), Capt. William D. Brown; La. Battery, Capt. Louis E. D'Aquin; Va. Battery (Courtney Art'y), Capt. J. W. Latimer; Va. Battery (Bedford Art'y), Lieut. Nathaniel Terry. Artillery loss: w, 8.

Total Confederate loss: killed, 241; wounded, 1120; missing, 4 = 1365. Estimated strength on the field at least 20,000.

‡ NOTE. In these tables the dash indicates that the name of the commanding officer has not been found in the "**Official Records.**" — EDITORS.

THE OPPOSING FORCES AT THE SECOND BULL RUN.

August 16th–September 2d, 1862.

The composition, losses, and strength of each army as here stated give the gist of all the data obtainable in the Official Records. K stands for killed; w for wounded; m w for mortally wounded; m for captured or missing; c for captured.

THE UNION FORCES.

ARMY OF VIRGINIA.—Major-General John Pope. Staff loss: m, 2.

Escort: A and C, 1st Ohio Cav., Capt. Nathan D. Menken. Loss: w, 1; m, 20 = 21.

FIRST ARMY CORPS, Maj.-Gen. Franz Sigel.

Escort: 1st Ind. Cav. (2 co's), Capt. Abram Sharra. Loss: w, 1; m, 1 = 2.

FIRST DIVISION, Brig.-Gen. Robert C. Schenck (w), Brig.-Gen. Julius Stahel. Staff loss: w, 1.

First Brigade, Brig.-Gen. Julius Stahel, Col. Adolphus Buschbeck: 8th N. Y., Lieut.-Col. Carl B. Hedterich; 41st N. Y., Lieut.-Col. Ernest W. Holmstedt; 45th N. Y., Lieut.-Col. Edward C. Wratislaw; 27th Pa., Col. Adolphus Buschbeck, Lieut.-Col. Lorenz Cantador; 2d N. Y. Battery, Capt. Louis Schirmer, Lieut. F. J. T. Blume. Brigade loss (incomplete): k, 40; w, 96; m, 33 = 169. *Second Brigade,* Col. Nathaniel C. McLean: 25th Ohio, Col. William P. Richardson; 55th Ohio, Col. John C. Lee; 73d Ohio, Col. Orland Smith; 75th Ohio, Maj. Robert Reilly; K, 1st Ohio Art'y, Lieut. George B. Haskin. Brigade loss: k, 57; w, 272; m, 105 = 434.

SECOND DIVISION, Brig.-Gen. Adolph von Steinwehr.

First Brigade, Col. John A. Koltes (k), Lieut.-Col. Gust. A. Muhleck: 29th N. Y., Col. Clemens Soest (w), Maj. Louis Hartmann; 68th N. Y., Lieut.-Col. John H. Kleefisch (m w); 73 Pa., Lieut.-Col. Gust. A. Muhleck. Brigade loss: k, 47; w, 294; m, 60 = 401.

THIRD DIVISION, Brig.-Gen. Carl Schurz.

First Brigade, Brig.-Gen. Henry Bohlen (k), Col. Alexander Schimmelfennig: 61st Ohio, Col. Newton Schleich, Lieut.-Col. Stephen J. McGroarty; 74th Pa., Maj. Franz Blessing; 8th W. Va., Capt. Hedgman Slack; F, Penn. Art'y, Capt. Robert B. Hampton. Brigade loss: k, 26; w, 96; m, 36 = 158. *Second Brigade,* Col. Wladimir Krzyzanowski: 54th N. Y., Lieut.-Col. Charles Ashby; 58th N. Y., Maj. William Henkel (w), Capt. Frederick Braun; 75th Pa., Lieut.-Col. Francis Mahler (w); L, 2d N. Y., Art'y, Capt. Jacob Roemer. Brigade loss: k, 48; w, 274; m, 50 = 372. *Unattached:* C, 3d W. Va. Cav., Capt. Jonathan Stahl; I, 1st Ohio Art'y, Capt. Hubert Dilger. Unattached loss: w, 4.

INDEPENDENT BRIGADE, Brig.-Gen. Robert H. Milroy.

2d W. Va., Col. George R. Latham; 3d W. Va., Col. David T. Hewes; 5th W. Va., Col. John L. Zeigler; 82d Ohio; Col. James Cantwell (k); C, E, and I, 1st W. Va. Cav., Maj. John S. Krepps; 12th Ohio Bat'y, Capt. Aaron C. Johnson. Brigade loss: k, 70; w, 286; m, 81 = 437.

CAVALRY BRIGADE, Col. John Beardsley.

1st Conn. (Bat'l'n), Capt. L. N. Middlebrook; 1st Md., Lieut.-Col. C. Wetschky; 4th N. Y., Lieut.-Col. Ferries Nazer; 9th N. Y., Maj. Charles McL. Knox; 6th Ohio, Col. William R. Lloyd. Brigade loss: k, 3; w, 15; m, 65 = 83.

RESERVE ARTILLERY, Capt. Frank Buell (k), Capt. Louis Schirmer.

I, 1st N. Y., Capt. Michael Wiedrich; 13th N. Y., Capt. Julius Dieckmann; C, W. Va., Lieut. Wallace Hill. Artillery Reserve loss: k, 4; w, 22 = 26.

SECOND ARMY CORPS, Maj.-Gen. Nathaniel P. Banks. (This corps, excepting its cavalry, was not engaged in any of the principal battles.)

FIRST DIVISION, Brig.-Gen. Alpheus S. Williams.

First Brigade, Brig.-Gen. Samuel W. Crawford; 5th Conn., Capt. James A. Betts; 10th Me., Col. George L. Beal; 28th N. Y., Capt. William H. H. Mapes; 46th Pa., Lieut.-Col. James L. Selfridge. Brigade loss: m, 15.

Third Brigade, Brig.-Gen. George H. Gordon: 2d Mass., Col. George L. Andrews; 27th Ind., Col. Silas Colgrove; 3d Wis., Col. Thomas H. Ruger.

SECOND DIVISION, Brig.-Gen. George S. Greene.

First Brigade, Col. Charles Candy, Col. John H. Patrick: 5th Ohio, Col. John H. Patrick, Maj. John Collins; 7th Ohio, Col. William R. Creighton, Capt. Frederick A.

Seymour, Capt. Orrin J. Crane; 29th Ohio, Capt. Wilbur F. Stevens, Capt. Jonas Schoonover, Lieut. Theron E. Winship; 66th Ohio, Lieut.-Col. Eugene Powell; 28th Pa., Col. Gabriel De Korponay. *Second Brigade,* Col. Matthew Schlaudecker, Col. Thomas B. Van Buren: 3d Md., Col. David P. De Witt; 102d N. Y., Col. Thomas B. Van Buren; 109th Pa., Col. Henry J. Stainrook; 111th Pa., Maj. Thomas M. Walker. Brigade loss: k, 2; w, 25; m, 3 = 30. *Third Brigade,* Col. James A. Tait; 3d Del., Col. William O. Redden, Lieut.-Col. Samuel H. Jenkins; 1st D. C., Lieut.-Col. Lemuel Towers, Capt. Marvin P. Fisher; 60th N. Y., Col. William B. Goodrich; 78th N. Y., Lieut.-Col. Jonathan Austin; Purnell Legion, Md., Col. William J. Leonard (c), Lieut.-Col. Benjamin L. Simpson. Brigade loss: k, 2; w, 11; m, 65 = 78. *Artillery,* Capt. Clermont L. Best: 4th Me., Capt. O'Neil W. Robinson, Jr.; M, 1st N. Y., Capt. George W. Cothran; 10th N. Y., Capt. John T. Bruen; E, Pa., Capt. Joseph M. Knap; F, 4th U. S., Lieut. Edward D. Muhlenberg.

CAVALRY BRIGADE, Brig.-Gen. John Buford.

1st Mich., Col. Thornton F. Brodhead (m w), Maj. Charles H. Town; 5th N. Y., Col. Othniel De Forest; 1st Vt., Col. Charles H. Tompkins; 1st W. Va., Lieut.-Col. Nathaniel P. Richmond. Brigade loss: k, 15; w, 35; m, 150 = 200.

THIRD ARMY CORPS, Maj.-Gen. Irvin McDowell.

FIRST DIVISION, Brig.-Gen. Rufus King, Brig.-Gen. John P. Hatch (w), Brig.-Gen. Abner Doubleday. Staff loss: w, 1.

First Brigade, Brig.-Gen. John P. Hatch, Col. Timothy Sullivan: 22d N. Y., Col. Walter Phelps, Jr.; 24th N. Y., Col. Timothy Sullivan; 30th N. Y., Col. Edward Frisby (k); 84th N. Y. (14th Militia), Lieut.-Col. Edward B. Fowler (w), Maj. William H. de Bevoise; 2d U. S. Sharp-shooters, Col. Henry A. V. Post. Brigade loss: k, 95; w, 382; m, 295 = 772. *Second Brigade,* Brig.-Gen. Abner Doubleday, Col. William P. Wainwright: 56th Pa., Col. Sullivan A. Meredith (w), Lieut.-Col. J. William Hofmann; 76th N. Y., Col. William P. Wainwright; 95th N. Y., Lieut.-Col. James B. Post. Brigade loss: k, 18; w, 192; m, 237 = 447. *Third Brigade,* Brig.-Gen. Marsena R. Patrick; 21st N. Y., Col. William F. Rogers; 23d N. Y., Lieut.-Col. Nirom M. Crane; 35th N. Y., Col. Newton B. Lord; 80th N. Y. (20th Militia), Col. George W. Pratt (m w), Lieut.-Col. Theodore B. Gates. Brigade loss: k, 56; w, 334; m, 178 = 568. *Fourth Brigade,* Brig.-Gen. John Gibbon: 2d Wis., Col. Edgar O'Connor (k), Lieut.-Col. Lucius Fairchild; 6th Wis., Col. Lysander Cutler (w), Lieut.-Col. Edward S. Bragg; 7th Wis., Col. William W. Robinson (w), Lieut.-Col. Charles A. Hamilton (w), Lieut.-Col. Lucius Fairchild; 19th Ind., Col. Solomon Meredith. Brigade loss: k, 148; w, 626; m, 120 = 894. *Artillery,* 1st N. H., Capt. George A. Gerrish (c), Lieut. Frederick M. Edgell; D, 1st R. I., Capt. J. Albert Monroe; L, 1st N. Y., Capt. John A. Reynolds; B, 4th U. S., Capt. Joseph B. Campbell. Artillery loss: k, 7; w, 25; m, 14 = 46.

SECOND DIVISION, Brig.-Gen. James B. Ricketts.

First Brigade, Brig.-Gen. Abram Duryea: 97th N. Y., Lieut.-Col. John P. Spofford; 104th N. Y., Maj. Lewis C. Skinner; 105th N. Y., Col. Howard Carroll; 107th Pa., Col. Thomas F. McCoy. Brigade loss: k, 29; w, 138; m, 224 = 391. *Second Brigade,* Brig.-Gen. Zealous B. Tower (w), Col. William H. Christian: 26th N. Y., Col. William H. Christian, Lieut.-Col. Richard H. Richardson; 94th N. Y., Col. Adrian R. Root (w); 88th Pa., Lieut.-Col. Joseph A. McLean (k), Maj. George W. Gile; 90th Pa., Col. Peter Lyle. Brigade loss: k, 66; w, 338; m, 292 = 696. *Third*

Brigade, Brig.-Gen. George L. Hartsuff, Col. John W. Stiles: 12th Mass., Col. Fletcher Webster (k), Lieut.-Col. Timothy M. Bryan, Jr.; 13th Mass., Col. Samuel H. Leonard; 83d N. Y. (9th Militia), Col. John W. Stiles, Lieut.-Col. William Atterbury; 11th Pa., Col. Richard Coulter. Brigade loss: k, 87; w, 305; m, 265 = 657. *Fourth Brigade*, Col. Joseph Thoburn (w): 7th Ind., Lieut.-Col. John F. Cheek; 84th Pa., Col. Samuel M. Bowman; 110th Pa., Col. William D. Lewis, Jr.; 1st W. Va., Lieut.-Col. Henry B. Hubbard. Brigade loss (incomplete): k, 5; w, 34; m, 75 = 114. *Artillery:* 2d Me., Capt. James A. Hall; 5th Me., Capt. G. F. Leppien; F, 1st Pa., Capt. Ezra W. Matthews; C, Pa., Capt. James Thompson. Artillery loss: k, 5; w, 30; m, 19 = 54.

CAVALRY BRIGADE, Brig.-Gen. George D. Bayard.

1st Me., Col. Samuel H. Allen; 2d N. Y., Col. J. Mansfield Davies; 1st N. J., Lieut.-Col. Joseph Kargé (w), Maj. Ivins D. Jones; 1st Pa., Col. Owen Jones; 1st R. I., Col. A. N. Duffié. Brigade loss: k, 13; w, 44; m, 70 = 127.

REYNOLDS'S DIVISION (temporarily attached), Brig.-Gen. John F. Reynolds.

First Brigade, Brig.-Gen. George G. Meade: 3d Pa. Reserves, Col. Horatio G. Sickel; 4th Pa. Reserves, Col. Albert L. Magilton; 7th Pa. Reserves, Lieut.-Col. Robert M. Henderson (w), Col. Henry C. Bolinger; 8th Pa. Reserves, Capt. William Lemon; 13th Pa. Reserves or 1st Rifles (6 co's), Col. Hugh W. McNeil. Brigade loss: k, 12; w, 96; m, 77 = 185. *Second Brigade*, Brig.-Gen. Truman Seymour: 1st Pa. Reserves, Col. R. Biddle Roberts; 2d Pa. Reserves, Col. William McCandless (w); 5th Pa. Reserves, Col. Joseph W. Fisher, Lieut.-Col. George Dare; 6th Pa. Reserves, Col. William Sinclair. Brigade loss: k, 13; w, 83; m, 42 = 138. *Third Brigade*, Brig.-Gen. Conrad F. Jackson, Col. Martin D. Hardin (w), Col. James T. Kirk (w), Lieut.-Col. Robert Anderson: 9th Pa. Reserves, Lieut.-Col. Robert Anderson, Maj. J. McK. Snodgrass; 10th Pa. Reserves, Col. James T. Kirk; 11th Pa. Reserves, Lieut.-Col. Samuel M. Jackson; 12th Pa. Reserves, Col. Martin D. Hardin, Capt. Richard Gustin. Brigade loss: k, 33; w, 172; m, 82 = 287. *Artillery*, Capt. Dunbar R. Ransom: A, 1st Pa., Capt. John G. Simpson; B, 1st Pa., Capt. James H. Cooper; G, 1st Pa., Capt. Mark Kerns (m w), Lieut. Frank P. Amsden; C, 5th U. S., Capt. Dunbar R. Ransom. Artillery loss: k, 8; w, 48; m, 10 = 66.

UNATTACHED: 3d Me. Battery (Pontonniers), Capt. James G. Swett; 16th Ind. Battery, Capt. Charles A. Naylor; E, 4th U. S. Art'y, Capt. Joseph C. Clark, Jr., 3d Ind. Cav. (detachment) ——; C, G, H, and I, 13th Pa. Reserves (1st Rifles), Lieut.-Col. Thomas L. Kane. Unattached loss: w, 5; m, 21 = 26.

RESERVE CORPS, Brig.-Gen. Samuel D. Sturgis.

Piatt's Brigade (temporarily attached to Fifth Army Corps August 27th-31st), Brig.-Gen. A. Sanders Piatt: 63d Ind. (4 co's), Lieut.-Col. John S. Williams; 86th N. Y., Col. Benajah P. Bailey. Brigade loss: k, 16; w, 84; m, 45 = 145. *Unattached:* 2d N. Y. H'y Art'y, Col. Gustav Waagner; 11th N. Y. Battery, Capt. Albert A. von Puttkammer; C, 1st N. Y. Art'y (detachment), Lieut. Samuel R. James. Unattached loss: w, 10; m, 67 = 77.

ARMY OF THE POTOMAC.

THIRD ARMY CORPS, Maj.-Gen. S. P. Heintzelman.

FIRST DIVISION, Maj.-Gen. Philip Kearny (k), Brig.-Gen. David B. Birney. Staff loss: k, 1; m, 1 = 2.

First Brigade, Brig.-Gen. John C. Robinson: 20th Ind., Col. William L. Brown (k), Maj. John Wheeler; 63d Pa., Col. Alexander Hays (w), Capt. James F. Ryan; 105th Pa., Lieut.-Col. Calvin A. Craig (w), Maj. Jacob W. Greenawalt. Brigade loss: k, 26; w, 166; m, 25 = 217. *Second Brigade*, Brig.-Gen. David B. Birney, Col. J. H. Hobart Ward: 3d Me., Capt. Moses B. Lakeman, Maj. Edwin Burt; 4th Me., Col. Elijah Walker; 1st N. Y., Maj. Edwin Burt, Capt. Joseph Yeamans; 38th N. Y., Col. J. H. Hobart Ward; 40th N. Y., Col. Thomas W. Egan; 101st N. Y., Lieut.-Col. Nelson A. Gesner; 57th Pa., Maj. William Birney. Brigade loss: k, 56; w, 459; m, 114 = 629. *Third Brigade*, Col. Orlando M. Poe: 37th N. Y., Col. Samuel B. Hayman; 99th Pa., Col. Asher S.

Leidy; 2d Mich., Lieut.-Col. Louis Dillman; 3d Mich., Col. Stephen G. Champlin, Maj. Byron R. Pierce; 5th Mich., Capt. William Wakenshaw. Brigade loss: k, 25; w, 115; m, 38 = 178. *Artillery:* E, 1st R. I., Capt. George E. Randolph; K, 1st U. S., Capt. William M. Graham. Artillery loss: k, 2; w, 1 = 3.

SECOND DIVISION, Maj.-Gen. Joseph Hooker, Brig.-Gen. Cuvier Grover.

First Brigade, Brig.-Gen. Cuvier Grover, Col. Robert Cowdin: 2d N. H., Col. Gilman Marston; 1st Mass., Col. Robert Cowdin, Capt. Clark B. Baldwin; 11th Mass., Col. William Blaisdell; 16th Mass., Maj. Gardner Banks; 26th Pa., Maj. Robert L. Bodine. Brigade loss: k, 55; w, 329; m, 103 = 487. *Second Brigade*, Col. Nelson Taylor; 70th N. Y., Capt. Charles L. Young; 71st N. Y., Lieut.-Col. Henry L. Potter (w), Capt. Owen Murphy; 72d N. Y., Capt. Harman J. Bliss; 73d N. Y., Capt. Alfred A. Donalds (m w), Capt. N. William Burns; 74th N. Y., Maj. Edward L. Price. Brigade loss: k, 47; w, 217; m, 65 = 329. *Third Brigade*, Col. Joseph B. Carr: 2d N. Y., Capt. Sidney W. Park; 5th N. J., Lieut.-Col. William J. Sewell; 6th N. J., Col. Gershom Mott (w), Lieut.-Col. George C. Burling; 7th N. J., Col. Joseph W. Revere; 8th N. J., Lieut.-Col. William Ward (w), Capt. John Tuite (k), Capt. George Hoffman, Capt. Oliver S. Johnson, Capt. Daniel Blauvelt, Jr.; 115th Pa., Lieut.-Col. Robert Thompson. Brigade loss: k, 48; w, 238; m, 107 = 393. *Unattached:* 6th Me. Battery, Capt. Freeman McGilvery. Loss: k, 4; w, 9; m, 5 = 18.

FIFTH ARMY CORPS, Maj.-Gen. Fitz-John Porter.

FIRST DIVISION, Maj.-Gen. George W. Morell.

First Brigade, Col. Charles W. Roberts: 2d Me., Maj. Daniel F. Sargent; 18th Mass., Capt. Stephen Thomas, Maj. Joseph Hayes; 22d Mass. (not in action), Capt. Mason W. Burt; 13th N. Y., Col. Elisha G. Marshall; 25th N. Y., Col. Charles A. Johnson; 1st Mich., Col. Horace S. Roberts (k), Capt. Emery W. Belton. Brigade loss: k, 103; w, 374; m, 99 = 576. *Second Brigade* (not in action), Brig.-Gen. Charles Griffin: 9th Mass., Col. Patrick R. Guiney; 32d Mass., Col. Francis J. Parker; 14th N. Y., Col. James McQuade; 62d Pa., Col. Jacob B. Sweitzer; 4th Mich., Col. Jonathan W. Childs. *Third Brigade*, Brig.-Gen. Daniel Butterfield (commanded First and Third Brigades in battle of August 30th), Col. Henry S. Lansing, Col. Henry A. Weeks (w), Col. James C. Rice: 12th N. Y., Col. Henry A. Weeks, Capt. Augustus I. Root (w), Capt. William Huson, Capt. Ira Wood; 17th N. Y., Col. Henry S. Lansing, Maj. W. T. C. Grower (w), Capt. John Vickers; 44th N. Y., Col. James C. Rice, Maj. Freeman Conner; 83d Pa., Lieut.-Col. Hugh S. Campbell (w), Maj. William H. Lamont (w), Capt. John Graham (w), Capt. Orpheus S. Woodward; 16th Mich., Capt. Thomas J. Barry (w), Capt. Henry H. Sibley. Brigade loss: k, 70; w, 357; m, 163 = 590. *Sharp-shooters:* 1st U. S., Col. Hiram Berdan. Loss: k, 5; w, 41; m, 15 = 61. *Artillery:* 3d Mass. (not in action), Capt. Augustus P. Martin; C, 1st R. I., Capt. Richard Waterman; D, 5th U. S., Lieut. Charles E. Hazlett. Artillery loss: w, 5; m, 1 = 6.

SECOND DIVISION, Brig.-Gen. George Sykes.

First Brigade, Lieut.-Col. Robert C. Buchanan: 3d U. S., Capt. John D. Wilkins; 4th U. S., Capt. Joseph B. Collins (w), Capt. Hiram Dryer; 12th U. S. (1st Battalion), Capt. Matthew M. Blunt; 14th U. S. (1st Battalion), Capt. John D. O'Connell (w), Capt. W. Harvey Brown; 14th U. S. (2d Battalion), Capt. David B. McKibbin. Brigade loss: k, 31; w, 189; m, 65 = 285. *Second Brigade*, Lieut.-Col. William Chapman: G, 1st U. S., Capt. Matthew R. Marston; 2d U. S., Maj. Charles S. Lovell; 6th U. S., Capt. Levi C. Bootes; 10th U. S., Maj. Charles S. Lovell; 11th U. S., Maj. De Lancey Floyd-Jones; 17th U. S., Maj. George L. Andrews. Brigade loss: k, 19; w, 159; m, 40 = 218. *Third Brigade*, Col. Gouverneur K. Warren: 5th N. Y., Capt. Cleveland Winslow; 10th N. Y., Col. John E. Bendix. Brigade loss: k, 102; w, 235; m, 75 = 412. *Artillery*, Capt. Stephen H. Weed: E and G, 1st U. S., Lieut. Alanson M. Randol; I, 5th U. S., Capt. Stephen H. Weed; K, 5th U. S., Capt. John R. Smead (k), Lieut. William E. Van Reed. Artillery loss: k, 1; w, 2 = 3.

FIRST BRIGADE, FIRST DIVISION, SIXTH ARMY CORPS (engaged only at Bull Run Bridge, August 27th), Brig.-Gen. George W. Taylor (m w), Col. Henry W. Brown.

1st N. J., Maj. William Henry, Jr.; 2d N. J., Col. Samuel L. Buck; 3d N. J., Col. Henry W. Brown; 4th N. J., Capt. Napoleon B. Aaronson, Capt. Thomas M. Fetters. Brigade loss: k, 9; w, 126; m, 204 = 339.

NINTH ARMY CORPS, Maj.-Gen. Jesse L. Reno.

FIRST DIVISION, Maj.-Gen. Isaac I. Stevens (k), Col. Benjamin C. Christ. Staff loss: k, 1.

First Brigade, Col. Benjamin C. Christ, Lieut.-Col. Frank Graves: 50th Pa., Lieut.-Col. Thomas S. Brenholtz (w), Maj. Edward Overton, Jr., 8th Mich., Lieut.-Col. Frank Graves, Capt. Ralph Ely. Brigade loss: k, 29; w, 175; m, 27 = 231. *Second Brigade*, Col. Daniel Leasure (w), Lieut.-Col. David A. Leckey; 46th N. Y. (5 co's), Col. Rudolph Rosa (w), Maj. Julius Parens; 100th Pa., Lieut. Col. David A. Leckey, Capt. James E. Cornelius (w), Capt. Hillery W. Squier. Brigade loss: k, 20; w, 133; m, 10 = 163. *Third Brigade*, Col. Addison Farnsworth (w), Lieut.-Col. David Morrison: 28th Mass., Maj. George W. Cartwright (w), Capt. Andrew P. Caraher; 79th N. Y., Maj. William St. George Elliot (w), Lieut.-Col. David Morrison. Brigade loss: k, 42; w, 267; m, 30 = 339. *Artillery*: 8th Mass., Capt. Asa M. Cook; E, 2d U. S., Lieut. Samuel N. Benjamin. Artillery loss: k, 3; w, 10 = 13.

SECOND DIVISION, Maj.-Gen. Jesse L. Reno.

First Brigade, Col. James Nagle: 6th N. H., Col. Simon G. Griffin; 48th Pa., Lieut.-Col. Joshua K. Sigfried; 2d Md., Lieut.-Col. J. Eugene Duryea. Brigade loss: k, 76; w, 259; m, 183 = 518. *Second Brigade*, Col. Edward Ferrero: 21st Mass., Col. William S. Clark; 51st N. Y., Lieut.-Col. Robert B. Potter; 51st Pa., Col. John F. Hartranft. Brigade loss: k, 33; w, 156; m, 69 = 258.

KANAWHA DIVISION—(En route to Pope from W. Va.)

First Provisional Brigade (engaged only at Bull Run Bridge, August 27th), Col. E. Parker Scammon: 11th Ohio, Maj. Lyman J. Jackson, Lieut.-Col. Augustus H. Coleman; 12th Ohio, Col. Carr B. White. Brigade loss: k, 14; w, 50; m, 42 = 106. *Unattached*, 30th Ohio, Lieut.-Col. Theodore Jones; 36th Ohio, Col. George Crook.

The loss of the Union army in the battles of August 29th and 30th is not separately reported. In all the combats of the campaign from the Rappahannock to the Potomac, the casualties amounted (approximately) to 1747 killed, 8452 wounded, and 4263 captured or missing = 14,462.

THE CONFEDERATE FORCES.

ARMY OF NORTHERN VIRGINIA — General Robert E. Lee.

RIGHT WING, OR LONGSTREET'S CORPS, Maj.-Gen. James Longstreet.

ANDERSON'S DIVISION, Maj.-Gen. Richard H. Anderson.

Armistead's Brigade, Brig.-Gen. Lewis A. Armistead: 9th Va., ——; 14th Va., ——; 38th Va., ——; 53d Va., ——; 57th Va., ——; 5th Va. Battalion, ——. Brigade loss: k, 2; w, 18 = 20. *Mahone's Brigade*, Brig.-Gen. William Mahone: 6th Va., ——; 12th Va., ——; 16th Va., ——; 41st Va., ——. Brigade loss: k, 38; w, 196 = 234. *Wright's Brigade*, Brig.-Gen. Ambrose R. Wright: 44th Ala., ——; 3d Ga., ——; 22d Ga., ——; 48th Ga., ——. Brigade loss: k, 32; w, 150; m, 8 = 190.

JONES'S DIVISION, Brig.-Gen. David R. Jones. Staff loss: m, 1.

Toombs's Brigade, Col. Henry L. Benning, Brig.-Gen. Robert Toombs: 2d Ga., Lieut.-Col. William R. Holmes; 15th Ga., Col. William T. Millican; 17th Ga., Maj. John H. Pickett (w), Capt. A. C. Jones (k), Capt. Hiram L. French; 20th Ga., Maj. J. D. Waddell. Brigade loss: k, 40; w, 327 = 367. *Drayton's Brigade*, Brig.-Gen. Thomas F. Drayton: 50th Ga., ——; 51st Ga., ——; 15th S. C., ——; Phillips's (Ga.) Legion, ——. Brigade loss: k, 13; w, 80 = 93. *Jones's Brigade*, Col. George T. Anderson: 1st Ga. (regulars), Maj. John D. Walker; 7th Ga., Col. W. T. Wilson (m w), 8th Ga., Lieut.-Col. John R. Towers; 9th Ga., Col. Benjamin Beck; 11th Ga., Lieut.-Col. William Luffman. Brigade loss: k, 103; w, 701; m, 6 = 809. ····

WILCOX'S DIVISION, Brig.-Gen. Cadmus M. Wilcox.

Wilcox's Brigade, Brig.-Gen. Cadmus M. Wilcox: 8th Ala., Maj. H. A. Herbert; 9th Ala., Maj. J. H. J. Williams; 10th Ala., Maj. John H. Caldwell; 11th Ala., Capt. J. C. C. Sanders; Va. Battery (Thomas Art'y), Capt. Edwin J. Anderson. Brigade loss: k, 9; w, 61 = 70. *Pryor's Brigade*, Brig.-Gen. Roger A. Pryor: 14th Ala., ——; 5th Fla., ——; 8th Fla., ——; 3d Va., ——. Brigade loss: k, 15; w, 76; m, 4 = 95. *Featherston's Brigade*, Brig.-Gen. Winfield S. Featherston, Col. Carnot Posey: 12th Miss., ——; 16th Miss., Col. Carnot Posey; 19th Miss., ——; 2d Miss. Battalion, ——; Va. Battery (Dixie Art'y), Capt. W. H. Chapman. Brigade loss: k, 26; w, 142 = 168.

HOOD'S DIVISION, Brig.-Gen. John B. Hood.

Hood's Brigade, Brig.-Gen. John B. Hood: 18th Ga., Col. William T. Wofford; Hampton (S. C.) Legion, Lieut.-Col. M. W. Gary; 1st Tex., Lieut.-Col. P. A. Work; 4th Tex., Lieut.-Col. B. F. Carter; 5th Tex., Col. J. B. Robertson (w), Capt. K. Bryan (w), Capt. I. N. M. Turner. Brigade loss: k, 75; w, 550; m, 13 = 638. *Whiting's Brigade*, Col. E. M. Law: 4th Ala., Lieut.-Col. O. K. McLemore; 2d Miss., Col. J. M. Stone; 11th Miss., Col. P. F. Liddell; 6th N. C., Maj. Robert F. Webb. Brigade loss: k, 56; w, 268 = 324. *Artillery*, Maj. B. W. Frobel; S. C. Battery (German Art'y), Capt. W. K. Bachman; S. C. Battery (Palmetto Art'y), Capt. Hugh R. Garden; N. C. Battery (Rowan Art'y), Capt. James Reilly. Artillery loss: k, 1; w, 9 = 10.

KEMPER'S DIVISION, Brig.-Gen. James L. Kemper.

Kemper's Brigade, Col. Montgomery D. Corse (w), Col. William R. Terry: 1st Va., Lieut.-Col. F. G. Skinner; 7th Va., Col. W. T. Patton (w); 11th Va., Maj. Adam Clement; 17th Va., Lieut.-Col. Morton Marye (w), Maj. Arthur Herbert; 24th Va., Col. William R. Terry. Brigade loss: k, 33; w, 240; m, 1 = 274. *Jenkins's Brigade*, Brig.-Gen. Micah Jenkins (w), Col. Joseph Walker: 1st S. C., Col. Thomas J. Glover (k); 2d S. C. (Rifles) ——; 5th S. C., ——; 6th S. C., ——; 4th S. C. Battalion, ——; Palmetto (S. C.) Sharp-shooters, Col. Joseph Walker. Brigade loss: k, 59; w, 408; m, 2 = 469. *Pickett's Brigade*, Col. Eppa Hunton: 8th Va., ——; 18th Va., ——; 19th Va., ——; 28th Va., ——; 56th Va., ——. Brigade loss: k, 21; w, 209; m, 4 = 234. *Evans's Independent Brigade*, Brig.-Gen. Nathan G. Evans (on Aug. 30th also in command of Hood's division), Col. P. F. Stevens: 17th S. C., Col. John H. Means (m w), Lieut.-Col. F. W. McMaster; 18th S. C., Col. J. M. Gadberry (k), Lieut.-Col. W. H. Wallace; 22d S. C., Col. S. D. Goodlett (w); 23d S. C., Col. H. L. Benbow (w), Capt. M. V. Bancroft; Holcombe (S. C.) Legion, Col. P. F. Stevens, Lieut.-Col. F. G. Palmer (w), Maj. W. J. Crawley; S. C. Battery (Macbeth Art'y), Capt. R. Boyce. Brigade loss: k, 133; w, 593; m, 8 = 734.

ARTILLERY: *Washington (La.) Artillery*, Col. John B. Walton: 1st Company, Capt. C. W. Squires; 2d Company, Capt. J. B. Richardson; 3d Company, Capt. M. B. Miller; 4th Company, Capt. B. F. Eshleman. Loss: k, 9; w, 23 = 32. *Lee's Battalion*, Col. Stephen D. Lee: Va. Battery, Capt. J. L. Eubank; Va. Battery (Grimes's), Lieut. Thomas J. Oakham; Va. Battery (Bedford Art'y), Capt. T. C. Jordan; Va., Battery, Capt. W. W. Parker; S. C. Battery (Rhett's), Lieut. William Elliott; Va. Battery, Capt. J. S. Taylor. Loss: w, 6. *Miscellaneous*: Va. Battery (Huger's), ——; Va. Battery (Leake's), ——; La. Battery (Donaldsonville Art'y), ——; Va. Battery (Moorman's) ——; Va. Battery (Loudoun Art'y), Capt. A. L. Rogers; Va. Battery (Fauquier Art'y), Capt. R. M. Stribling.

LEFT WING, OR JACKSON'S CORPS, Maj.-Gen. Thomas J. Jackson. Staff loss: w, 1.

FIRST (JACKSON'S) DIVISION, Brig.-Gen. William B. Taliaferro (w), Brig.-Gen. William E. Starke.

First Brigade, Col. W. S. H. Baylor (k), Col. A. J. Grigsby (w); 2d Va., Lieut.-Col. Lawson Botts (m w), Capt. J. W. Rowan, Capt. Rawley T. Colston; 4th Va., Lieut.-Col. R. D. Gardner; 5th Va., Maj. H. J. Williams; 27th Va., Col. A. J. Grigsby; 33d Va., Col. John F. Neff (k). Brigade loss: k, 65; w, 346 = 411. *Second Brigade*, Maj. John Seddon, Col. Bradley T. Johnson; 21st Va., Capt. William A. Witcher; 42d Va., Capt. John E. Penn; 48th Va., Lieut. Virginius Dabney (w), Capt. W. W. Goldsborough (w); 1st Va. (Irish) Battalion, Maj. John Seddon, Capt. O. C. Henderson. Brigade loss: k, 18; w, 102 = 120. *Third Brigade*, Col. Alexander G. Taliaferro; 47th Ala., Col. James W. Jackson; 48th Ala., Col. J. L. Sheffield; 10th Va., Lieut.-Col. S. T. Walker (w); 23d Va., ——; 37th Va., ——. Brigade loss: k, 22; w, 147 = 169. *Fourth Brigade*, Brig.-Gen. William E. Starke, Col. Leroy A. Stafford; 1st La., ——; 2d La., Col. J. M. Williams; 9th La., Col. Leroy A. Stafford; 10th La., ——; 15th La., Col. Edmund Pendleton; Coppens's (La.) Battalion, Maj. G. Coppens. Brigade loss: k, 110; w, 269; m, 6 = 385. *Artillery*, Maj. L. M. Shumaker; Md. Battery (Baltimore Art'y), Capt. J. B. Brockenbrough; Va. Battery, Capt. Joseph Carpenter; Va. Battery, (Hampden Art'y), Capt. William H. Caskie; Va. Battery, Capt. W. E. Cutshaw; Va. Battery (Rockbridge Art'y), Capt. William T. Poague; Va. Battery (Lee Art'y), Capt. Charles I. Raine; Va. Battery, Capt. W. H. Rice; Va. Battery (Danville Art'y), Capt. George W. Wooding. Artillery loss: k, 8; w, 13 = 21.

SECOND, OR LIGHT DIVISION, Major-General A. P. Hill.

Branch's Brigade, Brig.-Gen. L. O'B. Branch; 7th N. C., Capt. R. B. MacRae; 18th N. C., Lieut.-Col. T. J. Purdie; 28th N. C., Col. James H. Lane; 33d N. C., Col. Robert F. Hoke; 37th N. C., ——. Brigade loss: k, 44; w, 280; m, 3 = 327. *Pender's Brigade*, Brig.-Gen. William D. Pender; 16th N. C., Capt. L. W. Stowe (w); 22d N. C., Maj. C. C. Cole; 34th N. C., Col. Richard H. Riddick (m w); 38th N. C., Capt. John Ashford (w). Brigade loss: k, 26; w, 197 = 223. *Thomas's Brigade*, Col. Edward L. Thomas; 14th Ga., Col. R. W. Folsom; 35th Ga., ——; 45th Ga., Maj. W. L. Grice; 49th Ga., Lieut.-Col. S. M Manning. Brigade loss: k, 33; w, 199 = 232. *Artillery*, Lieut.-Col. R. L. Walker; Va. Battery (Fredericksburg Art'y), Capt. Carter M. Braxton; Va. Battery, Capt. W. G. Crenshaw; Va. Battery (Letcher Art'y), Capt. Greenlee Davidson; Va. Battery (Middlesex Art'y), Lieut. W. B. Hardy; N. C. Battery (Branch Art'y), Lieut. John R. Potts; S. C. Battery (Pee Dee Artillery), Capt. D. G. McIntosh; Va. Battery (Purcell Art'y), Capt. W. J. Pegram. Artillery loss: k, 4; w, 8 = 12. *Gregg's Brigade*, Brig.-Gen. Maxey Gregg; 1st S. C., Maj. Edward McCrady, Jr. (w), Capt. C. W. McCreary; 1st S. C. (Orr's Rifles), Col. J. Foster Marshall (k), Capt. Joseph J. Norton, Capt. G. McD. Miller, Capt. Joseph J. Norton; 12th S. C., Col. Dixon Barnes; 13th S. C., Col. O. E. Edwards (w), Capt. — Duncan; 14th S. C., Col. Samuel McGowan (w), Lieut.-Col. W. D. Simpson. Brigade loss: k, 116; w, 606 = 722. *Archer's Brigade*, Brig.-Gen. James J. Archer; 5th Ala. Battalion, Capt. Thomas Bush (k), Lieut. Charles M. Hooper; 19th Ga., Capt. F. M. Johnston; 1st Tenn. (Provisional Army), Col. Peter Turney; 7th Tenn., Maj. S. G. Shepard; 14th Tenn., Col. W. A. Forbes (m w), Maj. James W. Lockert. Brigade loss: k, 21; w, 213 = 234. *Field's Brigade*, Brig.-Gen. Charles W. Field (w), Col. J. M. Brockenbrough; 40th Va., Col. J. M. Brockenbrough; 47th Va., [Col. Robert M. Mayo (w)]; 55th Va., [Col. Frank Mallory]; 22d Va. Battalion, ——. Brigade loss: k, 15; w, 80 = 95.

THIRD DIVISION, Maj.-Gen. Richard S. Ewell (w), Brig.-Gen. A. R. Lawton. Staff loss: w, 1.

Lawton's Brigade, Brig.-Gen. A. R. Lawton, Col. M. Douglass; 13th Ga., Col. M. Douglass; 26th Ga., ——; 31st Ga., ——; 38th Ga., ——; 60th Ga., Maj. T. J. Berry; 61st Ga., ——. Brigade loss: k, 139; w, 368; m, 5 = 512. *Trimble's Brigade*, Brig.-Gen. Isaac R. Trimble (w), Capt. W. F. Brown (k); 15th Ala., Maj. A. A. Lowther; 12th Ga., Capt. W. F. Brown; 21st Ga., Capt. Thomas C. Glover; 21st N. C., Lieut.-Col. Saunders Fulton (k); 1st N. C. Battalion, ——. Brigade loss: k, 109; w, 331; m, 7 = 447. *Early's Brigade*, Brig.-Gen. Jubal A. Early; 13th Va., Col. James A. Walker; 25th Va., Col. George H. Smith (w); 31st Va., Col. John S. Hoffman; 44th Va., ——; 49th Va., Col. William Smith; 52d Va., ——; 58th Va., ——. Brigade loss: k, 29; w, 187; m, 4 = 220. *Hays's Brigade*, Col. Henry Forno (w), Col. H. B. Strong; 5th La., Maj. B. Menger; 6th La., Col. H. B. Strong; 7th La., ——; 8th La., Maj. T. D. Lewis; 14th La., ——. Brigade loss: k, 87; w, 263; m, 11 = 361. *Artillery*: Va. Battery (Staunton Art'y), Lieut. A. W. Garber; Md. Battery (Chesapeake Art'y), Capt. William D. Brown; La. Battery (La. Guard Art'y), Capt. L. E. D'Aquin; Md. Battery, Capt. W. F. Dement; Va. Battery, Capt. John R. Johnson; Va. Battery (Courtney Art'y), Capt. J. W. Latimer. Artillery loss: k, 6; w, 20; m, 1 = 27.

CAVALRY DIVISION, Maj.-Gen. James E. B. Stuart.

Robertson's Brigade, Brig.-Gen. Beverly H. Robertson; 2d Va., Col. Thomas T. Munford (w); 6th Va., Col. Thomas S. Flournoy; 7th Va., Col. William E. Jones, Capt. Samuel B. Myers; 12th Va., Col. A. W. Harman; 17th Va. Battalion, Maj. W. Patrick (m w). Brigade loss: k, 18; w, 78; m, 18 = 114. *Lee's Brigade*, Brig.-Gen. Fitzhugh Lee; 1st Va., Col. L. T. Brien; 3d Va., ——; 4th Va., Col. W. C. Wickham; 6th Va., Col. Thomas L. Rosser; 9th Va., Col. W. H. F. Lee. Brigade loss (not reported). *Artillery*: Va. Battery (Stuart Horse Art'y), Capt. John Pelham. Loss: k, 1; w, 6 = 6.

The losses sustained by Longstreet's corps are reported ("Official Records," Vol. XII., Pt. II., p. 568) as 663 killed, 4016 wounded, and 46 missing, in all 4725. Jackson reported his losses at 805 killed, 3547 wounded, and 35 missing, or a total of 4387 ("Official Records," Vol. XII., Pt II., p. 646), but the reports of his subordinate commanders aggregate 871 killed, 3713 wounded, and 45 missing = 4629. Adopting these latter figures as Jackson's loss, we have, after including the loss of 120 in Stuart's cavalry (less Fitzhugh Lee's brigade, not reported), a grand total of 1553 killed, 7812 wounded, and 100 missing = 9474.

Unquestionably the casualties given in these tables for both armies are too small, but they are the nearest approximation attainable from the records.

It is impossible to compute with precision the number of men actually present on the field of battle at Groveton and Bull Run. The official returns and reports are not only imperfect, but often contradictory. However, a careful study of the subject, based upon the best information obtainable, justifies the conclusion that the effective strength of the army under Pope's command was at least 63,000, and that of the Confederate army about 54,000 — of all arms. The computation of Pope's forces includes his own proper command (exclusive of Banks's corps, which did not reach the scene of action), Reno's corps, and the reinforcements received from the Army of the Potomac. The Confederate force has been estimated by some writers as low as 47,000. Others concede the number given above. Colonel William Allan, late chief-of-ordnance, Second Corps, Army of Northern Virginia, in a paper upon the subject, contributed to the Military Historical Society of Massachusetts, concludes that on the 28th of August, Pope had 70,000 men (including Banks's corps), and Lee about 49,000.

RAID ON A UNION BAGGAGE TRAIN BY STUART'S CAVALRY. FROM A WAR-TIME SKETCH.

JACKSON'S RAID AROUND POPE.

BY W. B. TALIAFERRO, MAJOR-GENERAL, C. S. A.

ON the morning of the 25th of August, 1862, Stonewall Jackson, with Ewell's and A. P. Hill's divisions and his own old division under my command, marched northward from Jeffersonton, Virginia, to cut Pope's communications and destroy his supplies. Quartermasters and commissaries, with their forage and subsistence stores, were left behind, their white tilted wagons parked conspicuously. The *impedimenta* which usually embarrass and delay a marching column had been reduced to a few ambulances and a limited ordnance train; three days' meager rations had been cooked and stowed away in haversacks and pockets; and tin cans and an occasional frying-pan constituted the entire camp-equipage. The men had rested and dried off, and as they marched out they exulted with the inspiration of the balmy summer atmosphere and the refreshing breezes which swept down from the Blue Mountains.

No man save one in that corps, whatever may have been his rank, knew our destination. The men said of Jackson that his piety expressed itself in obeying the injunction, "Let not thy left hand know what thy right hand doeth." No intelligence of intended Confederate movements ever reached the enemy by any slip of his. The orders to his division chiefs were like this: "March to a cross-road; a staff-officer there will inform you which fork to take; and so to the next fork, where you will find a courier with a sealed direction pointing out the road."

This extreme reticence was very uncomfortable and annoying to his subordinate commanders, and was sometimes carried too far; but it was the real secret of the reputation for ubiquity which he acquired, and which was so well expressed by General McClellan in one of his dispatches: "I am afraid of Jackson; he will turn up where least expected."

Naturally our destination was supposed to be Waterloo Bridge, there to force the passage of the river; but the road leading to Waterloo was passed and the northward march continued. The Rappahannock (locally the Hedgeman) is here confined in narrow limits by bold hills and rocky cliffs, and some miles above the bridge there is a road through these crossing the river at Hinson's Mills. The picturesque surroundings of the ford at this place and the cool bath into which the men plunged were not the less enjoyed because of the unexpected absence of opposition by the enemy; and after the inevitable delay which accompanies any crossing of a watercourse by an army, Jackson's corps stood on the same side of the river with the entire Federal army.

After crossing, Colonel Thomas T. Munford's 2d Virginia Cavalry picketed the roads leading in the direction of the enemy, whose whole force, now confronting Longstreet alone, was massed within lines drawn from Warrenton and Waterloo on the north to the Orange and Alexandria Railroad (now called the Midland) on the south. But Jackson's course was not directed toward the enemy. We were marching toward the lower Valley of Virginia, with our destination shrouded in mystery.

From the crossing at Hinson's Mills, Jackson's course still took the same direction—through the little village of Orlean, along the base of a small mountain which crops up in Fauquier County, and on to the little town of Salem, where his "foot cavalry," after a march of over twenty-six miles on a midsummer's day, rested for the night. At dawn on the 26th the route was resumed—this day at right angles with the direction of that of the preceding, and now, with faces set to the sunrise, the troops advanced toward the Bull Run Mountains, which loomed up across the pathway.

Thoroughfare Gap, of this range, is the outlet by which the Manassas Gap Railroad, passing from the Shenandoah Valley, penetrates the last mountain obstruction on its way to tide-water. Marching along the graded bed of this road, between the spurs and cliffs which rise on either side, and refreshed by the cooler atmosphere of the mountain elevation, the Confederate troops poured through the narrow pathway and streamed down into the plain below. Used to scanty diet, they had early learned the art of supplementing their slender commissariat, and the tempting corn-fields along which they passed were made to pay tribute.

At Gainesville, on the Warrenton and Alexandria turnpike, we were overtaken by Stuart, who, with Fitz Lee's and Robertson's brigades, had crossed the Rappahannock that morning and pursued nearly the same route with Jackson; and our subsequent movements were greatly aided and influenced by the admirable manner in which the cavalry was employed and managed by Stuart and his accomplished officers.

Late in the afternoon Ewell's division, preceded by Munford's cavalry, reached the Orange and Alexandria Railroad at Bristoe Station, the other two divisions being halted for the night a little short of that point. Munford, with his cavalry, dashed upon the station, dispersed a party of the same arm, and had a sharp skirmish with a company of infantry who took shelter in the houses; but he failed to stop a train which sped recklessly past, throwing aside the obstructions he had placed

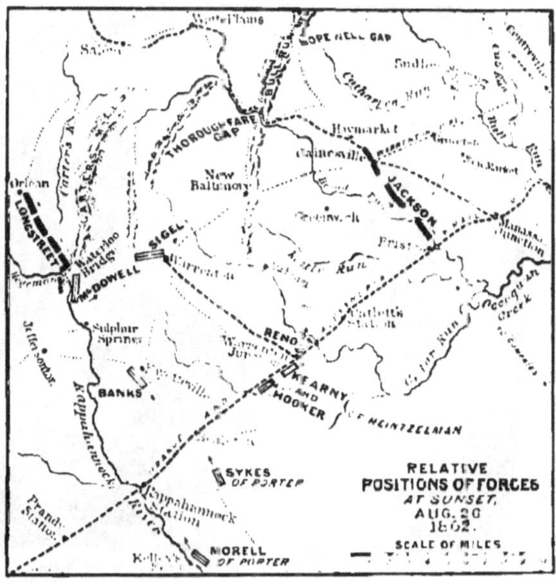

upon the track and effecting its escape. General Henry Forno's (Hays's) brigade, of General Ewell's division, however, quickly reënforcing him, two other trains and several prisoners were captured.

Wearied, as they were, with a march of over thirty miles, Jackson determined, nevertheless, to tax still further the powers of endurance of his men. At Manassas Junction was established a vast depot of quartermaster's, commissary, and ordnance stores; and it was also a "city of refuge" for many runaway negroes of all ages and of both sexes. The extent of the defenses, and of the force detailed for its protection, could not be known; but as it was far in the rear of the Federal army, not very distant from Alexandria, and directly on the line of communication and reënforcement, it was not probable that any large force had been detached for its protection. General Stonewall Jackson's habit in the valley had been to make enforced requisitions upon the Federal commissaries for his subsistence supplies; and the tempting opportunity of continuing this policy and rationing his hungry command, as well as inflicting almost irreparable loss upon the enemy, was not to be neglected. General Trimble volunteered to execute the enterprise with five hundred men, and his offer was readily accepted; but "to increase the prospect of success," Stuart, with a portion of his cavalry, was ordered to coöperate with him. The enemy were not taken by surprise, and opened with their artillery upon the first intimation of attack, but their force was too small; their cannon were taken at the point of the bayonet, and without the loss of a man killed, and with but fifteen wounded, the immense stores, eight guns, and three hundred prisoners fell into our

SUPPER AFTER A HARD MARCH.

hands.]　Early next morning A. P. Hill's division and mine were moved to the Junction, Ewell's remaining at Bristoe.

Our troops at Manassas had barely been placed in position before a gallant effort was made by General Taylor, with a New Jersey brigade, to drive off the supposed raiding party and recapture the stores; but, rushing upon overwhelming numbers, he lost his own life, two hundred prisoners, and the train that had transported them from Alexandria. The railroad bridge over Bull Run was destroyed, severing communication with Alexandria, the roads were picketed, and Fitz Lee's cavalry pushed forward as far as Fairfax Court House on the turnpike and Burke's Station on the railroad. The long march of over fifty-six miles in two days entitled Jackson's men to a holiday, and the day of rest at Manassas Junction was fully enjoyed. There was no

] The guns captured at Manassas Junction appear to have belonged to the 11th New York battery, Captain Albert A. von Puttkammer, who lost 6 guns; one section of Battery C, 1st New York Artillery, Lieutenant Samuel R. James, 2 guns. Part of one company of the 12th Pennsylvania Cavalry, which had been driven in from Bristoe, was captured. Captain von Puttkammer saved two of his guns and presently fell in with the advance of the 2d New York Heavy Artillery, Colonel Gustav Waagner (about 600 strong), which had been hurried forward from Washington. These forces, later in the morning, had a brief contest with Branch's brigade, moving on Union Mills at the head of A. P. Hill's division. Waagner's force was soon driven off, and in his retreat was harried by Fitzhugh Lee's cavalry from Centreville to Fairfax, where they met the 14th Massachusetts regiment (1st Massachusetts Heavy Artillery), Col. W. B. Greene, which had also been ordered forward. Colonel L. B. Pierce, 12th Pennsylvania Cavalry, was ill and in the hospital at Manassas; the rest of his regiment had been sent toward White Plains, and a portion of it seems to have encountered the advance of Stuart's cavalry at Hay Market and Gainesville; "the remains" of this regiment, as General McClellan describes them, were reunited near Alexandria.

Shortly after driving off Waagner's force, A. P. Hill's advance met and overpowered Taylor's New Jersey brigade of Slocum's division supported by part of Scammon's brigade of the Kanawha division. Taylor and Scammon were hurrying forward from Washington.—EDITORS.

lack or stint of good cheer, in the way of edibles, from canned meats to caramels.

Stonewall Jackson had now severed the communications of the enemy, broken down the bridges behind them, and destroyed their enormous reserve supplies. But this, which

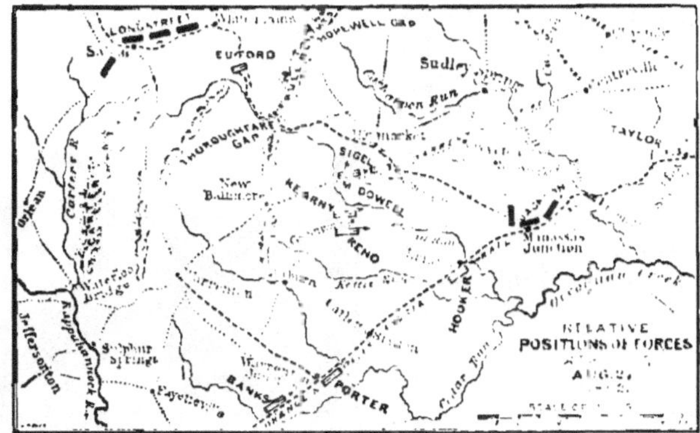

might have been accomplished by a raiding party, was by no means the only object of his enterprise; the object was beyond that—to deliver a stunning blow upon his adversary, if possible without hazard to himself. His plans, no doubt conditionally discussed with General Lee before he started on the expedition, were determined without hesitation at Manassas. He could throw himself north of Bull Run and await the coming of Pope,— who he believed would retreat along the line of the railroad and turnpike,—thus taking the chances of holding him in check until Longstreet came in to crush him from behind. The conditions of the problem were these: he must place himself on the enemy's flank, so as to avoid the full shock of his whole force if Longstreet should be delayed, and at the same time where he could himself strike effectively; he must remain within reach of Longstreet, in order to insure a more speedy concentration; and he must seek some point from which, in the event that Longstreet's advance should be barred, he might aid in removing the obstacle, or, in case of necessity, withdraw his corps and reunite it with the rest of the army behind the Bull Run Mountains.

The point that satisfied these requirements was west of Bull Run and north of the Warrenton turnpike, and within striking distance of Aldie Gap as the line of retreat. That position Jackson determined to occupy, and there was nothing to prevent or disconcert his plans. A glance at the map will show

that Jackson was really master of the situation—that neither General Lee nor himself had forced his command into a trap, but, on the contrary, he was at that time not even menaced; and if he had been, the gateways of retreat were wide open. His march had been made with such celerity, his flanks guarded with such consummate skill, that he was in no hurry to execute those tactical movements which he recognized as essential to his safety and to the delivery of his heaviest blows. On one flank, Fitz Lee was as near to Alexandria as to Manassas Junction; and, on the other, Munford and Rosser were in advance of Bristoe. Jackson was resting—as a man full of life and vigor, ready to start into action at the first touch—but he rested in the consciousness of security. The Federal commander, around whose flank and rear fourteen brigades of infantry, two of cavalry, and eighteen light batteries had passed, was also resting—but in profound ignorance. On the 26th he ordered Heintzel-

THE STONE BRIDGE, BULL RUN, FROM THE NORTH BANK.
FROM A SKETCH MADE IN 1884.

man "to send a regiment" from Warrenton to Manassas, "to repair the wires and protect the railroad." Aroused, however, on the evening of the 27th, to some appreciation of the condition of affairs, he sent one division (Hooker's) of Heintzelman's corps to Bristoe, which attacked the brigades of Lawton, Early, and Forno (Hays's) of Ewell's division, who successively retired, as they had been directed to do, with little loss, upon the main body at Manassas Junction.

At his leisure, Jackson now proceeded to execute his projected movements. A. P. Hill was ordered to Centreville, Ewell to cross Bull Run at Blackburn's Ford and follow the stream to the stone bridge, and my division by the Sudley road, to the left of the other routes, to the vicinity of Sudley Mills, north of the Warrenton pike, where the whole command was to be concentrated. The immense accumulation of stores and the captured trains were set on fire about midnight and destroyed ‡ [see p. 511]; and at night the troops took up their march, Jackson accompanying his old division then under my command. The night was starlit but moonless, and a slight mist or haze which settled about the earth made it difficult to distinguish objects at any distance. Still, little

‡ None of the Federal reports mention seeing the light of this great fire or that at Union Mills on the same night. — EDITORS.

encumbered by baggage, and with roads free from the blockade of trains, the march was made without serious impediment or difficulty. The enemy was again deceived. A. P. Hill's march to Centreville was mistaken for that of the whole command; Jackson was supposed to be between Bull Run and Washing-ton; and now, instead of a regiment, the whole Federal army was ordered to concentrate on Manassas for the pursuit.

Early on the morning of the 28th, Colonel Bradley T. Johnson, commanding a brigade of my division, was ordered down the Warrenton road toward Gainesville, with directions to picket the roads converging upon the

THE UNION MONUMENT NEAR THE "DEEP CUT."
FROM A SKETCH MADE IN 1884. (SEE MAPS, PP. 473, 509.)

turnpike near that place. Stuart had already placed a small cavalry force on this road and north of it, at Hay Market. Johnson, holding Groveton as his reserve, picketed the road as directed, pushed Captain George R. Gaither's troop of cavalry, which he found on picket, still farther on in the direction of Warrenton, and made dispositions to prevent surprise, and to check, if necessary, any advance of the enemy.

Ewell's division having now come up and united with the troops of my command, Jackson determined to rest and await further developments.

Captain Gaither had the good fortune to capture a courier conveying a dispatch from General McDowell to Generals Sigel and Reynolds, which revealed General Pope's intention of concentrating on Manassas Junction, Sigel being ordered to march on that point from Gainesville, with his right resting on the Manassas Gap Railroad; Reynolds, also from Gainesville, to keep his left on the Warrenton road; and King's division to move *en échelon* in support of the other two.

In the execution of this order, Reynolds's column struck Johnson's command; but after a short conflict, which was well sustained on both sides, the Federal commander, mistaking Johnson's force for a reconnoitering party, turned off to the right, on the road to Manassas. Johnson then, by order of General Stuart, took position, which he held for the rest of the day, north and west of the turnpike.

Johnson's messenger, bearing the captured order, found the Confederate headquarters established on the shady side of an old-fashioned worm fence, in the corners of which General Jackson and his two division commanders were profoundly sleeping after the fatigues of the preceding night, notwith-standing the intense heat of that August day. There was not so much as an ambulance at those headquarters. The headquarters' train was back beyond the Rappahannock (at Jeffersonton), with servants, camp-equipage, and all the arrangements for cooking and serving food. All the property of the gen-

THE "DEEP CUT." FROM A SKETCH MADE IN 1884.

If this picture were extended a little to the left it would include the Union monument. General Bradley T. Johnson, commanding a brigade in Jackson's old division, in his official report describes Porter's assault at this point on Saturday, August 30th, as follows:

"About 4 P. M. the movements of the enemy were suddenly developed in a decided manner. They stormed my position, deploying in the woods in brigade front and then charging in a run, line after line, brigade after brigade, up the hill on the thicket held by the 48th, and the railroad cut occupied by the 42d. . . . Before the railroad cut the fight was most obstinate. I saw a Federal flag hold its position for half an hour within ten yards of a flag of one of the regiments in the cut, and go down 6 or 8 times; and after the fight 100 dead men were lying 20 yards from the cut, some of them within two feet of it. The men fought until their ammunition was exhausted and then threw stones. Lieutenant —— —— of the battalion killed one with a stone, and I saw him after the fight with his skull fractured. Dr. Richard P. Johnson, on my volunteer staff, having no arms of any kind, was obliged to have recourse to this means of offense from the beginning. As line after line surged up the hill time after time, led up by their officers, they were dashed back on one another until the whole field was covered with a confused mass of struggling, running, routed Yankees." [See note to picture, p. 485.]

EDITORS.

eral, the staff, and of the headquarters' bureau, was strapped to the pommels and cantles of the saddles, and these formed the pillows of their weary owners.

The captured dispatch aroused Jackson like an electric shock. He was essentially a man of action; he rarely, if ever, hesitated; he never asked advice; he did not seem to reflect, or reason out a purpose; but he leaped by instinct and not by the slower process of ordinary ratiocination to a conclusion, and then as rapidly undertook its execution. He called no council to discuss the situation disclosed by this communication, although his ranking officers were almost at his side; he asked no conference, no expression of opinion; he made no suggestion, but simply, without a word except to repeat the language of the dispatch, turned to me and said, "Move your division and attack the enemy"; and to Ewell, "Support the attack." The slumbering soldiers sprang from the earth with the first summons. There was nothing for them to do but to form, and take their pieces. They were sleeping almost in ranks;

and by the time the horses of their officers were saddled, the long lines of infantry were moving to the anticipated battle-field.

The two divisions, after marching some distance to the north of the turnpike, finding no enemy, were halted and rested, and the prospect of an engagement on that afternoon [the 28th] seemed to disappear with the lengthening shadows. The enemy did not come — he could not be found — the Warrenton pike, along which it was supposed he would march, was in view — but it was as free from Federal soldiery as it had been two days before, when Jackson's men had streamed along its highway.

Ewell's division was in rear of mine, both lines fronting the turnpike. Beyond this road a pleasant farm-house, with shaded lawn and conspicuous dairy, invited the heated soldiers to its cool retreat and suggested tempting visions of milk and butter. Application was made by some of the men for permission to test the hospitality of the residents and the quality of their dairy products. They went and returned just as General Ewell happened to ride to the front. He heard their favorable report, and, laughingly suggesting that a canteen of buttermilk was a delicacy not to be despised on such an evening by the commander-in-chief himself, requested another party to procure for him the coveted luxury. As these men reached the farm-house a straggling party of the enemy, doubtless attracted by the same object, came in sight and made straight for what they supposed to be their comrades. A closer approach revealed the distinctive uniforms of enemies and brought about a brief but lively skirmish, from which both parties soon retired upon their respective friends — the Confederates, however, bearing off the *spolia opima.* General Ewell reaped the fruits of the contest, for he obtained and enjoyed his canteen of buttermilk.

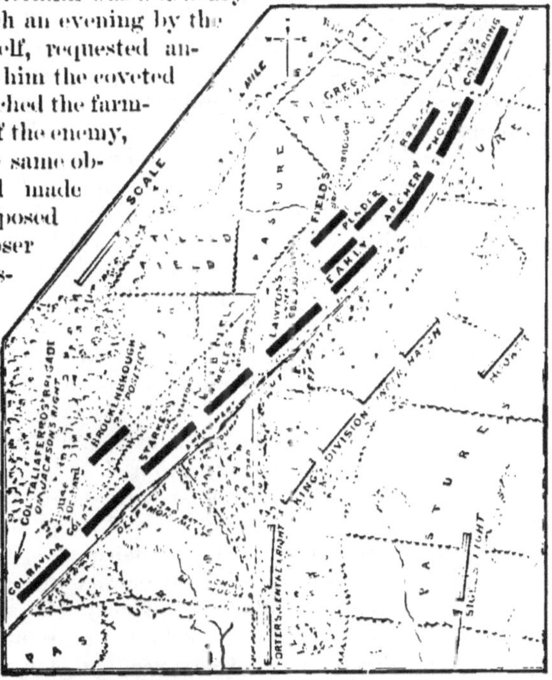

Shortly after this, then late in the afternoon, the Federal columns were discovered passing, and the Con-

JACKSON'S LINE ON THE AFTERNOON OF THE LAST DAY, AUGUST 30TH.

The topography is after General Beauregard's map, made from survey after the first battle of Bull Run. The deep cut and the embankment as far as the "Dump" were the scene of the fighting with stones, illustrated on p. 534. Here the unfinished railroad embankment is made of earth and blasted rock taken from the cut. The "Dump" was a break in the embankment, or rather a space which was never filled in; several hundred Union soldiers were buried near it. — EDITORS.

SUDLEY CHURCH, FROM THE SUDLEY SPRINGS ROAD. A HOSPITAL IN BOTH BULL RUN BATTLES, FROM A PHOTOGRAPH TAKEN SHORTLY BEFORE THE SECOND BATTLE.

federate line, formed parallel to the turnpike, moved rapidly forward to the attack. There was no disposition on the part of the Federals to avoid the onset, but, on the contrary, they met us half-way.

It was a sanguinary field; none was better contested during the war. The Federal artillery was admirably served, and at one time the annihilation of our batteries seemed inevitable, so destructive was the fire; but the Confederate guns, although forced to retire and seek new positions, responded with a determination and pluck unshaken by the fiery tempest they had encountered.

A farm-house, an orchard, a few stacks of hay, and a rotten "worm" fence were the only cover afforded to the opposing lines of infantry; it was a stand-up combat, dogged and unflinching, in a field almost bare. There were no wounds from spent balls; the confronting lines looked into each other's faces at deadly range, less than one hundred yards apart, and they stood as immovable as the painted heroes in a battle-piece. There was cover of woods not very far in rear of the lines on both sides, and brave men— with that instinct of self-preservation which is exhibited in the veteran soldier, who seizes every advantage of ground or obstacle—might have been justified in slowly seeking this shelter from the iron hail that smote them; but out in the sunlight, in the dying daylight, and under the stars, they stood, and although they could not advance, they would not retire. There was some discipline in this, but there was much more of true valor.

In this fight there was no manœuvring, and very little tactics—it was a question of endurance, and both endured.

The loss was unusually heavy on both sides. On ours, both division commanders, Ewell and myself, were seriously wounded, and several field-officers were killed or wounded. Federal reports state that "more than one-third of their commanders were left dead or wounded on the field," while Confederate accounts claim that the enemy slowly fell back about 9 o'clock at night, but the other side assert that they did not retire until 1 o'clock. It was dark, and the Confederates did not advance, and it may be called a drawn battle as a tribute due by either side to the gallantry of the other.

Five of Jackson's brigades took part in the conflict, Lawton's and Trimble's of Ewell's, and Starke's, Taliaferro's, and Baylor's, of Jackson's old division. Early's, Forno's, and Johnson's brigades were not engaged, nor were any of the brigades of General A. P. Hill's division. The Federal troops encountered were those of King's division, and consisted of the brigade of Gibbon and two regiments of Doubleday's brigade.↓

During our engagement at Groveton the white puffs in the air, seen away off to the Confederate right, and the sounds of sharp but distant explosions coming to our ears, foretold the passage of Thoroughfare Gap; and the next day, before noon, Longstreet's advance, under Hood, mingled their hurrahs with those of our men.‡ The march and the manœuvres of Jackson had been a success;⟍ the army was reunited, and ready, under its great head, to strike with both of its strong arms the blows he should direct.

↓ In this battle the right of the Confederate line was held by Taliaferro's brigade of Virginia and Alabama troops, commanded by Colonel Alexander G. Taliaferro, 23d Virginia; next on the left was Jackson's old brigade, all Virginians (lately commanded by General C. S. Winder, killed at Slaughter's [Cedar] Mountain),— officially designated as the "Stonewall," in honor of the steadiness and gallantry which it displayed on the same field [the First Bull Run] twelve months before, and which gained for their commander his well-known sobriquet,— now commanded by Colonel Baylor, 5th Virginia. Next came the Louisiana brigade, lately commanded by Colonel Stafford, and now by General William E. Starke, who took command about August 19th, and who was killed three weeks afterward at Antietam; then the Georgia brigade, commanded by General Alexander R. Lawton; and upon the extreme left General I. R. Trimble's brigade of Georgia, Mississippi, North Carolina, and Alabama troops. The batteries engaged were those of Wooding, Poague, and Carpenter, much outnumbered by the Federal guns, but, toward the close of the contest, ably supplemented by two pieces brought to their support by the "boy-major" Pelham, of Stuart's Horse Artillery, already famous for his skill and gallantry. Jackson ordered up twenty additional guns, but before they could be brought night and fatigue had closed the contest.— W. B. T.

‡ Jackson's force in this raid consisted of three divisions, as follows: Ewell's division, composed of the brigades of Lawton, Early, Hays (Forno commanding), and Trimble, with the batteries of Brown, Dement, Latimer, Balthis, and D'Aquin; Hill's division, of the brigades of Branch, Gregg, Field, Pender, Archer, and Thomas, with the batteries of Braxton, Latham, Crenshaw, McIntosh, Davidson, and Pegram; and Jackson's old division consisted of the brigades of Starke, Taliaferro (Col. A. G. Taliaferro commanding), Winder (Col. Baylor commanding), and Campbell (Major John Seddon commanding), with the batteries of Brockenbrough, Poague, Wooding, Carpenter, Caskie, and Raine. After the 26th, Colonel Bradley T. Johnson commanded Campbell's brigade. General Stuart, with the brigades of Fitz Lee and Robertson, coöperated with Jackson.— W. B. T.

⟍ The results of Jackson's raid on Manassas Junction were reported by General R. E. Lee to be — "eight pieces of artillery, with their horses and equipments, were taken. More than 300 prisoners, 175 horses, besides those belonging to the artillery, 200 new tents, and immense quantities of quartermaster's and commissary stores fell into our hands. . . . 50,000 pounds of bacon, 1000 barrels of corned beef, 2000 barrels of salt pork, and 2000 barrels of flour, besides other property of great value, were burned."— EDITORS.

RUINS OF THE HENRY HOUSE, BURNED DURING THE FIRST BATTLE OF BULL RUN. FROM A PHOTOGRAPH PROBABLY TAKEN IN MARCH, 1862.

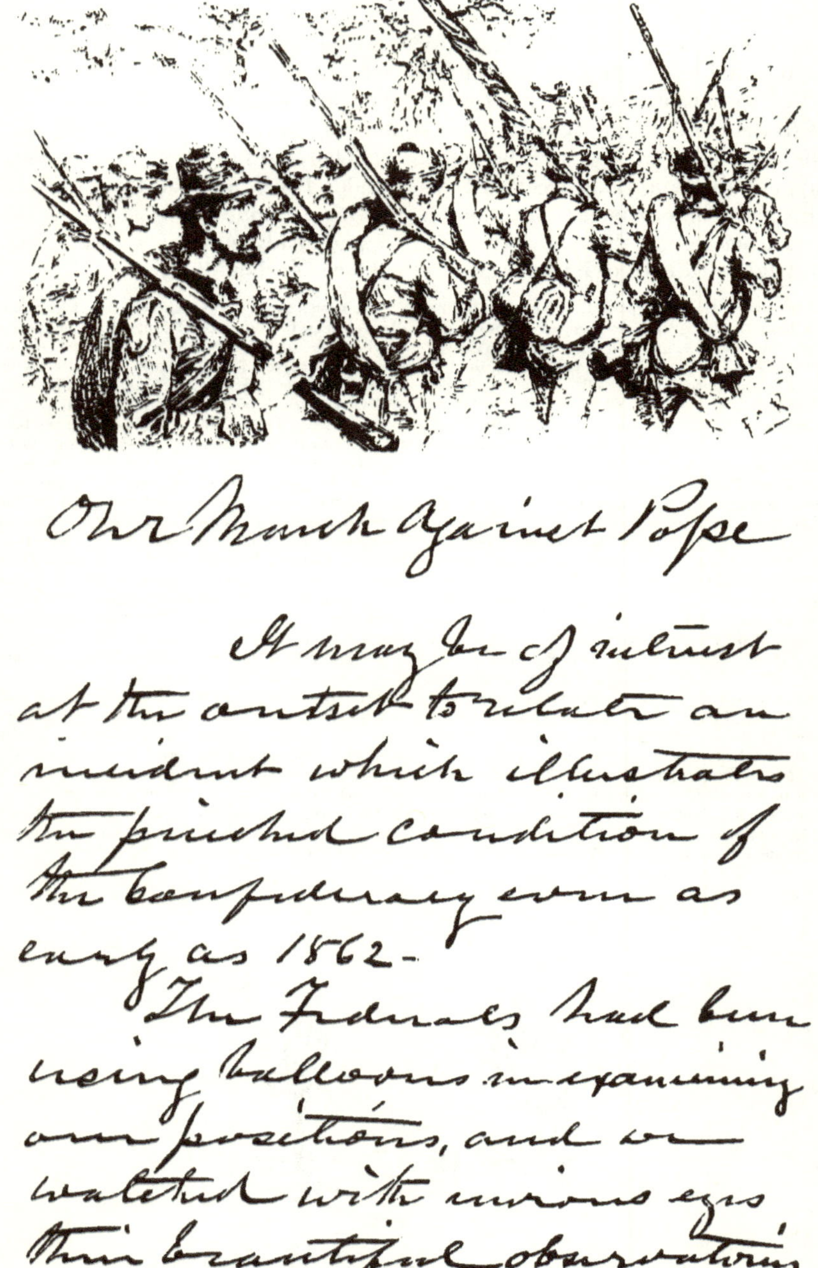

Our March Against Pope

It may be of interest at the outset to relate an incident which illustrates the pinched condition of the Confederacy even as early as 1862 —

The Federals had been using balloons in examining our positions, and we watched with curious eyes their beautiful observations

as they floated high up in the air, well out of the range of our guns. While
we were longing for the balloons that poverty denied us, a genius arose for
the occasion and suggested that we send out and gather together all the silk
dresses in the Confederacy and make a balloon. It was done, and soon we had
a great patchwork ship of many and varied hues which was ready for use in
the Seven Days' campaign. We had no gas except in Richmond, and it was
the custom to inflate the balloon there, tie it securely to an engine, and run
it down the York River Railroad to any point at which we desired to send it
up. One day it was on a steamer down the James when the tide went out
and left vessel and balloon high and dry on a bar. The Federals gathered
it in, and with it the last silk dress in the Confederacy. This capture was
the meanest trick of the war and one I have never yet forgiven.

By the Seven Days' fighting around Richmond General Lee frustrated
McClellan's plans for a siege. At the end of that campaign Lee retired to
Richmond and McClellan withdrew his forces to Westover Landing, where
intrenchments and gun-boats made him secure from attack. As his new position, thus guarded and protected by the navy, was not assailable, General Lee,
resuming the defensive at Richmond, resolved to strike out by his left in the
direction of Washington, with the idea that the Army of the Potomac might
be forced to abandon the James River, in defense of its own capital, threatened by this move.

Contemporaneously with our operations on the Chickahominy, the Washington authorities had been organizing the Army of Virginia of three efficient corps d'armée; and, continuing the search for a young Napoleon, had
assigned General Pope, fresh from the West, with his new laurels, to command
this select organization. This army, under its dashing leader, was at the same
time moving toward Richmond by the Orange and Alexandria Railway, so
that our move by the left had also in view the Army of Virginia, as the first
obstacle in the way of relief to Richmond—an obstacle to be removed, if possible, before it could be greatly reënforced from other commands.

The assignment of General John Pope to command was announced in Richmond three days after the orders were issued in Washington, and the flourish
of trumpets over the manner in which the campaign was to be conducted soon
followed. He was reported to have adopted a favorite expression of General
Worth's, "Headquarters in the saddle, sir!" and to be riding with as much
confidence as that old chieftain when searching the everglades of Florida for
the Seminole Indians.⏦ Lee had not known Pope intimately, but accepted
the popular opinion of him as a boastful man, quite ambitious to accomplish
great results, but unwilling to study closely and properly the means necessary
to gratify his desires in that direction. Pope was credited with other expressions, such as that he cared not for his rear; that he hoped in Virginia to see
the faces of the rebels, as in the West he had been able to see only their
backs.

When General Lee heard of these strange utterances his estimate of Pope
was considerably lessened. The high-sounding words seemed to come from

⏦ See General Pope's denial, p. 493; and the text of his address, p. 530.-- EDITORS.

LONGSTREET'S MARCH THROUGH THOROUGHFARE GAP.

a commander inexperienced in warfare. For centuries there has been among soldiers a maxim: "Don't despise your enemy." General Pope's words would seem to indicate great contempt for his enemy. Unfortunately for him our troops, at that time, were not so well clad that they cared to show their backs.

With the double purpose of drawing McClellan away from Westover, and of checking the advance of the new enemy then approaching from Washington by the Orange and Alexandria Railroad, General Lee sent Stonewall Jackson to Gordonsville, while I remained near Richmond to engage McClellan in case he should attempt an advance upon the Confederate capital. Jackson had his own division and that of General R. S. Ewell, and later A. P. Hill was sent to reënforce him. McDowell was already in coöperation with Pope, part of his command, however, being still at Fredericksburg. On the 9th of August Jackson encountered the enemy near Slaughter or Cedar Mountain. [See page 459.] There the battle of Cedar Run was fought and the Federals were repulsed. In this fight, about 5 o'clock in the afternoon, the Federals, by a well-executed move, were pressing the Confederates back, when the opportune approach of two brigades changed the scene, and a counter-attack from our side drove them back in disorder and left us masters of the field. We followed them some distance, but Jackson thought them too strongly reënforced for us to continue the pursuit and risk severe battle in a disjointed way; so, after caring for our wounded and dead, we retired to a position behind the Rapidan to await the arrival of General Lee with other forces. Thus on his first meeting with the Confederates in Virginia the new Federal commander went to the rear—a direction he was wholly unused to. At that time General Lee was feeling very certain that Richmond was in no immediate danger from an advance by McClellan's forces. He therefore began at once preparations for a vigorous campaign against Pope. Divisions under Generals R. H. Anderson, Lafayette McLaws, J. G. Walker, and D. H. Hill were left to watch McClellan, with instructions to follow the main body of the army as soon as the Federals were drawn away from Westover.

On the 13th of August my command was ordered to Gordonsville, and General Lee accompanied me there. Jackson's troops were stationed on the left of the Orange and Alexandria Railroad, and I went into camp on the right of Gordonsville. Northward was the Rapidan River, several miles distant.

Farther on, at Culpeper Court House, was the army of Pope, and farther still was the Rappahannock River. A little in advance of my position was Clark's Mountain, rising several hundred feet above the surrounding hills. With General Lee I proceeded to the mountain, and, climbing to its summit, we raised our glasses and turned them to the north. There, between the two rivers, clustering around Culpeper Court House, and perhaps fifteen miles away, we saw the flags of Pope's army floating placidly above the tops of the trees. From the summit of the mountain we beheld the enemy occupying ground so weak as to invite at-tack. Realizing the situation, General Lee determined on speedy work, and gave orders that his army should cross the Rapidan on the 18th and make battle. He was exceedingly anx-ious to move at once, before Pope could get reënforcements. For some reason not fully explained, our movements were delayed and we did not cross the Rapidan until the 20th. In the meantime a dispatch to General Stuart was captured by Pope, which gave information of our presence and contemplated advance. This, with information Pope already had, caused him to withdraw to a very strong position behind the Rappahannock River, and there, instead of at Culpeper Court House, where the attack was first

meant to be made, General Lee found him. I approached the Rappahannock at Kelly's Ford, and Jackson approached higher up at Beverly Ford, near the Orange and Alexandria Railroad bridge.

We reached the river on the morning of the 21st, without serious opposition, and found Pope in an almost unassailable position, with heavy reënforcements summoned to his aid. General Lee's intention was to force a passage and make the attack before Pope could concentrate. We hoped to be able to interpose, and to strike Pope before McClellan's reënforcements could reach him. We knew at that time that McClellan was withdrawing from Westover. I was preparing to force a passage at Kelly's Ford, when I received an order from General Lee to proceed to Beverly Ford and mask the movements of Jackson, who was to be sent up the river to cross by a left flank movement. On the 22d Jackson withdrew carefully and went on the proposed move. He sought an opportunity to cross farther up the stream, and succeeded in putting part of his command across at Warrenton Springs Ford and in occupying a position there. The flooding rains interrupted his operations, making the river past fording and crippling all attempts at forcing a passage. Jackson therefore withdrew his forces at night by a temporary bridge. As the lower fords become impassable by reason of the floods, the Federals seemed to concentrate against Jackson's efforts.

On the 23d I had quite a spirited artillery combat at Beverly Ford with a force of the enemy that had crossed at the railroad bridge near where I was stationed. The superior position and metal of the Federals gave them an advantage, which they improved by skillful practice. We had more guns, however, and by practice equally clever at length gained the advantage. A little before night the Federals withdrew from the combat.

Pending our movements south-west of the Rappahannock, General Stuart had been making an effort to go around Pope's army, but, fearing to remain on the Washington side of the river in the face of such floods as had come, recrossed with some important dispatches he had captured by a charge upon Pope's headquarters train [see p. 528]. This correspondence confirmed the information we already had, that the Federal army on the James under McClellan and the Federal troops in the Kanawha Valley under Cox had been ordered to reënforce Pope [see p. 278]. Upon receipt of that information, General Lee was more anxious than ever to cross at once. Pope, however, was on the alert, and Lee found he could not attack him to advantage in his stronghold behind the Rappahannock. Lee therefore decided to change his whole plan, and was gratified, on looking at the map, to find a very comfortable way of turning Pope out of his position. It was by moving Jackson off to our left, and far to the rear of the Federal army, while I remained in front with thirty thousand men to engage him in case he should offer to fight.

On the 25th Jackson crossed the Rappahannock at Hinson's Mill, four miles above Waterloo Bridge, and that night encamped at Salem. The next day he passed through Thoroughfare Gap and moved on by Gainesville, and when sunset came he was many miles in the rear of Pope's army, and between it and Washington. This daring move must have staggered the Federal commander. From the Rappahannock, Jackson had gone without serious opposition to within a stone's-throw of the field where the first battle of Manassas was fought. When he arrived at Bristoe Station, just before night, the greater part of the Federal guard at that point fled, and two trains of cars coming from the direction of Warrenton were captured. Jackson sent a force forward seven miles and captured Manassas Junction, taking eight pieces of artillery, a lot of prisoners, and great quantities of commissary and quartermaster's stores. He left a force at Bristoe Station and proceeded to the Junction, arriving there himself on the morning of the 27th.

During the afternoon the enemy attacked our troops at Bristoe Station, coming from the direction of Warrenton Junction in such force that it was evident Pope had discovered the situation and was moving with his entire army upon Jackson. The Confederates at the station withdrew, after a sharp engagement, and the Federals halted there. Jackson appropriated such of the supplies captured at Manassas as he could use, and burned the rest. He then moved over to a position north of the turnpike leading from Warrenton to Alexandria. There, on the old battle-field, Jackson waited for the Federals. On the evening of the 28th King's division came moving eastward down the turnpike and Jackson met them. A bloody fight ensued, lasting until 9 o'clock at night. The enemy withdrew, leaving the Confederates in possession of the field.

That same evening I arrived at Thoroughfare Gap. But I should say that during Jackson's march I had been engaging Pope at different points along the Rappahannock, to impress him with the idea that I was attempting to force a passage in his front. On the afternoon of the 26th, Pope's army broke away from its strong position to meet Jackson's daring and unexpected move. General Lee decided that I should follow at once, and asked whether I would prefer to force a passage of the river, now rapidly falling, or take the route by which Jackson had gone. From the crossing along the route to Warrenton were numerous strongly defensive positions where a small force could have detained me an uncertain length of time. I therefore decided to take Jackson's route, and on the 26th I started. On the 28th, just before night, I arrived at Thoroughfare Gap. As we approached, a report was made to me that the pass was unoccupied, and we went into bivouac on the west side of the mountain, sending a brigade under Anderson down to occupy the pass. As the Confederates neared the gap from one side, Ricketts's division of Federals approached from the other and took possession of the east side. Thoroughfare Gap is a rough pass in the Bull Run Mountains, at some points not more than a hundred yards wide. A turbid stream rushes over its rugged bottom, on both sides of which the mountain rises several hundred feet. On the north the face of the gap is almost perpendicular. The south face is less precipitous, but is covered with tangled mountain ivy and projecting bowlders, forming a position unassailable when occupied by a small infantry and artillery force. Up to this moment we had received reports from General Jackson, at regular intervals, assuring us of his successful operations, and of confidence in his ability to baffle all efforts of the enemy till we should reach him. This sudden interposition of a force at a mountain pass indicated a purpose on the part of the adversary to hold me in check, while overwhelming forces were being brought against Jackson. This placed us in a desperate strait; for we were within relieving distance, and must adopt prompt and vigorous measures that would burst through all opposition. Three miles north was Hopewell Gap, and it was necessary to get possession of this in advance of the Federals, in order to have that vantage-ground for a flank movement, at the same time that we forced our way by footpaths over the mountain heights at Thoroughfare Gap. During the night I sent Wilcox with three brigades through that pass, while Hood was climbing over the mountain at Thoroughfare by a trail. We had no trouble in getting over, and our apprehensions were relieved at the early dawn of the 29th by finding that Ricketts had given up the east side of the gap and was many

VIEW OF JACKSON'S POSITION AS SEEN FROM GROVETON CORNERS. FROM A RECENT PHOTOGRAPH.

The farthest ridge is the line of the unfinished railway. Jackson's center occupied the ground in the right of the picture. There, on elevated open ground, the front of a deep cut, stands the Union monument. [See map, p. 509.]

hours in advance of us, moving in the direction of Manassas Junction. His force, instead of marching around Jackson, could have been thrown against his right and rear. If Ricketts had made this move and the forces in front had coöperated with him, such an attack, well handled, might have given us serious trouble before I reached the field.

As we found the pass open at early dawn and a clean road in front, we marched leisurely to unite our forces on Manassas plains. Before reaching Gainesville we heard the artillery combat in front, and our men involuntarily quickened their steps. Our communications with Jackson were quite regular, and as he had not expressed a wish that we should hurry, our troops were allowed to take their natural swing under the inspiration of impending battle. As we approached the field the fire seemed to become more spirited, and gave additional impulse to our movements. According to the diary of the Washington Artillery we filed down the turnpike at Gainesville at 11:30 A. M.‡ The general impression was that we were there earlier; but this is the only record of time we made on the ground. We marched steadily from daylight till we reached the field, with the exception of an hour's halt to permit Stuart's cavalry to file from east to west of us. There were many of Jackson's men — several thousand — straggling at points along the road, who were taken for my men, and reported as such.

Passing through Gainesville we filed off to the left down the turnpike, and

‡ GAINESVILLE, GA., 8th January, 1886. My attention has just been called to a dispatch of the Federal General John Buford, written on August 29th, 1862, at 9:30 A. M., in which he gives information of my troops moving through Gainesville [Va.] some three-quarters of an hour before his note was written. This would place the head of my column at Gainesville about 9 A. M., and the line deployed and ready for battle at 12 M., which agrees with my recollection, and with my evidence in the F. J. Porter case. It seems that the Washington Artillery was halted some distance in rear to await my selection of the position to which it was assigned — hence the late hour (11:30) mentioned in the diary from which I have quoted above in fixing the hour of our arrival at Gainesville.—J. L. [In this connection see also the testimony of others, p. 527.]

soon came in sight of the troops held at bay by Jackson. Our line of march brought us in on the left and rear of the Federals. At sight of this favorable opportunity our artillery was ordered up, with the leading brigades for its support. Our advance was discovered, however, and the Federals withdrew from attack, retiring their left across the pike behind Groveton, and taking strong defensive ground. The battalion of Washington Artillery was thrown forward to a favorable position on Jackson's right, and from that point my line was deployed so as to extend it to the right some distance beyond the Manassas Gap Railroad. A Federal corps was reported to be at Manassas Junction that morning, and we trail-traced Ricketts's division from Thoroughfare Gap toward the same point; my line was now arranged for attack in front and also to guard against the force in the direction of the Junction. This preparation must have taken an hour—possibly more.

As soon as the troops were arranged, General Lee expressed his wish to have me attack. The change of position on the part of the Federals, however, involved sufficient delay for a reconnoissance on our part. To hasten matters I rode over in the direction of Brewer's Spring, east of the Hampton Cole House [see map, p. 482], to see the new position, and had a fair view of the Federal line, then extending some distance south of the turnpike. The position was not inviting, and I so reported to General Lee.

The two great armies were now face to face upon the memorable field of 1861; both in good defensible positions and both anxious to find a point for an entering wedge into the stronghold of the adversary. It appeared easy for us, except for the unknown quantity at Manassas Junction, to overleap the Federal left and strike a decisive blow. This force at the Junction was a thorn in our side which could not be ignored. General Lee was quite disappointed by my report against immediate attack along the turnpike, and insisted that by throwing some of the brigades beyond the Federal left their position would be broken up and a favorable field gained. While talking the matter over, General Stuart reported the advance of heavy forces from the direction of Manassas Junction against my right. It proved to be McDowell and Porter. I called over three brigades, under Wilcox, and prepared to receive the attack. Battle was not offered, and I reported to General Lee some time afterward that I did not think the force on my right was strong enough to attack us. General Lee urged me to go in, and of course I was anxious to meet his wishes. At the same time I wanted, more than anything else, to know that my troops had a chance to accomplish what they might undertake. The ground before me was greatly to the advantage of the Federals, but if the attack had come from them it would have been a favorable opportunity for me. After a short while McDowell moved toward the Federal right, leaving Porter in front of my right with nine thousand men. My estimate of his force, at the time, was ten thousand. General Lee, finding that attack was not likely, again became anxious to bring on the battle by attacking down the Groveton pike. I suggested that, the day being far spent, it might be as well to advance just before night upon a forced reconnoissance, get our troops into the most favorable positions, and have all things ready for battle at daylight the next morning. To this he reluctantly gave consent, and our plans were laid accordingly. Wilcox returned to position on the left of the turnpike. Orders were given for an advance, to be pursued under cover of night until the main position could be carefully examined. It so happened that an order to advance was issued on the other side at the same time, so that the encounter was something of a surprise on both sides. A very spirited engagement was the result, we being successful, so far at least as to carry our point, capturing a piece of artillery and making our reconnoissance before midnight. As none of the reports received of the Federal positions favored attack, I so explained to General Lee, and our forces were ordered back to their original positions. The gun which we had captured was ordered to be cut down, spiked, and left on the ground.

When Saturday the 30th broke, we were a little apprehensive that Pope was going to get away from us, and Pope was afraid that we were going to get away from him. He telegraphed to Washington that I was in full retreat and he was preparing to follow, while we, thinking he was trying to escape, were making arrangements for moving by our left across Bull Run, so as to get over on the Little River pike and

COLONEL W. S. H. BAYLOR, C. S. A., COMMANDING THE "STONEWALL" BRIGADE; KILLED AUGUST 30, 1862 — FROM A PHOTOGRAPH.

move down parallel to his lines and try to interpose between him and Washington. We had about completed our arrangements, and took it for granted that Pope would move out that night by the Warrenton and Centreville pike, and that we could move parallel with him along the Little River pike. General Lee was still anxious to give Pope battle on Manassas plains, but had given up the idea of attacking him in his strong position.

Shortly before nine on the 30th, Pope's artillery began to play a little, and not long afterward some of his infantry force was seen in motion. We did not understand that as an offer of battle, but merely as a display to cover his movements to the rear. Later a considerable force moved out and began to attack us on our left, extending and engaging the whole of Jackson's line. Evidently Pope supposed that I was gone, as he was ignoring me entirely. His whole army seemed to surge up against Jackson as if to crush him with an overwhelming mass. At the critical moment I happened to be riding to the front of my line to find a place where I might get in for my share of the battle. I reached a point a few rods in front of my line on the left of the pike where I could plainly see the Federals as they rushed in heavy masses against the obstinate ranks of the Confederate left. It was a grand display of well-organized attack, thoroughly concentrated and operating cleverly. So terrible was the onslaught that Jackson sent to me and begged for reïnforcements. About the same time I received an order from General Lee to the same effect. To retire from my advanced position in front of the Federals and get to Jackson would have taken an hour and a half. I had discovered a prominent position that commanded a view of the great struggle, and realizing the opportunity, I quickly ordered out three batteries, making twelve guns. Lieutenant Wm. H. Chapman's Dixie Battery of four guns was the first to report and was placed in position to rake the Federal ranks that seemed determined to break through Jackson's lines. In a moment a heavy fire of shot and shell was being poured into the thick columns of the enemy, and in ten minutes their stubborn masses began to waver and give back. For a moment there was chaos; then order returned and they re-formed, apparently to renew the attack. Meanwhile my other eight pieces reported to me, and from the crest of the little hill the fire of twelve guns cut them down. As the cannon thundered the ranks broke, only to be formed again with dogged determination. A third time the batteries tore the Federals to pieces, and as they fell back under this terrible fire, I sprung everything to the charge. My troops leaped forward with exultant yells, and all along the line we pushed forward. Farther and still farther back we pressed them, until at 10 o'clock at night we had the field; Pope was across Bull Run, and the victorious Confederates lay down on the battle-ground to sleep, while all around were strewn thousands—friend and foe, sleeping the last sleep together.

The next morning the Federals were in a strong position at Centreville. I sent a brigade across Bull Run under General Pryor and occupied a point over there near Centreville. As our troops proceeded to bury their dead, it began to rain, as it had done on the day after the first battle of Manassas. As soon as General Lee could make his preparations, he ordered Jackson to cross Bull Run near Sudley's and turn the position of the Federals occupying Centreville; and the next day, September 1st, I followed him. But the enemy discovered our turning movement, abandoned Centreville, and put out toward Washington. On the evening of September 1st Jackson encountered a part of the Federal force at Ox Hill [or Chantilly; see map, p. 450], and, attacking it, had quite a sharp engagement. I came up just before night and found his men retiring in a good deal of confusion. I asked Jackson what the situation was, and added that his men seemed to be pretty well dispersed. He said, "Yes, but I hope it will prove a victory."

I moved my troops out and occupied the lines where he had been, relieving the few men who were on picket. Just as we reached there General Kearny, a Federal officer, came along looking for his line, that had disappeared. It was raining in the woods, and was so late in the day that a Federal was not easily distinguished from a Confederate. Kearny did not seem to know that he was in the Confederate line, and our troops did not notice that he was a Federal. He began to inquire about some command, and in a moment or so the men saw that he was a Federal officer. At the same moment he realized where he was. He was called upon to surrender, but instead of doing so he wheeled his

VIEW FROM THE HENRY HILL DURING THE ATTACK UPON JACKSON, ABOUT FOUR O'CLOCK, AUGUST 30TH, FROM A SKETCH MADE AT THE TIME.

In the foreground Reynolds's division is marching to the defense of the left flank, where Milroy is fighting on Bald Hill. The stone house on the turnpike is seen in the hollow.— EDITORS.

horse, lay flat on the animal's neck, clapped spurs into his sides and dashed off. Instantly a half-dozen shots rang out, and before he had gone thirty steps he fell. He had been in the army all his life, and we knew him and respected him. His body was sent over the lines under a flag of truce. [See p. 538.] The forces we had been fighting at Ox Hill proved to be the rear-guard covering the retreat of the Federals into Washington.‡ They escaped and we abandoned further pursuit.

The entire Bull Run campaign up to Ox Hill was clever and brilliant. It was conceived entirely by General Lee, who held no such consultation over it as he had done in beginning the Seven Days' campaign. The movement around Pope was not as strong as it should have been. A skillful man could have concentrated against me or Jackson, and given us severe battles in detail. I suppose Pope tried to get too many men against Jackson before attacking. If he had been satisfied with a reasonable force he might have overwhelmed him.

General Pope, sanguine by nature, was not careful enough to keep himself informed about the movements of his enemy. At half-past four on the afternoon of the 29th, he issued an order for Porter to attack Jackson's right, supposing I was at Thoroughfare Gap, when in fact I had been in position since noon, and was anxiously awaiting attack. It has been said that General Stuart, by raising a dust in front of Porter, so impressed him that he did not offer battle. I know nothing of the truth of the story, and never heard of it till after the war. If from any such cause Porter was prevented from attacking me, it was to our disadvantage and delayed our victory twenty-four hours. Porter knew I was in his front. He had captured one or two of my men, which gave him information of my position before he actually saw me. If Porter had not appeared when he did I would have attacked by our right

‡ It appears from the official reports that the Union force encountered by Jackson at Chantilly (Ox Hill) was the advance of Pope's army, which had changed front in anticipation of attack down Little River Pike. (See pp. 492, 493.) — EDITORS.

early in the afternoon. In that event Porter would have had a fine opportunity to take me on the wing and strike a fearful blow. As it was, he was a check upon my move against Pope's main position. If I had advanced upon Pope I would have been under an enfilade fire from Porter's batteries, and if I had advanced upon Porter I would have been under a fire from the batteries on Pope's front as severe as the raking fire from my batteries the next day, when Pope was massed against Jackson. Had Porter attacked me between noon and night on the 29th, I should have received his nine thousand with about double that number. I would have held my line to receive the attack, and as soon as his line developed his strength I would have thrown three brigades

MAJOR GENERAL ROBERT H. MILROY.
FROM A PHOTOGRAPH.

forward beyond his extreme left. When my line of battle had broken up the attack, as it certainly would have done, these three brigades would have been thrown forward at the flank, and at the same time my main line would have pushed on in the pursuit. The result would have been Porter's retreat in confusion, and I might possibly have reached Pope's left and rear in time to cut him off. When his army was well concentrated on the 30th he was badly cut up and defeated. It does not seem unreasonable to conclude that attack on the 29th in his disjointed condition would have been attended with more disastrous results to him. If I had been attacked under the 4:30 order [see p. 475] the result might have been less damaging, as Porter would have had the night to cover his retreat, and the Federal army could have availed itself of the darkness to screen its move across Bull Run. But Porter's attack at night, if not followed by the back retreat of the army, would have drawn me around the Federal left and put me in a position for striking the next day.

Colonel Charles Marshall, of General Lee's staff, in his evidence before the Fitz John Porter Board, puts my forces on the 29th at 30,000. It is difficult to see how Porter with 9000 men was to march over 30,000 of the best soldiers the world ever knew. Any move that would have precipitated battle would have been to our advantage, as we were ready at all points and waiting for an opportunity to fight. The situation will be better understood when we reflect that the armies were too evenly balanced to admit mistakes on either side. I was waiting for an opportunity to get into the Federal lines close upon the heels of their own troops. The opportunity came on the 30th, but the

Federal army was then concentrated; had it come on the 29th I would have been greatly pleased.

It is proper to state that General Lee, upon hearing my guns on the 30th, sent me word that if I had anything better than reënforcing Jackson to pursue it, and soon afterward rode forward and joined me. Jackson did not respond with spirit to my move, so my men were subjected to a severe artillery fire from batteries in front of him. General Lee, seeing this, renewed his orders for Jackson to press on to the front. The fire still continued severe, however, and General Lee, who remained with me, was greatly exposed to it. As we could not persuade him to drop back behind it, I finally induced him to ride into a ravine which threw a traverse between us and the fire, which was more annoying than fire from the front.

On the 31st we were engaged in caring for our wounded and cleaning up the battle-field. General Lee was quite satisfied with the results of the campaign, though he had very little to say. He was not given to expressions of pride. Under all circumstances he was a moderate talker, and in everything was unassuming. His headquarters were exceedingly simple. He had his tents of the same kind as the other officers—perhaps a few more, to accommodate his larger staff. He made no display of position or rank. Only when he was specially engaged could a sentinel be seen at the door of his tent. On the march he usually had his headquarters near mine.

COLONEL FLETCHER WEBSTER.
FROM A PHOTOGRAPH.

Colonel Webster (son of Daniel Webster) commanded the 12th Massachusetts Volunteers (Ricketts's division) and was mortally wounded August 30th, in the defense of Bald Hill [see map, p. 482].

I was graduated with Pope at West Point. He was a handsome, dashing fellow, and a splendid cavalryman, sitting his horse beautifully. I think he stood at the head for riding. He did not apply himself to his books very closely. He studied about as much as I did, but knew his lessons better. We were graduated in 1842, but Pope saw little of active service till the opening of the Civil War. When he assumed command of the Army of Virginia he was in the prime of life, less than forty years old, and had lost little if any of the dash and grace of his youth. D. H. Hill, Lafayette McLaws, Mansfield Lovell, Gustavus W. Smith, R. H. Anderson, A. P. Stewart, and Earl Van Dorn were among the Confederate commanders who were graduated in the same class with me. Of the Federal commanders, there were of that class—besides Pope—Generals John Newton, W. S. Rosecrans, George Sykes, Abner Doubleday, and others less prominent. Stonewall Jackson came on four years after my class. General Lee had preceded us about fourteen years. General Ewell, who was hurt in this battle, was in the same class with Tecumseh Sherman and George H. Thomas. A truer soldier and nobler spirit than Ewell never drew sword.

"Jeb" Stuart was a very daring fellow and the best cavalryman America ever produced. At the Second Manassas, soon after we heard of the advance of McDowell and Porter, Stuart came up and made a report to General Lee. When he had done so General Lee said he had no orders at that moment, but he requested Stuart to wait awhile. Thereupon Stuart turned round in his tracks, lay down on the ground, put a stone under his head and instantly fell asleep. General Lee rode away and in an hour returned. Stuart was still sleeping. Lee asked for him, and Stuart sprang to his feet and said, "Here I am, General."

General Lee replied, "I want you to send a message to your troops over on the left to send a few more cavalry over to the right."

"I would better go myself," said Stuart, and with that he swung himself into the saddle and rode off at a rapid gallop, singing as loud as he could, 'Jine the cavalry.'"

General Toombs, our Georgia fire-eater, was given to criticising pretty severely all the officers of the regular army who had joined their fortunes with those of the Confederacy. He was hot-blooded and impatient, and chafed at the delays of the commanders in their preparations for battle. His general idea was that the troops went out to fight, and he thought they should be

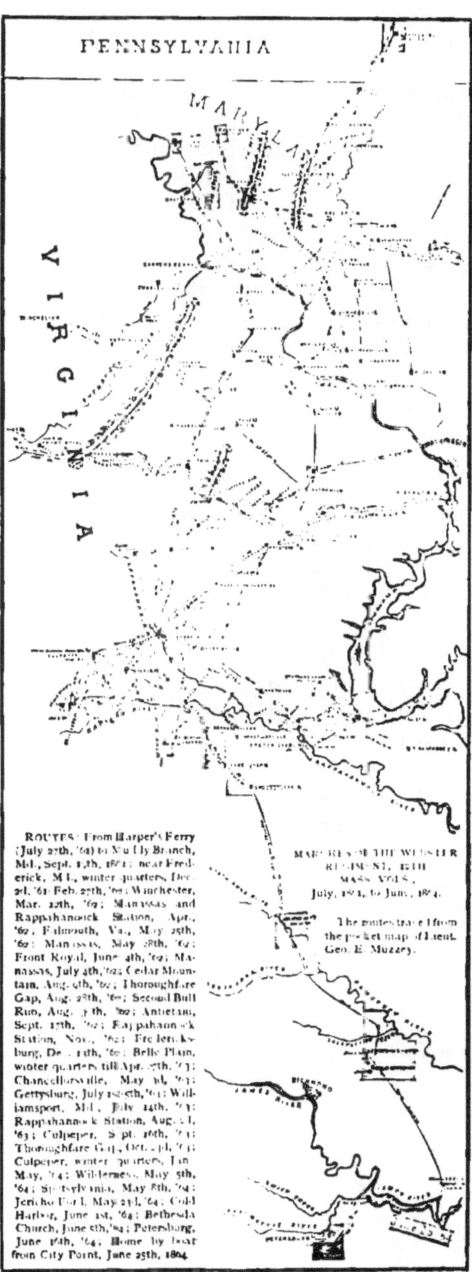

allowed to go at it at once. An incident that occurred in the second Manassas campaign will serve to illustrate his characteristic hot-headedness. As we were preparing to cross the Rapidan, Stuart sent me word that he had cut off a large cavalry force and had all the fords guarded except one. He asked that I detail a force to guard that point of escape. The work was assigned to the command under General Toombs, who was absent at the time. He had met a kindred spirit in the person of a wealthy Virginian named Morton, whom he had known in Congress, and was out dining with him. They were both good livers and loved to have their friends with them. In going back to his command General Toombs came upon his troops on the road and inquired what they were doing there. The explanation was made. Toombs had had a good dinner and felt independent. He said he would give the general to understand that he must consult him before sending his troops out to guard a ford, and thereupon he ordered them back to camp. As the mystified troops marched solemnly back, the matter was reported to me and I ordered Toombs under arrest. As we marched against Pope I allowed him to ride with his command, expecting that he would make some explanation of his conduct. He did not do so, and the next I heard of him he was stopping along the route and making stump-speeches to the troops and referring in anything but complimentary terms to the commander of his division. I then sent him back in arrest to Gordonsville, with instructions to confine himself to the limits of that town until further orders. He obeyed the command and went to Gordonsville. Just as I was leaving the Rappahannock, having received a long letter of apology from him, I directed him to join his command. As we were preparing for the charge at Manassas, Toombs arrived. He was riding rapidly, with his hat in his hand, and was very much excited. I was just sending a courier to his command with a dispatch.

"Let me carry it!" he exclaimed.

"With pleasure," I responded, and handed him the paper.

He put spurs to his horse and dashed off, accompanied by a courier. When he rode up and took command of his brigade there was wild enthusiasm, and, everything being ready, an exultant shout was sent up, and the men sprang to the charge. I had no more trouble with Toombs.

We were ever afterwards
warm personal friends

James Longstreet.

D. M. PERRY, sergeant in Company F, 76th New York (of Doubleday's brigade, King's division, McDowell's corps), wrote to the editors in 1886 to say that he was wounded in the attack made on the flank of King's division as it was passing Jackson's front on the evening of August 28th, was left on the field, was taken prisoner, hobbled off the next morning, and again fell into the hands of the enemy, Hood's men, of Longstreet's corps. By an ingenious device he managed to retain possession of his watch. He says:

"I awoke at 7 A. M., August 29th, by the Warrenton Pike, near Douglass's woods. A few yards away, under the trees, were several wounded comrades. . . . I made use of a broken musket as a crutch, and was well on my way to the shelter of the trees, when some one called out: 'Throw down that gun.' It was not until the order had been repeated that I was aware it was addressed to me. Looking round, I saw a company of the enemy's cavalry approaching. I dropped the gun, and they rode up and claimed us as prisoners.

"A few of the Confederates remained with us nearly two hours, and were then compelled to retire before Schenck's skirmishers, who passed through the woods, and remained west of us, possibly thirty minutes, when they in turn retired whence they came, followed by those of the enemy, with whom they exchanged a few shots. The enemy's skirmishers passed down the pike and through the field south of it, followed by the 2d Mississippi, of Hood's division, which halted a few yards east of us. The enemy now began to arrive in force, and occupied the woods. Hood's troops remained here from 11 A. M. until nearly sundown, when they went forward and engaged our troops under Hatch south-east of Groveton.

"This action between Hood and Hatch at sunset, August 29th, was fought east, rather than west of Groveton, as laid down on the map [p. 473], which would have been only a few yards from us, and within full view. The battle took place, I should think, at least a mile east of Douglass's woods. Participants in that action, who visited the field with me in October, 1883, were positive regarding the locality of the fight.

"My recollection of the time of Hood's arrival is concurred in by fellow-prisoners with whom I have recently corresponded. They say, '10 A. M., and the woods were full of the enemy's troops at 11 o'clock.'

"General Lee's headquarters during the 29th and 30th were on the elevation between Pageland lane and Meadowville lane [see p. 473], a few hundred yards west of us. When he moved on the 31st, the band stopped and played 'Dixie' for us in good old Southern style."

William R. Houghton, attorney-at-law, of Hayneville, Alabama, writes to the editors as follows:

"I belonged to Toombs's brigade of D. R. Jones's division, and we were ready to march from the eastern end of Thoroughfare Gap at daylight on the morning of the 29th of August, but other troops filing past occupied the road, so that we did not move until a little after sunrise. We moved at a quick pace, without halting, until we filed to the right of the road near Groveton. My recollection of the distance we marched is that it was eight or nine miles. At the time of our arrival some of Longstreet's troops who had preceded us were formed in two lines fronting toward Centreville, while Jones's division was deployed, facing more toward Manassas Station. I do not know the exact time of our arrival, but it could not have been later than 11 o'clock. My recollection is that it was earlier than the hour named, and that Jones's whole division, in addition to the two lines of men who had preceded us, was in position on very favorable ground before 11 o'clock in the day, and

between Porter's corps and Jackson's right flank. Before Porter could have attacked Jackson's right, it would have been necessary for him to remove or disperse this force, which must have been much larger than — if not double — his own. I volunteered for skirmish duty, and we remained in this position all the remainder of that day, and until about 4 o'clock in the afternoon of the 30th of August, at which time we advanced against the enemy, whose line was then at the Chinn house. I feel perfectly assured that we — that is, D. R. Jones's division of several thousand men — were in front of Porter all the day, 29th of August, and that General Pope is utterly mistaken when he says we were not."

General E. M. Law, then colonel of the 4th Alabama Regiment, commanding Whiting's brigade of Hood's division, has written us follows in the Philadelphia "Weekly Press":

"The true story of the forcing of Thoroughfare Gap has never been fully told. Bare allusions were made in some of the official reports to the fact that Hood's division was sent over the mountain by a trail north of the pass, and I have seen it stated that Hood was guided by a wood-chopper, who was familiar with the mountain. The facts are these: My brigade was leading the division when it reached the mountain. There I met General Hood, coming from the direction of the gap. He informed me that it was held on the other side in strong force by the enemy, and that Jones's division was unable to force it. He was accompanied by a man living in the vicinity, who, he said, would guide me by a trail across the mountain, a short distance above the gap. His own brigade was to follow mine. The head of my column was at once turned to the left, and, striking a slight trail, commenced the ascent. I had not gone half-way up the side of the mountain when my guide either missed the trail or it ran out. At any rate, he seemed to know as little as I did, and told me he could guide me no farther. Letting him go, I moved on through the tangled woods and huge rocks until the crest was reached. Here we were confronted by a natural wall of rock, which seemed impassable. Men were sent out on both sides to search for some opening through which we might pass, and a crevice was soon found several feet above our level, where the men could get through one at a time, the first one being lifted up by those behind, and each man as he got up lending a helping hand to the next. As I stood on the crest and heard the fighting in the gap below and the distant thundering of Jackson's battle at Manassas, I felt that the sound of each gun was a call for help, and the progress of the men, one by one, across the rocky barrier seemed painfully slow. In fact, they got through in an almost incredibly short time. As soon as the leading regiment was over, a skirmish line was pushed down the mountain, which on this side sloped gently, and presented few obstacles except a small ravine and stream which issued from the gap itself. The Federal batteries at the mouth of the gap soon came in sight. They were firing steadily but leisurely, and seemed as if they were there to stay. My whole brigade were soon over, the skirmishers in the meantime pressing forward upon the flank of the batteries, which were less than half a mile off. As they emerged into the open ground at the foot of the mountain and engaged the Federal skirmishers on the ravine already mentioned, there was a commotion among the batteries, which limbered up and rapidly moved off.

"It was now nearly dark. My skirmishers were pressing steadily forward, followed by the main line, when I received an order from a staff-officer of General Hood directing me to return at once to the gap by the way I had come — that the enemy was retiring. This was plain enough, but of what had caused him to retire Hood was at that time entirely ignorant. I remonstrated against the order, but was told that it was peremptory. I therefore had no choice but to move back, and march two miles and a half in the night to reach a point less than half a mile from where I had started. We passed through the gap and camped that night on the ground that Ricketts's troops had held in the afternoon. The second battle of Bull Run was practically decided at Thoroughfare Gap. Had McDowell's whole corps been assigned to the duty of keeping Longstreet on the west side of the Bull Run Mountains, it could, properly handled, have kept him there long enough to enable General Pope to crush Jackson with the other forces at his disposal.

"At sunrise the next morning we were on the march toward Manassas, Hood's division leading. A short delay was caused near Gainesville by the passage of a portion of Stuart's cavalry from left to right across our line of march; but before 10 o'clock the head of the column reached Jackson's battle-field, where heavy artillery firing was then going on. There have been many different statements as to the time of Longstreet's arrival at Manassas on the 29th of August. I am absolutely certain that Hood's division reached there not later than the time above stated. The distance to our camp of the previous night was under eight miles, and we marched steadily from 6 o'clock until we reached the field, with the exception of less than an hour's halt caused by the passage of the cavalry already referred to. At that time, in addition to the artillery firing, heavy skirmishing was in progress along Jackson's line, which was formed on the grading of an unfinished railroad running from Sudley Ford to a point near the Warrenton turnpike in rear (north-west) of Groveton. The line formed an acute angle with the pike, and the right wing was thrown back so as partially to face that road. Federal troops were moving on and to the south of the pike, around Jackson's right, when we arrived. Our division was thrown quickly into line across the road, one brigade on each side, and pressed these troops steadily back until Jackson's flank was cleared, when we took up a line on the ridge west of Groveton, slightly in advance of Jackson's right.

"The other troops of Longstreet's command were now rapidly coming up. Kemper, with three brigades, took position to the right of Hood, and D. R. Jones's division still farther to the right, extending the line a mile and a half south of the turnpike. Evans's brigade came up in rear of Hood, and Wilcox's three brigades were posted in rear of the interval between Longstreet's left and Jackson's right, the interval itself being occupied by Colonel Walton's battalion of Washington Artillery."

Colonel John S. Mosby, C. S. A., said, in 1887, in his lecture on "War Reminiscences":

"The reason that Jackson left Manassas was that Stuart had captured a dispatch showing that Pope was concentrating his army on that point. General Jackson says: 'General Stuart kept me advised of the movements of the enemy.' In a dispatch to Fitz John Porter, on the evening of the 27th, Pope ordered him to be at Bristoe at daylight the next morning to bag Jackson, who was then five miles off. General Pope says that Jackson made a mistake in leaving Manassas before he got there. If Jackson went there to be caught, it was. If Pope had reached the place at daylight he would have found nothing but a rear-guard of Stuart's cavalry. He has censured Porter for not getting there in time to bag Jackson. Pope himself arrived about noon. It happened that the evening before I rode off to a farmer's house to get some supper and slept under a tree in the yard. The next morning I returned to the Junction thinking our army was still there. I found the place deserted and as silent as the cities of the plain. So, if General Pope and Fitz John Porter had come at that time they might have caught *me*, that is, if their horses were faster than mine. . . . On the evening of the 28th, Longstreet drove Ricketts's division from Thoroughfare, and the head of his column bivouacked within about six miles of Jackson. During the fight I rode with Stuart toward Thoroughfare Gap. As Ricketts was then between him and Longstreet, Stuart sent a dispatch by a trusty messenger urging him [Longstreet] to press on to the support of Jackson."

And in a letter to the editors, referring to the above, Colonel Mosby says:

"You will also see that I make some new points in Fitz John Porter's case. I was a witness against him and was somewhat prejudiced against him by the unwise attacks his friends made on Stuart, and by being a particular friend of Colonel [T. C. H.] Smith, who preferred charges against Porter. You may remember that General Pope in his 'Century' article quotes Stuart's report to convict Porter: both sides have misunderstood it. Stuart is a conclusive witness for Porter. I took nothing in my lecture second-hand."

MARCHING ON MANASSAS.

BY W. ROY MASON, MAJOR, C. S. A.

ON the 23d of August, as our brigade (Field's, of Hill's division) was passing through an oak forest several miles from our starting-point in the morning, General Field and his staff riding leisurely at its head, we were hailed by General Fitzhugh Lee, who, with his staff, had alighted on one side of the road. He requested us to dismount, as he had something to show us. He then slipped behind a big oak-tree, and, in a moment or two, emerged dressed in the long blue cloak of a Federal general that reached nearly down to his feet, and wearing a Federal general's hat with its big plume. This masquerade was accompanied by a burst of jolly laughter from him that might have been heard for a hundred yards. We inquired as to what this meant, and he told us that the night before he had made a raid upon Pope's headquarters, near Catlett's Station, with orders to capture him. He had surrounded his tent, but

upon going in had found only the supper-table spread there, and near it a quartermaster [Major Charles N. Goulding] and one or two minor staff-officers, whom he took greatly by surprise.

Pope's cloak and hat were in the tent, and he was told that the general had taken them off on account of the heat, and had walked down through the woods to visit the headquarters of some other general,—where, they did not know. Being pressed for time, and anxious to retreat from a position that might soon become a dilemma, General Fitz Lee requested the quartermaster to open the military chest of his chief, which was found to contain (to the best of my recollection) $350,000 in greenbacks, after which, mounting the Federal officers behind three of his men, he prepared to go. ☆ He did not forget to take the supper from the table, however, or the uniform coat and hat from the chair.

☆ General Stuart reports that Fitzhugh Lee's command "charged the camp, capturing a large number of prisoners, particularly officers, and securing public property to a fabulous amount." Pope's uniform, his horses and equipments and money-chests were included in the enumeration of captures.— EDITORS.

Proceeding on our way, when we reached Manassas Plains on the morning of the 27th, a mile or a mile and a half from the Junction, our brigade in the van of Jackson's corps,—a staff-officer of General Fitz Lee's,—who had preceded us again after our late encounter,—rode back to explain the new situation.

He said that Fitz Lee had reached Manassas Junction at daybreak and made his appearance before the enemy. General George W. Taylor, of the U. S. army, commanding a brigade of Franklin's division advancing from Alexandria for the protection of the stores at Manassas Junction, supposing that Lee was making a mere cavalry reconnoissance, and not aware of the Confederate forces between General Pope and himself, had demanded Fitz Lee's unconditional surrender, adding that, as Pope was in the rear and his retreat was entirely cut off, there was no alternative. Lee returned him a facetious answer, requesting an hour to consider the question, supposing by that time that General Jackson would be up with him.

When we appeared from the woods which had concealed the infantry, General Taylor, still considering, when he saw us, that we were only a brigade of infantry that supported Lee's cavalry, advanced toward us in three lines of battle. We brought our batteries, four in number, to bear, the shot and shell from which began to plow through their ranks before we opened on them with our infantry. They closed up the gaps and marched toward us in the most perfect line of battle that I had seen during the war, and it was only when General Jackson's corps enveloped them front and flanks that they broke. General Taylor was mortally wounded, almost in the first onset, and his men were nearly all captured, or rendered *hors de combat*, as we chased them toward Washington for many miles.

That evening we took possession of the enormous commissary and quartermaster stores of the enemy.

The buildings that sheltered them were sheds reaching, as well as my memory serves me, for many hundred yards, and containing everything necessary to the equipment of an army, but, having only ambulances with us, we could carry away nothing but medical supplies, which we found in abundance. The first order that General Jackson issued was to knock out the heads of hundreds of barrels of whisky, wine, brandy, etc., intended for the army. I shall never forget the scene when this was done. Streams of spirits ran like water through the sands of Manassas, and the soldiers on hands and knees drank it greedily from the ground as it ran.

General C. W. Field and staff took possession of the Federal headquarters. When we reached them, we found spread upon the table, untouched, a breakfast of cold chicken, lamb, and biscuit, and coffee that by this time, had also grown cold. It had not been spread for us, but — "*Telle est la fortune de la guerre.*" There were also a barrel of cut sugar, a sack of Java coffee, and similar luxuries. There I found for the first time a bed with feather pillows and bolster, upon which I at once threw myself, begging to be allowed to rest, if but for ten minutes.

In a short time General A. P. Hill sent us an order to burn all the quartermaster and commissary stores with all the buildings, and requested me to superintend the execution of the order. It was with the greatest pain that I complied with this order, as there were so many things that we of the South absolutely required; but we had no wagons to transfer them. It must be remembered that we were within twenty miles of Washington, with Pope's enormous army between us and Longstreet's corps, which we had left at the Fauquier White Sulphur Springs.

Before I executed my order in burning the commissary and quartermaster stores, however, I took the bolster-case from the headquarters tent, filled it with cut sugar, and tied it at one end, and filled the pillow-case with Java coffee, and succeeded in strapping both behind my horse, for which small act of providence I was amply praised by General Field. I had hoped to get an ambulance to carry these, but was unfortunate enough to miss it.

As I before remarked, the army was far from being happy about its position, of which we knew the really critical nature, and just below us, a few miles over the plains, we could hear a terrific artillery fire. I became uneasy as it continued, and seeing General Jackson, who stood in the porch of one of the commissary depots, I proposed to General Field to let me go over and ask him if General Longstreet had passed through Thoroughfare Gap. Through this he must necessarily pass to reach us, and it was known to have been held by the enemy, and was, besides, a sort of second Pass of Thermopylæ in its difficulties. When I made this proposition to General Field, who was an old army officer, he replied promptly: "No, sir,— you cannot carry any such message from me to General Jackson."

"Well, Field, then I am going over to ask on my own account," I said.

"Then let it be distinctly understood"— was the answer — "that you don't go officially."

Walking over to where General Jackson stood, and saluting him, I remarked: "General, we are all of us desperately uneasy about Longstreet and the situation, and I have come over on my own account to ask the question: Has Longstreet passed Thoroughfare Gap successfully?" With a smile General Jackson replied: "Go back to your command, and say, 'Longstreet is through, and we are going to whip in the next battle.'"

JACKSON'S "FOOT-CAVALRY" AT THE SECOND BULL RUN.

BY ALLEN C. REDWOOD, 55TH VIRGINIA REGIMENT, C. S. A.

IN the operations of 1862, in Northern Virginia, the men of Jackson's corps have always claimed a peculiar proprietorship. The reorganization of the disrupted forces of Banks, Frémont, and McDowell under a new head seemed a direct challenge to the soldiers who had made the Valley Campaign, and the proclamation of General Pope / betokened to the "foot-cavalry" an infringement of their specialty, demanding emphatic rebuke. Some remnant of the old *esprit de corps* yet survives, and prompts this narrative.

After the check to Pope's advance at Cedar Mountain, on the 9th of August, and while we awaited the arrival of Longstreet's troops, A. P. Hill's division rested in camp at Crenshaw's farm. Our brigade (Field's) was rather a new one in organization and experience, most of us having "smelt powder" for the first time in the Seven Days before Richmond. We reached the field at Cedar Mountain too late to be more than slightly engaged, but on the 10th and 11th covered the leisurely retreat to Orange Court House without molestation. When, about a week later, Pope began to retreat in the direction of the Rappahannock, we did some sharp marching through Stevensburg and Brandy Station, but did not come up with him until he was over the river. While our artillery was dueling with him across the stream, I passed the time with my head in the scant shade of a sassafras bush by the roadside, with a chill and fever brought from the Chickahominy low-grounds.

For the next few days there was skirmishing at the fords, we moving up the south bank of the river, the enemy confronting us on the opposite side. The weather was very sultry, and the troops were much weakened by it,

/ The following is the full text of General Pope's address to his army:

"HEADQUARTERS ARMY OF VIRGINIA, WASHINGTON, D. C., July 14th, 1862. — To THE OFFICERS AND SOLDIERS OF THE ARMY OF VIRGINIA: By special assignment of the President of the United States, I have assumed the command of this army. I have spent two weeks in learning your whereabouts, your condition, and your wants, in preparing you for active operations, and in placing you in positions from which you can act promptly and to the purpose. These labors are nearly completed, and I am about to join you in the field.

"Let us understand each other. I have come to you from the West, where we have always seen the backs of our enemies; from an army whose business it has been to seek the adversary, and to beat him when he was found; whose policy has been attack and not defense. In but one instance has the enemy been able to place our Western armies in defensive attitude. I presume that I have been called here to pursue the same system and to lead you against the enemy. It is my purpose to do so, and that speedily. I am sure you long for an opportunity to win the distinction you are capable of achieving. That opportunity I shall endeavor to give you. Meantime I desire you to dismiss from your minds certain phrases, which I am sorry to find so much in vogue amongst you. I hear constantly of 'taking strong positions and holding them,' of 'lines of retreat,' and of 'bases of supplies.' Let us discard such ideas. The strongest position a soldier should desire to occupy is one from which he can most easily advance against the enemy. Let us study the probable lines of retreat of our opponents, and leave our own to take care of themselves. Let us look before us and not behind. Success and glory are in the advance, disaster and shame lurk in the rear. Let us act on this understanding, and it is safe to predict that your banners shall be inscribed with many a glorious deed and that your names will be dear to your countrymen forever.—JNO. POPE, Major-General, Commanding."

EDITORS.

and our rations of unsalted beef, eked out with green corn and unripe apples, formed a diet unsuited to soldiers on the march, and there was much straggling. I fell behind several times, but managed to catch up from day to day. Once some cavalry made a dash across the river at our train; I joined a party who, like myself, were separated from their commands, and we fought the enemy until Trimble's brigade, the rear-guard, came up.

We were then opposite the Warrenton Springs, and were making a great show of crossing, Early's brigade having been thrown over the river where it became smartly engaged. I have since heard that this officer remonstrated more than once at the service required of him, receiving each time in reply a peremptory order from Jackson "to hold his position." He finally retorted: "Oh! well, old Jube can *die* if *that's* what he wants, but tell General Jackson I'll be —— if this position *can* be held!"

The brigade moved off next morning, leaving me in the grip of the ague, which reported promptly for duty, and, thanks to a soaking overnight, got in its work most effectually. The fever did not let go until about sundown, when I made two feeble trips to carry my effects to the porch of a house about one hundred yards distant, where I passed the night without a blanket — mine having been stolen between the trips. I found a better one next morning thrown away in a field, and soon after came up with the command, in bivouac and breakfasting on some beef which had just been issued. Two ribs on a stump were indicated as my share, and I broiled them on the coals and made the first substantial meal I had eaten for forty-eight hours. This was interrupted by artillery fire from beyond the river,

CONFEDERATE CAMP-SERVANT ON THE MARCH.

and as I was taking my place in line, my colonel ordered me to the ambulance to recruit. Here I got a dose of Fowler's solution, "in lieu of quinine," and at the wagon-camp that day I fared better than for a long time before. Meanwhile they were having a hot time down at Waterloo Bridge, which the enemy's engineers were trying to burn, while some companies of sharp-shooters under Lieutenant Robert Healy of "ours"—whose rank was no measure of his services or merit—were disputing the attempt. A concentrated fire from the Federal batteries failed to dislodge the plucky riflemen, while our guns were now brought up, and some hard pounding ensued. But at sunset the bridge still stood, and I "spread down" for the night, under the pole of a wagon, fully expecting a serious fight on the morrow.

JACKSON'S TROOPS PILLAGING THE UNION DEPOT OF SUPPLIES AT MANASSAS JUNCTION.

I was roused by a courier's horse stepping on my leg, and found this rude waking meant orders to move. With no idea whither, we pulled out at half-past two in the morning, and for some time traveled by fields and "new cuts" in the woods, following no road, but by the growing dawn evidently keeping up the river. Now Hill's "Light Division" was to earn its name and qualify itself for membership in Jackson's corps. The hot August sun rose, clouds of choking dust enveloped the hurrying column, but on and on the march was pushed without relenting. Knapsacks had been left behind in the wagons, and haversacks were empty by noon; for the unsalted beef spoiled and was thrown away, and the column subsisted itself, without process of commissariat, upon green corn and apples from the fields and orchards along the route, devoured while marching; for there were no stated meal-times, and no systematic halts for rest. I recall a sumptuous banquet of "middling" bacon and "collards" which I was fortunate enough to obtain during the delay at Hinson's Mill where we forded the river, and the still more dainty fare of tea and biscuits, the bounty of some good maiden ladies at "The Plains," where our ambulance stopped some hours to repair a broken axle—the only episodes of the march which now stand out with distinctness. It was far on in the night when the column stopped, and the weary men dropped beside their stacked muskets and were instantly asleep, without so much as unrolling a blanket. A few hours of much-needed repose, and they were shaken up again long before "crack of day," and limped on in the darkness only half-awake. There was no mood for speech, nor breath to spare if there had been — only the shuffling tramp of the marching feet, the steady rumbling of wheels, the creak and rattle and clank of harness and accouterment, with an occasional order, uttered under the breath and always the same: "Close up! close up, men!"

All this time we had the vaguest notions as to our objective: at first we had expected to strike the enemy's flank, but as the march prolonged itself, a theory obtained that we were going to the Valley. But we threaded Thoroughfare Gap, heading eastward, and in the morning of the third day (August 27th) struck a railroad running north and south — Pope's "line of communication and supply." Manassas was ours.

What a prize it was! Here were long warehouses full of stores; cars loaded with boxes of new clothing *en route* to General Pope, but destined to adorn the "backs of his enemies"; camps, sutlers' shops — "no eating up" of good things. In view of the abundance, it was not an easy matter to determine what we should eat and drink and wherewithal we should be clothed; one was limited in his choice to only so much as he could personally transport, and the one thing needful in each individual case was not always readily found. However, as the day wore on, an equitable distribution of our wealth was effected by barter, upon a crude and irregular tariff in which the rule of supply and demand was somewhat complicated by fluctuating estimates of the imminence of marching orders. A mounted man would offer large odds in shirts or blankets for a pair of spurs or a bridle; and while in anxious quest of a pair of shoes I fell heir to a case of cavalry half-boots, which I would gladly have exchanged for the object of my search. For a change of underclothing and a pot of French mustard I owe grateful thanks to the major of the 12th Pennsylvania Cavalry, with regrets that I could not use his library. Whisky was, of course, at a high premium, but a keg of "lager" — a drink less popular then than now — went begging in our company.

But our brief holiday was drawing to a close, for by this time General Pope had some inkling of the disaster which lurked in his rear. When, some time after dark, having set fire to the remnant of the stores, we took the road to Centreville, our mystification as to Jackson's plans was complete. Could he actually be moving on Washington with his small force, or was he only seeking escape to the mountains? The glare of our big bonfire lighted up the country for miles, and was just dying out when we reached Centreville. The corduroy road had been full of pitfalls and stumbling-blocks, to some one of which our cracked axle had succumbed before we crossed Bull Run, and being on ahead, I did not know of the casualty until it was too late to save my personal belongings involved in the wreck. Thus suddenly reduced from affluence to poverty, just as the gray dawn revealed the features of the forlorn little hamlet, typical of this war-harried region, I had a distinct sense of being a long way from home. The night's march had seemed to put the

STARKE'S BRIGADE FIGHTING WITH STONES NEAR THE "DEEP CUT."   (SEE MAP, P. 509, AND NOTE, P. 536.)

climax to the endurance of the jaded troops. Such specters of men they were,—gaunt-cheeked and hollow-eyed, hair, beard, clothing, and accouterments covered with dust,—only their faces and hands, where mingled soil and sweat streaked and crusted the skin, showing any departure from the whitey-gray uniformity. The ranks were sadly thinned, too, by the stupendous work of the previous week. Our regiment, which had begun the campaign 1015 strong and had carried into action at Richmond 620, counted off that Thursday morning (August 28th) just 82 muskets! Such were the troops about to deliver battle on the already historic field of Manassas.

We were soon on the road again, heading west; we crossed Stone Bridge, and a short distance beyond, our ambulances halted, the brigade having entered some woods on the right of the road ahead,—going into camp, I thought. This pleasing delusion was soon dispelled by artillery firing in front, and our train was moved off through the fields to the right, out of range, and was parked near Sudley Church. Everything pointed to a battle next day; the customary hospital preparations were made, but few, if any, wounded came in that night, and I slept soundly, a thing to be grateful for. My bedfellow and I had decided to report for duty in the morning, knowing that every musket would be needed. I had picked up a good "Enfield" with the proper trappings, on the road from Centreville, to replace my own left in the abandoned ambulance; and having broken my chills, and gained strength from marching unencumbered, was fit for service—as much so as were the rest at least.

Friday morning early, we started in what we supposed to be the right direction, guided by the firing, which more and more betokened that the fight was on. Once we stopped for a few moments at a field-hospital to make inquiries, and were informed that our brigade was farther along to the right. General Ewell, who had lost his leg the evening before, was carried by on a stretcher while we were there. Very soon we heard sharp musketry over a low ridge which we had been skirting, and almost immediately we became involved with stragglers from that direction—Georgians, I think they were. It looked as if a whole line was giving way, and we hurried on to gain our own colors before it should grow too hot. The proverbial effect of bad company was soon apparent. We were halted by a Louisiana major, who was trying to rally these fragments upon his own command. My companion took the short cut out of the scrape by showing his "sick-permit," and was allowed to pass; mine, alas! had been left in my cartridge-box with my other belongings in that unlucky ambulance. The major was courteous but firm; he listened to my story with more attention than I could have expected, but attached my person all the same. "Better stay with us, my boy, and if you do your duty I'll make it right with your company officers when the fight's over. They won't find fault with you when they know you've been in with the 'Pelicans,'" he added, as he assigned me to company "F."

The command was as unlike my own as it was possible to conceive. Such a congress of nations only the cosmopolitan Crescent City could have sent forth, and the tongues of Babel seemed resurrected in its speech; English, German, French, and Spanish, all were represented, to say nothing of Doric brogue and local "gumbo." There was, moreover, a vehemence of utterance and gesture curiously at variance with the reticence of our Virginians. In point of fact, we burned little powder that day, and my promised distinction as a "Pelican" *pro tem.* was cheaply earned. The battalion did a good deal of counter-marching, and some skirmishing, but most of the time we were acting as support to a section of Cutshaw's battery. The tedium of this last service my companions relieved by games of "seven up," with a greasy, well-thumbed deck, and in smoking cigarettes, rolled with great dexterity, between the deals. Once, when a detail was ordered to go some distance under fire to fill the canteens of the company, a hand was dealt to determine who should go, and the decision was accepted by the loser without demur. Our numerous shifts of position completely confused what vague ideas I had of the situation, but we must have been near our extreme left at Sudley Church, and never very far from my own brigade, which was warmly engaged that day and the day following. | Toward evening we were again within sight of Sudley Church.

| A recent letter from Lieutenant Robert Healy, of the writer's regiment, the 55th Virginia, says: "Thursday night we slept on our arms: Friday, we charged a battery and took it, and in the evening got considerably worsted in an engagement with the enemy in a field on the left. Saturday morning we lay in reserve in the edge of the woods [see Brockenbrough's brigade on the map, p. 509]; about half-past two o'clock we received urgent orders to reïnforce a portion of our line in the center, which was about to give way. We proceeded at double-quick to a point in the woods

I could see the light of fires among the trees, as if cooking for the wounded was going on, and the idea occurred to me that there I could easily learn the exact position of my proper command. Once clear of my major and his polyglot " Pelicans," the rest would be plain sailing.

My flank movement was easily effected, and I suddenly found myself the *most* private soldier on that field; there seemed to be nobody else anywhere near. I passed a farm-house, which seemed to have been used as a hospital, and where I picked up a Zouave fez. Some cavalrymen were there, one of whom advised "me not to go down there," but as he gave no special reason and did not urge his views, I paid no heed to him, but went on my way down a long barren slope, ending in a small water-course at the bottom, beyond which the ground rose abruptly and was covered by small growth. The deepening twilight and strange solitude about me, with a remembrance of what had happened a year ago on this same ground, made me feel uncomfortably lonely. By this time I was close to the stream, and while noting the lay of the land on the opposite bank with regard to choice of a crossing-place, I became aware of a man observing me from the end of the cut above. I could not distinguish the color of his uniform, but the crown of his hat tapered suspiciously, I thought, and instinctively I dropped the butt of my rifle to the ground and reached behind me for a cartridge. "Come here!" he called;—his accent was worse than his hat. "Who are you?" I responded as I executed the movement of "tear cartridge." He laughed and then invited me to "come and see." Meanwhile I was trying to draw my rammer, but this operation was arrested by the dry click of several gunlocks, and I found myself covered by half a dozen rifles, and my friend of the steeple-crown, with less urbanity in his intonation, called out to me to "drop that." In our brief intercourse he had acquired a curious influence over me. I did so.

My captors were of Kearny's division, on picket. They told me they thought I was deserting until they saw me try to load. I could not account for their being where they were, and when they informed me that they had Jackson surrounded and that he must surrender next day, though I openly scouted the notion, I must own the weight of evidence seemed to be with them. The discussion of this and kindred topics was continued until a late hour that night with the sergeant of the guard at Kearny's headquarters, where I supped in unwonted luxury on hard-tack and "genuine" coffee, the sergeant explaining that the fare was no better because of our destruction of their supplies at the Junction. Kearny's orderly gave me a blanket, and so I passed the night. We were astir early in the morning (August 30th), and I saw Kearny as he

behind the deep cut, where we formed line. . . . We came in sight of the enemy when we had advanced a few yards, and were saluted with cannon. We pushed on, however, to the old railroad cut, in which most of Jackson's troops lay. The troops occupying this place had expended their ammunition and were defending themselves with rocks . . . which seemed to have been picked or blasted out of the bed of the railroad, chips and slivers of stone which many were collecting and others were throwing. Of course, such a defense would have been overcome in a very short time, but our arrival seemed to be almost simultaneous with that of the enemy. We had ammunition (twenty rounds to the man) and we attacked the enemy and drove them headlong down the hill, across the valley, and over the hill into the woods, when we were recalled by General Starke."—A. C. R.

DEATH OF GENERAL PHILIP KEARNY, SEPTEMBER 1, 1862.

passed with his staff to the front,—a spare, erect, military figure, looking every inch the fighter he was. He fell three days later, killed by some of my own brigade.*

* Captain James H. Haynes, 55th Virginia regiment, says he was on the skirmish line at Chantilly, in the edge of a brushy place with a clearing in front. It was raining heavily and growing dark when Kearny rode suddenly upon the line, and asked what troops they were. Seeing his mistake,

Near the Stone Bridge I found about 500 other prisoners, mostly stragglers picked up along the line of our march. Here my polite provost-sergeant turned me over to other guardians, and after drawing rations, hard-tack, coffee, and sugar, we took the road to Centreville. That thoroughfare was thronged with troops, trains, and batteries, and we had to stand a good deal of chaff on the way, at our forlorn appearance. We were a motley crowd enough, certainly, and it *did* look as if our friends in blue were having their return innings. More than once that day as I thought of the thin line I had left, I wondered how the boys were doing, for disturbing rumors came to us as we lay in a field near Centreville, exchanging rude badinage across the cordon of sentries surrounding us. Other prisoners came in from time to time who brought the same unvarying story, "Jackson hard-pressed — no news of Longstreet yet." So the day wore on. Toward evening there was a noticeable stir in the camps around us, a continual riding to and fro of couriers and orderlies, and now we thought we could hear more distinctly the deep-toned, jarring growl which had interjected itself at intervals all the afternoon through the trivial buzz about us. Watchful of indications, we noted, too, that the drift of wagons and ambulances was *from* the battle-field, and soon orders came for us to take the road in the same direction. The cannonading down the pike was sensibly nearer now, and at times we could catch even the roll of musketry, and once we thought we could distinguish, far off and faint, the prolonged, murmurous sound familiar to our ears as the charging shout of the gray people — but this may have been fancy. All the same, we gave tongue to the cry, and shouts of "Longstreet! Longstreet's at 'em, boys! Hurrah for Longstreet!" went up from our ranks, while the guards trudged beside us in sulky silence.

There is not much more to tell. An all-day march on Sunday through rain and mud brought us to Alexandria, where we were locked up for the night in a cotton-factory. Monday we embarked on a transport steamer, and the next evening were off Fort Monroe, where we got news of Pope's defeat. I was paroled and back in Richmond within ten days of my capture, and then and there learned how completely Jackson had made good the name of "Stonewall" on his baptismal battle-field.

he turned and started across the open ground to escape, but was fired on and killed. His body was brought into the lines and was recognized by General A. P. Hill, who said, sorrowfully, "Poor Kearny! he deserved a better death than this."

The next day General Lee ordered that the body be carried to the Federal lines, and in a note to General Pope he said: "The body of General Philip Kearny was brought from the field last night, and he was reported dead. I send it forward under a flag of truce, thinking the possession of his remains may be a consolation to his family."—A. C. R.

According to General A. P. Hill, Kearny fell in front of Thomas's brigade, but he also states that Brockenbrough's brigade held the skirmish line, and to this Captain Haynes's and Lieutenant Healy's regiment, the 55th Virginia, belonged.—EDITORS.

THE SIXTH CORPS AT THE SECOND BULL RUN.

BY WILLIAM B. FRANKLIN, MAJOR-GENERAL, U. S. V.

THE Sixth Corps left Harrison's Landing on the James River on August 16th, 1862, and arrived at Newport News on August 21st. On the 22d and 23d it embarked on transports for Aquia Creek. My impression is that Burnside's corps started first, landing at Aquia Creek; Porter's disembarked at Aquia Creek; Heintzelman's followed, landing at Alexandria; and the Sixth Corps followed Heintzelman's. As soon as I saw the infantry of the corps embarked at Newport News, leaving the chiefs of the quartermaster and subsistence departments and the chief of artillery to superintend the embarkation of the property for which they were responsible, with orders to hasten their departure to the utmost, I preceded the transports, and on Sunday, August 24th, about 2 o'clock, arrived at Aquia Creek, at which point I had orders to disembark and report to General McClellan. The wharves here were so encumbered with the artillery and stores that were already landed for the corps of Burnside and Porter, that McClellan directed me to have my corps landed at Alexandria, and to report upon my arrival to General Halleck. Still preceding the corps, I reported to General Halleck at Washington, arriving there about 4 o'clock P. M. The city was as quiet as though profound peace reigned; no one was at General Halleck's office to whom I could report, and I found him at his house. He told me that he felt under no apprehension about Pope's position, and that he doubted whether it would be necessary for me to go to the front at all; that in any event I could be of no use until my artillery and horses arrived — instancing the fact that Burnside had been much crippled, and had done little good so far, on account of the absence of his artillery. He directed me to go into camp in front of Alexandria, and reorganize the corps as the artillery and transportation reached the camp. The infantry arrived on Monday and Tuesday, the 25th and 26th, but no artillery horses, except sixteen, had arrived on Wednesday night.

The two division commanders and myself were constantly at work during this time, endeavoring to get horses. But we had no success, the answer to our demands always being that the teams then present were absolutely necessary to feed the troops in the forts from day to day, and that this duty was more important under the circumstances than that of providing transportation for artillery. Without transportation the artillery could not be used.

On Wednesday, the 27th, news having arrived that the enemy was at Centreville, Taylor's brigade of Slocum's division was sent there on the cars of the Orange and Alexandria Railroad to reconnoiter. It was received at the railroad bridge over Bull Run by a force of the enemy's artillery and infantry, and lost its gallant commander and many men. The brigade was withdrawn in safety in the face of a large force, four brigades of A. P. Hill's division, Jackson's corps. The order for this movement came from General Halleck. Thursday, the 28th, was employed in organizing such batteries as had arrived, with the horses, which now began to arrive slowly, and in attempting to collect a train for carrying provisions to General Pope's army. Little was accomplished, however. On Friday, the corps was started to the front with orders to communicate with General Pope, and at the same time to guard his communications with Alexandria. On the arrival of the leading division, commanded by General W. F. Smith, at Annandale, ten miles to the front, its commander reported to me that fugitives were constantly coming in, and reported a large force of the enemy near Fairfax Court House, six miles distant. As he had with him only ten rounds of ammunition for each gun, he considered it prudent to await further orders. General McClellan, upon learning this state of things, directed me to stop at Annandale for the night, and proceed the next morning at 6.

During the night more ammunition and provision wagons were collected, numbering about one hundred, and as I was starting in the morning at the designated time I received orders to delay my start until 8:30 A. M., to protect the train so formed. When I arrived at Fairfax Court House I detached a brigade of General Slocum's division and one battery to take position to guard the point where the Little River Turnpike joins the Warrenton pike between Centreville and Alexandria. The detachment of this brigade had an important effect upon the after events of the campaign, as will appear. Proceeding onwards toward Centreville I received, at 1:30 P. M., an order from General McClellan, directing me to join General Pope at once. The corps marched forward through Centreville toward Bull Run about three miles in front of Centreville, without stopping. Going to the front I found General Slocum's division formed across the road, in front of Cub Run, stopping what seemed to be an indiscriminate mass of men, horses, guns and wagons, all going pell-mell to the rear. As General Slocum expressed it, it was as bad as the Bull Run retreat of 1861. Officers of all grades, from brigadier-general down, were in the throng, but none of them exercised any authority. We gathered about three thousand in a yard near by. Presently a force of cavalry appeared to the left and front, about one mile off, and the fugitives, imagining that they were the enemy, ran to the rear as one man;—nothing could stop them.

General W. F. Smith's division was posted in a good position on hills in the vicinity, and shortly afterward Generals Pope and McDowell appeared, and I reported to General Pope. He directed me to return to Centreville, upon which place his army was falling back. The corps remained at Centreville during the 31st of August with the bulk of the army, the enormous trains in the meantime moving toward Washington. On the morning of that day, on my own responsibility, I sent a grand guard, consisting of the 5th Wisconsin infantry under Colonel Amasa Cobb, and a section of artillery, to the Cub Run Bridge, to guard the rear of the army. Large bodies of the enemy appeared in its front, but no attack was made on it. So far as I know, this was the only rear-guard between Pope and the enemy on the 31st of August.

On September 1st, the corps marched to Fairfax Court House with General Pope, and remained there until the evening of the 2d of September, when it moved back to the vicinity of Alexandria.

Colonel (afterward General) Torbert, who commanded the detachment left at Fairfax Court House on August 30th, reports that about 8 o'clock on the night of the 31st the enemy brought three pieces of artillery about three hundred yards from his pickets, and fired upon the trains then crowding the turnpike in his rear, causing great confusion. Torbert drove off the enemy's artillery, reported to General Pope, and on the next morning was reënforced by a brigade and two batteries. It appears from General J. E. B. Stuart's report of his operations that this attack was made by him. Had Colonel Torbert's brigade not been present to defend this very vulnerable point, Stuart's cavalry would easily have been in rear of the army that night; the trains would in all probability have been utterly destroyed, and another great disaster would have occurred. The wisdom of General McClellan's order, which directed me to guard General Pope's communications with Alexandria, was thus demonstrated.

HEINTZELMAN'S HEADQUARTERS AT ALEXANDRIA. FROM A SKETCH MADE SEPTEMBER 3, 1862.

WASHINGTON UNDER BANKS.

BY RICHARD B. IRWIN, LIEUTENANT-COLONEL AND ASSISTANT ADJUTANT-GENERAL, U. S. V.

"THE 27th and 28th" [of August], writes General F. A. Walker, in his admirable "History of the Second Army Corps," "were almost days of panic in Washington." These words mildly indicate the state into which affairs had fallen at the close of August and the opening of September, 1862, on the heels of General Pope's defeat in the Second Bull Run. Yet Washington was defended by not less than 110,000 men; for, in addition to the army which Pope was bringing back, beaten certainly, but by no means destroyed, there stood before the lines of Washington not less than 40,000 veterans who had not fired a shot in this campaign, and behind the lines 30,000 good men of the garrisons and the reserves of whom at least two-thirds were veterans in discipline, though all were untried in battle.

As General McClellan's staff rode in on the morning of the 2d of September, from their heart-rending exile on the Seminary heights, condemned there to hear in helpless idleness the awful thunder of Manassas and Chantilly, we made our way through the innumerable herd of stragglers,—mingled with an endless stream of wagons and ambulances, urged on by uncontrollable teamsters,—which presently poured into Washington, overflowed it, took possession of its streets and public places, and held high orgie. Disorder reigned unchecked and confusion was everywhere. The clerks in the departments, many of whom had been hurried toward the front to do service as nurses, were now hastily formed into companies and battalions for defense; the Government ordered the arms and ammunition at the arsenal and the money in the Treasury to be shipped to New York, and the banks followed the example; a gun-boat, with steam up, lay in the river off the White House, as if to announce to the army and

MAJOR-GENERAL W. F. BARRY, CHIEF-OF-ARTILLERY OF THE DEFENSES OF WASHINGTON, SEPTEMBER 1, 1862, TO MARCH 1, 1864. FROM A PHOTOGRAPH.

the inhabitants the impending flight of the Administration: It was at this juncture that the President, on his own responsibility, once more charged General McClellan with the defense of the capital.

The next day, the 3d of September, the President further confided to General Halleck ‡ the duty of preparing an army to take the field; but since Lee did not wait for this, McClellan could not; even before the President's order reached General Halleck the Confederate army had disappeared from the front of Washington and General McClellan was putting his troops in march to meet it.

On the afternoon of the 7th, 87,000 men were in motion, and General McClellan set out for

Rockville to put himself at their head. Almost at the last moment I was directed to remain in charge of the adjutant-general's department at his headquarters in Washington, to issue orders in his name and "to prevent the tail of the army from being cut off," and Lieutenant-Colonel Sawtelle was left in charge of the Quartermaster's Department, also with plenary authority, to see that the transportation and supplies went forward. On the same day, General Banks, who was reported confined to his bed, and unable to join his corps, was assigned to the immediate command of the defenses of Washington during McClellan's absence. The next day, General Banks assumed this command, having first obtained General McClellan's consent to my assignment as Assistant Adjutant-General, at the Headquarters of the Defenses, in addition to my other duties.‡ I thought then that this was a difficult position for a young captain of twenty-two; I think now that it would have been difficult for a field-marshal of sixty-two; certainly the arrangement could not have lasted an hour, but for the determination of all concerned to make it work, and to be deaf, blind, and dumb to everything not distinctly in front of us.

Everything was at once put in motion to carry out General McClellan's orders, of which the first point was to restore order.

The forces included the Third, Fifth, and Eleventh Army Corps, commanded respectively by Heintzelman, Fitz John Porter, and Sigel, covering the fortified line on the Virginia side and numbering about 47,000 for duty; the garrisons of the works, 15,000; Casey's provisional brigades of newly arriving regiments and the town guards, 11,000,—in all, 73,000,‡ with 120 field-pieces and about 500 heavy guns in position; in brief, nearly one half of McClellan's entire army; a force a fourth or a third larger than Lee's; indeed, to all appearance, the identical command designed for General McClellan himself, before the defense of the capital had made it necessary for him to resume operations in the field by the pursuit of Lee.

The improvised staff-officers were at once sent out to establish the picket lines, so broken and disconnected that virtually there were none. The troops were rapidly inspected, and their numbers, positions, and wants ascertained. With the three corps and the organized divisions this was simple enough, since their commanders had them in hand. For a few days the discoveries of scattered detachments were numerous and surprising; some only turned up after a check had been put on the commissary issues, and about ten days later, in the

---

‡ General McClellan seems never to have known of this order.—R. B. I.

‡ At this time General Banks was without a staff-officer. Colonel John S. Clark, A. D. C., Lieutenant-Colonel D. H. Strother, A. D. C. (the genial "Porte Crayon"), and others of his staff joined him presently. General Halleck also sent down many officers, as they happened to report to him for orders, and thus a curious yet very useful staff was soon collected, including several officers who afterward won deserved distinction; among them I recall Captains (afterward Major-General) Wesley Merritt and A. J. Alexander (afterward Brigadier-General) of the Cavalry; Captain (after-

ward Brevet Major-General) George W. Mindil, who had been Kearny's adjutant-general, one of the most gallant and accomplished officers of our (or any) branch of the volunteer service; Lieutenant (now Colonel) G. Norman Lieber, at present Acting Judge Advocate-General, and Drake DeKay, from Pope's staff. R. B. I.

‡ Rapidly augmented by new levies, these forces must have exceeded 80,000 before the dispatch of Porter's corps to Antietam, September 12th. The return for October 10th shows 79,535; for November 10th, 80,989. The lowest point was about 60,000 after Whipple's division left, October 17th. The actual effective strength would, as always, be a fifth or a sixth less.

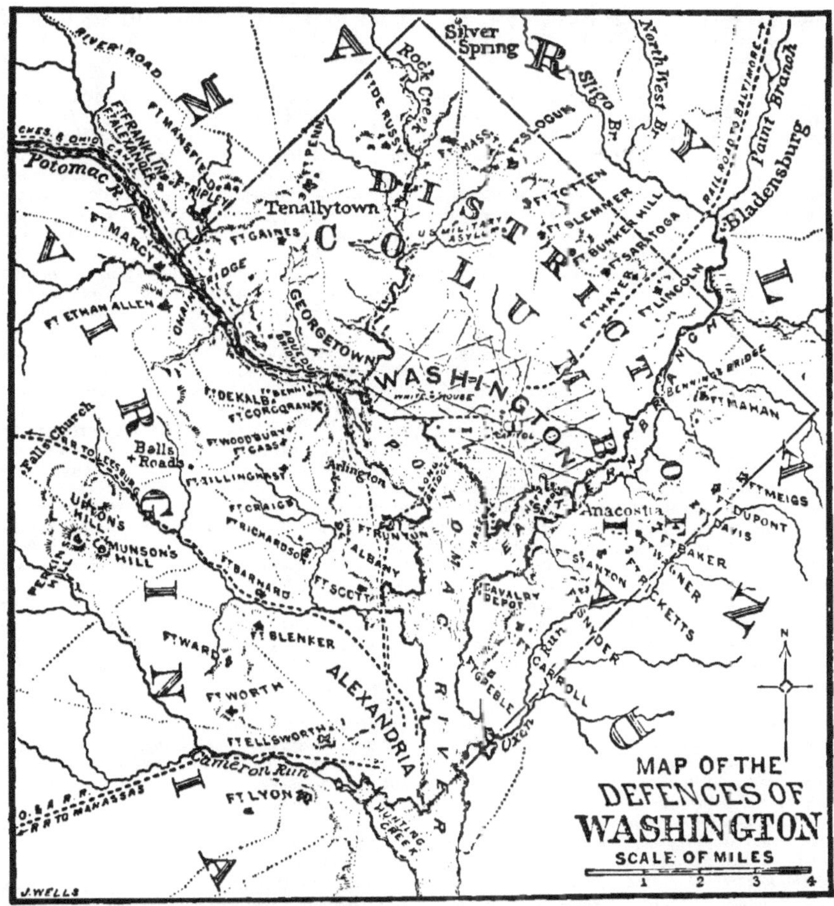

THE DEFENSES OF WASHINGTON DURING THE ANTIETAM CAMPAIGN, SEPTEMBER 1–20, 1862.

Extensive additions to the defenses of the west bank of the Potomac were made subsequently; these will be indicated hereafter on another map. Forts Alexander, Franklin, and Ripley were afterward united and called redoubts Davis, Kirby, and Cross, receiving later the name of Fort Sumner. Forts De Kalb, Massachusetts, Pennsylvania, and Blenker were afterward changed respectively to Strong, Stevens, Reno, and Reynolds.— EDITORS.

most insalubrious part of "the slashes" (now the fashionable quarter of the capital) I came upon a squadron of cavalry comfortably "waiting orders"— from anybody.

The stragglers were promptly gathered in, the hotels and bar-rooms were swept of officers of all grades "absent without leave," while heavy details of cavalry reduced to obedience even the unruly teamsters whose unbroken trains blocked the streets, and checked the reckless and senseless galloping of orderlies and other horsemen, who kept the foot-passengers in terror. Thus in two days order was restored, and it was afterward maintained.

There was quite an army of officers and men who had somehow become separated from their regiments. This happened often without any fault of their own, or with less than the frequent scoldings in general orders would have one believe. The number continued to be so enormous‡ as to be quite unmanageable by any existing method. There was already a convalescent camp near Alexandria, in charge of Colonel J. S. Belknap, of the 85th ... Under the ...

‡ General McClellan estimated the number of stragglers he met on the Centreville ... 2d at 20,000; Colonel Kelton those on the 1st at 30,000. Colonel Belknap estimates the number that ... hands before September 17th at 20,000.— R. B. I.

pressure of the moment, the name and place were made use of for the collection and organization of this army of the lost and strayed. Between the 17th of September, when the organization was completed, and the 30th, 17,343 convalescent stragglers, recruits, and paroled prisoners were thus taken care of; in October, 10,345; in November, 11,844, and in December, 12,238. The larger number were, of course, stragglers. At least one-third of the whole were unfit for duty, yet 16,176 were returned to the ranks during the first six weeks, 8226 in November, and 16,660 in December. The paroled and exchanged prisoners were afterward encamped separately, to the number of 3500 at one time, under Colonel Gabriel De Korponay, of the 28th Pennsylvania. As this camp was a clear innovation, the truly intolerable evils which it was intended to mitigate were forgotten the moment they ceased to press, and complaints came pouring in from every quarter. The reasonable ones were assiduously attended to, but of the other kind I recall two which came in company: one from a senator, saying that his constituents were so badly treated at the convalescent camp that they were driven to desert the service rather than remain there; the other from a corps commander, saying that his men were so well treated ("coddled" was the word) that they were deserting the colors in order to return. When it was seen that the camp must outlast the first emergency, arrangements were made to reorganize and remove it to a better place and to provide shelter against the coming winter, but these well-matured plans being set aside after General Banks left the department, such suffering ensued that in December the War Office gave peremptory orders to break up the camp; yet, as General Hunt aptly remarks of his Artillery Reserve, "such is the force of ideas" that these orders could never be carried out, and the camp remained, as it had begun, the offspring of necessity, a target for criticism, and a model for reluctant imitation.

General Casey was continued in the duty of receiving, organizing, and instructing the new regiments, forming them into "provisional brigades" and divisions; a service for which he was exactly fitted and in which he was ably assisted by Captain (afterward Lieutenant-Colonel) Robert N. Scott,[¶] as assistant adjutant-general. At this period not far from one hundred thousand men must have passed through this "dry nursery," as it was called.

General Barnard, as chief engineer of the defenses, with the full support of the Government (although Congress had, in a strange freak, forbidden it), set vigorously to work to complete and extend the fortifications, particularly on the north side and beyond the eastern branch, and to clear their front by felling the timber. Heavy details of new troops were furnished daily, and the men, carefully selected, easily and cheerfully got through an immense amount of work in an incredibly short time.[☆]

With the aid of General Barry as chief of artillery, and, among others, of Colonel R. O. Tyler, 1st Connecticut Heavy Artillery, the artillerists were instructed in their duties, and with the approval of the Government a permanent garrison was provided, formed of those splendid regiments of heavy artillery, each of twelve large companies, afterward known as the "heavies" of Grant's Virginia campaigns.

In the last three weeks of September there were sent to the Army of the Potomac in the field 36,000 men, in October, 29,000; in all, 65,000.[‡]

Frequent reconnoissances to the gaps of the Blue Ridge and to the Rapidan served to disturb the Confederate communications a little, to save us from needless "alarums and excursions," and incidentally to throw some strange lights on the dark ways of the Secret Service, whose reports we thus learned to believe in if possible less than ever.

Especially during General McClellan's active operations, we used to see the President rather often of an evening, when, as in earlier days, he would "just drop in" to ask, sometimes through a half-opened doorway, "Well, how does it look now?" One day in October, shortly after Stuart's raid into Maryland and Pennsylvania, on returning on board the *Martha Washington* from a review near Alexandria, when the President seemed in unusually high spirits and was conversing freely, some one (I think DeKay) suddenly asked: "Mr. President, what about McClellan?" Without looking at his questioner the President drew a ring on the deck with a stick or umbrella and said quietly: "When I was a boy we used to play a game, three times round and out. Stuart has been round him twice; if he goes round him once more, gentlemen, McClellan will be out!"

General Banks kept the President, as well as the Secretary of War, and, of course, the General-in-Chief and General McClellan, constantly and fully advised of everything, and managed by his tact, good judgment, and experience to retain the confidence of his superiors, without which, in the remarkable state of feeling and of faction then prevailing, no one could have done anything. The President felt that the capital was safe, that the forces in its front were in hand, ready for any service at any notice; that order had quietly replaced confusion, and was maintained without fuss or excitement. In his own words, he was not bothered all day and could sleep all night if he wanted to; and this it was that toward the end of October, when it had been decided to make a change in the Department of the Gulf, led him to offer the command to General Banks.

[¶] Distinguished after the war by his invaluable public services in the organization and editing of the "Official Records of the [War of the] Rebellion."—EDITORS.

[☆] It was [illegible] who [illegible] that, two years later, in his raid on Was'n I recall [illegible] brought up one evening; it was behind [illegible] Merritt[illegible] dawn revealed to him the familiar Greek cross of the Sixth Army Corps, and also the four-pointed star of the Nineteenth.—R. B. I.

[‡] Porter's corps (Morell and Humphreys), 15,500; [illegible] new regiments in a body, 18,500; Stoneman and Whipple, 15,000; together, 49,000; add convalescents and stragglers, 16,000.—R. B. I.

FROM THE PENINSULA TO ANTIETAM.ʲ

POSTHUMOUS NOTES BY GEORGE B. McCLELLAN, MAJOR-GENERAL, U. S. A.

IT is not proposed to give in this article a detailed account of the battles of South Mountain and Antietam, but simply a sketch of the general operations of the Maryland campaign of 1862 intended for general readers, especially for those whose memory does not extend back to those exciting days, and whose knowledge is derived from the meager accounts in so-called histories, too often intended to mislead and pander to party prejudices rather than to seek and record the truth.

A great battle can never be regarded as "a solitaire," a jewel to be admired or condemned for itself alone, and without reference to surrounding objects and circumstances. A battle is always one link in a long chain of events; the culmination of one series of manœuvres, and the starting-point of another series — therefore it can never be fully understood without reference to preceding and subsequent events.

Restricted as this narrative is intended to be, it is nevertheless necessary to preface it by a brief story of the antecedent circumstances.

In an article already published in "The Century" [May, 1885], I have narrated the events of the Peninsular campaign up to the time when, at the

---

ʲ After General McClellan had written the article on the Peninsular Campaign (published in "The Century" magazine for May, 1885 [see p. 160]), he was requested to write an account of the battle of Antietam, which he promised to do at his leisure. He had kept the promise in mind, and as occasion served had sketched introductory portions of the proposed article. In the morning after his sudden death, these manuscript pages were found on his table, with some others freshly written, possibly on the previous day or evening. There was also an unsealed note to one of the editors (in reply to one he had received), in which he said that he would at once proceed with the article and finish it.

It was his custom in writing for the press to make a rapid but complete sketch, often abbreviating words and leaving blanks for matter to be copied from documents, and then to rewrite the entire article for publication. It would seem that in this case he had first in mind the consideration stated in the second paragraph of the article, and had given his attention to the history of the army, from the close of the Seven Days' battles to the advance from Washington toward South Mountain and Antietam. There was no manuscript relating to later events. He had commenced what appears to be his final copy of this first portion of the article, but had completed only about three pages of foolscap, which extend in the print below to a place indicated.

It is an interesting fact that in this final copy the paragraph commencing with the words "So long as life lasts" was apparently the last written, being on a separate page and indicated by a letter A for insertion where it stands. This tribute of admiration for the army which loved him as he loved them was among the last thoughts, if it was not the very last, which his pen committed to paper.

Although this introduction to the account of Antietam is but his first sketch, and not in the final shape he would have given it for publication, it is so comprehensive and complete, and contains so much that is of historical importance, that his literary executor has considered it his duty to allow its publication in "The Century" in the form in which General McClellan left it, and thus as far as possible fulfill a promise made in the last hours of his life.

WILLIAM C. PRIME,
Literary Executor of General McClellan.

close of the Seven Days' battles, the Army of the Potomac was firmly established on its proper line of operations, the James River.

So long as life lasts the survivors of those glorious days will remember with quickened pulse the attitude of that army when it reached the goal for which it had striven with such transcendent heroism. Exhausted, depleted in numbers, bleeding at every pore, but still proud and defiant, and strong in the consciousness of a great feat of arms heroically accomplished, it stood ready to renew the struggle with undiminished ardor whenever its commander should give the word. It was one of those magnificent episodes which dignify a nation's history, and are fit subjects for the grandest efforts of the poet and the painter.

[Many years ago it was my good fortune, when in Europe, to make the acquaintance of a charming old Westphalian baron who was aide-de-camp to King Jerome in the days of his prosperity. In 1813 my friend was sent by his king with important dispatches to the Emperor, and, as it happened, arrived while the battle of Lutzen was in progress. He approached from the rear and for miles passed through crowds of stragglers, feeling no doubt that the battle was lost, and that he was about to witness the crushing defeat of the French. Still keeping on and on, he at last found the Emperor at the front, and to his great surprise discovered that the battle was won. Thus it very often happens in war that there are on each side two armies in the field, one of the fighting men with the colors, the other of stragglers and marauders in the rear; the relative strength of these two armies depends upon the state of discipline and the peculiar circumstances of the time.] ☫

At the close of such a series of battles and marches the returns of the killed, wounded, and missing by no means fully measure the temporary decrease of strength; there were also many thousands unfitted for duty for some days by illness, demoralization, and fatigue. The first thing to be done was to issue supplies from the vessels already sent to the James, and to allow the men some little time to rest and recover their strength after the great fatigue and nervous tension they had undergone.

In order to permit a small number to watch over the safety of the whole army, and at the same time to prepare the way for ulterior operations, so that when the army advanced again upon Richmond by either bank of the James its base of supplies might be secure with a small guard, the position was rapidly intrenched, the work being completed about the 10th of July.

Prior to the 10th of July two brigades of Shields's division, numbering about 5300 men, had joined the army, bringing its numbers for duty up to 89,549, officers and men, about the same strength as that with which it entered upon the siege of Yorktown, the reënforcements received in the shape of the divisions of Franklin and McCall, the brigades of Shields, and a few regiments from Fort Monroe having slightly more than made good the losses

---

☫ The paragraph inclosed by brackets was in the first sketch of the article, but was omitted by General McClellan in the final manuscript.— W. C. P.

in battle and by disease. But among these 89,000 for duty‡ on the 10th of July were included all the extra duty men employed as teamsters, and in the various administrative services, and, with the further deductions necessary for camp guards, guards of communications, depots and trains, flank detachments, etc., reduced the numbers actually available for offensive battle to not more than [60,000?]

A few days sufficed to give the men the necessary rest, and to renew the supplies exhausted on the march across the

FAC-SIMILE OF A PART OF GENERAL McCLELLAN'S LAST MANUSCRIPT. [SEE P. 546 AND FOOT-NOTE, P. 545.]

‡According to General McClellan's "Tri-monthly Return," dated July 10, 1862 ("Official Records," Vol. XI., Pt. III., p. 312), he would appear to be mistaken, above, in saying that the "89,000 for duty" included "all the extra duty men," for in the return he classifies (excluding the forces under Dix) 88,435 as "present for duty, equipped," at Harrison's Landing, and in the next column he accounts for 106,466 as the "aggregate present." Obviously there is no meaning in the return if the 88,435 "present for duty, equipped," did not exclude the 18,021 supposably extra duty men like teamsters, etc.) which made the difference between the "present for duty, equipped," and the 106,466 "aggregate present."—EDITORS.

Peninsula; the army was once more in condition to undertake any operation justified by its numbers, and was in an excellent position to advance by either bank of the James. [End of finished draft.]

. . . .

It was at last upon its true line of operations, which I had been unable to adopt at an earlier day in consequence of the Secretary of War's peremptory order of the 18th of May requiring the right wing to be extended to the north of Richmond in order to establish communication with General McDowell. General McDowell was then under orders to advance from Fredericksburg, but never came, because, in spite of his earnest protest, these orders were countermanded from Washington, and he was sent upon a fruitless expedition toward the Shenandoah instead of being permitted to join me, as he could have done, at the time of the affair of Hanover Court House.

I urged in vain that the Army of the Potomac should remain on the line of the James, and that it should resume the offensive as soon as reënforced to the full extent of the means in possession of the Government. Had the Army of the Potomac been permitted to remain on the line of the James, I would have crossed to the south bank of that river, and while engaging Lee's attention in front of Malvern, would have made a rapid movement in force on Petersburg, having gained which, I would have operated against Richmond and its communications from the west, having already gained those from the south.

Subsequent events proved that Lee did not move northward from Richmond with his army until assured that the Army of the Potomac was actually on its way to Fort Monroe; and they also proved that so long as the Army of the Potomac was on the James, Washington and Maryland would have been entirely safe under the protection of the fortifications and a comparatively small part of the troops then in that vicinity; so that Burnside's troops and a large part of the Union Army of Virginia might, with entire propriety, have been sent by water to join the army under my command, which—with detachments from the West—could easily have been brought up to more than 100,000 men disposable on the actual field of battle.

In spite of my most pressing and oft-repeated entreaties, the order was insisted upon for the abandonment of the Peninsula line and the return of the Army of the Potomac to Washington in order to support General Pope, who was in no danger so long as the Army of the Potomac remained on the James. With a heavy heart I relinquished the position gained at the cost of so much time and blood.

As an evidence of my good faith in opposing this movement it should be mentioned that General Halleck had assured me, verbally and in writing, that I was to command all the troops in front of Washington, including those of Generals Burnside and Pope—a promise that was not carried into effect.

As the different divisions of the Army of the Potomac reached Aquia Creek and the vicinity of Washington they were removed from my command, even to my personal escort and camp guard, so that on the 30th of August, in reply to a telegram from him, I telegraphed General Halleck from Alexandria, "I have no sharp-shooters except the guard around my camp. I have sent off every man but those, and will now send them with the train as you direct. I will also send my only remaining squadron of cavalry with General Sumner. I can do no more. You now have every man of the Army of the Potomac who is within my reach." I had already sent off even my headquarters wagons—so far as landed—with ammunition to the front.

On the same day I telegraphed to General Halleck, "I cannot express to you, etc." [The dispatch which General McClellan here indicates, as intending to insert when revising the manuscript, proceeds as follows:

"I cannot express to you the pain and mortification I have experienced to-day in listening to the distant sound of the firing of my men. As I can be of no further use here, I respectfully ask that if there is a possibility of the conflict being renewed to-morrow, I may be permitted to go to the scene of battle with my staff, merely to be with my own men, if nothing more; they will fight none the worse for my being with them. If it is not deemed best to intrust me with the command even of my own army, I simply ask to be permitted to share their fate on the field of battle. Please reply to this to-night.

"I have been engaged for the last few hours in doing what I can to make arrangements for the wounded. I have started out all the ambulances now landed. As I have sent my escort to the front, I would be glad to take some of Gregg's cavalry with me, if allowed to go.

"G. B. McCLELLAN, Major-General."

The dispatch was dated "Camp near Alexandria, Aug. 30th, 1862, 10:30 P. M." On the following day he received this answer:

"WASHINGTON, Aug. 31, 1862, 9:18 A. M.

"MAJOR-GENERAL McCLELLAN: I have just seen your telegram of 11:05 last night. The substance was stated to me when received, but I did not know that you asked for a reply immediately. I cannot answer without seeing the President, as General Pope is in command, by his orders, of the department.

"I think Couch's division should go forward as rapidly as possible, and find the battle-field.

"H. W. HALLECK, General-in-Chief."]

On the 1st of September I met General Halleck at his office in Washington, who by verbal order directed me to take charge of Washington and its defenses, but expressly prohibited me from exercising any control over the active troops under General Pope.

At this interview I informed General Halleck that from information received through one of my aides I was satisfied that affairs were not progressing favorably at the front, and urged him to go out in person to ascertain the exact state of the case. He declined doing this, but finally sent Colonel Kelton, his adjutant-general.

Next morning while at breakfast at an early hour I received a call from the President, accompanied by General Halleck.

The President informed me that Colonel Kelton had returned and represented the condition of affairs as much worse than I had stated to Halleck on the previous day; that there were thirty thousand stragglers on the roads; that the army was entirely defeated and falling back to Washington in confusion. He then said that he regarded Washington as lost, and asked me if I would, under the circumstances, consent to accept command of all the forces. Without one moment's hesitation and without making any conditions whatever, I at once said that I would accept the command and would stake my life that I would save the city. Both the President and Halleck again asserted that it was impossible to save the city, and I repeated my firm conviction that I could and would save it. They then left, the President verbally placing me in entire command of the city and of the troops falling back upon it from the front.

I at once sent for my staff-officers and dispatched them on various duties; some to the front with orders for the disposition of such corps as they met, others to see to the prompt forwarding of ammunition and supplies to meet the retreating troops. In a very short time I had made all the requisite preparations and was about to start to the front in person to assume command as far out as possible, when a message came to me from General Halleck informing me that it was the President's order that I should not assume command until the troops had reached the immediate vicinity of the fortifications. I therefore waited until the afternoon, when I rode out to Upton's Hill, the most advanced of the detached works covering the capital.

Soon after arriving there the head of Hatch's command of infantry arrived, immediately followed by Generals Pope and McDowell escorted by a regiment, or part of a regiment, of cavalry. I obtained what information I could from General Pope and dispatched the few remaining aides with me to meet the troops on the roads leading in on the left, with final orders to them, when quite a heavy distant artillery firing broke out in the direction of the Chantilly and Vienna road. Asking General Pope what that was, he replied it was probably an attack on Sumner, who commanded the rear-guard in that direction; in reply to another question he said that he thought it probably a serious affair. He and McDowell then asked if I had any objection to their proceeding to Washington. I said that they might do so, but that I was going to the firing. They then proceeded on with their escort while, with a single aide (Colonel Colburn) and three orderlies, I struck across country to intercept the column on our right by the shortest line. It was a little after dark when I reached the column.

I leave to others who were present the description of what then occurred: the frantic cheers of welcome that extended for miles along the column; the breaking of ranks and the wild appeals of the men that I should then and there take them back on the line of retreat and let them snatch victory out of defeat.↓ Let it suffice to say that before the day broke the troops were all in position to repulse attack, and that Washington was safe.

↓ In November, 1887, George Kimball of Boston wrote to the editors:

"Though a quarter of a century has passed since 'those darkest days of the war,' I still retain a vivid remembrance of the sudden and complete change which came upon the face of affairs when General McClellan was restored to command. At the time, I was serving in Company A, 12th Massachusetts Volunteers, attached to Ricketts's division of the First Army Corps. The announcement of McClellan's restoration came to us in the early evening of the 2d of September, 1862, just after reaching Hall's Hill, weary from long marching and well-nigh disheartened by recent reverses. The men were scattered about in groups, discussing the events of their ill-starred campaign, and indulging in comments that were decidedly uncomplimentary to those who had been responsible for its mismanagement. We did not know, of course, the exact significance of all that had happened, as we afterward learned it, but being mainly thinking men, we were able to form pretty shrewd guesses as to where the real difficulty lay. Suddenly, while these mournful consultations were in full blast, a mounted officer, dashing past our bivouac, reined up enough to shout, '"Little Mac" is back here on the road, boys!' The scene that followed can be more easily imagined than described. From extreme sadness we passed in a twinkling to a delirium of delight. A Deliverer had come. A real 'rainbow of promise' had appeared suddenly in the dark political sky. The feeling in our division upon the return of General McClellan had its counterpart in all the others, for the Army of the Potomac loved him as it never loved any other leader. In a few days we started upon

On the 3d it was clear that the enemy intended an invasion of Maryland and Pennsylvania by crossing the Upper Potomac; I therefore moved the Second, Ninth, and Twelfth Corps to the Maryland side of the Potomac in position to meet any attack upon the city on that side.

As soon as this was done I reported the fact to General Halleck, who asked what general I had placed in command of those three corps; I replied that I had made no such detail, as I should take command in person if the enemy appeared in that direction. He then said that my command included only the defenses of Washington and did not extend to any active column that might be moved out beyond the line of works; that no decision had yet been made as to the commander of the active army. He repeated the same thing on more than one occasion before the final advance to South Mountain and Antietam took place.

I should here state that the only published order ever issued in regard to the extent of my command after my interview with the President on the morning of the 2d‡ was the following:

> "WAR DEPARTMENT, ADJUTANT-GENERAL'S OFFICE,
>
> "WASHINGTON, September 2, 1862.
>
> "Major-General McClellan will have command of the fortifications of Washington and of all the troops for the defense of the capital.
>
> "By order of MAJOR-GENERAL HALLECK.\
>
> "E. D. TOWNSEND, *Assistant Adjutant-General.*"

A few days after this and before I went to the front, Secretary Seward came to my quarters one evening and asked my opinion of the condition of affairs at Harper's Ferry, remarking that he was not at ease on the subject. Harper's Ferry was not at that time in any sense under my control, but I told Mr. Seward that I regarded the arrangements there as exceedingly dangerous; that in my opinion the proper course was to abandon the position and unite the garrison (about ten thousand men) to the main army of operations,

that long march into Maryland, and whenever General McClellan appeared among his troops, from the crossing of the Potomac at Washington to the grapple with Lee at Antietam, it was the signal for the most spontaneous and enthusiastic cheering I ever listened to or participated in. Men threw their caps high into the air, and danced and frolicked like school-boys, so glad were they to get their old commander back again. It is true that McClellan had always been fortunate in being able to excite enthusiasm among his troops, but demonstrations at this time took on an added and noticeable emphasis from the fact that he had been recalled to command after what the army believed to be an unwise and unjust suspension. The climax seemed to be reached, however, at Middletown, where we first caught sight of the enemy. Here, upon our arrival, we found General McClellan sitting upon his horse in the road. The enemy occupied a gap in the South Mountain, a mile or two beyond. Reno and Hatch were fighting, and the smoke of their guns could be seen half-way up the mountain. As each organization passed the general, the men became apparently forgetful of everything but their love for him. They cheered and cheered again, until they became so hoarse they could cheer no longer. It seemed as if an intermission had been declared in order that a reception might be tendered to the general-in-chief. A great crowd continually surrounded him, and the most extravagant demonstrations were indulged in.

Hundreds even hugged the horse's legs and caressed his head and mane. While the troops were thus surging by, the general continually pointed with his finger to the gap in the mountain through which our path lay. It was like a great scene in a play, with the roar of the guns for an accompaniment. Another enthusiastic demonstration that I remember occurred in the afternoon of the 17th at Antietam, when the general rode along our line of battle. The cheers could not have been heartier than they were. General McClellan may have had opponents elsewhere; he had few, if any, among the soldiers whom he commanded." [See also p. 489.]

‡ On the 3d the President, by an order in his own handwriting, but signed by the Secretary of War, directed General Halleck to "organize an army for active operations . . . independent of the forces he may deem necessary for the defense of Washington, when such active army shall take the field." See "Washington under Banks," p. 542.—EDITORS.

\ In its original form, as it was first given to the newspapers and as it appeared in some of them, this order purported to be issued "by order of the Secretary of War."—EDITORS.

for the reason that its presence at Harper's Ferry would not hinder the enemy from crossing the Potomac; that if we were unsuccessful in the approaching battle, Harper's Ferry would be of no use to us and its garrison necessarily would be lost; that if we were successful we would immediately recover the post without any difficulty, while the addition of ten thousand men to the active army would be an important factor in securing success. I added that if it were determined to hold the position the existing arrangements were all wrong, as it would be easy for the enemy to surround and capture the garrison, and that the garrison ought, at least, to be withdrawn to the Maryland Heights, where they could resist attack until relieved.

The Secretary was much impressed by what I said, and asked me to accompany him to General Halleck and repeat my statement to him. I acquiesced, and we went together to General Halleck's quarters, where we found that he had retired for the night. But he received us in his bedroom, when, after a preliminary explanation by the Secretary as to the interview being at his request, I said to Halleck precisely what I had stated to Mr. Seward.

Halleck received my statement with ill-concealed contempt—said that everything was all right as it was; that my views were entirely erroneous, etc., and soon bowed us out, leaving matters at Harper's Ferry precisely as they were.

On the 7th of September, in addition to the three corps already mentioned (the Second, Ninth, and Twelfth), the First and Sixth Corps, Sykes's division of the Fifth Corps, and Couch's division of the Fourth Corps, were also on the Maryland side of the river; the First and Ninth Corps at Leesboro; the Second and Twelfth in front of Rockville; the Sixth Corps at Rockville; Couch's division at Offutt's Cross Roads; Sykes's division at Tenallytown.

As the time had now arrived for the army to advance, and I had received no orders to take command of it, but had been expressly told that the assignment of a commander had not been decided, I determined to solve the question for myself, and when I moved out from Washington with my staff and personal escort I left my card with *P. P. C.* written upon it, at the White House, War Office, and Secretary Seward's house, and went on my way. ☆

I was afterward accused of assuming command without authority, for nefarious purposes, and in fact I fought the battles of South Mountain and Antietam with a halter around my neck, for if the Army of the Potomac had been defeated and I had survived I would, no doubt, have been tried for assuming authority without orders, and, in the state of feeling which so unjustly condemned the innocent and most meritorious General F. J. Porter, I would probably have been condemned to death. I was fully aware of the risk I ran, but the path of duty was clear and I tried to follow it. It was absolutely necessary that Lee's army should be met, and in the state of affairs I have briefly described there could be no hesitation on my part as to doing it promptly. Very few in the Army of the Potomac doubted the favorable

☆ General McClellan's orders from the 1st to the 8th of September, inclusive, are dated "Headquarters, Washington." On the 9th he resumed the heading, "Headquarters, Army of the Potomac," at Rockville.—EDITORS.

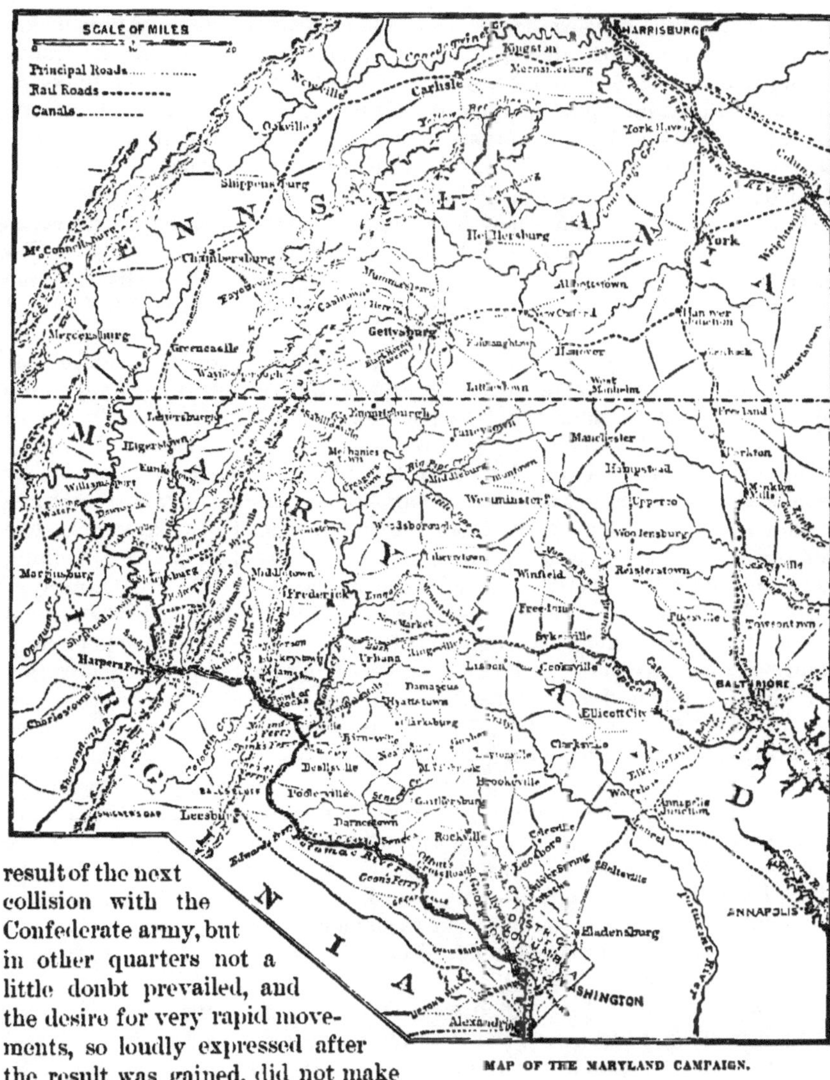

MAP OF THE MARYLAND CAMPAIGN.

result of the next collision with the Confederate army, but in other quarters not a little doubt prevailed, and the desire for very rapid movements, so loudly expressed after the result was gained, did not make itself heard during the movements preceding the battles; quite the contrary was the case, as I was more than once cautioned that I was moving too rashly and exposing the capital to an attack from the Virginia side.

As is well known, the result of General Pope's operations had not been favorable, and when I finally resumed command of the troops in and around Washington they were weary, disheartened, their organization impaired, their clothing, ammunition, and supplies in a pitiable condition.

The Army of the Potomac was thoroughly exhausted and depleted by its desperate fighting and severe marches in the unhealthy regions of the Chicka-hominy and afterward, during the second Bull Run campaign; its trains, administration services and supplies were disorganized or lacking in conse-quence of the rapidity and manner of its removal from the Peninsula as well as from the nature of its operations during the second Bull Run campaign. In the departure from the Peninsula, trains, supplies, cavalry, and artillery in many instances had necessarily been left at Fort Monroe and Yorktown for lack of vessels, as the important point was to remove the infantry divisions rapidly to the support of General Pope. The divisions of the Army of Vir-ginia were also exhausted and weakened, and their trains were disorganized and their supplies deficient by reason of the movements in which they had been engaged.

Had General Lee remained in front of Washington it would have been the part of wisdom to hold our own army quiet until its pressing wants were fully supplied, its organization was restored, and its ranks were filled with recruits — in brief, until it was prepared for a campaign. But as the enemy maintained the offensive and crossed the Upper Potomac to threaten or invade Pennsylvania, it became necessary to meet him at any cost notwith-standing the condition of the troops, to put a stop to the invasion, save Baltimore and Washington, and throw him back across the Potomac. Nothing but sheer necessity justified the advance of the Army of the Potomac to South Mountain and Antietam in its then condition, and it is to the eternal honor of the brave men who composed it that under such adverse circum-stances they gained those victories. The work of supply and reorganization was continued as best we might while on the march, and even after the close of the battles [September 14th–17th] so much remained to be done to place the army in condition for a campaign, that the delay which ensued was abso-lutely unavoidable, and the army could not have entered upon a new cam-paign one day earlier than it did. It must then be borne constantly in mind that the purpose of advancing from Washington was simply to meet the necessities of the moment by frustrating Lee's invasion of the Northern States, and, when that was accomplished, to push with the utmost rapidity the work of reorganization and supply so that a new campaign might be promptly inaugu-rated with the army in condition to prosecute it to a successful termination without intermission.

The advance from Washington was covered by the cavalry, under Gen-eral Pleasonton, which was pushed as far to the front as possible, and was soon in constant contact with the enemy's cavalry, with whom several well-conducted and successful affairs occurred.

Partly in order to move men freely and rapidly, partly in consequence of the lack of accurate information as to the exact position and intention of Lee's army, the troops advanced by three main roads: that part near the Potomac by Offutt's Cross Roads and the mouth of the Seneca; that by Rockville to Fred-erick, and that by Brookville and Urbana to New Market. We were then in condition to act according to the development of the enemy's plans and to con-centrate rapidly in any position. If Lee threatened our left flank by moving down the river road, or by crossing the Potomac at any of the fords from Coon's Ferry upward, there were enough troops on the river road to hold him in check until the rest of the army could move over to support them; if Lee took up a position behind the Seneca near Frederick the whole army could be rapidly concentrated in that direction to attack him in force; if he moved upon Baltimore the entire army could rapidly be thrown in his rear and his retreat would be cut off; if he moved by Gettysburg or Chambersburg upon York or Carlisle we were equally in position to throw ourselves in his rear.

The first requisite was to gain accurate information as to Lee's movements, and the second, to push the work of supply and reorganization as rapidly as possible.

General Lee and I knew each other well. In the days before the war we served together in Mexico, and we had commanded against each other in the Peninsula. I had the highest respect for his ability as a commander, and knew that he was a general not to be trifled with or carelessly afforded an opportunity of striking a fatal blow. Each of us naturally regarded his own army as the better, but each entertained the highest respect for the endurance, courage, and fighting qualities of the opposing army; and this feeling extended to the officers and men. It was perfectly natural under these circumstances that both of us should exercise a certain amount of caution,—I in my endeavors to ascertain Lee's strength, position, and intentions before I struck the fatal blow; he to abstain from any extended movements of invasion, and to hold his army well in hand until he could be satisfied as to the condition of the Army of the Potomac after its second Bull Run campaign, and as to the intentions of its commander.

. . . .

ROSTRUM IN THE NATIONAL CEMETERY AT SHARPSBURG. FROM A RECENT PHOTOGRAPH.

On Memorial Day, 1885, General McClellan addressed from this rostrum a large assembly of members of the "Grand Army of the Republic."— EDITORS.

BY DAVID L. THOMPSON, CO. G, 9TH NEW YORK VOLUNTEERS.

A DISORGANIZED PRIVATE. FROM A PHOTOGRAPH.

ON the 5th of September, 1862, Hawkins' Zouaves, as a part of Burnside's corps, from Fredericksburg, landed at Washington to assist in the defense of the capital, then threatened by Lee's first invasion of Maryland, and, as events proved, to join in the pursuit of the invaders. Here, in pursuance of a measure for shortening the baggage train which had lately been decided on, we were deprived of our Sibley tents — those cumbersome, conical caravansaries, in which eighteen men lie upon the ground with their feet toward the center.

Shelter tents came soon to replace the "Sibleys," and with them came marching orders — the army was moving west. At dusk we set up our new houses. A shelter or dog tent is like a bargain — it takes two to make it. Each man is provided with an oblong piece of thick, unbleached muslin about the length of a man — say six feet — and two-thirds as wide, bordered all round with buttons and button-holes alternately matching respectively the button-holes and buttons of his comrade's piece. To set it up, cut two crotched stakes, each about four feet long, point them at the uncrotched end, and drive them into the ground about six feet apart; cut a slender pole to lie horizontally from one crotch to the other, button the two pieces of muslin together and throw the resulting piece over the pole, drawing out the corners tight and pinning them down to the ground by means of little loops fastened in them. You will thus get a wedge-shaped structure — simply the two slopes of an ordinary roof — about three and a half feet high at its highest point, and open at both ends. This will accommodate two men, and in warm, pleasant weather is all that is needed. In rainy weather a third man is admitted. A piece of rope about four feet long is then tied to the top of one of the stakes and stretched out in the line of direction of the ridge pole, the free end being brought down to the ground and pinned there. The third man then buttons his piece of muslin to one slope of the roof, carries the other edge of the piece out around the tightened rope and brings it back to the edge of the other slope, to which it is buttoned. This third piece is shifted from one end of the tent to the other, according to the direction of the wind or storm. You thus get an extension to your tent in which knapsacks can be stored, leaving the rest of the space clear for sleeping purposes. This is large enough to accommodate three men lying side by side.

But will such a structure keep out rain? Certainly, just as your umbrella does — unless you touch it on the inside when it is soaked. If you do, the rain will come in, drop by drop, just where you have touched it. To keep the water from flowing in along the surface of the ground, dig a small trench about three inches deep all around the tent, close up, so that the rain shed from the roof will fall into it. Such a house is always with you potentially, for you carry the materials on your back and can snap your fingers at the baggage wagon. For three-fourths of the year it is all the shelter needed, as it keeps out rain, snow, and wind perfectly, being penetrable only by the cold.

We marched at last, and on the 12th of September entered Frederick, wondering all the way what the enemy meant. We of the ranks little suspected what sheaves he was gathering in at Harper's Ferry, behind the curtain of his main body. We guessed, however, as usual, and toward evening began to get our answer. He was right ahead, his rear-guard skirmishing with our advance. We came up at the close of the fight at Frederick, and, forming line of battle, went at double-quick through cornfields, potato patches, gardens, and backyards — the German washer-women of the 103d New York regiment going in with us on the run. It was only a measure of precaution, however, the cavalry having done what little there was to do in the way of driving out of the city a Confederate rear-guard not much inclined to stay. We pitched tents at once in the outskirts, and after a hearty supper went to explore the city.

The next morning the feeling of distrust which the night before had seemed to rule the place had disappeared, and a general holiday feeling took its place. The city was abloom with flags, houses were open everywhere, trays of food were set on the window-sills of nearly all the better class of houses, and the streets were filled with women dressed in their best, walking bareheaded, singing, and testifying in every way the general joy. September 13th in Frederick City was a bright one in memory for many a month after — a pleasant topic to discuss over many a camp-fire.

The next day our regiment went on a reconnoissance to a speck of a village, rather overweighted by its name, — Jefferson, — about eight miles from Frederick and on our left. Far up the mountain-side ahead of us we could see, in the fields confronting the edge of the woods that crowned the ridge, the scattered line of Rush's Lancers, their bright red pennons fluttering gayly from their spear heads.

We reached camp again about 10 o'clock at night, and found awaiting us marching orders for 2 o'clock the following morning. Late as it was, one of my tent-mates — an enterprising young fellow — started out on a foraging expedition, in pursuance of a vow made several days before to find something with which to vary his monotonous regimen of "hard-tack" and "salt horse." He "ran the guard"—an easy thing to do in the darkness and hubbub—and returned shortly after, struggling with a weight of miscellaneous plunder; a crock of butter, a quantity of apple-butter, some lard, a three-legged skillet weighing several pounds, and a live hen. It was a marvel how he managed to carry so much; but he was a rare gleaner always, with a comprehensive method that covered the ground. That night we had several immense flapjacks, the whole size of the pan; then, tethering the hen to one of the tent pegs, we went to sleep, to be roused an hour or so later by hearing our two-legged prize cackling and fluttering off in the darkness.

Up to the 10th the army had not marched so much as it had drifted, but from this point on our purpose seemed to grow more definite and the interest deepened steadily. There had been sporadic fighting through the day (the 13th), but it was over the hills to the west, and we heard nothing of it beyond those airy echoes that take the shape of rumor. Now, however, the ferment at the front, borne back by galloping orderlies, was swiftly leavening the mass. Occasionally, on our march we would pass a broken gun wheel or the bloated body of a slaughtered horse, and in various ways we knew that we were close upon the enemy, and that we could not now be long delayed. This would have been told us by the burden of our daily orders, always the same, to hold ourselves "in readiness to march at a moment's notice," with the stereotyped addendum, "three days' cooked rations and forty rounds." Every one lay down to sleep that night with a feeling of impending battle.

By daylight next morning we were in motion again—the whole army. The gathering of such a multitude is a swarm, its march a vast migration. It fills up every road leading in the same direction over a breadth of many miles, with long ammunition and supply trains disposed for safety along the inner roads, infantry and artillery next in order outwardly, feelers of cavalry all along its front and far out on its flanks; while behind, trailing along every road for miles (ravelings from the great square blanket which the enemy's cavalry, if active, snip off with ease), are the rabble of stragglers—laggards through sickness or exhaustion, squads of recruits, convalescents from the hospital, special duty men going up to rejoin their regiments. Each body has its route laid down for it each day, its time of starting set by watch, its place of bivouac or camp appointed, together with the hour of reaching it. If two roads come together, the corps that reaches the junction first moves on, while the other files out into the fields, stacks arms, builds fires, and boils its coffee. Stand, now, by the roadside while a corps is filing past. They march "route step," as it is called,—that is, not keeping time,—and four abreast, as a country road seldom permits a greater breadth, allowing for the aides and orderlies that gallop in either direction continually along the column. If the march has just begun, you hear the sound of voices everywhere, with roars of laughter in spots, marking the place of the company wag—generally some

Irishman, the action of whose tongue bears out his calling. Later on, when the weight of knapsack and musket begins to tell, these sounds die out; a sense of weariness and labor rises from the toiling masses streaming by, voiced only by the shuffle of a multitude of feet, the rubbing and straining of innumerable straps, and the flop of full canteens. So uniformly does the mass move on that it suggests a great machine, requiring only its directing mind. Yet such a mass, without experience in battle, would go to pieces before a moderately effective fire. Catch up a handful of snow and throw it, it flies to fluff; pack it, it strikes like stone. Here is the secret of organization—the aim and crown of drill, to make the units one, that when the crisis comes, the missile may be thoroughly compacted. Too much, however, has been claimed for theoretic discipline—not enough for intelligent individual action. No remark was oftener on the lips of officers during the war than this: "Obey orders! *I* do your thinking for you." But that soldier is the best whose good sense tells him when to be merely a part of a machine and when not.

The premonitions of the night were not fulfilled next day. That day—the 14th of September—we crossed the Catoctin range of mountains, reaching the summit about noon, and descended its western slope into the beautiful valley of Middletown. Half-way up the valley's western side we halted for a rest, and turned to look back on the moving host. It was a scene to linger in the memory. The valley in which Middletown lies is four or five miles wide, as I remember it, and runs almost due north and south between the parallel ranges of Catoctin and South Mountains. From where we stood the landscape lay below us, the eye commanding the opposite slope of the valley almost at point-blank. An hour before, from the same spot, it had been merely a scene of quiet pastoral beauty. All at once, along its eastern edge the heads of the columns began to appear, and grew and grew, pouring over the ridge and descending by every road, filling them completely and scarring the surface of the gentle landscape with the angry welts of war. By the farthest northern road—the farthest we could see—moved the baggage wagons, the line stretching from the bottom of the valley back to the top of the ridge, and beyond, only the canvas covers of the wagons revealing their character. We knew that each dot was a heavily loaded army wagon, drawn by six mules and occupying forty feet of road at least. Now they looked like white beads on a string. So far away were they that no motion was perceptible. The constant swelling of the end of the line down in the valley, where the teams turned into the fields to park, gave evidence that, in this way, it was being slowly reeled along the way. The troops were marching by two roads farther south. The Confederates fighting on the western summit must have seen them plainly. Half a mile beyond us the column broke abruptly, filing off into line of battle, right and left, across the fields. From that point backward and downward, across the valley and up the farther slope, it stretched with scarcely a gap, every curve and zigzag of the way defined more sharply by its somber presence. Here, too, on all the distant portions of the line, motion was imperceptible, but could be inferred from the casual glint of sunlight on a musket barrel miles away. It was 3 o'clock when we resumed our march, turning our backs upon the beautiful, impressive picture — each column a monstrous, crawling, blue-black snake, miles long, quilled with the silver slant of muskets at a "shoulder," its sluggish tail writhing slowly up over the distant eastern ridge, its bruised head weltering in the roar and smoke upon the crest above, where was being fought the battle of South Mountain.

We were now getting nearer to the danger line, the rattle of musketry going on incessantly in the edges of the woods and behind the low stone fences that seamed the mountain-side. Then we came upon the fringes of the contest — slightly wounded men scattered along the winding road on their way to the hospital, and now and then a squad of prisoners, wounded and unwounded together, going under guard to the rear.

The brigade was ordered to the left of the road to support a regular battery posted at the top of a steep slope, with a cornfield on the left, and twenty yards or so in front, a thin wood. We formed behind the battery and a little down the slope — the 89th on the left, the 9th next, then the 103d. We had been in position but a few minutes when a stir in front advised us of something unusual afoot, and the next moment the Confederates burst out of the woods and made a dash at the battery. We had just obeyed a hastily given order to lie down, when the bullets whistled over our heads, and fell far down the slope behind us. Then the guns opened at short range, fullshotted with grape and canister. The force of the charge was easily broken, for though it was vigorously made it was not sustained — perhaps was not intended to be, as the whole day's battle had been merely an effort of the enemy to check our advance till he could concentrate for a general engagement. As the Confederates came out of the woods their line touched ours on the extreme left only, and there at an acute angle, their men nearly treading on those of the 89th, who were on their faces in the cornfield, before they discovered them. At that instant the situation just there was ideally, cruelly advantageous to us. The Confederates stood before us not twenty feet away, the full intention of destruction on their faces — but helpless, with empty muskets. The 89th simply rose up and shot them down.

It was in this charge that I first heard the "rebel yell"; not the deep-breasted Northern cheer, given in unison and after a struggle, to signify an advantage gained, but a high shrill yelp, uttered without concert, and kept up continually when the fighting was approaching a climax, as an incentive to further effort. This charge ended the contest for the day on that part of the line. Pickets were set well forward in the woods, and we remained some time in position, waiting. How a trivial thing will often thrust itself upon the attention in a supreme moment was well exemplified here. All about us grew pennyroyal, bruised by the tramping of a hundred feet, and the smell of it has always been associated in my memory with that battle.

Before the sunlight faded, I walked over the narrow field. All around lay the Confederate dead — undersized men mostly, from the coast district of North Carolina, with sallow, hatchet faces, and clad in "butternut" — a color running all the way from a deep, coffee brown up to the whitish brown of ordinary dust. As I looked down on the poor, pinched faces, worn with marching and scant fare, all enmity died out. There was no "secession" in those rigid forms, nor in those fixed eyes staring blankly at the sky. Clearly it was not "their war." Some of our men primed their muskets afresh with the finer powder from the cartridge-boxes of the dead. With this exception, each remained untouched as he had fallen. Darkness came on rapidly, and it grew very chilly. As little could be done at that hour in the way of burial, we unrolled the blankets of the dead, spread them over the bodies, and then sat down in line, munching a little on our cooked rations in lieu of supper, and listening to the firing, which was kept up on the right, persistently. By 9 o'clock this ceased entirely. Drawing our blankets over us, we went to sleep, lying upon our arms in line as we had stood, living Yankee and dead Confederate side by side, and indistinguishable. — This was Sunday, the 14th of September.

The next morning, receiving no orders to march, we set to work collecting the arms and equipments scattered about the field, and burying the dead. The weather being fine, bowers were built in the woods — generally in fence corners — for such of the wounded as could not be moved with safety; others, after stimulants had been given, were helped down the mountain to the rude hospitals. Before we left the spot, some of the country people living thereabout, who had been scared away by the firing, ventured back, making big eyes at all they saw, and asking most ridiculous questions. One was, whether we were from Mexico! Those belated echoes, it seemed, were still sounding in the woods of Maryland.

THE BATTLE OF SOUTH MOUNTAIN, OR BOONSBORO'.

FIGHTING FOR TIME AT TURNER'S AND FOX'S GAPS.

BY DANIEL H. HILL, LIEUTENANT-GENERAL, C. S. A.

THE conflict of the 14th of September, 1862, is called at the North the battle of South Mountain, and at the South the battle of Boonsboro'. So many battle-fields of the Civil War bear double names that we cannot believe the duplication has been accidental. It is the unusual which impresses. The troops of the North came mainly from cities, towns, and villages, and were, therefore, impressed by some natural object near the scene of the conflict and named the battle from it. The soldiers from the South were chiefly from the country and were, therefore, impressed by some artificial object near the field of action. In one section the naming has been after the handiwork of God; in the other section it has been after the handiwork of man. Thus, the first passage of arms is called the battle of Bull Run at the North,—the name of a little stream. At the South it takes the name of Manassas, from a railroad station. The second battle on the same ground is called the Second Bull Run by the North, and the Second Manassas by the South. Stone's defeat is the battle of Ball's Bluff with the Federals, and the battle of Leesburg with the Confederates. The battle called by General Grant, Pittsburg Landing, a natural object, was named Shiloh, after a church, by his antagonist. Rosecrans called his first great fight with Bragg, the battle of Stone River, while Bragg named it after Murfreesboro', a village. So McClellan's battle of the Chickahominy,[*] a little river, was with Lee the battle of Cold Harbor, a tavern. The Federals speak of the battle of Pea Ridge, of the Ozark range of mountains, and the Confederates call it after Elk Horn, a country inn. The Union soldiers called the bloody battle three days after South Mountain from the little stream, Antietam, and the Southern troops named it after the village of Sharpsburg. Many instances might be given of this double naming by the opposing forces. According to the same law of the unusual, the war-songs of a people have generally been written by non-combatants. The bards who followed the banners of the feudal lords, sang of their exploits, and stimulated them and their retainers to deeds of high emprise, wore no armor and carried no swords. So, too, the impassioned orators, who roused our ancestors in 1776 with the thrilling cry, "Liberty or Death," never once put themselves in the way of a death by lead or steel, by musket-ball or bayonet stab. The noisy speakers of 1861, who fired the Northern heart and who fired the Southern heart, never did any other kind of *firing*.[‡]

The battle of South Mountain was one of extraordinary illusions and delusions. The Federals were under the self-imposed illusion that there was a

[*] Gaines's Mill.—EDITORS.

[‡] Of the political speakers of 1860 a number might be mentioned who afterward served, in some cases with distinction, in the respective armies; for example, Banks, Baker, Frank P. Blair, Jr., Logan, Garfield, Schurz, on the Union side; and Breckinridge, Toombs, Cobb, Floyd, and Pryor of the Confederates.—EDITORS.

very large force opposed to them, whereas there was only one weak division until late in the afternoon. They might have brushed it aside almost without halting, but for this illusion. It was a battle of delusions also, for, by moving about from point to point and meeting the foe wherever he presented himself, the Confederates deluded the Federals into the belief that the whole mountain was swarming with rebels. I will endeavor to explain the singular features of the battle and what caused them.

In the retirement of Lee's army from Frederick to Hagerstown and Boonsboro', my division constituted the rear-guard. It consisted of five brigades (Wise's brigade being left behind), and after the arrival at Boonsboro' was intrusted with guarding the wagon trains and parks of artillery belonging to the whole army. Longstreet's corps went to Hagerstown, thirteen miles from Boonsboro', and I was directed to distribute my five brigades so as not only to protect the wagons and guns, but also to watch all the roads leading from Harper's Ferry, in order to intercept the Federal forces that might make their escape before Jackson had completed the investment of that place. It required a considerable separation of my small command to accomplish these two objects, and my tent, which was pitched about the center of the five brigades, was not less than three miles from Turner's Gap on the National road crossing South Mountain.

During the forenoon of the 13th General Stuart, who was in an advance position at the gap in the Catoctin Mountain, east of Middletown, with our cavalry, sent a dispatch to me saying that he was followed by two brigades of Federal infantry, and asking me to send him a brigade to check the pursuit at South Mountain. I sent him the brigades of Colquitt and Garland, and the batteries of Bondurant and Lane, with four guns each. Pleasonton's Federal cavalry division came up to the mountain and pressed on till our infantry forces were displayed, when it returned without fighting. The Confederates, with more than half of Lee's army at Harper's Ferry, distant a march of two days, and with the remainder divided into two parts, thirteen miles from each other, were in good condition to be beaten in detail, scattered and captured. General Longstreet writes to me that he urged General Lee in the evening of the 13th to unite at Sharpsburg the troops which were then at Hagerstown and Boonsboro'. He said that he could effect more with one-third of his own corps, fresh and rested, than with the whole of it, when exhausted by a forced march to join their comrades. That night, finding that he could not rest, General Longstreet rose and wrote to his commander, presenting his views once more, favoring the abandonment of the defense of the mountain except by Stuart and the concentration at Sharpsburg.

I received a note about midnight of the 13th from General Lee saying that he was not satisfied with the condition of things on the turnpike or National road, and directing me to go in person to Turner's Gap the next morning and assist Stuart in its defense. In his official report General Lee says:

" Learning that Harper's Ferry had not surrendered and that the enemy was advancing more rapidly than was convenient from Fredericktown, I determined to return with Longstreet's command to the Blue Ridge to strengthen D. H. Hill's and Stuart's divisions engaged in holding the passes of the mountains, lest the enemy should fall upon McLaws's rear, drive him from the Maryland Heights, and thus relieve the garrison at Harper's Ferry."

This report and the note to me show that General Lee expected General Stuart to remain and help defend the pass on the 14th. But on reaching the Mountain House between daylight and sunrise that morning, I received a message from Stuart that he had gone to Crampton's Gap. [See map, p. 593.] He was too gallant a soldier to leave his post when a

RATIONS FROM THE STALK.

battle was imminent, and doubtless he believed that there was but a small Federal force on the National road.‡ I found Garland's brigade at the Mountain House and learned that Colquitt's was at the foot of the mountain on the east side. I found General Colquitt there without vedettes and without information of the Federals, but believing that they had retired. General Cox's Federal division was at that very time marching up the old Sharpsburg or Braddock's road, a mile to the south, seizing the heights on our right and establishing those heavy batteries which afterward commanded the pike and all the approaches to it. General Pleasonton, of the Federal cavalry, had learned the ground by the reconnoissance of the day before, and to him was intrusted the posting of the advance troops of Reno's corps on the south side of the pike. He says:

"I directed Scammon's brigade to move up the mountain on the left-hand road, gain the crest, and then move to the right, to the turnpike in the enemy's rear. At the same time I placed Gibson's battery and the heavy batteries in position to the left, covering the road on that side and obtaining a direct fire on the enemy's position in the gap."

This shows that Pleasonton knew that the Confederate forces were at the foot of the mountain. However, I brought Colquitt's brigade back to a point

‡ Generals Colquitt and Rosser have both written to me that General Stuart told them he had been followed by only a small Federal force.— D. H. H.

near the summit and placed the 23d and 28th Georgia regiments on the north side of the pike behind a stone-wall, which afforded an excellent fire upon the pike. The other three regiments, the 6th and 27th Georgia and the 13th Alabama, were posted on the south side of the pike, a little in advance of the wall and well protected by a dense wood. This brigade did not lose an inch of ground that day. The skirmishers were driven in, but the line of battle on both sides of the road was the same at 10 o'clock at night as it was at 9 o'clock in the morning. After posting Colquitt's brigade I went with Major Ratchford of my staff on a reconnoissance to our right. About three-fourths of a mile from the Mountain House we discovered, by the voices of command and the rumbling of wheels, that the old road and heights above it were occupied, and took it for granted that the occupation was by Federal troops. We did not see them, and I suppose we were not seen by them. Colonel T. L. Rosser of the cavalry had been sent that morning with his regiment and Pelham's artillery, by order of General Stuart, to seize Fox's Gap on the Braddock road. Cox had got to the heights first and confronted Rosser with a portion of his command, while the remainder of it could be plainly seen at the foot of the mountain. General Rosser writes to me that he reported the situation of things to Stuart, who was passing by on the east side of the mountain on his way south. He, Rosser, was not directed to report to me, and I did not suspect his presence. I do not know to this hour whether Ratchford and myself came near stumbling upon him or upon the enemy.

Returning through the woods we came upon a cabin, the owner of which was in the yard, surrounded by his children, and evidently expectant of something. The morning being cool, Ratchford was wearing a blue cloak which he had found at Seven Pines. In questioning the mountaineer about the roads I discovered that he thought we were Federals.

"The road on which *your* battery is," said he, "comes into the valley road near the church." This satisfied me that the enemy was on our right, and I asked him: "Are there any rebels on the pike?" "Yes; there are some about the Mountain House." I asked: "Are there many?" "Well, there are *several*; I don't know how many." "Who is in command?" "I don't know."

Just then a shell came hurtling through the woods, and a little girl began crying. Having a little one at home of about the same age, I could not forbear stopping a moment to say a few soothing words to the frightened child, before hurrying off to the work of death.

The firing had aroused that prompt and gallant soldier, General Garland, and his men were under arms when I reached the pike. I explained the situation briefly to him, directed him to sweep through the woods, reach the road, and hold it at all hazards, as the safety of Lee's large train depended upon its being held. He went off in high spirits and I never saw him again. I never knew a truer, better, braver man. Had he lived, his talents, pluck, energy, and purity of character must have put him in the front rank of his profession, whether in civil or military life.

After passing through the first belt of woods Garland found Rosser, and, conferring with him, determined to make his stand close to the junction of the roads, near the summit of the mountain (Fox's Gap). He had with him five regiments of infantry and Bondurant's battery of artillery—his infantry force being a little less than one thousand men, all North Carolinians. The 5th regiment was placed on the right of the road, with the 12th as its support; the 23d was posted behind a low stone-wall on the left of the 5th; then came the 20th and 13th. From the nature of the ground and the duty to be performed, the regiments were not in contact with each other, and the 13th was 250 yards to the left of the 20th. Fifty skirmishers of the 5th North Carolina soon encountered the 23d Ohio, deployed as skirmishers under Lieutenant-Colonel R. B. Hayes, afterward President of the United States, and the action began at 9 A. M. between Cox's division and Garland's brigade.

I will delay an account of the fight to give the strength of the forces engaged.♭ The Ninth Corps (Reno's) consisted of four divisions under Cox, Willcox, Sturgis, and Rodman; or eight brigades — Scammon and Crook (Cox); Christ and Welsh (Willcox); Nagle and Ferrero (Sturgis); and Fairchild and Harland (Rodman). It had 29 regiments of infantry, 3 companies of cavalry, and 8 batteries of artillery, 3 of them United States batteries of regulars under Benjamin, Clark, and Muhlenberg.♮

General Cox, who fought Garland, had six Ohio regiments under Brigadiers Scammon and Crook, and also the batteries of McMullin and Simmonds, and three companies of cavalry. The heavy batteries in position (20-pounder Parrotts) were of service to him also, in commanding the approaches to the scene of the conflict. The strength of the division is not given directly, but Scammon estimates his effectives at 1455. The other brigade was most likely equally strong, and I conclude that Cox's infantry, artillery, and cavalry reached three thousand. ☆ Garland's brigade is estimated at "scarce a thousand."

Scammon's brigade led the attack with great spirit. The 13th North Carolina, under Lieutenant-Colonel Ruffin, and the 20th, under Colonel Alfred Iverson, were furiously assailed on the left. Both regiments were under tried and true soldiers, and they received the assault calmly. Lieutenant Crome, of McMullin's battery, ran up a section of artillery by hand, and opened with effect upon the 20th North Carolina; but the skirmishers under Captain Atwell of that regiment killed the gallant officer while he was himself serving as a gunner. The section was abandoned, but the Confederates were unable to capture it. The effort seemed to be to turn the 13th; and Colonel Ruffin in vain urged General Garland to go to the other part of his line. But with Garland the post of danger was the post of honor. Judge Ruffin, in a recent letter to me, thus speaks of the fall of the hero:

" I said to him : ' General, why do you stay here ? you are in great danger.'

" To which he replied : ' I may as well be here as yourself.'

♭ See also Table of Opposing Forces in the Maryland Campaign, p. 598.— EDITORS.

♮ According to General Cox, until the arrival of Willcox with his division, about 2 o'clock, Cox's division and a portion of Pleasonton's cavalry were the only Union troops on the field. Sturgis arrived on the field about 3:30.— EDITORS

☆ In effect confirmed by General Cox.— EDITORS.

BRIGADIER-GENERAL SAMUEL GARLAND, JR., C. S. A., KILLED AT SOUTH MOUNTAIN. FROM A PHOTOGRAPH.

"I said: 'No, it is my duty to be here with my regiment, but you could better superintend your brigade from a safer position.'

"Just then I was shot in the hip, and as there was no field-officer then with the regiment, other than myself, I told him of my wound, and that it might disable me, and in that case I wished a field-officer to take my place. He turned and gave some order, which I have forgotten. In a moment I heard a groan, and looked and found him mortally wounded and writhing in pain. We continued to occupy this position for some time, when I sent my adjutant to the right to see what was going on (as the furious fighting had ceased in that direction). He returned and reported that the remainder of the brigade was gone and that the ground was occupied by the enemy. I then attempted to go to the left, hoping to come in contact with some portion of your command, but was again confronted by the enemy. I next tried to retreat to the rear, but to my dismay found myself entirely surrounded. The enemy in front was pressing us, and I saw but one way out, and that was to charge those in my front, repel them, if possible, and then, before they could recover, make a dash at those in my rear and cut my way out. This plan was successfully executed. I shall never forget the feelings of relief which I experienced when I first caught sight of you. You rode up to me, and, shaking my hand, said that you had given us up for lost and did not see how it was possible for us to have escaped. You then attached us to G. B. Anderson's brigade, which had come up in the meantime. . . . I remember one remark which you made just after congratulating me upon cutting my way out that surprised me very much. You said that you were greatly gratified to find that McClellan's whole army was in your front. As I knew how small your force was, I could not understand how it could be a source of pleasure to you to find yourself assailed by twenty times your number. In a moment you made it plain to me by saying that you had feared at first that McClellan's attack upon you was but a feint, and that with his main army he would cross the mountain at some of the lower gaps and would thus cut in between Jackson's corps and the forces under Lee."

A little before this I had seen from the lookout station near the Mountain House the vast army of McClellan spread out before me. The marching columns extended back far as eye could see in the distance; but many of the troops had already arrived and were in double lines of battle, and those advancing were taking up positions as fast as they arrived. It was a grand and glorious spectacle, and it was impossible to look at it without admiration. I had never seen so tremendous an army before, and I did not see one like it afterward. For though we confronted greater forces at Yorktown, Sharpsburg, Fredericksburg, and about Richmond under Grant, these were only partly seen, at most a corps at a time. But here four corps were in full view, one of which was on the mountain and almost within rifle-range. The sight inspired more satisfaction than discomfort; for though I knew that my little force could be brushed away as readily as the strong man can brush to one side the wasp or the hornet, I felt that General McClellan had made a mistake, and I hoped to be able to delay him until General Longstreet could come up and our trains could be extricated from their perilous position.

When two distinct roars of artillery were heard south of us that morning, I thought that the nearer one indicated that McClellan was forcing his way across some gap north of Harper's Ferry with a view of cutting Lee's army in two. I suppose that Stuart believed that this would be the movement of the enemy, and for this reason abandoned Turner's Gap and hastened to what he believed to be the point of danger. McClellan was too cautious a man for so daring a venture.] Had he made it, Jackson could have escaped across the Potomac, but the force under Lee in person (Longstreet's corps and my division) must have been caught. My division was very small and was embarrassed with the wagon trains and artillery of the whole army, save such as Jackson had taken with him. It must be remembered that the army now before McClellan had been constantly marching and fighting since the 25th of June. It had fought McClellan's army from Richmond to the James, and then had turned about and fought Pope's army, reënforced by parts of McClellan's, from the Rapidan to the Potomac. The order excusing barefooted men from marching into Maryland had sent thousands to the rear. Divisions had become smaller than brigades were when the fighting first began; brigades had become smaller than regiments, and regiments had become smaller than companies.‡ Dabney, a careful statistician, in his "Life of Jackson," estimates Lee's forces at Sharpsburg (Antietam) at 33,000 men, including the three arms of service.‖ Three of Longstreet's twelve brigades had gone to Harper's Ferry with Jackson. He (Longstreet) puts the strength of his nine brigades at Hagerstown on the morning of the 14th of September at thirteen thousand men. Accepting the correctness of his estimate for the present (though I expect to prove it to be too large), I find that Lee had under his immediate command that morning but eighteen thousand men.

McClellan gives his force at Sharpsburg at 87,164. Had he made the movement which Stuart and myself thought he was making, it was hardly possible for the little force under Lee in person to have escaped, encumbered as it was with wagon trains and reserve artillery. Forming his infantry into a solid column of attack, Lee might have cut a way through the five-fold force of his antagonist, but all the trains must have been lost,—an irreparable loss to the South. Frederick the Great's campaign against the allies

---

] See General Franklin's paper on the engagement at Crampton's Gap, p. 591.—EDITORS.

‡ Thus the 18th Virginia Regiment (p. 899, Vol. XIX., of the "Official Records") is put at 120 men; 56th Virginia Regiment at 80; 8th Virginia at 34; Hampton Legion (p. 931) at 77; 17th South Carolina Regiment at 59 (p. 940).—D. H. H.

‖ According to Thomas White, Chief Clerk in the Adjutant-General's Office at Lee's headquarters, General Lee had 33,000 *infantry* at Sharpsburg, or 41,500 of all arms. Adding 2000 for the previous casualties (only partly given), the total Confederate force on the 14th would appear to be 43,500, of which 15,000 were at Harper's Ferry, on the Virginia side, and 28,500 in Maryland.—EDITORS.

shows what he would have done had he been in command of the Federal army. But the American soldier preferred to do sure work rather than brilliant work, his natural caution being increased by the carping criticisms of his enemies.

Upon the fall of Garland, Colonel McRae, of the 5th North Carolina regiment, assumed command, and ordered the two regiments on the left to close in to the right. This order either was not received or it was found to be impossible of execution. The main attack was on the 23d North Carolina behind the stone-wall. The Federals had a plunging fire upon this regiment from the crest of a hill, higher than the wall, and only about fifty yards from it. The 12th North Carolina, a badly trained regiment, on that day under the command of a young captain, deserted the field.\ The 12th Ohio, actuated by a different impulse, made a charge upon Bondurant's battery and drove it off, failing, however, to capture it. The 30th Ohio advanced directly upon the stone-wall in their front, while a regiment moved upon the 23d North Carolina on each flank. Some of the 30th Ohio forced through a break in the wall, and bayonets and clubbed muskets were used freely for a few moments. Garland's brigade, demoralized by his death and by the furious assault on its center, now broke in confusion and retreated behind the mountain, leaving some two hundred prisoners of the 5th, 23d, and 20th North Carolina in the hands of the enemy. The brigade was too roughly handled to be of any further use that day. Rosser retired in better order, not, however, without having some of his men captured, and took up a position from which he could still fire upon the old road, and which he held until 10 o'clock that night.

General Cox, having beaten the force in his front, now showed a disposition to carry out General Pleasonton's instructions, and advance to the Mountain House by the road running south from it on the summit of the mountain. There was nothing to oppose him. My other three brigades had not come up; Colquitt's could not be taken from the pike except in the last extremity. So two guns were run down from the Mountain House and opened a brisk fire on the advancing foe. A line of dismounted staff-officers, couriers, teamsters, and cooks was formed behind the guns to give the appearance of battery supports. I do not remember ever to have experienced a feeling of greater *loneliness.* It seemed as though we were deserted by " all the world and the rest of mankind." Some of the advancing Federals encountered Colquitt's skirmishers under Captain Arnold, and fell back to their former positions.

General Cox seems not to have suspected that the defeat of Garland had cleared his front of every foe. He says in his report: " The enemy withdrew

\ Mr. R. V. Minor, of Oxford, North Carolina, a member of the 12th North Carolina regiment, writes to the editors that on the morning of the 14th of September his regiment numbered seventy-two men, and that they advanced along the mountain crest until they were in the midst of enemies. The commander, an inexperienced captain, then gave the order to " fire and fall back." The order was obeyed, but the fire was returned so promptly, at close range, that the withdrawal was attended with confusion. However, "thirty or forty" members of the 12th regiment halted on the line of the 13th North Carolina, of their own (Garland's) brigade. Lieutenant-Colonel T. Ruffin, Jr., commander of the 13th regiment, says in his report: " I feel it to be just that I should acknowledge the fact that we were joined by a small party of the 12th North Carolina regiment early in the morning, who continued with us throughout the day and rendered us very efficient aid."

their battery to a new position on a ridge more to the front and right, forming their infantry in support and moving columns toward both our flanks."

It was more than half an hour after the utter rout and dispersion of Garland's brigade when G. B. Anderson arrived at the head of his small but fine body of men. ☆ He made an effort to recover the ground lost by Garland, but failed and met a serious repulse. General Cox says of this attack: "The enemy made several attempts to retake the crest, advancing with great obstinacy and boldness."

Under the strange illusion that there was a large Confederate force on the mountain, the Federals withdrew to their first position in the morning to await the arrival of the other three divisions of Reno's corps. Willcox's arrived about noon, and Sturgis's and Rodman's between 3 and 4 o'clock, but there was no advance until 5 P. M. The falling back of Cox's division is alluded to by Colonel Ewing of Scammon's brigade and by Major Lyman J. Jackson of Crook's brigade. The former says: "We fell back to the original position until the general advance at 5 P. M." Major Jackson, after speaking of fighting the enemy behind a stone-wall with the coöperation of two other regiments, adds: "We then fell back to the hillside in the open fields, where we were out of reach of their guns, and remained here *with the rest of our brigade* until an advance was made against the enemy by the Pennsylvania and Rhode Island troops on our right."

After the arrival of his whole corps General Reno arranged his line of battle as follows: Cox's division on the left, resting on the batteries already in position; Willcox's on the right, supported by the division of Sturgis. Rodman's division was divided; Fairchild's brigade was sent to the extreme left to support the batteries, and Harland's was placed on the extreme right.

In the meantime Rodes and Ripley, of my division, reported to me for orders. Rodes was sent with his brigade of twelve hundred men to a commanding knoll north of the pike or National road. Ripley was directed to attach himself to G. B. Anderson's left. Anderson, being thus strengthened, and finding there was no enemy in his immediate front, sent out the 2d and 4th North Carolina regiments of his brigade on a reconnoissance to the front, right, and rear. Captain E. A. Osborne, commanding the skirmishers of the 4th North Carolina, discovered a brigade in an old field south of Fox's Gap, facing toward the turnpike and supporting a battery with its guns turned in the same direction. Captain Osborne hastened back to Colonel Grimes, commanding the regiment, and told him that they could deliver a flank fire upon the brigade before it could change its position to meet them. But a Federal

☆ General Hill in his official report thus describes the posting of his forces after the defeat of Garland: "There were two mountain roads practicable for artillery on the right of the main turnpike. The defense of the farther one had cost Garland his life. It was now intrusted to Colonel Rosser of the cavalry, who had reported to me, and who had artillery and dismounted sharp-shooters. General Anderson was intrusted with the care of the nearest and best road. Bondurant's battery was sent to aid him in its defense. The brigade of Colquitt was disposed on each side of the turnpike, and that with Lane's battery was judged adequate to the task. There was, however, a solitary peak on the left, which, if gained by the Yankees, would give them control of the ridge commanding the turnpike. I had a large number of guns from Cutts's artillery placed upon the hill . . . to sweep the approaches. . . . Rodes and Ripley came up soon after Anderson."— EDITORS.

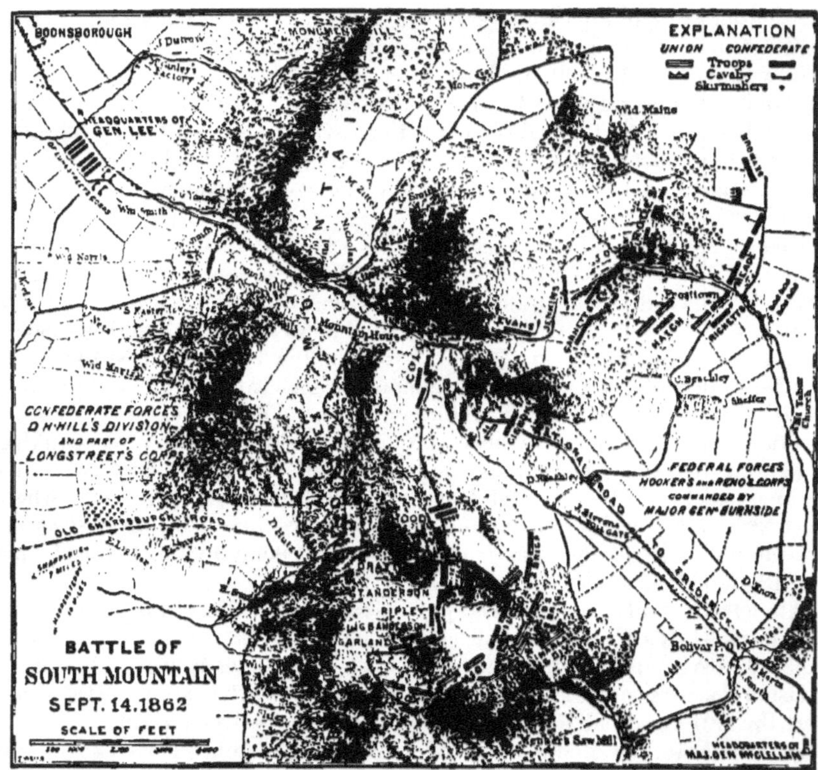

MAP OF THE POSITIONS AT FOX'S AND TURNER'S GAPS.

The fights of September 14th were so distinct as to time and place, and the positions of the troops were so often changed, that any single map would be misleading without analysis: (1) The early morning fight was mostly on the south side of Fox's Gap, between Cox's two Union brigades and Garland's brigade, the latter being assisted on its left by a part of Colquitt's brigade which was at Turner's Gap. By 10 o'clock Garland had been killed and his brigade routed. (2) Then Cox encountered G. B. Anderson's arriving brigade, repulsed it, and fell back to his position in the morning. (3) G. B. Anderson was then posted at Fox's Gap on both sides of the old Sharpsburg road. D. H. Hill's two other brigades came up toward noon, Ripley being joined to G. B. Anderson, and Rodes being sent to occupy a hill on the north side of Turner's Gap, near where Garnett is placed on the map. (4) About 2 o'clock, on the Union side, Cox's division was reinforced by the arriving divisions of Willcox, Sturgis, and Rodman; and Hooker's corps of three divisions was moving north of the National road by way of Mount Tabor Church (Hooker's headquarters) to flank the Confederate left. About the same time D. H. Hill's brigades at Fox's Gap were reinforced by Longstreet's brigades of G. T. Anderson, Drayton, Law, and Hood; and north of Turner's Gap three of Rodes's four regiments were sent still farther to the left. The defense was afterward strengthened by the posting of Longstreet's brigades of Garnett and Kemper, supported by Jenkins, on the hill first held by Rodes. Evans's brigade arrived later, and was of assistance to Rodes when the latter had been thrown back by Meade's flank movement. (5) The last severe engagements began at both gaps after 3 o'clock and lasted until after dark. Colquitt and Gibbon, in the center, joined desperately in the battle.— EDITORS.

scout had seen the captain, and the brigade was the first to open fire. The fight was, of course, brief, the regiment beating a hasty retreat. The brigade halted at the edge of the woods, probably believing that there was a concealed foe somewhere in the depths of the forest. This Federal brigade was, possibly, Benjamin C. Christ's of Willcox's division — the same which had made the successful flank movement in the previous fight. ☆

☆ This engagement is not mentioned by Cox, Willcox, or Christ. The Union brigade was more probably that of Colonel H. S. Fairchild, Rodman's division. See p. 558.— EDITORS.

About 3 : 30 P. M. the advance of Longstreet's command arrived and reported to me — one brigade under Colonel G. T. Anderson and one under General Drayton. They were attached to Ripley's left, and a forward movement was ordered. In half an hour or more I received a note from Ripley saying that he was progressing finely; so he was, to the rear of the mountain on the west side. Before he returned the fighting was over, and his brigade did not fire a shot that day. ☆ The Federal commander intrusted to General Burnside the management of the fight, but under his own eyes; Burnside ordered a general advance on both sides of the pike. The First Corps, under Hooker, was to attack on the north side of the National road, while the Ninth Corps, under Reno, was to move forward, as before, on the south side. Hooker's corps consisted of 3 divisions, 10 brigades, or 42 regiments, with 10 batteries of artillery and a battalion of cavalry. General Meade, a division commander, had under him the brigades of Seymour, Magilton, and Gallagher, containing 13 regiments with 4 batteries attached. General Hatch, division commander, had under him the brigades of Doubleday, Phelps, Patrick, and Gibbon — 17 regiments and 4 batteries. General Ricketts, division commander, had under him the brigades of Duryée, Christian, and Hartsuff — 12 regiments and 2 batteries. From the nature of the ground, none of the artillery of Hooker's corps could be used, except that which went directly up the pike with Gibbon's brigade and one battery (Cooper's) on the enemy's right.

The hour for the general advance is not specified in the reports. Some of the Federal officers, as we have seen, speak of the general advance at 5 P. M. General Sturgis says that he became engaged on the south side of the pike at 3 : 30 P. M. General Meade, on the north side, says that he moved toward the right at 2 P. M.,⚓ while General Ricketts, who took part in the same movement, says that he did not arrive at the foot of the mountain until 5 P. M. If General Meade was not mistaken as to the time of his starting, he must have been long delayed in the thick woods through which the first part of his march was made.

Here is probably the best place to explain the extraordinary caution of the Federals, which seemed so mysterious to us on that 14th of September. An

☆ In "The Century" magazine for December, 1886, page 308, was printed a letter from William L. De Rosset, Colonel of the 3d North Carolina regiment, in which, after stating that General Hill disclaims any intention of reflecting on Ripley's brigade in this statement, the writer says:

"The facts are these: He [General Hill] correctly states Ripley's manœuvres at Boonsboro' until we reached a position at the foot of the mountain, — on the west side, — when General Ripley said to me that we were entirely cut off from the rest of the army, except G. B. Anderson's brigade, which was on our right, and that he assumed the command of the two brigades, directing me to take command of the three regiments (Colonel Doles, with his 4th Georgia, having been detached and sent to a position on the north of the pike), and that he would remain near me, directing me at the same time to advance slowly up the mountain with a strong line of skirmishers in front. Upon reaching the summit, after toiling through the dense undergrowth of laurel, Major Thruston, in command of the skirmish line, reported troops in his front, a few minutes later confirming his first impression that they were G. B.

Anderson's brigade, presenting their flank and advancing toward his left. This was promptly reported through my adjutant to General Ripley, who directed me to withdraw to my original position, which having been accomplished, I was directed to hold my then position until further orders. After nightfall I moved forward, changing front to the left, a short distance, to the support of General Drayton, remaining there 'without drawing trigger' until we took up the line of march for Sharpsburg, about 10 to 12 at night. While, therefore, we accomplished nothing tangible, we were in position to do any duty for which we might be called."

EDITORS.

⚓ This is the hour at which General Meade says he received the order to move to the front, from the point where his division was halted beyond Middletown, at Catoctin creek. Meade turned off to the right, followed the old Hagerstown road to Mount Tabor Church, and then formed line at the foot of the mountain for the climb. Cooper's battery opened fire at 3 : 30. Hatch followed Meade, and Ricketts moved last. — EDITORS.

order of General Lee, made while at Frederick, directing Jackson to capture Harper's Ferry, and Longstreet and myself to go to Boonsboro', had fallen into the hands of the Federals, and had been carried to General McClellan. This order (known at the South as the Lost Dispatch) was addressed to me, but I proved twenty years ago that it could not have been lost through my neglect or carelessness.‡ The Federal commander gained two facts from the order, one of which was needless and the other misleading. He learned that Jackson had gone to Harper's Ferry — a truth that he must have learned from his own scouts and spies and the roar of artillery in his own ears: the cannonading could be distinctly heard at Frederick, and it told that *some one* was beleaguering Harper's Ferry. The misleading report was that Longstreet was at Boonsboro'.⚓ The map of the battle-field of South Mountain, prepared in 1872, ten years after the fight, by the United States Bureau of Engineers, represents ten regiments and one battalion under Longstreet at the foot of the mountain on the morning of the 14th of September, 1862. But Longstreet was then an ordinary day's march from that point. In fact, after the removal of Colquitt's brigade, about 7 A. M., there was not a Southern soldier at the foot of the mountain until 3 P. M., when Captain Park of the 12th Alabama Regiment was sent there with forty men. General McClellan in his report says: "It is believed that the force opposed to us at Turner's Gap consisted of D. H. Hill's corps (fifteen thousand) and a part if not the whole of Longstreet's, and perhaps a portion of Jackson's, — probably thirty thousand in all." ("Official Records," Volume XIX., Pt. I., p. 53.) The mistake of the Federal commander in regard to General Longstreet was natural, since he was misled by the Lost Dispatch. But it seems strange that the United States Engineers should repeat the blunder, with the light of history thrown for ten years upon all the incidents of the battle. It was incomprehensible to us of the losing side that the men who charged us so boldly and repulsed our attacks so successfully should let slip the fruits of victory and fall back as though defeated. The prisoners taken were from my division, but the victors seemed to think that Longstreet's men lay hidden somewhere in the depths of those mysterious forests. Thus it was that a thin line of men extending for miles along the crest of the mountain could afford protection for so many hours to Lee's trains and artillery and could delay the Federal advance until Longstreet's command did come up, and, joining with mine, saved the two wings of the army from being cut in two. But for the mistake about the position of our forces, McClellan could have captured Lee's trains and artillery and interposed between Jackson and Longstreet before noon on that 14th of September. The losing of the dispatch was the saving of Lee's army.

---

‡ In a private letter to the editors, dated Feb. 24th, 1888, General Hill says: "I went into Maryland under Jackson's command. I was under his command when Lee's order was issued. It was proper that I should receive that order through Jackson and not through Lee. I have now before me the order received from Jackson. . . . My adjutant-general made affidavit, twenty years ago, that no order was received at our office from General Lee. But an order from Lee's office, directed to me, was lost and fell into McClellan's hands. Did the courier lose it? Did Lee's own staff-officers lose it? I do not know." See also pp. 603 and 664. — EDITORS.

⚓ "Special Orders No. 191," which was the "lost order," sent Longstreet to Boonsboro'. It was afterward modified by General Lee so as to place Longstreet at Hagerstown. — EDITORS.

About 4 P. M. I saw what appeared to be two Federal brigades emerge from the woods south of Colquitt's position and form in an open field nearly at right angles to each other — one brigade facing toward the pike, and the other facing the general direction of the mountain. This inverted V-like formation was similar to that of the 1st Mississippi Regiment at Buena Vista. If it was made anywhere else during the Civil War, I never heard of it. The V afforded a fine target from the pike, and I directed Captain Lane to open on it with his battery. His firing was wild, not a shot hitting the mark. The heavy batteries promptly replied, showing such excellent practice that Lane's guns were soon silenced. A small force in the edge of the woods on the west side of the old field opened fire upon the V. The Federals changed their formation, and, advancing in line of battle, brushed away their assailants and plunged into the woods, when heavy firing began which lasted possibly half an hour.

I suppose that the Federal force which I saw was the division of General Sturgis, ǂ and that he left behind Harland's brigade of Rodman's division to guard his flank in his advance, since Harland reports that he had no casualties. General Sturgis claims that he swept everything before him. So do his comrades who fought on his left. On the other hand, General Hood, who came up a short time before this advance, with the brigades of Wofford and Law, claims that he checked and drove back the Federals. G. T. Anderson reports that only his skirmishers were engaged. The surviving officers under G. B. Anderson (who was killed at Sharpsburg, and left no report) say that the same thing was true of their brigade in the afternoon. Ripley's brigade was not engaged at all. About dusk the 2d and 13th North Carolina Regiments attacked Fairchild's brigade and the batteries protected by it on the extreme Federal left, and were repulsed disastrously. Generals Burnside and Willcox say that the fight was continued until 10 o'clock at night. Hood was mistaken, then, in thinking that he had driven back the Federal advance. The opposing lines were close together at nightfall, and the firing between the skirmishers was kept up till a late hour. Equally erroneous is the claim that any Confederates were driven except Drayton's small brigade. We held the crests of the mountain, on the National road and the old Sharpsburg road, until Lee's order for withdrawal was given. General Reno, the Federal corps commander on our right, was killed at 7 P. M., in Wise's field, where the fight began at 9 o'clock in the morning. But on our left a commanding hill was lost before night. Batteries placed upon it next morning, acting in concert with the heavy batteries placed on our right by General Pleasonton before we were aware of his presence, would have made any position untenable on the pike or the crest of the mountain. I made that statement to General Lee about 9 P. M., when he consulted with Longstreet and myself in regard to renewing the fight the next morning. Longstreet concurred in this view, remarking that I knew the ground and the situation better than he did.

General Hooker detached Gibbon's brigade, consisting of three Wisconsin

ǂ Probably Willcox's division, with its right refused to avoid the enfilading fire from the batteries on the mountain.— EDITORS.

FOX'S GAP.—THE APPROACH TO WISE'S FIELD.

This sketch and the one on the next page (from photographs made in 1885) may be regarded as parts of one picture. The old Sharpsburg or Braddock road lies between the stone-wall and the rail fence. The left distance shows the Middletown valley and the Catoctin range, from which Reno approached.— EDITORS.

regiments and one Indiana regiment, from Hatch's division, and directed it to move directly up the pike with a section of artillery. Then the divisions of Meade and Hatch were formed on the north side of the pike, with the division of Ricketts in supporting distance in rear. A belt of woods had to be passed through, and then it was open field all the way to the summit, and the two detached peaks were in full view upon which the devoted little band of Rodes was posted — the 12th Alabama Regiment on one, and the 3d, 5th, 6th, and 26th Alabama regiments on the other. Under the illusion that there were ten regiments and one battalion of Longstreet's command in those woods, the progress through them was slow, but, when once cleared, the advance was steady and made almost with the precision of movement of a parade day. Captain Robert E. Park, of Macon, Georgia, who commanded the forty skirmishers in the woods, thinks that he delayed the Federal advance for a long time.‡

It is not more improbable that a few active skirmishers north of the pike should prove an obstacle to progress through the forest there, than that a

‡ Captain Park writes:

"After passing through Boonsboro', *en route* to the scene of action, we met the dead body of the gallant General Garland, when an order from General D. H. Hill, through General R. E. Rodes, to Colonel B. B. Gayle of the 12th Alabama, directed that skirmishers should be deployed in front. Colonel Gayle hurriedly ordered captains of companies to send four men each to the front to report to Lieutenant R. E. Park as sharp-shooters, and I promptly reported for orders; was directed to carry my squad of forty men to the foot of South Mountain, 'and keep the enemy back as long as possible.' I hastily deployed the men, and we moved down the mountain-side. On our way down we could see the enemy, in two lines of battle, in the valley below, advancing, preceded only a few steps by their dense line of skirmishers. I concealed my men behind trees, rocks, and bushes, and cautioned them to aim well before firing. We awaited with beating hearts the sure and steady approach of the 'Pennsylvania Bucktails,' who were directly in my front, and soon near enough to fire upon. I gave the command, 'Fire,' and forty guns were almost simultaneously emptied with deadly effect, and the surviving skirmishers rushed back pell-mell to their main line, disordering it greatly. The solid, well-drilled line soon rallied, and advanced steadily forward, and my small party, as soon as they were near enough, fired again, and nearly every bullet did fatal work. At least thirty men must have been killed or wounded at the second fire, and perhaps more at the first. Though checked for some minutes, the enemy again advanced, their officers earnestly exhorting them with 'close up' and 'forward.' I directed my men to fall back slowly, and to fire from everything which would screen them from observation. I had lost only four men wounded up to this time, but six or eight more became demoralized and, despite my commands, entreaties, and threats, left me and hastily fled to the rear. With the brave

FOX'S GAP—WISE'S FIELD AS SEEN FROM THE PASTURE NORTH OF THE ROAD.

The stump in the middle of the field beyond the wall is near where Reno fell. Part of the struggle was for the wooded crest on the left of the field. The house is Wise's, at the crossing of the ridge and Old Sharpsburg roads. [See map, p. 568.] The Confederates here were posted behind a stone-wall. The well at Wise's house was filled with the Confederate dead.— EDITORS.

division on the south side should hesitate to penetrate a forest from which their foes had been completely driven. The success of the Federals on the north side was due to the fact that after getting through the belt of woods at the foot of the mountain, they saw exactly what was before them. The lack of complete success south of the pike was owing to the thick woods on that side, which were supposed to be full of hidden enemies. In the battle of South Mountain the imaginary foes of the Lost Dispatch were worth more to us than ten thousand men.

The advance of Hatch's division in three lines, a brigade in each, was as grand and imposing as that of Meade's division. Hatch's general and field officers were on horseback, his colors were all flying, and the alignment of his men seemed to be perfectly preserved. General Hooker, looking at the steady and precise movement from the foot of the mountain, describes it as a beautiful sight. From the top of the mountain the sight was grand and sublime, but the elements of the pretty and the picturesque did not enter into it. Doubtless the Hebrew poet whose idea of the awe-inspiring is expressed by

squad which remained, we retreated slowly, firing as rapidly as we could load, and doing fatal work with every step. The advance was very slow and cautious. It was about 3 o'clock when we had opened fire at the foot of the mountain, and now the sun was rapidly setting. Corporal Myers, of Mobile, at my request, aimed at and shot an exposed officer, receiving himself a terrible wound as he did so. I raised him tenderly, gave him water, and reluctantly was about to abandon him to his fate, when a dozen muskets were pointed at me, and I was ordered to surrender. There was a deep ravine to our left, and the 3d Alabama skirmishers having fallen back, the Federals had got in my rear, and at the same time had closed upon me in front. If I had not stopped with Myers I might have escaped capture, but I was mortified and humiliated by the necessity of yielding myself a prisoner. Certain death was the only alternative. The enemy pushed forward after my capture, and came upon Colonel Gayle and the rear support. Colonel Gayle was ordered to surrender, but, drawing his pistol and firing it in their faces, he exclaimed: 'We are flanked, boys, but let's die in our tracks.' and continued to fire until he was literally riddled by bullets

" I was accompanied to the rear by three Federal soldiers, and could but notice, as I walked down the mountain, the great execution done by my little squad as shown by the dead and wounded lying all along the route. At the foot of the mountain ambulances were being loaded. From what I saw and gathered from my captors, my little party committed fearful havoc, and the Federals imagined that several divisions of Lee's army confronted them. . . . I was carried before some prominent officer (have heard it was General Hatch), who questioned me about my regiment, brigade, division, number of troops, etc. The information I gave could not have benefited him much."   D. H. H.

the phrase, "terrible as an army with banners," had his view of the enemy from the top of a mountain.

There was not a single Confederate soldier to oppose the advance of General Hatch. I got some guns from the reserve artillery of Colonel Cutts to fire at the three lines; but owing to the little practice of the gunners and to the large angles of depression, the cannonade was as harmless as blank-cartridge salutes in honor of a militia general. While these ineffective missiles were flying, which the enemy did not honor by so much as a dodge, Longstreet came up in person with three small brigades, and assumed direction of affairs. He sent the brigade of Evans under Colonel Stevens to the aid of Rodes's men, sorely pressed and well-nigh exhausted. The brigade of Pickett (under Garnett) and that of Kemper were hurried forward to meet and check Hatch, advancing, hitherto, without opposition.

General Meade had moved the brigade of Seymour to the right to take Rodes's position in reverse, while the brigades of Magilton and Gallagher went straight to the front. Meade was one of our most dreaded foes; he was always in deadly earnest, and he eschewed all trifling. He had under him brigade commanders, officers, and soldiers worthy of his leadership. In his onward sweep the peak upon which the 12th Alabama was posted was passed, the gallant Colonel Gayle was killed, and his regiment was routed and dispersed. The four other regiments of Rodes made such heroic resistance that Meade, believing his division about to be flanked, sent for and obtained Duryée's brigade of Ricketts's division. It was pitiable to see the gallant but hopeless struggle of those Alabamians against such mighty odds. Rodes claimed to have fought for three hours without support; but an over-estimate of time under such circumstances is usual and natural. He lost 61 killed, 157 wounded, and 204 missing (captured), or more than one-third of his brigade. His supports [Evans's brigade] fought gallantly and saved him from being entirely surrounded, but they got on the ground too late to effect anything else. Evans's brigade under Stevens had been wasted by two campaigns and was small when it left Hagerstown that morning, and many had fallen out on the hot and dusty forced march. Of the four regiments in the brigade, we find in Volume XIX. of the "Official Records" only the report of one, the 17th South Carolina regiment under Colonel McMaster. That says that 141 men entered the fight on South Mountain, and of these 7 are reported killed, 37 wounded, and 17 missing (captured). Colonel McMaster writes to me that his was the largest regiment in the brigade; so the brigade must have been about 550 strong. General Meade says in his report that he lost 397 men, or ten per cent. of his division. As he received the support of Duryée before or about the time that Rodes got the aid of Stevens, he fought Rodes with the advantage all the while of three to one.

When Ripley came up, as before described, the pressure was all at Fox's Gap. He was sent in there and his brigade was uselessly employed by him in marching and counter-marching. Had it been sent to strengthen Rodes the key of the position might not have been lost. But the vainest of all speculations and regrets are about "the might have been."

Meade encamped that night on the commanding eminence which he had won.

The strength of the two brigades sent to check General Hatch did not exceed eight hundred men, as I will show presently. They must have performed prodigies of valor, and their praises can best be spoken in the words of their enemies. General Patrick, commanding the leading Federal brigade, tells of a race between his men and a strong force of the enemy for the possession of a fence. Patrick won the race and delivered his fire from the fence, picking off the cannoneers at some of our guns. General Hatch was wounded at this fence, and the command devolved on General Doubleday. The latter speaks of lying down behind the fence and allowing the enemy to charge up to within fifteen paces, whereupon he opened a deadly fire. Colonel Wainwright, who succeeded Doubleday in command of his brigade, was also wounded here, and Colonel Hofmann assumed command of it. Colonel Hofmann tells us that the ammunition of the brigade was just giving out when Ricketts relieved Doubleday. Several of the reports speak of the "superior force of the enemy." General Ricketts says that "he relieved Doubleday hard-pressed and nearly out of ammunition." Before Ricketts came in person with Hartsuff's brigade, he had sent Christian's brigade to the assistance of Doubleday. The brigades of Kemper and Pickett (the latter under Garnett) must have fought valiantly, else such results could not have been achieved. General Doubleday's report contains this curious story: "I learned from a wounded prisoner that we were engaged with four to five thousand under the immediate command of General Pickett, with heavy masses in their vicinity. He stated also that Longstreet in vain tried to rally the men, calling them his pets and using every effort to induce them to renew the attack." Of course, the old rebel knew that Pickett was not there in person and that there were no heavy masses in the vicinity. The astonishing thing is that General Doubleday should believe that there were 4000 or 5000 men before him under the immediate command of Pickett. But Doubleday's belief of the story is a tribute to the efficiency of the 800 men who fought a division of 3500 men (the number reported by Hatch after Gibbon had been detached), and fought it so vigorously that two brigades were sent to its assistance.

Jenkins's brigade, under Walker, came up at dusk, too late to be in the fight; but it went in on the right of Garnett and took part in the irregular firing which was kept up till a late hour. Colonel Walker's report shows a loss of 3 killed and 29 wounded, which proves that he was but slightly engaged. The tired men of both sides lay down at last to rest within a hundred yards of each other. But now Gibbon was putting in earnest work on the pike. He had a choice brigade, strong in numbers and strong in the pluck of his men, all from the North-west, where habitually good fighters are reared. He had pushed forward cautiously in the afternoon with the 7th Wisconsin regiment, followed by the 6th on the north side of the pike and the 19th Indiana, supported by the 2d Wisconsin, on the south side. The ten imaginary regiments of the Lost Dispatch retarded his progress through the woods; and at one time, believing that the 7th Wisconsin was about to be

VIEW FROM TURNER'S GAP, LOOKING SOUTH-EAST [SEE MAP, P. 568]. FROM A PHOTOGRAPH TAKEN IN 1886.

The point of view is a little to the left of the Mountain House, now the home of Mrs. Dahlgren, widow of Admiral Dahlgren. Rodes was first posted on the hill, the slope of which is seen on the left; Gibbon was farther down the road in the hollow. The white patch on the mountain to the south (on the right) is Wise's field at Fox's Gap, where Reno and Garland were killed.— EDITORS.

turned on its right flank, he sent the 6th to its assistance. There were only a few skirmishers on his right, but the Lost Dispatch made him believe otherwise. About 9 P. M. the stone-wall was reached, and several gallant efforts were made in vain to carry it. When each repulse was followed by the "rebel" yells, the young men on my staff would cry out: "Hurrah for Georgia! Georgia is having a free fight." The Western men had met in the 23d and 28th Georgia regiments men as brave as themselves and far more advantageously posted. Colonel Bragg, of the 6th Wisconsin, says in his report: "We sat down in the dark to wait another attack, but the enemy was no more seen." At midnight Gorman's brigade of Sumner's corps relieved Gibbon's.

General Gibbon reports officially 318 men killed and wounded—a loss sustained almost entirely, I think, at the stone-wall. The colonel of the 7th Wisconsin reports a loss of 147 men in killed and wounded out of 375 muskets carried into action. This shows that he had brave men and that he encountered brave men. From his report we infer that Gibbon had fifteen hundred men. On our side Colquitt had 1100 men, and lost less than 100, owing to the admirable position in which he had been placed.

And now in regard to the numbers engaged. Longstreet sent to my aid 8 brigades,—5 belonging to the division of D. R. Jones, consisting of the brigades of Drayton, Pickett, Jenkins, G. T. Anderson, and Kemper; and 3 belonging to an extemporized division of N. G. Evans, including the brigades of Evans, Hood, and Law. On page 886, Part I., Volume XIX. of the "Official Records," Jones says that after Toombs joined him from Hagerstown, his 6 brigades numbered at Sharpsburg 2430 men; i. e., an average of 405 men to each brigade. Now all Longstreet's officers and men know that the ranks were fuller at Sharpsburg than at South Mountain, because there were more stragglers in the forced march from Hagerstown to the battle-field of the 14th of September than there were casualties in the battle. \ The above average would give 810 as the number of men in the two brigades which confronted the division of Hatch aided by two brigades from Ricketts. But it is well known that the Virginia brigades were unusually small, because of the heavy draughts upon them for cavalry, artillery, and local service. Between pages 894 and 902, Volume XIX., we have the strength at South Mountain of four of the five regiments of Pickett's brigade given officially,—the 19th Regiment, 150 men; 18th Regiment, 120 men; 56th Regiment, 80 men; 8th Regiment, 34 men. The strength of the other regiment, the 28th, is not given; but, assuming that it was 96, the average of the other four regiments, we have 480 as the number of men in Pickett's brigade at South Mountain. But the report of the colonel of the 56th shows that he was turned off with his 80 muskets, and did not go in with his brigade; so that Garnett had in the battle but 400 of Pickett's men. From Kemper's brigade we have but one report giving the strength of a regiment, and that comes from Colonel Corse of the 17th Virginia. He says that at Sharpsburg he had 6 officers and 49 privates in his regiment. A calculation based upon this report would show that Kemper's brigade was smaller than Pickett's.

On page 907 we have the only report from Jenkins's brigade which gives any intimation of its strength. There the 1st South Carolina regiment is said to have 106 men at Sharpsburg. It is possible the five regiments of this brigade numbered 530 in that battle. It is true that it was considerably larger at Sharpsburg than at South Mountain, because the stragglers from the Hagerstown march much more than made up for the small loss (32) in the battle of the 14th. But with due allowance for that gain, the brigade must have been 450 strong at South Mountain. It is evident, then, that Kemper's brigade fell below 400 at South Mountain; otherwise, the brigade average in Jones's division would have exceeded 406.

Longstreet thinks that he had four thousand men at South Mountain. His estimate is too high, according to the records as I find them. Accepting

\ In his official report General Hill, after stating his force on the morning of the 14th as "less than 5000 men," says: "My ranks had been diminished by some additional straggling, and the morning of the 17th [Antietam] I had but 3000 infantry." Adding to this number General Hill's losses on September 14th at Fox's and Turner's Gaps, and we have 3934 as his strength in the battle of South Mountain, without counting these additional stragglers.—EDITORS.

BRIGADIER-GENERAL GEORGE B. ANDERSON, C. S. A., KILLED AT ANTIETAM. FROM AN OIL PORTRAIT.

his numbers, I would place 2200 at Fox's Gap and 1800 north of Turner's Gap. Colquitt fought mainly and Rodes entirely with Hooker's corps. Adding the 2200 men of these two brigades to Longstreet's 1800, we have 4000 as the number opposed to Hooker. ☆

General McClellan puts the strength of the two attacking corps at thirty thousand. His figures are substantially corroborated by the reports of his subordinates, — division, brigade, and regimental commanders. They indicate, moreover, that there had been great straggling in the Federal army, as well as in our own. On p. 97, General Ingalls, chief quartermaster, reports, October 1st, 1862, means of transporation for 13,707 men in the First Corps; for 12,860 men in the Ninth Corps . . . . and for 127,818 men in the entire Army of the Potomac.‡ This was after the wastage of the two

---

☆ According to the estimate of Mr. Thomas White, chief clerk of the adjutant-general's office at General Lee's headquarters, who had charge of the field returns during the war, the effective strength of the Confederate forces at South Mountain, or Boonsboro', was: Longstreet, 8000; D. H. Hill, 7000,—total, 15,000. According to Colonel W. H. Taylor, adjutant-general of the Army of Northern Virginia, Hill had "less than 5000"; 6 brigades of Longstreet engaged numbered 4000,— total, 9000 (with 2 of Longstreet's brigades not engaged and not included). In his official report, General D. H. Hill says "the division numbered less than 5000 men on the morning of September 14th"; of his 5 brigades, Rodes's is stated to have numbered 1200, and Garland's "scarce 1000 men." The Union returns quoted show the whole number of officers and men of all arms present for duty without deduction. It to the strength of the First and Ninth Corps on the 20th of September we add the previous losses, these numbers will show as follows: First Corps, 15,750; Ninth Corps, 13,972. Deduct one-fifth, 5944, for non-effectives,—total available Union force, 23,778. Total available Confederate force, according to Mr. White, 15,000; according to Colonel Taylor, 9000, plus the two reserve brigades of Longstreet, whose strength he does not give.— EDITORS.

‡ The return of the Army of the Potomac for September 30th shows a total present for duty of 98,774 officers and men, including 5714 cavalry and headquarters guard. General Ingalls's statement, partly estimated as shown on its face (he counts cavalry 7000, it being actually 4543), is obviously in error in the figures, 30,026, set down for the Fifth Corps, which the return shows to have had 17,268 for duty, and 31,688 *present and absent.*— EDITORS.

battles (14th and 17th of September), reported on page 204 as amounting to 15,203.

General Hooker was well pleased with the work of his corps. He says in his report: " When the advantages of the enemy's position are considered, and his preponderating numbers, the forcing of the passage of South Mountain will be classed among the most brilliant and satisfactory achievements of this army, and its principal glory will be awarded to the First Corps." Undoubtedly that corps had gained important positions, but it is difficult to see how 4000 men could preponderate in numbers over 13,707. Hooker's division and brigade commanders, who had been well up under musketry fire, do not speak in such glowing terms of the victory. The reports of the stubborn fighters in the Federal army on both sides of the pike are models of modest propriety. This is especially so with those who bore the heat and burden of the day,— Meade, Hatch, Cox, Willcox, Scammon, Crook, Gibbon, Ewing, Gallagher, Magilton, Phelps, White, Jackson, Callis, Bragg, and others.

In regard to the casualties of the opposing forces, the losses in killed and wounded were greater on the Federal side than on the Confederate, because the one thin line of the latter fired at the dense masses of the former, sometimes in two lines, and sometimes in three. But from their weakness the Confederates took no prisoners, while they lost over four hundred within the enveloping ranks of their enemies. The revised statement of Federal losses in Volume XIX. gives the casualties in the First Corps as 923; of the Ninth Corps as 889,—total 1812, infantry and artillery; and to this number is added one cavalryman, how killed is not explained.

I lost two brigadiers and a large number of regimental commanders within three days, so that my division reports are very meager. Of the five brigades, there is a statistical report from that of Rodes alone. By means of a very extensive correspondence I have ascertained the casualties as nearly as they can be reached at this late day:

	Killed and Wounded.	*Missing.*
Rodes	218	204
Colquitt	92	7
Garland	100	200
Anderson	84	29
Ripley	0	0
	494	440

Longstreet's loss must have been less than mine, as he had but four small brigades seriously engaged. Walker reports only thirty-two casualties in Jenkins's brigade; G. T. Anderson had none. Hood speaks lightly of the fight of the two brigades under him. The exact losses can, however, never be known.

In the foregoing table reference is had to prisoners taken in battle. Some of our wearied men slipped off in the woods to sleep, and were not aroused when the orders came to fall back. Colonel Parker of the 30th North Carolina regiment, a brave and efficient officer, writes to me that he could hardly keep his men awake even when the deadly missiles were flying among them. This is in confirmation of what General Hood, in charge of the rear-guard, told me when I passed him after daylight on the 15th. He said that he found it difficult to arouse and push on the tired men, who had fallen out by the wayside to get a few minutes' sleep.

If the battle of South Mountain was fought to prevent the advance of McClellan, it was a failure on the part of the Confederates. If it was fought to save Lee's trains and artillery, and to reunite his scattered forces, it was a Confederate success. The former view was taken by the President of the United States, for he telegraphed to General McClellan on the 15th of September: "God bless you and all with you. Destroy the rebel army, if possible."

But, from whatever standpoint it may be looked at, the battle of South Mountain must be of interest to the military reader as showing the effect of a hallucination in enabling 9000 men to hold 30,000 at bay for so many hours, in robbing victory of its fruits, and in inspiring the victors with such caution that a simple ruse turned them back in their triumphal career.

MAJOR-GENERAL R. E. RODES, C. S. A.
FROM A PHOTOGRAPH.

Every battle-field of the Civil War beheld the deadly conflict of former friends with each other. South Mountain may be taken as a specimen of this unnatural and horrible state of things. The last time I ever saw Generals McClellan and Reno was in 1848, at the table of General G. W. Smith, in the city of Mexico. Generals Meade and Scammon had both been instructors while I was at West Point. Colonel Magilton, commanding a brigade in Meade's division, had been a lieutenant in my company in the Mexican war. General John Gibbon (whose brigade pressed up the pike on the 14th of September) and his brother Lardner had been "best men" at my wedding. They were from North Carolina; one brother took the Northern side, while the other took the Southern.

There is another view of the picture, however. If we had to be beaten it was better to be beaten by former friends. Every true soldier loves to have "a foeman worthy of his steel." Every true man likes to attribute high qualities to those who were once friends, though now alienated for a time. The temporary estrangement cannot obliterate the recollection of noble traits of character. Some one attempted to condole with Tom Yearwood, a famous old South Carolina bully, upon the beating given him by his own son. "Hush up," said old Tom. "I am glad that no one but my own flesh and blood had a hand in my drubbing."

The sons of the South struck her many heavy blows. Farragut, of Tennessee, rose, as a reward of merit, to the highest rank in the Federal navy. A large number of his associates were from the South. In the Federal army there were of Southern blood and lineage Generals Thomas, Sykes, Reno,

Newtown, J. J. Reynolds, Canby, Ord, Brannan, William Nelson, Crittenden, Blair, R. W. Johnson, T. J. Wood, N. B. Buford, Terrill, Graham [Lawrence P.], Davidson, Cooke, Alexander, Getty, French, Frémont, Pope, Hunter. Some of these doubtless served the South better by the side they took; most of them were fine, and some superb, officers.

Moreover, the South had three hundred thousand of her sons in the Federal army in subordinate capacities.‡ Her armies surrendered when a Southern-born President and a Southern-born Vice-President were at the head of the United States Government. That the wounds of defeat and humiliation have been so soon healed has been owing largely to this balm to mortified pride. The sting of shame to Frenchmen is that their magnificent capital was captured by, and their splendid armies were surrendered to, soldiers of an alien race and religion. On the other hand, the civil wars in England have left no bitter memories behind them. Compare this forgetfulness of civil strife in England with the bitterness which Ireland still feels over her subjugation; compare it with the fact that the Roman occupation of England for five hundred years made no impression upon the language of the natives, so little intercourse was there between them and their conquerors; compare it with the fact that for four hundred years after the Norman conquest there was no fusion between the Norman and Saxon tongues. In truth, all history teaches that the humiliation of defeat by a foreign foe is felt for ages, while that of defeat by the same race is temporary and soon forgotten. The late Civil War was relieved of very much of its sectional character by the presence of so many Southerners in the Union armies. Therefore, it will be in the United States as in all the unsectional civil wars of the world's history in which race and religion were not involved,—the waves of oblivion will roll over the bitter recollections of the strife. But we trust that fragrant forever will be the memory of deeds of heroism, patience, fortitude, self-denial, and constancy to principle, whether those deeds were performed by the wearers of the blue or of the gray.

‡ According to a printed statement dated at the "Adjutant-General's Office, Washington, November 9th, 1880," the slave-holding States furnished troops to the Union army as follows: Delaware, 12,284; Maryland, 46,638; West Virginia, 32,068; District of Columbia, 16,534: Missouri, 109,111; Kentucky, 75,760; Tennessee, 31,092; Arkansas, 8289; North Carolina, 3156; Alabama, 2576; Florida, 1290; Louisiana, 5224; Mississippi, 545; Texas, 1965,—total, 316,532. This sum includes colored troops, but their number is not stated. The territory in actual rebellion also furnished 94,337 colored soldiers, recruited at various stations and not accredited to States. The so-called Northern, or free, States furnished to the Union army 2,419,150 men. — EDITORS.

FROM A PHOTOGRAPH.

582

FORCING FOX'S GAP AND TURNER'S GAP.

BY JACOB D. COX, MAJOR-GENERAL, U. S. V.

ON the 5th of September, 1862, the Kanawha Division was ordered by McClellan to report to General Burnside, commanding the Right Wing of the Army of the Potomac.[/] We left Upton's Hill early on the morning of the 6th, crossed the river, and marched through Washington to Leesboro, Maryland, where the First Corps [⚓] (Hooker's) and the Ninth Corps [↓] (Burnside's, under Reno), constituting the right wing, were assembling. Our formal assignment to the Ninth Corps was made a day or two later. On the 8th, the division was ordered to take the advance and marched to Brookville; on the 9th to Goshen; on the 11th to Ridgeville, and on the 12th, shortly after noon, to Frederick City, being the first to enter that place, and driving out the Confederate rear-guard of cavalry under General Wade Hampton. The insignificant skirmish which occurred there had a considerable influence upon the battle of the 14th, in an indirect way. The enemy's cavalry had been driven from the banks of the Monocacy River and retired into the town. The division, consisting of two brigades (Moor's and Scammon's), had crossed at the stone bridge on the National road, and Moor's, deployed on both sides of the turn-pike, advanced upon the city. Colonel Moor himself, with a troop of cavalry and a single cannon, was in the road. An impertinent criticism upon the speed of his movement, volunteered by a young staff-officer from corps head-

[/] For an account of the transfer of the Kanawha Division from West Virginia to the Potomac, see p. 281. The division was not engaged in the second battle of Bull Run; but two regiments of Scammon's brigade were under fire at Bull Run Bridge, near Union Mills, August 27th.— EDITORS.

[⚓] Confusion in the numbers of the First and Twelfth Corps is found in the records and correspondence. In the Army of Virginia, Sigel's corps (Eleventh) had been designated as First, Banks's (Twelfth) had been Second, and McDowell's (First) had been Third. In the Maryland campaign Hooker was assigned to McDowell's, which was sometimes called First and sometimes Third. Mansfield was assigned to Banks's. The proper designations after the consolidation of the armies were First and Twelfth. Reno had been assigned to the First, but McClellan got authority to change it, and gave that corps to Hooker, sending Reno back to the Ninth ("Official Records," XIX., Pt. II., pp. 197, 198, 279, 349).— J. D. C.

[↓] The Ninth Corps, created July 22d, 1862, was composed of the command that Burnside brought from North Carolina.— EDITORS.

quarters, stung Moor into dashing ahead at a gallop, with his escort and staff, and the gun. Just at the outskirts of the town the road turns to the left among the houses, and cannot be seen. While we were wondering at the charge by the brigade commander and his escort, he came to the turn of the road: there was a quick, sharp rattling of carbines, and Hampton's Legion was atop of the little party. There was one discharge of the cannon, and some of the brigade staff and the escort came back in disorder. I ordered up quickly the 11th Ohio, of Scammon's brigade, which was in column in the road, and they dashed into the town at a charge with fixed bayonets. The enemy's cavalry had not waited for them, but had retreated out of the place by the Hagerstown road. Moor had been ridden down, unhorsed, and captured. The artillerymen had unlimbered their gun, pointed it, and the gunner stood with the lanyard in his hand, when he was struck by a rushing horse; the gun was fired by the concussion, but at the same moment it was capsized into the ditch by the impact of the cavalry column. The enemy had no time to right the gun or carry it off, nor to stop for prisoners. They forced Moor on another horse and turned tail as the charging lines of infantry came up on right and left, together with the column in the road, for there had not been a moment's pause in the advance. Those who have a fancy for learning how Munchausen could have told this story are referred to the narrative of Major Heros Von Borcke, of J. E. B. Stuart's staff. Moor's capture, however, had consequences, as we shall see. His brigade passed to the command of Colonel George Crook, of the 36th Ohio.

Frederick was a loyal city, and as Hampton's cavalry went out at one end of the street and our infantry came in at the other, while the carbine smoke and the smell of powder still lingered, the closed window-shutters of the houses flew open, the sashes went up, the windows were filled with ladies waving their handkerchiefs and the national flag, and the men came to the column with fruits and refreshments for the marching soldiers.

We encamped just beyond the town. Pleasonton's cavalry, which had advanced by a different road (the one leading through Urbana), was sent forward next morning (September 13th) to reconnoiter the passes of Catoctin Mountain, and Rodman's division of our corps went as his support. Through some misunderstanding, Rodman did not advance on the Hagerstown road beyond Catoctin Mountain, but moved toward Franklin's line of march upon Crampton's Gap (southward). About noon of the 13th, I was ordered to march with my division to Middletown, on the National road leading to Hagerstown. McClellan himself met me as my column moved out of town, and told me of the misunderstanding in Rodman's orders, adding, that if I met him on the march I should take his division also along with me. I did not meet him, but his division returned to Frederick that night. The other two divisions of our corps crossed the Catoctin in the evening, and camped near the western base of the mountain. My own camp for the night was pitched on the western side of the village of Middletown.

The Catoctin or Middletown valley is beautifully included between Catoctin Mountain and South Mountain, two ranges of the Blue Ridge, running north-

east and south-west. The valley is 6 or
8 miles wide, and the National road, as
it goes north-westward, crosses South
Mountain at a depression called Turner's Gap. The old Sharpsburg road
leaves the turnpike a little west of Middletown, turns to the left, and crosses
the mountain at Fox's Gap, about a
mile from Turner's. The mountain
crests are about 1300 feet above the
Catoctin valley, and the "gaps" are
from 200 to 300 feet lower than the
summits near them. ⚓ These summits
are like scattered and somewhat irregular hills upon the high rounded surface of the mountain-top. They are
wooded, but along the south-easterly
slopes, quite near the top of the mountain, are small farms with meadows
and cultivated fields.

MAJOR-GENERAL JESSE L. RENO, KILLED AT
FOX'S GAP. FROM A PHOTOGRAPH.

In the evening of the 13th I was ordered to support General Pleasonton in
his cavalry reconnoissance to be made toward Turner's Gap in the morning.
He had already been reënforced by Benjamin's and Gibson's batteries from
the corps. The notion that Pleasonton was authorized to put the infantry in
position for an expected battle is wholly a mistake. No battle was expected
at Turner's Gap. Lee's order, of which a copy had fallen into McClellan's
hands, directed the concentration of the forces under Longstreet and D.
H. Hill at Boonsboro', where they were to be joined by those under Jackson
as soon as Harper's Ferry should be taken. McClellan's orders and correspondence show that he expected a battle at Boonsboro', but not at South
Mountain or east of it. Pleasonton had found a rear-guard at Turner's
Gap, but the support of a single brigade of infantry was assumed to be
enough to enable his cavalry to clear the way. Pleasonton asked for
one brigade of infantry to report to him for the purpose stated, and
I detailed the brigade under command of Colonel E. P. Scammon. At
6 o'clock in the morning of Sunday, September 14th, he marched out of
camp at Middletown. His brigade consisted of the 12th, 23d, and 30th
Ohio regiments; that of Crook, which was left in camp, was made up of
the 11th, 28th, and 36th Ohio, and each brigade was nearly fifteen hundred
strong. Two batteries of artillery and a squadron of cavalry also belonged
to the division.

I was myself on the road when Scammon marched out, and was riding forward with him to learn how Pleasonton intended to use the troops, when, just
as we crossed Catoctin Creek, I was surprised to see Colonel Moor standing

⚓ These elevations are from the official map made by the U. S. Engineers.—J. D. C.

at the roadside. With astonishment, I rode to him and asked how he came there. He said he had been taken as prisoner beyond the mountain, but had been paroled the evening before, and was now finding his way back to us on foot. "But where are *you* going?" said he. I answered that Scammon's brigade was going to support Pleasonton in a reconnoissance into the gap. Moor made an involuntary start, saying, "My God! be careful"; then, checking himself, said, "But I am paroled!" and turned away.

I galloped to Scammon and told him that I should follow him in close support with Crook's brigade, and as I went back along the column I spoke to each regimental commander, warning them to be prepared for anything, big or little,—it might be a skirmish, it might be a battle. Hurrying back to the camp, I ordered Crook to turn out his brigade prepared to march at once. I then wrote a dispatch to General Reno, saying I suspected we should find the enemy in force on the mountain-top, and should go forward with both brigades instead of sending one. Starting a courier with this, I rode forward to find Pleasonton, who was about a mile in front of my camp, where the old Sharpsburg road leaves the turnpike. I found that he was convinced that the enemy's position in the gap was too strong to be carried by a direct attack, and that he had determined to let his horsemen demonstrate on the main road, supporting the batteries, one of which at least (Benjamin's) was of 20-pounder Parrott guns, while Scammon should march by the Sharpsburg road and try to reach the flank of the force on the summit. Telling him of my suspicion as to the enemy, I also informed him that I had determined to support Scammon with Crook, and if it became necessary to fight with the whole division I should do so, in which case I should assume the responsibility myself as his senior officer. To this he cordially assented.

One of my batteries contained a section of 20-pounder Parrotts, and as these were too heavy to take up the rough mountain road, I ordered them to go into action beside Benjamin's battery, near the turnpike, and to remain with it till further orders. Our artillery at this time was occupying a knoll about half a mile in front of the forks of the road, and was exchanging shots with a battery of the enemy well up toward the gap. It was about half-past 7 o'clock when Crook's column filed off on the old Sharpsburg road, Scammon having perhaps half an hour's start. We had fully two miles to go before we should reach the place where our attack was made, and, as it was a pretty steep road, the men marched slowly with frequent rests. On our way up we were overtaken by my courier who had returned from Reno with approval of my action, and the assurance that the rest of the Ninth Corps would come forward to my support. [See map, p. 568.]

At about half a mile from the summit, at Fox's Gap, the enemy had opened upon Scammon with case shot from the edge of the timber above the open fields, and the latter had judiciously turned off upon a country road leading still farther to the left and nearly parallel to the ridge above. Here I overtook him, his brigade being formed in line, under cover of the timber, facing open pasture fields, having a stone-wall along the upper side, with the forest again beyond this. Crook was brought up close in his rear. The ascent and the formation of the division had occupied more than an hour, and it was now about 9 o'clock. Bayonets were fixed, and at the word the lines charged forward with loud hurrahs. The enemy opened with musketry and shrapnel; our men fell fast, but they kept up their pace, and in a few moments they were on and over the wall, the center of Garland's North Carolina brigade breaking before them. They hung on a little longer at right and left, and for some time it was a fierce mêlée, hand to hand, but the Ohio boys were the victors. We found that there was a country road behind the wall on top of the ridge, and the cover of the forest had enabled the enemy's guns to get away toward our right. The 11th Ohio was sent from Crook's brigade beyond Scammon's left, where part of the enemy's force held a hill and summit higher than the ridge at the stone-wall. This seems to have been held by Rosser's cavalry with a battery. The 36th Ohio was, in similar manner, sent beyond Scammon's right. The whole line again sprung forward. The high knoll on the left was carried, the enemy's center was completely broken and driven down the mountain, while on the right our men pushed the routed Carolinians beyond the Sharpsburg road, through Wise's fields, and up the slope of the crest toward the Mountain House at Turner's Gap. The regiment on the enemy's extreme right had been cut off from the others and retreated south-westwardly down the mountain toward Rohrersville. Those on their left had made such resistance as they could till they were supported by Anderson's brigade, which hurried to their assistance. The cavalry also took refuge on a wooded hill west of the Mountain House. Although Garland's line had been broken in the first charge, the rallying and fighting had been stubborn for more than an hour. Our position was now diagonally across the mountain-top, the shape of the ridges making our formation a hollow curve with our right too much in the air, where it was exposed to a severe artillery fire, not only from the batteries near the Mountain House but from one on a high hill north of the turnpike. The batteries with Pleasonton did their best to assist us, and were admirably served. We had several hundred prisoners in our hands, and learned from them that D. H. Hill's division, consisting of five brigades, was opposed to us, and that Longstreet was said to be in near support. Our own losses had not been trifling, and it seemed wise to contract our lines a little, so that we might have some reserve and hold the crest we had won till the rest of the Ninth Corps should arrive. Our left and center were strongly posted, but the right was partly across Fox's Gap, at the edge of the woods beyond Wise's house, around which there had been a fierce struggle. The 30th and 36th were therefore brought back to the crest on the hither side of the gap, where we still commanded the Sharpsburg road, and making the 30th our right flank, the 36th and the 28th were put in second line. My right thus occupied the woods looking northward into Wise's fields. About noon the combat was reduced to one of artillery, and the enemy's guns had so completely the range of the sloping fields behind us that their canister shot cut long furrows in the sod, with a noise like the cutting of a melon rind.

Willcox's division reported to me at about 2 o'clock, and would have been up considerably earlier but for a mistake in the delivery of a message to him, in consequence of which he moved first toward the hill on the north of the turnpike (afterward carried by Hooker's corps), until he was recalled and given the right direction by Reno, who had arrived at Pleasonton's headquarters. As he went into position on my right, the artillery fire from the crest beyond the turnpike annoyed him, and to avoid being enfiladed by it, he formed with his right thrown back nearly at right angles to the front and facing toward the turnpike. We were not long left idle. Longstreet's divisions had been arriving on the field faster than ours, and made a most determined effort to push us back from the ridge we held. I sent two regiments of Willcox's to extend my left, which was in danger of being turned. Their strongest attack fell upon the angle of Willcox's command, and for a little while there was some confusion there, due to the raking artillery fire which came from the right; but Willcox soon reformed his lines, and after a very bloody contest, pushed across the Sharpsburg road, through Wise's fields, and into the wooded slope beyond. Along the front of the Kanawha Division the line was steadily maintained and the enemy was repulsed with severe loss. At nearly 4 o'clock, Sturgis's division arrived and

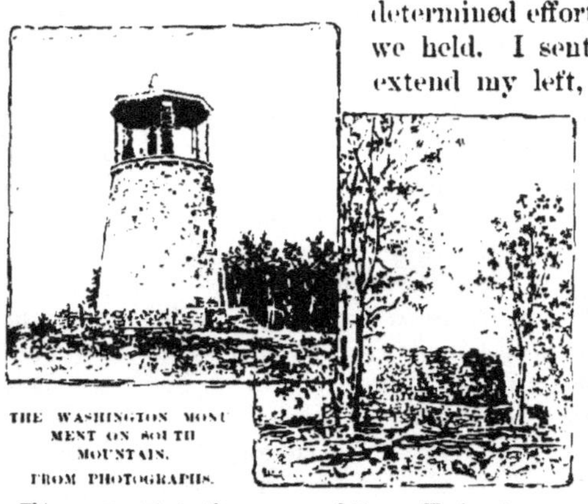

THE WASHINGTON MONUMENT ON SOUTH MOUNTAIN.

FROM PHOTOGRAPHS.

This monument, to the memory of George Washington, was first erected by the citizens of Boonsboro' and vicinity in 1827. It stands on the summit, a mile and a half north of Turner's Gap (see map, p. 568). Originally it was twenty feet high. In its tumble-down condition, as seen on the right of the picture, it served as one of the Union signal stations during the battle of Antietam. In 1882 the monument was rebuilt, as seen on the left of the picture, by the Odd Fellows of Boonsboro'. The present height of the tower, including the observatory, is forty feet.—EDITORS.

relieved the left wing of Willcox's division, the latter taking ground a little more to the right and rear. Rodman was the last to arrive, and as part of Longstreet's corps again threatened to pass beyond my left flank, I sent Fairchild's brigade to extend the line in that direction, the rest of that division going to the support of Sturgis and Willcox. During all this time there was sharp fighting all along the front, the struggle being on the part of the Confederates to drive back our center and left, where we held the highest summits of the mountain, and on our part to push forward our right so as to gain the one elevation they still held on our side of the National road, at the Mountain House. On the other side of the turnpike Hooker had by this time deployed, and his corps was fighting its way up the mountain side there.

McClellan, Burnside, and Reno had come, soon after Willcox's division, to the knoll in the valley which had been Pleasonton's position, and from that point, a central one in the midst of curving hills, had issued their orders. The Ninth Corps troops, as they came up the mountain, had reported to me for position, as I was senior on the line. Soon after the arrival of Rodman's division, the order came to advance the whole line, so as to complete the dislodgment of the enemy from the remaining summit at the Mountain House. At the center and left the advance was not difficult, for we held the ridge and pushed our opponents down the mountain. But the right had still to climb, and the ground there was rough and rocky, a fortress in itself and stoutly held. Good progress was made by both Sturgis and Willcox, but the fastness at the Mountain House had not been carried when darkness fell upon the field. A little before sunset, Reno came up in person, anxious to know why the right could not get forward quite to the summit. After a few moments' conversation with me he passed on to Sturgis; it seemed to me he was hardly gone before he was brought back upon a stretcher, dead. He had gone to the skirmish line to examine for himself the situation there, and had been shot down by the enemy posted among the rocks and trees. There was more or less firing in that part of the field till late in the evening, but when morning dawned, the Confederates had abandoned the last foothold above Turner's Gap.

On the north of the National road the First Corps under Hooker had been opposed by one of Hill's brigades and four of Longstreet's, and had gradually worked its way along the old Hagerstown road, crossing the heights in that direction after dark in the evening. Gibbon's brigade had advanced along the National road, crowding up quite close to Turner's Gap, and engaging the enemy under Colquitt in a lively combat. It has been my purpose, however, to limit any detailed account to what occurred under my own eye.

The peculiar character of the battle had been that it grew out of what was intended for a mere reconnoissance. The Kanawha Division had carried the crest at Fox's Gap early in the forenoon, while the rest of the army was miles away. General Hill has since argued that only part of his division could oppose us; but his brigades were all on the mountain summit within easy support of each other, and they had the day before them. It was five hours from the time of our first charge to the arrival of our first supports, and it was not till 3 o'clock in the afternoon that Hooker's corps reached the eastern base of the mountain and began its deployment north of the National road. Our effort was to attack the weak end of the Confederate line, and we succeeded in putting a stronger force there than that which opposed us. It is for our opponent to explain how we were permitted to do it. The two brigades of the Kanawha Division numbered less than three thousand men. Hill's division was five thousand strong, even by the Confederate method of counting their effectives, which should be increased nearly one-fifth to compare properly with our reports. In addition to these, Stuart had the principal part of the Confederate cavalry on this line, and they were not idle spectators. Part of Lee's and Hampton's brigades were certainly there, and probably the whole of Lee's. With less than half the numerical strength which was opposed to it, therefore, the Kanawha Division had carried the summit, advancing to the charge for the most part over open ground in a storm of musketry and artillery fire, and had held the crests they had gained through the livelong day, in spite of all efforts to retake them. The Ninth and the First Corps were deployed about 4 o'clock in the afternoon, and from that time till dark the proportions of the combat were enlarged to a battle which raged along two miles of mountain summits. The casualties in the Ninth Corps had been 889, of which 356 were in the Kanawha Division, which also captured some 600 of the enemy and sent them to the rear under guard. Reno on the National side and Garland on the Confederate were the officers of highest rank who were killed; but the wounded included a long list of distinguished men, among whom was Lieutenant-Colonel Rutherford B. Hayes (afterward President), who fell severely wounded in the early morning struggle on our left, where, also, Garland died, vainly trying to stay the rout of his brigade as our men covered the mountain-top.↓

On Monday morning our first duty was to bury the dead and to see that the wounded in our field-hospitals were sent back to Middletown where the general hospital had been established. During the forenoon we received orders to march toward Sharpsburg, but the road was already occupied by other troops, and when the head of my division reached it, at the place where the fight in front of Willcox's division had been most severe, we were halted for two or three hours till the corps which had the right of way should pass. Then we turned our faces toward the Antietam.

↓ General Hooker, commander of the First Corps, in his report, thus describes the action on the right of the Union Army, for the control of Turner's Gap:

"In front of us was South Mountain, the crest of the spinal ridge of which was held by the enemy in considerable force. Its slopes are precipitous, rugged, and wooded, and difficult of access to an infantry force even in absence of a foe in front. . . . Meade moved forward with great vigor and soon became engaged, driving everything before him. Every step of his advance was resisted stubbornly by a numerous enemy, and, besides, he had great natural obstacles to overcome which impeded his advance, but did not check it. . . . At this moment word was received that the enemy were attempting to turn Meade's right, when Duryée's brigade, of Ricketts's division, was dispatched to thwart it, and reached there in good time to render substantial aid in this, and also in assisting their comrades in crowning the summit with our arms. This was taken possession of in fine style between sundown and dark, and from that moment the battle was won. . . . Meantime Hatch had pressed into the forest on the left, and, after driving in their advanced pickets, encountered a heavy fire from the enemy massed in his front. The struggle became violent and protracted, his troops displaying the finest courage and determination. . . . Hatch being outnumbered, sorely pressed, and almost out of ammunition, Christian's brigade, of Ricketts's division, was ordered forward to strengthen him, and in this rendered good service. On this part of the field the resistance of the enemy was continued until after dark, and only subsided on his being driven from his position. It being very dark, our troops were directed to remain in position, and Hartsuff's brigade [of Ricketts's division] was brought up and formed a line across the valley, connecting with Meade's left and Hatch's right, and all were directed to sleep on their arms."

Brigadier-General John Gibbon reports:

". . . My brigade was detached from the division and ordered to report for duty to Major-General Burnside. Late in the afternoon I was ordered to move up the Hagerstown turnpike (National road) with my brigade and one section of Gibbon's battery to attack the position of the enemy in the gorge. The 7th Wisconsin and the 19th Indiana were placed respectively on the right and left of the turnpike, to advance by the head of the company, preceded by two companies of skirmishers from the 6th and 2d Wisconsin, and, followed by these regiments, formed in double column at half distance, the section of the battery under Lieutenant Stewart, 4th Artillery, keeping on the pike a little in rear of the first line. The skirmishers soon became engaged and were supported by the leading regiments, while our guns moved forward on the turnpike until within range of the enemy's guns which were firing on our column from the top of the gorge, when they opened with good effect. My men steadily advanced on the enemy posted in the woods and behind stone-walls, driving him before them until he was reënforced by three additional regiments, making five in all opposed to us. Seeing we were likely to be outflanked on our right, I directed Lieutenant-Colonel Bragg, of the 6th Wisconsin, to enter the wood on his right and deploy his regiment on the right of the 7th. This was successfully accomplished, while the 19th Indiana, supported by the 2d Wisconsin, deployed, and, swinging around parallel to the turnpike, took the enemy in the flank. Thus the fight continued till long after dark, Stewart using his guns with good effect over the heads of our own men. My men, with their ammunition nearly exhausted, held all the ground they had taken. . . ."

The Confederate troops opposed to Meade appear to have been Rodes's brigade, of D. H. Hill's division, supported by Jenkins's, of D. R. Jones's division, while Hatch's advance appears to have been resisted by Kemper's and Garnett's brigades, of D. R. Jones's division, supported by Evans's independent brigade. Colquitt's brigade, of D. H. Hill's division, held the main turnpike against Gibbon.—EDITORS.

CAVALRY SKIRMISHERS.

NOTES ON CRAMPTON'S GAP AND ANTIETAM.

BY WM. B. FRANKLIN, MAJOR-GENERAL, U. S. V.

BETWEEN the 2d and 6th of September, the Sixth Corps remained in camp near Alexandria and collected horses and transportation for ammunition and provisions, which were gradually disembarked. On the latter date it marched to Tenallytown, beyond Georgetown, D. C., crossing the Potomac by the Long Bridge, and beginning the Maryland campaign. Its daily marches thereafter, to the date of the battle of Antietam, were regulated by orders from General McClellan, who, in turn, was in direct communication with Washington. It appears from the telegraphic correspondence which was carried on between Halleck and McClellan, that while the latter believed that General Lee's object was the invasion of Pennsylvania, the former could not divest himself of the notion that Lee was about to play the Union army some slippery trick by turning its left, getting between it and Washington and Baltimore, and then taking each city by a *coup-de-main*.

The following are extracts from some of General Halleck's dispatches:

SEPT. 9.—". . . I think we must be very cautious about stripping too much the forts on the Virginia side. It may be the enemy's object to draw off the mass of our forces, and then attempt to attack from the Virginia side of the Potomac."

SEPT. 11.—"I think the main force of the enemy is in your front; more troops can be spared from here."]

SEPT. 13.—"I am of opinion that the enemy will send a small column toward Pennsylvania, so as to draw your forces in that direction: then suddenly move on Washington with the forces south of the Potomac, and those he may cross over."

]General McClellan states that he received the dispatch in this form, but as printed in the "Official Records," Vol. XIX., Pt. II., p. 253, the sentence reads: "If the main force of the enemy is in your front, more troops can be spared from here."—EDITORS.

SEPT. 14. - "Scouts report a large force still on Virginia side of the Potomac, near Leesburg. If so, I fear you are exposing your left flank, and that the enemy can cross in your rear."

SEPT. 16.— "I fear now more than ever that they [the enemy] will recross at Harper's Ferry, or below, and turn your left, thus cutting you off from Washington. . . ."

On September 12th, Mr. Lincoln telegraphed General McClellan that he believed the enemy was recrossing the Potomac, and said, "Please do not let him get off without being hurt."

These dispatches demonstrate that it was McClellan's duty as a subordinate to move slowly and cautiously in his advance, although he believed that the whole of Lee's army was in his front. And during the whole Maryland campaign his army was nearer Washington than was Lee's.

On or before September 7th, General McClellan advised that Harper's Ferry should be evacuated *via* Hagerstown, so as to hold the Cumberland Valley against an advance toward Harrisburg, and on the 10th of September he asked that the garrison at Harper's Ferry should be ordered to join him. General Halleck in answer to the last request stated, "There is no way for Colonel Miles to join you at present; his only chance is to defend his works till you can open communication with him." Yet during the night of September 14th two regiments of cavalry marched out of Harper's Ferry to Hagerstown without meeting any enemy; and the whole infantry and field-artillery force of the garrison might have escaped before the 14th had General McClellan's advice of September 7th and 10th been followed. So the Sixth Corps moved by easy marches toward the Blue Ridge, under daily orders from the commanding general, and on the 14th of September fought the battle of Crampton's Gap, gaining the completest victory gained up to that time by any part of the Army of the Potomac.

While Burnside and Hooker were forcing Turner's Gap to open the direct road to Hagerstown, I was ordered to move by Crampton's Gap, five miles farther south, and gain Rohrersville, in order to cut off McLaws and R. H. Anderson on Maryland Heights, and to relieve Harper's Ferry. About noon on the 14th of September, the head of my column, Slocum's division, came upon Munford's brigade of cavalry, comprising the 2d and 12th Virginia regiments, with Chew's battery and a section of the Portsmouth battery of naval howitzers, supported by two regiments of Mahone's brigade of R. H. Anderson's division, under Colonel William A. Parham. General McLaws had also posted the remainder of Mahone's brigade and the brigades of Semmes and Cobb of his own division within supporting distance, and ordered General Howell Cobb to take command and to hold the pass against us. With the remainder of Anderson's division and his own, General McLaws occupied Maryland Heights, distant five miles. I quote from my official report of the action which ensued:

"The enemy was strongly posted on both sides of the road, which made a steep ascent through a narrow defile, wooded on both sides and offering great advantages of cover and position. Their advance was posted near the base of the mountain, in the rear of a stone-wall, stretching to the right of the road at a point where the ascent was gradual and for the most part over open fields. Eight guns had been stationed on the road and at points on the sides and summit of the mountain to the left of the pass. It was evident that the position could be carried

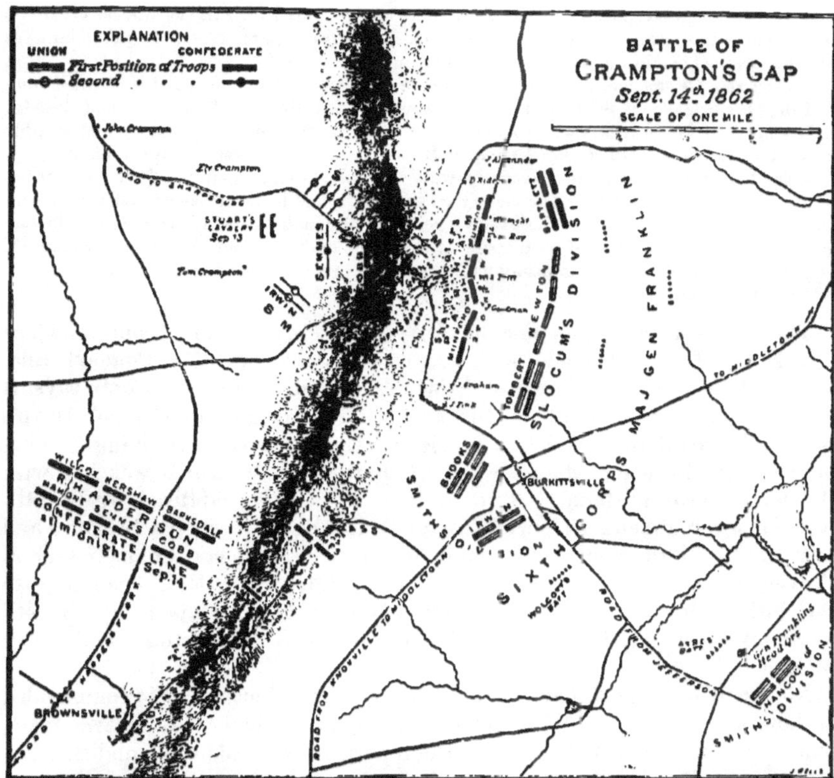

The Confederate sharp-shooters were behind their main line on higher ground, protected by trees and bowlders. After Parham's troops retired, Cobb, who had just reached the field, assumed command.— EDITORS.

only by an infantry attack. Accordingly, I directed Major-General Slocum to advance his division through the village of Burkittsville and commence the attack upon the right. Wolcott's 1st Maryland Battery was stationed on the left and to the rear of the village, and maintained a steady fire on the positions of the enemy until they were assailed and carried by our troops. Smith's division was placed in reserve on the east side of the village, and held in readiness to coöperate with General Slocum or support his attack as occasion might require. Captain Ayres's battery of this division was posted on a commanding ground to the left of the reserves, and kept up an uninterrupted fire on the principal battery of the enemy until the latter was driven from its position.

"The advance of General Slocum was made with admirable steadiness through a well-directed fire from the batteries on the mountain, the brigade of Colonel Bartlett taking the lead, and followed at proper intervals by the brigades of General Newton and Colonel Torbert. Upon fully determining the enemy's position, the skirmishers were withdrawn and Colonel Bartlett became engaged along his entire line. He maintained his ground steadily under a severe fire for some time at a manifest disadvantage, until reënforced by two regiments of General Newton's brigade upon his right, and the brigade of Colonel Torbert and the two remaining regiments of Newton's on his left. The line of battle thus formed, an immediate charge was ordered, and most gallantly executed. The men swept forward with a cheer, over the stone-wall, dislodging the enemy, and pursuing him up the mountain-side to the crest of the hill and down the opposite slope. This single charge, sustained as it was over a great distance, and on a rough ascent of unusual steepness, was decisive. The enemy was driven in the utmost confusion from a position of strength and allowed no opportunity for even an attempt to rally, until the pass was cleared and in the possession of our troops.

"When the division under General Slocum first became actively engaged, I directed General Brooks's brigade, of Smith's division, to advance upon the left of the road and dislodge the enemy from the woods upon Slocum's flank. The movement was promptly and steadily made under a severe artillery fire. General Brooks occupied the woods after a slight resistance, and then advanced, simultaneously with General Slocum, rapidly and in good order, to the crest of the mountain. The victory was complete, and its achievement followed so rapidly upon the first attack that the enemy's reserves, although pushed forward at the double-quick, arrived but in time to participate in the flight and add confusion to the rout. 400 prisoners, from 17 different organizations, 700 stand of arms, 1 piece of artillery, and 3 stand of colors were captured." . . .

The gun was a 12-pounder howitzer belonging to the Troup artillery attached to Cobb's brigade, and was captured by the 95th Pennsylvania, Colonel Gustavus W. Town, of Newton's brigade. General Cobb says it was "lost by an accident to the axle," but according to Colonel Town's report the artillerists fled before his advance, "merely disabling it temporarily by throwing off one wheel from the limber, which was left with the horses near at hand." Two of the colors were captured by the 4th New Jersey regiment, Colonel William B. Hatch, of Torbert's brigade, and one by the 16th New York, commanded by Lieutenant-Colonel Joel J. Seaver, of Bartlett's brigade. A fourth stand of colors, belonging to the 16th Virginia regiment, of Mahone's brigade, was taken by the 4th Vermont regiment, Lieutenant-Colonel Charles B. Stoughton, of Brooks's brigade.

No report appears to have been made by Colonel Parham, who commanded Mahone's brigade, nor by his division commander, General R. H. Anderson, who was wounded at Antietam, but the reports of Generals Cobb and Semmes and Colonel Munford sufficiently indicate the effect of our advance upon the forces under their command. Munford, who had eight guns, his two regiments of cavalry dismounted, and Mahone's brigade, was driven from his position behind a stone-wall at the foot of the pass. Cobb now came to his support, dividing his brigade to the right and left, but too late to change the result. One regiment, the 10th Georgia, of Semmes's brigade, also joined in Parham's defense, while the remaining three regiments, with nine guns of Manly's, Macon's, and Page's batteries, were posted for the defense of Burkittsville Gap, about a mile below toward our left, where the artillery is described, in the Confederate reports, as having done "good service." General Cobb says:

"As I was marching the last of the column, I received a message from you [McLaws] . . . that I must hold the gap if it cost the life of every man in my command. . . . Two of my regiments were sent to the right and two to the left to meet these movements of the enemy. In this we were successful, until the center gave way, pressed by fresh troops of the enemy and increased numbers. Up to this time the troops had fought well and maintained their ground against greatly superior forces. The 10th Georgia regiment, of General Semmes's brigade, had been ordered to the gap from their position at the foot of the mountain and participated in the battle with great courage and energy. After the lines were broken, all my efforts to rally the troops were unsuccessful."

A BATTERY GOING INTO ACTION.

General Semmes, who hurried forward to offer his assistance to General Cobb, thus describes the scene he witnessed on the Confederate side of the crest:

"Arriving at the base of and soon after commencing the ascent of the mountain at Crampton's Gap, I encountered fugitives from the battle-field and endeavored to turn them back. Proceeding farther up the mountain, the troops were met pouring down the road and through the wood in great disorder, where I found General Cobb and his staff, at the imminent risk of their lives, using every effort to check and rally them. I immediately joined my efforts, and those of my staff who were with me, to General Cobb's, and coöperated with him for a considerable time in the vain effort to rally the men."

General McLaws moved Wilcox's brigade of R. H. Anderson's, and later Kershaw's and Barksdale's brigades of his own division, to the support of Cobb, but not in time to take part in the engagement. The report of General McLaws shows that he accurately appreciated the effect of our success in completely shutting up his command on Maryland Heights until the surrender of Harper's Ferry opened the door for him to cross into Virginia. Accepting the estimate of Mr. Thomas White, who was chief clerk in the adjutant-general's office at General Lee's headquarters, and had charge of the returns, the whole available force under McLaws was 8000 men, and mine, on the basis of the last returns, 12,300. Couch's division (7219 men) of the Fourth Corps did not reach the field of the 14th until the fighting was over, and was detached from my command early the next morning. But these figures are at least one-fifth, if not one-fourth, beyond the actual effective strength. General Cobb estimates the Confederate forces actually engaged at 2200. Mine can hardly have exceeded 6500; heavy odds, indeed, but so are stone walls and a steep mountain pass. My losses were 533. The losses in Parham's (Mahone's) brigade, spoken of as heavy, are not reported; those in Cobb's and Semmes's brigades are given as 749.

At the end of the fight, after nightfall, the division of the corps which had borne the brunt of the fight (Slocum's), was, as it were, astride of the mountain. Of the other division (Smith's), the brigades of Brooks and Irwin were on the mountain, the reserve under Hancock being at the eastern base. Couch's division reported to me at 10 P. M.⌋ Early the next morning, Smith's division was sent into Pleasant Valley, west of the Blue Ridge, to begin the movement toward Harper's Ferry. Couch's division was sent, by order of the commanding general, to occupy Rohrersville. Slocum was to support Smith.

As I was crossing the mountain about 7 A. M., on September 15th, I had a good view of the enemy's force below, which seemed to be well posted on hills stretching across the valley, which is at this place about two miles wide. When I reached General Smith we made an examination of the position, and concluded that it would be suicidal to attack it. The whole breadth of the valley was occupied, and batteries swept the only approaches to the position. We estimated the force as quite as large as ours, and it was in a position which, properly defended, would have required a much greater force than ours to have carried. I am unable to give the numbers, but McLaws, in his report of the operations of the day, states that he formed the line across the valley with the brigades of Kershaw and Barksdale, except one regiment and two guns of the latter, and the "remnants" of the brigades of Cobb, Semmes, Mahone, and Wilcox, which he afterward states were very small.

The only force available for an attack would have been Smith's division of about 4500 men, Slocum's division being in no condition for a fight that day. Reading between the lines of General McLaws's report, he seems to have been disgusted that I did not attack him. The evidence before the court of inquiry on the surrender of Harper's Ferry shows that the white flag was shown at 7:30 A. M., on the 15th, and the firing ceased about one hour afterward. It is evident, therefore, that a fight between General McLaws's force and mine could have had no effect upon the surrender of Harper's Ferry. Success on my part would have drawn me farther away from the army and would have brought me in dangerous nearness to Jackson's force, already set free by the surrender. McLaws's supports were three and a half miles from him, while my force was seven miles from the main army.

Later on that day the enemy withdrew from Pleasant Valley and Harper's Ferry toward Sharpsburg. Couch's division joined me, and the corps remained stationary without orders from McClellan until the evening of the 16th, when I was ordered to march the next morning to join the army and to send Couch's division to occupy Maryland Heights. Accordingly the corps started at 5:30 A. M., and the advance reached the field of Antietam at 10 A. M., about twelve miles distant from the starting-point.

⌋ In October, 1862, when Mr. Lincoln visited the army, he came through Crampton's Gap; he told me that he was astonished to see and hear of what we had done there. He thanked me for it, and said that he had not understood it before. He was in all respects very kind and complimentary.— W. B. F.

General Smith's division arrived first and was immediately brought into action in the vicinity of the Dunker Church, repelling a strong attack made by the enemy at this point. The details of the part borne by the corps in the battle are graphically given in the official reports.

While awaiting the arrival of Slocum, I went to the right, held by Sumner. I found him at the head of his troops, but much depressed. He told me that his whole corps was exhausted and could do nothing more that day. It was lying in line of battle partly in a wood from which it had driven the enemy that morning. About three hundred yards in its front, across an open field, was a wood nearer the bank of the river, strongly held by the enemy. The corps had been driven back from an attack on this wood with great loss.

When General Slocum arrived I placed two brigades of his division on General Sumner's left and was awaiting the arrival of his third brigade, which was to be in reserve. With the two brigades I intended to

FROM A PHOTOGRAPH TAKEN BEFORE THE WAR.

make an attack on the wood referred to, and General Sumner was informed of my intention. The two brigades were ready to move. Just as the third brigade arrived, General Sumner rode up and directed me not to make the attack, giving as a reason for his order, that if I were defeated the right would be entirely routed, mine being the only troops left on the right that had any life in them. Major Hammerstein, of McClellan's staff, was near, and I requested him to inform General McClellan of the state of affairs, and that I thought the attack ought to be made. Shortly afterward McClellan rode up, and, after hearing the statements of Sumner and myself, decided that as the day had gone so well on the other parts of the line it would be unsafe to risk anything on the right. Of course, no advance was made by the division.

Later in the day General McClellan came again to my headquarters, and there was pointed out to him a hill on the right, commanding the wood, and it was proposed that the hill should be occupied by our artillery early the next morning, and that after shelling the wood, the attack should be made by the whole corps from the position then held by it. He assented to this, and it was understood that the attack was to be made. During the night, however, the order was countermanded. I met him about 9 o'clock on the morning of the 18th. He informed me that he countermanded the order because fifteen thousand Pennsylvania troops would soon arrive, and that upon their arrival the attack would be ordered. The troops, however, did not arrive, and the order was not renewed that day. On the 19th the corps entered the wood, expecting a fight, but the enemy had slipped off during the night.

THE OPPOSING FORCES IN THE MARYLAND CAMPAIGN.

The composition, losses, and strength of each army as here stated give the gist of all the data obtainable in the Official Records. K stands for killed; w for wounded, m w for mortally wounded; m for captured or missing; c for captured.

THE UNION ARMY.

(On September 14th, the right wing of this army, consisting of the First and Ninth Corps, was commanded by Maj.-Gen. A. E. Burnside; the center, composed of the Second and Twelfth Corps, by Maj.-Gen. Edwin V. Sumner; and the left wing, comprising the Sixth Corps and Couch's division of the Fourth Corps, by Maj.-Gen. W. B. Franklin.)

ARMY OF THE POTOMAC.—Major-General George B. McClellan.

Escort, Capt. James B. McIntyre: Oneida (N. Y.) Cav., Capt. Daniel P. Mann; A, 4th U. S. Cav., Lieut. Thomas H. McCormick; E, 4th U. S. Cav., Capt. James B. McIntyre. *Regular Engineer Battalion*, Capt. James C. Duane. *Provost Guard*, Maj. William H. Wood: 2d U. S. Cav. (4 co's) Capt. George A. Gordon; 8th U. S. Inf. (4 co's), Capt. Royal T. Frank; G, 19th U. S. Inf., Capt. Edmund L. Smith; H, 19th U. S. Inf., Capt. Henry S. Welton. *Headquarters Guard*, Maj. Granville O. Haller: 93d N. Y., Lieut.-Col. Benjamin C. Butler. *Quartermaster's Guard:* 1st U. S. Cav. (4 co's), Capt. Marcus A. Reno.

FIRST ARMY CORPS, Maj.-Gen. Joseph Hooker (w), Brig.-Gen. George G. Meade. Staff loss: Antietam, w, 1.

Escort: 2d N. Y. Cav. (4 co's), Capt. John E. Naylor.

FIRST DIVISION, Brig.-Gen. Rufus King, Brig.-Gen. John P. Hatch (w), Brig.-Gen. Abner Doubleday. Staff loss: South Mountain, w, 1.

First Brigade, Col. Walter Phelps, Jr.: 22d N. Y., Lieut.-Col. John McKie, Jr.; 24th N. Y., Capt. John D. O'Brian (w); 30th N. Y., Col. William M. Searing; 84th N. Y. (14th Militia), Maj. William H. de Bevoise: 2d U. S. Sharp-shooters, Col. Henry A. V. Post (w). Brigade loss: South Mountain, k, 20; w, 67; m, 8 = 95. Antietam, k, 30; w, 120; m, 4 = 154. *Second Brigade*, Brig.-Gen. Abner Doubleday, Col. William P. Wainwright (w), Lieut.-Col. J. William Hofmann: 7th Ind., Maj. Ira G. Grover; 76th N. Y., Col. William P. Wainwright, Capt. John W. Young; 95th N. Y., Maj. Edward Pye; 56th Pa., Lieut.-Col. J. William Hofmann, Capt. Frederick Williams. Brigade loss: South Mountain, k, 3; w, 52; m, 4 = 59. Antietam, w, 10. *Third Brigade*, Brig.-Gen. Marsena R. Patrick: 21st N. Y., Col. William F. Rogers; 23d N. Y., Col. Henry C. Hoffman; 35th N. Y., Col. Newton B. Lord; 80th N. Y. (20th Militia), Lieut.-Col. Theodore B. Gates. Brigade loss: South Mountain, k, 3; w, 19; m, 1 = 23. Antietam, k, 30; w, 187; m, 17 = 234. *Fourth Brigade*, Brig.-Gen. John Gibbon: 19th Ind., Col. Solomon Meredith, Lieut.-Col. Alois O. Bachman (k), Capt. William W. Dudley: 2d Wis., Col. Lucius Fairchild, Lieut.-Col. Thomas S. Allen (w); 6th Wis., Lieut.-Col. Edward S. Bragg (w), Maj. Rufus R. Dawes; 7th Wis., Capt. John B. Callis. Brigade loss: South Mountain, k, 37; w, 251; m, 30 = 318. Antietam, k, 68; w, 275; m, 6 = 349. *Artillery*, Capt. J. Albert Monroe: 1st N. H., Lieut. Frederick M. Edgell; D, 1st R. I., Capt. J. Albert Monroe; L, 1st N. Y., Capt. John A. Reynolds; B, 4th U. S., Capt. Joseph B. Campbell (w), Lieut. James Stewart. Artillery loss: Antietam, k, 12; w, 46; m, 8 = 66.

SECOND DIVISION, Brig.-Gen. James B. Ricketts.

First Brigade, Brig.-Gen. Abram Duryee: 97th N. Y., Maj. Charles Northrup; 104th N. Y., Maj. Lewis C. Skinner; 105th N. Y., Col. Howard Carroll; 107th Pa., Capt. James MacThomson. Brigade loss: South Mountain, k, 5; w, 16 = 21. Antietam, k, 59; w, 233; m, 35 = 327. *Second Brigade*, Col. William A. Christian, Col. Peter Lyle (w): 26th N. Y., Lieut.-Col. Richard H. Richardson; 94th N. Y., Lieut.-Col. Calvin Littlefield; 88th Pa., Lieut.-Col. George W. Gile (w), Capt. Henry R. Myers; 90th Pa., Col. Peter Lyle, Lieut.-Col. William A. Leech. Brigade loss: South Mountain, k, 2; w, 6 = 8. Antietam, k, 28; w, 197; m, 29 = 254. *Third Brigade*, Brig.-Gen. George L. Hartsuff (w), Col. Richard Coulter: 12th Mass., Maj. Elisha Burbank (m w), Capt. Benjamin F. Cook; 13th Mass., Maj. J. Parker Gould; 83d N. Y. (9th Militia), Lieut.-Col. William Atterbury; 11th Pa., Col. Richard Coulter, Capt. David M. Cook. Brigade loss: South Mountain, k, 2; w, 4 = 6. Antietam, k, 82; w, 497; m, 20 = 599. *Artillery:* F, 1st Pa., Capt. Ezra W. Matthews; C, Pa., Capt. James Thompson. Artillery loss: Antietam, k, 3; w, 19; m, 2 = 24.

THIRD DIVISION (Pa. Reserves), Brig.-Gen. George G. Meade, Brig.-Gen. Truman Seymour.

First Brigade, Brig.-Gen. Truman Seymour, Col. R. Biddle Roberts: 1st Pa., Col. R. Biddle Roberts, Capt. William C. Talley; 2d Pa., Capt. James N. Byrnes; 5th Pa., Col. Joseph W. Fisher; 6th Pa., Col. William Sinclair; 13th Pa. (1st Rifles), Col. Hugh W. McNeil (k), Capt. Dennis McGee. Brigade loss: South Mountain, k, 38; w, 133 = 171. Antietam, k, 24; w, 131 = 155. *Second Brigade*, Col. Albert L. Magilton: 3d Pa., Lieut.-Col. John Clark; 4th Pa., Maj. John Nyce; 7th Pa., Col. Henry C. Bolinger (w), Maj. Chauncey A. Lyman; 8th Pa., Maj. Silas M. Baily. Brigade loss: South Mountain, k, 25; w, 63; m, 1 = 89. Antietam, k, 41; w, 181 = 222. *Third Brigade*, Col. Thomas F. Gallagher (w), Lieut.-Col. Robert Anderson: 9th Pa., Lieut.-Col. Robert Anderson, Capt. Samuel B. Dick; 10th Pa., Lieut.-Col. Adoniram J. Warner (w), Capt. Jonathan P. Smith; 11th Pa., Lieut.-Col. Samuel M. Jackson; 12th Pa., Capt. Richard Gustin. Brigade loss: South Mountain, k, 32; w, 100 = 132. Antietam, k, 37; w, 136; m, 2 = 175. *Artillery:* A, 1st Pa., Lieut. John G. Simpson; B, 1st Pa., Capt. James H. Cooper; C, 5th U. S., Capt. Dunbar R. Ransom. Artillery loss: Antietam, k, 3; w, 18 = 21.

SECOND ARMY CORPS, Maj.-Gen. Edwin V. Sumner. Staff loss: Antietam, w, 2.

Escort: D and K, 6th N. Y. Cav., Capts. Henry W. Lyon and Riley Johnson. Loss: Antietam, w, 1.

FIRST DIVISION, Maj.-Gen. Israel B. Richardson (m w), Brig.-Gen. John C. Caldwell, Brig.-Gen. Winfield S. Hancock. Staff loss: Antietam, w, 2.

First Brigade, Brig.-Gen. John C. Caldwell: 5th N. H., Col. Edward E. Cross; 7th N. Y., Capt. Chas. Brestel; 61st and 64th N. Y., Col. Francis C. Barlow (w), Lieut.-Col. Nelson A. Miles; 81st Pa., Maj. H. Boyd McKeen. Brigade loss: Antietam, k, 44; w, 268; m, 2 = 314. *Second Brigade*, Brig.-Gen. Thomas F. Meagher, Col. John Burke: 29th Mass., Lieut.-Col. Joseph H. Barnes; 63d N. Y., Col. John Burke, Lieut.-Col. Henry Fowler (w), Maj. Richard C. Bentley (w), Capt. Joseph O'Neill; 69th N. Y., Lieut.-Col. James Kelly (w), Maj. James Cavanagh; 88th N. Y., Lieut.-Col. Patrick Kelly. Brigade loss: Antietam, k, 113; w, 422; m, 5 = 540. *Third Brigade*, Col. John R. Brooke: 2d Del., Capt. David L. Stricker; 52d N. Y., Col. Paul Frank; 57th N. Y., Lieut.-Col. Philip J. Parisen (k), Maj. Alford B. Chapman; 66th N. Y., Capt. Julius Wehle, Lieut.-Col. James H. Bull; 53d Pa., Lieut.-Col. Richards McMichael. Brigade loss: Antietam, k, 52; w, 244; m, 9 = 305. *Artillery:* B, 1st N. Y., Capt. Rufus D. Pettit; A and C, 4th U. S., Lieut. Evan Thomas. Artillery loss: Antietam, k, 1; w, 3 = 4.

SECOND DIVISION, Maj.-Gen. John Sedgwick (w), Brig.-Gen. Oliver O. Howard. Staff loss: Antietam, w, 2.

First Brigade, Brig.-Gen. Willis A. Gorman: 15th Mass., Lieut.-Col. John W. Kimball; 1st Minn., Col. Alfred Sully; 34th N. Y., Col. James A. Suiter; 82d N. Y. (2d Militia), Col. Henry W. Hudson; 1st Co. Mass. Sharp-shooters, Capt. John Saunders (k); 2d Co. Minn. Sharp-shooters, Capt. William F. Russell. Brigade loss: Antietam, k, 134; w, 639; m, 67 = 740. *Second Brigade,*

"

Brig.-Gen. Oliver O. Howard, Col. Joshua T. Owen, Col. De Witt C. Baxter: 69th Pa., Col. Joshua T. Owen; 71st Pa., Col. Isaac J. Wistar (w), Lieut. Richard P. Smith, Capt. Enoch E. Lewis; 72d Pa., Col. De Witt C. Baxter; 106th Pa., Col. Turner G. Morehead. Brigade loss: Antietam, k, 93; w, 379; m, 73 = 545. *Third Brigade*, Brig.-Gen. Napoleon J. T. Dana (w), Col. Norman J. Hall: 19th Mass., Col. Edward W. Hinks (w), Lieut.-Col. Arthur F. Devereux (w); 20th Mass., Col. William R. Lee; 7th Mich., Col. Norman J. Hall, Capt. Charles J. Hunt; 42d N. Y., Lieut.-Col. George N. Bomford, Maj. James E. Mallon; 59th N. Y., Col. Wm. L. Tidball. Brigade loss: Antietam, k, 142; w, 652; m, 104 = 898. *Artillery:* A, 1st R. I., Capt. John A. Tompkins; I, 1st U. S., Lieut. George A. Woodruff. Artillery loss: Antietam, k, 4; w, 21 = 25. THIRD DIVISION, Brig.-Gen. William H. French.

First Brigade, Brig.-Gen. Nathan Kimball: 14th Ind., Col. William Harrow; 8th Ohio, Lieut.-Col. Franklin Sawyer; 132d Pa., Col. Richard A. Oakford (k), Lieut.-Col. Vincent M. Wilcox; 7th W. Va., Col. Joseph Snider. Brigade loss: Antietam, k, 121; w, 510; m, 8 = 639. *Second Brigade*, Col. Dwight Morris: 14th Conn., Lieut.-Col. Sanford H. Perkins; 108th N. Y., Col. Oliver H. Palmer; 130th Pa., Col. Henry I. Zinn. Brigade loss: Antietam, k, 78; w, 356; m, 95 = 529. *Third Brigade*, Brig.-Gen. Max Weber (w), Col. John W. Andrews: 1st Del., Col. John W. Andrews, Lieut.-Col. Oliver Hopkinson (w); 5th Md., Maj. Leopold Blumenberg (w), Capt. E. F. M. Faehtz; 4th N. Y., Lieut.-Col. John D. MacGregor. Brigade loss: Antietam, k, 100; w, 449; m, 33 = 582. UNATTACHED ARTILLERY: G, 1st N. Y., Capt. John D. Frank; B, 1st R. I., Capt. John G. Hazard; G, 1st R. I., Capt. C. D. Owen. Artillery loss: Antietam, k, 1; w, 9 = 10.

FOURTH ARMY CORPS.

FIRST DIVISION (attached to Sixth Army Corps), Maj.-Gen. Darius N. Couch.

First Brigade, Brig.-Gen. Charles Devens, Jr.: 7th Mass., Col. David A. Russell; 10th Mass., Col. Henry L. Eustis; 36th N. Y., Col. William H. Browne; 2d R. I., Col. Frank Wheaton. *Second Brigade*, Brig.-Gen. Albion P. Howe: 62d N. Y., Col. David J. Nevin; 93d Pa., Col. James M. McCarter; 98th Pa., Col. John F. Ballier; 102d Pa., Col. Thomas A. Rowley; 139th Pa., Col. Frank H. Collier. *Third Brigade*, Brig.-Gen. John Cochrane: 65th N. Y., Col. Alexander Shaler; 67th N. Y., Col. Julius W. Adams; 122d N. Y., Col. Silas Titus; 23d Pa., Col. Thomas H. Neill; 61st Pa., Col. George C. Spear; 82d Pa., Col. David H. Williams. Brigade loss: Antietam (Sept. 18th), w, 9. *Artillery:* 3d N. Y., Capt. William Stuart; C, 1st Pa., Capt. Jeremiah McCarthy; D, 1st Pa., Capt. Michael Hall; G, 2d U. S., Lieut. J. H. Butler.

FIFTH ARMY CORPS, Maj.-Gen. Fitz John Porter.

Escort: Detachment 1st Me. Cav., Capt. George J. Summat.

FIRST DIVISION, Maj.-Gen. George W. Morell.

First Brigade, Col. James Barnes: 2d Me., Col. Charles W. Roberts; 18th Mass., Lieut.-Col. Joseph Hayes; 22d Mass., Lieut.-Col. William S. Tilton; 1st Mich., Capt. Emory W. Belton; 13th N. Y., Col. Elisha G. Marshall; 25th N. Y., Col. Charles A. Johnson; 118th Pa., Col. Charles M. Prevost; 2d Co. Mass. Sharp-shooters, Capt. Lewis E. Wentworth. Brigade loss: Shepherdstown, k, 66; w, 125; m, 130 = 321. *Second Brigade*, Brig.-Gen. Charles Griffin: 2d D. C., Col. Charles M. Alexander; 9th Mass., Col. Patrick R. Guiney; 32d Mass., Col. Francis J. Parker; 4th Mich., Col. Jonathan W. Childs; 14th N. Y., Col. James McQuade; 62d Pa., Col. Jacob B. Sweitzer. Brigade loss: Shepherdstown, k, 1; w, 10 = 11. *Third Brigade*, Col. T. B. W. Stockton: 20th Me., Col. Adelbert Ames; 16th Mich., Lieut.-Col. Norval E. Welch; 12th N. Y., Capt. William Huson; 17th N. Y., Lieut.-Col. Nelson B. Bartram; 44th N. Y., Maj. Freeman Conner; 83d Pa., Capt. Orpheus S. Woodward; Brady's Co. Mich. Sharp-shooters, Lieut. Jonas H. Titus, Jr. Brigade loss: Shepherdstown, w, 7. *Artillery:* 3d Mass., Capt. Augustus P. Martin; C, 1st R. I., Capt. Richard Waterman; D, 5th U. S., Lieut. Charles E. Hazlett. Artillery loss: Shepherdstown, m, 1. *Sharp-shooters:* 1st U. S., Capt. John B. Isler. Loss: Shepherdstown, k, 2; w, 5 = 7.

SECOND DIVISION, Brig.-Gen. George Sykes.

First Brigade, Lieut.-Col. Robert C. Buchanan: 3d U. S., Capt. John D. Wilkins; 4th U. S., Capt. Hiram Dryer; 12th U. S. (1st Battalion), Capt. Matthew M. Blunt; 12th U. S. (2d Battalion), Capt. Thomas M. Anderson; 14th U. S. (1st Battalion), Capt. W. Harvey Brown; 14th U. S. (2d Battalion), Capt. David B. McKibbin. Brigade loss: Antietam, k, 4; w, 35 = 39. *Second Brigade*, Maj. Charles S. Lovell: 1st and 6th U. S., Capt. Levi C. Bootes; 2d and 10th U. S., Capt. John S. Poland; 11th U. S., Capt. De Lancey Floyd-Jones; 17th U. S., Maj. George L. Andrews. Brigade loss: Antietam, k, 8; w, 47; m, 1 = 56; Shepherdstown, k, 1; w, 8 = 9. *Third Brigade*, Col. Gouverneur K. Warren: 5th N. Y., Capt. Cleveland Winslow; 10th N. Y., Lieut.-Col. John W. Marshall. Brigade loss: Shepherdstown, w, 1. *Artillery:* E and G, 1st U. S., Lieut. Alanson M. Randol; I, 5th U. S., Capt. Stephen H. Weed; K, 5th U. S., Lieut. William E. Van Reed. Artillery loss: Antietam, w, 3. Shepherdstown, k, 1; w, 2 = 3.

THIRD DIVISION (reached the field of Antietam Sept. 18th), Brig.-Gen. Andrew A. Humphreys.

First Brigade, Brig.-Gen. Erastus B. Tyler: 91st Pa., Col. Edgar M. Gregory; 126th Pa., Col. James G. Elder; 129th Pa., Col. Jacob G. Frick; 134th Pa., Col. Matthew S. Quay. *Second Brigade*, Col. Peter H. Allabach: 123d Pa., Col. John B. Clark; 131st Pa., Lieut.-Col. William B. Shaut; 133d Pa., Col. Franklin B. Speakman; 155th Pa., Col. Edward J. Allen. *Artillery:* C, 1st N. Y., Capt. Almont Barnes; L, 1st Ohio, Capt. Lucius N. Robinson. ARTILLERY RESERVE, Lieut.-Col. William Hays:

A, B, C, and D, 1st Battalion N. Y., Lieuts. Bernhard Wever and Alfred von Kleiser, and Capts. Robert Langner and Charles Kusserow; 5th N. Y., Capt. Elijah D. Taft; K, 1st U. S., Capt. William M. Graham; G, 4th U. S., Lieut. Marcus P. Miller. Artillery loss: Antietam, k, 5; w, 5; m, 1 = 11.

SIXTH ARMY CORPS, Maj.-Gen. William B. Franklin.

Escort: B and G, 6th Pa. Cav., Capt. H. P. Muirheid. FIRST DIVISION, Maj.-Gen. Henry W. Slocum.

First Brigade, Col. A. T. A. Torbert: 1st N. J., Lieut.-Col. Mark W. Collet; 2d N. J., Col. Samuel L. Buck; 3d N. J., Col. Henry W. Brown; 4th N. J., Col. William B. Hatch. Brigade loss: Crampton's Pass, k, 38; w, 134 = 172. Antietam, k, 2; w, 17 = 19. *Second Brigade*, Col. Joseph J. Bartlett: 5th Me., Col. Nathaniel J. Jackson; 16th N. Y., Lieut.-Col. Joel J. Seaver; 27th N. Y., Lieut.-Col. Alexander D. Adams; 96th Pa., Col. Henry L. Cake. Brigade loss: Crampton's Pass, k, 50; w, 167 = 217. Antietam, k, 1; w, 8 = 9. *Third Brigade*, Brig.-Gen. John Newton: 18th N. Y., Lieut.-Col. George R. Myers; 31st N. Y., Lieut.-Col. Francis E. Pinto; 32d N. Y., Col. Roderick Matheson (m w), Maj. George F. Lemon (m w); 95th Pa., Col. Gustavus W. Town. Brigade loss: Crampton's Pass, k, 24; w, 98; m, 2 = 124. Antietam, k, 1; w, 20 = 21. *Artillery*, Capt. Emory Upton: A, Md., Capt. John W. Wolcott; 1st Mass., Capt. Josiah Porter; 1st N. J., Capt. William Hexamer; D, 2d U. S., Lieut. Edward B. Williston. Artillery loss: Antietam, k, 1; w, 13; m, 2 = 16.

SECOND DIVISION, Maj.-Gen. William F. Smith.

First Brigade, Brig.-Gen. Winfield S. Hancock, Col. Amasa Cobb: 6th Me., Col. Hiram Burnham; 43d N. Y., Maj. John Wilson; 49th Pa., Lieut.-Col. William Brisbane; 137th Pa., Col. Henry M. Bossert; 5th Wis., Col. Amasa Cobb. Brigade loss: Antietam, w, 6. *Second Brigade*, Brig.-Gen. W. T. H. Brooks: 2d Vt., Maj. James H. Walbridge; 3d Vt., Col. Breed N. Hyde; 4th Vt., Lieut.-Col. Charles B. Stoughton; 5th Vt., Col. Lewis A. Grant; 6th Vt., Maj. Oscar L. Tuttle. Brigade loss: Crampton's Pass, k, 1; w, 18 = 19. Antietam, k, 1; w, 24 = 25. *Third Brigade*, Col. William H. Irwin: 7th Me., Maj. Thomas W. Hyde; 20th N. Y., Col. Ernest von Vegesack; 33d N. Y., Lieut.-Col. Joseph W. Corning; 49th N. Y., Lieut.-Col. William C. Alberger (w), Maj. George W. Johnson; 77th N. Y., Capt. Nathan S. Babcock. Brigade loss: Antietam, k, 64; w, 247; m, 31 = 342. *Artillery*, Capt. Romeyn B. Ayres: B, Md., Lieut. Theodore J. Vanneman; 1st N. Y., Capt. Andrew Cowan; F, 5th U. S., Lieut. Leonard Martin.

NINTH ARMY CORPS, Maj.-Gen. Ambrose E. Burnside (commanded the right wing of the army at South Mountain and exercised general command on the left at Antietam), Maj.-Gen. Jesse L. Reno (k), Brig. Gen. Jacob D. Cox. Staff loss: South Mountain, k, 1.

Escort: G, 1st Me. Cav., Capt. Zebulon B. Blethen.

FIRST DIVISION, Brig.-Gen. Orlando B. Willcox.

First Brigade, Col. Benjamin C. Christ: 28th Mass., Capt. Andrew P. Caraher; 17th Mich., Col. William H. Withington; 79th N. Y., Lieut.-Col. David Morrison; 50th Pa., Maj. Edward Overton (w), Capt. William H. Diehl. Brigade loss: South Mountain, k, 26; w, 136 = 162. Antietam, k, 43; w, 198; m, 3 = 244. *Second Brigade,* Col. Thomas Welsh: 8th Mich. (transferred to First Brigade, Sept. 16th), Lieut.-Col. Frank Graves, Maj. Ralph Ely; 46th N. Y., Lieut.-Col. Joseph Gerhardt; 45th Pa., Lieut.-Col. John I. Curtin; 100th Pa., Lieut.-Col. David A. Leckey. Brigade loss: South Mountain, k, 37; w, 151 = 188. Antietam, k, 3; w, 86; m, 4 = 93. *Artillery:* 8th Mass., Capt. Asa M. Cook; E, 2d U. S., Lieut. Samuel N. Benjamin. Artillery loss: South Mountain, k, 1; w, 4 = 5. Antietam, w, 1.

SECOND DIVISION, Brig.-Gen. Samuel D. Sturgis.

First Brigade, Brig.-Gen. James Nagle: 2d Md., Lieut.-Col. J. Eugene Duryea; 6th N. H., Col. Simon G. Griffin; 9th N. H., Col. Enoch Q. Fellows; 48th Pa., Lieut.-Col. Joshua K. Sigfried. Brigade loss: South Mountain, w, 34; m, 7 = 41. Antietam, k, 39; w, 160; m, 6 = 204. *Second Brigade,* Brig.-Gen. Edward Ferrero: 21st Mass., Col. William S. Clark; 35th Mass., Col. Edward A. Wild (w), Lieut.-Col. Sumner Carruth (w); 51st N.Y., Col. Robert B. Potter; 51st Pa., Col. John F. Hartranft. Brigade loss: South Mountain, k, 10; w, 83; m, 23 = 116. Antietam, k, 95; w, 368; m, 6 = 469. *Artillery:* D, Pa., Capt. George W. Durell; E, 4th U. S., Capt. Joseph C. Clark, Jr. Artillery loss: Antietam, k, 2; w, 4 = 6.

THIRD DIVISION, Brig.-Gen. Isaac P. Rodman (m w). Staff loss: Antietam, w, 1.

First Brigade, Col. Harrison S. Fairchild: 9th N. Y., Lieut.-Col. Edgar A. Kimball; 89th N. Y., Maj. Edward Jardine; 103d N. Y., Maj. Benjamin Ringold. Brigade loss: South Mountain, k, 2; w, 18 = 20. Antietam, k, 87; w, 321; m, 47 = 455. *Second Brigade,* Col. Edward Harland: 8th Conn., Lieut.-Col. Hiram Appelman (w), Maj. John E. Ward; 11th Conn., Col. Henry W. Kingsbury (k); 16th Conn., Col. Francis Beach; 4th R. I., Col. William H. P. Steere (w), Lieut.-Col. Joseph B. Curtis. Brigade loss: Antietam, k, 133; w, 462; m, 23 = 618. *Artillery:* A, 5th U. S., Lieut. Charles P. Muhlenberg. Loss: Antietam, w, 3.

KANAWHA DIVISION, Brig.-Gen. Jacob D. Cox, Col. Eliakim P. Scammon.

First Brigade, Col. Eliakim P. Scammon, Col. Hugh Ewing: 12th Ohio, Col. Carr B. White; 23d Ohio, Lieut.-Col. Rutherford B. Hayes (w), Maj. James M. Comly; 30th Ohio, Col. Hugh Ewing, Lieut.-Col. Theodore Jones (c), Maj. George H. Hildt; 1st Ohio Battery, Capt. James R. McMullin; Gilmore's Co., W. Va. Cav., Lieut. James Abraham; Harrison's Co., W. Va. Cav., Lieut. Dennis Delaney. Brigade loss: South Mountain, k, 63; w, 201; m, 8 = 272. Antietam, k, 28; w, 134; m, 20 = 182. *Second Brigade,* Col. Augustus Moor (c), Col. George Crook: 11th Ohio, Lieut.-Col. Augustus H. Coleman (k), Maj. Lyman J. Jackson; 28th Ohio, Lieut.-Col. Gottfried Becker; 36th Ohio, Col. George Crook, Lieut.-Col. Melvin Clarke (k), Maj. E. B. Andrews; Chicago (Ill.) Dragoons, Capt. Frederick Schambeck; Ky. Battery, Capt. Seth J. Simmonds. Brigade loss: South Mountain, k, 17; w, 64; m, 3 = 84. Antietam, k, 8; w, 58; m, 7 = 73.

UNATTACHED TROOPS: 6th N. Y. Cav. (8 co's), Col. Thomas C. Devin; 3d Co. Ohio Cav., Lieut. Jonas Seamen; L and M, 3d U. S. Art'y, Capt. John Edwards, Jr.

TWELFTH ARMY CORPS, Maj.-Gen. Joseph K. F. Mansfield (k), Brig.-Gen. Alpheus S. Williams. Staff loss: Antietam, k, 1.

Escort: L, 1st Mich. Cav., Capt. Melvin Brewer.

FIRST DIVISION, Brig.-Gen. Alpheus S. Williams, Brig.-Gen. Samuel W. Crawford (w), Brig.-Gen. George H. Gordon. Staff loss: Antietam, w, 1.

First Brigade, Brig.-Gen. Samuel W. Crawford, Col. Joseph F. Knipe: 10th Me., Col. George L. Beal (w); 28th N. Y., Capt. William H. H. Mapes; 46th Pa., Col. Joseph F. Knipe, Lieut.-Col. James L. Selfridge; 124th Pa., Col. Joseph W. Hawley (w), Maj. Isaac L. Haldeman; 125th Pa., Col. Jacob Higgins; 128th Pa., Col. Samuel Croasdale (k), Lieut.-Col. William W. Hammersly (w), Maj. Joel B. Wanner. Brigade loss: Antietam, k, 88; w, 315; m, 27 = 430. *Third Brigade,* Brig.-Gen. George H. Gordon, Col. Thomas H. Ruger (w): 27th Ind., Col. Silas Colgrove; 2d Mass., Col. George L. Andrews; 13th N. J., Col. Ezra A. Carman; 107th N. Y., Col. R. B. Van Valkenburgh; Pa. Zouaves d'Afrique; 3d Wis., Col. Thomas H. Ruger. Brigade loss: Antietam, k, 71; w, 548; m, 27 = 646.

SECOND DIVISION, Brig.-Gen. George S. Greene.

First Brigade, Lieut.-Col. Hector Tyndale (w), Maj. Orrin J. Crane: 5th Ohio, Maj. John Collins; 7th Ohio, Maj. Orrin J. Crane, Capt. Frederick A. Seymour; 66th Ohio, Lieut.-Col. Eugene Powell (w); 28th Pa., Maj. Ario Pardee, Jr. Brigade loss: Antietam, k, 61; w, 308; m, 7 = 376. *Second Brigade,* Col. Henry J. Stainrook: 3d Md., Lieut.-Col. Joseph M. Sudsburg; 102d N. Y., Lieut.-Col. James C. Lane; 111th Pa., Maj. Thomas M. Walker. Brigade loss: Antietam, k, 32; w, 128; m, 16 = 176. *Third Brigade,* Col. William B. Goodrich (k), Lieut.-Col. Jonathan Austin; 3d Del., Maj. Arthur Maginnis (w), Capt. William J. McKaig; Purnell (Md.) Legion, Lieut.-Col. Benjamin L. Simpson; 60th N. Y., Lieut.-Col. Charles R. Brundage; 78th N. Y., Lieut.-Col. Jonathan Austin, Capt. Henry R. Stagg. Brigade loss: Antietam, k, 21; w, 71; m, 7 = 99. *Artillery,* Capt. Clermont L. Best: 4th Me., Capt. O'Neil W. Robinson; 6th Me., Capt. Freeman McGilvery; M, 1st N. Y., Capt. George W. Cothran; 10th N. Y., Capt. John T. Bruen; E, Pa., Capt. Joseph M. Knap; F, Pa., Capt. R. B. Hampton; F, 4th U. S., Lieut. E. D. Muhlenberg. Artillery loss: Antietam, k, 1; w, 15; m, 1 = 17.

CAVALRY DIVISION, Brig.-Gen. Alfred Pleasonton.

First Brigade, Maj. Charles J. Whiting: 5th U. S., Capt. Joseph H. McArthur; 6th U. S., Capt. William P. Sanders. Brigade loss: Antietam, w, 1. *Second Brigade,* Col. John F. Farnsworth: 8th Ill., Maj. William H. Medill; 3d Ind., Maj. George H. Chapman; 1st Mass., Capt. Casper Crowninshield; 8th Pa., Capt. Peter Keenan. Brigade loss: Antietam, w, 6. *Third Brigade,* Col. Richard H. Rush: 4th Pa., Col. James H. Childs (k), Lieut.-Col. James K. Kerr; 6th Pa., Lieut.-Col. C. Ross Smith. Brigade loss: Antietam, k, 3; w, 10 = 13. *Fourth Brigade,* Col. Andrew T. McReynolds: 1st N. Y., Maj. Alonzo W. Adams; 12th Pa., Maj. James A. Congdon. *Fifth Brigade,* Col. Benjamin F. Davis: 8th N. Y., Col. Benjamin F. Davis; 3d Pa., Lieut.-Col. Samuel W. Owen. *Unattached,* 15th Pa. (detachment), Col. William J. Palmer. Loss: Antietam, k, 1.

The total loss of the Union Army in the three principal engagements of the campaign was as follows:

	Killed.	Wounded.	Captured or missing.	Total.
South Mountain....	325	1403	85	1813
Crampton's Pass....	113	418	2	533
Antietam..........	2108	9549	753	12,410

The casualties during the entire campaign, from September 3d to 20th (exclusive of Miles's force at Harper's Ferry, for which see page 618), aggregated 2629 killed, 11,583 wounded, and 991 captured or missing = 15,203.

THE CONFEDERATE ARMY.
General Robert E. Lee.

LONGSTREET'S COMMAND, Maj.-Gen. James Longstreet. Staff loss (in the campaign): w, 2.

McLAWS'S DIVISION, Maj.-Gen. Lafayette McLaws. Staff loss (in the campaign): k, 1.

Kershaw's Brigade, Brig.-Gen. Joseph B. Kershaw: 2d S. C., Col. John D. Kennedy (w), Maj. Franklin Gaillard; 3d S. C., Col. James D. Nance; 7th S. C., Col. D. Wyatt Aiken (w), Capt. John S. Hard; 8th S. C., Col.

John W. Heuagan, Lieut.-Col. A. J. Hoole. Brigade loss (in the campaign): k, 90; w, 455; m, 6 = 551. *Cobb's Brigade*, Brig.-Gen. Howell Cobb, Lieut.-Col. C. C. Sanders, Lieut.-Col. William MacRae: 16th Ga., ——; ☆ 24th Ga., Lieut.-Col. C. C. Sanders, Maj. R. E. McMillan; Cobb's (Ga.) Legion, ——; 15th N. C., Lieut.-Col. William MacRae. Brigade loss (in the campaign): k, 76; w, 318, m, 452 = 846. *Semmes's Brigade*, Brig.-Gen. Paul J. Semmes: 10th Ga., Maj. Willis C. Holt (w), Capt. P. H. Loud; 53d Ga., Lieut.-Col. Thomas Sloan (w), Capt. S. W. Marshborne; 15th Va., Capt. E. M. Morrison (w), Capt. Edward J. Willis; 32d Va., Col. E. B. Montague. Brigade loss (in the campaign): k, 56; w, 274; m, 43 = 373. *Barksdale's Brigade*, Brig.-Gen. William Barksdale: 13th Miss., Lieut.-Col. Kennon McElroy (w); 17th Miss., Lieut.-Col. John C. Fiser; 18th Miss., Maj. J. C. Campbell (w), Lieut.-Col. William H. Luse; 21st Miss., Capt. John Sims, Col. Benjamin G. Humphreys. Brigade loss (in the campaign): k, 35; w, 272; m, 4 = 311. *Artillery*, Maj. S. P. Hamilton, Col. Henry C. Cabell: N. C. Battery, Capt. Basil C. Manly; Ga. Battery (Pulaski Art'y), Capt. John P. W. Read; Va. Battery (Richmond Fayette Art'y), Capt. M. C. Macon; Va. Battery (1st Co. Richmond Howitzers), Capt. E. S. McCarthy; Ga. Battery (Troup Art'y), Capt. H. H. Carlton. (Loss of the artillery included with that of the brigades to which attached.)

ANDERSON'S DIVISION, Maj.-Gen. Richard H. Anderson (w), Brig.-Gen. Roger A. Pryor. Staff loss (in the campaign): w, 1.

Wilcox's Brigade, Col. Alfred Cumming: 8th Ala., ——; 9th Ala., ——; 10th Ala., ——; 11th Ala., ——. Brigade loss (in the campaign): k, 34; w, 181; m, 29 = 244. *Mahone's Brigade*, Col. W. A. Parham: 6th Va., ——; 12th Va., ——; 16th Va., ——; 41st Va., ——; 61st Va., ——. Brigade loss (in the campaign): k, 8; w, 92; m, 127 = 227. *Featherston's Brigade*, Col. Carnot Posey: 12th Miss., ——; 16th Miss., Capt. A. M. Feltus; 19th Miss., ——; 2d Miss. Battalion, ——. Brigade loss (in the campaign): k, 45; w, 238; m, 36 = 319. *Armistead's Brigade*, Brig.-Gen. Lewis A. Armistead, Col. J. G. Hodges: 9th Va., ——; 14th Va., Col. J. G. Hodges; 38th Va., ——; 53d Va., ——; 57th Va., ——. Brigade loss (in the campaign): k, 5; w, 29; m, 1 = 35. *Pryor's Brigade*, Brig.-Gen. Roger A. Pryor: 14th Ala., ——; 2d Fla., ——; 8th Fla., ——; 3d Va., ——. Brigade loss (in the campaign): k, 48; w, 285; m, 49 = 382. *Wright's Brigade*, Brig.-Gen. Ambrose R. Wright: 44th Ala., ——; 3d Ga., ——; 22d Ga., ——; 48th Ga., ——. Brigade loss (in the campaign): k, 32; w, 192; m, 34 = 258. *Artillery*, Maj. J. S. Saunders: La. Battery (Donaldsville Art'y), Capt. Victor Maurin; Va. Battery (Huger's); Va. Battery, Lieut. C. R. Phelps; Va. Battery (Thompson's or Grimes's). (Loss of artillery not separately reported.)

JONES'S DIVISION, Brig.-Gen. David R. Jones.

Toombs's Brigade, Brig.-Gen. R. Toombs (in temporary command of a division), Col. Henry L. Benning: 2d Ga., Lieut.-Col. William R Holmes (k), Maj. Skidmore Harris (w); 15th Ga., Col. William T. Millican (k); 17th Ga., Capt. J. A. McGregor; 20th Ga., Col. John B. Cumming. Brigade loss (in the campaign): k, 16; w, 122; m, 22 = 160. *Drayton's Brigade*, Brig.-Gen. Thomas F. Drayton: 50th Ga., Lieut.-Col. F. Kearse; 51st Ga., ——; 15th S. C., Col. W. D. De Saussure. Brigade loss (in the campaign): k, 82; w, 280; m, 179 = 541. *Pickett's Brigade*, Brig.-Gen. Richard B. Garnett: 8th Va., Col. Eppa Hunton; 18th Va., Maj. George C. Cabell; 19th Va., Col. J. B. Strange (m w), Capt. John L. Cochran, Lieut. William N. Wood; 28th Va., Capt. W. L. Wingfield; 56th Va., Col. William D. Stuart, Capt. John B. McPhail. Brigade loss (in the campaign): k, 30; w, 199; m, 32 = 261. *Kemper's Brigade*, Brig.-Gen. James L. Kemper: 1st Va., ——; 7th Va., ——; 11th Va., Maj. Adam Clement; 17th Va., Col. Montgomery D. Corse (w), Maj. Arthur Herbert; 24th Va., ——. Brigade loss (in the campaign): k, 15; w, 102; m, 27 = 144. *Jenkins's Brigade*, Col. Joseph Walker: 1st S. C., Lieut.-Col. D. Livingston (w); 2d S. C. (rifles), ——; 5th S. C., Capt. T. C. Beckham; 6th S. C., Lieut.-Col. J. M. Steedman, Capt. E. B. Cantey (w); 4th S. C. Battalion, ——; Palmetto (S. C.) Sharp-shooters, ——. Brigade loss (in the campaign): k, 27; w, 196; m, 12 = 235. *Anderson's Brigade*, Col. George T. Anderson: 1st Ga. (Regulars), Col. William J. Magill; 7th Ga., ——; 8th Ga., ——; 9th Ga., ——; 11th Ga., Maj. F. H. Little; Va. Battery (Wise Art'y), Capt. J. S. Brown (w). Brigade loss (in the campaign): k, 8; w, 80; m, 6 = 94.

WALKER'S DIVISION, Brig.-Gen. John G. Walker.

Walker's Brigade, Col. Van H. Manning (w), Col. E. D. Hall: 3d Ark., Capt. John W. Reedy; 27th N. C., Col. John R. Cooke; 46th N. C., Col. E. D. Hall, Lieut.-Col. William A. Jenkins; 48th N. C., Col. R. C. Hill; 30th Va., ——; Va. Battery, Capt. Thomas B. French. Brigade loss (in the campaign): k, 140; w, 684; m, 93 = 917. *Ransom's Brigade*, Brig.-Gen. Robert Ransom, Jr.: 24th N. C., Lieut.-Col. John L. Harris; 25th N. C., Col. H. M. Rutledge; 35th N. C., Col. M. W. Ransom; 49th N. C., Lieut.-Col. Lee M. McAfee; Va. Battery, Capt. James R. Branch. Brigade loss (in the campaign): k, 41; w, 141; m, 4 = 186.

HOOD'S DIVISION, Brig.-Gen. John B. Hood

Hood's Brigade, Col. W. T. Wofford: 18th Ga., Lieut.-Col. S. Z. Ruff; Hampton (S. C.) Legion, Lieut.-Col. M. W. Gary; 1st Tex., Lieut.-Col. P. A. Work; 4th Tex., Lieut.-Col. B. F. Carter; 5th Tex., Capt. Ike N. M. Turner. Brigade loss (in the campaign): k, 69; w, 417; m, 62 = 548. *Law's Brigade*, Col. E. McIver Law: 4th Ala., Lieut.-Col. O. K. McLemore (m w), Capt. L. H. Scruggs (w); 2d Miss., Col. J. M. Stone (w), 11th Miss., Col. P. F. Liddell (m w), Lieut.-Col. S. F. Butler (w); 6th N. C., Maj. Robert F. Webb (w). Brigade loss (in the campaign): k, 53; w, 386; m, 25 = 464. *Artillery*, Maj. B. W. Frobel: S. C. Battery (German Art'y), Capt. W. K. Bachman; S. C. Battery (Palmetto Art'y), Capt. H. R. Garden; N. C. Battery (Rowan Art'y), Capt. James Reilly. Artillery loss (in the campaign): k, 4; w, 19 = 23.

EVANS'S BRIGADE, Brig.-Gen. Nathan G. Evans (in temporary command of a division), Col. P. F. Stevens: 17th S. C., Col. F. W. McMaster; 18th S. C., Col. W. H. Wallace; 22d S. C., Lieut.-Col. Thomas C. Watkins (k), Maj. M. Hilton; 23d S. C., Capt. S. A. Durham (w), Lieut. E. R. White; Holcombe's (S. C.) Legion, ——; S. C. Battery (Macbeth Art'y), Capt. R. Boyce. Brigade loss (in the campaign): k, 40; w, 185; m, 65 = 290.

ARTILLERY. *Washington (La.) Artillery*, Col. J. B. Walton: 1st Co., Capt. C. W. Squires; 2d Co., Capt. J. B. Richardson; 3d Co., Capt. M. B. Miller; 4th Co., Capt. B. F. Eshleman. Loss (in campaign): k, 4; w, 28; m, 2, = 34. *Lee's Battalion*, Col. S. D. Lee: Va. Battery (Ashland Art'y), Capt. Pichegru Woolfolk, Jr.; Va. Battery (Bedford Art'y), Capt. T. C. Jordan; S. C. Battery (Brooks's Art'y), Lieut. William Elliott; Va. Battery, Capt. J. L. Eubank; La. Battery (Madison Light Art'y), Capt. Geo. V. Moody; Va. Battery, Capt. W. W. Parker. Loss (in the campaign): k, 11; w, 75 = 86.

JACKSON'S COMMAND, Maj.-Gen. T. J. Jackson.

EWELL'S DIVISION, Brig.-Gen. A. R. Lawton (w), Brig.-Gen. Jubal A. Early. Staff loss: Antietam w, 2.

Lawton's Brigade, Col. M. Douglass (k), Maj. J. H. Lowe, Col. John H. Lamar: 13th Ga., ——; 26th Ga., ——; 31st Ga., Lieut.-Col. J. T. Crowder; 38th Ga., ——; 60th Ga., ——; 61st Ga., Col. John H. Lamar. Brigade loss: Antietam, k, 106; w, 440; m, 21 = 567. Shepherdstown, w, 7. *Early's Brigade*, Brig.-Gen. Jubal A. Early, Col. William Smith (w): 13th Va., Capt. F. V. Winston; 25th Va., ——; 31st Va., ——; 44th Va., ——; 49th Va., Col. William Smith; 52d Va., Col. M. G. Harman; 58th Va., ——. Brigade loss: Antietam, k, 18; w, 167; m, 9 = 194. *Trimble's Brigade*, Col. James A. Walker (w): 15th Ala., Capt. I. B. Feagin; 12th Ga., Capt. James G. Rodgers (k); 21st Ga., Maj. Thomas C. Glover (w); 21st N. C. (1st N. C. Battalion attached), Capt. F. P. Miller (k); Va. Battery, Capt. John R. Johnson. Brigade loss: Antietam, k, 27; w, 202; m, 8 = 237. Shepherdstown, w, 1.

Hays's Brigade, Col. H. B. Strong, Brig.-Gen. Harry T. Hays: 5th La., ——; 6th La., Col. H. B. Strong (k); 7th La., ——; 8th La., ——; 14th La., ——; La. Battery, Capt. Louis E. D'Aquin. Brigade loss: Antietam, k, 45;

w, 289; m, 2 = 336. *Artillery,* Maj. A. R. Courtney: 1st Md. Battery, Capt. William F. Dement; Md. Battery (Chesapeake Art'y), Capt. William D. Brown; Va. Battery (Courtney Art'y), Capt. J. W. Latimer; Va. Battery (Staunton Art'y), Lieut. A. W. Garber. Artillery not engaged at Antietam.

LIGHT DIVISION, Maj.-Gen. Ambrose P. Hill.

Branch's Brigade, Brig.-Gen. L. O'B. Branch (k), Col. James H. Lane; 7th N. C., ——; 18th N. C., Lieut.-Col. T. J. Purdie; 28th N. C., Col. James H. Lane; 33d N. C., ; 37th N. C., ——. Brigade loss: Harper's Ferry, w, 4. Antietam, k, 21; w, 79; m, 4 = 104. Shepherdstown, k, 3; w, 71 = 74. *Gregg's Brigade,* Brig.-Gen. Maxcy Gregg (w); 1st S. C. (Prov. Army), Col. D. H Hamilton; 1st S. C. (Rifles), Lieut.-Col. James M. Perrin (w); 12th S C., Col. Dixon Barnes (k), Maj. W. H. McCorkle; 13th S. C., Col. O. E. Edwards; 14th S. C., Lieut.-Col. W. D. Simpson. Brigade loss: Antietam, k, 28; w, 135; m, 2 = 165. Shepherdstown, k, 10; w, 53 = 63. *Field's Brigade,* Col. J M. Brockenbrough; 40th Va., ——; 47th Va., ——; 55th Va., ——; 22d Va. Battalion, ——. Brigade loss not separately reported. *Archer's Brigade,* Brig.-Gen. James J. Archer, Col. Peter Turney; 5th Ala. Battalion, Capt. Charles M. Hooper; 19th Ga., Maj. James H. Neal, Capt. F. M. Johnston; 1st Tenn. (Prov. Army), Col. Peter Turney; 7th Tenn., Maj. S. G. Shepard, Lieut. G. A. Howard; 14th Tenn., Lieut.-Col. J. W. Lockert, Col. William McComb (w). Brigade loss: Harper's Ferry, k, 1; w, 22 = 23. Antietam, k, 15; w, 90 = 105. Shepherdstown, k, 6; w, 49 = 55. *Pender's Brigade,* Brig.-Gen. William D. Pender; 16th N. C., Lieut.-Col. W. A. Stowe; 23d N. C., Maj. C. C. Cole; 34th N. C., ——; 38th N. C., ——. Brigade loss: Harper's Ferry, k, 2; w, 20 = 22. Antietam, k, 2; w, 28 = 30. Shepherdstown, k, 8; w, 55 = 63. *Thomas's Brigade,* Col. Edward L. Thomas; 14th Ga., Col. R. W. Folsom; 35th Ga., ——; 45th Ga., Maj. W. L. Grice; 49th Ga., Lieut.-Col. S. M. Manning. Brigade not at Antietam; losses elsewhere not separately reported. *Artillery,* Lieut.-Col. R. L. Walker; Va. Battery, Capt. William G. Crenshaw; Va. Battery (Fredericksburg Art'y), Capt. Carter M. Braxton, Lieut. E. A. Marye; Va. Battery (Letcher Art'y), Capt. Greenlee Davidson; Va. Battery (Purcell Art'y), Capt. W. J. Pegram (w); S. C. Battery (Pee Dee Art'y), Capt. D. G. McIntosh. Artillery loss not separately reported. Division loss (in the campaign): k, 99; w, 605; m, 6 = 710. JACKSON'S DIVISION, Brig.-Gen. John R. Jones (w), Brig.-Gen. William E. Starke (k), Col. A. J. Grigsby. Staff loss: Antietam, k, 1; m, 1 = 2.

Winder's Brigade, Col. A. J. Grigsby, Lieut.-Col. R. D. Gardner, Maj. H. J. Williams; 2d Va. (detached at Martinsburg), Capt. R. T. Colston; 4th Va., Lieut.-Col. R. D. Gardner; 5th Va., Maj. H. J. Williams; 27th Va., Capt. Frank C. Wilson; 33d Va., Capt. Jacob B. Golladay, Lieut. David H. Walton. Brigade loss: Antietam, k, 11; w, 77 = 88. *Taliaferro's Brigade,* Col. E. T. H. Warren, Col. James W. Jackson, Col. James L. Sheffield; 47th Ala., Col. James W. Jackson; 48th Ala., Col. James L. Sheffield; 10th Va., ——; 23d Va., ——; 37th Va., ——. Brigade loss: Antietam, k, 41; w, 132 = 173. *Jones's Brigade,* Col. Bradley T. Johnson, Capt. John E. Penn (w), Capt. A. C. Page (w), Capt. R. W. Withers; 21st Va., Capt. A. C. Page; 42d Va., Capt. R. W. Withers; 48th Va., Capt. John H. Candler; 1st Va. Battalion, Lieut. C. A. Davidson. Brigade loss not separately reported. *Starke's Brigade,* Brig.-Gen. William E. Starke, Col. Leroy A. Stafford (w), Col. Edmund Pendleton; 1st La., Lieut.-Col. M. Nolan (w); 2d La., Col. J. M. Williams (w); 9th La., Col. Leroy A. Stafford; 10th La., Capt. H. D. Monier; 15th La., Col. Edmund Pendleton; 1st La. Battalion (Zouaves), Lieut.-Col. G. Coppens. Brigade loss (partial): Antietam, k, 81; w, 189; m, 17 = 287. *Artillery,* Maj. L. M. Shumaker; Md. Battery Baltimore Battery), Capt. J. B. Brockenbrough; Va. Battery (Alleghany Art'y), Capt. Joseph Carpenter; Va. Battery (Danville Art'y), Capt. George W. Wooding; Va. Battery (Hampden Art'y), Capt. William H. Caskie; Va. Battery (Lee Battery), Capt. Charles I. Raine; Va. Battery (Rockbridge Art'y), Capt. W. T. Poague. Artillery loss not separately reported.

HILL'S DIVISION, Maj.-Gen. Daniel H. Hill.

Ripley's Brigade, Brig.-Gen. Roswell S. Ripley (w), Col. George Doles; 4th Ga., Col. George Doles; 44th Ga., Capt. John C. Key; 1st N. C., Lieut.-Col. Hamilton A. Brown; 3d N. C., Col. William L. De Rosset (w). Brigade loss: South Mountain and Antietam, k, 110; w, 506; m, 124 = 740. *Rodes's Brigade,* Brig.-Gen. R. E. Rodes (w); 3d Ala., Col. C. A. Battle; 5th Ala., Maj. E. L. Hobson; 6th Ala., Col. J. B. Gordon (w), Lieut.-Col. J. N. Lightfoot (w); 12th Ala., Col. B. B. Gayle (k); 26th Ala., Col. E. A. O'Neal (w). Brigade loss: South Mountain, k, 61; w, 157; m, 204 = 422. Antietam, k, 50; w, 132; m, 21 = 203. *Garland's Brigade,* Brig.-Gen. Samuel Garland, Jr., (k), Col. D. K. McRae (w); 5th N. C., Col. D. K. McRae, Capt. Thomas M. Garrett; 12th N. C., Capt. S. Snow; 13th N. C., Lieut.-Col. Thomas Ruffin, Jr. (w), Capt. J. H. Hyman; 20th N. C., Col. Alfred Iverson; 23d N. C., Col. Daniel H. Christie. Brigade loss: South Mountain and Antietam, k, 46; w, 210; m, 187 = 443. *Anderson's Brigade,* Brig.-Gen. George B. Anderson (m w), Col. R. T. Bennett (w); 2d N. C., Col. C. C. Tew (k), Capt. G. M. Roberts; 4th N. C., Col. Bryan Grimes, Capt. W. T. Marsh (k), Capt. D. P. Latham (k); 14th N. C., Col. R. T. Bennett, Lieut.-Col. William A. Johnston (w); 30th N. C., Col. F. M. Parker (w), Maj. William W. Sillers. Brigade loss: South Mountain and Antietam, k, 64; w, 229; m, 202 = 565. *Colquitt's Brigade,* Col. A. H. Colquitt; 13th Ala., Col. B. D. Fry (w), Lieut.-Col. W. H. Betts (w); 6th Ga., Lieut.-Col. J. M. Newton (k); 23d Ga., Col. W. P. Barclay (k); 27th Ga., Col. Levi B. Smith (k); 28th Ga., Maj. Tully Graybill, Capt. N. J. Garrison (w). Brigade loss: South Mountain and Antietam, k, 129; w, 518; m, 184 = 831. *Artillery,* Maj. S. F Pierson: Ala. Battery, Capt. R. A. Hardaway; Ala. Battery (Jeff Davis Art'y), Capt. J. W. Bondurant; Va. Battery, Capt. William B. Jones; Va. Battery (King William Art'y), Capt. Thomas H. Carter. Brigade loss: South Mountain and Antietam, k, 4; w, 30; m, 3 = 37.

RESERVE ARTILLERY, Brig.-Gen. William N. Pendleton.

Brown's Battalion (1st Va. Art'y), Col. J. Thompson Brown: Powhatan Art'y, Capt. Willis J. Dance; 2d Co. Richmond Howitzers, Capt. D. Watson; 3d Co. Richmond Howitzers, Capt. Benjamin H. Smith, Jr.; Salem Art'y, Capt. A. Hupp; Williamsburg Art'y, Capt. John A. Coke. *Cutts's Battalion,* Lieut.-Col. A. S. Cutts: Ga. Battery, Capt. James Ap Blackshear; Ga. Battery (Irwin Art'y), Capt. John Lane; N. C. Battery, Capt. W. P. Lloyd; Ga. Battery, Capt. G. M. Patterson; Ga. Battery, Capt. H. M. Ross. *Jones's Battalion,* Maj. H. P. Jones: Va. Battery (Morris Art'y), Capt. R. C. M. Page; Va. Battery (Orange Art'y), Capt. Jefferson Peyton; Va. Battery (Turner's); Va. Battery, Capt. A Wimbish. *Nelson's Battalion,* Maj. William Nelson: Va. Battery (Amherst Art'y), Capt. T. J. Kirkpatrick; Va. Battery (Fluvanna Art'y), Capt. John J. Ancell; Va. Battery, Capt. Charles T. Huckstep; Va. Battery, Capt. Marmaduke Johnson; Ga. Battery (Milledge Art'y), Capt. John Milledge. *Miscellaneous:* Va. Battery, Capt. W. E. Cutshaw; Va. Battery (Dixie Art'y), Capt. W. H. Chapman; Va. Battery (Magruder Art'y), Capt. T. J. Page, Jr.; Va. Battery, Capt. W. H. Rice.

CAVALRY, Maj.-Gen. James E. B. Stuart.

Hampton's Brigade, Brig.-Gen. Wade Hampton: 1st N. C., Col. L. S. Baker; 2d S. C., Col. M. C. Butler; 10th Va., ——; Cobb's (Ga.) Legion, Lieut.-Col. P. M. B. Young (w), Maj. William G. Delony; Jeff. Davis (Miss.) Legion, Lieut.-Col. W. T. Martin. *Lee's Brigade,* Brig.-Gen. Fitzhugh Lee: 1st Va., Lieut.-Col. L. T. Brien; 3d Va., Lieut.-Col. John T. Thornton (m w); 4th Va., Col. W. C. Wickham; 5th Va., Col. Thomas L. Rosser; 9th Va., ——. *Robertson's Brigade,* Col. Thomas T. Munford; 2d Va., Lieut.-Col. Richard H. Burks; 7th Va., Capt. S. B. Myers; 12th Va., Col. A. W. Harman. *Horse Artillery:* Va. Battery, Capt. R. P. Chew; S. C. Battery, Capt. J. F. Hart; Va. Battery, Capt. John Pelham. Cavalry and Horse Artillery loss (in the campaign): k, 10; w, 45; m, 6 = 61.

According to the report of Lee's medical director (Dr. Guild), there was a loss of 1567 killed and 8724 wounded in the battles of South Mountain, Crampton's Pass, Harper's Ferry, Sharpsburg (or Antietam), and Shepherdstown. Dr. Guild does not give the number of missing and prisoners, and he also omits the casualties in Jones's brigade of Jackson's division, Rodes's brigade of D. H. Hill's division, and the whole of A. P. Hill's division. The corps and division commanders report 1890 killed, 9770 wounded, and 2304 captured or missing during the campaign, making a total of 13,964. Estimating four-fifths of these for the battle of Antietam, we have the following comparative result in that engagement:

	Killed.	Wounded.	Captured or Missing.	Total.
Union Army	... 2108	9549	753	12,410
Confederate Army	... 1512	7816	1844	11,172

There is not the slightest reason for doubting that many of the "missing" of Lee's army were killed, and that if the number could be ascertained, it would materially increase that class of casualties. General McClellan (Vol. XIX., Pt. 1, p. 67, "Official Records"), says that "about 2700 of the enemy's dead were . . . counted and buried upon the battle-field of Antietam"; also, that "a portion of their dead had been previously buried by the enemy."

RELATIVE STRENGTH OF THE ARMIES.

According to McClellan's report the number of combatants in his command was 87,164; but the brunt of the battle was borne by not above 60,000 men.

Comparing the *available* strength of the two armies, undoubtedly McClellan's doubled that of Lee's. In his official report General Lee says, "This great battle was fought by less than 40,000 men on our side."

THE FINDING OF LEE'S LOST ORDER.

BY SILAS COLGROVE, BREVET BRIGADIER-GENERAL, U. S. V.

IN reply to your request for the particulars of the finding of General Lee's lost dispatch, "Special Orders No. 191," and the manner in which it reached General McClellan, I beg leave to submit the following account:

The Twelfth Army Corps arrived at Frederick, Maryland, about noon on the 13th of September, 1862. The 27th Indiana Volunteers, of which I was colonel at that date, belonged to the Third Brigade, First Division, of that corps.

We stacked arms on the same ground that had been occupied by General D. H. Hill's division the evening before.

Within a very few minutes after halting, the order was brought to me by First Sergeant John M. Bloss and Private B. W. Mitchell, of Company F, 27th Indiana Volunteers, who stated that it was found by Private Mitchell near where they had stacked arms. When I received the order it was wrapped around three cigars, and Private Mitchell stated that it was in that condition when found by him. [See p. 664.]

General A. S. Williams was in command of our division. I immediately took the order to his headquarters, and delivered it to Colonel S. E. Pittman, General Williams's adjutant-general.

The order was signed by Colonel Chilton, General Lee's adjutant-general, and the signature was at once recognized by Colonel Pittman, who had served with Colonel Chilton at Detroit, Michigan, before the war, and was acquainted with his handwriting. It was at once taken to General McClellan's headquarters by Colonel Pittman. It was a general order giving directions for the movement of General Lee's entire army, designating the route and objective point of each corps. Within an hour after finding the dispatch, General McClellan's whole army was on the move, and the enemy were overtaken next day, the 14th, at South Mountain, and the battle of that name was fought. During the night of the 14th General Lee's army fell back toward the Potomac River, General McClellan following the next day. On the 16th they were overtaken again, and the battle of Antietam was fought mainly on the 17th. General D. H. Hill says in his article in the May "Century," that the battle of South Mountain was fought in order to give General Lee time to move his trains, which were then parked in the neighborhood of Boonsboro'. It is evident from General Lee's movements from the time he left Frederick City, that he intended to recross the Potomac without hazarding a battle in Maryland, and had it not been for the finding of this lost order, the battle of South Mountain, and probably that of Antietam, would not have been fought.

For confirmation of the above statements in regard to the finding of the dispatch, you are respectfully referred to Colonel Samuel E. Pittman, of Detroit, Michigan, and Captain John M. Bloss, of Muncie, Indiana.

WASHINGTON, D. C., June 2d, 1886.

NOTE.— Mr. W. A. Mitchell, the son of Private Mitchell, who, as General Silas Colgrove describes above, was the finder of Lee's order, writes to say that his father was severely wounded at Antietam. After eight months in hospital he completed his term of enlistment, three years, and three years after his discharge died at his home in Bartholomew, Indiana. As his family were then destitute, some efforts are said to have been made to procure a pension for the widow, but General Colgrove in a letter to the editor of the "Century," dated Washington, November 15th, 1886, states that "neither the soldier nor the widow has ever filed a claim for pension, and any seeming failure of recognition is not due to neglect on the part of the Pension Office."

The following letter from General McClellan to the son is of interest:

"TRENTON, NEW JERSEY, November 18th, 1879. W. A. MITCHELL, ESQ., LA CYGNE, KANSAS.— DEAR SIR: Your letter of the 9th inst. has reached me. I cannot, at this interval of time, recall the name of the finder of the papers to which you refer; it is doubtful whether I ever knew the name. All that I can say is that on or about the 13th of September, 1862,— just before the battles of South Mountain and Antietam,— there was handed to me by a member of my staff a copy (original) of one of General Lee's orders of march, directed to General D. H. Hill, which order developed General Lee's intended operations for the next few days, and was of very great service to me in enabling me to direct the movements of my own troops accordingly. This order was stated to have been found on one of the abandoned camp-grounds of the Confederate troops by a private soldier, and, as I think, of an Indiana regiment. Whoever found the order in question and transmitted it to the headquarters showed intelligence and deserved marked reward, for he rendered an infinite service. The widow of that soldier should have her pension without a day's delay. Regretting that it is not in my power to give the name of the finder of the order, I am very truly yours, GEO. B. MCCLELLAN." EDITORS.

JACKSON'S CAPTURE OF HARPER'S FERRY.[1]

BY JOHN G. WALKER, MAJOR-GENERAL, C. S. A.

WHEN General Lee began his campaign against Pope I was in command of a division (of three brigades) which was not a part of either of the two corps of the Army of Northern Virginia. I was left on the James for the defense of Richmond, but after the evacuation of Harrison's Landing by McClellan's army [August 14th to 20th], the Confederate capital being no longer threatened, I was ordered by the Secretary of War to leave one of my brigades at Richmond and proceed with the other two to join General Lee in the field. Leaving Daniel's brigade on the James, I marched northward with my old brigade, the strongest and the one which had seen most service, at that time commanded by Colonel Van H. Manning, and with the brigade of General Robert Ransom.

It was our hope that we should overtake General Lee in time to take part in the fight with Pope; but when we reached the field of Bull Run we found it strewn with the still unburied dead of Pope's army, and learned that Lee was pushing for the fords of the Upper Potomac. Following him rapidly, on the night of the 6th of September my division reached the vicinity of Leesburg, and the next morning crossed the Potomac at Cheek's Ford, at the mouth of the Monocacy, and about three miles above White's Ford, where Stonewall Jackson had crossed.

At Cheek's Ford I overtook G. B. Anderson's brigade of D. H. Hill's division and crossed into Maryland with it. The next day we reached the neighborhood of Frederick. I went at once to General Lee, who was alone. After listening to my report, he said that as I had a division which would often, perhaps, be ordered on detached service, an intelligent performance of my duty might require a knowledge of the ulterior purposes and objects of the campaign.

"Here," said he, tracing with his finger on a large map, "is the line of our communications, from Rapidan Station to Manassas, thence to Frederick. It is too near the Potomac, and is liable to be cut any day by the enemy's cavalry. I have therefore given orders to move the line back into the Valley of Virginia, by way of Staunton, Harrisonburg, and Winchester, entering Maryland at Shepherdstown. [See map, p. 553.]

"I wish you to return to the mouth of the Monocacy and effectually destroy the aqueduct of the Chesapeake and Ohio canal. By the time that is accomplished you will receive orders to coöperate in the capture of Harper's Ferry, and you will not return here, but, after the capture of Harper's Ferry, will rejoin us at Hagerstown, where the army will be concentrated. My information is that there are between 10,000 and 12,000 men at Harper's Ferry, and 3000 at Martinsburg. The latter may escape toward Cumberland, but I think the chances are that they will take refuge at Harper's Ferry and be captured.

[1] For other Harper's Ferry pictures, see Vol. I., pp. 115 to 120, and Vol. II., p. 155.—EDITORS.

"

"Besides the men and material of war which we shall capture at Harper's Ferry, the position is necessary to us, not to garrison and hold, but because in the hands of the enemy it would be a break in our new line of communications with Richmond.

"A few days' rest at Hagerstown will be of great service to our men. Hundreds of them are barefooted, and nearly all of them are ragged. I hope to get shoes and clothing for the most needy. But the best of it will be that the short delay will enable us to get up our stragglers — not stragglers from a shirking disposition, but simply from inability to keep up with their commands. ⚓ I believe there are not less than from eight to ten thousand of them between here and Rapidan Station. Besides these we shall be able to get a large number of recruits who have been accumulating at Richmond for some weeks. I have now requested that they be sent forward to join us. They ought to reach us at Hagerstown. We shall then have a very good army, and," he smilingly added, "one that I think will be able to give a good account of itself.

"In ten days from now," he continued, "if the military situation is then what I confidently expect it to be after the capture of Harper's Ferry, I shall concentrate the army at Hagerstown, effectually destroy the Baltimore and Ohio road, and march to this point," placing his finger at Harrisburg, Pennsylvania. "That is the objective point of the campaign. You remember, no doubt, the long bridge of the Pennsylvania railroad over the Susquehanna, a few miles west of Harrisburg. Well, I wish effectually to destroy that bridge, which will disable the Pennsylvania railroad for a long time. With the Baltimore and Ohio in our possession, and the Pennsylvania railroad broken up, there will remain to the enemy but one route of communication with the West, and that very circuitous, by way of the Lakes. After that I can turn my attention to Philadelphia, Baltimore, or Washington, as may seem best for our interests."

I was very much astonished at this announcement, and I suppose he observed it, for he turned to me and said:

"You doubtless regard it hazardous to leave McClellan practically on my line of communication, and to march into the heart of the enemy's country?" I admitted that such a thought had occurred to me.

"Are you acquainted with General McClellan?" he inquired. I replied that we had served together in the Mexican war, under General Scott, but that I had seen but little of him since that time.

⚓ During the Maryland campaign the Federals as well as the Confederates were greatly weakened by straggling. On October 7th, twenty days after the battle of Antietam, General Halleck, in a letter to General McClellan, said:

"Straggling is the great curse of the army, and must be checked by severe measures. . . . I think, myself, that shooting them while in the act of straggling from their commands, is the only effective remedy that can be applied. If you apply the remedy you will be sustained here. . . . The country is becoming very impatient at the want of activity of your army, and we must push it on. . . . There is a decided want of legs in our troops. . . . The real difficulty is they are not sufficiently exercised in marching; they lie still in camp too long. After a hard march one day is time enough to rest. Lying still beyond that time does not rest the men. If we compare the average distances marched per month by our troops for the last year, with that of the rebels, or with European armies in the field, we will see why our troops march no better. They are not sufficiently exercised to make them good and efficient soldiers." EDITORS.

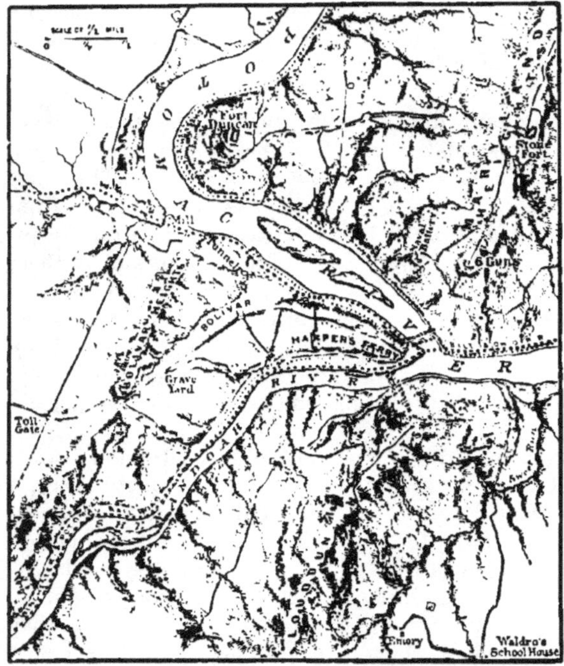

MAP OF THE DEFENSES AND APPROACHES OF HARPER'S FERRY.

"He is an able general but a very cautious one. His enemies among his own people think him too much so. His army is in a very demoralized and chaotic condition, and will not be prepared for offensive operations —or he will not think it so—for three or four weeks. Before that time I hope to be on the Susquehanna."

Our conversation was interrupted at this point by the arrival of Stonewall Jackson, and after a few minutes Lee and Jackson turned to the subject of the capture of Harper's Ferry. I remember Jackson seemed in high spirits, and even indulged in a little mild pleasantry about his long neglect of his friends in "the Valley," General Lee replying that Jackson had "some friends" in that region who would not, he feared, be delighted to see him.

The arrival of a party of ladies from Frederick and vicinity, to pay their respects to Lee and Jackson, put an end to the conversation, and soon after I took my departure.

Retracing our steps toward the Potomac, at 10 P. M. of the 9th my division arrived at the aqueduct which conveys the waters of the Chesapeake and Ohio canal across the Monocacy. The attempted work of destruction began, but so admirably was the aqueduct constructed and cemented that it was found to be virtually a solid mass of granite. Not a seam or crevice could be discovered in which to insert the point of a crow-bar, and the only resource was in blasting. But the drills furnished to my engineer were too dull and the granite too hard, and after several hours of zealous but ineffectual effort the attempt had to be abandoned. Dynamite had not then been invented, so we were foiled in our purpose, and about 3 o'clock A. M. of the 10th went into bivouac about two miles and a half west of the Monocacy.

Late in the afternoon a courier from General Lee delivered me a copy of his famous "Special Orders No. 191," directing me to coöperate with Jackson and McLaws in the capture of Harper's Ferry. That order contained the most precise and detailed information respecting the position, at its date, of every portion of the Confederate army,— where it would be during the next five or six days at least,—and inferentially revealed the ulterior designs of the Confederate commander. Possessed of the information it contained, the Federal general would be enabled to throw the weight of his whole force on that small portion of the Confederate army then with Lee, before Jackson, McLaws, and Walker could effect the capture of Harper's Ferry and go to its assistance.

General McClellan did get possession, on the 13th of September, of a copy of this order, addressed to General D. H. Hill. In what manner this happened is not positively known. General Bradley T. Johnson says that there is a tradition in Frederick that General Hill was seen to drop a paper in the streets of that town, which was supposed to be the order in question. The Comte de Paris says it was found in a house in Frederick which had been occupied by General Hill. But General Hill informed me, two years after the war, that he never received the order, and never knew of its existence until he read it in McClellan's report.‡

To whatever circumstance General McClellan owed its possession, it certainly enabled him to thwart General Lee's designs for the invasion of Pennsylvania, or a movement upon Washington. But that he obtained all the advantages he might have done will hardly be contended for by General McClellan's warmest admirer. By the exercise of greater energy he might easily have crushed Lee on the afternoon of the 15th or early on the 16th, before the arrival of Jackson from Harper's Ferry. On receiving my copy of the order I was so impressed with the disastrous consequence which might result from its loss that I pinned it securely in an inside pocket. In speaking with General Longstreet on this subject afterward, he remarked that the same thought had occurred to him, and that, as an absolutely sure precaution, he memorized the order and then "chewed it up."

Informed of the presence of a superior Federal force at Cheek's Ford, where I was ordered to pass the Potomac, and learning that the crossing at the Point of Rocks was practicable, I moved my division to that place and succeeded in landing everything safe on the Virginia shore by daylight of the 11th.

About the same time a heavy rain set in, and as the men were much exhausted by their night march, I put them into bivouac. I would here remark that the Army of Northern Virginia had long since discarded their tents, capacious trunks, carpet-bags, bowie-knives, mill-saw swords, and six-shooters, and had reduced their "kits" to the simplest elements and smallest dimensions.

Resuming our march on the morning of the 12th, we reached Hillsboro' and halted for the night. During the night I was sent for from the village inn by a woman who claimed my attendance on the ground that she was just from Washington, and had very important information to give me. Answering the call, I found seated in the hotel parlor a young woman of perhaps twenty-five, of rather prepossessing appearance, who claimed to have left

‡ See General D. H. Hill's statement, p. 570; General Colgrove's, p. 603, and the text of the order, p. 604.—EDITORS.

VIEW FROM WALKER'S POSITION ON LOUDOUN HEIGHTS OF THE UNION CAMP AND POSITION ON MARYLAND HEIGHTS, FROM A WAR-TIME SKETCH.

Washington the morning before, with important information from "our friends" in the Federal capital which she could communicate only to General Lee himself, and wished to know from me where he could be found. I saw at once that I had to do with a Federal spy; but as I did not wish to be encumbered with a woman prisoner, I professed ignorance of General Lee's whereabouts and advised her to remain quietly at the hotel, as I should, no doubt, have some information for her the next morning. Before resuming our march the next day I sent her under guard to Leesburg, directing the provost marshal at that place to hold her for three or four days and then release her.

Resuming the march at daylight on the 13th, we reached the foot of Loudoun Heights about 10 o'clock. Here I was joined by a detachment of signal men and Captain White's company of Maryland cavalry. I detached two regiments,—the 27th North Carolina and 30th Virginia,—under Colonel J. R. Cooke, directing him to ascend Loudoun Mountain and take possession of the heights, but, in case he found no enemy, not to reveal his presence to the garrison of Harper's Ferry. I sent with him the men of the Signal Corps, with orders to open communication if possible with Jackson, whose force ought to be in the neighborhood, coming from the west. I then disposed of the remainder of the division around the point of the mountain, where it abuts on the Potomac.

About 2 P. M. Colonel Cooke reported that he had taken unopposed possession of Loudoun Heights, but that he had seen nothing of Jackson, yet from the movements of the Federals he thought he was close at hand. By 8 o'clock the next morning five long-range Parrott rifles were on the top of the mountain in a masked position, but ready to open fire. About half-past 10 o'clock my signal party succeeded in informing Jackson of my position and my readiness to attack.

At a reunion of the Association of the Army of Northern Virginia held at Richmond on October 23d, 1884, in an address delivered by General Bradley T. Johnson, occurs this passage:

"McLaws, having constructed a road up Maryland Heights and placed his artillery in position during the 14th, while fighting was going on at Crampton's Gap and Turner's Gap, signaled to Jackson that he was ready; whereupon Jackson signaled the order both to McLaws and Walker—'Fire at such positions of the enemy as will be most effective.'"

I am, of course, ignorant of what Jackson may have signaled McLaws, but it is certain that I received no such order. On the contrary, as soon as he was informed that McLaws was in possession of Maryland Heights, Jackson signaled me substantially the following dispatch: "Harper's Ferry is now completely invested. I shall summon its commander to surrender. Should he refuse I shall give him twenty-four hours to remove the non-combatants, and then carry the place by assault. *Do not fire unless forced to."* ‡

Jackson at this time had, of course, no reason to suspect that McClellan was advancing in force, and doubtless supposed, as we all did, that we should have abundant leisure to rejoin General Lee at Hagerstown. But about noon I signaled to Jackson that an action seemed to be in progress at Crampton's Gap, that the enemy had made his appearance in Pleasant Valley in rear of McLaws, and that I had no doubt McClellan was advancing in force.

To this message Jackson replied that it was, he thought, no more than a cavalry affair between Stuart and Pleasonton. It was now about half-past 12 and every minute the sound of artillery in the direction of South Mountain was growing louder, which left no doubt on my mind of the advance of the whole Federal army. If this were the case, it was certain that General Lee would be in fearful peril should the capture of Harper's Ferry be much longer delayed. I thereupon asked permission to open fire, but receiving no reply, I determined to be "forced." For this purpose I placed the two North Carolina regiments under Colonel (afterward Major-General, and now U. S. Senator) M. W. Ransom, which had relieved those under Cooke, in line of battle in full view of the Federal batteries on Bolivar Heights. As I expected, they at once opened a heavy, but harmless, fire upon my regiments, which afforded me the wished-for pretext. Withdrawing the infantry to the safe side of the mountain, I directed my batteries to reply.

It is possible that some of my military readers may question the propriety of my course, and allege that it amounted virtually to disobedience of orders.

‡ See statements by General Bradley T. Johnson, p. 615, and Colonel H. Kyd Douglas, p. 617.— EDITORS.

This I freely admit, but plead the dire urgency of the case. Had Jackson compromised himself by agreeing to allow the Federal commander twenty-four hours, as he proposed, General Lee would undoubtedly have been driven into the Potomac before any portion of the Confederate force around Harper's Ferry could have reënforced him. The trouble was that Jackson could not be made to believe that McClellan's whole army was in movement.

I never knew whether or not Jackson actually made a formal demand for the surrender of the Federal garrison, but I had his own word for it that he intended to do so. Besides, such a course was in harmony with the humanity of his generous nature, and with his constant practice of doing as little harm as possible to non-combatants.

About an hour after my batteries opened fire those of A. P. Hill and Lawton followed suit, and about 3 o'clock those of McLaws. But the range from Maryland Heights being too great, the fire of McLaws's guns was ineffective, the shells bursting in mid-air without reaching the enemy. From my position on Loudoun Heights my guns had a plunging fire on the Federal batteries a thousand feet below and did great execution. By 5 o'clock our combined fire had silenced all the opposing batteries except one or two guns east of Bolivar Heights, which kept up a plucky but feeble response until night put a stop to the combat.

During the night of the 14th–15th, Major (afterward Brigadier-General) R. Lindsay Walker, chief of artillery of A. P. Hill's division, succeeded in crossing the Shenandoah with several batteries, and placing them in such a position on the slope of Loudoun Mountain, far below me, as to command the enemy's works. McLaws got his batteries into position nearer the enemy, and at daylight of the 15th the batteries of our five divisions were pouring their fire on the doomed garrison. The fire of my batteries, however, was at random, as the enemy's position was entirely concealed by a dense fog clinging to the sides of the mountain far below. But my artillerists trained their guns by the previous day's experience and delivered their fire through the fog.

The Federal batteries replied promptly, and for more than an hour maintained a spirited fire; but after that time it grew more and more feeble until about 8 o'clock, when it ceased altogether, and the garrison surrendered. Owing to the fog I was ignorant of what had taken place, but surmising it, I soon ordered my batteries to cease firing. Those of Lawton, however, continued some minutes later. This happened unfortunately, as Colonel Dixon S. Miles, the Federal commander, was at this time mortally wounded by a fragment of shell while waving a white flag in token of surrender.

It was pleasing to us, perched upon the top of the mountain, to know that more than twelve thousand "boys in blue" below us were stacking arms. Such a situation has its pathetic side too, for after the first feeling of exultation has passed there comes one of sympathy for the humiliation of the brave men, who are no longer enemies, but unfortunate fellow-soldiers.

Some hours later, accompanied by two of my staff, I rode into Harper's Ferry, and we were interested in seeing our tattered Confederates fraternizing in the most cordial manner with their well-dressed prisoners. I was introduced by General A. P. Hill to Federal Brigadier-General White. He explained to me that although of superior rank to Colonel Miles he had declined to assume command of the garrison, since he was at Harper's Ferry by accident — "an unfortunate accident too," he added.

I am of the opinion that it would have been practicable for Colonel Miles to have escaped with the infantry of his garrison during the night of the 14th–15th, as did a body of thirteen hundred cavalry under Colonel "Grimes" Davis. \ This enterprising young officer crossed his cavalry to the Maryland side of the Potomac over the pontoon bridge, and followed the road on the berme side of the Chesapeake and Ohio canal, leading north to Sharpsburg. Mention of this very meritorious action is made in neither Federal nor Confederate accounts of the capture of Harper's Ferry that have fallen under my notice. ☆   There is a strong probability that the infantry of the garrison could have done the same. It should be stated that Davis not only escaped capture, but that he passed through Sharpsburg at daylight of the 15th, | and in crossing the Hagerstown and Williamsport road he destroyed the greater part of Longstreet's reserve ordnance trains. ‡   This escape of Davis from Harper's Ferry and Forrest's escape from Fort Donelson under very similar circumstances show what a bold subordinate may achieve after his superior has lost heart.

No sooner had the surrender of Harper's Ferry been assured than my division took up its line of march to join General Lee. At 2 A. M. of the 16th my advance overtook the rear of Jackson's force, and about 8 o'clock in the morning [of the day of the battle], after seeing our commands safe across the river at the ford below Shepherdstown, Jackson and myself went forward together toward Sharpsburg. As we rode along I mentioned my *ruse* in opening fire on Harper's Ferry. Knowing the strictness of Jackson's ideas in regard to military obedience, I felt a little doubtful as to what he would say. When I had finished my confession he was silent for some minutes, and then remarked: "It was just as well as it was; but I could not believe that the fire you reported indicated the advance of McClellan in force. It seemed more likely to be merely a cavalry affair." Then after an interval of silence, as if to himself, he continued: "I thought I knew McClellan" (they were classmates at West Point), "but this movement of his puzzles me."

\ Colonel Benjamin F. Davis of the 8th New York Cavalry, familiarly known at West Point and among his old army associates as "Grimes" Davis. He was killed at Beverly Ford, June 9th, 1863. For some interesting details of his escape from Harper's Ferry and subsequent march, see page 613.—EDITORS.

☆ Mentioned by General McClellan.—EDITORS.

| According to a paper read by Captain William M. Luff, 12th Illinois Cavalry, before the Illinois Commandery of the Loyal Legion, the hour was 10 P. M. of the 14th.—EDITORS.

‡ Narrowly missing an encounter with the Reserve Artillery under General William N. Pendleton, which crossed Davis's track about eight miles north of Sharpsburg, about sunrise on the 15th. General Pendleton says Davis was "perhaps less than an hour ahead of us," and speaks of the large wagon train then passing, which he took immediate measures to protect.—EDITORS.

BY JULIUS WHITE, BRIGADIER-GENERAL, U. S. V.

ON the 8th of September, 1862, being then in command of the Union forces at Martinsburg, Virginia, about 2500 of all arms, I reported to General Wool at Baltimore, commanding the Department, that the enemy was approaching from the north in a force estimated at 15,000 to 20,000, and asked for instructions. General Wool replied:

"If 20,000 men should attack you, you will of course fall back. Harper's Ferry would be the best position I could recommend." . . .

After reconnoissance, and some skirmishing with the enemy's advance [Sept. 11th], demonstrating that his force was too large to be opposed with success, especially as there were no defenses at Martinsburg, the post, in accordance with General Wool's views, was evacuated, and on the 12th Harper's Ferry was reached.

Upon my reporting to Colonel Miles, the officer in command, he showed me the following dispatch:

"WASHINGTON, D. C., Sept. 7th, 1862. COLONEL MILES, Harper's Ferry: Our army [McClellan's] is in motion; it is important that Harper's Ferry be held to the latest moment. The Government has the utmost confidence in you, and is ready to give you full credit for the defense it expects you to make. H. W. HALLECK, General-in-Chief."

In view of the foregoing dispatch, and of the fact that I had been ordered from Harper's Ferry to the command at Martinsburg a few days before by General Wool, it was manifest that the authorities intended to retain Colonel Miles in command—very properly so, as he was an officer of forty years' experience.

The defenses of Harper's Ferry, if worthy of the name, comprised a small work on the crest of Maryland Heights called Stone Fort; another well down the western slope, where a battery of heavy naval guns was established; and a line of intrench-ments terminating at a work near the Potomac called Fort Duncan,—but this line was not occupied except at the upper end. [See map, p. 606.]

On Bolivar Heights a line of rifle-pits extended from near the Potomac southward to the Charlestown road, where a small work for the protection of artillery was situated.

In the rear of this line eastward, and in the upper part of the town, was an earth-work known as Camp Hill. Loudoun Heights (east of the Shenandoah) were not occupied by our troops.

The troops constituting the garrison were originally disposed by Colonel Miles as follows: on Maryland Heights, about 2000; on Bolivar Heights, from the Potomac to the Charlestown road, thence at a right angle to the Shenandoah, a distance in all of at least a mile and a half, 7000 men; in the work at Camp Hill, about 800; while the remainder, about 1000, guarded the bridges and other points on the rivers.

The distance from Maryland Heights to the nearest point on Bolivar Heights by way of the pontoon bridge was two and a quarter miles; to the intersection of the Charlestown road, three miles. Thus the principal points to be defended were not within supporting distance of each other in case of assault, nor was either of them properly fortified.

On the 13th the divisions of Generals McLaws and R. H. Anderson, by order of General Lee, reached Maryland Heights, and attacked the force stationed there, under Colonel Ford, who after some fighting abandoned the position—as he stated, by order of Colonel Miles; the latter, however, denied having given such an order. Be this as it may, it is certain that the enemy could easily have taken it with the force at his command whenever he chose.

On the same day General Walker, with a force of the enemy estimated at eight thousand, had taken possession of Loudoun Heights, and General Jackson with a much larger force had reached a position in front of Bolivar Heights—thus completing the investment of Harper's Ferry.

It has generally been considered that Colonel Miles should have tried to hold Maryland Heights (on the north side of the Potomac), even if it became necessary to mass his whole force there. The reasons given by him to the writer for not doing so were: (1) That his orders required him to hold Harper's Ferry, and this would be a violation of such orders; (2) that water would be inaccessible. Moreover, it was manifest that if the town of Harper's Ferry and the defensive line on Bolivar Heights were evacuated, the entire forces of the enemy on the Virginia side of the Potomac would recross to the north side, enveloping our small force and at the same time concentrating Lee's entire army in front of McClellan; while we should have given up the river-crossing, which, as the contending armies were then placed, constituted the only strategic value of Harper's Ferry.

Whether this view was correct or not, it is a fact that the maintenance of the line on Bolivar Heights till the morning of September 15th prevented the presence of the divisions of Generals A. P. Hill, McLaws, and Anderson with Lee, until the 17th, the day of Antietam, being four full days after General McClellan had received a copy of General Lee's orders directing the movement against Harper's Ferry, and disclosing the fact that fully one-third of his army was south of the Potomac, and much more than that, including the force under General McLaws, engaged in the movement against Harper's Ferry. Distinguished officers of the Confederate army [Generals Longstreet and Walker and Colonel Douglas, see pp. 604, 620, 663] describe the situation of that part of Lee's army north of the Potomac during the 14th, 15th, and 16th of September as one of "imminent peril," "very serious," etc., etc., virtually admitting that it might then have been defeated.

Thus it will be seen that there were two sides to the question whether Maryland Heights was the key to Harper's Ferry under the then existing circumstances, and that the detention of the Confederate forces around that place was prolonged, instead of abbreviated, by the continued occupation of Bolivar Heights by Colonel Miles.

In the afternoon of the 14th General Jackson moved forward with a view to occupy the ridge which is a prolongation of Bolivar Heights south of the Charlestown road and descends toward the Shenandoah River.

To oppose this movement troops were advanced, but after a spirited engagement it was manifest that we could not prevent his establishment in the position sought, and at night our force was withdrawn within the lines of defense.

During the evening of the 13th a consultation took place between the writer, then temporarily in command of the cavalry, Colonel B. F. Davis of the 8th New York, and Lieutenant-Colonel Hasbrouck Davis of the 12th Illinois, at which it was agreed that the mounted force could be of little use in the defense — that the horses and equipments would be of great value to the enemy if captured, and that an attempt to reach McClellan ought therefore to be made.

This proposition, made by Colonel B. F. Davis, was warmly seconded by Colonel Davis of the 12th Illinois. The question whether the whole force might not also escape was considered, but was negatived on the ground that infantry and artillery could not march fast enough to succeed. Besides, Colonel Miles considered that he had no right under his orders to evacuate the post.

After some hesitation and some sharp words between Colonels Miles and B. F. Davis, the former issued the order directing the cavalry to move out on the evening of the 14th, under the general command of the senior officer, Colonel Arno Voss, of the 12th Illinois.

Under the inspiration and immediate direction of the two Davises, who rode together at the head of the column, the escaping force accomplished the brilliant achievement of reaching the Union lines without the loss of a man, capturing on the way a Confederate ammunition train of 97 wagons and its escort of 600 men.

Graphic accounts of this daring and successful exploit have been published by Major Thomas Bell of the 8th New York, Major W. M. Luff of the 12th Illinois, and Sergeant Pettengill of the 1st Rhode Island Cavalry — all of whom were participants, and I regret that the limits of this article do not permit the recital here.

There were other incidents in the history of the events under consideration highly creditable to the troops constituting the garrison of Harper's Ferry. General Kershaw's report to General McLaws of the capture of Maryland Heights, on the 13th, states that he met with a "most obstinate resistance" from our force stationed there, "a fierce fire being kept up at a distance of one hundred yards," and it was not till he had sent General Barksdale's brigade to attack the works in rear that the heights were evacuated.

The fighting with Jackson's advance in front of Bolivar Heights, on the afternoon of the 14th and on the morning of the 15th, by the troops posted in that quarter, was deliberate, systematic, and plucky. The artillery was admirably handled, and if there had been anything like an equality of position, its effect would have been more decided. It would be invidious to specify the action of certain brigades, regiments, or batteries, but common justice to these troops requires that the foregoing statement of their service be made.

Soon after daylight on the morning of the 15th fire was opened by the enemy's artillery, comprising nearly or quite fifty pieces. Those established at the southern extremity of Bolivar Heights completely enfiladed that part of our line extending from the Charlestown road northward to the Potomac; those placed on the south-western slope of Loudoun Heights, and on the west side of the Shenandoah near by, delivered their fire at an acute angle to our line, being half enfilade; those at or near the crest of Loudoun Heights took us in reverse; and still others in the valley beyond Bolivar Heights fired directly at our front.

The fire was chiefly converged upon the batteries we had established at and near the intersection of Bolivar Heights and the Charlestown road, that being the point upon which it was manifest that General Jackson would deliver the expected assault.

The writer, being in command of the forces in this quarter, ordered the massing of the artillery there and the movements of the regiments holding Camp Hill to the front. These orders, as I afterward learned, were countermanded by Colonel Miles, who deemed it necessary to retain a force near the river-crossing; at all events the order was not executed.

The artillery fire continued until half-past 8 in the morning, when it was apparent the assault might be expected immediately. At this time Colonel Miles visited the work at the Charlestown road and said to the writer that the situation seemed hopeless, and that the place might as well be surrendered without further sacrifice of life. It was replied that such a step should only be taken upon the judgment of a council of war; whereupon Colonel Miles called the commanders of brigades together, who, after consultation, and with great reluctance on the part of some, voted unanimously for capitulation if honorable terms could be obtained, for the following reasons:

First. The officer commanding had lost all confidence in his ability further to defend the place, and was the first to advise surrender.

Second. There was no reason to hope that the attenuated line on Bolivar Heights could be maintained, even for half an hour, against the greatly superior force massed for the assault, supported if necessary by an attack on our rear by Generals Walker and McLaws.

Third. Great as was the disparity in numbers, the disparity in position was greater. Harper's Ferry and Bolivar Heights were dominated by Maryland and Loudoun Heights, and the other positions held by the enemy's artillery. The crest of Maryland Heights is at an elevation of 1060 feet; the southern point, nearest Harper's Ferry, 649 feet; Loudoun Heights, 954 feet. The south-western slope of the latter and the grounds near by, west of the Shenandoah, where batteries of the enemy were placed, were 300 to 600 feet high. The elevation of Bolivar Heights is about 300 feet, while Camp Hill and the town of Harper's Ferry are still lower. Thus all our movements of men or guns during the engagements of the 14th and 15th, as well as the effect of their own plunging fire, were plainly visible from the enemy's signal-station on Loudoun Heights. No effective reply could be made to the fire from these elevated positions, no suitable defenses existed from which to resist the assault, and there was no opportunity on the morning of the 15th to change our position, even if there had been a better one to occupy.

Fourth. To await the assault, then impending, with no hope of even a temporary successful resistance, did not seem to justify the sacrifice of life consequent upon such a course — the situation being regarded as one of the unfortunate chances of war, unavoidable under existing circumstances.

I was appointed by Colonel Miles commissioner to arrange the terms of capitulation, and at the urgent request of other officers I accepted the unwelcome duty, in the hope of obtaining honorable conditions. Immediately after the council broke up Colonel Miles was mortally wounded; he died the next day.

As commissioner I was received very courteously by the Confederate officers, and the terms of capitulation agreed upon with General A. P. Hill provided that all private property of individuals and the side-arms of officers should be retained by them. Refugees, of whom there were a considerable number, were not to be treated as prisoners, except such, if any, as were deserters from the Confederate army. There were none of this class. All the Union troops were immediately paroled, not to serve again until regularly exchanged. A number of the prominent officers of the Confederate army spoke of our situation as hopeless from the hour when the investment was completed.

Harper's Ferry is not defensible by a force inferior to that attacking it, unless the surrounding heights be well fortified, and each of them held by a force sufficient to maintain itself unsupported by the others. It was this which doubtless prompted the advice given by General McClellan to General Halleck, before the investment, that the garrison be withdrawn.

The battle of South Mountain was fought by General McClellan, on the 14th of September, against a force of the enemy not more than two-thirds as large as that encountered by him at Antietam.

After the mountain passes had been carried, if a prompt advance down Pleasant Valley had been made by his largely preponderating force, there seems good reason to believe that Harper's Ferry would have been relieved, the river-crossing at that place secured, the reunion of Lee's army, separated as it was by the Potomac, rendered difficult, if not impossible, and the capture or dispersion of a large part of it probable.

The orders issued by General McClellan to General Franklin, commanding the Sixth Corps, on the night of the 13th, announced his purpose to do these very things, and directed that Crampton's Gap — the pass nearest Harper's Ferry — be carried at whatever cost. The enemy in front of General Franklin was then to be "cut off, destroyed, or captured, and Harper's Ferry relieved." The dispatch concludes with the remark: "My general idea is to cut the enemy in two, and beat him in detail." The column to be thus interposed between the enemy and Harper's Ferry consisted of General Franklin's corps only — subsequently reënforced by General Couch's division of the Fourth Corps. The imminent peril of Harper's Ferry had been known to General McClellan from the inception of the campaign. He had advised the withdrawal of the garrison, and had predicted its loss if left there, before he left Washington.

No direct measures were taken by him, however, for the relief of the post, until after his receipt on the 13th of General Lee's order detaching a large part of his army for its capture, which force had then completed its investment. Early on the morning of the 14th General McClellan had been informed by Colonel Miles, through Major Russell of the 1st Maryland Cavalry, who, with great courage and tact, had made his way during the night through the enemy's lines, that Harper's Ferry could not be held more than forty-eight hours — from the time the courier left — viz., till the 15th.

Thus the time within which to relieve that post had been reduced to the minimum, so that success depended upon the prompt and vigorous advance of a force large enough to readily overcome such of the enemy as stood in the way. Unfortunately, General Franklin's command was not sufficient to accomplish this vitally important purpose.

After receiving the orders, he was not able to get his command into action until midday of the 14th, and met with such determined resistance that it was not until near nightfall, and after a loss of more than five hundred in killed and wounded, that he had forced the pass and found himself on the west side of the mountain in Pleasant Valley, confronted by an increased force of the enemy, with plenty of artillery advantageously posted.

The attack on Turner's Gap by the main body of the army, although successful, did not result, as General McClellan had expected, in relieving General Franklin of the enemy in his front; and the latter, as shown in his dispatches of the morning of the 15th, declined to attack unless reënforced.

But the time within which it was possible to relieve Harper's Ferry had then passed, even if the place had been held during the whole of that day.

During the afternoon of the 14th our guns at Harper's Ferry, engaged with Jackson's forces, were cheeringly responded to by those of General Franklin at Crampton's Gap; but after 4 o'clock of that day, and on the morning of the 15th, there was no sound of conflict in that direction, and the hope of relief from McClellan, which the proximity of the firing had inspired, was abandoned. Harper's Ferry was doomed, and as affecting this result, it did not matter whether the garrison occupied the town or either of the adjacent heights, nor whether the surrender took place before or after an assault, *because it was surrounded by the whole of Lee's army.*

I must not be understood as presuming to criticise the conduct of this campaign by General McClellan. The object of this article, as before stated, is only to relate the historical facts bearing upon the subject in hand; therefore, no commentary is made upon the questions whether his advice that the garrison of Harper's Ferry be withdrawn should have been adopted, whether he might have marched his army toward Harper's Ferry faster, or whether he might and should have detached a larger force for the purposes indicated in his orders to General Franklin. Manifestly it was his design to relieve that post, but the measures taken did not succeed.

It has been often asserted that Harper's Ferry might have held out a day or two longer, but of those who have claimed that it could have been longer held, no one has yet, so far as the writer is informed, stated *how* a garrison mostly of recruits under fire for the first time could have successfully defended an area of three square miles, assailed from all sides by veterans three times their number, posted, with artillery, in positions commanding the whole field. The writer, with due deference, expresses the opinion that the force under Jackson could have carried the place by assault within an hour after his arrival before it, or at any time thereafter prior to the surrender, in spite of any resistance which under the circumstances could have been made.[+]

STONEWALL JACKSON'S INTENTIONS AT HARPER'S FERRY.

I. BY BRADLEY T. JOHNSON, BRIGADIER-GENERAL, C. S. A.

MAJOR-GENERAL J. G. WALKER, in his interesting paper in "The Century" [June, 1886], states that after he had occupied Loudoun Heights on September 14th, he received a dispatch from General Jackson, by signal, substantially as follows: "Harper's Ferry is now completely invested. I shall summon its commander to surrender. Should he refuse, I will give him twenty-four hours to remove the non-combatants, and then carry the place by assault. Do not fire unless forced to." [See p. 609.]

Referring to the statement made by me in an address before the Association of the Army of Northern Virginia, October 23d, 1884, that on the 14th of September General Jackson signaled the order to both McLaws and Walker, "Fire at such positions of the enemy as will be most effective," General Walker says: "I am, of course, ignorant of what Jackson may have signaled McLaws, but it is certain I received no such order." General Walker then goes on to show that Jackson determined to give the commanding officer of Harper's Ferry twenty-four hours before he carried the place; that he, General Walker, was satisfied that the delay of twenty-four hours would be fatal to General Lee,—as it would have been; that, therefore, against orders not to fire until he was forced to, he determined to be forced; and that he secured this end by the display of two North Carolina regiments, under Colonel M. W. Ransom, in line of battle on Loudoun Heights, in full view of the Federal batteries on Bolivar Heights. As he expected, he says, "they at once opened a heavy but harmless fire upon my regiments, which afforded me the wished-for pretext. Withdrawing the infantry to the safe side of the mountain, I directed my batteries to reply."

Thus it would appear that General Walker forced the attack on Harper's Ferry, and prevented the delay of twenty-four hours which General Jackson proposed to give; and that to this prompt attack was due the capture of Harper's Ferry, and the salvation of that part of the Army of Northern Virginia which, with Lee, Longstreet, and D. H. Hill, was waiting at Sharpsburg the reduction of the force at the former place, and the reënforcement of Lee by Jackson, McLaws, and Walker after Harper's Ferry had fallen. Twenty-four hours' delay would have postponed the fall of Harper's Ferry, and the battle of the 17th would have been fought by Longstreet and D. H. Hill alone, who would have been destroyed by McClellan before Jackson could have come up.

I prepared the address before the Association of the Army of Northern Virginia after careful study of the records and reports of both sides, and all accessible accounts of the battle of Sharpsburg, and believe every statement made by me can be substantiated by the record, or by the statements of eye-witnesses. Unless General Walker has a copy of the dispatch referred to by him, I respectfully submit that his recollection is in error; that no intention was ever entertained by Jackson of giving twenty-four hours' delay; and that General Jackson himself gave the order to Walker and McLaws to open fire, exactly as stated by me.

The reasons for believing that General Walker is mistaken in thinking that he ever received the order referred to by him, or one in any way intimating an intention of giving twenty-four hours'

[+] The report of the Military Commission censured Colonels Miles and Ford and Major Baird. It affirmed that there was nothing in the conduct of Colonels D'Utassy and Trimble to call for censure; and that General Julius White merited the approbation of the Commission, adding, "He appears from the evidence to have acted with decided capability and courage."— EDITORS.

delay, seem to me to be conclusive. Colonel H. Kyd Douglas was aide-de-camp to Jackson, and occupied, particularly in that campaign, peculiarly confidential relations to him. His home was near Sharpsburg and Shepherdstown, the scene of operations, and he probably knew as much of General Jackson's intentions as any man living. He tells me he never heard of any such projected delay. The "lost order" No. 191 — from General Lee to Jackson, Walker, and McLaws — specially directs Walker and McLaws to be in position on Loudoun and Maryland Heights respectively by Friday morning, September 12th, and Jackson to take possession of the Baltimore and Ohio railroad by Friday morning and "intercept such of the enemy as may attempt to escape from Harper's Ferry." Jackson's advance division reached the vicinity of Harper's Ferry during Saturday forenoon, the 13th; Walker and McLaws reached the designated points Saturday night, but were not in position for offensive action until September 14th.

Now, when the army was moving to the positions assigned by "Special Orders No. 191," it was a matter of common knowledge that McClellan's advance was in contact with our rear. Hampton had a sharp affair in the streets of Frederick late on the 12th. Fitz Lee, hanging on to the advance, located McClellan and reported his presence to Stuart, who held the mountain pass over Catoctin at Hagan's. During the 13th Stuart delayed the advance of the Federal infantry through Middletown Valley by sturdily defending the practicable points on the National road.

On the 14th, when, according to General Walker, Jackson, then a day late, proposed to give the commander of Harper's Ferry twenty-four hours' delay, and General Walker, in order to prevent that delay, drew the fire of the Federal guns on him on Loudoun Heights, Franklin's corps attacked Crampton's Gap about noon, and after a sharp defense drove Munford through the mountain pass. Now Crampton's Gap is in full sight of Loudoun Heights, not four miles off as the crow flies, and is in rear of McLaws's position on Maryland Heights. Jackson then knew that McClellan was thundering in his rear. Walker and McLaws could see the battle and hear the guns at Crampton's, and Walker could also see the fight at South Mountain.

It would have been contrary to every known characteristic of the chief of the "Foot Cavalry" for him to have given his adversary twenty-four hours' breathing-time, under any circumstances, anywhere, and utterly impossible for him to have done so under these circumstances at this time.

General Jackson did send General Walker an order by signal: "I do not desire any of the batteries to open until all are ready on both sides of the river, except you should find it necessary, of which you must judge for yourself. I will let you know when to open all the batteries."

In the War Records office may be seen the report of Captain J. L. Bartlett, signal officer of Jackson's corps. It contains the order to Walker and McLaws quoted by me in my address: "Fire at such positions of the enemy as will be most

effective." This order General Walker does not recollect to have received. It certainly was sent by Captain Bartlett to Walker's signal officer, and just as certainly received by the latter. It is hardly possible that so important an order, at such a time, should not have been forwarded by the signal officer to General Walker. The following order was also sent from Captain Bartlett's signal-station to General Walker's officer on Loudoun Heights:

"*Special Orders*   HEADQUARTERS VALLEY DISTRICT,
No. ——   September 14, 1862.

"1. To-day Major-General McLaws will attack so as to sweep with his artillery the ground occupied by the enemy, take his batteries in reverse, and otherwise operate against him as circumstances may justify.

"2. Brigadier-General Walker will take in reverse the battery on the turnpike, and also sweep with his artillery the ground occupied by the enemy, and silence the battery on the island in the Shenandoah, should he find a battery there.

"3. Major-General A. P. Hill will move along the left bank of the Shenandoah, and thus turn the enemy's left flank and enter Harper's Ferry.

"4. Brigadier-General Lawton will move along the turnpike for the purpose of supporting General Hill and otherwise operating against the enemy on the left of General Hill.

"5. Brigadier-General Jones will, with one of his brigades and a battery of artillery, make a demonstration against the enemy's right; the remaining part of his division will constitute the reserve and move along the turnpike.

"By order of Major-General Jackson:

"WILLIAM L. JACKSON,
"Acting Assistant Adjutant-General."

Captain Bartlett, after reporting all messages and orders sent through his station, among which were the foregoing, says, "If any other dispatches or orders were sent at Harper's Ferry, it was done at other posts than mine."

Now, there was no signal officer except Captain Bartlett attached to Jackson's headquarters, communicating with Loudoun Heights, and his report thus shows all the orders sent by Jackson to Walker. The one quoted by General Walker is not among them; the one quoted by me is. Therefore, inasmuch as it appears that the investing force under Jackson was twenty-four hours behind the time fixed by General Lee for completing the investment of Harper's Ferry, and that Generals Jackson and McLaws knew that McClellan had been in Frederick on the 12th, only twenty miles off; and that McClellan was actually attacking at Crampton's, three or four miles from Harper's Ferry; and that Lee, Longstreet, and D. H. Hill were then north of the Potomac, and in imminent danger of being cut off from the rest of the army at Harper's Ferry; and that General Jackson did, in fact, send the order, cited by me, to Walker and McLaws to fire at such positions of the enemy as would be most effective, and did, in fact, as soon as his troops were in position, completing the investment, issue an order of battle for the assault on Harper's Ferry: taking all these facts into consideration, we must believe that General Walker is mistaken as to the order he thinks he received, and that General Jackson never issued such order, nor entertained the idea of delaying the attack.

II. BY HENRY KYD DOUGLAS, COLONEL, C. S. A.

IN his article in "The Century" for June, 1885, on "Harper's Ferry and Sharpsburg," General John G. Walker said, in substance, that General Jackson, after Harper's Ferry was invested, informed him that he intended to summon the Federal commander to surrender, and, should he refuse, then to give him twenty-four hours to remove the non-combatants before making an assault; but that he, General Walker, being better advised as to the movements of General McClellan, became impatient of the delay, and by a piece of mild strategy *forced* the assault, and thereby hastened the surrender of Harper's Ferry, saved Jackson from being "compromised," and Lee from being driven into the Potomac. [See pp. 604–611.]

With the help of such notes as I have, confirming my recollection, and the official reports corroborating them, I will briefly examine General Walker's statement.

I think I may safely assume that General Jackson, being in immediate communication, by signal, with General McLaws (who was in contact with the enemy), and with General Lee both by signal through McLaws and by a constant line of couriers, knew at least as much about the movements of General McClellan and the situation of the rest of our army as General Walker, on Loudoun Heights, could possibly know.

Jackson reached Harper's Ferry on Saturday, September 13th, and immediately shut up his side of the pen. McLaws and Walker were not yet in position, their delay being doubtless unavoidable. Let us see whether Jackson was in danger of compromising himself by want of activity. The next day at 7:20 A. M., in anticipation that McLaws and Walker would soon be ready, he sent to McLaws a characteristic letter of instructions. As will appear, a copy of this letter was doubtless sent to Walker, and will help to explain one of the errors into which he has fallen. That letter looks to quick work. But although Jackson was ready, there were obstacles in the way of immediate action. General Jackson says that, separated by the Potomac and Shenandoah from McLaws and Walker, he resorted to signals, "and that before the necessary orders were thus transmitted the day was far advanced." General A. P. Hill says, in effect, that it was afternoon before the signals from Maryland and Loudoun Heights notified Jackson that "all was ready," and then Jackson ordered him against the enemy. General McLaws says the morning of the 14th was occupied cutting a road for artillery, and that by 2 P. M. he had four pieces in position on Maryland Heights. General Walker says that at half-past 10 he succeeded in notifying Jackson that he was ready, and Captain Bartlett, the signal officer of Jackson, reports to the same effect. Jackson then ordered Walker to "wait" for McLaws. Every one at headquarters knew how impatient General Jackson was at the unavoidable loss of time. He had written the McLaws letter very early in the morning, and in further preparation for prompt and decisive action he dictated to Colonel Jackson his "special order"

for the attack, and as soon as it was practicable issued it. It speaks for itself. He also issued his joint order to McLaws and Walker — "Fire at such positions of the enemy as will be most effective." Walker opened fire about 1 P. M. — whether shortly before or shortly after this joint order does not appear, and is of little importance. McLaws began about 2 P. M. He says Walker and Jackson were both at it before him. Hill moved promptly, and did enough of work that afternoon and night, as he says, "to seal the fate of Harper's Ferry," with the assistance of McLaws and Walker. At 3 o'clock the next morning I was sent by General Jackson to direct the movement of Jones's division at first dawn, and at daylight everybody was in action, and Harper's Ferry speedily surrendered. In energy, Jackson at Harper's Ferry simply paralleled himself; he could do no more. "Let the work be done thoroughly," he had said to McLaws; and it was.

Was General Jackson pushed to this activity by General Walker, and would he otherwise have given Colonel Miles twenty-four hours to remove non-combatants before assault, and thus have imperiled General Lee beyond hope? I will treat this question soberly, as becomes the gravity of General Walker's statement and his regard for General Jackson's reputation. But, as the matter now presents itself, I will submit the reasons for thinking General Walker is mistaken in regard to the dispatch he says he received from General Jackson respecting the twenty-four hours' delay. It is known now that Jackson never did summon the enemy to surrender, and in his report he makes no mention of such a purpose. I find in my notes this item in regard to the 14th: "It was late in the afternoon when McLaws was ready for action — too late to effect anything on that day. Preparations were made for an assault early the next morning. I am not aware that General Jackson made any demand for the surrender of the garrison." There is nothing in the reports of Hill, McLaws, Jones, or Walker, touching the matter of a contemplated demand for surrender, or any delay by reason thereof. Captain Bartlett's report as signal officer — the only one known to have sent signal dispatches between Jackson and Walker — contains no such order as the one quoted by General Walker. If such a message had been sent to Walker, it would, of course, have been sent also to Hill and McLaws, and they make no mention of it. It could not have gone to McLaws except through Bartlett, and he surely would have made a note of it. General Walker says it was after Jackson was informed that McLaws was in possession of Maryland Heights that the dispatch was sent to him. This was not earlier than 2 P. M., and before that time Walker had opened fire, and Jackson had issued the joint order, "Fire," etc., and had followed it up with his specific "special order," prepared beforehand. In fact, General Jackson knew the urgency of the situation better than General Walker, and it is simply incredible that he contemplated a delay of twenty-four hours for any purpose. General Walker must be mistaken. It does not follow, however, that he has no ground for his mistake. I have said that the substance of Jackson's early letter to McLaws must have been sent to Walker. That letter looks to an attack by Walker on an island battery in the Shenandoah, and during the morning a dispatch to Jackson from Loudoun Heights says: "Walker can't get position to bear on island."—showing that Walker had in some way been instructed with regard to it. (It would seem that Jackson's "special order" must have been prepared in the morning and before the receipt of the dispatch from Walker, for in it he gives instructions to Walker touching that island battery.) In the McLaws letter, Jackson speaks of a flag of truce to get out non-combatants should the enemy not surrender; but the spirit of that letter is against any delay. I remember the question of a demand for surrender was vaguely talked of at headquarters by the staff. It is likely they got the idea from the McLaws letter, for I never heard the general [Jackson] say anything on the subject, and every indication was against any delay in making the assault. I merely throw out the suggestion to account for the error of memory into which I think General Walker has fallen. Whatever purpose General Jackson at first had to demand a surrender or to consider non-combatants, his ruling anxiety was for the speedy fall of Harper's Ferry. It may be that a little reflection satisfied him, after writing the McLaws letter, that the citizens of the town would be in little danger from the firing of McLaws and Walker at the enemy on Bolivar Heights, and that he dismissed that consideration from his mind. If this humane purpose ever took definite shape in his intentions, there was never any occasion to execute it, and it would now be of little consequence had not General Walker attempted to give it such strange form and significance.

THE OPPOSING FORCES AT HARPER'S FERRY, VA.

September 12–15, 1862.

The composition, losses, and strength of each army as here stated give the gist of all the data obtainable in the Official Records. K stands for killed; w for wounded; m w for mortally wounded; m for captured or missing; c for captured.

THE UNION FORCES.

Col. Dixon S. Miles (m w), Brig.-Gen. Julius White.

Brigade Commanders: Colonels F. G. D'Utassy, William H. Trimble, Thomas H. Ford, and William G. Ward. *Troops:* 12th Ill. Cav., Col. Arno Voss; M, 2d Ill. Art'y, Capt. John C. Phillips; 65th Ill., Col. Daniel Cameron; 15th Ind. Battery, Capt. John C. H. von Sehlen; Ind. Battery, Capt. Silas F. Rigby; 1st Md. Cav. (detachment), Capt. Charles H. Russell; Battalion Md. Cav., Maj. Henry A. Cole; 1st Md., P. H. Brigade, Col. William P. Maulsby; 3d Md., P. H. Brigade, Lieut.-Col. Stephen W. Downey; 8th N. Y. Cav., Col. Benjamin F. Davis; A, 5th N. Y. H. Art'y, Capt. John H. Graham; F, 5th N. Y. H. Art'y, Capt. Eugene McGrath; 12th N. Y. (militia), Col. William G. Ward; 39th N. Y., Maj. Hugo Hildebrandt; 111th N. Y., Col. Jesse Segoine; 115th N. Y., Col. Simeon Sammon; 125th N. Y., Col. George L. Willard; 126th N. Y., Col. Eliakim Sherrill (w), Maj. William H. Baird; Ohio Battery, Capt. Benjamin F. Potts; 32d Ohio, Maj. Sylvester M. Hewitt; 60th Ohio, Lieut.-Col. Noah H. Hixon; 87th Ohio, Col. Henry B. Banning; 7th Squadron R. I. Cav., Maj. Augustus W. Corliss; 9th Vermont, Col. George J. Stannard.

The total Union loss in the actions on Maryland Heights and at Harper's Ferry and Bolivar Heights was 44 killed, 173 wounded, and 12,520 captured = 12,737. (Most of the wounded were probably counted among the captured.)

The Confederate force employed at Harper's Ferry consisted of the commands of Generals Jackson, McLaws (including R. H. Anderson's division), and Walker. For composition of these forces in detail, see pp. 600–602.

THE HISTORICAL BASIS OF WHITTIER'S "BARBARA FRIETCHIE."

BY GEORGE O. SEILHEIMER.[*]

THAT Barbara Frietchie lived is not denied. That she died at the advanced age of 96 years and is buried in the burial-ground of the German Reformed Church in Frederick is also true.

There is only one account of Stonewall Jackson's entry into Frederick, and that was written by a Union army surgeon who was in charge of the hospital there at the time. "Jackson I did not get a look at to recognize him," the doctor wrote on the 21st of September, "though I must have seen him, as I witnessed the passage of all the troops through the town." Not a word about Barbara Frietchie and this incident. Dr. Oliver Wendell Holmes, too, was in Frederick soon afterward, on his way to find his son, reported mortally wounded at Antietam. Such a story, had it been true, could scarcely have failed to reach his ears, and he would undoubtedly have told it in his delightful chapter of war reminiscences, "My Hunt for the Captain," had he heard it. Barbara Frietchie had a flag, and it is now in the possession of Mrs. Handschue and her daughter, Mrs. Abbott, of Frederick. Mrs. Handschue was the niece and adopted daughter of Mrs. Frietchie, and the flag came to her as part of her inheritance, a cup out of which General Washington drank tea when he spent a night in Frederick in 1791 being among the Frietchie heirlooms. This flag which Mrs. Handschue and her daughter so religiously preserve is torn, but the banner was not rent with seam and gash from a rifle-blast; it is torn — only this and nothing more. That Mrs. Frietchie did not wave the flag at Jackson's men Mrs. Handschue positively affirms. The flag-waving act was done, however, by Mrs. Mary S. Quantrell, another Frederick woman; but Jackson took no notice of it, and

[*] Condensed from a contribution to the "Philadelphia *Times*" for July 21st, 1886.— EDITORS.

as Mrs. Quantrell was not fortunate enough to find a poet to celebrate her deed she never became famous.

Colonel Henry Kyd Douglas, who was with General Jackson every minute of his stay in Frederick, declares in an article in "The Century" for June, 1886, that Jackson never saw Barbara Frietchie, and that Barbara never saw Jackson. This story is borne out by Mrs. Frietchie's relatives.

As already said, Barbara Frietchie had a flag and she waved it, not on the 6th to Jackson's men, but on the 12th to Burnside's. Here is the story as told by Mrs. Abbott, Mrs. Hanshew's daughter:

"Jackson and his men had been in Frederick and had left a short time before. We were glad that the rebels had gone and that our troops came. My mother and I lived almost opposite aunt's place. She and my mother's cousin, Harriet Yoner, lived together. Mother said I should go and see aunt and tell her not to be frightened. You know that aunt was then almost ninety-six years old. When I reached aunt's place she knew as much as I did about matters, and cousin Harriet was with her. They were on the front porch, and aunt was leaning on the cane she always carried. When the troops marched along aunt waved her hand, and cheer after cheer went up from the men as they saw her. Some even ran into the yard. 'God bless you, old lady.' 'Let me take you by the hand.' 'May you live long, you dear old soul,' cried one after the other, as they rushed into the yard. Aunt being rather feeble, and in order to save her as much as we could, cousin Harriet Yoner said, 'Aunt ought to have a flag to wave.' The flag was hidden in the family Bible, and cousin Harriet got it and gave it to aunt. Then she waved the flag to the men and they cheered her as they went by. She was very patriotic and the troops all knew of her. The day before General Reno was killed he came to see aunt and had a talk with her."

The manner in which the Frietchie legend originated was very simple. A Frederick lady visited Washington some time after the accession of 1862 and spoke of the open sympathy and valor of Barbara Frietchie. The story was told again and again, and it was never lost in the telling. Mr. Whittier received his first knowledge of it from Mrs. E. D. E. N. Southworth, the novelist, who is a resident of Washington. When Mrs. Southworth wrote to Mr. Whittier concerning Barbara, she inclosed a newspaper slip reciting the circumstances of Barbara Frietchie's action when Lee entered Frederick.

When Mr. Whittier wrote the poem, he followed as closely as possible the account sent him at the time. He has a cane made from the timber of Barbara's house — a present from Dr. Steiner, a member of the Senate of Maryland. The flag with which Barbara Frietchie gave a hearty welcome to Burnside's troops has but thirty-four stars, is small, of silk, and attached to a staff probably a yard in length.

Barbara Frietchie was born at Lancaster, Pennsylvania. Her maiden name was Hauer. She was born December 3d, 1766, her parents being Nicholas and Catharine Hauer. She went to Frederick in early life, where she married John C. Frietchie, a glover, in 1806. She died December 18th, 1862, Mr. Frietchie having died in 1849. In 1868 the waters of Carroll Creek rose to such a height that they nearly wrecked the old home of the heroine of Whittier's poem.

* Writing to the editor of "The Century" on the 10th of June, 1886, Mr. Whittier said: "The poem 'Barbara Frietchie' was written in good faith. The story was no invention of mine. It came to me from sources which I regarded as entirely reliable; it had been published in newspapers, and had gained public credence in Washington and Maryland before my poem was written. I had no reason to doubt its accuracy then, and I am still constrained to believe that it had foundation in fact. If I thought otherwise I should not hesitate to express it. I have no pride of authorship to interfere with my allegiance to truth." Mr. Whittier, writing March 4th, 1885, informs us further that he also received letters from several other responsible persons wholly or partially confirming the story, among whom was the late Dorothea L. Dix." — Editors

UNION HOSPITAL IN A BARN NEAR ANTIETAM CREEK. AFTER A SKETCH MADE AT THE TIME.

STONEWALL JACKSON IN MARYLAND.

BY HENRY KYD DOUGLAS, COLONEL, C. S. A.

ROASTING GREEN CORN AT THE CAMP-FIRE.

ON the 3d of September, 1862, the Federal army under General Pope having been confounded, General Lee turned his columns toward the Potomac, with Stonewall Jackson in front. On the 5th of September Jackson crossed the Potomac at White's Ford, a few miles beyond Leesburg. The passage of the river by the troops marching in fours, well closed up, the laughing, shouting, and singing, as a brass band in front played "Maryland, my Maryland," was a memorable experience. The Marylanders in the corps imparted much of their enthusiasm to the other troops, but we were not long in finding out that if General Lee had hopes that the decimated regiments of his army would be filled by the sons of Maryland he was doomed to a speedy and unqualified disappointment. However, before we had been in Maryland many hours, one enthusiastic citizen presented Jackson with a gigantic gray mare. She was a little heavy and awkward for a war-horse, but as the general's "Little Sorrel" had a few days before been temporarily stolen, the present was a timely one, and he was not disposed to "look a gift horse in the mouth." Yet the present proved almost a Trojan horse to him, for the next morning when he mounted his new steed and touched her with his spur the loyal and undisciplined beast reared straight into the air, and, standing erect for a moment, threw herself backward, horse and rider rolling upon the ground. The general was stunned and severely bruised, and lay upon the ground for some time before he could be removed. He was then placed in an ambulance, where he rode during the day's march, having turned his command over to his brother-in-law, General D. H. Hill, the officer next in rank.

Early that day the army went into camp near Frederick, and Generals Lee, Longstreet, Jackson, and for a time "Jeb" Stuart, had their headquarters near one another in Best's grove. Hither in crowds came the good people of Frederick, especially the ladies, as to a fair. General Jackson, still suffering from his hurt, kept to his tent, busying himself with maps and official papers, and declined to see visitors. Once, however, when he had been called to General Lee's tent, two young girls waylaid him, paralyzed him with smiles and embraces and questions, and then jumped into

<hr>

"We had been faring very badly since we left Manassas Junction, having had only one meal that included bread and coffee. Our diet had been green corn, with beef without salt, roasted on the end of ramrods. We heard with delight of the 'plenty' to be had in Maryland; judge of our disappointment when, about 2 o'clock at night, we were marched into a dank clover-field and the order came down the line, 'Men, go into that corn-field and get your rations — and be ready to march at 5 in the morning. Don't burn any of these fence-rails.' Of course we obeyed orders as to the corn, but, the rails suffered."— Extract from a letter written by Lieut. Robert Healy, of Jackson's corps.

JACKSON'S MEN WADING THE POTOMAC AT WHITE'S FORD. ⚓

their carriage and drove off rapidly, leaving him there, cap in hand, bowing, blushing, and speechless. But once safe in his tent he was seen no more that day. The next evening, Sunday, he went into Frederick for the first time to attend church, and there being no service in the Presbyterian Church he went to the German Reformed. As usual he fell asleep, but this time more soundly than was his wont. His head sunk upon his breast, his cap dropped from his hands to the floor, the prayers of the congregation did not disturb him, and only the choir and the deep-toned organ awakened him. Afterward I learned that the minister was credited with much loyalty and courage because he had prayed for the President of the United States in the very presence of Stonewall Jackson. Well, the general didn't hear the prayer, and if he had he would doubtless have felt like replying as General Ewell did, when asked at Carlisle, Pennsylvania, if he would permit the usual prayer for President Lincoln—"Certainly: I'm sure he needs it."

General Lee believed that Harper's Ferry would be evacuated as soon as he interposed between it and Washington. But he did not know that Halleck, and not McClellan, held command of it. When he found that it was not

⚓ Lieutenant Robert Healy, of the 55th Virginia, in Stonewall Jackson's command, tells the following incident of the march into Maryland: "The day before the corps waded the Potomac at White's Ford, they marched through Leesburg, where an old lady with upraised hands, and with tears in her eyes exclaimed: 'The Lord bless your dirty ragged souls!' Lieutenant Healy adds: 'Don't think we were any dirtier than the rest, but it was our luck to get the blessing.'"— EDITORS.

evacuated he knew some one had blundered, and took steps to capture the garrison and stores. On Tuesday, the 9th, he issued an order, directing General Jackson to move the next morning, cross the Potomac near Sharpsburg, and envelop Harper's Ferry on the Virginia side. In the same order he directed General McLaws to march on Harper's Ferry by way of Middletown and seize Maryland Heights, and General Walker to cross the Potomac below Harper's Ferry and take Loudoun Heights, all to be in position on the 12th, except Jackson, who was first to capture, if possible, the troops at Martinsburg.

Early on the 10th Jackson was off. In Frederick he asked for a map of Chambersburg and its vicinity, and made many irrelevant inquiries about roads and localities in the direction of Pennsylvania. To his staff, who knew what little value these inquiries had, his questions only illustrated his well-known motto, "Mystery, mystery is the secret of success." I was then assistant inspector-general on his staff, and also acting aide-de-camp. It was my turn this day to be intrusted with the knowledge of his purpose. Having finished this public inquiry, he took me aside, and after asking me about the different fords of the Potomac between Williamsport and Harper's Ferry, told me that he was ordered to capture the garrison at Harper's Ferry, and would cross either at Williamsport or Shepherdstown, as the enemy might or might not withdraw from Martinsburg. I did not then know of General Lee's order.

The troops being on the march, the general and staff rode rapidly out of town and took the head of the column. Just a few words here in regard to Mr. Whittier's touching poem, "Barbara Frietchie." An old woman, by that now immortal name, did live in Frederick in those days, but she never saw General Jackson, and General Jackson never saw "Barbara Frietchie." I was with him every minute of the time he was in that city,—he was there only twice,—and nothing like the scene so graphically described by the poet ever happened. Mr. Whittier must have been misinformed as to the incident. [See p. 619.— Editors.]

On the march that day, the captain of the cavalry advance, just ahead, had instructions to let no civilian go to the front, and we entered each village we passed before the inhabitants knew of our coming. In Middletown two very pretty girls, with ribbons of red, white, and blue floating from their hair, and small Union flags in their hands, rushed out of a house as we passed, came to the curbstone, and with much laughter waved their flags defiantly in the face of the general. He bowed and raised his hat, and, turning with his quiet smile to his staff, said: "We evidently have no friends in this town." And this is about the way he would have treated Barbara Frietchie!

Having crossed South Mountain, at Turner's Gap, the command encamped for the night within a mile of Boonsboro'. Here General Jackson must determine whether he would go on to Williamsport or turn toward Shepherdstown. I at once rode into the village with a cavalryman to make some inquiries, but we ran into a squadron of Federal cavalry, who without ceremony proceeded to make war upon us. We retraced our steps, and although we did not stand upon the order of our going, a squad of them escorted us out of town with great rapidity. When I tried a couple of Parthian shots at them with my revolver, they returned them with interest, and shot a hole in my new hat, which, with the beautiful plume that a lady in Frederick had placed there, rolled in the dust. This was of little moment, but at the end of the town, reaching the top of the hill, we discovered, just over it, General Jackson, walking slowly toward us, leading his horse. There was but one thing to do. Fortunately the chase had become less vigorous, and, with a cry of command to unseen troops, we turned and charged the enemy. They, suspecting trouble, turned and fled, while the general quickly galloped to the rear. I recovered my hat and plume, and as I returned to camp I picked up the gloves which the general had dropped in mounting, and took them to him. Although he had sent a regiment of infantry to the front as soon as he went back, the only allusion he made to the incident was to express the opinion that I had a very fast horse.

The next morning, having learned that the Federal troops still occupied Martinsburg, General Jackson took the direct road to Williamsport. He there forded the Potomac, the troops now singing, and the bands playing, "Carry me back to ole Virginny!" We marched on Martinsburg. General A. P. Hill took the direct turnpike, while Jackson, with the rest of his command, followed a side road, so as to approach Martinsburg from the west, and encamped four miles from the town. His object was to drive General White, who occupied Martinsburg, toward Harper's Ferry, and thus "corral" all the Federal troops in that military pen. As the Comte de Paris puts it, he "organized a kind of grand hunting match through the lower valley of Virginia, driving all the Federal detachments before him and forcing them to crowd into the blind alley of Harper's Ferry." Fatigued by the day's march, Jackson was persuaded by his host of the night to drink a whisky toddy — the only glass of spirits I ever saw him take. While mixing it leisurely, he remarked that he believed he liked the taste of whisky and brandy more than any soldier in the army; that they were more palatable to him than the most fragrant coffee, and for that reason, with others, he rarely tasted them.

The next morning the Confederates entered Martinsburg. Here the general was welcomed with great enthusiasm, and a great crowd hastened to the hotel to greet him. At first he shut himself up in a room to write dispatches, but the demonstration became so persistent that he ordered the door to be opened. The crowd, chiefly ladies, rushed in and embarrassed the general with every possible outburst of affection, to which he could only reply, "Thank you, you're very kind." He gave them his autograph in books and on scraps of paper, cut a button from his coat for a little girl, and then submitted patiently to an attack by the others, who soon stripped the coat of nearly all the remaining buttons. But when they looked beseechingly at his hair, which was thin, he drew the line there, and managed to close the interview. These blandishments did not delay his movements, however, for in the afternoon he was off again.

A GLIMPSE OF STONEWALL JACKSON.

On the 13th he invested Bolivar Heights and Harper's Ferry. On this day General McClellan came into possession, by carelessness or accident, of General Lee's order of the 9th, and he was thus notified of the division of the Confederate army and the intention to capture Harper's Ferry. From this moment General Lee's army was in peril, imminent in proportion to the promptness with which the Federal commander might use the knowledge he thus obtained. The plans of the latter were quickly and skillfully made. Had they been executed more rapidly, or had Jackson been slower and less sure, the result must have been a disastrous one to us. But military critics disposed to censure General McClellan for not being equal to his opportunities should credit him with the embarrassment of his position. He had not been in command of this army two weeks. It was a large army, but a heterogeneous one, with many old troops dispirited by recent defeat, and many new troops that had never been under fire. With such an army a general as cautious as McClellan does not take great risks, nor put the safety of his army rashly "to the touch, to win or lose it all." General McClellan was inclined by nature to magnify the forces of the enemy, and had he known General Lee's weakness he would have ventured more. Yet when we remember what Pope had done and suffered just before, and what happened to Burnside and Hooker not long after, their friends can hardly sit in judgment upon McClellan.

On the afternoon of the 13th Colonel Miles, in command at Harper's Ferry, made the fatal mistake of withdrawing his troops from Maryland Heights, and giving them up to McLaws. Napier has said, "He who wars walks in a mist through which the keenest eyes cannot always discern the right path." But it does seem that Colonel Miles might have known that to abandon these heights under the circumstances was simply suicidal.♦

Jackson met with so much delay in opening communication with McLaws and Walker, and ascertaining whether they were in position, that much of the 14th was consumed. But late in the afternoon A. P. Hill gained a foothold, with little resistance, well up on the enemy's left, and established some artillery at the base of Loudoun Heights and across the Shenandoah, so as to take the Federal line on Bolivar Heights in rear. (General Hill had been placed under arrest by General Jackson, before crossing the Potomac into Maryland, for disobedience of orders, and the command of his division devolved upon General Branch, who was killed a few days later at Antietam. Believing a battle imminent, General Hill requested General Jackson to reinstate him in command of his division until the approaching engagement was over. No one could appreciate such an appeal more keenly than General Jackson, and he at once restored General Hill to his command. The work the Light Division did at Harper's Ferry and Sharpsburg proved the wisdom of Hill's request and of Jackson's compliance with it.)

During the 14th, while Jackson was fixing his clamps on Harper's Ferry, McClellan was pushing against Lee's divided forces at Turner's Gap. Hooker and Reno, under Burnside and under the eye of General McClellan, were fighting the battle of South Mountain against D. H. Hill and Longstreet. Here Reno and Garland were killed on opposite sides, and night ended the contest before it was decided. At the same time Franklin was forcing his way through Crampton's Gap, driving out Howell Cobb commanding his own brigade and one regiment of Semmes's brigade, both of McLaws's division, Parham's brigade of R. H. Anderson's division, and two regiments of Stuart's cavalry under Colonel Munford. The military complications were losing their simplicity. Being advised of these movements, Jackson saw that his work must be done speedily. On Monday morning, at 3 o'clock, he sent me to the left to move Jones forward at first dawn, and to open on Bolivar Heights with all his artillery. This feint was executed promptly and produced confusion on the enemy's right. Troops were moved to strengthen it. Then the guns from Maryland and Loudoun Heights opened fire, and very soon, off on our right, the battle-flags of A. P. Hill rose on Bolivar Heights, and Harper's Ferry was doomed. Returning, I found General Jackson at the church in the wood on the Bolivar and Halltown turnpike, and just as I joined him a white flag was raised on Bolivar and all the firing ceased.

<hr>

♦ General Julius White says in his report ("Official Records," Vol. XIX., Pt. I., p. 523): "It will be noticed that Colonel Ford claims to have been ordered by Colonel Miles to evacuate the heights. Colonel Miles, however, denied to me ever having given such an order, but said he gave orders that if it became necessary to abandon the heights the guns were to be spiked and dismounted." See also General White's statement. p. 612.—Editors.

LIEUTENANT-GENERAL AMBROSE P. HILL, C. S. A. FROM A PHOTOGRAPH.

Under instructions from General Jackson, I rode up the pike and into the enemy's lines to ascertain the purpose of the white flag. Near the top of the hill I met General White and staff and told him my mission. He replied that Colonel Miles had been mortally wounded, that he was in command and desired to have an interview with General Jackson. Just then General Hill came up from the direction of his line, and at his request I conducted them to General Jackson, whom I found sitting on his horse where I had left him. He was not, as the Comte de Paris says, leaning against a tree asleep, but exceedingly wide-awake. The contrast in appearances there presented was striking. General White, riding a handsome black horse, was carefully dressed and had on untarnished gloves, boots, and sword. His staff were equally comely in costume. On the other hand, General Jackson was the dingiest, worst-dressed, and worst-mounted general that a warrior who cared for good looks and style would wish to surrender to. The surrender was unconditional, and then General Jackson turned the matter over to General A. P. Hill, who allowed General White the same liberal terms that Grant afterward gave Lee at Appomattox.‡

‡ Of the expectations of Jackson's men, Lieutenant Robert Healy says, in a letter written in 1886:

"On the evening of the 14th we took position within six hundred yards of a Federal fort on Bolivar Heights. We lay that night in a deep ravine, perpendicular to the Shenandoah. The next morning by dawn I crept up the hill to see how the land lay. A few strides brought me to the edge of an abatis which extended solidly for two hundred yards, a narrow bare field being between the abatis and the foot of the fort, which was garnished with thirty guns. They were searching the abatis lazily

The fruits of the surrender were 12,520 prisoners ("Official Records"), 13,000 arms, 73 pieces of artillery, and several hundred wagons.

General Jackson, after sending a brief dispatch to General Lee announcing the capitulation, rode up to Bolivar and down into Harper's Ferry. The curiosity in the Union army to see him was so great that the soldiers lined the sides of the road. Many of them uncovered as he passed, and he invariably returned the salute. One man had an echo of response all about him when he said aloud: "Boys, he's not much for looks, but if we'd had him we wouldn't have been caught in this trap!"

General Jackson lost little time in contemplating his victory. When night came, he started for Shepherdstown with J. R. Jones and Lawton, leaving directions to McLaws and Walker to follow the next morning. He left A. P. Hill behind to finish up with Harper's Ferry. His first order had been to take position at Shepherdstown to cover Lee's crossing into Virginia, but, whether at his own suggestion or not, the order was changed, and after daylight on the 16th he crossed the Potomac there and joined Longstreet at Sharpsburg. General McClellan had, by that time, nearly all his army in position on the east bank of the Antietam, and General Lee was occupying the irregular range of high ground to the west of it, with the Potomac in his rear. Except some sparring between Hooker and Hood on our left, the 16th was allowed to pass without battle, fortunately for us. In the new dispositions of that evening, Jackson was placed on the left of Lee's army. [See map, p. 636.]

The first onset, early on the morning of the 17th, told what the day would be. The impatient Hooker, with the divisions of Meade, Doubleday, and Ricketts, struck the first blow, and Jackson's old division caught it and struck back again. Between such foes the battle soon waxed hot. Step by step and marking each step with dead, the thin Confederate line was pushed back to the wood around the Dunker Church. Here Lawton, Starke (commanding in place of Jones, already wounded), and D. H. Hill with part of his division, engaged Meade. And now in turn the Federals halted and fell back, and left their dead by Dunker Church. Next Mansfield entered the fight, and beat with resistless might on Jackson's people. The battle here grew angry and bloody. Starke was killed, Lawton wounded, and nearly all their general and field officers had fallen; the sullen Confederate line again fell back, killing Mansfield and wounding Hooker, Crawford, and Hartsuff.

And now D. H. Hill led in the rest of his division; Hood also took part, to the right and left, front and rear of Dunker Church. The Federal line was again driven back, while artillery added its din to the incessant

with grape-shot, which flew uncomfortably near at times. I thought I had never seen a more dangerous trap in my life. The order had been given that we were to charge at sunrise. I went back, and Austin Brockenbrough asked, 'How is it?' 'Well,' said I, 'we'll say our prayers and go in like men.' 'Not as bad as that?' 'Every bit; see for yourself.' He went up and came back looking very grave. Meanwhile, from the east, north-west, and north-east our cannon opened and were answered by the Federal guns from Bolivar Heights. We were down in a ravine; we could see nothing; we could only hear. Presently, along our line came the words, 'Prepare to charge!' We moved steadily up the hill; the sun had just risen; some one said: 'Colonel, what is that on the fort?' 'Halt,' cried the colonel, 'they have surrendered.' A glad shout burst from ten thousand men. We got into the place as soon as we could, but the way was so difficult it took us a half hour." EDITORS.

rattle of musketry. Then Sumner, with the fresh division of Sedgwick, re-formed the Federal line and renewed the offensive. Hood was driven back, and Hill partly; the Dunker Church wood was passed, the field south of it entered, and the Confederate left turned. Just then McLaws, hurrying from Harper's Ferry, came upon the field, and hurled his men against the victorious Sedgwick. He drove Sedgwick back into the Dunker wood and beyond it, into the open ground. Farther to our right, the pendulum of battle had been swinging to and fro, with D. H. Hill and R. H. Anderson hammering away at French and Richardson, until the sunken road became historic as "bloody lane." Richardson was mortally wounded and Hancock assumed command of his division.

For a while there was a lull in the storm. It was early in the day, but hours are fearfully long in battle. About noon Franklin, with Slocum and W. F. Smith, marched upon the field to join the unequal contest. Smith tried his luck and was repulsed. Sumner then ordered a halt. Jackson's fight was over, and a strange silence reigned around Dunker Church.

General Lee had not visited the left that day. As usual he trusted to Jackson to fight his own battle and work out salvation in his own way. How well he did it, against the ablest and fiercest of McClellan's lieutenants, history has told.

BRIGADIER-GENERAL WILLIAM E. STARKE. FROM A TINTYPE.

In the cannonade which began with dawn of the 17th, General J. R. Jones, commanding the left division of Jackson, was stunned and injured by a shell which exploded directly over his head. General Starke was directed to take command of the division, which he led against Hooker, and a half-hour later he fell pierced by three minie-balls. Of that terrible struggle Stonewall Jackson says in his report: "The carnage on both sides was terrific. At this early hour General Starke was killed. Colonel Douglass, commanding Lawton's brigade, was also killed. General Lawton, commanding division, and Colonel Walker, commanding brigade, were severely wounded. More than half of the brigades of Lawton and Hays were either killed or wounded, and more than a third of Trimble's, and all the regimental commanders in those brigades, except two, were killed or wounded."— EDITORS.

During all this time Longstreet, stripped of his troops,—sent to the help of Jackson,—held the right almost alone, with his eye on the center. He was now called into active work on his own front, for there were no unfought troops in Lee's army at Sharpsburg; every soldier on that field tasted battle.

General Burnside, with his corps of fourteen thousand men, had been lying all day beyond the bridge which now bears his name. Ordered to cross at 8 o'clock he managed to get over at 1, and by 3 was ready to advance. \ He

moved against the hill which D. R. Jones held with his little division of
2500 men. Longstreet was watching this advance. Jackson was at General
Lee's headquarters on a knoll in rear of Sharpsburg. A. P. Hill was coming,
but had not arrived, and it was apparent that Burnside must be stayed, if
at all, with artillery. One of the sections, transferred to the right from
Jackson at the request of General Lee, was of the Rockbridge Artillery, and
as it galloped by, the youngest son of the general-in-chief, Robert E. Lee, Jr.,
a private at the guns, black with the grime and powder of a long day's
fight, stopped a moment to salute his father and then rushed after his gun.
Where else in this war was the son of a commanding general a private in the
ranks?

Going to put this section in place, I saw Burnside's heavy line move up
the hill, and the earth seemed to tremble beneath their tread. It was a splendid and fearful sight, but for them to beat back Jones's feeble line was scarcely
war. The artillery tore, but did not stay them. They pressed forward until
Sharpsburg was uncovered and Lee's line of retreat was at their mercy. But
then, just then, A. P. Hill, picturesque in his red battle-shirt, with 3 of his
brigades, 2500 men, who had marched that day 17 miles from Harper's Ferry
and had waded the Potomac, appeared upon the scene. Tired and footsore,
the men forgot their woes in that supreme moment, and with no breathing
time braced themselves to meet the coming shock. They met it and stayed it.
The blue line staggered and hesitated, and, hesitating, was lost. At the critical moment A. P. Hill was always at his strongest. Quickly advancing his
battle-flags, his line moved forward, Jones's troops rallied on him, and in the
din of musketry and artillery on either flank the Federals broke over the field.
Hill did not wait for his other brigades, but held the vantage gained until Burnside was driven back to the Antietam and under the shelter of heavy guns.
The day was done. Again A. P. Hill, as at Manassas, Harper's Ferry, and
elsewhere, had struck with the right hand of Mars. No wonder that both Lee
and Jackson, when, in the delirium of their last moments on earth, they
stood again to battle, saw the form of A. P. Hill leading his columns on;
but it is a wonder and a shame that the grave of this valiant Virginian
in Hollywood cemetery has not a stone to mark it and keep it from
oblivion.

The battle at Sharpsburg was the result of unforeseen circumstances and
not of deliberate purpose. It was one of the bloodiest of the war, and a defeat
for both armies. The prestige of the day was with Lee, but when on the
night of the 18th he recrossed into Virginia, although, as the Comte de Paris
says, he "left not a single trophy of his nocturnal retreat in the hands of the
enemy," he left the prestige of the result with McClellan. And yet when it
is known that General McClellan had 87,000 troops at hand, and General
Lee fought the battle with less than 35,000,♦ an army depleted by battles,
weakened by privations, broken down by marching, and "ruined by straggling," it was unquestionably on the Confederate side the best-fought battle
of the war.

♦ See notes on pp. 565 and 603 as to the strength of the forces on each side.— EDITORS.

THE BATTLE OF ANTIETAM.

BY JACOB D. COX, MAJOR-GENERAL, U. S. V.

IT was not till some time past noon of the 15th of September that, the way
being clear for the Ninth Corps at South Mountain, we marched through
Fox's gap to the Boonsboro' and Sharpsburg turnpike, and along this road till
we came up in rear of Sumner's command. Hooker's corps, which was part
of the right wing (Burnside's), had been in the advance, and had moved off
from the turnpike to the right near Keedysville. I was with the Kanawha
Division, assuming that my temporary command of the corps ended with
the battle on the mountain. When we approached the line of hills bordering the Antietam, we received orders to turn off the road to the left, and
halted our battalions closed in mass. It was now about 3 o'clock in the afternoon. McClellan, as it seemed, had just reached the field, and was surrounded
by a group of his principal officers, most of whom I had never seen before.
I rode up with General Burnside, dismounted, and was very cordially greeted
by General McClellan. He and Burnside were evidently on terms of most
intimate friendship and familiarity. He introduced me to the officers I had
not known before, referring pleasantly to my service with him in Ohio and
West Virginia, putting me upon an easy footing with them in a very agreeable
and genial way.

We walked up the slope of the ridge before us, and looking westward from
its crest the whole field of the coming battle was before us. Immediately in
front the Antietam wound through the hollow, the hills rising gently on both
sides. In the background on our left was the village of Sharpsburg, with fields

inclosed by stone fences in front of it. At its right was a bit of wood (since known as the West Wood), with the little Dunker Church standing out white and sharp against it. Farther to the right and left the scene was closed in by wooded ridges with open farm lands between, the whole making as pleasing and prosperous a landscape as can easily be imagined. We made a large group as we stood upon the hill, and it was not long before we attracted the enemy's attention. A puff of white smoke from a knoll on the right of the Sharpsburg road was followed by the screaming of a shell over our heads. McClellan directed that all but one or two should retire behind the ridge, while he continued the reconnoissance, walking slowly to the right. I noted with satisfaction the cool and business-like air with which he made his examination under fire. The Confederate artillery was answered by a battery, and a lively cannonade ensued on both sides, though without any noticeable effect. The enemy's position was revealed, and he was evidently in force on both sides of the turnpike in front of Sharpsburg, covered by the undulations of the rolling ground which hid his infantry from our sight.

UNION SIGNAL STATION ON ELK MOUNTAIN, FIVE OR SIX MILES SOUTH-EAST OF SHARPSBURG. FROM A PHOTOGRAPH.

The examination of the enemy's position and the discussion of it continued till near the close of the day. Orders were then given for the Ninth Corps to move to the left, keeping off the road, which was occupied by other troops. We moved through fields and farm lands, an hour's march in the dusk of the evening, going into bivouac about a mile south of the Sharpsburg bridge, and in rear of the hills bordering the Antietam.

On Tuesday, September 16th, we confidently expected a battle, and I kept with my division. In the afternoon I saw General Burnside, and learned from him that McClellan had determined to let Hooker make a movement on our extreme right to turn Lee's position. Burnside's manner in speaking of this implied that he thought it was done at Hooker's solicitation and through his desire, openly evinced, to be independent in command.

I urged Burnside to assume the immediate command of the corps and allow me to lead only my own division. He objected that as he had been announced as commander of the right wing of the army composed of two corps (his own and Hooker's), he was unwilling to waive his precedence or to assume that Hooker was detached for anything more than a temporary purpose. I pointed out that Reno's staff had been granted leave of absence to

DOUBLEDAY'S DIVISION OF HOOKER'S CORPS CROSSING THE UPPER FORDS OF THE ANTIETAM.
FROM A SKETCH MADE AT THE TIME.

take the body of their chief to Washington, and that my division staff was too small for corps duty; but he met this by saying that he would use his staff for this purpose and help me in every way he could, till the crisis of the campaign should be over.

The 16th passed without serious fighting, though there was desultory cannonading and picket firing. It was hard to restrain our men from showing themselves on the crest of the long ridge in front of us, and whenever they did so they drew the fire from some of the enemy's batteries, to which ours would respond. In the afternoon McClellan reconnoitered the line of the Antietam near us, Burnside being with him. As the result of this we were ordered to change our positions at nightfall, staff-officers being sent to guide each division to its new camp. Rodman's division went half a mile to the left, where a country road led to a ford in a great bend in the Antietam curving deeply into the enemy's side of the stream.⸗ Sturgis's division was placed on the sides of the road leading to the stone bridge, since known as Burnside's Bridge (below the Sharpsburg bridge). Willcox's was put in reserve in rear of Sturgis. My own division was divided, Scammon's brigade going with Rodman, and Crook's going with Sturgis. Crook was ordered to take the advance in crossing the bridge, in case we should be ordered to attack.

⸗ The information obtained from the neighborhood was that no fords of the Antietam were passable at that time, except one about half-way between the two upper bridges and another less than half a mile below Burnside's Bridge. We, however, found during the engagement another ford a short distance above Burnside's Bridge. The inquiry and reconnoissance for the fords was made by engineer officers of the general staff, and our orders were based on their reports.—J. D. C.

This selection was made by Burnside himself, as a compliment to the division for the vigor of its assault at South Mountain. While we were moving, we heard Hooker's guns far off on the right and front, and the cannonade continued an hour or more after it became dark.

The morning of Wednesday, the 17th, broke fresh and fair. The men were astir at dawn, getting breakfast and preparing for a day of battle. The artillery opened on both sides as soon as it was fairly light, and the positions which had been assigned us in the dusk of the evening were found to be exposed in some places to the direct fire of the Confederate guns, Rodman's division suffering more than the others. Fairchild's brigade alone reported thirty-six casualties before they could find cover. It was not till 7 o'clock that orders came to advance toward the creek as far as could be done without exposing the men to unnecessary loss. Rodman was directed to acquaint himself with the situation of the ford in front of him, and Sturgis to seek the best means of approach to the stone bridge. All were then to remain in readiness to obey further orders.

When these arrangements had been made, I rode to the position Burnside had selected for himself, which was upon a high knoll north-east of the Burnside Bridge, near a hay-stack which was a prominent landmark. Near by was Benjamin's battery of 20-pounder Parrotts, and a little farther still to the right, on the same ridge, General Sturgis had sent in Durell's battery. These were exchanging shots with the enemy's guns opposite, and had the advantage in range and weight of metal.

Whatever the reason, McClellan had adopted a plan of battle which practically reduced Sumner and Burnside to the command of one corps each, while Hooker had been sent far off on the right front, followed later by Mansfield, but without organizing the right wing as a unit so that one commander could give his whole attention to handling it with vigor. In his preliminary report, made before he was relieved from command, McClellan says:

" The design was to make the main attack upon the enemy's left —at least to create a diversion in favor of the main attack, with the hope of something more, by assailing the enemy's right — and, as soon as one or both of the flank movements were fully successful, to attack their center with any reserve I might then have in hand."

McClellan's report covering his whole career in the war, dated August 4th, 1863 (and published February, 1864, after warm controversies had arisen and he had become a political character), modifies the above statement in some important particulars. It says:

" My plan for the impending general engagement was to attack the enemy's left with the corps of Hooker and Mansfield, supported by Sumner's, and if necessary by Franklin's, and as soon as matters looked favorably there to move the corps of Burnside against the enemy's extreme right upon the ridge running to the south and rear of Sharpsburg, and having carried their position, to press along the crest toward our right, and whenever either of these flank movements should be successful, to advance our center with all the forces then disposable."

The opinion I got from Burnside as to the part the Ninth Corps was to take was fairly consistent with the design first quoted, viz., that when the attack by Sumner, Hooker, and Franklin should be progressing favorably, we were

THE SHARPSBURG BRIDGE OVER THE ANTIETAM.
FROM A WAR-TIME PHOTOGRAPH.

"to create a diversion in favor of the main attack, with the hope of something more." It would also appear probable that Hooker's movement was at first intended to be made by his corps alone, taken up by Sumner's two corps as soon as he was ready to attack, and shared in by Franklin if he reached the field in time, thus making a simultaneous oblique attack from our right by the whole army except Porter's corps, which was in reserve, and the Ninth Corps, which was to create the "diversion" on our left and prevent the enemy from stripping his right to reënforce his left. It is hardly disputable that this would have been a better plan than the one actually carried out. Certainly the assumption that the Ninth Corps could cross the Antietam alone at the only place on the field where the Confederates had their line immediately upon the stream which must be crossed under fire by two narrow heads of column, and could then turn to the right along the high ground occupied by the hostile army before that army had been broken or seriously shaken elsewhere, is one which would hardly be made till time had dimmed the remembrance of the actual positions of Lee's divisions upon the field.

The evidence that the plan did not originally include the wide separation of two corps to the right, to make the extended turning movement, is found in

Hooker's incomplete report, and in the wide interval in time between the marching of his corps and that of Mansfield. Hooker was ordered to cross the Antietam at about 2 o'clock in the afternoon of the 16th by the bridge in front of Keedysville and the ford below it. He says that after his troops were over and in march, he rode back to McClellan, who told him that he might call for reënforcements and that when they came they should be under his command. Somewhat later McClellan rode forward with his staff to observe the progress making, and Hooker again urged the necessity of reënforcements. Yet Sumner did not receive orders to send Mansfield to support Hooker till evening, and the Twelfth Corps marched only half an hour before midnight, reaching its bivouac, about a mile and a half in rear of that of Hooker, at 2 A. M. of the 17th. Sumner was also ordered to be in readiness to march with the Second Corps an hour before day, but his orders to move did not reach him till nearly half-past 7 in the morning. By this time, Hooker had fought his battle, had been repulsed, and later in the morning was carried wounded from the field. Mansfield had fallen before his corps was deployed, and General Alpheus S. Williams who succeeded him was fighting a losing battle at all points but one — where Greene's division held the East Wood.

After crossing the Antietam, Hooker had shaped his course to the westward, aiming to reach the ridge upon which the Hagerstown turnpike runs, and which is the dominant feature of the landscape. This ridge is some two

GERMAN REFORMED CHURCH IN KEEDYSVILLE, USED AS A UNION HOSPITAL. FROM A PHOTOGRAPH TAKEN IN 1886.

miles distant from the Antietam, and for the first mile of the way no resistance was met. However, Hooker's progress had been observed by the enemy, and Hood's two brigades were taken from the center and passed to the left of D. H. Hill. Here they occupied an open wood (since known as the East Wood), north-east of the Dunker Church. Hooker was now trying to approach the Confederate positions, Meade's division of the Pennsylvania Reserves being in the advance. A sharp skirmishing combat ensued and artillery was also brought into action on both sides, the engagement continuing till after dark. On our side Seymour's brigade had been chiefly engaged, and had felt the enemy so vigorously that Hood supposed he had repulsed a serious effort to take the wood. Hooker was, however, aiming to pass quite beyond the flank, and kept his other divisions north of the hollow beyond the wood, and upon the ridge which reaches the turnpike near the largest reëntrant bend of the Potomac, which is here only half a mile distant. Here he bivouacked upon the northern slopes of the ridge, Doubleday's division resting with its

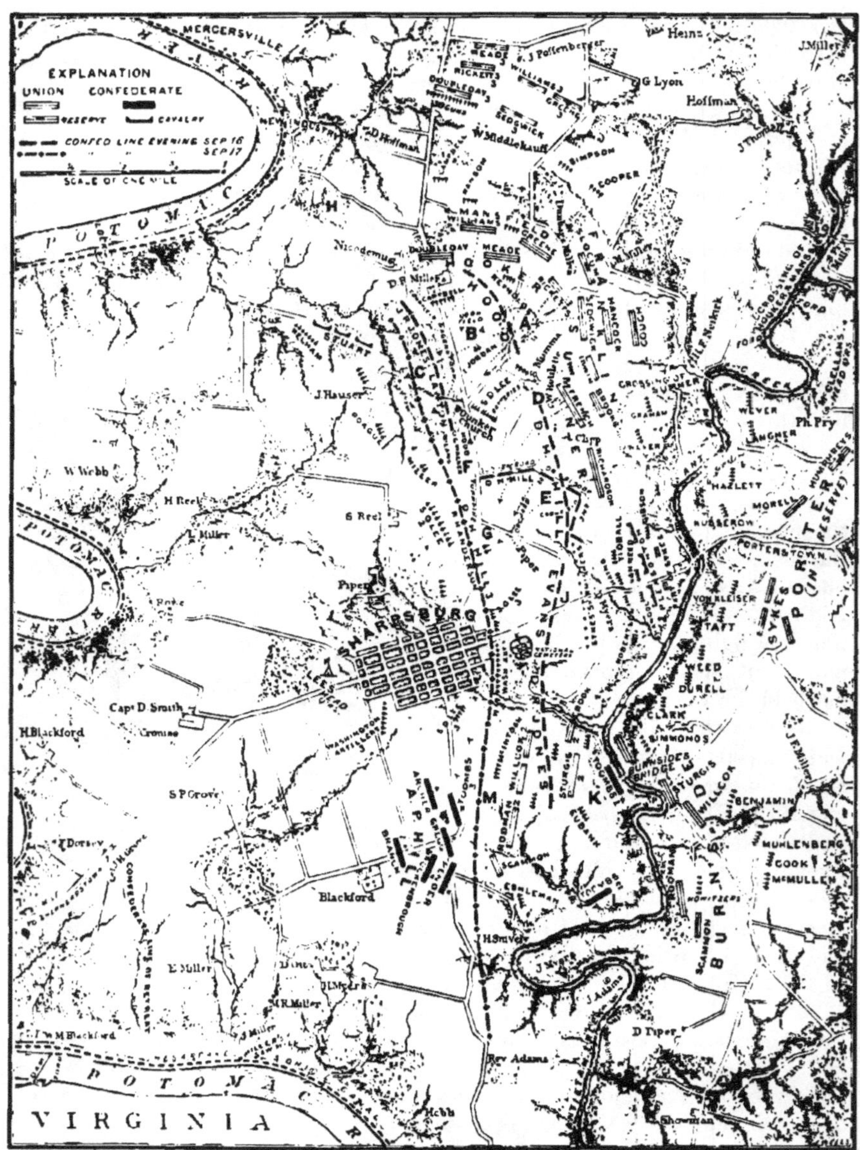

THE FIELD OF ANTIETAM.

On the afternoon of September 16th, Hooker's corps crossed at the two fords and the bridge north of McClellan's headquarters.

A.— From near sunset till dark Hooker engaged Hood's division (of Longstreet's corps) about the "East Wood," marked A on the map. Hood was relieved by two brigades of Jackson's corps, which was in and behind the Dunker Church wood (or West Wood), C.

B.— At dawn on the 17th, Hooker and Jackson began a terrible contest which raged in and about the famous corn-field, B, and in the woods, A and C. Jackson's reserves regained the corn-field. Hartsuff's brigade, of Hooker's corps, and Mansfield's corps charged through the corn-field into the Dunker Church wood, General Mansfield being mortally wounded in front of the East Wood.

right upon the turnpike, Ricketts's division upon the left of Doubleday, and Meade covering the front of both with the skirmishers of Seymour's brigade. Between Meade's skirmishers and the ridge were the farm-house and barn of J. Poffenberger on the east of the road, where Hooker made his own quarters for the night. Half a mile farther in front was the farm of D. R. Miller, the dwelling on the east, and the barn surrounded by stacks on the west of the road. ⚓ Mansfield's corps, marching as it did late in the night, kept farther to the right than Hooker's, but moved on a nearly parallel course and bivouacked upon the farm of another J. Poffenberger near the road which, branching from the Hagerstown turnpike at the Dunker Church, intersects the one running from Keedysville through Smoketown to the same turnpike about a mile north of Hooker's position.

On the Confederate side, Hood's division had been so severely handled that it was replaced by Jackson's (commanded by J. R. Jones), which, with Ewell's, had been led to the field from Harper's Ferry by Jackson, reaching Sharpsburg in the afternoon of the 16th. These divisions were formed on the left of D. H. Hill and almost at right angles to his line, crossing the turnpike and facing northward. Hood's division, on being relieved, was placed in reserve near the Dunker Church, and spent part of the night in cooking rations, of which its supply had been short for a day or two. The combatants on both sides slept upon their arms, well knowing that the dawn would bring bloody work.

When day broke on Wednesday morning, the 17th, Hooker, looking south from the Poffenberger farm along the turnpike, saw a gently rolling landscape, of which the commanding point was the Dunker Church, whose white brick walls appeared on the west side of the road backed by the foliage of the West Wood, which came toward him, filling a slight hollow which ran parallel to the turnpike, with a single row of fields between. Beyond the Miller house and barns, the ground dipped into a little depression. Beyond this was seen a large corn-field between the East Wood and the turnpike, rising again

Jackson, with the aid of Hood, and a part of D. H. Hill's division, again cleared the Dunker Church wood. J. G. Walker's division, taken from the extreme right of the Confederate line, charged in support of Jackson and Hood.

C.—Sumner's corps formed line of battle in the center, Sedgwick's division facing the East Wood, through which it charged over the corn-field again, and through Dunker Church wood to the edge of the fields beyond. McLaws's division (of Longstreet's corps), just arrived from Harper's Ferry, assisted in driving out Sedgwick, who was forced to retreat northward by the Hagerstown pike.

D.—About the time that Sedgwick charged, French and Richardson, of Sumner's corps, dislodged D. H. Hill's line from Roulette's house

E.—Hill re-formed in the sunken road, since known as the "Bloody Lane," where his position was carried by French and Richardson, the latter being mortally wounded in the corn-field, E.

F.—Irwin and Brooks, of Franklin's corps, moved to the support of French and Richardson. At the point F. Irwin's brigade was repelled.

G.—D. H. Hill, reënforced by R. H. Anderson's division of Longstreet's corps, fought for the ground about Piper's house.

H.—Stuart attempted a flank movement north of the Dunker Church wood, but was driven back by the thirty guns under Doubleday.

J.—Pleasonton, with a part of his cavalry and several batteries, crossed the Boonsboro' bridge as a flank support to Richardson, and to Burnside on the south. Several battalions of regulars from Porter's corps came to his assistance and made their way well up to the hill which is now the National Cemetery.

K.—Toombs (of Longstreet) had defended the lower bridge until Burnside moved Rodman and Scammon to the fords below.

L.—Then Toombs hurried south to protect the Confederate flank. Sturgis and Crook charged across the Burnside Bridge and gained the heights. Toombs was driven away from the fords.

M.—After 3 o'clock, Burnside's lines, being re-formed, completed the defeat of D. R. Jones's division (of Longstreet), and on the right gained the outskirts of Sharpsburg. Toombs, and the arriving brigades of A. P. Hill, of Jackson's corps, saved the village and regained a part of the lost ground.— EDITORS.

⚓ Hooker's unfinished report says he slept in the barn of D. R. Miller, but he places it on the east of the road, and the spot is fully identified as Poffenberger's by General Gibbon, who commanded the right brigade, and by Major Rufus R. Dawes (afterward Brevet Brigadier-General), both of whom subsequently visited the field and determined the positions.— J. D. C.

to the higher level. There was, however, another small dip beyond, which could not be seen from Hooker's position; and on the second ridge, near the church, and extending across the turnpike eastward into the East Wood, could be seen the Confederate line of gray, partly sheltered by piles of rails taken from the fences. They seemed to Hooker to be at the farther side of the corn-field and at the top of the first rise of ground beyond Miller's. It was plain that the high ground about the little white church was the key of the enemy's position, and if that could be carried Hooker's task would be well done.

The Confederates opened the engagement by a rapid fire from a battery near the East Wood as soon as it was light, and Hooker answered the challenge by an immediate order for his line to advance. Doubleday's division was in two lines, Gibbon's and Phelps's brigades in front, supported by Patrick and Hofmann. Gibbon had the right and guided upon the turnpike. Patrick held a small wood in his rear, which is upon both sides of the road a

THE PRY HOUSE, GENERAL McCLELLAN'S HEADQUARTERS AT THE BATTLE OF ANTIETAM. FROM A PHOTOGRAPH TAKEN IN 1886.

little north of Miller's house. Some of Meade's men were supposed to be in the northernmost extension of the West Wood, and thus to cover Gibbon's right flank as he advanced. Part of Battery B, 4th United States Artillery (Gibbon's own battery), was run forward to Miller's barn and stack-yard on the right of the road, and fired over the heads of the advancing regiments. Other batteries were similarly placed more to the left. The line moved swiftly forward through Miller's orchard and kitchen garden, breaking through a stout picket fence on the near side, down into the moist ground of the hollow, and up through the corn, which was higher than their heads, and shut out every-thing from view. At the southern side of the field they came to a low fence, beyond which was an open field, at the farther side of which was the enemy's line. But Gibbon's right, covered by the corn, had outmarched the left, which had been exposed to a terrible fire, and the direction taken had been a little oblique, so that the right wing of the 6th Wisconsin, the flanking regiment, had crossed the turnpike and was suddenly assailed by a sharp fire from the West Wood on its flank. They swung back into the road, lying down along the high, stout post-and-rail fence, keeping up their fire by shooting between the rails. Leaving this little band to protect their right, the main line, which had come up on the left, leaped the fence at the south edge of the corn-field and charged across the open at the enemy in front. But the concentrated fire of artillery and musketry was more than they could bear. Men fell by scores and hundreds, and the thinned lines gave way and ran for the shelter of the corn. They were rallied in the hollow on the north side of the field. The enemy had rapidly extended his left under cover of the West Wood, and now made a dash at the right flank and at Gibbon's exposed guns. His men on the right faced by that flank and followed him bravely, though with little order, in a dash at the Confederates, who were swarming out of the wood. The gunners double-charged the cannon with canister, and under a terrible fire of both artillery and rifles the enemy broke and sought shelter.

Patrick's brigade had come up in support of Gibbon, and was sent across the turnpike into the West Wood to cover that flank. They pushed forward, the enemy retiring, until they were in advance of the principal line in the corn-field, upon which the Confederates were now advancing. Patrick faced his men to the left, parallel to the edge of the wood and to the turnpike, and poured his fire into the flank of the enemy, following it by a charge through the field and up to the fence along the road. Again the Confederates were driven back, but only to push in again by way of these woods, forcing Patrick to resume his original line of front and to retire to the cover of a ledge at right angles to the road near Gibbon's guns.

Farther to the left Phelps's and Hofmann's brigades had had similar experience, pushing forward nearly to the Confederate lines, and being driven back with great loss when they charged over open ground against the enemy. Ricketts's division entered the edge of the East Wood; but here, at the salient angle, where D. H. Hill and Lawton joined, the enemy held the position stubbornly, and the repulse of Doubleday's division made Ricketts glad to hold even the edge of the East Wood, as the right of the line was driven back.

It was now about 7 o'clock, and Mansfield's corps (the Twelfth) was approaching, for that officer had called his men to arms at the first sound of Hooker's battle and had marched to his support. The corps consisted of two divisions, Williams's and Greene's. It contained a number of new and undrilled regiments, and in hastening to the field in columns of battalions in mass, proper intervals for deployment had not been preserved, and time was necessarily lost before the troops could be put in line. General Mansfield fell mortally wounded before the deployment was complete, and the command devolved on General Williams. Williams had only time to take the most general directions from Hooker, when the latter also was wounded.‡ The Twelfth Corps attack

‡Of the early morning fight in the corn-field, General Hooker says in his report:

"We had not proceeded far before I discovered that a heavy force of the enemy had taken possession of a corn-field (I have since learned about a thirty-acre field), in my immediate front, and from the sun's rays falling on their bayonets projecting above the corn could see

MAJOR-GENERAL JOSEPH K. F. MANSFIELD. ☆
FROM A PHOTOGRAPH.

seems to have been made obliquely to that of Hooker, and facing more to the westward, for General Williams speaks of the post-and-rail fences along the turnpike being a great obstruction in their front. Greene's division, on his left, moved along the ridge leading to the East Wood, taking as the guide for his extreme left the line of the burning house of Mumma, which had been set on fire by D. H. Hill's men. Doubleday, in his report, notices this change of direction of Williams's division, which had relieved him, and says Williams's brigades were swept away by a fire from their left and front, from behind rocky ledges they could not see.‡ Our officers were deceived in part as to the extent and direction of the enemy's line by the fact that the Confederate cavalry commander, Stuart, had occupied a commanding hill west of the pike and beyond our right flank, and from this position, which, in fact, was considerably detached from the Confederate line, he used his batteries with such effect as to produce the belief that a continuous line extended from this point to the Dunker Church.↘ Our true lines of attack were convergent ones, the right sweeping southward along the pike and through the narrow strip of the West Wood, while the division

that the field was filled with the enemy, with arms in their hands, standing apparently at 'support arms.' Instructions were immediately given for the assemblage of all of my spare batteries near at hand, of which I think there were five or six, to spring into battery on the right of this field, and to open with canister at once. In the time I am writing every stalk of corn in the northern and greater part of the field was cut as closely as could have been done with a knife, and the slain lay in rows precisely as they had stood in their ranks a few moments before.

"It was never my fortune to witness a more bloody, dismal battle-field. Those that escaped fled in the opposite direction from our advance, and sought refuge behind the trees, fences, and stone ledges nearly on a line with the Dunker Church, etc., as there was no resisting this torrent of death-dealing missives. . . . The whole morning had been one of unusual animation to me and fraught with the grandest events. The conduct of my troops was sublime, and the occasion almost lifted me to the skies, and its memories will ever remain near me. My command followed the fugitives closely until we had passed the corn-field a quarter of a mile or more, when I was removed from my saddle in the act of falling out of it from loss of blood, having previously been struck without my knowledge."

EDITORS.

‡ Both in the West and East Wood and on the ground south of the East Wood the Confederates were protected by outcroppings of rocks, which served as natural breastworks.— EDITORS.

↘ Stuart says he had batteries from all parts of Jackson's command, and mentions Poague's, Pegram's, and Carrington's, besides Pelham's which was attached to the cavalry. He also says he was supported part of the time by Early's brigade; afterward by one regiment of it, the 13th Virginia.— EDITORS.

☆ General Mansfield was mortally wounded early in the action. In the "History of the 1st, 10th, 29th Maine Regiments," Major John M. Gould, who was Adjutant of the 10th Maine regiment, at Antietam, in Crawford's First Brigade, of A. S. Williams's First Division, of Mansfield's Twelfth Corps, gives the following circumstantial account of this event:

"The Confederate force in our front showed no colors. They appeared to be somewhat detached from and in advance of the main rebel line, and were about where the

SUMNER'S ADVANCE.—FRENCH'S DIVISION CLOSING IN UPON ROULETTE'S BARNS AND HOUSE—RICHARDSON'S DIVISION CONTINUING THE LINE FAR TO THE LEFT. FROM A SKETCH MADE AT THE TIME.

which drove the enemy from the East Wood should move upon the commanding ground around the church. This error of direction was repeated with disastrous effect a little later, when Sumner came on the ground with Sedgwick's corps.

When Mansfield's corps came on the field, Meade, who succeeded Hooker, ‡ withdrew the First Corps to the ridge north of Poffenberger's, where it had bivouacked the night before. It had suffered severely, having lost 2470 in killed and wounded, but it was still further depleted by straggling, so that

left of General Duryée's brigade might be supposed to have retreated. To General Mansfield we appeared to be firing into Duryea's troops; therefore he beckoned to us to cease firing, and as this was the very last thing we proposed to do, the few who saw him did not understand what his motions meant, and so no attention was paid to him. He now rode down the hill from the 128th Pennsylvania, and passing quickly through H, A, K, E, I, G, and D of the 10th Maine, ordering them to cease firing, he halted in front of C, at the earnest remonstrances of Captain Jordan and Sergeant Burnham, who asked him to see the gray coats of the enemy, and pointed out particular men of them who were then aiming their rifles at us and at him. The general was convinced, and remarked ‘Yes, yes, you are right,’ and was almost instantly hit. He turned and attempted to put his horse over the rails, but the animal had also been severely wounded and could not go over. Thereupon the general dismounted, and a gust of wind blowing open his coat we saw that he was wounded in the body. Sergeant Joe Merritt, Storer Knight, and I took the general to the rear, assisted for a while by a negro cook from Hooker's corps. We put the general into an ambulance in the woods in front of which we had deployed, and noticed that General Gordon was just at that moment posting the 107th New York in their front edge."

Colonel Jacob Higgins, 125th Pennsylvania regiment, commanding the brigade after Crawford was wounded, reports that some of his men carried General Mansfield "off the field on their muskets until a blanket was procured." General George H. Gordon, commanding the Third Brigade of this division, which formed on Crawford's left, reports that "General Mansfield had been mortally wounded . . . while making a bold reconnoissance of the woods through which we had just dashed."— EDITORS.

‡ The order assigning Meade to command is dated 1:25 P. M.— EDITORS.

MAJOR-GENERAL ISRAEL B. RICHARDSON. FROM A PHOTOGRAPH.

Referring in his report to the incidents accompanying General Richardson's fall, General Caldwell says: "The enemy made one more effort to break my line, and this time the attack was made in the center. Colonel Barlow [General Francis C.], hearing firing to his left, on our old front, immediately moved to the left and formed in line with the rest of the brigade. The whole brigade then moved forward in line, driving the enemy entirely out of the corn-field [see E on the map] and through the orchard beyond, the enemy firing grape and canister from two brass pieces in the orchard to our front, and shell and spherical-case shot from a battery on our right. While leading his men forward under the fire, Colonel Barlow fell dangerously wounded by a grape shot in the groin. By command of General Richardson I halted the brigade, and, drawing back the line, restored it near the edge of the corn-field. It was now 1 o'clock P. M. Here we lay exposed to a heavy artillery fire, by which General Richardson was severely wounded. The fall of General Richardson (General Meagher having been previously borne from the field) left me in command of the division, which I formed in line, awaiting the enemy's attack. Not long after, I was relieved of the command by General Hancock, who had been assigned to the command of the division by General McClellan." General Richardson was carried to Pry's house, McClellan's headquarters, where he died November 3d.— EDITORS.

Meade reported less than 7000 men with the colors that evening. Its organization was preserved, however, and the story that it was utterly dispersed was a mistake.

Greene's division, on the left of the Twelfth Corps, profited by the hard fighting of those who had preceded it, and was able to drive the enemy quite out of the East Wood and across the open fields between it and the Dunker Church. Greene even succeeded, about the time of Sumner's advance, in getting a foothold about the Dunker Church itself, which he held for some time.‡ But the fighting of Hooker's and Mansfield's men, though lacking unity of force and of purpose, had cost the enemy dear. J. R. Jones, who commanded Jackson's division, had been wounded; Starke, who succeeded Jones, was killed; Lawton, who followed Starke, was wounded. Ewell's division, commanded by Early, had suffered hardly less. Hood was sent back into the fight to relieve Lawton, and had been reënforced by the brigades of Ripley, Colquitt, and McRae (Garland's), from D. H. Hill's division. When Greene reached the Dunker Church, therefore, the Confederates on that wing had suffered more fearfully than our own men. Nearly half their numbers were killed and wounded, and Jackson's famous "Stonewall" division was so completely disorganized that only a handful of men under Colonels Grigsby and Stafford remained and attached themselves to Early's command. Of the division under Early, his own brigade was all that retained much strength, and this, posted among the rocks in the West Wood and vigorously supported by Stuart's horse artillery on the flank, was all that covered the left of Lee's army. Could Hooker and Mansfield have attacked together,—or, still better, could Sumner's Second Corps have marched before day and united with the first onset,—Lee's left must inevitably have been crushed long before the Confederate divisions of McLaws, Walker, and A. P. Hill could have reached the field. It is this failure to carry out any intelligible plan which the historian must regard as the unpardonable military fault on the National side. To account for the hours between 4 and 8 on that morning, is the most serious responsibility of the National commander.

Sumner's Second Corps was now approaching the scene of action, or rather two divisions of it—Sedgwick's and French's—Richardson's being still delayed ↓ till his place could be filled by Porter's troops, the strange tardiness in sending orders being noticeable in regard to every part of the army. Sumner met Hooker, who was being carried from the field, and the few words he could exchange with the wounded general were enough to make him feel the need of haste, but not sufficient to give him any clear idea of the position.

Both Sedgwick and French marched their divisions by the right flank, in three columns, a brigade in each column, Sedgwick leading. They crossed the Antietam by Hooker's route, but did not march as far to the north-west as Hooker had done. When the center of the corps was opposite the Dunker Church, and nearly east of it, the change of direction was given; the troops faced to their proper front and advanced in line of battle in three lines, fully deployed, and 60 or 70 yards apart, Sumner himself being in rear of Sedgwick's first line, and near its left. When they approached the position held by Greene's division at Dunker Church, French kept on so as to form on Greene's left, while Sedgwick, under Sumner's immediate lead, diverged somewhat to the right, passing through the East Wood, crossing the turnpike on the right of Greene and of the Dunker Church, and plunged into the West Wood. At this point there were absolutely no Confederate troops in front of them. Early was

---

‡ Until he was driven out, about 1:30, according to Generals Williams and Greene.—EDITORS.

↓ Sumner says Richardson came about an hour later. Howard, who succeeded Sedgwick, says his division moved "about 7." French says he followed "about 7:30." Hancock, who succeeded Richardson, says that officer received his orders "about 9:30."—EDITORS.

SCENE AT THE RUINS OF MUMMA'S HOUSE AND BARNS. FROM A SKETCH MADE AT THE TIME.

These buildings were fired early in the morning by D. H. Hill's men, who feared they would become a point of vantage to the Union forces. The sketch was made after the advance of French to the sunken road. Presumably, the battery firing upon the Confederate line to the right of that road is the First Rhode Island Light Artillery; for Captain John A. Tompkins, of Battery A, says, in his report, that he placed his pieces on a knoll "directly in front of some burning ruins," and opened fire upon a battery in front. "At 9:30," he continues, "the enemy appeared upon my right front with a large column, apparently designing to charge the battery. I was not aware of their approach until the head of the column gained the brow of a hill about sixty yards from the right gun of the battery. The pieces were immediately obliqued to the right and a sharp fire of canister opened upon them, causing them to retire in confusion, leaving the ground covered with their dead and wounded, and abandoning one of their battle-flags, which was secured by a regiment which came up on my right after the enemy had retreated. The enemy now opened a fire upon us from a battery in front, and also from one on the right near the white school-house [Dunker Church]. Two guns were directed to reply to the battery on the right, while the fire of the rest was directed upon the guns in front, which were silenced in about twenty minutes, and one of their caissons blown up." At noon, Tompkins was relieved by Battery G.— EDITORS.

farther to the right, opposing Williams's division of the Twelfth Corps, and now made haste under cover of the woods to pass around Sedgwick's right and to get in front of him to oppose his progress. This led to a lively skirmishing fight in which Early was making as great a demonstration as possible, but with no chance of solid success. At this very moment, however, McLaws's and Walker's divisions came upon the field, marching rapidly from Harper's Ferry. Walker charged headlong upon the left flank of Sedgwick's lines, which were soon thrown into confusion, and McLaws, passing by Walker's left, also threw his division diagonally upon the already broken and retreating lines of Sumner. Taken at such a disadvantage, these had never a chance; and in spite of the heroic bravery of Sumner and Sedgwick, with most of their officers (Sedgwick being severely wounded), the division was driven off to the north with terrible losses, carrying along in the rout part of Williams's men of the Twelfth Corps, who had been holding Early at bay. All these troops were rallied at the ridge on the Poffenberger farm, where Hooker's corps had already taken position. Here some thirty cannon of both corps were concentrated, and, supported by the organized parts of all three of the corps which had fought upon this part of the field, easily repulsed all efforts of Jackson and Stuart to resume the aggressive or to pass between them and the Potomac. Sumner himself did not accompany the routed troops to this position, but as soon as it was plain that the division could not be rallied, he galloped off to put himself in communication with French and with the headquarters of the army and try to retrieve the misfortune. From the flag-station east of the East Wood he signaled to McClellan: "Reënforcements are badly wanted. Our troops are giving way." It was between 9 and 10 o'clock when Sumner entered the West Wood, and in fifteen minutes, or a little more, the one-sided combat was over. ⸿

The enemy now concentrated upon Greene at the Dunker Church, and after a stubborn resistance he too was driven back across the turnpike and the open ground to the edge of the East Wood. Here, by the aid of several batteries gallantly handled, he defeated the subsequent effort to dislodge him. French had come up on his left, and both his batteries and the numerous ones on the Poffenberger hill swept the open ground and the corn-field over which Hooker had fought, and he was able to make good his position. The enemy was content to regain the high ground near the church, and French's attack upon D. H. Hill was now attracting their attention.

The battle on the extreme right was thus ended before 10 o'clock in the morning, and there was no more serious fighting north of the Dunker Church. French advanced on Greene's left, over the open farm lands, and after a fierce combat about the Roulette and Clipp farm buildings, drove D. H. Hill's division from them. Richardson's division came up on French's left soon after, and foot by foot, field by field, from hill to hill and from fence to fence, the enemy was pressed back, till after several hours of fighting the sunken road, since known as "Bloody Lane," was in our hands, piled full of the Confederate dead who had defended it with their lives. Richardson had been mortally wounded, and Hancock had been sent from Franklin's corps to command the division. Barlow had been conspicuous in the thickest of the fight, and after a series of brilliant actions was carried off desperately wounded. On the Confederate side equal courage had been shown and a magnificent tenacity exhibited. But it is not my purpose to describe the battle in detail. I limit

---

⸿ Sumner's principal-attack was made, as I have already indicated, at right angles to that of Hooker. He had thus crossed the line of Hooker's movement both in the latter's advance and retreat. Greene's division was the only part of the Twelfth Corps troops he saw, and he led Sedgwick's men to the right of these. Ignorant, as he necessarily was, of what had occurred before, he assumed that he formed on the extreme right of the Twelfth Corps, and that he fronted in the same direction as Hooker had done. This misconception of the situation led him into another error. He had seen only a few stragglers and wounded men of Hooker's corps on the line of his own advance, and hence concluded that the First Corps was completely dispersed and its division and brigade organizations broke up. He not only gave this report to McClellan at the time, but reiterated it later in his statement before the Committee on the Conduct of the War. The truth was that he had marched westward more than half a mile south of the Poffenberger hill, where Meade was with the sadly diminished but still organized First Corps, and half that distance south of the Miller farm buildings, near which Williams's division of the Twelfth Corps held the ground along the turnpike till they were carried away in the disordered retreat of Sedgwick's men toward the right. Sedgwick had gone in, therefore, between Greene and Williams, of the Twelfth Corps, and the four divisions of the two corps alternated in their order from left to right, thus: French, Greene, Sedgwick, Williams.—J. D. C.

myself to such an outline as may make clear my interpretation of the larger features of the engagement and its essential plan.

The head of Franklin's corps (the Sixth) had arrived about 10 o'clock and taken the position near the Sharpsburg Bridge which Sumner had occupied. Before noon Smith's and Slocum's divisions were ordered to Sumner's assistance, and early in the afternoon Irwin and Brooks, of Smith's, advanced to the charge and relieved Greene's division and part of French's, holding the line from Bloody Lane by the Clipp, Roulette, and Mumma houses to the East Wood and the ridge in front. Here Smith and Slocum remained till Lee retreated, Smith's division repelling a sharp attack. French and Richardson's battle may be considered as ended at 1 or 2 o'clock.

It seems to me very clear that about 10 o'clock in the morning was the great crisis in this battle. The sudden and complete rout of Sedgwick's division was not easily accounted for, and with McClellan's theory of the enormous superiority of Lee's numbers, it looked as if the Confederate general had massed overwhelming forces on our right. Sumner's notion that Hooker's corps was utterly dispersed was naturally accepted, and McClellan limited his hopes to holding on at the East Wood and the Poffenberger hill where Sedgwick's batteries were massed and supported by the troops that had

CHARGE OF IRWIN'S BRIGADE (SMITH'S DIVISION) AT THE DUNKER CHURCH. FROM A SKETCH MADE AT THE TIME.

General Wm. F. Smith, commanding the Second Division of Franklin's corps, went to the assistance of French. On getting into position, for the most part to the right of French, General Smith, in his report, says: "Finding that the enemy were advancing, I ordered forward the Third Brigade (Colonel Irwin's), who, passing through the regular battery then commanded by Lieutenant Thomas (Fourth Artillery), charged upon the enemy and drove them gallantly until abreast the little church at the point of woods, the possession of which had been so fiercely contested. At this point a severe flank fire from the woods was received." The brigade rallied behind the crest of a slope, and remained in an advanced position until the next day.— EDITORS.

GENERAL VIEW OF THE BATTLE OF ANTIETAM. FROM A SKETCH MADE AT THE TIME.

This sketch was made on the hill behind McClellan's headquarters, which is seen in the hollow on the left. Sumner's corps is seen in line of battle in the middle-ground, and Franklin's is advancing in column to his support. The smoke in the left background is from a bursting Confederate caisson. The column of smoke is from the burning house and barn of S. Mumma, who gave the ground on which the Dunker Church stands, and after whom, in the Confederate reports, the church is frequently called "St. Mumma's." On the right is the East Wood, in which is seen the smoke of the conflict between Mansfield and Jackson.— EDITORS.

been rallied there. Franklin's corps as it came on the field was detained to support the threatened right center, and McClellan determined to help it further by a demonstration upon the extreme left by the Ninth Corps. At this time, therefore (10 A. M.), he gave his order to Burnside to try to cross the Antietam and attack the enemy, thus creating a diversion in favor of our hard-pressed right. \ Facts within my own recollection strongly sustain

\ Here, as in regard to the time at which Sumner was ordered to march to Hooker's support, is a disputed question of fact. In his official report, McClellan says he ordered Burnside to make this attack at 8 o'clock, and from the day that the latter relieved McClellan in command of the army, and especially after the battle of Fredericksburg, a hot partisan effort was made to hold Burnside responsible for the lack of complete success at Antietam as well as for the repulse upon the Rappahannock. I think I understand the limitations of Burnside's abilities as a general, but I have had, ever since the battle itself, a profound conviction that the current criticisms upon him in relation to the battle of Antietam were unjust. Burnside's official report declares that he received the order to advance at 10 o'clock. This report was dated on the 30th of September, within two weeks of the battle, and at a time when public discussion of the incomplete results of the battle was animated. It was made after he had in his hands my own report as his immediate subordinate, in which I had given about 9 o'clock as my remembrance of the time,

As I directed the details of the action at the bridge in obedience to this order, it would have been easy for him to have accepted the hour named by me, for I should have been answerable for any delay in execution after that time. But he believed he knew the time at which the order came to him upon the hill-top overlooking the field, and no officer in the whole army has a better established reputation for candor and freedom from any wish to avoid full personal responsibility for his acts. It was not till quite lately that I saw a copy of his report or learned its contents, although I enjoyed his personal friendship down to the time of his death. He was content to have stated the fact as he knew it, and did not feel the need of debating it. Several circumstances have satisfied me that his accuracy in giving the hour was greater than my own. McClellan's preliminary report (dated October 16th, 1862) explicitly states that the order to Burnside to attack was "communicated to him at 10 o'clock A. M." This exact agreement with General Burnside would ordinarily be conclusive in itself.— J. D. C.

GENERAL M°CLELLAN RIDING THE LINE OF BATTLE AT ANTIETAM. FROM A SKETCH MADE AT THE TIME.

General McClellan rode his black horse, "Daniel Webster," which, on account of the difficulty of keeping pace with him, was better known to the staff as "that devil Dan."— EDITORS.

this view that the hour was 10 A. M. I have mentioned the hill above the Burnside Bridge where Burnside took his position, and to which I went after the preliminary orders for the day had been issued. There I remained until the order of attack came, anxiously watching what we could see at the right, and noting the effect of the fire of the heavy guns of Benjamin's battery.

From that point we could see nothing that occurred beyond the Dunker Church, for the East and West Woods, with farm-houses and orchards between, made an impenetrable screen. But as the morning wore on we saw lines of troops advancing from our right upon the other side of the Antietam, and engaging the enemy between us and the East Wood. The Confederate lines facing them now rose into view. From our position we looked, as it were, down between the opposing lines as if they had been the sides of a street, and as the fire opened we saw wounded men carried to the rear and stragglers making off. Our lines halted, and we were tortured with anxiety as we speculated whether our men would charge or retreat. The enemy occupied lines of fences and stone-walls, and their batteries made gaps in the National ranks. Our long-range guns were immediately turned in that direction, and we cheered every well-aimed shot. One of our shells blew up a caisson close to the Confederate line. This contest was going on, and it was yet uncertain which would succeed, when one of McClellan's staff ☆ rode up with an order to Burnside. The latter turned to me, saying we were ordered to make our

☆ Colonel D. B. Sackett, who says he got the order from McClellan about 9 o'clock.— EDITORS.

attack. I left the hill-top at once to give personal supervision to the movement ordered, and did not return to it, and my knowledge by actual vision of what occurred on the right ceased. The manner in which we had waited, the free discussion of what was occurring under our eyes and of our relation to it, the public receipt of the order by Burnside in the usual and business-like form, all forbid the supposition that this was any reiteration of a former order. It was immediately transmitted to me without delay or discussion, further than to inform us that things were not going altogether well on the right, and that it was hoped our attack would be of assistance to that wing. If then we can determine whose troops we saw engaged, we shall know something of the time of day; for there has been a general agreement reached as to the hours of movement during the forenoon on the right. The official map settles this. No lines of our troops were engaged in the direction of Bloody Lane and the Roulette farm-house, and between the latter and our station on the hill, till French's division made its attack. We saw them distinctly on the hither side of the farm buildings, upon the open ground, considerably nearer to us than the Dunker Church or the East Wood. In number we took them to be a corps. The place, the circumstances, all fix it beyond controversy that they were French's men, or French's and Richardson's. No others fought on that part of the field until Franklin went to their assistance at noon or later. The incident of their advance and the explosion of the caisson was illustrated by the pencil of the artist, Forbes, on the spot [see p. 647], and placed by him at the time Franklin's head of column was approaching from Rohrersville, which was about 10 o'clock. ☆

McClellan truly said, in his original report, that the task of carrying the bridge in front of Burnside was a difficult one. The depth of the valley and the shape of its curve made it impossible to reach the enemy's position at the bridge by artillery fire from the hill-tops on our side. Not so from the enemy's position, for the curve of the valley was such that it was perfectly enfiladed near the bridge by the Confederate batteries at the position now occupied by the national cemetery. [See map, p. 636.] The Confederate defense of the passage was intrusted to D. R. Jones's division of four brigades, which was the one Longstreet himself had disciplined and led till he was assigned to a larger command. Toombs's brigade was placed in advance, occupying the defenses of the bridge itself and the wooded slopes above, while the other brigades supported him, covered by the ridges which looked down upon the valley. The division batteries were supplemented by others from the reserve, and the valley, the bridge, and the ford below were under the direct and powerful fire of shot and shell from the Confederate cannon. Toombs speaks in his report in a characteristic way of his brigade

☆ It will not be wondered at, therefore, if to my mind the story of the 8 o'clock order is an instance of the way in which an erroneous memory is based upon the desire to make the facts accord with a theory. The actual time must have been as much later than 9 o'clock as the period during which, with absorbed attention, we had been watching the battle on the right,—a period, it is safe to say, much longer than it seemed to us. The judgment of the hour, 9 o'clock, which I gave in my report, was merely my impression from passing events, for I hastened at once to my own duties without thinking to look at my watch, while the cumulative evidence seems to prove conclusively that the time stated by Burnside, and by McClellan himself in his original report, is correct.—J. D. C.

holding back Burnside's corps; but his force, thus strongly supported, was as large as could be disposed of at the head of the bridge, and abundantly large for resistance to any that could be brought against it. Our advance upon the bridge could only be made by a narrow column, showing a front of eight men at most. But the front which Toombs deployed behind his defenses was three or four hundred yards both above and below the bridge. He himself says in his report:

BRIGADIER-GENERAL ISAAC P. RODMAN, MORTALLY WOUNDED AT ANTIETAM. FROM A PHOTOGRAPH.

"From the nature of the ground on the other side, the enemy were compelled to approach mainly by the road which led up the river for near three hundred paces parallel with my line of battle and distant therefrom from fifty to a hundred and fifty feet, thus exposing his flank to a destructive fire the most of that distance."

Under such circumstances, I do not hesitate to affirm that the Confederate position was virtually impregnable to a direct attack over the bridge, for the column approaching it was not only exposed at pistol-range to the perfectly covered infantry of the enemy and to two batteries which were assigned to the special duty of supporting Toombs, and which had the exact range of the little valley with their shrapnel, but if it should succeed in reaching the bridge its charge across it must be made under a fire plowing through its length, the head of the column melting away as it advanced, so that, as every soldier knows, it could show no front strong enough to make an impression upon the enemy's breastworks, even if it should reach the other side. As a desperate sort of diversion in favor of the right wing, it might be justifiable; but I believe that no officer or man who knew the actual situation at that bridge thinks a serious attack upon it was any part of McClellan's original plan. Yet, in his detailed official report, instead of speaking of it as the difficult task the original report had called it, he treats it as little different from a parade or march across, which might have been done in half an hour.

Burnside's view of the matter was that the front attack at the bridge was so difficult that the passage by the ford below must be an important factor in the task; for if Rodman's division should succeed in getting across there, at the bend in the Antietam, he would come up in rear of Toombs, and either the whole of D. R. Jones's division would have to advance to meet Rodman, or Toombs must abandon the bridge. In this I certainly concurred, and Rodman was ordered to push rapidly for the ford. It is important to remember, however, that Walker's Confederate division had been posted during the earlier morning to hold that part of the Antietam line, and it was probably from him that Rodman suffered the first casualties which occurred in his ranks. But, as we have seen, Walker had been called away by Lee only an hour before, and had made the hasty march by the rear of Sharpsburg, to fall upon Sedgwick. If, therefore, Rodman had been sent to cross at 8 o'clock, it is safe to say that his column fording the stream in the face of Walker's deployed division would never have reached the farther bank,—a contingency that McClellan did not consider when arguing long afterward the favorable results that might have followed an earlier attack. As Rodman died upon the field, no full report for his division was made, and we only know that he met with some resistance from both infantry and artillery; that the winding of the stream made his march longer than he anticipated, and that, in fact, he only approached the rear of Toombs's position from that direction about the time when our last and successful charge upon the bridge was made, between noon and 1 o'clock.

The attacks at Burnside's Bridge were made under my own eye. Sturgis's division occupied the center of our line, with Crook's brigade of the Kanawha Division on his right front, and Willcox's division in reserve, as I have already stated. Crook's position was somewhat above the bridge, but it was thought that by advancing part of Sturgis's men to the brow of the hill they could cover the advance of Crook, and that the latter could make a straight dash down the hill to our end of the bridge. The orders were accordingly given, and Crook advanced, covered by the 11th Connecticut (of Rodman), under Colonel Kingsbury, deployed as skirmishers. In passing over the spurs of the hills, Crook came out on the bank of the stream above the bridge and found himself under a heavy fire. He faced the enemy and returned the fire, getting such cover for his men as he could and trying to drive off or silence his opponents. The engagement was one in which the Antietam prevented the combatants from coming to close quarters, but it was none the less vigorously continued with musketry fire. Crook reported that his hands were full, and that he could not approach closer to the bridge. But later in the contest, and about the time that the successful charge at the bridge was made, he got five companies of the 28th Ohio over by a ford above. Sturgis ordered forward an attacking column from Nagle's brigade, supported and covered by Ferrero's brigade, which took position in a field of corn on one of the lower slopes of the hill opposite the head of the bridge. The whole front was carefully covered with skirmishers, and our batteries on the heights overhead were ordered to keep down the fire of the enemy's artillery. Nagle's effort was gallantly made, but it failed, and his men were forced to seek cover behind the spur of the hill from which they had advanced. We were constantly hoping to hear something from Rodman's advance by the ford, and would gladly have waited for some more certain knowledge of his progress, but at this time McClellan's sense of the necessity of relieving the right was such that he was sending reiterated orders to push the assault. Not only were these forwarded to me, but to give added weight to my instructions Burnside sent direct to Sturgis urgent messages to carry the bridge at all hazards. I directed Sturgis to take two regiments from Ferrero's brigade, which had not

THE CHARGE ACROSS THE BURNSIDE BRIDGE. FROM A SKETCH MADE AT THE TIME.

In his report General Sturgis describes as follows the charge across the bridge:

"Orders arrived from General Burnside to carry the bridge at all hazards. I then selected the Fifty-first New York and the Fifty-first Pennsylvania from the second Brigade, and directed them to charge with the bayonet. They started on their mission of death full of enthusiasm, and, taking a route less exposed than the regiments [Second Maryland and Sixth New Hampshire] which had made the effort before them, rushed at a double-quick over the slope leading to the bridge and over the bridge itself, with an impetuosity which the enemy could not resist; and the Stars and Stripes were planted on the opposite bank at 1 o'clock P. M., amid the most enthusiastic cheering from every part of the field from where they could be seen."

been engaged, and make a column by moving them by the flank, the one left in front and the other right in front, side by side, so that when they passed the bridge they could turn to left and right, forming line as they advanced on the run. He chose the 51st New York, Colonel Robert B. Potter, and the 51st Pennsylvania, Colonel John F. Hartranft (both names afterward greatly distinguished), and both officers and men were made to feel the necessity of success. At the same time Crook succeeded in bringing a light howitzer of Simmonds's mixed battery down from the hill-tops, and placed it where it had a point-blank fire on the farther end of the bridge. The howitzer was one we had captured in West Virginia, and had been added to the battery, which was partly made up of heavy rifled Parrott guns. When everything was ready, a heavy skirmishing fire was opened all along the bank, the howitzer threw in double charges of canister, the two regiments charged up the road in column with fixed bayonets, and in scarcely more time than it takes to tell it, the bridge was passed and Toombs's brigade fled through the woods and over the top of the hill. The charging regiments were advanced in line to the crest above the bridge as soon as they were deployed, and the rest of Sturgis's division, with Crook's brigade, were immediately brought over to strengthen the line. These were soon joined by Rodman's division with Scammon's brigade, which had crossed at the ford, and whose presence on that side of the stream had no doubt made the final struggle of Toombs's men less obstinate than it would otherwise have been, the fear of being taken in rear having always a strong moral effect upon even the best of troops. It was now about 1 o'clock, and nearly three hours had been spent in a bitter and bloody contest across the narrow stream. The successive efforts to carry the bridge had been made as closely following each other as possible. Each had been a fierce combat, in which the men, with wonderful courage, had not easily accepted defeat, and even when not able to cross the bridge had made use of the walls at the end, the fences, and every tree and stone as cover, while they strove to reach with their fire their well-protected and nearly concealed opponents. The lulls in the fighting had been short, and only to prepare new efforts. The severity of the work was attested by our losses, which, before the crossing was won, exceeded five hundred men and included some of our best officers, such as Colonel Kingsbury, of the 11th Connecticut; Lieutenant-Colonel Bell, of the 51st Pennsylvania, and Lieutenant-Colonel Coleman, of the 11th Ohio, two of them commanding regiments. The proportion of casualties to the number engaged was much greater than common, for the nature of the task required that comparatively few troops should be exposed at once, the others remaining under cover.

Our first task was to prepare to hold the height we had gained against the return assault of the enemy which we expected, and to reply to the destructive fire from the enemy's abundant artillery. The light batteries were brought over and distributed in the line. The men were made to lie down behind the crest to save them from the concentrated artillery fire which the enemy opened upon us as soon as Toombs's regiments succeeded in reaching their main line. But McClellan's anticipation of an overwhelming attack upon his right was so strong that he determined still to press our advance, and sent orders accordingly. The ammunition of Sturgis's and Crook's men had been nearly exhausted, and it was imperative that they should be freshly supplied before entering into another engagement. Sturgis also reported his men so exhausted by their efforts as to be unfit for an immediate advance. On this I sent to Burnside the request that Willcox's division be sent over, with an ammunition train, and that Sturgis's division be replaced by the fresh troops, remaining, however, on the west side of the stream as support to the others. This was done as rapidly as was practicable, where everything had to pass down the steep hill road and through so narrow a defile as the bridge. Still, it was 3 o'clock before these changes and further preparations could be made. Burnside had personally striven to hasten them, and had come over to the west bank to consult and to hurry matters, and took his share of personal peril, for he came at a time when the ammunition wagons were delivering cartridges, and the road where they were, at the end of the bridge, was in the range of the enemy's constant and accurate fire. It is proper to mention this because it has been said that he did not cross the stream. The criticisms made by McClellan as to the time occupied in these changes and movements will not seem

BURNSIDE'S ATTACK UPON SHARPSBURG.   FROM A SKETCH MADE AT THE TIME.

In this attack Willcox's division (the right of the line) charged into the village. Colonel Fairchild, commanding a brigade in Rodman's division, on the left of the line (which included Hawkins's Zouaves, seen at the stone-wall in the picture), describes as follows in his report the advance upon Sharpsburg after the hill above the bridge had been gained: "We continued to advance to the opposite hill under a tremendous fire from the enemy's batteries, up steep embankments. Arriving near a stone fence, the enemy — a brigade composed of South Carolina and Georgia regiments — opened on us with musketry. After returning their fire I immediately ordered a charge, which the whole brigade gallantly responded to, moving with alacrity and steadiness. Arriving at the fence, behind which the enemy were awaiting us, receiving their fire, losing large numbers of our men, we charged over the fence, dislodging them and driving them from their positions down the hill toward the village, a stand of regimental colors belonging to a South Carolina regiment being taken by Private Thomas Hare, Company D, 89th New York Volunteers, who was afterward killed. We continued to pursue the enemy down the hill. Discovering that they were massing fresh troops on our left, I went back and requested General Rodman to bring up rapidly the Second Brigade to our support, which he did, they engaging the enemy, he soon afterward falling badly wounded. . . . The large force advancing on our left flank compelled us to retire from the position, which we could have held had we been properly supported."

foreible, if one will compare them with any similar movements on the field; such as Mansfield's to support Hooker, or Sumner's or Franklin's to reach the scene of action. About this, however, there is fair room for difference of opinion; what I personally know is that it would have been folly to advance again before Willcox had relieved Sturgis, and that as soon as the fresh troops reported and could be put in line, the order to advance was given. McClellan is in accord with all other witnesses in declaring that when the movement began, the conduct of the troops was gallant beyond criticism.

Willcox's division formed the right, Christ's brigade being north and Welsh's brigade south of the road leading from the bridge to Sharpsburg. Crook's brigade of the Kanawha Division supported Willcox. Rodman's division formed on the left, Harland's brigade having the position on the flank, and Fairchild's uniting with Willcox at the center. Scammon's brigade of the Kanawha Division was the reserve for Rodman on the extreme left. Sturgis's division remained and held the crest of the hill above the bridge. About half the batteries of the divisions accompanied the movement, the rest being in position on the hill-tops east of the Antietam. The advance necessarily followed the high ground toward Sharpsburg, and as the enemy made strongest resistance toward our right, the movement curved in that direction, the six brigades of D. R. Jones's Confederate division being deployed diagonally across our front, holding the stone fences and crests of the cross ridges and aided by abundant artillery, in which arm the enemy was particularly strong. The battle was a fierce one from the moment Willcox's men showed themselves on the open ground. Christ's brigade, taking advantage of all the cover the trees and inequalities of surface gave them, pushed on along the depression in which the road ran, a section of artillery keeping pace with them in the road. The direction of movement brought all the brigades of the first line in échelon, but Welsh soon fought his way up beside Christ, and they, together, drove the enemy successively from the fields and farm-yards till they reached the edge of the village. Upon the elevation on the right of the road was an orchard in which the shattered and diminished force of Jones made a final stand, but Willcox concentrated his artillery fire upon it, and his infantry was able to push forward and occupy it. They now partly occupied the town of Sharpsburg, and held the high ground commanding it on the south-east, where the national cemetery now is. The struggle had been long and bloody. It was half-past 4 in the afternoon, and ammunition had again run low, for the wagons had not been able to accompany the movement. Willcox paused for his men to take breath again, and to fetch up some cartridges; but meanwhile affairs were taking a serious turn on the left.

As Rodman's division went forward, he found the enemy before him seemingly detached from Willcox's opponents, and occupying ridges upon his left front, so that he was not able to keep his own connection with Willcox in the swinging movement to the right. Still, he made good progress in the face of stubborn resistance, though finding the enemy constantly developing more to his left, and the interval between him and Willcox widening. In fact his movement became practically by column of brigades. The view of the field to the south was now obstructed by fields of tall Indian corn, and under this cover Confederate troops approached the flank in line of battle. Scammon's officers in the reserve saw them as soon as Rodman's brigades écheloned, as these were toward the front and right. This hostile force proved to be A. P. Hill's division of six brigades, the last of Jackson's force to leave Harper's Ferry, and which had reached Sharpsburg since noon. Those first seen by Scammon's men were dressed in the National blue uniforms which they had captured at Harper's Ferry, and it was assumed that they were part of our own forces till they began to fire. Scammon quickly changed front to the left, drove back the enemy before him, and occupied a line of stone fences, which he held until he was withdrawn from it. Harland's brigade was partly moving in the corn-fields. One of his regiments was new, having been organized only three weeks, and the brigade had somewhat lost its order and connection when the sudden attack came. Rodman directed Colonel Harland to lead the right of the brigade, while he himself attempted to bring the left into position.

In performing this duty he fell mortally wounded, and the brigade broke in confusion after a brief effort of its right wing to hold on. Fairchild, also, now received the fire on his left, and was forced to fall back and change front.

Being at the center when this break occurred on the left, I saw that it would be impossible to continue the movement to the right, and sent instant orders to Willcox and Crook to retire the left of their line, and to Sturgis to come forward into the gap made in Rodman's. The troops on the right swung back in perfect order; Scammon's brigade hung on at its stone-wall with unflinching tenacity till Sturgis had formed on the curving hill in rear of them, and Rodman's had found refuge behind. Willcox's left, then united with Sturgis and Scammon, was withdrawn to a new position on the left flank of the whole line. That these manœuvres on the field were really performed in good order is demonstrated by the fact that, although the break in Rodman's line was a bad one, the enemy was not able to capture many prisoners, the whole number of missing, out of the 2340 casualties which the Ninth Corps suffered in the battle, being 115, which includes wounded men unable to leave the field. The enemy were not lacking in bold efforts to take advantage of the check we had received, but were repulsed with severe punishment, and as the day declined were content to entrench themselves along the line of the road leading from Sharpsburg to the Potomac at the mouth of the Antietam, half a mile in our front. The men of the Ninth Corps lay that night upon their arms, the line being one which rested with both flanks near the Antietam, and curved outward upon the rolling hill-tops which covered the bridge and commanded the plateau between us and the enemy. With my staff I lay upon the ground behind the troops, holding our horses by the bridles as we rested, for our orderlies were so exhausted that we could not deny them the same chance for a little broken slumber.

The conduct of the battle on the left has given rise to several criticisms, among which the most prominent has been that Porter's corps, which lay in reserve, was not put in at the same time with the Ninth Corps. ∫ McClellan

---

∫ Captain Thomas M. Anderson, in 1886 Lieutenant-Colonel of the 9th Infantry, U. S. A., wrote to the editors in that year:

"At the battle of Antietam I commanded one of the battalions of Sykes's division of regulars, held in reserve on the north of Antietam creek near the stone bridge. Three of our battalions were on the south side of the creek, deployed as skirmishers in front of Sharpsburg. At the time A. P. Hill began to force Burnside back upon the left, I was talking with Colonel Buchanan, our brigade commander, when an orderly brought him a note from Captain (now Colonel) Blunt, who was the senior officer with the battalions of our brigade beyond the creek. The note, as I remember, stated in effect that Captain Dryer, commanding the 4th Infantry, had ridden into the enemy's lines, and upon returning had reported that there were but one Confederate battery and two regiments in front of Sharpsburg, connecting the wings of Lee's army.' Dryer was one of the coolest and bravest officers in our service, and on his report Blunt asked instructions. We learned afterward that Dryer proposed that he, Blunt, and Brown, commanding the 4th, 12th, and 14th Infantries, should charge the enemy in Sharpsburg instanter. But Blunt preferred asking for orders. Colonel Buchanan sent the note to Sykes, who was at the time talking with General McClellan and Fitz John Porter, about a hundred and fifty yards from us. They were sitting on their horses between Taft's and Weed's batteries a little to our left. I saw the note passed from one to the other in the group, but could not, of course, hear what was said.

"We received no orders to advance, however, although the advance of a single brigade at the time (sunset) would have cut Lee's army in two.

"After the war, I asked General Sykes why our reserves did not advance upon receiving Dryer's report. He answered that he remembered the circumstance very well and that he thought McClellan was inclined to order in the Fifth Corps, but that when he spoke of doing so Fitz John Porter said: 'Remember, General! I command the last reserve of the last Army of the Republic.'"

' General Fitz John Porter writes to say that no such note as "Captain Dryer's report" was seen by him, and that no such discussion as to the opportunity for using the "reserve" took place between him and General McClellan. General Porter says that nearly all of his Fifth Corps (according to McClellan's report, 12,900 strong), instead of being idle at that critical hour, had been sent to reënforce the right and left wings, leaving of the Fifth Corps to defend the center a force "but then four thousand strong," according to General Porter's report.— EDITORS.

answered this by saying that he did not think it prudent to divest the center of all reserve troops.⸸ No doubt a single strong division marching beyond the left flank of the Ninth Corps would have so occupied A. P. Hill's division that our movement into Sharpsburg could not have been checked, and, assisted by the advance of Sumner and Franklin on the right, apparently would have made certain the complete rout of Lee. As troops are put in reserve, not to diminish the army, but to be used in a pinch, I am deeply convinced that McClellan's refusal to use them on the left was the result of his continued conviction through all the day after Sedgwick's defeat, that Lee was overwhelmingly superior in force, and was preparing to return a crushing blow upon our right flank. He was keeping something in hand to cover a retreat, if that wing should be driven back. Except in this way, also, I am at a loss to account for the inaction of our right during the whole of our engagement on the left. Looking at our part of the battle as only a strong diversion to prevent or delay Lee's

PRESIDENT LINCOLN IN GENERAL McCLELLAN'S TENT AT ANTIETAM AFTER THE BATTLE. FROM A PHOTOGRAPH.

following up his success against Hooker and the rest, it is intelligible. I certainly so understood it at the time, as my report witnesses, and McClellan's preliminary report supports this view. If he had been impatient to have our attack delivered earlier, he had reason for double impatience that Franklin's fresh troops should assail Lee's left simultaneously with ours, unless he regarded action there as hopeless, and looked upon our movement as a sort of forlorn-hope to keep Lee from following up his advantages.

But even these are not all the troublesome questions requiring an answer. Couch's division had been left north-east of Maryland Heights to observe Jackson's command, supposed still to be in Harper's Ferry. Why could it not have come up on our left as well as A. P. Hill's division, which was the last of

⸸ At this time Sykes and Griffin, of Porter's corps, had been advanced, and part of their troops were actively engaged. — EDITORS.

the Confederate troops to leave the Ferry, there being nothing to observe after it was gone? Couch's division, coming with equal pace with Hill's on the other side of the river, would have answered our needs as well as one from Porter's corps. Hill came, but Couch did not. Yet even then, a regiment of horse watching that flank and scouring the country as we swung it forward would have developed Hill's presence and enabled the commanding general either to stop our movement or to take the available means to support it; but the cavalry was put to no such use; it occupied the center of the whole line, only its artillery being engaged during the day. It would have been invaluable to Hooker in the morning as it would have been to us in the afternoon. McClellan had marched from Frederick City with the information that Lee's army was divided, Jackson being detached with a large force to take Harper's Ferry. He had put Lee's strength at 120,000 men. Assuming that there was still danger that Jackson might come upon our left with a large force, and that Lee had proven strong enough without Jackson to repulse three corps on our right and right center, McClellan might have regarded his own army as divided also for the purpose of meeting both opponents, and his cavalry would have been upon the flank of the part with which he was attacking Lee; Porter would have been in position to help either part in an extremity, or to cover a retreat, and Burnside would have been the only subordinate available to check Lee's apparent success. Will any other hypothesis intelligibly account for McClellan's dispositions and orders? The error in the above assumption would be that McClellan estimated Lee's troops at nearly double their actual numbers, and that what was taken for proof of Lee's superiority in force on the field was a series of partial reverses which resulted directly from the piecemeal and disjointed way in which McClellan's morning attacks had been made.

The same explanation is the most satisfactory one that I can give for the inaction of Thursday, the 18th of September. Could McClellan have known the desperate condition of most of Lee's brigades he would have known that his own were in much better case, badly as they had suffered. I do not doubt that most of his subordinates discouraged the resumption of the attack, for the rooted belief in Lee's preponderance of numbers had been chronic in the army during the whole year. That belief was based upon the inconceivably mistaken reports of the secret service organization, accepted at headquarters, given to the War Department at Washington as a reason for incessant demands of reënforcements, and permeating downward through the whole organization till the error was accepted as truth by officers and men, and became a factor in their morale which can hardly be over-estimated. The result was that Lee retreated unmolested on the night of the 18th, and that what might have been a real and decisive success was a drawn battle in which our chief claim to victory was the possession of the field.

The Ninth Corps occupied its position on the heights west of the Antietam without further molestation, except an irritating picket firing, till the Confederate army retreated. But the position was one in which no shelter from the weather could be had; nor could any cooking be done; and the troops were short of rations. Late in the afternoon of Thursday, Morell's division of

GENERAL M'CLELLAN AND PRESIDENT LINCOLN AT ANTIETAM. FROM A PHOTOGRAPH.

The Proclamation of Emancipation was published September 22d, three days after the withdrawal of Lee to Virginia, and was communicated to the army officially on September 24th.

On October 1st President Lincoln visited the army to see for himself if it was in no condition to pursue Lee into Virginia. General McClellan says in his general report: "His Excellency the President honored the Army of the Potomac with a visit, and remained several days, during which he went through the different encampments, reviewed the troops, and went over the battle-fields of South Mountain and Antietam. I had the opportunity during this visit to describe to him the operations of the army since the time it left Washington, and gave him my reasons for not following the enemy after he crossed the Potomac." In "McClellan's Own Story" he says that the President "more than once assured me that he was fully satisfied with my whole course from the beginning; that the only fault he could possibly find was, that I was too prone to be sure that everything was ready before acting, but that my actions were all right when I started. I said to him that I thought a few experiments with those who acted before they were ready would probably convince him that in the end I consumed less time than they did."

After the President's return to Washington, October 5th, Halleck telegraphed to McClellan under date of October 6th: "The President directs that you cross the Potomac and give battle to the enemy or drive him south," etc.

On October 7th McClellan, in "General Orders No. 163," referred to the Proclamation of Emancipation. He warned the army of the danger to military discipline of heated political discussions, and reminded them that the "remedy for political errors, if any are committed, is to be found only in the action of the people at the polls." On October 5th General McClellan had said, in a letter to his wife [see "McClellan's Own Story," p. 655], "Mr. Aspinwall [W. H., of New York] is decidedly of the opinion that it is my duty to submit to the President's proclamation and quietly continue doing my duty as a soldier. I presume he is right, and am at least sure that he is honest in his opinion. I shall surely give his views full consideration."—EDITORS.

Porter's corps was ordered to report to Burnside to relieve the picket line and some of the regiments in the most exposed position. One brigade was sent over the Antietam for this purpose,‡ and a few of the Ninth Corps regiments were enabled to withdraw far enough to cook some rations of which they had been in need for twenty-four hours. Harland's brigade of Rodman's division had been taken to the east side of the stream on the evening of the 17th to be reorganized.

‡ Porter in his report says that Morell took the place of the whole Ninth Corps. In this he is entirely mistaken, as the reports from Morell's division show.—J. D. C.

WITH BURNSIDE AT ANTIETAM. ☆

BY DAVID L. THOMPSON, CO. G, 9TH N. Y. VOLS.

ON THE LINE OF A SCATTERED FENCE AT ANTIETAM. FROM A PHOTOGRAPH.

AT Antietam our corps — the Ninth, under Burnside — was on the extreme left, opposite the stone bridge. Our brigade stole into position about half-past 10 o'clock on the night of the 16th. No lights were permitted, and all conversation was carried on in whispers. As the regiment was moving past the 103d New York to get to its place, there occurred, on a small scale and without serious results, one of those unaccountable panics often noticed in crowds, by which each man, however brave individually, merges his individuality for the moment, and surrenders to an utterly causeless fear. When everything was at its darkest and stealthiest one of the 103d stumbled over the regimental dog, and, in trying to avoid treading on it, staggered against a stack of muskets and knocked them over. The giving way of the two or three men upon whom they fell was communicated to others in a sort of wave movement of constantly increasing magnitude, reinforced by the ever-present apprehension of attack, till two regiments were in confusion. In a few seconds order was restored, and we went on to our place in the line — a field of thin corn sloping toward the creek, where we sat down on the plowed ground and watched for a while the dull glare on the sky of the Confederate camp-fires behind the hills. We were hungry, of course, but, as no fires were allowed, we could only mix our ground coffee and sugar in our hands and eat them dry. I think we were the more easily inclined to this crude disposal of our rations from a feeling that for many of us the need of drawing them would cease forever with the following day.

All through the evening the shifting and placing had gone on, the moving masses being dimly descried in the strange half lights of earth and sky. There was something weirdly impressive yet unreal in the gradual drawing together of those whispering armies under cover of the night — something of awe and dread, as always in the secret preparation for momentous deeds. By 11 o'clock the whole line, four miles or more in length, was sleeping, each corps apprised of its appointed task, each battery in place.

It is astonishing how soon, and by what slight causes, regularity of formation and movement are lost in actual battle. Disintegration begins with the first shot. To the book-soldier all order seems destroyed, months of drill apparently going for nothing in a few minutes. Next after the most powerful factor in this derangement — the enemy — come natural obstacles and the inequalities of the ground. One of the commonest is a patch of trees. An advancing line lags there inevitably, the rest of the line swinging around insensibly, with the view of keeping the alignment, and so losing direction. The struggle for the possession of such a point is sure to be persistent. Wounded men crawl to a wood for shelter, broken troops reform behind it, a battery planted in its edge will stick there after other parts of the line have given way. Often a slight rise of ground in an open field, not noticeable a thousand yards away, becomes, in the keep of a stubborn regiment, a powerful head-land against which the waves of battle roll and break, requiring new dispositions and much time to clear it. A stronger fortress than a casual railroad embankment often proves, it would be difficult to find; and as for a sunken road, what possibilities of victory or disaster lie in that obstruction, let Waterloo and Fredericksburg bear witness.

At Antietam it was a low, rocky ledge, prefaced by a corn-field. There were woods, too, and knolls, and there were other corn-fields; but the student of that battle knows one corn-field only — *the* corn-field, now historic, lying a quarter of a mile north of Dunker Church, and east of and bordering the Hagerstown road. About it and across it, to and fro, the waves of battle swung almost from the first, till by 10 o'clock in the

☆ See p. 556.—EDITORS.

morning, when the struggle was over, hundreds of men lay dead among its peaceful blades.

While these things were happening on the right, the left was not without its excitement. A Confederate battery discovered our position in our corn-field, as soon as it was light enough to see, and began to shell us. As the range became better we were moved back and ordered to boil coffee in the protection of a hollow. The general plan of battle appears to have been to break through the Confederate left, following up the advantage with a constantly increasing force, sweep him away from the fords, and so crowd his whole army down into the narrow peninsula formed by the Potomac and Antietam Creek. Even the non-military eye, however, can see that the tendency of such a plan would be to bring the two armies upon concentric arcs, the inner and shorter of which must be held by the enemy, affording him the opportunity for reënforcement by interior lines — an immense advantage only to be counteracted by the utmost activity on our part, who must attack vigorously where attacking at all, and where not, imminently threaten. Certainly there was no imminence in the threat of our center or left — none whatever of the left, only a vague consciousness of whose existence even seems to have been in the enemy's mind, for he flouted us all the morning with hardly more than a meager skirmish line, while his coming troops, as fast as they arrived upon the ground, were sent off to the Dunker Church.

So the morning wore away, and the fighting on the right ceased entirely. That was fresh anxiety — the scales were turning perhaps, but which way? About noon the battle began afresh. This must have been Franklin's men of the Sixth Corps, for the firing was nearer, and they came up behind the center. Suddenly a stir beginning far up on the right, and running like a wave along the line, brought the regiment to its feet. A silence fell on every one at once, for each felt that the momentous "now" had come. Just as we started I saw, with a little shock, a line-officer take out his watch to note the hour, as though the affair beyond the creek were a business appointment which he was going to keep.

When we reached the brow of the hill the fringe of trees along the creek screened the fighting entirely, and we were deployed as skirmishers under their cover. We sat there two hours. All that time the rest of the corps had been moving over the stone bridge and going into position on the other side of the creek. Then we were ordered over at a ford which had been found below the bridge, where the water was waist-deep. One man was shot in mid-stream. At the foot of the slope on the opposite side the line was formed and we moved up through the thin woods. Reaching the level we lay down behind a battery which seemed to have been disabled. There, if anywhere, I should have remembered that I was soaking wet from my waist down. So great was the excitement, however, that I have never been able to recall it. Here some of the men, going to the rear for water, discovered in the ashes of some hay-ricks which

had been fired by our shells the charred remains of several Confederates. After long waiting it became noised along the line that we were to take a battery that was at work several hundred yards ahead on the top of a hill. This narrowed the field and brought us to consider the work before us more attentively.

Right across our front, two hundred feet or so away, ran a country road bordered on each side by a snake fence. Beyond this road stretched a plowed field several hundred feet in length, sloping up to the battery, which was hidden in a corn-field. A stone fence, breast-high, inclosed the field on the left, and behind it lay a regiment of Confederates, who would be directly on our flank if we should attempt the slope. The prospect was far from encouraging, but the order came to get ready for the attempt.

Our knapsacks were left on the ground behind us. At the word a rush was made for the fences. The line was so disordered by the time the second fence was passed that we hurried forward to a shallow undulation a few feet ahead, and lay down among the furrows to re-form, doing so by crawling up into line. A hundred feet or so ahead was a similar undulation to which we ran for a second shelter. The battery, which at first had not seemed to notice us, now, apprised of its danger, opened fire upon us. We were getting ready now for the charge proper, but were still lying on our faces. Lieutenant-Colonel Kimball was ramping up and down the line. The discreet regiment behind the fence was silent. Now and then a bullet from them cut the air over our heads, but generally they were reserving their fire for that better shot which they knew they would get in a few minutes. The battery, however, whose shots at first went over our heads, had depressed its guns so as to shave the surface of the ground. Its fire was beginning to tell. I remember looking behind and seeing an officer riding diagonally across the field — a most inviting target — instinctively bending his head down over his horse's neck, as though he were riding through driving rain. While my eye was on him I saw, between me and him, a rolled overcoat with its straps on bound into the air and fall among the furrows. One of the enemy's grape-shot had plowed a groove in the skull of a young fellow and had cut his overcoat from his shoulders. He never stirred from his position, but lay there face downward — a dreadful spectacle. A moment after, I heard a man cursing a comrade for lying on him heavily. He was cursing a dying man. As the range grew better, the firing became more rapid, the situation desperate and exasperating to the last degree. Human nature was on the rack, and there burst forth from it the most vehement, terrible swearing I have ever heard. Certainly the joy of conflict was not ours that day. The suspense was only for a moment, however, for the order to charge came just after. Whether the regiment was thrown into disorder or not, I never knew. I only remember that as we rose and started all the fire that had been held back so long was loosed. In a second the air was full of the hiss of bullets and the hurtle of grape-shot. The mental strain was so great that I saw at that moment the singular effect mentioned, I think, in the life of Goethe on a similar occasion — the whole landscape for an instant turned slightly red. I see again, as I saw it then in a flash, a man just in front of me drop his musket and throw up his hands, stung into vigorous swearing by a bullet behind the ear. Many men fell going up the hill, but it seemed to be all over in a moment, and I found myself passing a hollow where a dozen wounded men lay —

MAJOR-GENERAL JOHN G. WALKER, C. S. A. FROM A PHOTOGRAPH.

among them our sergeant-major, who was calling me to come down. He had caught sight of the blanket rolled across my back, and called me to unroll it and help to carry from the field one of our wounded lieutenants.

When I returned from obeying this summons the regiment (?) was not to be seen. It had gone in on the run, what there was left of it, and had disappeared in the corn-field about the battery. There was nothing to do but lie there and await developments. Nearly all the men in the hollow were wounded, one man — a recruit named Devlin, I think — frightfully so, his arm being cut short off. He lived a few minutes only. All were calling for water, of course, but none was to be had. We lay there till dusk,— perhaps an hour, when the fighting ceased. During that hour, while the bullets snipped the leaves from a young locust-tree growing at the edge of the hollow and powdered us with the fragments, we had time to speculate on many things — among others, on the impatience with which men clamor, in dull times, to be led into a fight. We heard all through the war that the army "was eager to be led against the enemy." It must have been so, for truthful correspondents said so, and editors confirmed it. But when you came to hunt for this particular itch, it was always the next regiment that had it. The truth is, when bullets are whacking against tree-trunks and solid shot are

cracking skulls like egg-shells, the consuming passion in the breast of the average man is to get out of the way. Between the physical fear of going forward and the moral fear of turning back, there is a predicament of exceptional awkwardness from which a hidden hole in the ground would be a wonderfully welcome outlet.

Night fell, preventing further struggle. Of 600 men of the regiment who crossed the creek at 3 o'clock that afternoon, 45 were killed and 176 wounded. The Confederates held possession of that part of the field over which we had moved, and just after dusk they sent out detachments to collect arms and bring in prisoners. When they came to our hollow all the unwounded and slightly wounded there were marched to the rear — prisoners of the 15th Georgia. We slept on the ground that night without protection of any kind; for, with a recklessness quite common throughout the war, we had thrown away every incumbrance on going into the fight. The weather, however, was warm and pleasant, and there was little discomfort.

The next morning we were marched — about six hundred of us, fragments of a dozen different commands — to the Potomac, passing through Sharpsburg. We crossed the Potomac by the Shepherdstown ford, and bivouacked in the yard of a house near the river, remaining there all day. The next morning (the 19th) shells began to come from over the river, and we were started on the road to Richmond with a mixed guard of cavalry and infantry. When we reached Winchester we were quartered for a night in the court-house yard, where we were beset by a motley crew who were eager to exchange the produce of the region for greenbacks.

On the road between Shepherdstown and Winchester we fell in with the Maryland Battalion — a meeting I have always remembered with pleasure. They were marching to the front by companies, spaced apart about 300 or 400 feet. We were an ungainly, draggled lot, about as far removed as well could be from any claim to ceremonious courtesy; yet each company, as it passed, gave us the military salute of shouldered arms. They were noticeable, at that early stage of the war, as the only organization we saw that wore the regulation Confederate gray, all other troops having assumed a sort of revised regulation uniform of homespun butternut — a significant witness, we thought, to the efficacy of the blockade.

From Winchester we were marched to Staunton, where we were put on board cattle-cars and forwarded at night, by way of Gordonsville, to Richmond, where we entered Libby Prison. We were not treated with special severity, for Libby was not at that time the hissing it afterward became. Our time there, also, was not long. Only nine days after we entered it we were sent away, going by steamer to Camp Parole, at Annapolis. From that place I went home without ceremony, reporting my address to my company officers. Three weeks afterward they advised me that I was exchanged — which meant that I was again, legally and technically, food for powder.

THE INVASION OF MARYLAND.

BY JAMES LONGSTREET, LIEUTENANT-GENERAL, C. S. A.

WHEN the Second Bull Run campaign closed we had the most brilliant prospects the Confederates ever had. We then possessed an army which, had it been kept together, the Federals would never have dared attack. With such a splendid victory behind us, and such bright prospects ahead, the question arose as to whether or not we should go into Maryland. General Lee, on account of our short supplies, hesitated a little, but I reminded him of my experience in Mexico, where sometimes we were obliged to live two or three days on green corn. I told him we could not starve at that season of the year so long as the fields were loaded with "roasting ears." Finally he determined to go on, and accordingly crossed the river and went to Frederick City. On the 6th of September some of our cavalry, moving toward Harper's Ferry, became engaged with some of the Federal artillery near there. General Lee proposed that I should organize a force, and surround the garrison and capture it. I objected, and urged that our troops were worn with marching and were on short rations, and that it would be a bad idea to divide our forces while we were in the enemy's country, where he could get information, in six or eight hours, of any movement we might make. The Federal army, though beaten at the Second Manassas, was not disorganized, and it would certainly come out to look for us, and we should guard against being caught in such a condition. Our army consisted of a superior quality of soldiers, but it was in no condition to divide in the enemy's country. I urged that we should keep it well in hand, recruit our strength, and get up supplies, and then we could do anything we pleased. General Lee made no reply to this, and I supposed the Harper's Ferry scheme was abandoned. A day or two after we had reached Frederick City, I went up to General Lee's tent and found the front walls closed. I inquired for the general, and he, recognizing my voice, asked me to come in. I went in and found Jackson there. The two were discussing the move against Harper's Ferry, both heartily approving it. They had gone so far that it seemed useless for me to offer any further opposition, and I only suggested that Lee should use his entire army in the move instead of sending off a large portion of it to Hagerstown as he intended to do. General Lee so far changed the wording of his order as to require me to halt at Boonsboro' with General D. H. Hill; Jackson being ordered to Harper's Ferry *via* Bolivar Heights, on the south side; McLaws by the Maryland Heights on the north, and Walker, *via* Loudoun Heights, from the south-east. This was afterward changed, and I was sent on to Hagerstown, leaving D. H. Hill alone at South Mountain.

The movement against Harper's Ferry began on the 10th. Jackson made a wide, sweeping march around the Ferry, passing the Potomac at Williamsport, and moving from there on toward Martinsburg, and turning thence upon Harper's Ferry to make his attack by Bolivar Heights. McLaws made a hurried march to reach Maryland Heights before Jackson could get in position, and succeeded in doing so. With Maryland Heights in our possession the Federals could not hold their position there. McLaws put 200 or 300 men to each piece of his artillery and carried it up the heights, and was in position when Jackson came on the heights opposite. Simultaneously Walker appeared upon Loudoun Heights, south of the Potomac and east of the Shenandoah, thus completing the combination against the Federal garrison. The surrender of the Ferry and the twelve thousand Federal troops there was a matter of only a short time.

If the Confederates had been able to stop with that, they might have been well contented with their month's campaign. They had had a series of successes and no defeats; but the division of the army to make this attack on Harper's Ferry was a fatal error, as the subsequent events showed.

While a part of the army had gone toward Harper's Ferry I had moved up to Hagerstown. In the meantime Pope had been relieved and McClellan was in command of the army, and with ninety thousand refreshed troops was marching forth to avenge the Second Manassas. The situation was a very serious one for us. McClellan was close upon us. As we moved out of Frederick he came on and occupied that place, and there he came across a lost copy of the order assigning position to the several commands in the Harper's Ferry move.

This "lost order" has been the subject of much severe comment by Virginians who have written of the war. It was addressed to D. H. Hill, and they charged that its loss was due to him, and that the failure of the campaign was the result of the lost order. As General Hill has proved that he never received the order at his headquarters it must have been lost by some one else.] Ordinarily, upon getting possession of such an order, the adversary

---

] See General Hill's statement on p. 570, and General Colgrove's on p. 603. The following is the text of the "lost order" as quoted by General McClellan in his official report:

"SPECIAL ORDERS, } HEADQUARTERS, ARMY
No. 191. } OF NORTHERN VIRGINIA, }
September 9th, 1862. }

"The army will resume its march to-morrow, taking the Hagerstown road. General Jackson's command will form the advance, and after passing Middletown, with such portions as he may select, take the route toward Sharpsburg, cross the Potomac at the most convenient point, and by Friday night take possession of the Baltimore and Ohio Railroad, capture such of the enemy as may be at Martinsburg, and intercept such as may attempt to escape from Harper's Ferry.

"General Longstreet's command will pursue the same road as far as Boonsboro', where it will halt with the reserve, supply, and baggage trains of the army.

"General McLaws, with his own division and that of General R. H. Anderson, will follow General Longstreet; on reaching Middletown he will take the route to Harper's Ferry, and by Friday morning possess himself of the Maryland Heights and endeavor to capture the enemy at Harper's Ferry and vicinity.

"General Walker, with his division after accomplishing the object in which he is now engaged, will cross the Potomac at Check's ford, ascend its right bank to Lovettsville, take possession of Loudoun Heights, if practicable, by Friday morning, Keyes's ford on his left, and the road between the end of the mountain and the Potomac on his right. He will, as far as practicable, coöperate with General McLaws and General Jackson in intercepting the retreat of the enemy.

"General D. H. Hill's division will form the rear-guard of the army, pursuing the road taken by the main body. The reserve artillery, ordnance, and supply trains, etc., will precede General Hill.

"General Stuart will detach a squadron of cavalry to accompany the commands of Generals Longstreet, Jackson, and McLaws, and, with the main body of the cavalry, will cover the route of the army and bring up all stragglers that may have been left behind.

"The commands of Generals Jackson, McLaws, and Walker, after accomplishing the objects for which they have been detached, will join the main body of the army at Boonsboro' or Hagerstown.

"Each regiment on the march will habitually carry its axes in the regimental ordnance-wagons, for use of the men at their encampments, to procure wood, etc. By command of General R. E. Lee.

"R. H. CHILTON, Assistant Adjutant-General.
"MAJOR-GENERAL D. H. HILL, Commanding Division."

Comparison of the above with the copy of the order as printed among the Confederate Correspondence ("Official Records," Volume XIX., Part II., p. 603) shows that the latter contains two paragraphs, omitted above. In the first paragraph the officers and men of Lee's army are prohibited from visiting Fredericktown except on written permission; and in the second paragraph directions are given for the transportation of the sick and disabled to Winchester.—EDITORS.

would take it as a *ruse de guerre*, but it seems that General McClellan gave it his confidence, and made his dispositions accordingly. He planned his attack upon D. H. Hill under the impression that I was there with 12 brigades, 9 of which were really at Hagerstown, while R. H. Anderson's division was on Maryland Heights with General McLaws. Had McClellan exercised due diligence in seeking information from his own resources, he would have known better the situation at South Mountain and could have enveloped General D. H. Hill's division on the afternoon of the 13th, or early on the morning of the 14th, and then

THE OLD LUTHERAN CHURCH, SHARPSBURG. FROM A WAR-TIME PHOTOGRAPH.

The church stands at the east end of the village, on Main street, and was a Federal hospital after the battle. Burnside's skirmishers gained a hold in the first cross-street below the church, where there was considerable fighting. On the hill in the extreme distance Main street becomes the Shepherdstown road, by which the Confederates retreated.—EDITORS.

turned upon McLaws at Maryland Heights, before I could have reached either point. As it was, McClellan, after finding the order, moved with more confidence on toward South Mountain, where D. H. Hill was stationed as a Confederate rear-guard with five thousand men under his command. As I have stated, my command was at Hagerstown, thirteen miles farther on. General Lee was with me, and on the night of the 13th we received information that McClellan was at the foot of South Mountain with his great army. General Lee ordered me to march back to the mountain early the next morning. I suggested that, instead of meeting McClellan there, we withdraw Hill and unite my forces and Hill's at Sharpsburg, at the same time explaining that Sharpsburg was a strong defensive position from which we could strike the flank or rear of any force that might be sent to the relief of Harper's Ferry. I endeavored to show him that by making a forced march to Hill my troops would be in an exhausted condition and could not make a proper battle. Lee listened patiently enough, but did not change his plans, and directed that I should go back the next day and make a stand at the mountain. After lying down, my mind was still on the battle of the next day, and I was so impressed with the thought that it would be impossible for us to do anything at South Mountain with the fragments of a worn and exhausted army, that I rose and, striking a light, wrote a note to General Lee, urging him to order Hill away and concentrate at Sharpsburg. To that note I got no answer, and the next morning I marched as directed, leaving General Toombs, as ordered by General Lee, at Hagerstown to guard our trains and supplies.

We marched as hurriedly as we could over a hot and dusty road, and reached the mountain about 3 o'clock in the afternoon, with the troops much scattered and worn. In riding up the mountain to join General Hill I discovered that everything was in such disjointed condition that it would be impossible for my troops and Hill's to hold the mountain against such forces as McClellan had there, and wrote a note to General Lee, in which I stated that fact, and cautioned him to make his arrangements to retire that night. We got as many troops up as we could, and by putting in detachments here and there managed to hold McClellan in check until night, when Lee ordered the withdrawal to Sharpsburg.

On the afternoon of the 15th of September my command and Hill's crossed the Antietam Creek, and took position in front of Sharpsburg, my command filing into position on the right of the Sharpsburg and Boonsboro' turnpike, and D. H. Hill's division on the left. Soon after getting into position we found our left, at Dunker Church, the weak point, and Hood, with two brigades, was changed from my right to guard this point, leaving General D. H. Hill between the parts of my command.

That night, after we heard of the fall of Harper's Ferry, General Lee ordered Stonewall Jackson to march to Sharpsburg as rapidly as he could come. Then it was that we should have retired from Sharpsburg and gone to the Virginia side of the Potomac.

The moral effect of our move into Maryland had been lost by our discomfiture at South Mountain, and it was then evident we could not hope to concentrate

LEE'S HEADQUARTERS IN SHARPSBURG. FROM A PHOTOGRAPH.

This house, which was the residence of Jacob H. Grove, is noted in Sharpsburg as the place where Lee held a conference with Longstreet and D. H. Hill. But Lee's headquarters tents were pitched in a small grove on the right of the Shepherdstown road, just outside the town.— EDITORS.

SOUTH-EASTERN STRETCH OF THE SUNKEN ROAD, OR "BLOODY LANE." (SEE MAP, P. 636.) FROM A PHOTOGRAPH TAKEN IN 1885.

in time to do more than make a respectable retreat, whereas by retiring before the battle we could have claimed a very successful campaign.

On the forenoon of the 15th, the blue uniforms of the Federals appeared among the trees that crowned the heights on the eastern bank of the Antietam. The number increased, and larger and larger grew the field of blue until it seemed to stretch as far as the eye could see, and from the tops of the mountains down to the edges of the stream gathered the great army of McClellan. It was an awe-inspiring spectacle as this grand force settled down in sight of the Confederates, then shattered by battles and scattered by long and tiresome marches. On the 16th Jackson came and took position with part of his command on my left. Before night the Federals attacked my left and gave us a severe fight, principally against Hood's division, but we drove them back, holding well our ground. After nightfall Hood was relieved from the position on the left, ordered to replenish his ammunition, and be ready to resume his first position on my right in the morning. General Jackson's forces, who relieved Hood, were extended to our left, reaching well back toward the Potomac, where most of our cavalry was. Toombs had joined us with two of his regiments, and was placed as guard on the bridge on my right. Hooker, who had thrown his corps against my left in the afternoon, was reënforced by the corps of Sumner and Mansfield. Sykes's division was also drawn into position for the impending battle. Burnside was over against my right, threatening the passage of the Antietam at that point. On the morning of the 17th the Federals were in good position along the Antietam, stretching up and down and across it to our left for three miles. They had a good position for their guns, which were of the most approved make and metal. Our position overcrowded theirs a little, but our guns were inferior and our ammunition was very imperfect.

THE SUNKEN ROAD, OR "BLOODY LANE."
FROM A PHOTOGRAPH TAKEN SINCE THE WAR.

This view is from the second bend in the lane, looking toward the Hagerstown pike, the Dunker Church wood appearing in the background. In the foreground Richardson crossed to the left into the cornfield near Piper's house. The house in the middle ground, erected since the war, marks the scene of French's hard fight after passing Roulette's house.—EDITORS.

Back of McClellan's line was a high ridge upon which was his signal station overlooking every point of our field. D. R. Jones's brigades of my command deployed on the right of the Sharpsburg pike, while Hood's brigades awaited orders. D. H. Hill was on the left extending toward the Hagerstown-Sharpsburg pike, and Jackson extended out from Hill's left toward the Potomac. The battle opened heavily with the attacks of the corps of Hooker, Mansfield, and Sumner against our left center, which consisted of Jackson's right and D. H. Hill's left. So severe and persistent were these attacks that I was obliged to send Hood to support our center. The Federals forced us back a little, however, and held this part of our position to the end of the day's work. With new troops and renewed efforts McClellan continued his attacks upon this point from time to time, while he brought his forces to bear against other points. The line swayed forward and back like a rope exposed to rushing currents. A force too heavy to be withstood would strike and drive in a weak point till we could collect a few fragments, and in turn force back the advance till our lost ground was recovered. A heroic effort was made by D. H. Hill, who collected some fragments and led a charge to drive back and recover our lost ground at the center. He soon found that his little band was too much exposed on its left flank and was obliged to abandon the attempt. Thus the battle ebbed and flowed with terrific slaughter on both sides.

The Federals fought with wonderful bravery and the Confederates clung to their ground with heroic courage as hour after hour they were mown down like grass. The fresh troops of McClellan literally tore into shreds the already ragged army of Lee, but the Confederates never gave back.

I remember at one time they were surging up against us with fearful

THE SUNKEN ROAD, LOOKING EAST FROM ROULETTE'S LANE. FROM A PHOTOGRAPH TAKEN IN 1885.

numbers. I was occupying the left over by Hood, whose ammunition gave out. He retired to get a fresh supply. Soon after the Federals moved up against us in great masses.

We were under the crest of a hill occupying a position that ought to have been held by from four to six brigades. The only troops there were Cooke's regiment of North Carolina infantry, and they were without a cartridge. As I rode along the line with my staff I saw two pieces of the Washington Artillery (Miller's battery), but there were not enough men to man them. The gunners had been either killed or wounded. This was a fearful situation for the Confederate center. I put my staff-officers to the guns while I held their horses. It was easy to see that if the Federals broke through our line there, the Confederate army would be cut in two and probably destroyed, for we were already

CONFEDERATE DEAD (OF D. H. HILL'S DIVISION) IN THE SUNKEN ROAD.
FROM A PHOTOGRAPH.

badly whipped and were only holding our ground by sheer force of desperation. Cooke sent me word that his ammunition was out. I replied that he must hold his position as long as he had a man left. He responded that he would show his colors as long as there was a man alive to hold them up. We loaded up our little guns with canister and sent a rattle of hail into the Federals as they came up over the crest of the hill.

That little battery shot harder and faster, with a sort of human energy, as though it realized that it was to hold the thousands of Federals at bay or the battle was lost. So warm was the reception we gave them that they dodged back behind the crest of the hill. We sought to make them believe we had many batteries before them. As the Federals would come up they would see the colors of the North Carolina regiment waving placidly and then would receive a shower of canister. We made it lively while it lasted. In the meantime General Chilton, General Lee's chief of staff, made his way to me and asked, "Where are the troops you are holding your line with?" I pointed to my two pieces and to Cooke's regiment, and replied, "There they are; but that regiment hasn't a cartridge."

Chilton's eyes popped as though they would come out of his head; he struck spurs to his horse and away he went to General Lee. I suppose he made some remarkable report, although I did not see General Lee again until night. After a little a shot came across the Federal front, plowing the ground in a parallel line. Another and another, each nearer and nearer their line. This enfilade fire, so distressing to soldiers, was from a battery on D. H. Hill's line, and it soon beat back the attacking column.

Meanwhile, R. H. Anderson and Hood came to our support and gave us more confidence. It was a little while only until another assault was made against D. H. Hill, and extending far over toward our left, where McLaws and Walker were supporting Jackson. In this desperate effort the lines seemed to swing back and forth for many minutes, but at last they settled down to their respective positions, the Confederates holding with a desperation which seemed to say, "We are here to die."

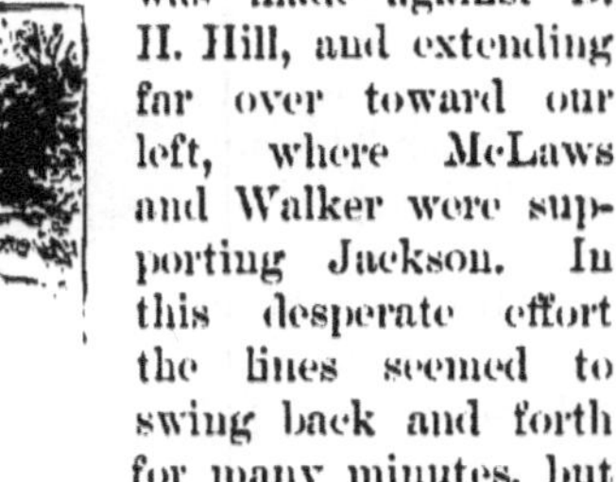

Meantime General Lee was over toward our right, where Burnside was trying to cross to the attack. Toombs, who had been assigned as guard at that point, did handsome service. His troops were footsore and worn from marching, and he had only four hundred men to meet the Ninth Corps. The little band fought bravely, but the Federals were pressing them slowly back. The delay that Toombs caused saved that part of the battle, however, for at the last moment A. P. Hill came in to reënforce him, and D. H. Hill discovered a good place for a battery and opened with it. Thus the Confederates were enabled to drive the Federals back, and when night settled down the army of Lee was still in possession of the field. But it was dearly bought, for thousands of brave soldiers were dead on the field and many gallant commands were torn as a forest in a cyclone. It was heart-rending to see how Lee's army had been slashed by the day's fighting.

ROULETTE'S FARM.

1.—View of William Roulette's farm-house. 2.—Roulette's spring-house, in which Confederate prisoners were confined during the battle. 3.—Roulette's spring, a copious fountain which refreshed many thirsty soldiers of both armies.

Nearly one-fourth of the troops who went into the battle were killed or wounded. We were so badly crushed that at the close of the day ten thousand fresh troops could have come in and taken Lee's army and everything it had. But McClellan did not know it, and [apparently] feared, when Burnside was pressed back, that Sharpsburg was a Confederate victory, and that he would have to retire. As it was, when night settled down both armies were content to stay where they were.

During the progress of the battle of Sharpsburg General Lee and I were
riding along my line and D. H. Hill's, when we received a report of movements of the enemy and started up the ridge to make a reconnoissance.
General Lee and I dismounted, but Hill declined to do so. I said to Hill,
"If you insist on riding up there and drawing the fire, give us a little interval
so that we may not be in the line of the fire when they open upon you."
General Lee and I stood on
the top of the crest with our
glasses, looking at the movements of the Federals on the
rear left. After a moment I
turned my glass to the right—
the Federal left. As I did so,
I noticed a puff of white smoke
from the mouth of a cannon.
"There is a shot for you," I said
to General Hill. The gunner
was a mile away, and the cannon-shot came whisking through
the air for three or four seconds
and took off the front legs of
the horse that Hill sat on and
let the animal down upon his
stumps. The horse's head was

AFTER THE BATTLE — POSITION OF THE CONFEDERATE
BATTERIES IN FRONT OF DUNKER CHURCH.
FROM A PHOTOGRAPH.

so low and his croup so high that Hill was in a most ludicrous position.
With one foot in the stirrup he made several efforts to get the other leg over
the croup, but failed. Finally we prevailed upon him to try the other end of
the horse, and he got down. He had a third horse shot under him before the
close of the battle. That shot at Hill was the second best shot I ever saw.
The best was at Yorktown. There a Federal officer came out in front of our
line, and sitting down to his little platting table began to make a map.
One of our officers carefully sighted a gun, touched it off, and dropped a
shell into the hands of the man at the little table.↓

When the battle was over and night was gathering, I started to Lee's
headquarters to make my report. In going through the town I passed a
house that had been set afire and was still burning. The family was in great
distress, and I stopped to do what I could for them. By that I was detained
until after the other officers had reached headquarters and made their reports.

↓Major Alfred A. Woodhull, Surgeon, U. S. A.,
wrote from David's Island, N. Y., July 16th,
1886:

"General Longstreet's 'best shot' was undoubtedly
the shell that shattered the plane table that First
Lieutenant Orlando G. Wagner, Topographical Engineer, was using in front of Yorktown, when he was
mortally wounded, precisely as described. He died
April 21st, 1862.

"Early on the morning of September 17th, 1862 (about
8 or 9 o'clock), I was standing near the guns of Captain
Stephen H. Weed, 5th Artillery, when a small group
came in sight, directly in our front, about a mile away.
There was no firing of any importance at that time on
our left, and Captain Weed, who was a superb artillerist
himself, aimed and fired at the single mounted man and
struck the horse. I witnessed the shot, and have no
doubt it was the one General Longstreet commemorates
as the 'second best.' My recollection is that the horse
was gray, and I had the impression that the party was
somewhat to the left (south) of the turnpike. General
Longstreet kindly writes me that he cannot now recall
the hour, but that there was little firing at the time, and
that the place 'was about twenty feet from the Boonsboro' pike, north.'" EDITORS.

My delay caused some apprehension on the part of General Lee that I had been hurt; in fact, such a report had been sent him. When I rode up and dismounted he seemed much relieved, and, coming to me very hurriedly for one of his dignified manner, threw his arms upon my shoulders and said:

"Here is my old war-horse at last."

When all the reports were in, General Lee decided that he would not be prepared the next day for offensive battle, and would prepare only for defense, as we had been doing.

The next day [the 18th] the Federals failed to advance, and both armies remained in position. During the day some of the

FIELD-HOSPITALS OF FRENCH'S DIVISION AT ANTIETAM. FROM A PHOTOGRAPH.

These pictures, according to a letter received by the editors from Dr. Samuel Sexton (8th Ohio), represent two field-hospitals established for the use of French's division at Antietam. The upper one was in charge of Dr. Sexton, who sent back the wounded men under his care at the front to this place during the battle, and afterward organized a hospital for all of the wounded soldiers found there,— utilizing for that purpose two or three barns, and erecting, besides, a number of shelters (shown in the cut) out of Virginia split-rails, set up on end in two parallel rows, meeting at the top, where they were secured. The sheds thus made were afterward thatched with straw, and could accommodate about 10 or 15 men each.

The lower picture shows an adjacent hospital for wounded Confederate prisoners, which was in charge of Dr. Anson Hurd of the 14th Indiana, who is seen standing on the right.

Federals came over under a flag of truce to look after their dead and wounded. The following night we withdrew, passing the Potomac with our entire army. After we had crossed, the Federals made a show of pursuit, and a force of about fifteen hundred crossed the river and gave a considerable amount of trouble to the command under Pendleton. A. P. Hill was sent back with his division, and attacked the Federals who had crossed the river in pursuit of us. His lines extended beyond theirs, and he drove them back in great confusion. Some sprang over the bluffs of the river and were killed; some were drowned and others were shot.↓

Proceeding on our march, we went to Bunker Hill, where we remained for several days. A report was made of a Federal advance, but it turned out to be only a party of cavalry and amounted to nothing. As soon as the cavalry

↓ Major Alfred A. Woodhull, Surgeon, U. S. A., wrote from David's Island, N. Y., July 21st, 1886, concerning this movement:

"Early Saturday, September 20th, Major Charles S. Lovell, 10th Infantry, crossed to reconnoiter with the Second Brigade (regulars), of Sykes's division, and other troops followed. On our ascent to the plateau we passed some abandoned artillery, but met with no opposition until nearly a mile from the bank, where a long infantry

BLACKFORD'S, OR BOTELER'S, FORD, FROM THE MARYLAND SIDE. FROM A RECENT PHOTOGRAPH.

This picture, taken from the tow-path of the Chesapeake and Ohio Canal, shows the ford below Shepherdstown by which Lee's army retreated after Antietam, the cliff on the Virginia side being the scene of the disaster to the 118th Pennsylvania, or Corn Exchange, regiment. When Porter's corps arrived at the Potomac in pursuit, on September 19th, Confederate artillery on the cliffs disputed the passage. A small Union force, under General Griffin, moved across the river in face of a warm fire, and, scaling the heights, captured several pieces of artillery. This attacking party was recalled during the night. Next morning, the 20th, two brigades of Sykes's division crossed and gained the heights on the left by the cement mill, while one brigade of Morell's division advanced to the right toward Shepherdstown and ascended the heights by way of the ravine. The 118th Pennsylvania formed beyond the crest and abreast of the dam. Soon the Confederates attacked with spirit. The Union forces were withdrawn without much loss, except to the 118th Pennsylvania, which was a new regiment, numbering 737 men, and had been armed, as it proved, with defective rifles. They made a stout resistance, until ordered to retreat, when most of the men fled down the precipitous face of the bluff and thence across the river, some crossing on the dam, the top of which was then dry. They were also under fire in crossing; and out of 363 in killed, wounded, and captured at this place, the 118th Pennsylvania lost 269.

retired we moved back and camped around Winchester, where we remained until some time in October. Our stragglers continued to come in until November, which shows how many we had lost by severe marches.

The great mistake of the campaign was the division of Lee's army. If General Lee had kept his forces together, he could not have suffered defeat.

line was confronted unexpectedly. Major Lovell had been informed that cavalry was to cross before us at daylight, but we were then found to be in advance, and the cavalry which was to feel the way was in our rear, and being useless was at once withdrawn. The overlapping size of the advancing force in front, its manifest effort to envelop our left flank as well, and the probability of its extension beyond our right, compelled an immediate return, which was effected with steadiness, while skirmishing. Infantry reinforcements that had crossed the river were simultaneously withdrawn, but on the right the 118th Pennsylvania, known as the "Corn Exchange" regiment, suffered severely, especially in one wing, where it was said at the time that there was a misapprehension of orders. When our men were in the stream there were dropping shots, but there was no direct infantry fire of importance. A fierce Union artillery fire was kept up to cover the retreat of our right, which indeed lost heavily. But there was no such slaughter as the Confederate reports announced. I think A. P. Hill put it at 3000, and said the Potomac was blue with the Yankee dead. Had the cavalry really been in advance, the reconnoissance could have been accomplished with comparative ease. I was a medical officer attached to the infantry, and, acting as an aide for Major Lovell, had opportunity to witness what is here stated." EDITORS.

At Sharpsburg he had hardly 37,000 men,‡ who were in poor condition for battle, while McClellan had about 87,000, who were fresh and strong.

The next year, when on our way to Gettysburg, there was the same situation of affairs at Harper's Ferry, but we let it alone.

General Lee was not satisfied with the result of the Maryland campaign, and seemed inclined to attribute the failure to the Lost Dispatch; though I believe he was more inclined to attribute the loss of the dispatch to the fault of a courier or to other negligence than that of the officer to whom it was directed.

Our men came in so rapidly after the battle that renewed hope of gathering his army in great strength soon caused Lee to look for other and new prospects, and to lose sight of the lost campaign. But at Sharpsburg was sprung the keystone of the arch upon which the Confederate cause rested. Jackson was quite satisfied with the campaign, as the Virginia papers made him the hero of Harper's Ferry, although the greater danger was with McLaws, whose service was the severer and more important. Lee lost nearly 20,000 by straggling in this campaign,—almost twice as many as were captured at Harper's Ferry.

The battle casualties of Jackson's command from the Rappahannock to the Potomac, according to the "Official Records," were 4629, while mine, including those of R. H. Anderson's division, were 4725, making in all, 9354. That taken from the army of 55,000 at the Second Manassas left a force of 45,646 moving across the Potomac. To that number must be added the forces that joined us; namely, D. H. Hill with 5000, McLaws with 4000, and Walker with 2000. Thus Lee's army on entering Maryland was made up of nearly 57,000 men, exclusive of artillery and cavalry. As we had but 37,000 at Sharpsburg, our losses in the several engagements after we crossed the Potomac, *including stragglers*, reached nearly 20,000. Our casualties in the affairs of the Maryland campaign, including Sharpsburg, were 13,964. Estimating the casualties in the Maryland campaign preceding Sharpsburg at 2000, it will be seen that we lost at Sharpsburg 11,000 to 12,000. Only a glance at these figures is necessary to impress one with the number of those who were unable to stand the long and rapid marches, and fell by the wayside, viz., 8000 to 9000. The Virginians who have written of the war have often charged the loss of the Maryland campaign to "laggards." It is unkind to apply such a term to our soldiers, who were as patient, courageous, and chivalrous as any ever marshaled into phalanx. Many were just out of the hospitals, and many more were crippled by injuries received in battle. They were marching without sufficient food or clothing, with their muskets, ammunition, provisions, and in fact their all, packed upon their backs. They struggled along with bleeding feet, tramping rugged mountain roads through a heated season. Such soldiers should not be called "laggards" by their countrymen. Let them have their well-earned honors though the fame of others suffer thereby.

<hr>

‡ This was Lee's estimate as stated to me at the time. It is much above the estimate of those who have since written of this campaign. Colonel Charles Marshall, in his evidence in the Fitz John Porter case, gives our forces at the Second Manassas on August 29th as 50,000, not including artillery or cavalry. R. H. Anderson joined me on the night of August 29th, with over 4000.—J. L.

Lee says officially that "Antietam was fought with less than 40,000 men on our side."—EDITORS.

SHARPSBURG.‡

BY JOHN G. WALKER, MAJOR-GENERAL, C. S. A.

A LITTLE past the hour of noon on the 16th of September, 1862, General "Stonewall" Jackson and myself reached General Lee's headquarters at Sharpsburg and reported the arrival of our commands. I am thus particular in noting the hour of the arrival of my division for the reason that some writers have fallen into the error of mentioning my arrival as coincident with that of McLaws's division, which was some twenty-two hours later.

The thought of General Lee's perilous situation, with the Potomac River in his rear, confronting, with his small force, McClellan's vast army, had haunted me through the long hours of the night's march, and I expected to find General Lee anxious and careworn. Anxious enough, no doubt, he was; but there was nothing in his look or manner to indicate it. On the contrary, he was calm, dignified, and even cheerful. If he had had a well-equipped army of a hundred thousand veterans at his back, he could not have appeared more composed and confident. On shaking hands with us, he simply expressed his satisfaction with the result of our operations at Harper's Ferry, and with our timely arrival at Sharpsburg; adding that with our reënforcement he felt confident of being able to hold his ground until the arrival of the divisions of R. H. Anderson, McLaws, and A. P. Hill, which were still behind, and which did not arrive until the next day.

At four in the afternoon I received an order from General Lee to move at 3 o'clock the next morning, and take position with my division on the extreme right of his line of battle, so as to cover a ford of the Antietam, and to lend a hand, in case of necessity, to General Toombs, whose brigade was guarding the bridge over the Antietam called by Federal writers "Burnside's Bridge."

‡ For an account of the part taken by General Walker's division in the operations leading to the surrender of Harper's Ferry, see pp. 605 to 611. — EDITORS.

BURNSIDE'S BRIDGE — I.

This picture, after a photograph taken in 1885, is a view of the Confederate position from the slope of the hill occupied by the Union batteries before a crossing was effected. At the time of the battle the buildings had not been erected, and the Confederate hill-side was covered with trees. A Confederate battery on the left enfiladed the crossing. Union sharp-shooters took advantage of the stone-wall on the right of the approach to the bridge. The continuation of the road to Sharpsburg is seen on the right across the bridge.— EDITORS.

At daybreak on the 17th I took the position assigned me, forming my line of battle on the crest of a ridge in front of the ford just mentioned. The ground, from my position to the creek, distant about five hundred yards, sloped gradually down to the crossing, just below which there was a wooded, bluff-like hill commanding the approach to the ford from the east.✝ Here I posted a battalion of skirmishers.

While these dispositions, after a careful reconnoissance of the ground on both sides of the Antietam, were being made, the booming of artillery, at some distance on my left, warned us that the battle had begun. As the morning wore on the firing grew heavier and heavier, until Elk Mountain, to the eastward, gave back an incessant echo.

About 9 o'clock an order was brought by a staff-officer of General Lee, directing me to hurry to the left to reënforce Jackson, who was being hard pressed. Hastily recalling my skirmishers, I hurried forward, left in front, along the rear of the whole Confederate line of battle. As I passed what is now known as Cemetery Hill, I saw General Lee standing erect and calm, with a field-glass to his eye, his fine form sharply outlined against the sky, and I

✝ The ford by which Rodman crossed after Walker's forces were withdrawn.— EDITORS.

BURNSIDE'S BRIDGE — II.

This picture, after a photograph taken in 1880, is a view of the Union position from the hill where Confederate artillery was planted to enfilade the bridge. From a point below, the 2d Maryland and the 6th New Hampshire charged up the road, but they were swept by such a murderous fire that only a few reached the bridge and sought shelter behind the stone-wall above. Subsequently, the bridge was carried by the 51st Pennsylvania and the 51st New York, charging from the pines on the hillside. see p. 632 .— EDITORS.

thought I had never seen a nobler figure. He seemed quite unconscious that the enemy's shells were exploding around and beyond him.

To those who have not been witnesses of a great battle like this, where more than a hundred thousand men, armed with all the appliances of modern science and skill, are engaged in the work of slaughtering each other, it is impossible by the power of words to convey an adequate idea of its terrible sublimity. The constant booming of cannon, the ceaseless rattle and roar of musketry, the glimpses of galloping horsemen and marching infantry, now seen, now lost in the smoke, adding weirdness to terror, all together make up a combination of sights and sounds wholly indescribable.

Opposite the rear of Longstreet's position I overtook General Ripley, of D. H. Hill's division, who, after having had dressed a serious wound in the neck, was returning to the command of his brigade, then hotly engaged. From him I obtained some information of the progress of the battle in the center.

Hurrying on, I was soon met by a staff-officer, who informed me that it was General Jackson's wish that I should go to the assistance of Hood, who was hard pressed and almost out of ammunition, adding that if I found the

Federals in possession of the wood on the Hagerstown road, I must drive them out, as it was the key of the battle-field.

He further explained that there was between the wood, just referred to, and the left of D. H. Hill's position, a gap of at least a third of a mile, and that I must leave a part of my command to fill it, and to support the reserve batteries under Colonel Stephen D. Lee which would also occupy the gap.

For this purpose I detached the 27th North Carolina and the 3d Arkansas of Manning's brigade, and placed them under the orders of Colonel John R. Cooke, of the former regiment. ‡

Moving forward, we soon reached the rear of Hood's position, and there, forming line of battle with Ransom on the left, we moved forward to Hood's relief, supported by McLaws's division, which at that moment (10:30 A. M.) arrived from Harper's Ferry. By this time the Federals [under Sedgwick] had forced Hood's men out of the wood, and were in possession of the key of the battle-field. To regain this position and restore our line was now the task before us. This we soon accomplished, but only after perhaps the severest struggle of the day.

The Federals contended for every foot of the ground, but, driven from rock to rock, from tree to tree, of the "West Wood," after a bloody struggle of some thirty minutes, Sedgwick's forces were pressed back into the open fields beyond, and, being there exposed to the fire of S. D. Lee's artillery, broke and fled in great disorder back to the cover of the "East Wood," beyond the Hagerstown road.

My loss in this attack was heavy, including the gallant Colonel Van H. Manning, commanding Walker's brigade, who fell severely wounded. The regiment which suffered most was the 30th Virginia. In the ardor of their pursuit of the enemy through the wood, the Virginians followed three hundred yards into the open, where they were fearfully cut up by the Federal batteries; they only saved themselves from annihilation by a timely retreat to the cover of the wood.

This ended the attempt of the Federals to drive Jackson from his position by infantry attacks. Their artillery, however, continued throughout the day to pour a heavy fire upon him, but with little effect. Our position was a most advantageous one. The space between it and the "East Wood," occupied by

‡ These are the troops spoken of in General D. H. Hill's report as "Walker's," who assisted in the repulse of Federal General French, later in the day. As the main body of my division was some distance to the left of the corn-fields where Cooke's regiments were posted, General Palfrey [in his volume "The Antietam and Fredericksburg," p. 94] expresses some uncertainty as to General Hill's meaning.—J. G. W.

See also General Longstreet, p. 669.—EDITORS.

the Federals, consisted of meadows and corn-fields, intersected by fences, and in passing over the ground their attacking columns were exposed to the fire of our batteries. Seventy or eighty yards in front of our position, and parallel with it, was a ridge, which, although slight, was sufficient to cover our men as they lay down among the trees and bowlders which covered the ground. The projectiles from the Federal batteries, striking this ridge, passed harmlessly over our heads, shattering the branches of the trees and tumbling them down in showers upon our men. Occasionally a shell would explode above us and send its hissing fragments in the midst of us, but our loss from this cause was surprisingly small.

The Federal infantry assaults having ceased, about half-past twelve I sought Jackson to report that from the front of my position in the wood I thought I had observed a movement of the enemy, as if to pass through the gap where I had posted Colonel Cooke's two regiments. I found Jackson in rear of Barksdale's brigade, under an apple-tree, sitting on his horse, with one leg thrown carelessly over the pommel of his saddle, plucking and eating the fruit. Without

CONFEDERATE DEAD ON THE WEST SIDE OF THE HAGERSTOWN ROAD OPPOSITE THE CORN-FIELD. FROM A PHOTOGRAPH.

making any reply to my report, he asked me abruptly: "Can you spare me a regiment and a battery?" I replied that Colonel Hill's 48th North Carolina, a very strong regiment, was in reserve, and could be spared, and that I could also give him both French's and Branch's batteries, but that they were without long-range ammunition, which had been exhausted at Harper's Ferry.

Jackson then went on to say that, owing to the nature of the ground, General Stuart's cavalry could take no part in the battle and were in the rear, but that Stuart himself had reported for such duty as he could perform.

Jackson added that he wished to make up, from the different commands on our left, a force of four or five thousand men, and give them to Stuart, with orders to turn the enemy's right, and attack him in the rear; that I must give orders to my division to advance to the front, and attack the enemy as soon as I should hear Stuart's guns—and that our whole left wing would move to the attack at the same time. Then, replacing his foot in the stirrup, he said with great emphasis: "We'll drive McClellan into the Potomac."

After giving orders for the regiment and batteries to report to Stuart, I galloped down the line where I had posted Cooke, but found that General Longstreet, having observed the danger from General French's formidable attack, had ordered Cooke forward, and that (together with D. H. Hill's division)

NORTH-WEST ANGLE OF THE "EAST WOOD" AND THE CORN-FIELD. FROM A SKETCH MADE AT THE TIME.

When the artist sketched this scene he was told that the guns in the corn-field belonged to a Maryland battery (Union), which was firing into the Dunker Church wood beyond. Most of the dead and wounded in this angle of the "East Wood" were Confederates. One of them, under the large tree at the left, had bound his shattered leg with corn-stalks and leaves to stop the flow of blood. He asked for water, of which there was none, and then begged the artist to remove his dead comrade, who was lying partly upon him, which was done. He wanted to be carried out of the woods, because he expected his friends to return and fight for them again. At the right was a tall young Georgian with a shattered ankle, sitting at the feet of one of the dead, who, he said, was his father.— EDITORS.

he was then closely engaged. Soon returning to my command, I repeated General Jackson's order to my brigade commanders and directed them to listen for the sound of Stuart's guns. We all confidently expected to hear the welcome sound by 2 o'clock, at least, and as that hour approached every ear was on the alert. Napoleon at Waterloo did not listen more intently for the sound of Grouchy's fire than did we for Stuart's. Two o'clock came, but nothing was heard of Stuart. Half-past two and then three, and still Stuart made no sign.

About half-past three a staff-officer of General Longstreet brought me an order from that general to advance and attack the enemy in my front. As the execution of this order would materially interfere with Jackson's plans, I thought it my duty before beginning the movement to communicate with General Longstreet personally. I found him in rear of the position in which I had posted Cooke in the morning, and upon informing him of Jackson's intentions, he withdrew his order.

While we were discussing this subject, Jackson himself joined us with the information of Stuart's failure to turn the Federal right, for the reason that he had found it securely *posted on the Potomac.* Upon my expressing surprise at this statement, Jackson replied that he also had been surprised, as he had supposed the Potomac much farther away; but he remarked that Stuart had an excellent eye for topography, and it must be as he represented. He added: "It is a great pity,— we should have driven McClellan into the Potomac."

By this time, with staff-officers, couriers, etc., we were a mounted group of some ten or a dozen persons, presenting so tempting a target that a Federal battery, at a distance of five hundred yards, opened fire upon us, but with no other result, strange to say, than the slaughter of the horse of one of my couriers.

The attempt of the Federals to penetrate our center, and its repulse by D. H. Hill, materially assisted by Colonel John R. Cooke's two regiments of my division,‡ ended infantry operations on our portion of the field for the day. The batteries, however, continued to pound away at each other until dark.

Late in the afternoon the direction of the firing on our extreme right was most alarming,—indicating, as it did, that the Federal left had forced a crossing of the Antietam, and that it must be perilously near our only line of retreat to the Potomac, at Shepherdstown. Could it be that A. P. Hill had come up and had been repulsed? If so, we had lost the day.

We hoped that A. P. Hill was still behind, but within striking distance. Soon the sound of musketry, which had almost ceased, roared out again with increased volume, indicating that fresh troops had been brought up, on one side or the other. For thirty minutes the sound of the firing came steadily from the same direction; then it seemed to recede eastward, and finally to die away almost entirely. We knew then that Hill *was* up; that the Federals had been driven back, and that the Confederate army had narrowly escaped defeat.

As night closed down, the firing along the whole line ceased; one of the bloodiest and most hotly contested battles of the war had been fought. The men of my division — worn out by a week's incessant marching and fighting by day and night —dropped down where they were, and could with difficulty be roused, even to take their cooked rations, brought up from our camp in the rear.

But there was little sleep for the ambulance corps; and all night long their lanterns could be seen flashing about the battle-field while they were searching for and bringing in the wounded, of friend and foe alike. In company with General Barksdale of Mississippi, whose brigade was on my left, I rode over that part of the battle-field where our own troops had been engaged, to see that none of the wounded had been overlooked. While passing along a worm fence, in the darkness, we heard a feeble voice almost under our horses' feet : " Don't let your horses t-r-e-a-d on m-e !" We at once pulled up, and peering over the pommels of our saddles into the darkness, we could distinguish the dim outlines of a human form extended across our path. "Who are you?" we inquired. "I belong to the 20th Mas-sa-chu-setts rig-i-ment," answered the voice; "I can't move — I think my back's broken." We sent for an ambulance and gave orders to care for the poor fellow, who was one of Sedgwick's men. This was but one of the very many instances of human suffering we encountered that night.

During the whole of the 18th the two armies rested in the positions which they had occupied at the close of the battle. There was a tacit truce, and Federal and Confederate burying-parties passed freely between the lines.

‡ The gallant conduct of Colonel Cooke on this occasion deservedly won for him promotion to the grade of brigadier-general. His losses in this engagement were terrible. In his own regiment, the 27th North Carolina, out of 26 commissioned officers who went into action, 18 were killed or wounded. In the 3d Arkansas the losses were equally great.— J. G. W.

We had fought an indecisive battle, and although we were, perhaps, in as good a condition to renew the struggle as the enemy were, General Lee recognized the fact that his ulterior plans had been thwarted by this premature engagement, and after a consultation with his corps commanders he determined to withdraw from Maryland. At dark on the night of the 18th the rearward movement began; and a little after sunrise of the next morning the entire Confederate army had safely recrossed the Potomac at Shepherdstown.

Detained in superintending the removal of a number of the wounded of my division, I was among the last to cross the Potomac. As I rode into the river I passed General Lee, sitting on his horse in the stream, watching the crossing of the wagons and artillery. Returning my greeting, he inquired as to what was still behind. There was nothing but the wagons containing my wounded, and a battery of artillery, all of which were near at hand, and I told him so. "Thank God!" I heard him say as I rode on.

UNION BURIAL PARTY AT ANTIETAM. FROM A PHOTOGRAPH.

ANTIETAM SCENES.

BY CHARLES CARLETON COFFIN.

THE cannon were thundering when at early morn, September 17th, 1862, I mounted my horse at Hagerstown, where I had arrived the preceding day, as an army correspondent, upon its evacuation by the Confederates. The people of the town, aroused by the cannonade, were at the windows of the houses or in the streets, standing in groups, listening to the reverberations rolling along the valley. The wind was south-west, the clouds hanging low and sweeping the tree-tops on South Mountain.

The cannonade, reverberating from cloud to mountain and from mountain to cloud, became a continuous roar, like the unbroken roll of a thunder-storm. The breeze, being in our direction, made the battle seem much nearer than it was. I was fully seven miles from Hooker's battle-field.

I turned down the Hagerstown and Sharpsburg turnpike at a brisk gallop, although I knew that Lee's army was in possession of the thoroughfare by the toll-gate which then stood about two miles north of Sharpsburg. A citizen who had left his home, to be beyond harm during the battle, had given me the information. The thought uppermost in my mind was to gain the left flank of the Confederate army, mingle with the citizens, and so witness the battle from the Confederate side. It would be a grand accomplishment if successful.

It would give me a splendid opportunity to see the make-up of the Confederate army. It would be like going behind the scenes of a theater. I was in citizen's dress, splashed with mud, and wore a dilapidated hat.

While wondering what would be the outcome of the venture, I came upon a group of farmers, who were listening with dazed countenances to the uproar momentarily increasing in volume. It was no longer alone the boom of the batteries, but a rattle of musketry—at first like pattering drops upon a roof; then a roll, crash, roar, and rush, like a mighty ocean billow upon the shore, chafing the pebbles, wave on wave,— with deep and heavy explosions of the batteries, like the crashing of thunderbolts. I think the currents of air must have had something to do with the effect of sound. The farmers were walking about nervously, undecided, evidently, whether to flee or to remain.

"I wouldn't go down the pike if I were you," said one, addressing me. "You will ride right into the Rebs."

"That is just where I would like to go."

"You can't pass yourself off for a Reb; they'll see, the instant they set eyes on you, that you are a Yank. They'll gobble you up and take you to Richmond," said the second.

No doubt I acted wisely in leaving the turnpike and riding to gain the right flank of the Union line. A short distance and I came upon a Confederate soldier lying beneath a tree. He doubtless supposed that I was a cavalryman, and raised his hand as if to implore me not to shoot him. His face was pale and haggard, and he had dropped from the ranks through sheer exhaustion. I left the poor fellow with the conviction that he never again would see his Southern home.

A mile farther on and I came upon the driftwood of McClellan's army. Every army has its driftwood soldiers — valiant at the mess-table, brave in the story around the bivouac fire, but faint of heart when battle begins. Some of them were old skulkers, others fresh recruits, with bright uniforms, who had volunteered under the pressure of enthusiasm. This was their first battle and was not what they had pictured a battle to be.

"Where does this road lead to?" asked one with white lips.

"To Hagerstown. But where are you going?"

"Oh, our division has been ordered to Hagerstown," was the reply as they hastened on.

Ammunition trains were winding up the hill from the road leading to Keedysville. Striking across the fields, I soon came upon the grounds on Hoffman's farm selected for the field-hospitals. Even at that hour of the morning it was an appalling sight. The wounded were lying in rows awaiting their turn at the surgeons' tables. The hospital stewards had a corps of men distributing straw over the field for their comfort.

Turning from the scenes of the hospital, I ascended the hill and came upon the men who had been the first to sweep across the Hagerstown pike, past the toll-gate, and into the Dunker Church woods, only to be hurled back by Jackson,

who had established his line in a strong position behind outcropping limestone ledges.

"There are not many of us left," was the mournful remark of an officer.

I learned the story of the morning's engagement, and then rode to the line of batteries on the ridge by the house of J. Poffenberger; if my memory serves me there were thirty guns in position there pointing south-west. There was a lull in the strife. All was quiet in the woods along the turnpike, and in the corn-field beyond D. R. Miller's house,—so quiet that I thought I would ride on to the front line, not knowing that the brigade lying upon the ground near the cannon was the advanced line of the army. I rode through Poffenberger's door-yard, and noticed that a Confederate cannon-shot had ripped through the building; another had upset a hive of bees, and the angry insects had taken their revenge on the soldiers. I walked my horse down the pike past the toll-gate.

"Hold on!" It was the peremptory hail of a Union soldier crouching under the fence by the roadside. "Where are you going?"

"I thought I would go out to the front!"

"The front! you have passed it. This is the picket line. If you know what is good for yourself, you'll skedaddle mighty quick. The Rebs are in the corn right out there."

I acted upon the timely advice and retreated to a more respectful distance; and none too soon, for a moment later the uproar began again — solid shot tearing through the woods and crashing among the trees, and shells exploding in unexpected places. I recall a round shot that came ricochetting over the ground, cutting little furrows, tossing the earth into the air, as the plow of the locomotive turns its white furrow after a snow-storm. Its speed gradually diminished and a soldier was about to catch it, as if he were at a game of baseball, but a united yell of "Look out!" "Don't!" "Take care!" "Hold on!" caused him to desist. Had he attempted it, he would have been knocked over instantly.

Turning from the conflict on the right, I rode down the line, toward the center, forded the Antietam and ascended the hill east of it to the large square mansion of Mr. Pry, where General McClellan had established his headquarters. The general was sitting in an arm-chair in front of the house. His staff were about him; their horses, saddled and bridled, were hitched to the trees and fences. Stakes had been driven in the earth in front of the house, to which were strapped the headquarters telescopes, through which a view of the operations and movements of the two armies could be obtained.

It was a commanding situation. The panorama included fully two-thirds of the battle-field, from the woods by the Dunker Church southward to the hills below Sharpsburg.

The Fifth Corps, under Fitz John Porter, was behind the ridge extending south toward the bridge, where the artillery of the Ninth Corps was thundering. Porter, I remember, was with McClellan, watching the movements of the troops across the Antietam — French's and Richardson's divisions, which were forming in the fields east of Roulette's and Mumma's houses. What a splendid sight it was! How beautifully the lines deployed! The clouds which had hung low all the morning had lifted, and the sun was shining through the rifts, its bright beams falling on the flags and glinting from gun-barrel and bayonet. Upon the crest of the hill south of the Dunker Church, I could see Confederates on horseback, galloping, evidently with orders; for, a few moments later, there was another gleam in the sunshine from the bayonets of their troops, who were apparently getting into position to resist the threatened movement of French and Richardson.

Memory recalls the advance of the line of men in blue across the meadow east of Roulette's. They reach the spacious barn, which divides the line of men as a rock parts the current of a river, flowing around it, but uniting beyond. The orchard around the house screens the movement in part. I see the blue uniforms beneath the apple-trees. The line halts for alignment. The skirmishers are in advance. There are isolated puffs of smoke, and then the Confederate skirmishers scamper up the hill and disappear. Up the slope moves the line to the top of a knoll. Ah! what a crash! A white cloud, gleams of lightning, a yell, a hurrah, and then up in the corn-field a great commotion, men firing into each other's faces, the Confederate line breaking, the ground strewn with prostrate forms. The Confederate line in " Bloody lane " has been annihilated, the center pierced.

Just here McClellan lost a great opportunity. It was the plain dictate of common sense that then was the time when Porter's eleven thousand should have been sent across the Antietam and thrown like a thunderbolt upon the enemy. It was so plain that the rank and file saw it. " Now is the time " was the universal comment. But not a soldier stirred from his position. McClellan saw it, but issued no order. All through the day most of the Fifth Corps remained in reserve.

The battle was in the main fought by divisions — one after another. There was no concerted action, no hammering all along the line at the same time. Heavy blows were given, but they were not followed up. It has been said that McClellan's excuse for not throwing in Porter's corps at that moment was the reason given by Napoleon at Borodino when asked why he did not at a certain moment put in the Imperial Guard: " If I am defeated to-day, where is my army for to-morrow?" There was no parallel between Antietam and Borodino. The moment had come for dividing Lee's army at its center and crushing it back upon the Potomac in utter rout. A. P. Hill, on his way from Harper's Ferry to join Lee, was at that moment fording the Potomac at Shepherdstown. This General McClellan did not know, but the fact was before him that French and Richardson had pierced the Confederate center.

With the falling back of the Confederates I went up past Roulette's house to the sunken road. The hillside was dotted with prostrate forms of men in blue, but in the sunken road, what a ghastly spectacle! The Confederates had gone down as the grass falls before the scythe. Words are inadequate to portray the scene. Resolution and energy still lingered in the pallid cheeks, in the set teeth, in the gripping hand. I recall a soldier with the cartridge between his thumb and finger, the end of the cartridge bitten off, and the paper between his teeth when the bullet had pierced his heart, and the machinery of life — all the muscles and nerves — had come to a standstill. A young lieutenant had fallen while trying to rally his men; his hand was still firmly grasping his sword, and determination was visible in every line of his face. I counted fourteen bodies lying together, literally in a heap, amid the corn rows on the hillside. The broad, green leaves were sprinkled and stained with blood.

The close of the battle presented a magnificent spectacle as the artillery of both armies came into play. The arrival of A. P. Hill had a stimulating effect upon Lee's veterans, while the carrying of the bridge and the work accomplished by French's and Richardson's divisions in the center gave great encouragement to the Union army. It was plain that Lee was economical in the use of artillery ammunition. In fact, he had a short supply. The engagements at Gainesville, Groveton, Bull Run, Chantilly, Harper's Ferry, and South Mountain had depleted his ammunition-chests, and supply trains had not reached him from the west side of the Potomac.

Far up on the Union right, as well as in the center, the Union batteries were pounding. I recall a remarkable scene. The sun was going down,— its disc red and large as seen through the murky battle-cloud. One of Sumner's batteries was directly in line toward the sun, on the crest of the ridge north of the smoking ruins of Mumma's house and barn, and there was one piece of which the gunners, as they rammed home the cartridge, seemed to be standing in the sun. Beyond, hid from view by the distance and the low-hanging branches of the oaks by the Dunker Church, the Confederate guns were flashing. Immediately north of Sharpsburg, and along the hill in front, now the National Cemetery, Longstreet's cannon were in play. Half-way up the hill were Burnside's men sending out a continuous flame, with A. P. Hill's veterans confronting them. All the country was flaming and smoking; shells were bursting above the contending lines; Burnside was asking for reënforcements. How quickly Porter's eleven thousand could have rushed across Antietam bridge with no Confederates to oppose them, swept up the hillside and forced themselves like a wedge between Longstreet and A. P. Hill!—but McClellan had only Miller's battery to send him! The sun went down; the thunder died away, the musketry ceased, bivouac fires gleamed out as if a great city had lighted its lamps.

When the soldiers are seeking rest, the work of the army correspondent begins. All through the day eyes and ears have been open. The note-book is scrawled with characters intelligible to him if read at once, but wholly meaningless a few hours later. He must grope his way along the lines in the darkness, visit the hospitals, hear the narratives of all, eliminate error, get at the probable truth, keeping ever in mind that each general thinks his brigade, each colonel his regiment, every captain his company, did most of the fighting. While thus visiting the lines, I heard a song rising on the night air sweet and plaintive:

Do they miss me at home, do they miss me?
'Twould be an assurance most dear
To know that this moment some lov'd one
Were saying, 'I wish he were here';
To feel that the group at the fireside
Were thinking of me, as I roam.
Oh, yes, 'twould be joy beyond measure
To know that they miss me at home."

Both before and after a battle, sad and solemn thoughts come to the soldier. Before the conflict they are of apprehension; after the strife there is a sense of relief; but the thinned ranks, the knowledge that the comrade who stood by your side in the morning never will stand there again, bring inexpressible sadness. The soldiers, with thoughts far away, were apprehensive that the conflict of the day was but a prelude to another struggle more fierce and bloody in the morning. They were in position and lying on their arms, ready to renew the battle at daylight; but day dawned and the cannon were silent. The troops were in line, yet there was no order to advance. I could hear now and then the isolated shots of the pickets. I could see that Lee had contracted his line between Dunker Church and Sharpsburg. His cannon were in position, his troops in line. Everybody knew that Franklin's corps was comparatively fresh; that McClellan had 29,000 men who either had as yet not fired a musket or had been only slightly engaged. Why did he not attack? No one could tell.

Riding up to the right, I found that hostilities had ceased; that the ambulance corps of both armies were gathering up the wounded in the field near the Dunker Church. ☆ Going out over the ground where the tides had ebbed and flowed, I

found it thickly strewn with dead. I recall a Union soldier lying near the Dunker Church with his face turned upward, and his pocket Bible open upon his breast. I lifted the volume and read the words: "Though I walk through the valley of the shadow of death, I will fear no evil; for Thou art with me. Thy rod and Thy staff, they comfort me." Upon the fly-leaf were the words: "We hope and pray that you may be permitted by a kind Providence, after the war is over, to return."

Near by stood a wounded battery-horse and a shattered caisson belonging to one of Hood's batteries. The animal had eaten every blade of grass within reach. No human being ever looked more imploringly for help than that dumb animal, wounded beyond the possibility of moving, yet resolutely standing, as if knowing that lying down would be the end.

The assumed armistice came to an end, the pickets stood in hostile attitude once more, but the day wore away and no orders were issued for a renewal of the attack. Another morning, and Lee was beyond the Potomac. I galloped along the lines where his army had stood, and saw the wreck and ruin of battle. I recall the body of a Confederate sharp-shooter, lying in the forks of a tree by the roadside, between the Dunker Church and Sharpsburg. Shells had exploded in the streets of Sharpsburg. The horses of a Confederate battery had gone down in a heap in the public square.

Porter's corps was passing through the town. McClellan and his staff came galloping up the hill. Porter's men swung their hats and gave a cheer; but few hurrahs came from the other corps—none from Hooker's. A change had come over the army. The complacent look which I had seen upon McClellan's countenance on the 17th, as if all were going well, had disappeared. There was a troubled look instead—a manifest awakening to the fact that his great opportunity had gone by. Lee had slipped through his fingers.

☆ Surgeon Jonathan Letterman, Medical Director, Army of the Potomac, reports as follows upon the work of his department on the field: "Immediately after the retreat of the enemy from the field of Antietam, measures were taken to have all the Confederate wounded gathered in from the field, over which they lay scattered in all directions, and from the houses and barns in the rear of their lines, and placed under such circumstances as would permit of their being properly attended to, and at such points as would enable their removal to be effected to Frederick, and thence to Baltimore and Fortress Monroe to their own lines. They were removed as rapidly as their recovery would permit. . . . There were many cases both on our right and left whose wounds were so serious that their lives would be endangered by their removal; and to have every opportunity afforded them for recovery, the Antietam hospital, consisting of hospital tents and capable of comfortably accommodating nearly six hundred cases, was established at a place called Smoketown, near Keedysville, for those who were wounded on our right, and a similar hospital, but not so capacious,—the Locust Spring hospital,—was established in the rear of the Fifth Corps for those cases which occurred on our left. To one or other of these hospitals all the wounded were carried whose wounds were of such a character as to forbid their re-

moval to Frederick or elsewhere. . . . Immediately after the battle a great many citizens came within our lines in order to remove their relatives or friends who had been injured, and in a great many instances when the life of the man depended upon his remaining at rest. It was impossible to make them understand that they were better where they were, and that a removal would probably be done only with the sacrifice of life. Their minds seemed bent on having them in a house. If that could be accomplished, all would, in their opinion, be well. No greater mistake could exist, and the results of that battle only added additional evidence of the absolute necessity of a full supply of pure air, constantly renewed—a supply which cannot be obtained in the most perfectly constructed building. Within a few yards a marked contrast could be seen between the wounded in houses and barns and in the open air. Those in houses progressed less favorably than those in the barns, those in barns less favorably than those in the open air, although all were in other respects treated alike. The capacious barns, abundantly provided with hay and straw, the delightful weather with which we were favored, and the kindness exhibited by the people afforded increased facilities to the medical department for taking care of the wounded thrown upon it by that battle . . . ."—EDITORS.

A WOMAN'S RECOLLECTIONS OF ANTIETAM.

BY MARY BEDINGER MITCHELL.

SEPTEMBER, 1862, was in the skies of the almanac, but August still reigned in ours; it was hot and dusty. The railroads in the Shenandoah Valley had been torn up, the bridges had been destroyed, communication had been made difficult, and Shepherdstown, cornered by the bend of the Potomac, lay as if forgotten in the bottom of somebody's pocket. We were without news or knowledge, except when some chance traveler would repeat the last wild and uncertain rumor that he had heard. We had passed an exciting summer. Winchester had changed hands more than once; we had been "in the Confederacy" and out of it again, and were now waiting, in an exasperating state of ignorance and suspense, for the next move in the great game.

It was a saying with us that Shepherdstown was just nine miles from everywhere. It was, in fact, about that distance from Martinsburg and Harper's Ferry — oft-mentioned names — and from Williamsport, where the armies so often crossed, both to and from Maryland. It was off the direct road between those places and lay, as I said, at the foot of a great sweep in the river, and five miles from the nearest station on the Baltimore and Ohio railroad. As no trains were running now, this was of little consequence; what was more important was that a turnpike road — unusually fine for that region of stiff, red clay — led in almost a straight line for thirty miles to Winchester on the south, and stretched northward, beyond the Potomac, twenty miles to Hagerstown. Two years later it was the scene of "Sheridan's ride." Before the days of steam this had been part of the old posting-road between the Valley towns and Pennsylvania, and we had boasted a very substantial bridge. This had been burned early in the war, and only the massive stone piers remained; but a mile and a half down the Potomac was the ford, and the road that led to it lay partly above and partly along the face of rocky and precipitous cliffs. It was narrow and stony, and especially in one place, around the foot of "Mount

Misery," was very steep and difficult for vehicles. It was, moreover, entirely commanded by the hills on the Maryland side, but it was the ford over which some part of the Confederate army passed every year, and in 1863 was used by the main body of infantry on the way to Gettysburg. Beyond the river were the Cumberland Canal and its willow-fringed tow-path, from which rose the soft and rounded outlines of the hills that from their farther slopes looked down upon the battle-field of Antietam. On clear days we could see the fort at Harper's Ferry without a glass, and the flag flying over it, a mere speck against the sky, and we could hear the gun that was fired every evening at sunset.

Shepherdstown's only access to the river was through a narrow gorge, the bed of a small tributary of the Potomac, that was made to do much duty as it slipped cheerily over its rocks and furnished power for several mills and factories, most of them at that time silent. Here were also three or four stone warehouses, huge empty structures, testifying mutely that the town had once had a business. The road to the bridge led through this cleft, down an indescribably steep street skirting the stream's ravine to whose sides the mills and factories clung in most extraordinary fashion; but it was always a marvel how anything heavier than a wheelbarrow could be pulled up its tedious length, or how any vehicle could be driven down without plunging into the water at the bottom.

In this odd little borough, then, we were waiting "developments," hearing first that "our men" were coming, and then that they were not coming, when suddenly, on Saturday, the 13th of September, early in the morning, we found ourselves surrounded by a hungry horde of lean and dusty tatterdemalions, who seemed to rise from the ground at our feet. I did not know where they came from, or to whose command they belonged; I have since been informed that General Jackson recrossed into Virginia at Williamsport, and hastened to Harper's Ferry by the shortest roads. These would take him some four miles south of us, and our haggard apparitions were perhaps a part of his force. They were stragglers, at all events,—professional, some of them, but some worn out by the incessant strain of that summer. When I say that they were hungry, I convey no impression of the gaunt starvation that looked from their cavernous eyes. All day they crowded to the doors of our houses, with always the same drawling complaint: " I've been a-marchin' an' a-fightin' for six weeks stiddy, and I ain't had n-a-r-thin' to eat 'cept green apples an' green cawn, an' I wish you'd please to gimme a bite to eat."

Their looks bore out their statements, and when they told us they had "clean gin out," we believed them, and went to get what we had. They could be seen afterward asleep in every fence corner, and under every tree, but after a night's rest they "pulled themselves together" somehow and disappeared as suddenly as they had come. Possibly they went back to their commands, possibly they only moved on to repeat the same tale elsewhere. I know nothing of numbers, nor what force was or was not engaged in any battle, but I saw the troops march past us every summer for four years, and I know something of the appearance of a marching army, both Union and Southern. There are always stragglers, of course, but never before or after did I see anything comparable to the demoralized state of the Confederates at this time. Never were want and exhaustion more visibly put before my eyes, and that they could march or fight at all seemed incredible.

As I remember, the next morning — it was Sunday, September 14th — we were awakened by heavy firing at two points on the mountains. We were expecting the bombardment of Harper's Ferry, and knew that Jackson was before it. Many of our friends were with him, and our interest there was so intense that we sat watching the bellowing and smoking Heights, for a long time, before we became aware that the same phenomena were to be noticed in the north. From our windows both points could be observed, and we could not tell which to watch more keenly. We knew almost nothing except that there was fighting, that it must be very heavy, and that our friends were surely in it somewhere, but whether at South Mountain or Harper's Ferry we had no means of discovering. I remember how the day wore on, how we staid at the windows until we could not endure the suspense; how we walked about and came back to them; and how finally, when night fell, it seemed cruel and preposterous to go to bed still ignorant of the result.

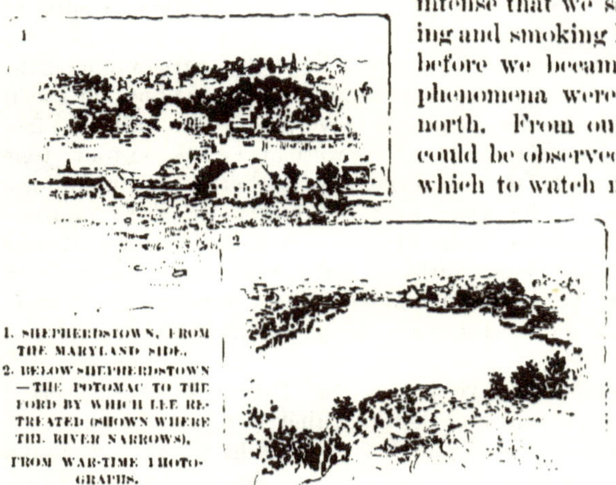

1. SHEPHERDSTOWN, FROM THE MARYLAND SIDE.

2. BELOW SHEPHERDSTOWN — THE POTOMAC TO THE FORD BY WHICH LEE RETREATED (SHOWN WHERE THE RIVER NARROWS).

FROM WAR-TIME PHOTO-GRAPHS.

Monday afternoon, about 2 or 3 o'clock, when we were sitting about in disconsolate fashion, distracted by the contradictory rumors, our negro cook rushed into the room with eyes shining and face working with excitement. She had been down in "de ten-acre lot to pick a few years ob cawn," and she had seen a long train of wagons coming up from the ford, and "dey is full ob wounded men, and de blood runnin' outen dem dat deep," measuring on her outstretched arm to the shoulder. This horrible picture sent us flying to town, where we found the streets already crowded, the people all astir, and the foremost wagons, of what seemed an endless line, discharging their piteous burdens. The scene speedily became ghastly, but fortunately we could not stay to look at it. There were no preparations, no accommodations — the men could not be left in the street — what was to be done?

A Federal soldier once said to me, "I was always sorry for your wounded; they never seemed to get any care." The remark was extreme, but there was much justice in it. There was little mitigation of hardship to our unfortunate armies. We were fond of calling them Spartans, and they were but too truly called upon to endure a Spartan system of neglect and privation. They were generally ill-fed and ill-cared for. It would have been possible at this time, one would think, to send a courier back to inform the town and bespeak what comforts it could provide for the approaching wounded; but here they were, unannounced, on the brick pavements, and the first thing was to find roofs to cover them. Men ran for keys and opened the shops, long empty, and the unused rooms; other people got brooms and stirred up the dust of ages; then swarms of children began to appear with bundles of hay and straw, taken from anybody's stable. These were hastily disposed in heaps, and covered with blankets—the soldiers' own, or blankets begged or borrowed. On these improvised beds the sufferers were placed, and the next question was how properly to dress their wounds. No surgeons were to be seen. A few men, detailed as nurses, had come, but they were incompetent, of course. Our women set bravely to work and washed away the blood or stanched it as well as they could, where the jolting of the long rough ride had disarranged the hasty binding done upon the battle-field. But what did they know of wounds beyond a cut finger, or a boil? Yet they bandaged and bathed, with a devotion that went far to make up for their inexperience. Then there was the hunt for bandages. Every housekeeper ransacked her stores and brought forth things new and old. I saw one girl, in despair for a strip of cloth, look about helplessly, and then rip off the hem of her white petticoat. The doctors came up, by and by, or I suppose they did, for some amputating was done—rough surgery, you may be sure. The women helped, holding the instruments and the basins, and trying to soothe or strengthen. They stood to their work nobly; the emergency brought out all their strength to meet it.

One girl who had been working very hard helping the men on the sidewalks, and dressing wounds afterward in a close, hot room, told me that at one time the sights and smells (these last were fearful) so overcame her that she could only stagger to the staircase, where she hung, half conscious, over the banisters, saying to herself, "Oh, I hope if I faint some one will kick me into a corner and let me lie there!" She did not faint, but went back to her work in a few moments, and through the whole of what followed was one of the most indefatigable and useful. She was one of many; even children did their part.

It became a grave question how to feed so many unexpected guests. The news spread rapidly, and the people from the country neighborhoods came pouring in to help, expecting to stay with friends who had already given up every spare bed and every inch of room where beds could be put up. Virginia houses are very elastic, but ours were strained to their utmost. Fortunately some of the farmers' wives had been thoughtful enough to bring supplies of linen, and some bread and fruit, and when our wants became better known other contributions flowed in; but when all was done it was not enough.

We worked far into the night that Monday, went to bed late, and rose early next morning. Tuesday brought fresh wagon-loads of wounded, and would have brought despair, except that they were accompanied by an apology for a commissariat. Soon more reliable sources of supply were organized among our country friends. Some doctors also arrived, who—with a few honorable exceptions—might as well have staid away. The remembrance of that worthless body of officials stirs me to wrath. Two or three worked conscientiously and hard, and they did all the medical work, except what was done by our own town physicians. In strong contrast was the conduct of the common men detailed as nurses. They were as gentle as they knew how to be, and very obliging and untiring. Of course they were uncouth and often rough, but with the wounded dying about us every day, and with the necessity that we were under for the first few days, of removing those who died at once that others not yet quite dead might take their places, there was no time to be fastidious; it required all our efforts to be simply decent, and we sometimes failed in that.

We fed our men as well as we could from every available source, and often had some difficulty in feeding ourselves. The townspeople were very hospitable, and we were invited here and there, but could not always go, or hesitated, knowing every house was full. I remember once, that having breakfasted upon a single roll and having worked hard among sickening details, about 4 o'clock I turned wolfishly ravenous and ran to a friend's house down the street. When I got there I was almost too faint to speak, but my friend looked at me and disappeared in silence, coming back in a moment with a plate of hot soup. What luxury! I sat down then and there on the front doorstep and devoured the soup as if I had been without food for a week.

It was known on Tuesday that Harper's Ferry had been taken, but it was growing evident that South Mountain had not been a victory. We had heard from some of our friends, but not from all, and what we did hear was often most unsatisfactory and tantalizing. For instance, we would be told that some one whom we loved had been seen standing with his battery, had left his gun an instant to shake hands and send a message, and had then stepped back to position, while our civilian informant had come away for safety, and the smoke of conflict had hidden battery and all from view. As night drew nearer, whispers of a great battle to be fought the next day grew louder, and we shuddered at the prospect, for battles had come to mean to us, as they never had before, blood, wounds, and death.

On the 17th of September cloudy skies looked down upon the two armies facing each other on the fields of Maryland. It seems to me now that the roar of that day began with the light, and all through its long and dragging hours its thunder formed a background to our pain and terror. If we had been in doubt as to our friends' whereabouts on Sunday, there was no room for doubt now. There was no sitting at the windows now and counting discharges of guns, or watching the curling smoke. We went about our work with pale faces and trembling hands, yet trying to appear composed for the sake of our patients, who were much excited. We could hear the incessant explosions of artillery, the shrieking whistles of the shells, and the sharper, deadlier, more thrilling roll of musketry; while every now and then the echo of some charging cheer would come, borne by the wind, and as the human voice pierced that demoniacal clangor we would catch our breath and listen, and try not to sob, and turn back to the forlorn hospitals, to the suffering at our feet and before our eyes, while imagination fainted at thought of those other scenes hidden from us beyond the Potomac.

On our side of the river there were noise, confusion, dust; throngs of stragglers; horsemen galloping about; wagons blocking each other, and teamsters wrangling; and a continued din of shouting, swearing, and rumbling, in the midst of which men were dying, fresh wounded arriving, surgeons amputating limbs and dressing wounds, women going in and out with bandages, lint, medicines, food. An ever-present sense of anguish, dread, pity, and, I fear, hatred—these are my recollections of Antietam.

When night came we could still hear the sullen guns and hoarse, indefinite murmurs that succeeded the day's turmoil. That night was dark and lowering and the air heavy and dull. Across the river innumerable camp-fires were blazing, and we could but too well imagine the scenes that they were lighting. We sat in silence, looking into each other's tired faces. There were no impatient words, few tears; only silence, and a drawing close together, as if for comfort. We were almost hopeless, yet clung with desperation to the thought that we were hoping. But in our hearts we could not believe that anything human could have escaped from that appalling fire. On Thursday the two armies lay idly facing each other, but we could not be idle. The wounded continued to arrive until the town was quite unable to hold all the disabled and suffering. They filled every building and overflowed into the country round, into farm-houses, barns, corn-cribs, cabins,—wherever four walls and a roof were found together. Those able to travel were sent on to Winchester and other towns back from the river, but their departure seemed to make no appreciable difference. There were six churches, and they were all full; the Odd Fellows' Hall, the Freemasons', the little Town Council room, the barn-like place known as the Drill Room, all the private houses after their capacity, the shops and empty buildings, the school-houses,—every inch of space, and yet the cry was for room.

The unfinished Town Hall had stood in naked ugliness for many a long day. Somebody threw a few rough boards across the beams, placed piles of straw over them, laid down single planks to walk upon, and lo, it was a hospital at once. The stone warehouses down in the ravine and by the river had been passed by, because low and damp and undesirable as sanitariums, but now their doors and windows were thrown wide, and, with barely time allowed to sweep them, they were all occupied,—even the "old blue factory," an antiquated, crazy, dismal building of blue stucco that peeled off in great blotches, which had been shut up for years, and was in the last stages of dilapidation.

On Thursday night we heard more than usual sounds of disturbance and movement, and in the morning we found the Confederate army in full retreat. General Lee crossed the Potomac under cover of the darkness, and when the day broke the greater part of his force—or the more orderly portion of it—had gone on toward Kearneysville and Leetown. General McClellan followed to the river, and without crossing got a battery in position on Douglas's Hill, and began to shell the retreating army and, in consequence, the town. What before was confusion grew worse; the retreat became a stampede. The battery may not have done a very great deal of execution, but it made a fearful noise. It is curious how much louder guns sound when they are pointed at you than when turned the other way! And the shell, with its long-drawn screeching, though no doubt less terrifying than the singing minie-ball, has a way of making one's hair stand on end. Then, too, every one who has had any experience in such things, knows how infectious fear is, how it grows when yielded to, and how, when you once begin to run, it soon seems impossible to run fast enough; whereas, if you can manage to stand your ground, the alarm lessens and sometimes disappears.

Some one suggested that yellow was the hospital color, and immediately everybody who could lay hands upon a yellow rag hoisted it over the house. The whole town was a hospital; there was scarcely a building that could not with truth seek protection under that plea, and the fantastic little strips were soon flaunting their ineffectual remonstrance from every roof-tree and chimney. When this specific failed the excitement became wild and ungovernable. It would have been ludicrous had it not produced so much suffering. The danger was less than it seemed, for McClellan, after all, was not bombarding the town, but the army, and most of the shells flew over us and exploded in the fields; but aim cannot be always sure, and enough shells fell short to convince the terrified citizens that their homes were about to be battered down over their ears. The better people kept some outward coolness, with perhaps a feeling of "*noblesse oblige*"; but the poorer classes acted as if the town were already in a blaze, and rushed from their houses with their families and household goods to make their way into the country. The road was thronged, the streets blocked; men were vociferating, women crying, children screaming; wagons, ambulances, guns, caissons, horsemen, footmen, all mingled—nay, even wedged and jammed together—in one struggling, shouting mass. The negroes were the worst, and with faces of a ghastly ash-color, and staring eyes, they swarmed into the fields, carrying their babies, their clothes, their pots and kettles, fleeing from the wrath behind them. The comparison to a hornet's nest attacked by boys is not a good one, for there was no "fight" shown; but a disturbed ant-hill is altogether inadequate. They fled widely and camped out of range, nor would they venture back for days.

Had this been all, we could afford to laugh now, but there was another side to the picture that lent it an intensely painful aspect. It was the hurrying crowds of wounded. Ah me! those maimed and bleeding fugitives! When the firing commenced the hospitals began to empty. All who were able to pull one foot after another, or could bribe or beg comrades to carry them, left in haste. In vain we implored them to stay; in vain we showed them the folly, the suicide, of the attempt; in vain we argued, cajoled, threatened, ridiculed; pointed out that we were remaining and that there was less danger here than on the road. There is no sense or reason in a panic. The cannon were bellowing upon Douglas's Hill, the shells whistling and shrieking, the air full of shouts and cries; we had to scream to make ourselves heard. The men replied that the "Yankees" were crossing; that the town was to be burned; that *we* could not be made prisoners, but they could; that, anyhow, they were going as far as they could walk, or be carried. And go they did. Men with cloths about their heads went hatless in the sun, men with cloths about their feet limped shoeless on the stony road; men with arms in slings, without arms, with one leg, with bandaged sides and backs; men in ambulances, wagons, carts, wheelbarrows, men carried on stretchers or supported on the shoulder of some self-denying comrade—all who could crawl went, and went to almost certain death. They could not go far, they dropped off into the country houses, where they were received with as much kindness as it was possible to ask for; but their wounds had become inflamed, their frames were weakened by fright and over-exertion: erysipelas, mortification, gangrene set in; and long rows of nameless graves still bear witness to the results.

Our hospitals did not remain empty. It was but a portion who could get off in any manner, and their places were soon taken by others, who had remained nearer the battle-field, had attempted to follow the retreat, but, having reached Shepherdstown, could go no farther. We had plenty to do, but all that day we went about with hearts bursting with rage and shame, and breaking with pity and grief for the needless, needless waste of life. The amateur nurses all stood firm, and managed to be cheerful for the sake of keeping their men quiet, but they could not be without fear. One who had no thought of leaving her post desired to send her sister—a mere child—out of harm's way. She, therefore, told her to go to their home, about half a mile distant, and ask their mother for some yellow cloth that was in the house, thinking, of course, that the mother would never permit the girl to come back into the town. But she miscalculated. The child accepted the commission as a sacred trust, forced her way out over the crowded road, where the danger was more real than in the town itself, reached home, and made her request. The house had its own flag flying, for it was directly in range and full of wounded. Perhaps for this reason the mother was less anxious to keep her daughter with her; perhaps in the hurry and excitement she allowed herself to be persuaded that it was really necessary to get that strip of yellow flannel into Shepherdstown as soon as possible. At all events, she made no difficulty, but with streaming tears kissed the girl, and saw her set out to go alone, half a mile through a panic-stricken rabble, under the fire of a battery and into a town whose escape from conflagration was at best not assured. To come out had been comparatively easy, for she was going with the stream. The return was a different matter. The turbulent tide had now to be stemmed. Yet she managed to work her way along, now in the road, now in the field, slipping between the wagon wheels, and once, at least, crawling under a stretcher. No one had noticed her coming out, she was but one of the crowd; and now most were too busy with their own safety to pay much heed to anything else. Still, as her face seemed alone set toward the town, she attracted some attention. One or two spoke to her. Now it was, "Look-a here, little gal! don't you know you're a-goin' the wrong way?" One man looked at the yellow thing she had slung across her shoulder and said, with an approving nod:

"That's right, that's right; save the wounded if ye kin." She meant to do it, and finally reached her sister, breathless but triumphant, with as proud a sense of duty done as if her futile errand had been the deliverance of a city.

I have said that there was less danger than appeared, but it must not be supposed that there was none. A friend who worked chiefly in the old blue factory had asked me to bring her a bowl of gruel that some one had promised to make for one of her patients. I had just taken it to her, and she was walking across the floor with the bowl in her hands, when a shell crashed through a corner of the wall and passed out at the opposite end of the building, shaking the rookery to its foundations, filling the room with dust and plaster, and throwing her upon her knees to the floor. The wounded screamed, and had they not been entirely unable to move, not a man would have been left in the building. But it was found that no one was hurt, and things proceeded as before. I asked her afterward if she was frightened. She said yes, when it was over, but her chief thought at the time was to save the gruel, for the man needed it, and it had been very hard to find any one composed enough to make it. I am glad to be able to say that he got his gruel in spite of bombs. That factory was struck twice. A school-house, full of wounded, and one or two other buildings were hit, but I believe no serious damage was done.

On Saturday morning there was a fight at the ford. The negroes were still encamped in the fields, though some, finding that the town was yet standing, ventured back on various errands during the day. What we feared were the stragglers and hangers-on and nondescripts that circle round an army like the great buzzards we shuddered to see wheeling silently over us. The people were still excited, anticipating the Federal crossing and dreading a repetition of the bombardment or an encounter in the streets. Some parties of Confederate cavalry rode through, and it is possible that a body of infantry remained drawn up in readiness on one of the hills during the morning, but I remember no large force of troops at any time on that day.

About noon, or a little after, we were told that General McClellan's advance had been checked, and that it was not believed he would attempt to cross the river at once—a surmise that proved to be correct. The country grew more composed. General Lee lay near Leetown, some seven miles south of us, and General McClellan rested quietly in Maryland. On Sunday we were able to have some short church services for our wounded, cut still shorter, I regret to say, by reports that the "Yankees" were crossing. Such reports continued to harass us, especially as we feared the capture of our friends, who would often ride down to see us during the day, but who seldom ventured to spend a night so near the river. We presently passed into debatable land, when we were in the Confederacy in the morning, in the Union after dinner, and on neutral ground at night. We lived through a disturbed and eventful autumn, subject to continual "alarms and excursions," but when this Saturday came to an end, the most trying and tempestuous week of the war for Shepherdstown was over.

THE CASE OF FITZ JOHN PORTER.

BY RICHARD B. IRWIN, LIEUTENANT-COLONEL AND ASSISTANT ADJUTANT-GENERAL, U. S. V.

WITHOUT going into the intricacies of allegation, evidence, and argument on one side or the other of this many-sided controversy, some account of the proceedings and conclusions of the military tribunals appointed for its investigation seems necessary. These tribunals were four in number: First, a Court of Inquiry, ordered by the President September 5th, 1862, and which met and was finally dissolved on the 15th, without taking any action; second, the Military Commission, convened November 17th, 1862; third, the Court-martial, appointed November 25th, which sentenced General Porter to be cashiered; fourth, the Board of Officers, appointed by President Hayes April 12th, 1878, and upon whose report, reversing the findings of the court-martial, General Porter was finally reinstated in the service.

In his report of September 3d, 1862, General Pope made certain representations unfavorable to Generals Porter, Franklin, and Griffin. On the 5th, by the same order that relieved General Pope from command, the President directed that Generals Porter, Franklin, and Griffin "be relieved from their respective commands until the charges against them can be investigated by a court of inquiry." This order appears to have been suspended the next day at General McClellan's request, and was never executed, all three of the generals named remaining on duty; but on the 5th of November, by the same order that removed General McClellan from command of the Army of the Potomac, the President again directed that General Porter be relieved from command of the Fifth Corps; and this order, issued by Halleck on the 10th, was put in force on the 12th.

The Court of Inquiry, appointed on the 5th of September, was ordered to inquire into the charges preferred by General Pope against Generals Franklin, Porter, and Griffin. The detail consisted of Major-General George Cadwalader, Brigadier-Generals Silas Casey and J. K. F. Mansfield, with Colonel Joseph Holt as Judge-Advocate, and this commission met on the 6th and 8th, adjourned and was dissolved without action, General Mansfield being ordered into the field on the day last named, and Generals Franklin, Porter, and Griffin being already there.

On the 17th of November a military commission was appointed by the General-in-Chief to examine and report on charges preferred against General Porter by General Pope.

A military commission is a tribunal constituted to try civil cases when the functions of the ordinary courts of law are suspended by the state of war. Its authority rests entirely upon the supreme will of the commander. Its jurisdiction is wholly outside the articles of war by which the army itself is exclusively governed. When the soldier is arraigned before such a commission, it is for offenses for which, in time of peace, he would be tried by the civil authorities. The proceeding first contemplated would therefore, at first sight, appear to have been of a character unusual in armies and altogether different from that afterward pursued; however, the distinction was not always strictly regarded during this war, purely military cases being more than once brought before a commission, sitting really as a court of inquiry, as in the Harper's Ferry case, and in the investigation as to "the operations of the army under the command of Major-General D. C. Buell, in Kentucky and Tennessee," and punishment even inflicted, as in the former, without charges, or arraignment, and without other trial.

No charges preferred against General Porter by General Pope have been found, save in his official reports of September 3d, 1862, and January 27th, 1863; and General Pope testified before the court-martial that he had in fact preferred none. In his letter to General Halleck of September 30th, 1862, General Pope speaks of "having laid before the Government the conduct of McClellan, Porter, and Griffin," and of being "not disposed to push the matter farther unless the silence of the Government . . . and the restoration of these officers without trial to their commands, coupled with my banishment to a distant and unimportant department, render it necessary as an act of justice to myself." In his reply, October 10th, Halleck says: "Again you complain that Porter and Griffin have not been tried on your charges against them. You know that a court was ordered for their trial and that it was suspended because all officers were required in the field. A new court has been ordered, and they are to be tried and the grounds of your charges to be fully investigated."

On November 25th, 1862, the military commission, having simply met and adjourned, was dissolved and the court-martial appointed. General Porter was now placed in arrest.

As finally constituted the court consisted of Major-Generals David Hunter and E. A. Hitchcock, and Brigadier-Generals Rufus King, B. M. Prentiss, James B. Ricketts, Silas Casey, James A. Garfield, N. B. Buford, and J. P. Slough, with Colonel Joseph Holt, Judge-Advocate-General of the Army, as Judge-Advocate.

The charges exhibited to the court were found to have been preferred by Brigadier-General Benjamin S. Roberts, Inspector-General on General Pope's staff at the time of the occurrences. The first charge, laid under the ninth article of war, alleged five instances of "disobedience of orders"; the second charge, laid under the fifty-second article of war, contained four allegations covering two acts of misbehavior in the presence of the enemy on the 29th and 30th.

The court found the accused guilty of having disobeyed three of General Pope's orders — that of August 27th, to march on Bristoe at 1 A. M.; the "joint order" on the morning of the 29th, to "move toward Gainesville"; and the order dated 4:30 that afternoon, "to push forward into action at once on the enemy's right flank"; guilty, also, of having "shamefully disobeyed" the latter order, and of having retreated without any attempt to engage the enemy; but not guilty of having permitted Griffin's and Piatt's brigades to leave the battle-field and go to Centreville. The charge of having feebly attacked the enemy on the 30th was withdrawn.

In substance the charges on which Porter was convicted were two,— that he disobeyed General Pope's order to march at 1 A. M. on the 28th, and that, in disobedience of orders, he failed to attack, but retreated, on the 29th. Upon the former we shall not dwell, since even upon the first trial it was shown that Porter delayed only two hours, on account of the darkness of the night, that he marched at 3, that nothing turned upon his delay,

that McDowell, Kearny, and Reno, with less distance to cover, under orders substantially similar, were similarly delayed. The vital point remains whether Porter did or did not disobey his orders and fail in his duty by not attacking on the 29th, and by retreating.

The sentence of the court-martial delivered on the 10th of January, 1863, was that General Porter "be cashiered and be forever disqualified from holding any office of trust or profit under the Government of the United States." On the 21st of January this sentence was approved by President Lincoln.

During the next fifteen years General Porter continually applied for a rehearing, in the light of evidence newly discovered or not available at the time of his trial.

On the 12th of April, 1878, President Hayes appointed a board of officers, consisting of Major-General John M. Schofield, Brigadier-General Alfred H. Terry, and Colonel George W. Getty, to examine the new evidence in connection with the old.

The new evidence consisted largely of the testimony and the official reports of the Confederate officers serving in the Army of Northern Virginia at the second battle of Bull Run, supplemented by new and accurate maps of the field of battle. None of this information, from the nature of the case, was, or could have been, before the court-martial. By it, if established, an entirely new light was thrown upon the circumstances as they existed in Porter's front on the 29th of August.

General Pope's orders of the 29th, which Porter was charged with disobeying, were as follows, the first, known as the "joint order," having reached him about or shortly after noon:

"GENERALS McDOWELL AND PORTER: You will please move forward with your joint commands toward Gainesville. I sent General Porter written orders to that effect an hour and a half ago. Heintzelman, Sigel, and Reno are moving on the Warrenton turnpike, and must now be not far from Gainesville. [†] I desire that as soon as communication is established between this force and your own, the whole command shall halt. It may be necessary to fall back behind Bull Run at Centreville to-night. I presume it will be so, on account of our supplies. If any considerable advantages are to be gained by departing from this order it will not be strictly carried out. One thing must be had in view, that the troops must occupy a position from which they can reach Bull Run to-night or by morning. The indications are that the whole force of the enemy is moving in this direction at a pace that will bring them here by to-morrow night or the next day."

General McDowell almost immediately withdrew King's division, marched it round in the rear by the Sudley Springs road, did not connect or again communicate with Porter during the day, and only brought King's division into action, on the right, at 6:15 P. M.

Porter's right was not in connection or communication with Reynolds, who held the left of the main line. Between them was a very wide gap, hid-

---

moving on Gainesville from Manassas Junction, and will come in on your left. They have about twenty thousand men. The command must return to this place (Centreville) to-night or by morning on account of subsistence and forage."

den by a wood through which Generals McDowell and Porter were unable to pass on horseback, and in which messengers sent by Porter to communicate with McDowell and others were captured by the enemy.

The second order did not reach General Porter till 6:30 P. M., and before the dispositions immediately ordered to execute it could be completed, darkness interposed. It read:

> "August 29th, 1862 — 4:30 P. M.
>
> "MAJOR-GENERAL PORTER:
>
> "Your line of march brings you in on the enemy's right flank. I desire you to push forward into action at once on the enemy's flank and, if possible, on his rear, keeping your right in communication with General Reynolds. The enemy is massed in the woods in front of us, but can be shelled out as soon as you engage their flank. Keep heavy reserves and use your batteries, keeping well closed to your right all the time. In case you are obliged to fall back, do so to your right and rear, so as to keep you in close communication with the right wing."

Both orders are based upon the supposition that the enemy was Jackson; that Longstreet was not there, and would not arrive till the night of the 30th or the 31st, and that Jackson was to be attacked in front and flank or rear and crushed before Longstreet joined him.

When McDowell came upon the rear of Porter's troops near Bethlehem Church he had just received Buford's dispatch of 9:30 A. M. forwarded by Ricketts at 11:30 A. M. ☆ This told of Longstreet's passage through Gainesville before 9:30; it reached McDowell after 11:30. When McDowell joined Porter he found him at the head of his troops, advancing; therefore, when Porter arrived on the crest of the hills which descend to Dawkin's Branch, his advance encountered Longstreet's, already in occupation of the opposite slope.

The board of officers say in their report:

> "General Porter's conduct was adjudged [by the court-martial] upon the assumption that not more than one division under Longstreet had arrived on the field, and that Porter had no considerable force in his front.
>
> "The fact is that Longstreet, with *four* divisions of 25,000 ‡ men, was there on the field before Porter arrived with his two divisions of 9000 men; that the Confederate general-in-chief was there in person at least two or three hours before the commander of the Army of Virginia himself arrived on the field, and that Porter with his two divisions saved the Army of Virginia that day from the disaster naturally due to the enemy's earlier preparations for battle.
>
> "If the 4:30 order had been promptly delivered a very grave responsibility would have devolved upon General Porter. The order was based upon conditions which were essentially erroneous and upon expectations which could not possibly be realized. . . .
>
> "What General Porter actually did do . . . now seems to have been only the simple necessary action which an intelligent soldier had no choice but to take. It is not possible that any court-martial could have condemned such conduct if it had been correctly understood. On the contrary, that conduct was obedient, subordinate, faithful, and judicious. It saved the Union army from disaster on the 29th of August."

The board accordingly recommended to President Hayes to set aside the findings and sentence of the court-martial and to restore Porter to his rank in the service from the date of his dismissal.

In the absence of legislation, President Hayes considered himself as without power to act, and on the 5th of June, 1879, he submitted the proceedings and conclusions of the board for the action of Congress.

On the 4th of May, 1882, President Arthur, by letters patent, remitted so much of the sentence of the court as had not been fully executed, and thus relieved General Porter from the continuing disqualification to hold office.

On the 1st of July, 1886, President Cleveland approved an act "for the relief of Fitz John Porter" which had been passed in the House of Representatives on the 18th of February by a vote of 171 to 113, and in the Senate on the 25th of June by a vote of 30 to 17. In accordance with the provisions of this act, on the 5th of August Porter was once more commissioned as colonel of infantry in the army of the United States, to rank from May 14th, 1861, but without back pay; and on August 7th he was placed on the retired list.

☆ Ricketts's dispatch was not produced in evidence. It strongly confirms Surgeon R. O. Abbott's statement that it was "between 12 and 1 o'clock, toward 1," when he delivered one copy of the "joint order" to Porter, after delivering the other to General McDowell.— R. B. I.

‡ According to Col. Marshall of Gen. Lee's staff, 30,000.

CANBY'S SERVICES IN THE NEW MEXICAN CAMPAIGN.

BY LATHAM ANDERSON, BREVET BRIGADIER-GENERAL, U. S. V.

THE account in this work by Captain Pettis of "The Confederate Invasion of New Mexico and Arizona," ‡ is accurate as to most details. It is open to criticism, however, in two particulars: it fails to recognize the political as well as the military importance of the campaign, and it does injustice to General Canby.

The remote and unimportant territory of New Mexico was not the real objective of this invasion. The Confederate leaders were striking at much higher game — no less than the conquest of California, Sonora, Chihuahua, New Mexico, Arizona, and Utah — and, above all, the possession of the gold supply of the Pacific coast, a source of strength considered by Mr. Lincoln to be essential to the successful prosecution of the war.

The truth of this view will be apparent when we consider what the relative positions of the two governments would have been had Sibley succeeded in his enterprise. The Confederacy would have controlled the Gulf of California and the two finest harbors on the Pacific coast with a coast-line of 1200 or 1500 miles. The conquest alone of this vast domain, in all probability, would have insured the recognition of the Confederacy by the European powers. Owing to the remoteness of this

---

‡ For Captain Pettis's article and accompanying maps, see Vol. II., p. 103. EDITORS.

coast it would have been impossible for us to have effectually blockaded it. In fact the Confederates could have overpowered us in the Pacific Ocean, as all the advantages of position and materials would have been on their side. Finally, the current of gold, that, according to Mr. Lincoln, formed the life-blood of our financial credit, would have been diverted from Washington to Richmond. What then would have been the relative quotations of "Greenbacks" and "Graybacks"? Unquestionably the Confederate paper would have been worth at least as much as ours, and the oceans would have swarmed with *Alabamas*. But it may be asked, to what extent would Sibley's conquest of New Mexico have contributed to this result? If it would have rendered the conquest of California probable, then it was one of the most momentous campaigns of the war. If the reverse were true, then it was a series of insignificant skirmishes, devoid of military or political significance. The capture of Forts Craig and Union with their garrisons and supplies would have rendered highly probable the successful accomplishment of the entire plan of Sibley's campaign. Southerners and Southern sympathizers were scattered throughout the Western mountain regions. They preponderated strongly in Southern New Mexico, Arizona, and Southern California.

In the coast and river towns and cities of California, the Confederates formed a powerful faction. Had Sibley's conquest of New Mexico been complete, he would have captured 6000 or 8000 stand of arms and 25 or 30 pieces of artillery. Hardly miners and frontier desperadoes would have flocked to his standard from all parts of the Rocky Mountains. He could have entered California with at least twice as many men as he brought into New Mexico. As a matter of course, the entire Mormon population of Utah, Arizona, and California would have joined him joyfully, and would have furnished him most efficient aid. In the meantime the California Secessionists would not have been idle. Although General George Wright and the Unionists would have been too enterprising to enable them to effect any complete or systematic organization, a fierce guerrilla warfare would certainly have been inaugurated all over the central and southern parts of the State as soon as it was known that Sibley's victorious army was approaching. Unaided they could have accomplished nothing. The National forces had absolute control of the situation. The forts in San Francisco harbor, the arsenal at Benicia, the Mare Island navy-yard, and whatever naval force there was on the coast were all in Union hands, under the custody of a nucleus (small, it is true) of regular troops. Moreover, the Union volunteers, with whom the enemy would have had to contend, were unsurpassed as fighting material. But with an invading army of 6000 or 8000 men across the Colorado, flushed with victory and well supplied with small arms, artillery, ammunition, and transportation, the situation would have been materially changed. The Government,

in order to maintain its prestige, must have continually protected many points from attack. It would thus have been compelled to divide and weaken its forces. The California desert constitutes a serious obstacle to an invading army; but, in this instance, the Confederates and their natural allies, the Mormons, preponderated so largely in that region that they could have maintained control of all the water-holes on the desert, and thus could have prevented Union scouts from observing and reporting promptly the movements of the invading army. Our forces probably could not have received notice of the route of the invading column in time to concentrate upon the Tejon Pass. Simultaneously with the arrival of the Confederate column, diversion by guerrilla attacks at various points throughout the State could, and, no doubt, would, have been made so as to compel a still further weakening of our forces at the main point of attack. Owing to all these causes it would have been impossible for the Union commander to meet Sibley with equal forces. For the Union army defeat under these circumstances in Southern California would have been defeat in an enemy's country, and it would have been very difficult for it to escape capture had it been routed. However superb the material of which the California volunteers were composed,[†] they were raw troops and would have been confronted by larger numbers of men, many of them already seasoned to war in a victorious campaign, who would, moreover, have been compelled to fight with desperation because they had the desert at their backs. It is true the fortunes of war are uncertain, and none of these things might have happened; but, in view of the above facts, the probabilities seem altogether in favor of the success of the Confederates, backed by an army which had conquered New Mexico and Arizona. Hence, in view of the situation in California and of the momentous consequences of its capture by the Confederates, the conflict in New Mexico should be regarded as one of the decisive campaigns of the war. The soundness and brilliancy of General Canby's management rendered it decisive in our favor. For the invading column the result was practically annihilation, unless the reports brought into our lines were gross exaggerations. It is to be hoped that this discussion may elicit from some of the survivors of Sibley's column a detailed account of that retreat.

Soon after Canby assumed command of the department, and before he had time to get it fairly in hand, he was confronted with the appalling disaster of San Augustine Springs. This was quickly followed by the intelligence that two expeditions were forming to attack him,—one in Northern Texas under Van Dorn, to enter by the Canadian route against Fort Union; the other at San Antonio, under Sibley, intended to reënforce Baylor at El Paso. He was therefore compelled to keep a strong force at Fort Union, another at Fort Craig, and to hold a third at an intermediate point

---

[†] A remarkable march through the hostile Indian country of Arizona to join Canby was made by eleven companies of infantry, two of cavalry, and two batteries, under Colonel J. H. Carleton, which were dispatched by

General George Wright, commanding the Department of the Pacific, overland from Southern California. The column started April 13th, 1862, and arrived at Santa Fé September 20th.— EDITORS.

whence he could succor the division first attacked. This prevented him from acting aggressively against Baylor early in the campaign. After Sibley had passed Fort Craig, Canby called a meeting of his senior officers and outlined to them his plan of campaign, which was to follow the enemy closely in his march up the valley, harass him in front, flanks, and rear with the irregular troops and cavalry—burn or remove all supplies in his front, but avoid a general engagement, except where the position was strongly in our favor. The numerous adobe villages along the line gave admirable opportunities for carrying out this plan at intervals of a few miles. Canby had no confidence in the capacity of the New Mexico volunteers to face the Texans in the open field, and the results fully confirmed his judgment on that point. But the adobe villages could be quickly loop-holed and converted into admirable defenses for raw troops. By placing the New Mexicans in these improvised fortresses, and using the regulars and Colorado volunteers aggressively in the open parts of the line, the efficiency of his force would have been doubled. Should the enemy refuse to attack us in any of these strong positions until he passed Albuquerque, Canby could then form a junction with the reënforcements at Fort Union, and Sibley's fate would have been sealed. The late Major H. R. Selden, who was present at the meeting, is the writer's authority for this outline of Canby's intended plan of campaign. This plan was marred at the very outset by the impetuosity of that rash old fighter, Lieutenant-Colonel B. S. Roberts, who, at Valverde, January 21st, precipitated a decisive engagement with the enemy, where the latter had the advantage of position. It must be said in justice to Colonel Roberts, however, that had not two of his subordinates shown a lack of their commander's dash, the result of that day's battle would have been different. Mr. Pettis intimates that all went well on the field until Canby arrived. Such was not the case. Roberts had failed to dislodge the enemy from his strong position behind the sand hills. Had it not been for the fatal gap in our center, the Texan assault on McRae's battery could not have been made, as the attacking column would have been taken in flank by our center. That gap was caused by Colonel Miguel Pino's 2d New Mexican Regiment remaining under the river-bank and refusing to move forward into line. For this, of course, Canby was not responsible. His plan of pivoting on his left and doubling up the enemy's left flank so as to sweep him out of his natural intrenchment was an admirable one.

After the reverse at Valverde nothing remained for Canby but to strive for a junction with the troops at Fort Union. In this he was thwarted for a time by the fact that Colonel John P. Slough, against his instructions, brought on a decisive engagement with the enemy at Cañon Glorieta on the 28th of March. Slough's main force was driven from the field, and the defeat would have been a disastrous one had not the flanking party, under Major Chivington, of the 1st Colorado Volunteers, and Captain W. H. Lewis, 5th U. S. Infantry, succeeded in destroying the Texan train. The rumor is said to have spread among the Texans that they were being attacked in rear by Canby's column. This caused a panic among part of their force, and prevented an effective pursuit of Slough's defeated troops.

After the junction with the troops from Fort Union, and the overtaking and surprising of the enemy at Peralta, on the 15th of April, Canby had it in his power to capture the entire column. But this was impracticable, because he could not have fed his prisoners. The country was stripped of provisions of all sorts, his own troops were on short rations, and he was at Peralta, one thousand miles from his base of supplies. His only alternative was to force the Texans into their disastrous retreat.

The account of the battle of Valverde in Greeley's "American Conflict" is erroneous in two important statements. First, speaking of the fighting in the morning he says: "The day wore on with more noise than execution, until 2 P. M." As a matter of fact our losses in the morning were heavier than in the evening, when most of the casualties were confined to McRae's Battery. Also Mr. Greeley states: "Our supporting infantry, twice or three the Texans in number, and including more than man for man of regulars, shamefully withstood every entreaty to charge, and the Colorado volunteers vied with the regulars in this infamous flight." There were only one thousand regulars in the field altogether, and the bulk of them were on the extreme right, out of supporting distance of the battery. In the morning fight the single company of Colorado volunteers behaved admirably, showing as much steadiness as old regulars.

CANBY AT VALVERDE.

BY A. W. EVANS, LIEUTENANT-COLONEL, U. S. A.

COLONEL CANBY reached the field of Valverde in the afternoon, during the lull, proceeding to the position of McRae's battery. One or two shots were fired from it after his arrival without eliciting a reply. After consultation and examination of the position, he moved that battery about two hundred yards to the left and directed the placing of its supports, which had hardly—if at all—got completely into position when the Texan charge was made. It was a surprise, and the attacking force (picked men) was superior in numbers to the supports of the battery—certainly to the regulars in support. Hall's battery (its commander is now Major R. H. Hall, 22d U. S. Infantry) was an extempore one of two 24-pounders, one of which was disabled in the course of the day by the breaking of its trail, and was taken off the field. His position was on the extreme right, down the river, a mile from McRae, with a great gap between. Neither Captain Wingate's battalion nor Colonel Carson's regiment was in support of him. They were nearer McRae. Just before the charge upon the latter Major Duncan sent up for reënforcements, announcing that a charge was about to be made upon him; and Carson's regiment and Company H, 7th Infantry, Captain Ingraham, were sent, but did not reach him in time, or only got half-way. One of McRae's caissons (possibly a limber-box, but I think the former) was blown up in the fight,—it was said, by one of his sergeants firing his pistol into it to prevent its capture, but this is not authenticated. The New Mexican volunteers in support broke early, and caused much confusion. It was reported that the muzzles of the cannon had been elevated for distant firing, and that in the flurry they were not depressed, thus firing over the heads of the approaching enemy. The ammunition was, I think, only round shot and spherical case; there was no grape.

That the Union troops were successful in the morning under Colonel Roberts and were defeated in the evening under Colonel Canby was the fortune of war. It is not always correct to argue *post hoc, propter hoc*. The result would probably have been the same if the commanders had been reversed, or if Colonel Canby had remained at Fort Craig.

SIBLEY'S NEW MEXICAN CAMPAIGN.—ITS OBJECTS AND THE CAUSES OF ITS FAILURE.

BY T. T. TEEL, MAJOR, C. S. A.

THE object of his campaign in New Mexico was explained in detail by General H. H. Sibley to the writer in a conversation which occurred just after the former had assumed command of the army. His plans were in substance as follows: While in the United States army and stationed in Arizona, he had acquired full information as to the resources of that Territory and of New Mexico; and as to the condition of the United States forces in those Territories, the quantity of Government stores, supplies, transportation, etc. He had informed President Davis of these things, and had submitted to him the plan of campaign. President Davis had authorized him to enlist three regiments in Texas, to constitute a brigade to be mounted and mustered into the service, with such arms as could be obtained in Texas, and, upon arriving in New Mexico, the brigade was to be furnished with arms and equipments out of the supply already captured or that might be captured. His campaign was to be self-sustaining; President Davis knew that Colonel John R. Baylor, with less than five hundred troops, had captured large supplies and was in possession of all of Arizona and the lower part of New Mexico; Sibley was to utilize the results of Baylor's successes, make Mesilla the base of operations, and with the enlistment of men from New Mexico, California, Arizona, and Colorado form an army which would effect the ultimate aim of the campaign, for there were scattered all over the Western States and Territories Southern men who were anxiously awaiting an opportunity to join the Confederate army. Upon the arrival of his brigade at Mesilla, Sibley was to open negotiations with the governors of Chihuahua, Sonora, and Lower California, for supplies, etc. *The objective aim and design of the campaign was the conquest of California*, and as soon as the Confederate army should occupy the Territory of New Mexico, an army of advance would be organized, and "On to San Francisco" would be the watchword; California had to be conquered, so that there would be an outlet for slavery, the boundaries of the Confederacy, as they then existed, including none of the Territories, but with New Mexico, Arizona, California, and Utah there would be plenty of room for the extension of slavery, which would greatly strengthen the Confederate States. If the Confederates succeeded in occupying California, New Mexico, and Arizona, negotiations to secure Chihuahua, Sonora, and Lower California, either by purchase or by conquest, would be opened; the state of affairs in Mexico made it an easy thing to take those States, and the Mexican President would be glad to get rid of them and at the same time improve his exchequer. In addition to all this, General Sibley intimated that there was a secret understanding between the Mexican and the Confederate authorities, and that, as soon as our occupation of the said states was assured, a transfer of those Mexican states would be made to the Confederacy. Juarez, the President of the Republic (so called), was then in the City of Mexico with a small army under his command, hardly sufficient to keep him in his position. That date (1862) was the darkest hour in the annals of our sister republic, but it was the brightest of the Confederacy, and General Sibley thought that he would have little difficulty in consummating the ends so devoutly wished by the Confederate Government.

The direct cause of our discomfiture and the failure of our campaign was the want of supplies of all kinds for the use of our army. The territory which we occupied was no storehouse. Colonel Canby's order to destroy everything that would be of use to the Confederates had been fully enforced. Thus we were situated in the very heart of the enemy's country, with well-equipped forces in our front and rear.

General Sibley was not a good administrative officer. He did not husband his resources, and was too prone to let the morrow take care of itself. But for this the expedition never would have been undertaken, nor would he have left the enemy between him and his base of supplies, a mistake which he made at Fort Craig. The other reasons for the failure of the campaign were want of supplies, ammunition, discipline, and confidence. Under such circumstances failure was inevitable. Had Colonel John R. Baylor continued to command, the result might have been different.

OPERATIONS IN NORTH ALABAMA.

BY DON CARLOS BUELL, MAJOR-GENERAL, U. S. V.

THE instructions‡ which I left behind for the regulation of affairs in Tennessee, when I started from Nashville for Savannah prior to the battle of Shiloh, constituted an important part in the plan of campaign, but could not be made absolute with reference to military operations which depended so much on undetermined conditions. For East Tennessee, General George W. Morgan, the officer assigned to the command of a column operating in that direction from Kentucky, was instructed, as a first step, to take Cumberland Gap if practicable, or to hold the enemy in check on that line if his force should prove insufficient to advance. The force left in Middle Tennessee was to preserve internal order there, keep open the communications of the army, repel invasion, and occupy the Memphis and Charleston railroad when the opportunity offered. The two latter objects were chiefly intrusted to General O. M. Mitchel. Only the instructions to him,⚹ and his action under them, can here be remarked upon.

These instructions placed General Mitchel, in the beginning, mainly at Fayetteville, Tennessee, twenty-eight miles north of Huntsville, Alabama, and explained to him how his position was to be used according to circumstances; among other things to concentrate his force at Huntsville or Decatur — the occupation of the Memphis and Charleston railroad through those points having been all the time distinctly understood as a standing object, and discussed in the conversations referred to in the instructions.‖ One division, with three field-batteries (18 pieces) of artillery, a regiment of cavalry, and two companies of engineer troops, in all about 8000 effective men, constituted his command; and he was told that in case of necessity the remainder of the force in Middle Tennessee would be placed under his orders. The general dispositions included a few regiments for the immediate protection of Nashville, under the command of General Ebenezer Dumont, who besides was charged with the communications of the army, in certain respects. A regiment was also designated as a provost-guard for Nashville, with orders to answer the demands of the military governor, Andrew Johnson, for the enforcement of his authority. The fine regiment (51st Ohio) of Colonel Stanley Matthews, now a justice of the United States Supreme Court, was selected for that position, on account of the efficient and judicious character of its commander. Governor Johnson was not pleased with the limited power thus arranged for himself. He wanted a much larger force under his control, and the records exhibit earnest protests from him to the President and Secretary of War against the defenseless condition in which he considered that I had left him.

Under the instructions given to Mitchel, that officer, after hearing of the victory at Shiloh (April 7th, 1862), marched from Fayetteville at noon on the 10th of April, and reached Huntsville at 6 A. M. on the 11th, capturing, as he reports, about 200 prisoners, 15 locomotives, and other rolling-stock and

‡ See "Official Records," Vol. X., Pt. II., pp. 47, 54, 71, 75, 86. ⚹ Page 71. ‖ Pages 37 and 60.

"

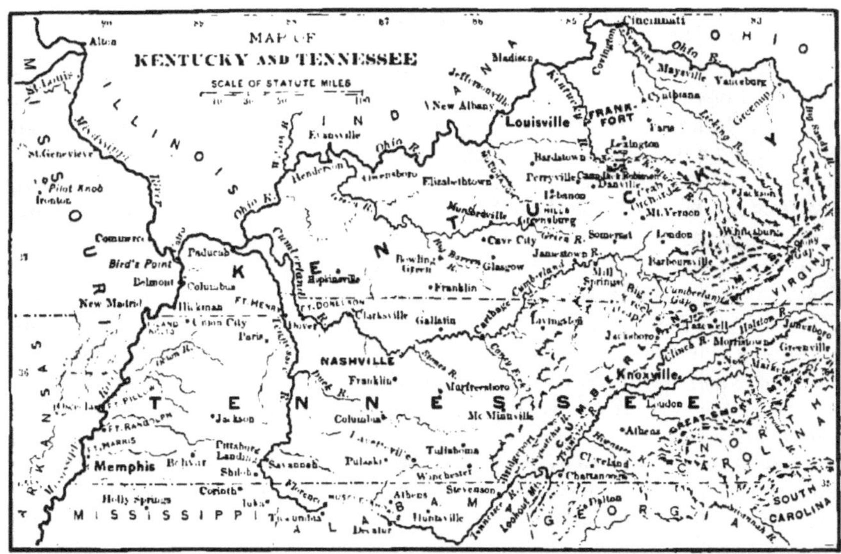

public property. On the 12th, expeditions were sent eastward to within four miles of the bridge over the Tennessee River at Bridgeport, destroying bridges in that direction and capturing five more locomotives; and westward to the Decatur bridge, twenty miles from Huntsville. Reporting these last movements on the 12th, General Mitchel says: "We have nothing more to do in this region, having fully accomplished all that was ordered."

These operations of course stopped the enemy's railroad communications through North Alabama. On the 13th a brigade under Colonel John B. Turchin was started to Tuscumbia (thirty miles west of Decatur), where it arrived about the 17th, and where I furnished it with supplies by water. It encountered no enemy, and was recalled by Mitchel on the 24th, upon a rumor that it was threatened from Corinth. As soon as it crossed again to the north side of the Tennessee the Decatur bridge was burned. As a reconnoitering measure, this expedition was well enough. The evil of it, as it turned out, was in the injury which resulted to the line of railroad — the destruction of the Decatur bridge by Mitchel himself, and other bridges by the enemy. Nothing could be more unwise than Mitchel's idea that the brigade should be reënforced from the main army so as to hold Tuscumbia, while Beauregard was at Corinth, fifty miles distant, with railroad communication, and Halleck not yet prepared to march against him from Pittsburg Landing.

On the 1st of May Mitchel reports from Huntsville to the Secretary of War, with whom he had established a correspondence: "On yesterday (properly the 29th of April), the enemy having cut our wires and attacked during the night one of our brigades, I deemed it my duty to head in person the expedition against Bridgeport," and he describes what was done. The expedition was under the command of Colonel Joshua W. Sill, a capable young officer, afterward killed at Stone's River. Mitchel represents the force of the enemy, by report, at 5000 infantry and one regiment of cavalry; and again at five regiments of infantry and 1800 cavalry. The enemy reports 450 raw infantry, 150 cavalry, and two old iron field-pieces drawn by hand. There was virtually no resistance. Sill had one man killed, and the enemy reports two men slightly wounded in retiring. The Confederates withdrew as the Federals advanced. The 50 men that remained a moment at the bridge-head retreated rapidly across at the first shot, and the whole force, after burning 450 feet at the east end of the bridge, continued the retreat, leaving behind the two iron guns. The blast which the enemy had prepared for blowing up a span at the west end failed to do its work. Mitchel reports the following incident in this affair: "A body of 40 or 50 cavalry came dashing through a wheat-field in full sight just below the bridge, supposing our troops to be theirs, and advanced to within 400 yards. Our cavalry dashed after them, while our artillery opened fire. *How many escaped I do not know.*" The enemy reports "10 or 12" of his cavalry scouts in that position, probably afraid to venture on the bridge, which was about to be destroyed. As neither the enemy nor Mitchel reports any of them killed or captured, the presumption is that *all* escaped. Mitchel at Huntsville, on May 1st, closes his report of this affair as follows: "This campaign is ended, and I can now occupy Huntsville in perfect security, while all of Alabama north of the Tennessee floats no flag but that of the Union." Thus far no resistance had been encountered, but Mitchel's movements had been well conceived and vigorous, and made a good appearance. Stanton answered his glowing dispatches naturally: "Your spirited operations afford great satisfaction to the President."

Three days after Mitchel's dispatch as quoted, he telegraphed Stanton, May 4th, in explanation of some unexpected developments of the enemy, and says:

"I shall soon have watchful guards among the slaves on the plantations from Bridgeport to Florence, and all who communicate to me valuable information I have promised the protection of my government. Should my course in this particular be disapproved, it would be impossible for me to hold my position. I must abandon the line of railway, and Northern Alabama falls back into the hands of the enemy. No reënforcements have been sent to me, and I am promised none except a regiment of cavalry and a company of scouts, neither of which have reached me. I should esteem it a great military and political misfortune to be compelled to yield up one inch of the territory we have conquered." [And again the same day, May 4th]: "I have promised protection to the slaves who have given me valuable assistance and information. If the government disapproves of what I have done, I must receive heavy reënforcements or abandon my position."

The only visible or actual ground for this sudden change from easy assurance to anxious uncertainty, was the appearance of the Confederate John Morgan on the road from Decatur to Nashville on the 2d of May with a force which Mitchel reports at 600 cavalry, including Scott's attack at Athens, and by which some careless detachments were surprised and captured. Without tarrying, Morgan continued his passage into Kentucky. He was overtaken and defeated with some loss, at Lebanon, Tennessee, by a force under General Dumont not under Mitchel's command. Morgan was promptly succeeded in Middle Tennessee by small bands of cavalry, which gave Mitchel great

MAJOR-GENERAL ORMSBY M. MITCHEL.
FROM A PHOTOGRAPH.

uneasiness and caused considerable harassment by operating on the railroads, and firing into guards and trains. It was a foretaste of what was to be experienced on a much larger scale and to a much wider extent, when the army entered North Alabama to advance into East Tennessee in July.

On the 7th of May Mitchel was authorized to employ the whole of the available force in Middle Tennessee, amounting to about 16,000 men, including what he had before. There was a considerable display of activity. A movement of two columns under General James S. Negley and Colonel William H. Lytle, about the 14th of May, interrupted the crossing of a body of Confederate cavalry, 1750 strong, under Colonel Wirt Adams from the south to the north side of the Tennessee at Lamb's ferry below Decatur. The Federals had one man killed in these operations. Adams, with 850 men, moved north of Huntsville to the Nashville and Chattanooga railroad in the vicinity of Manchester. Toward the last of May quite a large expedition was organized, to which the dispatches ascribe different objects at different times.

Sometimes it is to repel a heavy force that is supposed to be invading Middle Tennessee from Chattanooga. Sometimes it is to attack Chattanooga, which it is at last reported as having attacked. It embraced, according to Mitchel's report, at least 6000 men, under the command of General Negley. A portion of it under Negley surprised Adams's cavalry at Sweeden's Cove near the railroad, compelling it to make a precipitate retreat, and capturing some camp-equipage and supplies. Negley had two men killed and seven wounded in this affair. He then advanced to the river opposite Chattanooga. A sharp fire with field-artillery was opened upon the trenches and the town, and the enemy was reported as driven out. Negley had been authorized "to take the town in case he deemed it prudent," but he had no means of crossing the river, and for the want of supplies could not have remained forty-eight hours if he had crossed, or even have held his position on the north side. His supplies were already virtually exhausted, and he was ordered back by Mitchel, June 9th, ostensibly on the ground that an imaginary force was threatening Nashville in his rear. A better reason was that he was there without any ulterior purpose, and without adequate means for advancing or remaining.

General Mitchel deprecated this withdrawal because, as he says: "If we fall back we open the door to pour in troops at the exact point they (the enemy) are already determined to use, and if we once commence to fall back it is difficult to determine when we can halt"; and in reporting his action he says: "I am quite certain the enemy will follow." The next day he concludes that the invading force, with reference to which this formidable expedition was set on foot, did not exist. Negley had one man wounded opposite Chattanooga.

The destruction of the Bridgeport and Decatur bridges was not contrary to my orders under certain conditions. General Mitchel's position was an isolated one. It happened that the Confederate force in East Tennessee at the moment was small, but the resources of the enemy were not well understood at that early period. By the road to the east Mitchel was exposed to whatever force the enemy might be capable of sending against him, and he was not within reach of prompt succor even if the troops for that purpose could be spared from the main army on the west side of the Tennessee. Very soon, therefore, after his arrival at Huntsville, he was authorized to destroy the Bridgeport bridge. But the orders, though ample, were not imperative, as he evidently understood, for in reporting his expedition of the 29th of April, he took credit to his command for partially rescuing the bridge from destruction by the enemy. He says: "We can now hold it or destroy it as may be ordered." He did not report that upon the withdrawal of his force the bridge was totally burned by his order. That action was unnecessary, the bridge having been already sufficiently disabled by the enemy.

There was no necessity for the burning of the Decatur bridge. Mitchel had been instructed to destroy it in case he should be forced to retire from his position in North Alabama, a contingency of which he frequently expressed apprehension; but while he remained, the bridge was so completely under his control as to render its destruction unnecessary until the last moment. On April 25th Mitchel reported: "I have determined to withdraw my troops to the north side of the river, and, if necessary to our safety, to destroy the Decatur bridge." I never censured him for these acts, and do not now censure him. I only mean to make a proper account of them. Channels of communication in the field of operations of hostile armies, if not guarded, will generally be obstructed by one side or the other, and it is seldom that their importance in advance of actual use will warrant the means requisite for their preservation. These are matters of judgment at the moment, and ought not to be too narrowly criticised. A measure which proved in the end to have been superfluous, or even hurtful, may with the evidence at the time have seemed entirely advisable.

A far more serious fault was the habitual lawlessness that prevailed in a portion of General Mitchel's command. He has described it himself in a dispatch to the Secretary of War: "The most terrible outrages — robberies, rapes, arsons, and plunderings — are being committed by lawless brigands and vagabonds connected with the army"; and he asks for authority to visit the punishment of death upon the offenders. The authority was granted, but nobody was punished. Not only straggling individuals, but a whole brigade, under the open authority of its commander, could engage in these acts. Mitchel's refinement would be shocked by brutality under any circumstances, but he could not apply the means of repression when his command was the offender and the people of the country were the victims; and when a body of respectable citizens appealed to him for protection and justice in a case which was of undisputed atrocity, he answered them: "I cannot arraign before a court, civil or military, a brigade, and I most deeply regret that a portion at least of your time had not been occupied in searching for the testimony which would have fixed the charge of pillage and plunder upon some individual officer or soldier under my command!" This was to the inhabitants of a town in which he had previously reported the existence of a strong Union sentiment, and which had been given up by one of his brigade commanders to indiscriminate sack.✠ These disorders do not appear to have prevailed in the portion of the command immediately under Mitchel's eye.

The conditions which were found to exist when I arrived at Huntsville about the last of June were certainly not gratifying. The discipline of the command demanded vindication; the troops to a considerable extent were scattered, and their whereabouts unknown; the cavalry was broken down by marchings and counter-marchings that seemed not to have been well considered; a treatment partly authoritative and partly riotous, resulting from imperfect discipline and an injudicious temper on the part of the commander of the troops, had embittered even that portion of the population that would have been friendly or passive; no supplies had been provided for the army on its arrival from Corinth; substantially nothing had been done as ordered to repair the railroads to Nashville, though some steps had been taken, and the wagon train was worn down in hauling cotton for speculators. The measures that were necessary to remedy this state of affairs—the frequent calls upon General Mitchel for information, the arrest and trial of offenders whose flagrant crimes he had condoned or neglected, the breaking up of Turchin's ungoverned brigade, the orders with reference to the use of public transportation for private purposes, and other reformatory measures—seemed unavoidably to reflect upon Mitchel, and no doubt he felt them keenly, though that was in no manner their object. The records show, however, that he had been preparing the way for a transfer to the east, though I knew nothing of it at the time. I had been in Huntsville three days, when I received a letter from him tendering the resignation of his commission, and I was requested to forward it to the War Department. I sent for him in a friendly spirit to dissuade him, but I found him avowedly in a very wounded frame of mind, and apparently fixed in his purpose. I therefore said to him, "Very well; I am sorry to have you go, but if you desire I will forward your letter, and recommend that you be assigned some other duty. I cannot approve your resignation. It is not necessary that you should sacrifice your commission merely because you do not wish to serve under my command." And I forwarded his letter with an endorsement to that effect. The letter must now be on file in the War Department. The very next day orders, dated 9:20 A. M., were received by telegraph for him to repair to Washington, and he started immediately. The day after his departure I was surprised to

---

✠ See the official order promulgating the trial and dismissal of Colonel Turchin. Several other officers were tried and variously punished by the same court for similar disorders.—D. C. B.

be shown the original of a dispatch from him to the War Department, on file in the telegraph office, saying that, finding it impossible to serve his country longer under his present commander, he had forwarded his unconditional resignation, and he solicited leave of absence for twenty days. If a leave of absence was his object, he knew I could grant it as well as the Secretary of War.

Upon the whole, it is difficult to find satisfaction in an attentive study of General Mitchel's proceedings during the period referred to. The first occupation of the Memphis and Charleston railroad in April was well executed; but everywhere the pleasing impression of an apparently vigorous action is marred by exaggeration and false coloring, and inconsistency and self-seeking. The most trivial occurrence is reported with the flourish of a great battle; an old flat-boat in which he had rigged the machinery of a saw-mill, incapable of harming anything or resisting anything, is called a *gun-boat* and named the *Tennessee*, which he reports he has extemporized, and hopes will arrive in time to take part in the fight at Chattanooga, where he hopes also to receive 600 prisoners. At one moment he is appealing to be transferred to the Army of the Potomac, in order that he may have more active service; and almost in the same breath he is threatened by an overwhelming force, and is broken down by his responsibilities, and by his unceasing watchfulness night and day.

But in spite of his peculiarities, General Mitchel was a valuable officer. He was a graduate of West Point, about fifty-five years of age, a man of good bearing and pure morals, of considerable culture, and some reputation in science, having been employed as a teacher of science in a Cincinnati college, and having lectured and published entertainingly on astronomy. He was energetic in a certain way, and had some qualification from practical experience, as well as by education, in railroad construction and management, which was often useful in the war. He was not insubordinate, but was restless in ordinary service, ambitious in an ostentatious way, and by temperament unsuited to an important independent command. Until the publication of volumes X. and XVI. of the "Official Records" I knew nothing of the account which Mitchel after he went to Washington was called upon to render of his administration in North Alabama, in regard to discipline and cotton trading. He answered earnestly and no doubt satisfactorily. He had at the time reported to the War Department the use of Government transportation for getting out cotton for traders, but he did not report it to me.

Whitelaw Reid, in his sketch of him in "Ohio in the War," no doubt on Mitchel's authority, gives me a credit to which I am not entitled, as having said to Mitchel at Huntsville that I would myself resign rather than that the country should be deprived of his valuable services. General Mitchel was at last assigned to a sort of local command at Hilton Head, South Carolina, and died there from yellow fever under circumstances which inspired general sympathy, within a very few months after his departure from Huntsville.

Postscript.—The foregoing notes were in the hands of the editors of this work when there appeared a biography of General Mitchel written by his son (Boston: Houghton, Mifflin & Co.) This biography as well as a book called "Daring and Suffering," by the Rev. William Pittenger, attach great importance to the expedition under Andrews against the Georgia railroad. [See pp. 709, 716.] There is in Pittenger's book an express assumption not adopted in the Mitchel biography, that this project was a part of a comprehensive plan of invasion devised by Mitchel, but it rests on no evidence whatever. In moving upon Huntsville Mitchel was totally unprepared for the supposed enterprise, and instead of turning his column to the east to take advantage of the occasion promptly, as he must have done if he would have availed himself of it at all, be at once spread his force to the right and left to secure both flanks — on his left destroying bridges which would have been necessary for the execution of the alleged plan; and on the right taking steps to open communication with the army before Corinth. It is not improbable, however, that he hoped that Andrews's work would give greater security to an advance upon Huntsville.

The military portion of the Mitchel biography shows on his part an unhappy misconception of his official functions, and breathes a general accent of complaint that his ability was fettered and his usefulness thwarted by the faults of his superiors. He was continually falling under hindrances and vexations which were the fruit of his vague impulses and erroneous notions of the military situation and of his relations to it. To Secretary Chase he chafes that he had hoped he "would be allowed to march on Chattanooga and Knoxville," and now fears that his line is to be abandoned; but his propositions, if they may be so called, are never submitted to his commanding officer, with information and reasons that might bring them to fruition if they deserved it. Having opened a direct correspondence with the Secretary of War, he uses the privilege to criticise the measures of his commanding officer, nominates a military governor for North Alabama, and wants authority to send rebel citizens to Northern prisons. He complains to Secretary Stanton that his "is the first instance in the history of war where a general has been deprived of the command of his own lines of supply and communication," never, apparently, realizing that in the independent sense he is not a general at all, but only the commander of a detachment for a specific subordinate duty. The demoralizing effect of his surreptitious intercourse with Washington, encouraged by Secretary Stanton, and some of it withheld from the official files but brought to light after twenty-five years in the biography, is to be seen in the whole of Mitchel's career in North Alabama, and it followed him after his departure.

In a long report evidently suggested by conversations and called for by the Secretary of War, Mitchel makes the statement, July 7th, that one month before, evidently referring to Negley's expedition, he could have been "permanently established in Chattanooga." His dispatches from June 7th to the 22d explain the importance he attached to the occupation of Chattanooga and the difficulties which prevented him from seizing it. No censure is meant to be applied to General Mitchel for not seizing Chattanooga at any time, but his dispatches alluded to above and his report of July 7th show that his action was not consistent with his profession, and that his representations misled the Government and the public with reference to the responsibility of others, and the feasibility of an operation which upon his own judgment he had abandoned.

I have no recollection of ever having been at General Mitchel's quarters at Huntsville. It is not improbable, however, that on my arrival I was met by him and invited to his quarters. His son and biographer describes a scene as having occurred there on the day of my arrival: A map upon a pine-table under a tree, and on opposite sides "the two commanders," as he expresses it, one being the commander of the army and the other a subordinate officer belonging to it, consulting over a plan of campaign — "the one having the power for decision, the other being simply adviser." After many hours, during which one talked much, and the other "was, as usual, uncommunicative," no conclusion was reached. The commander of the army "rolled up his maps and withdrew." The next day, says the biographer, "the consultation was renewed at General Buell's headquarters, and the next for three successive days." "General Mitchel pleaded with General Buell for a quick occupation of the territory east." "At length," says the biographer, "Mitchel induced Buell to go to Bridgeport" to look over the ground, saying, "I will have a train ready for you to-morrow morning at 7 o'clock," "but Buell declined to go so soon." Whereupon, Mitchel gave up the struggle, and retiring to his tent telegraphed to the Secretary of War: "Finding it impossible to serve my country longer under my present commander, I have to-day forwarded through him my unconditional resignation, and respectfully solicit leave of absence for twenty days." A copy of this dispatch, the biographer adds, he sent to General Buell. The biographer then quotes "two documents," written, as he says, "within a day or two of each other," "to show how differently two men can look upon the same subject." The second in citation, though the first in date, is the report called for by Secretary Stanton and made by General Mitchel on the 7th of July, probably the next day after his arrival in Washington. It does not appear among the published war records, and I learn of its existence through the biography for the first time. It gives a so-called plan of campaign which it states that the writer, General Mitchel, had urged upon me. No plan of campaign was proposed to me by General Mitchel, and no such controversy, or discussion, or series of consultations as would be inferred from the biography, ever occurred between us.

General Mitchel failed to obtain from the War Department the recognition which he desired. The official records show in part, and a study of his son's publication will indicate more fully, by what means and with what effect his influence entered, as it nevertheless did, into the channels of public opinion and the councils of the Government. They may also explain the true cause of his many disappointments. The merely individual bearing of the inquiry, however, is now of little consequence.— D. C. BUELL.

THE LOCOMOTIVE CHASE IN GEORGIA.

BY THE REV. WILLIAM PITTENGER, 2D OHIO VOLUNTEERS, ONE OF THE RAIDERS.

THE railroad raid in Georgia in the spring of 1862 has always been considered to rank high among the striking and novel events of the civil war. At that time General O. M. Mitchel, under whose authority it was organized [see pp. 708, 716], commanded Union forces in Middle Tennessee, consisting of a division of Buell's Army. The Confederates were concentrating at Corinth, Miss., and Grant and Buell were advancing by different routes toward that point. Mitchel's orders required him to protect Nashville and the country around, but allowed him latitude in the disposition of his division, which, with detachments and garrisons, numbered nearly seventeen thousand men. His attention had long been turned toward the liberation of East Tennessee, which he knew President Lincoln also earnestly desired, and which would, if achieved, strike a most damaging blow at the resources of the Rebellion. A Union army once in possession of East Tennessee would have the inestimable advantage, found nowhere else in the South, of operating in the midst of a friendly population, and having at hand abundant supplies of all kinds. Mitchel had no reason to believe that Corinth would detain the Union armies much longer than Fort Donelson had done, and was satisfied that as soon as it had been captured, the next movement would be eastward toward Chattanooga, thus throwing his own division in advance. He determined, therefore, to press into the heart of the enemy's country as far as possible, occupying strategical points before they were adequately defended.

On the 8th of April, 1862,— the day after the battle of Pittsburg Landing, of which, however, Mitchel had received no intelligence,— he marched swiftly southward from Shelbyville and seized Huntsville, in Alabama, on the 11th of April, and then sent a detachment westward over the Memphis and Charleston railroad to open railway communication with the Union army at Pittsburg Landing.

Another detachment, commanded by Mitchel in person, advanced on the same day 70 miles by rail directly into the enemy's territory, arriving unchecked within 30 miles of Chattanooga. In two hours' time he could have reached that point, the most important position in the West, with 2000 men. Why did he not go? The story of the railroad raid is the answer.

The night before breaking camp at Shelbyville, Mitchel sent an expedition secretly into the heart of Georgia to cut the railroad communications of Chattanooga to the south and east. The fortune of this attempt had a most important bearing upon his movements, and will now be narrated.

In the employ of General Buell was a spy, named James J. Andrews, who had rendered valuable services [see p. 716] in the first year of the war, and had secured the confidence of the Union commanders. In March, 1862, Buell had sent him secretly with eight men to burn the bridges west of Chattanooga; but the failure of expected coöperation defeated the plan, and Andrews, after visiting Atlanta, and inspecting the whole of the enemy's lines in that vicinity and northward, had returned, ambitious to make another attempt. His plans for the second raid were submitted to Mitchel, and on the eve of the movement from Shelbyville to Huntsville, the latter authorized him to take twenty-

<hr>

↑ See "Official Records," Volume X., Part I., pp. 630–639 [For a detailed account by the present writer, see "Daring and Suffering," War Publishing Co., N. Y.]

four men, secretly enter the enemy's territory, and, by means of capturing a train, burn the bridges on the northern part of the Georgia State railroad, and also one on the East Tennessee railroad where it approaches the Georgia State line, thus completely isolating Chattanooga, which was then virtually ungarrisoned.

The soldiers for this expedition, of whom the writer was one, were selected from the three Ohio

JAMES J. ANDREWS.   FROM A PHOTOGRAPH.

regiments belonging to General J. W. Sill's brigade, being simply told that they were wanted for secret and very dangerous service. So far as known not a man chosen declined the perilous honor. Our uniforms were exchanged for ordinary Southern dress, and all arms, except revolvers, were left in camp. On the 7th of April, by the roadside about a mile east of Shelbyville, in the late twilight, we met our leader. Taking us a little way from the road he quietly placed before us the outlines of the romantic and adventurous plan, which was: to break into small detachments of three or four, journey eastward into the mountains, and then work southward, traveling by rail after we were well within the Confederate lines, and finally meet Andrews at Marietta, Georgia, more than 200 miles away, the evening of the third day after the start. When questioned, we were to profess ourselves Kentuckians going to join the Southern army.

On the journey we were a good deal annoyed by the swollen streams and the muddy roads consequent on three days of almost ceaseless rain. Andrews was led to believe that Mitchel's column would be inevitably delayed, and as we were expected to destroy the bridges the very day that Huntsville was entered, he took the responsibility of sending word to our different groups that our attempt would be postponed one day — from Friday to Saturday, April 12th. This was a natural but a most lamentable error of judgment.

One of the men was belated and did not join us at all. Two others were very soon captured by the enemy, and though their true character was not detected, they were forced into the Southern army, and two, who reached Marietta, failed to report at the rendezvous. Thus, when we assembled, very early in the morning, in Andrews's room at the Marietta Hotel for final consultation before the blow was struck, we were but twenty, including our leader. All preliminary difficulties had been easily overcome, and we were in good spirits. But some serious obstacles had been revealed on our ride from Chattanooga to Marietta the previous evening. ⚓ The railroad was found to be crowded with trains, and many soldiers were among the passengers. Then the station — Big Shanty — at which the capture was to be effected had recently been made a Confederate camp. To succeed in our enterprise it would be necessary first to capture the engine in a guarded camp, with soldiers standing around as spectators, and then to run it from 100 to 200 miles through the enemy's country, and to deceive or overpower all trains that should be met — a large contract for twenty men! Some of our party thought the chances of success so slight, under existing circumstances, that they urged the abandonment of the whole enterprise. But Andrews declared his purpose to succeed or die, offering to each man, however, the privilege of withdrawing from the attempt — an offer no one was in the least disposed to accept. Final instructions were then given, and we hurried to the ticket office in time for the northward bound mail train, and purchased tickets for different stations along the line in the direction of Chattanooga.

Our ride as passengers was but eight miles. We swept swiftly around the base of Kenesaw Mountain, and soon saw the tents of the forces camped at Big Shanty (now Kenesaw Station) gleam white in the morning mist. Here we were to stop for breakfast and attempt the seizure of the train. The morning was raw and gloomy, and a rain, which fell all day, had already begun. It was a painfully thrilling moment! We were but twenty, with an army about us and a long and difficult road before us crowded with enemies. In an instant we were to throw off the disguise which had been our only protection, and trust our leader's genius and our own efforts for safety and success. Fortunately we had no time for giving way to reflections and conjectures which could only unfit us for the stern task ahead.

When we stopped, the conductor, engineer, and many of the passengers hurried to breakfast, leaving the train unguarded. Now was the moment of action! Ascertaining that there was nothing to prevent a rapid start, Andrews, our two engineers, Brown and Knight, and the fireman hurried forward, uncoupling a section of the train consisting of three empty baggage or box cars, the locomotive and tender. The engineers and fireman sprung into the cab of the engine, while Andrews, with

⚓ The different detachments reached the Georgia State railroad at Chattanooga, and traveled as ordinary passengers on trains running southward. — EDITORS.

BIG SHANTY (NOW KENESAW) STATION. FROM A WAR-TIME SKETCH.

hand on the rail and foot on the step, waited to see that the remainder of the band had gained entrance into the rear box car. This seemed difficult and slow, though it really consumed but a few seconds, for the car stood on a considerable bank, and the first who came were pitched in by their comrades, while these, in turn, dragged in the others, and the door was instantly closed. A sentinel, with musket in hand, stood not a dozen feet from the engine watching the whole proceeding, but before he or any of the soldiers and guards around could make up their minds to interfere, all was done, and Andrews, with a nod to his engineer, stepped on board. The valve was pulled wide open, and for a moment the wheels of the "General" slipped around ineffectively; then, with a bound that jerked the soldiers in the box car from their feet, the little train darted away, leaving the camp and station in the wildest uproar and confusion. The first step of the enterprise was triumphantly accomplished.

According to the time-table, of which Andrews had secured a copy, there were two trains to be met. These presented no serious hindrance to our attaining high speed, for we could tell just where to expect them. There was also a local freight not down on the time-table, but which could not be far distant. Any danger of collision with it could be avoided by running according to the schedule of the captured train until it was passed; then, at the highest possible speed, we would run to the Oostenaula and Chickamauga bridges, lay them in ashes, and pass on through Chattanooga to Mitchel, at Huntsville, or wherever eastward of that point he might be found, arriving long before the close of the day. It was a brilliant prospect, and, so far as human estimates can determine, it would have been realized had the day been Friday instead of Saturday. On Friday every train had been on time, the day dry, and the road in perfect order. Now the road was in disorder, every train far behind time, and two "extras" were approaching us. But of these unfavorable conditions we knew nothing, and pressed confidently forward.

We stopped frequently, at one point tore up the track, cut telegraph wires, and loaded on crossties to be used in bridge burning. Wood and water were taken without difficulty, Andrews telling, very coolly, the story to which he adhered throughout the run, namely, that he was an agent of General Beauregard's running an impressed powder train through to that officer at Corinth. We had no good instruments for track-raising, as we had intended rather to depend upon fire; but the amount of time spent in taking up a rail was not material at this stage of our journey, as we easily kept on the time of our captured train. There was a wonderful exhilaration in passing swiftly by towns and stations through the heart of an enemy's country in this manner. It possessed just enough of the spice of danger—in this part of the run—to render it thoroughly enjoyable. The slightest accident to our engine, however, or a miscarriage in any part of our programme, would have completely changed the conditions.

At Etowah Station we found the "Yonah," an old locomotive owned by an iron company, standing with steam up; but not wishing to alarm the enemy till the local freight had been safely met, we left it unharmed. Kingston, thirty miles from the starting-point, was safely reached. A train from Rome, Ga., on a branch road, had just arrived and was waiting for the morning mail—our train. We learned that the local freight would soon come also, and, taking the side track, waited for it. When it arrived, however, Andrews saw to his surprise and chagrin that it bore a red flag, indicating another train not far behind. Stepping to the conductor, he boldly asked, "What does it mean that the road is blocked in this manner when I have orders to take this powder to Beauregard without a minute's delay?" The answer was interesting but not reassuring: "Mitchel has captured Huntsville and is said to be coming to Chattanooga, and we are getting everything out

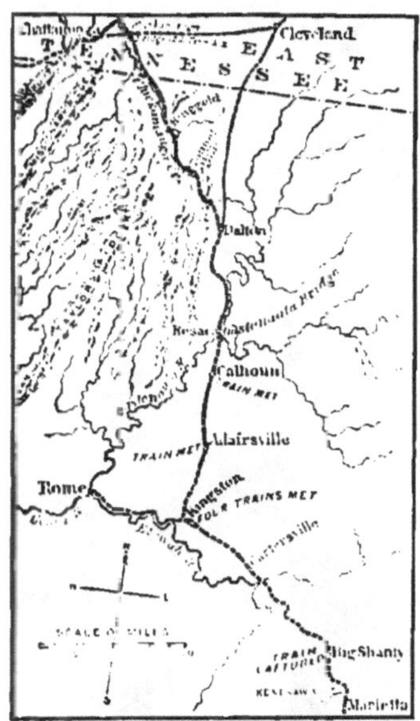

THE RAILROAD FROM MARIETTA TO CHATTANOOGA.

of there." He was asked by Andrews to pull his train a long way down the track out of the way, and promptly obeyed.

It seemed an exceedingly long time before the expected "extra" arrived; and when it did come it bore another red flag! The reason given was that the "local," being too great for one engine, had been made up in two sections, and the second section would doubtless be along in a short time. This was terribly vexatious; yet there seemed nothing to do but wait. To start out between the sections of an extra train would be to court destruction. There were already three trains around us, and their many passengers, and others, were growing very curious about the mysterious train which had arrived on the time of the morning mail, manned by strangers. *For an hour and five minutes* from the time of arrival at Kingston, we remained in this most critical position. The sixteen of us who were shut up tightly in a box car, personating Beauregard's ammunition,— hearing sounds outside, but unable to distinguish words,— had perhaps the most trying position. Andrews sent us, by one of the engineers, a cautious warning to be ready to fight in case the uneasiness of the crowd around led them to make any investigation, while he himself kept near the station to prevent the sending off of any alarming telegram. So intolerable was our suspense that the order for a deadly conflict would have been felt as a relief. But the assurance of Andrews quieted the crowd until the whistle of the expected train from the north was heard; then, as it glided up to the depot, past the end of our side track, we were off without more words.

But unexpected danger had arisen behind us. Out of the panic at Big Shanty two men emerged, determined, if possible, to foil the unknown captors of their train. There was no telegraph station, and no locomotive at hand with which to follow; but the conductor of the train, W. A. Fuller, and

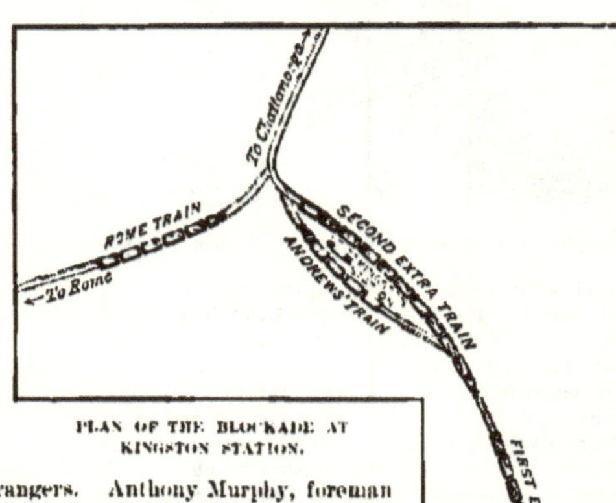

PLAN OF THE BLOCKADE AT KINGSTON STATION.

Anthony Murphy, foreman of the Atlanta railway machine shops, who happened to be on board of Fuller's train, started on foot after us as hard as they could run! Finding a hand-car they mounted it and pushed forward till they neared Etowah, where they ran on the break we had made in the road and were precipitated down the embankment into the ditch. Continuing with more caution, they reached Etowah and found the "Yonah," which was at once pressed into service, loaded with soldiers who were at hand, and hurried with flying wheels toward Kingston. Fuller prepared to fight at that point, for he knew of the tangle of extra trains, and of the lateness of the regular trains, and did not think we would be able to pass. We had been gone only four minutes when he arrived and found himself stopped by three long, heavy trains of cars headed in the wrong direction. To move them out of the way so as to pass would cause a delay he was little inclined to afford — would indeed have almost certainly given us the victory. So, abandoning his engine, he, with Murphy, ran across to the Rome train, and, uncoupling the engine and one car, pushed forward with about forty armed men. As the Rome branch connected with the main road above the depot, he encountered no hindrance, and it was now a fair race. We were not many minutes ahead.

Four miles from Kingston we again stopped and cut the telegraph. While trying to take up a rail at this point, we were greatly startled. One end of the rail was loosened and eight of us were pulling at it, when distant, but distinct, we heard the whistle of a pursuing engine! With a frantic pull we broke the rail and all tumbled over the embankment with the effort. We moved on, and at Adairsville we found a mixed train (freight and passenger) waiting, but there was an express on the road that had not yet arrived. We could afford no more

CAPTAIN WM. A. FULLER, C. S. A., LEADER OF THE PURSUIT. FROM AN AMBROTYPE.

delay, and set out for the next station, Calhoun, at terrible speed, hoping to reach that point before the express, which was behind time, should arrive. The nine miles which we had to travel were left behind in less than the same number of minutes! The express was just pulling out, but, hearing our whistle, backed before us until we were able to take the side track; it stopped, however, in such a manner as completely to close up the other end of the switch. The two trains, side by side, almost touched each other, and our precipitate arrival caused natural suspicion. Many searching questions were asked which had to be answered before we could get the opportunity of proceeding. We, in the box car, could hear the altercation and were almost sure that a fight would be necessary before the conductor would consent to "pull up" in order to let us out. Here, again, our position was most critical, for the pursuers were rapidly approaching.

PURSUERS OFF THE TRACK.

Fuller and Murphy saw the obstruction of the broken rail, in time to prevent wreck, by reversing their engine; but the hindrance was for the present insuperable. Leaving all their men behind, they started for a second foot-race. Before they had gone far they met the train we had passed at Adairsville and turned it back after us. At Adairsville they dropped the cars, and, with locomotive and tender loaded with armed men, they drove forward at the highest speed possible. They knew that we were not many minutes ahead, and trusted to overhaul us before the express train could be safely passed.

But Andrews had told the powder story again, with all his skill, and had added a direct request in peremptory form to have the way opened before him, which the Confederate conductor did not see fit to resist; and just before the pursuers arrived at Calhoun we were again under way. Stopping once more to cut wires and tear up the track, we felt a thrill of exhilaration to which we had long been strangers. The track was now clear before us to Chattanooga; and even west of that city we had good reason to believe that we would find no other train in the way till we had reached Mitchel's lines. If one rail could now be lifted we would be in a few minutes at Oostenaula bridge, and, that burned, the rest of the task would be little more than simple manual labor, with the enemy absolutely powerless. We worked with a will.

But in a moment the tables were turned! Not far behind we heard the scream of a locomotive bearing down upon us at lightning speed! The men on board were in plain sight and well armed! Two minutes—perhaps one—would have removed the rail at which we were toiling; then the game would have been in our own hands, for there was no other locomotive beyond that could be turned back after us. But the most desperate efforts were in vain. The rail was simply bent, and we hurried to our engine and darted away, while remorselessly after us thundered the enemy.

Now the contestants were in clear view, and a most exciting race followed. Wishing to gain a little time for the burning of the Oostenaula bridge we dropped one car, and shortly after, another; but they were "picked up" and pushed ahead to Resaca station. We were obliged to run over the high trestles and covered bridge at that point without a pause. This was the first failure in the work assigned us.

The Confederates could not overtake and stop us on the road, but their aim was to keep close behind so that we might not be able to damage the road or take in wood or water. In the former they succeeded, but not the latter. Both engines were put at the highest rate of speed. We were obliged to cut the wire after every station passed, in order that an alarm might not be sent ahead, and we constantly strove to throw our pursuer off the track or to obstruct the road permanently in some way so that we might be able to burn the Chickamauga bridges, still ahead. The chances seemed good that Fuller and Murphy would be wrecked. We broke out the end of our last box car and dropped cross-ties on the track as we ran, thus checking their progress and getting far enough ahead to take in wood and water at two separate stations. Several times we almost lifted a rail, but each time the coming of the Confederates, within rifle range, compelled us to desist and speed on. Our worst hindrance was the rain. The previous day (Friday) had been clear, with a high wind, and on such a day fire would have been easily and tremendously effective. But to-day a bridge could be burned only with abundance of fuel and careful nursing.

Thus we sped on, mile after mile, in this fearful chase, around curves and past stations in seemingly endless perspective. Whenever we lost sight of the enemy beyond a curve we hoped that some of our obstructions had been effective in throwing him from the track and that we would see him no more; but at each long reach backward the smoke was again seen, and the shrill whistle was like the scream of a bird of prey. The time could not have been so very long, for the terrible speed was rapidly devouring the distance, but with our nerves strained to the highest tension each minute seemed an hour. On several occasions the escape of the enemy from wreck seemed little less than miraculous. At one point a rail

THE PURSUERS PUSHING THE BURNING CAR FROM THE BRIDGE.

was placed across the track so skillfully on a curve that it was not seen till the train ran upon it at full speed. Fuller says that they were terribly jolted, and seemed to bounce altogether from the track, but lighted on the rails in safety. Some of the Confederates wished to leave a train which was driven at such a reckless rate, but their wishes were not gratified.

Before reaching Dalton we urged Andrews to turn and attack the enemy, laying an ambush so as to get into close quarters that our revolvers might be on equal terms with their guns. I have little doubt that if this had been carried out it would have succeeded. But Andrews — whether because he thought the chance of wrecking or obstructing the enemy still good, or feared that the country ahead had been alarmed by a telegram around the Confederacy by the way of Richmond —

merely gave the plan his sanction without making any attempt to carry it into execution.

Dalton was passed without difficulty, and beyond we stopped again to cut wires and obstruct the track. It happened that a regiment was encamped not a hundred yards away, but they did not molest us. Fuller had written a dispatch to Chattanooga, and dropped a man with orders to have it forwarded instantly while he pushed on to save the bridges. Part of the message got through and created a wild panic in Chattanooga, although it did not materially influence our fortunes. Our supply of fuel was now very short, and without getting rid of our pursuer long enough to take in more, it was evident that we could not run as far as Chattanooga.

While cutting the wire we made an attempt to get up another rail, but the enemy, as usual, were too quick for us. We had no tool for this purpose except a wedge pointed iron bar. Two or three bent iron claws for pulling out spikes would have given us such superiority, that, down to almost the last of our run, we would have been able to escape and to burn all the Chickamauga bridges. But it had not been our intention to rely on this mode of obstruction — an emergency only rendered necessary by our unexpected delay and the pouring rain.

We made no attempt to damage the long tunnel north of Dalton, as our enemies had greatly dreaded. The last hope of the raid was now staked upon an effort of a different kind. A few more obstructions were dropped on the track and our speed was increased so that we soon forged a considerable distance ahead. The side and end boards of the last car were torn into shreds, all available fuel was piled upon it, and blazing brands were brought back from the engine. By the time we approached a long covered bridge the fire in the car was fairly started. We uncoupled it in the middle of the bridge, and with painful suspense awaited the issue. Oh, for a few minutes till the work of conflagration was fairly begun! There was still steam-pressure enough in our boiler to carry us to the next wood-yard, where we could have replenished our fuel, by force if necessary, so as to run as near to Chattanooga as was deemed prudent. We did not know of the telegraph message which the pursuers had sent ahead. But, alas! the minutes were not given. Before the bridge was extensively fired the enemy was upon us. They pushed right into the smoke and drove the burning car before them to the next side-track.

With no car left, and no fuel, the last scrap having been thrown into the engine or upon the burning car, and with no obstruction to drop on the track, our situation was indeed desperate.

But it might still be possible to save ourselves if we left the train in a body and took a direct

END OF THE RUN — THE STOLEN ENGINE, THE "GENERAL" ABANDONED.

course toward the Union lines. Confederate pursuers with whom I have since conversed have agreed on two points — that we could have escaped in the manner here pointed out; and that an attack on the pursuing train would likely have been successful. But Andrews thought otherwise, at least in relation to the former plan, and ordered us to jump from the locomotive, and, dispersing in the woods, each endeavor to save himself.

The question is often asked, "Why did you not reverse your engine and thus wreck the one following?" Wanton injury was no part of our plan, and we could not afford to throw away our engine till the last extremity. When the raiders were jumping off, however, the engine was reversed and driven back, but by that time the steam was so nearly exhausted that the Confederate engine had no difficulty in reversing and receiving the shock without injury. Both were soon at a stand-still, and the Confederates, reënforced by a party from a train which soon arrived on the scene, — the express passenger, which had been turned back at Calhoun, — continued the chase on foot.

It is easy now to understand why Mitchel paused thirty miles west of Chattanooga. The Andrews raiders had been forced to stop eighteen miles south of the same town, and no flying train met Mitchel with tidings that all the railroad communications of Chattanooga were destroyed, and that the town was in a panic and undefended.

A few words will give the sequel to this remarkable enterprise. The hunt for the fugitive raiders was prompt, energetic, and successful. Several were captured the same day, and all but two within a week. Even these two were overtaken and brought back, when they supposed that they were virtually out of danger. Two who had reached Marietta, but had failed to board the train (J. R. Porter,‡ Co. C, 21st Ohio, and Martin J. Hawkins,‡ Co. A, 33d Ohio), were identified and added to the band of prisoners. Now follows the saddest part of the story. Being in citizens' dress within an enemy's lines, the whole party were held as spies. A court-martial was convened, and the leader and seven out of the remaining twenty-one were condemned and executed. ☆ The others were

MEMORIAL DAY AT CHATTANOOGA, 1883. GRAVES OF ANDREWS AND HIS COMPANIONS.

☆ The participants in the raid were: James J. Andrews,* Leader; William Campbell,* a civilian who volunteered to accompany the raiders; George D. Wilson,* Co. B, 2d Ohio; Marion A. Ross,* Co. A, 2d Ohio; Perry G. Shadrack,* Co. K, 2d Ohio; Samuel Slavens,* 33d Ohio; Samuel Robinson,* Co. G, 33d Ohio; John Scott,* Co. K, 21st Ohio; Wilson W. Brown,† Co. F, 21st Ohio; William Knight,† Co. E, 21st Ohio; Mark Wood,† Co. C, 21st Ohio; James A. Wilson,† Co. C, 21st Ohio; John Wollam,†Co. C, 33d Ohio; D. A. Dorsey,† Co. H, 33d Ohio; Jacob Parrott,‡ Co. K, 33d Ohio; Robert Buffum,‡ Co. H, 21st Ohio; William Bensinger,‡ Co. G, 21st Ohio; William Reddick,‡ Co. B, 33d Ohio; E. H. Mason,‡ Co. K, 21st Ohio; William Pittenger,‡ Co. G, 2d Ohio.— EDITORS

* Executed.　　† Escaped.　　‡ Exchanged.

never brought to trial, probably because of the advance of Union forces and the consequent confusion into which the affairs of the Departments of East Tennessee and Georgia were thrown. Of the remaining fourteen, eight succeeded, by a bold effort,—attacking their guard in broad daylight,—in making their escape from Atlanta, Ga., and ultimately in reaching the North. The other six, who shared in this effort, but were recaptured, remained prisoners until the latter part of March, 1863, when they were exchanged through a special arrangement made by Secretary Stanton. All the survivors of this expedition received medals and promotion. The pursuers also received expressions of gratitude from their fellow Confederates, notably from the Governor and Legislature of Georgia.

NOTES ON THE LOCOMOTIVE CHASE.

BY JAMES B. FRY, BREVET MAJOR-GENERAL, U. S. A.

Two expeditions to burn bridges near Chattanooga were sent from the Union lines early in 1862. The first was authorized by General D. C. Buell, commanding the Army of the Ohio, who had seized Nashville in the latter part of February, and was about marching south-westward to join Grant at Savannah on the Tennessee River. Buell was not unmindful of the advantage of breaking, west of Chattanooga, the railroad which led the Confederate forces from the east and south to his flank and also directly connected them with Corinth, against which Halleck was moving. A spy by the name of Andrews, who was in Buell's service, represented early in March that with a party of six trusty men he could destroy the bridges between Chattanooga and Bridgeport, and also the important bridge over the Tennessee, at the latter place, and thus effectually prevent the enemy from using that route, either to reënforce Corinth or to return to Middle Tennessee. Buell had received but little benefit from Andrews's services † and did not encourage the proposition, but in consequence mainly of the confidence and urgency of the spy, he finally directed me, his chief of staff, to confer fully with Andrews and use my discretion as to authorizing and organizing the enterprise. On the strength of Andrews's assurance that an engineer running a regular train over the road was in our interest and would use his locomotive for the purpose, I sanctioned and arranged the expedition. General Mitchel was directed to furnish six men, if volunteers for the service could be found—that is all he had to do with the original expedition. Of this operation General Buell wrote, August 5th, 1863, to the Adjutant-General of the army as follows:

"SIR: In the 'Official Gazette' of the 21st ultimo, I see a report of Judge-Advocate General Holt, dated the 27th of March, relative to an expedition set on foot in April, 1862, under the authority and direction (as the report says) of General O. M. Mitchel, the object of which was to destroy the communication on the Georgia State railroad between Atlanta and Chattanooga. The expedition was set on foot under my authority, the plan was arranged between Mr. Andrews, whom I had had in

employment from shortly after assuming command in Kentucky, and my chief of staff, Colonel James B. Fry, and General Mitchel had nothing to do either with its conception or execution, except to furnish from his command the soldiers who took part in it. He was directed to furnish 6; instead of that he sent 22. Had he conformed to the instructions given him, it would have been better, the chances of success would have been greater, and in any event several lives would have been saved. The report speaks of the plan as an emanation of genius, and of the results which it promised as absolutely sublime. It may be proper, therefore, to say that this statement is made for the sake of truth, and not to call attention to the extravagant colors in which it has been presented. Very respectfully your obedient servant,

"D. C. BUELL, Major-General."

General Buell was speaking here of the first expedition,—the one he authorized. In relation to the merits of this scheme it may be said that at the time perhaps the object was of sufficient importance to offset the probabilities of failure and the risk to the men engaged. But at best the undertaking was hardly commendable. Buell, basing no plans on the success of it, marched with the main body of his army for the field of Shiloh, without knowing the result. The effort failed, and when Andrews returned, early in April, he found Mitchel in command below Nashville, and reported to him in Buell's absence. Thereupon Mitchel, on the 7th of April, 1862, set on foot the second expedition. This expedition also failed, and with distressingly disastrous consequences to those engaged in it. The Confederates were fully aware of the importance of holding Chattanooga, and from my knowledge of the military situation at the time, the military commanders concerned, and the course of events afterward, I do not hesitate to express the opinion that if the raiders had succeeded in destroying every bridge on their proposed route it would have produced no important effect upon Mitchel's military operations, and that he would not have taken, certainly would not have held, Chattanooga. Hence it is my opinion that Mitchel's bridge-burners took desperate chances to accomplish objects of no substantial advantage. ‖

† General Buell writes, March, 1898: "Andrews came into my employment in the capacity of a spy. Having traffic in quinine, etc., as an excuse for his movements, he made one trip and returned without information of any value. He started on another at a critical period, full of important facts. While the crisis was pending I expected him every day. He returned only after I entered Nashville, and then the current of events had told all he knew. . . . I had little confidence in his usefulness, apprehending that he thought more of his traffic than of the object for which he was engaged. When he proposed to attempt the destruction of bridges I did not assent. . . . He, however, interested my chief of staff, and at the request of the latter I consented to the arrangement that was completed between them."—J. B. F.

‖ General Buell writes: "The damage could only have been partial and temporary; and no condition of the contending forces then existed upon which the obstruction could have exerted any decisive influence."—J. B. F.

WITH PRICE EAST OF THE MISSISSIPPI.

BY COLONEL THOMAS L. SNEAD.

BEAUREGARD, withdrawing his army in good order from the field of Shiloh, took position once more within the defenses of Corinth, and called for help to stay the advance of Halleck's fast-gathering forces. Of the 40,000 men who had followed Johnston out to battle, 30,000 were again in the trenches on the 9th of April, 1862. Van Dorn, after his defeat at Pea Ridge, was hastening to join them from the trans-Mississippi with the remainder of the Army of the West more than twenty thousand strong. Its advance under Price was even now embarking on the White River of Arkansas, and would be at Corinth in less than a week. Kirby Smith ‡ sent his every available regiment from East Tennessee, and Pemberton ‖ every man that could be spared from the coasts of Carolina and Georgia. The armies which had been assembled for the defense of New Orleans and Pensacola had already been sent to Corinth, and had fought at Shiloh. The President telegraphed on the 10th of April to the governors of South Carolina, Georgia, Alabama,

‡ See (Vol. I., p. 262) Colonel Snead's paper on "The First Year of the War in Missouri," of which this is a continuation.— EDITORS.

‡ Major-General E. Kirby Smith, who, as a brigadier-general, had commanded a brigade in General J. E. Johnston's Army of the Shenandoah at the battle of Bull Run (where he was wounded), and afterward a division in the Army of Northern Virginia, assumed command of the District of East Tennessee (afterward raised to a Department), with headquarters at Knoxville, on the 8th of March, 1862.— EDITORS.

‖ Major-General John C. Pemberton at this time commanded the Confederate Department of South Carolina, with headquarters at Charleston, South Carolina.— EDITORS.

Mississippi, and Louisiana, "Beauregard must have reënforcements to meet the vast accumulation of the enemy before him. The necessity is imminent, the case of vital importance. Send forward to Corinth all the armed men that you can furnish." The Confederate Congress supported all this activity by enacting in haste on the 22d of April a stringent law for conscripting every white male between the ages of 18 and 35.

Halleck was at St. Louis, getting ready in his elaborate way to go to the Tennessee, when he was startled by learning that Grant had been attacked at Shiloh and had barely escaped a great disaster. Hastening to the front, he assumed command in person of the forces in the field on the 11th of April, and proceeded to execute deliberately his long-conceived plan of campaign.

Preëminently cautious by nature, and the more cautious now because he was sure of ultimate success, and averse always to the unnecessary shedding of human blood, Halleck, instead of advancing boldly against Beauregard as Grant would have done and risking all upon the hazard of a battle whose issue would have been uncertain, first fortified his position on the left bank of the Tennessee, and then began to strengthen his army by bringing to it all the available forces of his immense Department.

Pope was recalled from before Fort Pillow, which he was preparing to attack, and reached the Tennessee with the Army of the Mississippi on the 21st of April. He came flushed with his victories at New Madrid and at Island No. Ten — the last of which Halleck pronounced "a splendid achievement, exceeding in boldness and brilliancy all other operations of the war," and one that "would be memorable in military history and admired by future generations." Halleck did not then know how weakly the place had been defended by the officer to whom Beauregard had intrusted its defense.

Though the main body of the army with which Curtis had defeated Van Dorn at Elkhorn was still dragging itself slowly over the mountains, or floundering through the swamps of Arkansas, it, too, sent reënforcements to the Tennessee.

At length, toward the last of April, Halleck had assembled on the banks of the Tennessee an army of one hundred thousand men.

Remarkable and imposing as this great army was for its numbers and the excellence of its *personnel*, it was still more remarkable for its array of distinguished leaders. Among them were the future generals-in-chief of the armies of the United States,— Halleck himself, and after him the three most successful of all the soldiers that fought for the Union — Grant, Sherman, and Sheridan; and with them were George H. Thomas, whom Greeley believed to be the greatest soldier of them all, and Buell, and Pope, and Rosecrans, and many others that rose to high command. With it, but not of it, were also the great War Governor of Indiana, Oliver P. Morton, and the Assistant Secretary of War, Colonel Thomas A. Scott, the railway king of the future, who had come to advise and assist Halleck; while in commands more or less important were McClernand, Palmer, Oglesby, Hurlbut, John A. Logan, and Colonel Robert G. Ingersoll, Illinoisians all.

THE 31ST OHIO VOLUNTEERS BUILDING BREASTWORKS BEFORE CORINTH IN MAY, 1862.
FROM A LITHOGRAPH

Halleck, before advancing, reorganized his army. Having little faith in Grant, he assigned him to the merely honorary position of second in command of the forces—a position analogous to and as unimportant as that of Vice-President. George H. Thomas was transferred with his division from Buell's army to Grant's—the Army of the Tennessee—and put in command of that army, which formed the right wing of the forces. Buell with the Army of the Ohio occupied the center, and Pope with the Army of the Mississippi the left.

Moving cautiously, and intrenching every time that he halted, Halleck by the middle of May approached within four miles of Corinth, some twenty miles from the Tennessee. He then seized and fortified a line extending from the Mobile and Ohio railroad on the north-west to and beyond Farmington on the south-east—some five miles or more in length—and began to mount his heavy siege guns. By the 25th of May he was almost ready to open with these upon the Confederates, some of whose intrenchments were hardly a thousand yards in his front.

Halleck's force now amounted to more than 110,000 fighting men. Beauregard's army had long ago reached its maximum, and was fast wasting away with disease. Of the 80,000 officers and men who were at Corinth, 18,000 were in the hospitals, and of the rest there were very few whose health was not affected by the pestilential air and unwholesome water of that swamp-surrounded village. Of those that were fit for duty, 5000 were on detached service and 4000 were on extra duty. There were "present for duty" 53,000 officers and men. One-third of them belonged to the Army of the West, and two-thirds to the Army of the Mississippi. The latter was commanded by

Bragg and the former by Van Dorn. Polk, Hardee, and Breckinridge commanded corps in the Army of the Mississippi.

On the 25th of May General Beauregard called his subordinate commanders together—namely, Bragg, Van Dorn, Polk, Hardee, Breckinridge, and Price‡—to discuss the propriety of evacuating Corinth. The matter was fully debated, particularly by General Hardee, who urged, with great good sense, that Corinth should be forthwith abandoned and the army withdrawn southward along the line of the Mobile and Ohio railroad. The necessity for this course had indeed become apparent to every one, and Beauregard issued the appropriate orders the same night.

It was none too soon, for Halleck would be ready within two or three days to open with shot and shell from his great guns, and to attack the weak defenses of the Confederates with an overwhelming force. He was also extending his line so as to flank Beauregard on the south and west, and to cut the railroad behind the Confederates.

The evacuation was conducted with the utmost secrecy. The troops were ordered to the front with three days' cooked rations in their haversacks, and told that they were about to attack the enemy. The sick were then sent to the rear, and all military stores and supplies were removed by the railways which were still at Beauregard's service. That the army was about to retreat was known to very few of its officers till the 29th. During that night there was a great running of cars, and the Confederates were ordered to cheer whenever a train arrived, so as to delude Halleck into believing that they were being reënforced. Before daybreak of the 30th all of Beauregard's forces except his cavalry had been withdrawn from Corinth.

Halleck had been completely deceived. Pope telegraphed him a few lines before daybreak (May 30th): "The enemy are reënforcing heavily in my front and on my left. The cars are running constantly, and the cheering is immense every time that they unload in front of me. I have no doubt that I shall be attacked in heavy force at daylight." Halleck thereupon ordered Grant to hold the reserve, and Buell the center, in readiness to reënforce Pope. It was not until 5 o'clock in the morning that any one, except some war correspondents,‖ even suspected that the Confederates were retreating, and it was nearly 7 when the first Union troops entered the town and learned that Beauregard had certainly escaped. His army was then safe behind the Tuscumbia.

---

‡ It may be of interest to mention that General Price regarded Beauregard as the fittest of these officers for a great command.—T. L. S.

‖ General Pope's dispatch here quoted is dated May 30th, 1:20 A. M. At 6 A. M. he reported "a succession of loud explosions," adding that "everything indicates evacuation and retreat." At 5 A. M. Brigadier-General William Nelson had reported: "The prisoner who accompanies this states that the enemy have gone, and the town to me appears to be on fire." General Grant mentions, in his "Memoirs," Vol. I. p. 379, that, "probably on the 28th of May, General John A. Logan . . . said to me that the enemy had been evacuating for several days, and that, if allowed, he could go into Corinth with his brigade. Trains of cars were heard coming into and going out of Corinth constantly. Some of the men who had been engaged in various capacities on railroads before the war, claimed that they could tell by putting their ears to the rail, not only which way the trains were moving, but which trains were loaded and which were empty. They said loaded trains had been going out for several days and empty ones coming in. Subsequent events proved the correctness of their judgment."—EDITORS.

GENERAL POPE'S ENCAMPMENT BEFORE CORINTH IN MAY, 1862.

The camps, beginning at the left, are those of the 8th Wisconsin, 27th Illinois, 10th Michigan, 14th Michigan, 42d Illinois, 16th Illinois, 27th Ohio, 51st Illinois, 22d Illinois, and 39th Ohio. In the middle distance, on the right, are seen Captain Williams's siege guns. The flag marks General Pope's headquarters.

Pope's forces went in pursuit. Before night (May 30th) he reported that he had captured hundreds of barrels of beef, several hundred wagons, and seven thousand stand of arms, which Price and Van Dorn, in their haste to get away, had abandoned. Two days later (June 1st) he reported that Colonel Elliott, with a brigade of cavalry (one regiment of which was commanded by Sheridan), had, among other things done at and near Booneville on the 30th of May, destroyed 10,000 stand of small arms, 3 pieces of artillery, a great quantity of clothing and ammunition, and had paroled 2000 prisoners, who could not keep up with his cavalry; and on the 3d of June he reported "the woods for miles are full of stragglers from the enemy, who are coming in in squads. Not less than ten thousand men are thus scattered about, who will come in within a day or two."

The next day (June 4th) Halleck telegraphed to Washington:

"General Pope with 40,000 men is 30 miles south of Corinth, pushing the enemy hard. He already reports 10,000 prisoners and deserters from the enemy, and 15,000 stand of arms captured. . . . A farmer says that when Beauregard learned that Colonel Elliott had cut the railroad on his line of retreat he became frantic, and told his men to save themselves the best they could." ⸋

At that very time (June 4th) Pope himself was within 4 miles of Halleck's headquarters; Beauregard with his entire army was still within 27 miles of Corinth, and nobody was pushing him. He had already been there several days, and he remained there three or four days longer. Price and Van Dorn had *not* abandoned any wagons, nor had they abandoned any arms. Colonel Elliott had destroyed about 2000 muskets at Booneville, and had found about

⸋ General Pope afterward denied having made any such report, and complained that General Halleck's dispatch had done him injustice. See his correspondence with General Halleck, July 3d–5th, 1865, in the "Official Records," Vol. X., Pt. II., pp. 635–637. See also General Halleck's telegram to the Secretary of War, July 3d, 1862, claiming that he had "telegraphed the exact language of General Pope" ("Official Records," Vol. X., Pt. I., p. 671). No dispatch from General Pope containing this "exact language" appears in the "Official Records."—EDITORS.

2000 sick men there and several hundred stragglers. But he did not carry off a single prisoner, nor did he parole one.

Beauregard, far from being frantic with alarm and despair, assumed such a threatening attitude on the 4th that Halleck, at Pope's request, ordered Buell to the front by forced marches, with twenty thousand men to reënforce him. Reaching Booneville the next day, Buell assumed command of the combined force, amounting to about sixty thousand men, and on the 8th ordered a reconnoissance in force to be made the next morning, in order to ascertain the strength and position of the enemy.

Beauregard was already on his way to Tupelo, 25 miles farther south, and 52 miles from Corinth. Pope fired a parting shot at him by telegraphing to Halleck:

"They have lost by desertion of the Tennessee, Kentucky and Arkansas regiments near 20,000 men, since they left Corinth. All the regiments yet left from these States passed down closely guarded on both sides by Mississippi and Alabama troops."

The "Official Records" show that Beauregard lost less than 4000 on the retreat from Corinth, and many of these came in after a few days. The Army of the West, and notably Price's division, mustered more men "present for duty" the day after it reached Tupelo than when it began its retreat from Corinth.

By the series of operations which Halleck had directed since he assumed command at St. Louis in November, 1861, the Confederates had now been driven out of Missouri, north Arkansas, Kentucky, and all of western and middle Tennessee, and had lost every city and stronghold on the Mississippi except Vicksburg. No wonder that the Government was so well pleased with him that on the 8th of June, 1862, it extended his command over the whole of Kentucky and Tennessee, so that he might have abundant means to conduct the new campaign upon which he had determined, with Chattanooga as its first objective.

He began straightway to prepare for it by sending Buell's army back into middle Tennessee, and by making such disposition of his forces in western Tennessee as would assure the safety of that part of his command and of the country west of the Mississippi. In the midst of these preparations the President, whose confidence in McClellan had been greatly shaken by the latter's reverses before Richmond, appointed Halleck (July 11th) general-in-chief, and ordered him to repair forthwith to Washington. Halleck, before leaving, put Grant in command of all the troops west of the Tennessee, including those at Columbus and Cairo; ordering him, however, to send Hovey's division to Helena to reënforce Curtis, and Thomas into middle Tennessee to rejoin Buell.

As soon as Beauregard, whose health had been seriously impaired, was satisfied that Halleck did not intend to attack him at Tupelo, he turned over the command of his army temporarily to Bragg (June 17th) and went to Mobile. When the President learned this fact he relieved Beauregard, and assigned Bragg to the command of the Department.

While Halleck at Corinth and Bragg at Tupelo were engaged in the congenial business of reorganizing and disciplining their armies, a cavalry engagement took place near Booneville which, though only an affair of outposts, is worth relating, because it brought into conspicuous notice a young officer of rare merit and singular good fortune—Philip H. Sheridan. At the beginning of 1862 he was still but a captain of infantry, on duty as quartermaster and commissary of the army with which Curtis was marching against Price in Missouri. He had come to Corinth with Halleck, and was still doing duty there as quartermaster when, on the 25th of May, he was made colonel of the 2d Michigan Cavalry. Within forty-eight hours he went with Elliott on what Pope says was "the first cavalry raid of the war," and participated in the attack upon Booneville (May 30th). He was now fairly started in his new career. On the 1st of July he was in command of a brigade consisting of two cavalry regiments, and had just established his headquarters at Booneville.

Bragg, who was sending a division of infantry to Ripley, Miss., had ordered Chalmers (June 30th) to take some 1200 or 1500 cavalry, and to cover the movement of this infantry by making a feint upon Rienzi. In executing this order Chalmers encountered Sheridan (July 1st), and a stubborn engagement took place. It lasted from 8:30 in the morning till late in the afternoon, when, Sheridan having been reënforced by infantry and artillery, Chalmers retired.

Rosecrans (who, in June, upon Pope's transfer to the East, had succeeded him in the command of the Army of the Mississippi, to which Sheridan's brigade belonged) issued an order declaring that "the coolness, determination, and fearless gallantry displayed by Colonel Sheridan and the officers and men of his command in this action deserved the thanks and admiration of the army," and telegraphed Halleck: "More cavalry massed under such an officer would be of great use to us. Sheridan ought to be made a brigadier. He would not be a stampeding general." Halleck at once asked the President to promote him "for gallant conduct in battle"; and soon afterward Generals Rosecrans, J. C. Sullivan, Gordon Granger, Elliott, and Asboth telegraphed to Halleck (then in Washington): "The undersigned respectfully beg that you will obtain the promotion of Sheridan. *He is worth his weight in gold.*" He was eventually promoted to the rank of brigadier-general, his commission dating from this fight with Chalmers on July 1st.

When the army had got into camp at Tupelo, and it was apparent that hostilities would not be resumed immediately, General Price went to Richmond in order to persuade the President to send him and the Missourians back to the trans-Mississippi. Beauregard, Bragg, and Van Dorn all advised that this be done; and Van Dorn, who was still in nominal command of the country west of the Mississippi, generously urged the President to assign General Price to that command, saying, in a private letter to Mr. Davis, that as "the love of the people of Missouri was so strong for General Price, and his prestige as a commander so great there, wisdom would seem to dictate that he be put at the head of affairs in the West."

All along the route to Richmond crowds testified their great admiration for Price. At Richmond, the capital of his native State, he was fêted and honored, even in the midst of the great anxiety which was felt in the dangerous presence of McClellan's great army within sight of the capital. The General Assembly gave him a formal reception, and the people manifested for him their respect and affection.

Not so the President. He received the general courteously, but he had been strongly prejudiced against him; he had little confidence in any soldier who had not been educated at West Point, and he had been told again and again, by those who did not know the difference between a drill-sergeant and a general, that Price was not a disciplinarian, and that his army was a mere mob. I do not blame Mr. Davis for believing it, for some of the men who told these things were men of high degree,—generals, congressmen, statesmen, and many of them, I am sorry to have to add, Missourians.

President Davis asked Price to express his opinions and wishes in writing. This the general did, as he did everything, plainly, sensibly, and modestly, asking for himself nothing but permission to return with his Missourians to Arkansas, there to rally around these veterans an army with which to gain possession of their own State.

This letter was submitted to the President, who, after a few days, sent for the general. The details of this final interview, at which the Secretary of War and myself were also present, are deeply impressed upon my memory. After discussing the matter awhile, the President said that he had determined not to let the general and the Missourians return to the trans-Mississippi.

"Well, Mr. President," said General Price, with the utmost respect and courtesy of manner, "Well, Mr. President, if you will not let me serve *you*, I will nevertheless serve my *country*. You cannot prevent me from doing that. I will send you my resignation, and go back to Missouri and raise another army there without your assistance, and fight again under the flag of Missouri, and win new victories for the South in spite of the Government."

No one who ever encountered Jefferson Davis in authority, especially when he was President, can ever forget the measured articulation with which he gave force to words addressed to one who presumed to oppose his wishes or to refuse obedience to his will. And now he had been defied in the very Executive Chamber of the Confederacy by a wild Western chieftain, whom he had himself raised from insignificance as a major-general of the Missouri militia to the height of major-general in the provisional army of the Confederate States. His eye flashed with anger as he glanced to the general's flushed face, and his tone was contemptuous, as he replied with measured slowness: "Your resignation will be promptly accepted, General; and if you do go back to Missouri and raise another army, and win victories for the South, or do it any service at all, no one will be more *pleased* than myself, or," after a pause which was intended to emphasize, and did emphasize, the words that followed, "more *surprised*."

"Then I will surprise you, sir," said the general, bringing his clenched fist down upon the table with a violence which set the inkstands and everything upon it a-dancing; and out he went, indignant and furious, to return to his hotel and forward his resignation. The next day Price was informed that the President, instead of accepting his resignation, would instruct Bragg to send the Missourians to the trans-Mississippi as soon as it could safely be done.

Leaving Richmond while the Seven Days' battles were still being fought within sight of the capital, General Price arrived at Tupelo on the 2d of July. On reporting to Bragg, the latter told him that he could not spare him or the Missouri troops just then, but would give him command of the Army of the West, since Van Dorn had been sent by order of the President to relieve Lovell in the command at Vicksburg, then threatened by Farragut's fleet.

Halleck, as has been said, began to move his army toward Chattanooga immediately after occupying Corinth. One of his last acts, before laying down his Western command in order to assume the position of general-in-chief, was to order Grant to send Thomas's division eastward to Buell. This was done in obedience to the wishes of President Lincoln, who telegraphed him on the 30th of June not to do anything which would force him "to give up, or weaken, or delay the expedition against Chattanooga. To take and hold the railroad at or east of Cleveland, in east Tennessee, is, I think, fully as important as the taking and holding of Richmond."

The Confederate Government also recognized the vital importance of Chattanooga and reorganized its Western commands accordingly. The country west of the Mississippi was erected into a separate military department, and Bragg was assigned to the command of all the country lying between the Mississippi and Virginia. This was done on the 18th of July, and Bragg at once determined to transfer the bulk of his forces to Chattanooga, and, assuming the offensive before Buell was ready to oppose him, to push boldly through Tennessee into Kentucky, and call upon the people of those States to rise and help him to drive the enemy beyond the Ohio.

To this end he made his dispositions. Van Dorn was assigned to the command of the District of the Mississippi lying along the eastern bank of that river, and ordered to defend Vicksburg, to keep open communication with the trans-Mississippi, and at the same time to prevent the Union armies from occupying the north-eastern part of the State of Mississippi. Forney was left in command of the district of the Gulf. Price was placed in command of the District of the Tennessee, with orders to hold the line of the Mobile and Ohio railroad, and, above all, to watch Grant and prevent him from sending reënforcements to Buell in middle Tennessee. Kirby Smith was directed to get ready to move from Knoxville, and Humphrey Marshall out of Western Virginia into Kentucky. Polk was "Second in command of the forces"; Hardee was put in immediate command of the Army of the Mississippi, now thoroughly reorganized. On July 21st this army started for Chattanooga, the infantry being sent by rail *via* Mobile. To cover the movement, Bragg sent Wheeler with his cavalry on a raid into west Tennessee. ☆

☆ The Confederate cavalry brigade, at this time commanded by Colonel Joseph Wheeler, consisted at first of parts of the 1st Alabama and 1st Kentucky regiments; afterward of the 3d Georgia, 1st Kentucky, and 8th Texas regiments and 9th Tennessee battalion.—EDITORS.

Price was left with the Army of the West at Tupelo. At the time when Price assumed command of this army it consisted of two divisions of infantry, a light battery for each brigade, and a small force of cavalry. One division was commanded by Brigadier-General Henry Little, and the other by Brigadier-General Dabney H. Maury. The strength of the two was about 15,000 officers and men, but of these nearly 4000 were sick or on extra duty; there were, therefore, about 11,000 "present for duty."

As the cavalry of the Army of the West had been dismounted in Arkansas when about to be moved to Corinth, Price's mounted force consisted of only a few fractional regiments and independent companies, which, all together, could not muster one thousand men for duty. One of his first cares was to organize this force efficiently. The difficulty of the task was increased by the fact that the men were scattered in all directions on picket duty; and, moreover, they had never been accustomed to act together. With the consent of Bragg he assigned Frank C. Armstrong, who had lately been elected colonel of the 3d Louisiana infantry (one of the best regiments in the service), to the command of the cavalry, with the provisional rank of brigadier-general; and Armstrong quickly brought it to a high state of discipline and efficiency.

On leaving Tupelo, Bragg ordered other troops within the district to report to Price, whose "effective" force was thus raised to about fifteen thousand.

Hardee left Tupelo on the 29th of July, and during the next week all of the Army of the Mississippi was on its way to Chattanooga. Price at once began to get ready to move toward Corinth, in order, by threatening that place, to keep Grant from reënforcing Buell. As, however, he knew that he would have to encounter a force of at least thirty thousand men, he did not dare to make any serious advance without the coöperation of Van Dorn, to whom he therefore wrote, on the 31st of July (sending the letter by Dr. Blackburn, one of his volunteer aides, since Governor of Kentucky), that he would himself be ready within a few days to move against Grant with fifteen thousand effectives, and would gladly place himself and them under his command if he would, with his own available force, coöperate in the proposed movement.

Unfortunately Van Dorn at Vicksburg did not have any available force at that time, or for many weeks afterward. With the assistance of the gun-boat *Arkansas* he had demonstrated to Farragut the impracticability of taking Vicksburg without the coöperation of a large land force, and had caused him to return to New Orleans with his fleet, and Davis's and Ellet's to retire up the river, and on July 27th, the very day on which Farragut withdrew, he ordered Breckinridge to proceed at once to Baton Rouge with five thousand picked men and occupy that place.⸸ A series of misadventures had followed that expedition, and Van Dorn, far from being able to coöperate with Price in a forward movement, was himself in great want of reënforcements for Breckinridge, and implored Price to send that officer a brigade.

Now it had so happened that when General Hardee was leaving Tupelo on the 29th of July he sent for me (I being at that time chief of staff of the District of the Tennessee), and said that he had just learned of Van Dorn's expe-

⸸ For accounts of operations about Vicksburg see Vol. III. of this work.—EDITORS.

MAP OF THE CORINTH AND IUKA REGION.

dition against Baton Rouge; that he feared that it would lead Van Dorn into other adventures which would overtask his strength, and that Van Dorn would then call on General Price to help him. "Now," said he, "when this happens, as it surely will, I want you to say to General Price, for me, that the success of General Bragg's movement into Tennessee and Kentucky depends greatly upon his (Price's) ability to keep Grant from reënforcing Buell, and consequently that General Bragg would sternly disapprove the sending of any reënforcements whatever to Van Dorn. Say to General Price that I know that General Bragg expects him to keep his men well in hand, and ready to move northward at a moment's notice."

Simultaneously with Van Dorn's request for reënforcements came a telegram from Bragg (August 2d) saying that Grant had been reënforcing Buell, and that "the road was open for him (Price) into west Tennessee." Price therefore replied to Van Dorn that in view of Bragg's telegram, and considering the very important relations which the Army of the West bore to that in east Tennessee, he could not send any of his troops to Breckinridge, but must concentrate them for a forward movement.

"The enemy [said he] is still transferring his troops from Corinth and its vicinity eastward. He will, by the end of this week, have reduced the force to its minimum. We should be quick to take advantage of this, for he will soon begin to get in reënforcements under the late call for volunteers. . . . Every consideration makes it important that I shall move forward without a day's unnecessary delay. I earnestly desire your coöperation in such a movement, and will, as I have before said, gladly place my army and myself under your command in that contingency."

Bragg, to whom Price forwarded a copy of this correspondence, warmly approved Price's conduct, and ordered Van Dorn (August 11th) to coöperate with Price. Price meanwhile went vigorously to work to get ready for active operations. An efficient officer, who had been sent to Richmond for funds, came back with enough to pay off the troops and to purchase an abundance of supplies of every kind. Transportation was collected, more than enough, and the roads in our front were all put in order. Three active and intelligent officers who had been sent to Richmond for the purpose, brought back with them improved arms sufficient to supply the wants of the troops in camp, and also to arm five thousand exchanged prisoners whom Bragg had ordered to Price, but whom Van Dorn, with Mr. Davis's consent, intercepted on the way.

On the 4th of September Price telegraphed to Van Dorn: "I state for your information that I can put in the field an effective total of 13,000 infantry, 3000 cavalry, and 800 artillerymen; that they are supplied with transportation and ammunition as prescribed in General Bragg's last general orders; that subsistence has been provided to October 1st; that the commissary trains will transport seven days' provisions; and that I will have arms for all my troops, including those exchanged prisoners that Bragg has ordered sent to me."

Not only were these men well armed and equipped, well fed, well clothed, and well provided with everything that an army in the field needed, but they were thoroughly organized, drilled, and disciplined. July 24th, just before leaving Tupelo, Bragg reviewed them for the first time. When Price's old division, to the command of which Little had succeeded, had passed in review, and Little was about to resume his place at its head, Bragg turned to Little and said: "You had the reputation of having one of the finest companies in the old army. General, this is certainly as fine a division as I have ever seen." And it was.⚓ But however brave and well-disciplined his men, Price did not dare to throw them against the fortifications of Corinth, defended by twice their own number commanded by Grant and Rosecrans.

All that he could do was to send Armstrong with his cavalry into west Tennessee to harass Grant, and bring back such information as he could get.

⚓ What manner of men they were that constituted it no one who has not shared their fortunes, their hardships, and their dangers in camp, on the march, and upon the field of battle, can ever know. There lie before me now two yellowing bits of coarse paper which throw some light upon their humanity. While at Richmond during the Seven Days' battles around that city, the general and those of us that were with him had seen the long files of wounded that came or were brought day by day to the crowded hospitals. Naturally, when we got back to the army we spoke of these things to the men. Within less than forty-eight hours the chaplain of Erwin's battalion was on his way to Richmond with $2350, which the officers and men of that battalion were sending to the relief of the wounded of Lee's army. A day or two afterward Colonel Gates, of the 1st Missouri Cavalry, sent a similar contribution. These men, it must be remembered, had been away from their homes for almost a year, serving much the greater part of that time without pay, and clothing themselves besides. Nor was this money depreciated currency, but it was just as good as any United States Treasury notes. Other regiments did likewise, but the record of their humanity has been lost.—T. L. S.

DWELLINGS IN IUKA. FROM PHOTOGRAPHS TAKEN IN 1884.

1. General George H. Thomas's headquarters. 2. Female seminary, used as a hospital. 3. General Price's headquarters. 4. Iuka Springs. 5. Methodist Church, used as a hospital. 6. General Rosecrans's headquarters. 7. General Grant's headquarters.

Taking 1600 men, Armstrong reached Holly Springs on the 26th of August, and having been reënforced there by 1100 men under Jackson, struck for Bolivar, Tennessee. There he encountered and defeated a force under Colonel Leggett, who, in his report of this affair, says that after fighting for seven hours with "less than 900" he "drove from the field over 6000." Armstrong then crossed the Hatchie and cut the railroad between Bolivar and Jackson. He then turned back to Tupelo. On the way he met a force under Colonel Dennis, whose brigade commander, General L. F. Ross, reported that with 800 men he met Armstrong, 6000 strong, and won "the most brilliant victory of the war"; that he himself lost only 5 men, but that "Armstrong left 179 dead upon the field." This is his *official* report; but the fact is that during the whole expedition Armstrong lost only one hundred and fifteen men killed, wounded, and missing.

Van Dorn, having brought Breckinridge and most of his men back to Jackson, Miss., announced, on the 24th of August, that he was ready to coöperate with General Price in an aggressive campaign. He proposed to move through western Tennessee into Kentucky, and thence to Paducah and "wherever circumstances might dictate." But he was not ready to move, and there was no possibility that he could get ready for two weeks to come.

On the 1st of September Bragg telegraphed Price that Buell was in full retreat upon Nashville, and that he must watch Rosecrans and prevent their junction; or, if he should escape, follow him closely. Price consequently told Van Dorn that he could wait for him no longer, but must move in three days. Van Dorn replied that he would be ready to move from Holly Springs on the 12th, but wanted men, arms, and wagons. Upon Price's refusal to give them he asked the President to order Price to do it, and also to give him command of Price and his army. After some hesitation, the President, without consulting General Bragg, or knowing the special instructions which Bragg had given to Van Dorn and Price, ordered Van Dorn by telegraph (September 11th) to assume command of both armies, and thereby unknowingly struck Bragg a heavier blow than any which he had yet received from the enemy.

Price, not knowing what had been done, was on the march to Iuka, intending to move thence into middle Tennessee, if, on reaching that place, he should find that Rosecrans had gone to Nashville, as Bragg believed. His cavalry under Armstrong entered the town on the 13th, but withdrew when the enemy appeared in force.

Moving by moonlight that night with his infantry and artillery,

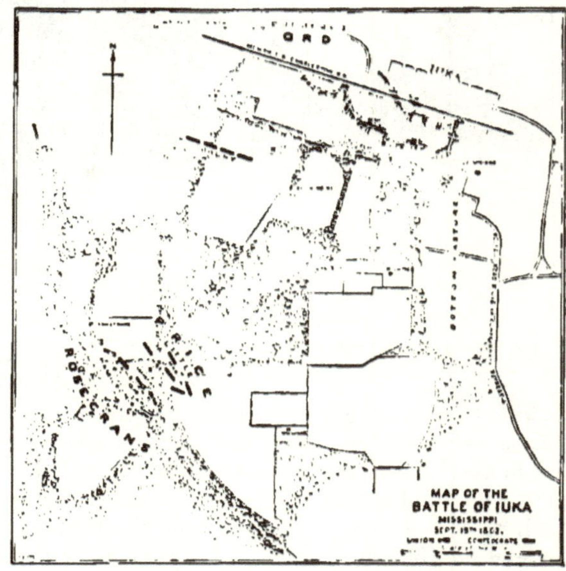

Price entered Iuka the next morning (September 14th), and quietly took possession,—the Union garrison retiring without offering any resistance, and abandoning a large amount of supplies which added greatly to the happiness of the Confederates.

Price learned as soon as he got into Iuka that though Rosecrans had sent three divisions of his army [E. A. Paine's, Jeff. C. Davis's, and Gordon Granger's] to Buell, he was himself still west of Iuka with two divisions. After some hesitation he felt that it was his duty not to go to Nashville, but to look after Rosecrans and what was left of his army; accordingly he telegraphed Van Dorn that as Rosecrans had gone to Corinth he would turn back and coöperate with Van Dorn in an attack upon that place. Hardly had he done this when Price received a telegram from Bragg urging him to hasten to Nashville. [See map, p. 702.]

This is what Price ought to have done. It is what Halleck, Grant, and Rosecrans feared that he would do. Rosecrans telegraphed Grant that he "had better watch the Old Woodpecker" (alluding to that bird's skill in deceiving its

BRIGADIER-GENERAL HENRY LITTLE, C. S. A., KILLED AT IUKA. FROM A PHOTOGRAPH.

enemies), "or he would get away from them." Halleck telegraphed (September 17th): "Do everything in your power to prevent Price from crossing the Tennessee River. A junction of Price and Bragg in Tennessee would be most disastrous. They should be fought while separate." Grant replied that he "would do everything in his power to prevent such a catastrophe," and began at once to concentrate his forces against Price. Ord was pushed forward to Burnsville, where Grant established his own headquarters, and Rosecrans was ordered to concentrate his two divisions at Jacinto, and to move thence upon Iuka, in order to flank Price and cut off his retreat.

Hurlbut, who was at Bolivar, was at the same time ordered to make a strong demonstration toward Grand Junction, near which place Van Dorn had at last arrived with about 10,000 effectives. In order to deceive Van Dorn, and to keep him from helping Price by an attack upon Corinth, Hurlbut was told to make a great fuss, and to let it leak out that he was expecting heavy reënforcements from Columbus, and that as soon as they came, he, Sherman and Steele were going to make a dash for Grenada and the Yazoo country.‡

On the 18th of September, Ord with about 6500 men was advanced to within 6 miles of Iuka and directed to be ready to attack the next morning;

‡ On the 19th of September, 1862, General Grant telegraphed to General Halleck that before leaving Corinth he had sent instructions to General Hurlbut as indicated in the text. Meanwhile General Grant had received General Halleck's orders of September 18th to make the very movement up the Yazoo that Hurlbut had been told to feign.— EDITORS.

but Grant, having learned that Rosecrans could not reach Iuka till the afternoon, instructed Ord not to attack till he heard Rosecrans's guns.

There was yet time for Price to obey Bragg's order and hurry to Nashville. Once across the defiles of Bear Creek, he would have been safe from pursuit, for Grant would hardly have ventured to lay open west Tennessee to the advance of Van Dorn, who was now waiting for an opportunity to enter it. Price was still undecided what to do in view of this latest order from Bragg, when, during the night of the 18th, one of Van Dorn's staff arrived, bringing the intelligence that Van Dorn had been directed by the President to take command of Price and the Army of the West. This staff-officer was also authorized to concert with General Price the movements by which the junction of the two armies should be effected. This settled the matter. Orders were issued to load the wagons and get the troops ready to move the next morning at daybreak toward Baldwyn, on the Mobile and Ohio railroad.

While preparations for this movement were being made, Price learned about 2 P. M. (September 19th) that his pickets on the Jacinto road had been driven in, and that Rosecrans was advancing on that road in force. All of Price's infantry and artillery was at that time in front of Ord, from which direction Price expected to be attacked.

Little was hastily ordered to send Hébert's brigade to the left, toward Rosecrans. It came forward on the instant, Price himself taking it to the front. Hamilton's division of Rosecrans's corps was by this time within a mile and a half of the center of the town. Seeing that he was greatly outnumbered, Price ordered Little to send up another brigade, and Martin's was quickly on the ground. The fight had already begun and was being waged with great severity. Price now ordered Little to bring up the rest of his division. After starting the men forward, Little himself galloped to the front and joined General Price in the thickest of the fight. While they were consulting, a minie-ball, crashing through Little's forehead, killed him instantly.

MAJOR-GENERAL C. S. HAMILTON.
FROM A PHOTOGRAPH.

Hamilton was already giving way. Price pushed him the more vigorously, and, capturing 9 of his guns, drove him back about 600 yards. Hamilton was now reënforced by Stanley's division. About the same time the rest of Little's division reached the field,—too late, however, to take part in the battle, for it was already dark. The Confederate division bivouacked upon the ground from which Hamilton had been driven.

General Price returned sorrowfully to town, for he had lost his most trusted lieutenant,—the very best division commander I have ever known,—Henry Little. He, nevertheless, resolved to renew the battle at daylight, and was confident of victory. Maury was ordered to move his division to the front of Rosecrans, and Armstrong and Wirt Adams were directed to occupy with the cavalry the positions in front of Ord, so as to cover the movement of our troops from that front to the front of Rosecrans, and also to hinder the advance of the Federals upon our right. General Price then went to the house of a friend, instead of to his own quarters, and told me not to let him be disturbed till an hour before day.

After burying Little by torchlight, I returned to headquarters, determined to remain awake all night. Some time after midnight Hébert, who had succeeded to the command of Little's division, came in and said that his brigade was so badly cut up and was so much disheartened by the death of Little that he was apprehensive of the morrow. While he was still there, Maury came in and said that he was convinced that Grant would attack us in overwhelming force in the morning, brush our cavalry out of his way, destroy our trains, and assail us in rear. Wirt Adams, who came in next, sustained Maury's views, and all of them insisted upon seeing General Price. I was still hesitating what to do when one of Van Dorn's staff arrived with important dispatches from Van Dorn, and asked to see the general. I hesitated no longer, but took them to his lodgings. It was nearly dawn, and he thought I had come to call him to battle. Great was his disappointment when he ascertained the true cause of our coming. He tried to convince his generals that their apprehensions were groundless, and that a victory was in their grasp, but they would not be convinced. Unwilling to give battle when all of his chief officers were so averse to it, he reluctantly directed them to carry out the orders which had been issued the preceding morning for the withdrawal of the army to Baldwyn. The trains had already been loaded and were ready to leave. They were put in motion instantly, and toward sunrise the troops followed. Every wagon, all the valuable captured stores, and all the sick and wounded that were fit to be moved, were brought away safely. Maury's division left the town about 8 A. M., and Armstrong brought up the rear with the cavalry.

Between Burnsville, where Grant was on the 19th, and the battle-field of that day, there lay a densely wooded country, much of it an impassable swamp, and it was only by making a long circuit that Rosecrans could communicate with him. The wind, too, happened during the battle to be blowing away from Burnsville. It was, therefore, not till half-past 8 o'clock the next morning that Grant knew that a battle had been fought.‡ Hastening to the front, he directed Ord to push forward. Rosecrans had meanwhile entered the town. Grant sent Hamilton's and Stanley's divisions with some cavalry in pursuit. The cavalry came up with Price's rear-guard in the afternoon, but

---

‡ In his "Memoirs" (Vol. I., p. 412), Grant says: "The wind was still blowing hard and in the wrong direction to transmit sound toward either Ord or me. Neither he nor I nor any one in either command heard a gun that was fired on the battle-field."— EDITORS.

having been roughly handled and driven back by McCulloch's regiment of Missouri cavalry, supported by Colonel Rogers's regiment of Texas sharp-shooters and Bledsoe's battery, the pursuit was abandoned and the Confederates reached Baldwyn without further interruption.

In the battle of Iuka only two brigades of Price's army were engaged, Hébert's and Adams's brigades of Little's division. They were composed exclusively of troops from Mississippi, Alabama, Louisiana, Arkansas, and Texas, and one Missouri battery. The aggregate strength of both brigades was 3179 officers and men. Their loss was 86 killed and 408 wounded [see also p. 736]. In addition to these, about 200 of the Confederate sick were left at Iuka and on the road. Price's loss, therefore, was about 700.

Rosecrans's column, according to his own report, was 9000 strong, but the brunt of the battle fell upon two brigades of Hamilton's division. The Union loss was 141 killed, 613 wounded, and 36 missing; total, 790.

Rosecrans says that Price's loss was 1438; and Hamilton states "boldly," to use his own expression, that he, "with a force of not more than 2800 men, met and conquered a rebel force of 11,000 on a field chosen by Price." General Grant, in his report of the battle written a month afterward, discards these exaggerations of Rosecrans and Hamilton.

THE BATTLE OF IUKA.

BY C. S. HAMILTON, MAJOR-GENERAL, U. S. V.

IUKA is a little village on the Memphis and Charleston railway, in northern Mississippi, about thirty miles east of Corinth. In September, 1862, the Confederate authorities, to prevent reënforcements being sent by the Federal commander in Mississippi to Buell in Kentucky, sent General Sterling Price with his army corps to Iuka. A regiment of Union troops stationed at Iuka evacuated the place, leaving a considerable quantity of army stores, as also quite an amount of cotton. The latter was destroyed, the former made use of, and Price settled down, apparently at his leisure, under the nose of Grant's force, whose headquarters were at Corinth. As soon as definite information was had of this position of Price, Grant took immediate steps to beat him up. A combined attack was planned, by which Rosecrans with his two divisions (Hamilton's and Stanley's) was to move on Iuka from the south, while Ord, with a similar column, was to approach Iuka from the west. This he did, taking position within about six miles of the village, where he was to await Rosecrans's attack.

From Iuka southward ran two parallel roads, some two miles distant from each other — the most eastern known as the Fulton road, the western as the Tuscumbia. Grant's plan contemplated an approach on Iuka by way of the Fulton road, at least in part, with a view of cutting off the escape of Price by that road. Rosecrans, however, for reasons of his own, decided on taking the Tuscumbia road with his whole force, thus leaving the Fulton road open.

A rapid march from Jacinto (Hamilton's division leading, Sanborn's brigade in the advance) brought Rosecrans's column to Barnett's by noon. Hamilton, who had expected to march upon the Fulton road from that point, was furnished with a guide, and directed to continue his march on the Tuscumbia road without further instructions.

About 4 P. M. the guide gave notice that the column was within about two miles of Iuka. In fact, we were on the eve of a battle, and it is well here to note the strength and position of the opposing forces. On the Union side was Hamilton's division of 2 brigades (Sanborn's and Sullivan's) of 5 regiments and a battery each. Stanley's division was following along the same road, but as yet was some distance in the rear. It also had 2 brigades of 5 regiments each, but only 3 of these regiments reached the field in time to take any part in the conflict.

At the moment the guide gave notice of our nearness to Iuka, the whole of the leading division was halted in the road in exactly the order they had been marching. The head of the column had just finished ascending a long hill, from the top of which the ground sloped in undulations toward the front. A few hundred yards ahead, in line of battle, the enemy lay concealed in the woods. Hébert's brigade of 6 regiments lay athwart the road by which we were approaching; Martin's brigade of 4 regiments had been divided, and 2 of these regiments were thrown on the right of the Confederate line and 2 on the left, making 10 regiments in line of battle. At the commencement of the conflict, the other 2 brigades which had been ordered up had arrived on the field, making the whole strength of Little's division, 18 regiments, ready for action before a gun had been fired.

On the halting of my troops, the battalion of skirmishers was pushed rapidly forward in the direction of Iuka. An advance of four hundred yards brought them in the immediate presence of the enemy. I was immediately in rear of the skirmishers, and taking in the situation at a glance dashed back to the head of the column. If this should become enveloped by the enemy, a rout was inevitable, and our force would be doubled back on itself. I threw the leading regiment, the 5th Iowa, across the road, moving it a short distance to the right, and ordered up the nearest battery, which was placed in position on the road, and to the left of the first regiment in position. Colonel Sanborn was active in bringing up other regiments, and getting them into line. Just as the first regiment was placed, the enemy opened one of his batteries with canister. The charge passed over our heads, doing no damage beyond bringing down a shower of twigs and leaves. The Confederates were in line ready for action. Why they did not move forward and attack us at once is not understood. Their delay, which enabled us to form the nearest three regiments in line of battle before the attack began, was our salvation. An earlier attack would have enveloped the head of the column, and brought a disastrous rout.

Meantime not a moment was lost. A second regiment, and a third, with all the rapidity that men could exercise, were added to our little line; and while the Confederates were moving to the front, we had managed to get a battle line of three regiments into position. It was then the storm of battle opened. The opposing infantry lines were within close musketry shot. Our battery was handled with energy, and dealt death to the enemy. The Confederate batteries had ceased firing, their line of fire having been covered by the advance of their infantry. Our own infantry held their ground nobly against the overwhelming force moving against them, and we were enabled to add another regiment to the line of battle. At the first musketry fire of the enemy, most of the horses of our battery were killed, and the pieces could not be removed from the field. The fight became an infantry duel. I never saw a hotter or more destructive engagement. General Price says in his official report, "The fight began, and was waged with a severity I have never seen surpassed."

The regiments of Sanborn's brigade were in the front line. Sullivan's brigade was divided — a regiment thrown to the right flank, and one to the left — the remaining two being placed in rear of Sanborn's center as a reënforcement. Thus was every regiment of my command doing duty on the field. Stanley's division seemed long in coming up. The Confederate lines had moved forward, concentrating their fire on our little front, and stretching out their wings to the right and left, as though we were to be taken in at once. Our men stood their ground bravely, yielding nothing for a long time; but the pressure began to grow severe, and I feared we might be driven from our ground. Thinking General Rosecrans was in the rear, where he could hurry up the troops of Stanley's division, I dispatched an aide with the request that General Rosecrans would come forward far enough to confer with me. All the while the battle waxed hotter and more furious. The dead lay in lines along the regiments, while some of our troops gave signs of yielding. I dispatched another officer, the only one in reach, for General Rosecrans. He happened to be one of General Rosecrans's staff, and at my request he started to bear the message to his general. Our troops, as yet, had not given way. The battery under Sears was doing noble service, but had lost nearly half its men. Sanborn's brigade was held by him to their work like Roman veterans, but without help we could not much longer hold out. I dispatched my adjutant-general, Captain Sawyer, and a short time later another aide, Lieutenant Wheeler, with messages for General Rosecrans, saying that I considered it imperative he should come forward to see me, and should hurry forward fresh troops. ‡

Stanley's division had now reached the vicinity of the battle-field, and General Stanley came instantly to the front, directing the division to follow as rapidly as possible. It was time, for our line had begun to give way slowly. It had been formed on the crest of the hill (up which we had come, and which sloped to our rear), and in falling back had been arrested just below the brow of the hill, where it maintained the fight. Other regiments were yielding ground slowly, but were readily stopped by the united exertions of Stanley, Sanborn, and myself. The falling back of the troops had exposed the battery, into which the Confederates had entered. A short time later, however, a desperate rally was made, and they were driven back from the battery; but returning with renewed strength, our troops were again forced below the brow of the hill. Here three of Stanley's regiments reached the field, and were pushed to the right of the line, where they made good the places of troops that had fallen to the rear. They fought bravely under Colonels Mower, Boomer, and Holman, but the fire was too deadly, and they in turn were forced back. It was growing dark. The smoke of battle added to the coming night, and it was soon too dark to distinguish the gray from the blue uniform. The storm of battle gradually lulled to entire quiet.

Our troops bivouacked on the slope of the hill. The Confederates, for several hours, were occupied with burying their dead and removing their wounded.

A consultation between General Rosecrans and his division commanders resulted in a rearrangement of the troops early in the night, and every-

<hr>

‡ Rosecrans in his official report says: "About this time [referring to a time subsequent to the capture and recovery of Sears's battery] it was deemed prudent to order up the first brigade of Stanley's division." This shows that Stanley had reached the vicinity of the battle-field, but for some reason no one had ordered him to the front.—C. S. H.

thing was made ready for battle in the morning. The enemy, however, left the vicinity of the field during the night, leaving the battery which had been the object of such a sanguinary struggle but a short distance to the rear, and near their first line of battle.

The Fulton road being open, there was nothing to interfere with the enemy's escape. A pursuit was made the following day — but a pursuit of a defeated enemy can amount to little in a country like that of northern Mississippi, heavily wooded, and with narrow roads, when the enemy has time enough to get his artillery and trains in front of his infantry. To make an effective pursuit, it must be so close on the heels of the battle that trains, artillery, and troops can be made to blockade the roads by being mixed in an indiscriminate mass.

On the following day, September 21st, our troops were back in their old encampments at Jacinto. Just two weeks later, the same divisions and brigades were measured against each other on the field of Corinth.

THE OPPOSING FORCES AT IUKA, MISS.
September 19th, 1862.

The composition, losses, and strength of each army as here stated give the gist of all the data obtainable in the Official Records. K stands for killed; w for wounded; m w for mortally wounded; m for captured or missing; c for captured.

THE UNION FORCES.
ARMY OF THE MISSISSIPPI. — Major-General William S. Rosecrans.

SECOND DIVISION, Brig.-Gen. David S. Stanley.

First Brigade, Col. John W. Fuller: 27th Ohio, Major Zephaniah S. Spaulding; 39th Ohio, Col. Alfred W. Gilbert; 43d Ohio, Col. J. L. Kirby Smith; 63d Ohio, Col. John W. Sprague; M, 1st Mo. Art'y, Capt. Albert M. Powell; 8th Wis. Battery (section), Lieut. John D. McLean; F, 2d U. S. Art'y, Capt. Thomas D. Maurice. Brigade loss: w, 8. *Second Brigade*, Col. Joseph A. Mower: 26th Ill., Major Robert A. Gillmore; 47th Ill., Lieut.-Col. William A. Thrush; 11th Mo., Major Andrew J. Weber; 8th Wis., Lieut.-Col. George W. Robbins; 2d Iowa Battery, Capt. Nelson T. Spoor; 3d Mich. Battery, Capt. Alex W. Dees. Brigade loss: k, 8; w, 81; m, 4 = 93. THIRD DIVISION, Brig.-Gen. C. S. Hamilton. Staff loss: w, 2.

Escort: C, 5th Mo. Cav., Capt. Albert Borcherdt (w). Loss: k, 1; w, 2 = 3.

First Brigade, Col. John B. Sanborn: 48th Ind., Col. Norman Eddy (w), Lieut.-Col. De Witt C. Rugg; 5th Iowa, Col. Charles L. Matthies; 16th Iowa, Col. Alexander Chambers (w), Lieut.-Col. Add. H. Sanders; 4th Minn., Capt. Ebenezer Le Gro; 26th Mo., Col. George B. Boomer (w); 11th Ohio Battery, Lieut. Cyrus Sears (w). Brigade loss: k, 127; w, 434; m, 27 = 588. *Second Brigade*, Brig.-Gen. Jeremiah C. Sullivan: 10th Iowa, Col. Nicholas Perczel; 17th Iowa, Col. John W. Rankin (injured), Capt. Samson M. Archer (w), Capt. John L. Young; 10th Mo., Col. Samuel A. Holmes; E, 24th Mo., Capt. Lafayette M. Rice; 80th Ohio, Lieut.-Col. Matthias H. Bartilson (w), Major Richard Lanning; 12th Wis. Battery, Lieut. Lorenzo D. Immell. Brigade loss: k, 5; w, 76; m, 5 = 86.

CAVALRY DIVISION, Col. John K. Mizner: 2d Iowa, Col. Edward Hatch; B and E, 7th Kans., Capt. Frederick Swoyer; 3d Mich., Capt. Lyman G. Willcox. Division loss: w, 9. *Unattached:* Jenks's Co., Ill. Cav., Capt. Albert Jenks. Loss: w, 1.

Total loss of the Union Army: killed, 141; wounded, 613; captured or missing, 36 = 790.

General Rosecrans says ("Official Records," Vol. XVII., Pt. I., p. 74) that "we moved from Jacinto at 6 A. M., with 9000 men, on Price's forces at Iuka. After a march of 18 miles attacked them at 4:30 P. M. . . . with less than half our forces in action." Meanwhile the command of General E. O. C. Ord, comprising the divisions of Davies, Ross, and McArthur, numbering about 8000 men, was marching from Corinth direct on Iuka, and was within four or five miles of the battle-field on the 19th (see map, p. 730). The entire Union force near Iuka, including Ord, was about 17,000 men.

THE CONFEDERATE FORCES.
ARMY OF THE WEST. — Major-General Sterling Price.

FIRST DIVISION, Brig.-Gen. Henry Little (k).

First Brigade, Col. Elijah Gates: 16th Ark., ——; 2d Mo., Col. Francis M. Cockrell; 3d Mo., Col. James A. Pritchard; 5th Mo., ——; 1st Mo. (dismounted cavalry), Lieut.-Col. W. D. Maupin; Mo. Battery, Capt. William Wade. Brigade loss: w, 10. *Second Brigade*, Brig.-Gen. Louis Hébert: 14th Ark., ——; 17th Ark., Lieut.-Col. John Griffith; 3d La., Lieut.-Col. J. B. Gilmore (w); 40th Miss., Col. W. Bruce Colbert; 1st Tex. Legion (dismounted cavalry), Col. John W. Whitfield (w), Lieut.-Col. E. R. Hawkins; 3d Tex. (dismounted cavalry), Col. H. P. Mabry (w); St. Louis (Mo.) Battery, Capt. William E. Dawson; Clark (Mo.) Battery, Lieut. J. L. Faris. Brigade loss: k, 63; w, 305; m, 40 = 408. *Third Brigade*, Brig.-Gen. Martin E. Green: 7th Miss. Battalion, Lieut.-Col. J. S. Terral; 43d Miss., Col. W. H. Moore; 4th Mo., Col. A. MacFarlane; 6th Mo., Col. Eugene Erwin; 3d Mo. (dismounted cavalry), ——; Mo. Battery, Capt. Henry Guibor; Mo. Battery, Capt. John C. Landis. *Fourth Brigade*, Col. John D. Martin; 37th Ala., Col. James F. Dowdell (w); 36th Miss., Col. W. W. Witherspoon; 37th Miss., Col. Robert McLain; 38th Miss., Col. F. W. Adams. Brigade loss: k, 22; w, 95 = 117.

CAVALRY, Brig.-Gen. Frank C. Armstrong: Miss. regiment, Col. Wirt Adams; 2d Ark., Col. W. F. Slemons; 2d Mo., Col. Robert McCulloch; 1st Miss. Partisan Rangers, Col. W. C. Falkner. Loss not reported.

Total Confederate loss: killed, 85; wounded, 410; captured or missing, 40 = 535.

The battle was fought on the Confederate side by Little's division, and mainly by the brigades of Hébert and Martin, numbering 3179 men. But the effective strength of Price's entire command is estimated at about 14,000, including Dabney H. Maury's division, of three brigades, which, during the 19th, was held near Iuka in readiness to confront Ord.

THE BATTLE OF CORINTH.

BY WILLIAM S. ROSECRANS, MAJOR-GENERAL, U. S. V., BREVET MAJOR-GENERAL, U. S. A.

THE battle of Corinth, Miss., which is often confounded in public memory with our advance, under Halleck, from Pittsburg Landing in April and May, 1862, was fought on the 3d and 4th of October, of that year, between the combined forces of Generals Earl Van Dorn and Sterling Price of the Confederacy, and the Union divisions of Generals David S. Stanley, Charles S. Hamilton, Thomas A. Davies, and Thomas J. McKean, under myself as commander of the Third Division of the District of West Tennessee.

The Confederate evacuation of Corinth occurred on the 30th of May, General Beauregard withdrawing his army to Tupelo, where, June 27th, he was succeeded in the command by General Braxton Bragg. Halleck occupied Corinth on the day of its evacuation, and May 31st instructed General Buell, commanding the Army of the Ohio, to repair the Memphis and Charleston railway in the direction of Chattanooga—a movement to which, on June 11th, Halleck gave the objective of "Chattanooga and Cleveland and Dalton"; the ultimate purpose being to take possession of east Tennessee, in coöperation with General G. W. Morgan. To counteract these plans. General Bragg began, on June 27th, the transfer of a large portion of his army to Chattanooga by rail, via Mobile, and about the middle of August set out on the northward movement which terminated only within sight of the Ohio River. The Confederate forces in Mississippi were left under command of Generals Van Dorn and Price. About the middle of July General Halleck was called to Washington to discharge the duties of General-in-chief. He left the District of West Tennessee and the territory held in northern Mississippi under the command of General Grant. In August, by Halleck's orders, General Grant sent E. A. Paine's and Jeff. C. Davis's divisions across the Tennessee to strengthen Buell, who was moving northward through middle Tennessee, to meet Bragg. One of these divisions garrisoned Nashville while the other marched with Buell after Bragg into Kentucky.

In the early days of September, after the disaster of the "Second Bull Run," the friends of the Union watched with almost breathless anxiety the advance of Lee into Maryland, of Bragg into Kentucky, and the hurrying of the Army of the Potomac northward from Washington, to get between Lee and the cities of Washington, Baltimore, and Philadelphia. The suspense lest McClellan should not be in time to head off Lee—lest Buell should not arrive in time to prevent Bragg from taking Louisville or assaulting Cincinnati, was fearful.

At this time I was stationed at Corinth with the "Army of the Mississippi," having succeeded General Pope in that command on the 11th of June. We were in the District of West Tennessee, commanded by General Grant. Under the idea that I would reënforce Buell, General Sterling Price, who, during July and August, had been on the Mobile and Ohio railway near Guntown and Baldwyn, Miss., with 15,000 to 20,000 men, moved up to Iuka about the 12th of September, intending to follow me; and, as he reported, "finding that General Rosecrans had not crossed the Tennessee River," he "concluded to withdraw from Iuka toward my [his] old encampment." His "withdrawal" was after the hot battle of Iuka on September 19th, two days after the battle of Antietam which had caused Lee's "withdrawal" from Maryland.

During the month of August General Price had been conferring with General Van Dorn, commanding all the Confederate troops in Mississippi except Price's, to form a combined movement to expel the Union forces from northern Mississippi and western Tennessee, and to plant their flags on the banks of the Lower Ohio, while Bragg was to do the like on that river in Kentucky. General Earl Van Dorn, an able and enterprising commander, after disposing his forces to hold the Mississippi from Grand Gulf up toward Memphis, late in September, with Lovell's division, a little over 8000 men, came up to Ripley, Mississippi, where, on the 28th of September, he was joined by General Price, with Hébert's and Maury's divisions, numbering 13,863 effective infantry, artillery, and cavalry.

This concentration, following the precipitate "withdrawal" of Price from Iuka, portended mischief to the Union forces in west Tennessee, numbering some forty to fifty thousand effectives, scattered over the district occupying the vicinity of the Memphis and Charleston railway from Iuka to Memphis, a stretch of about a hundred and fifteen miles, and located at interior positions on the Ohio and Mississippi from Paducah to Columbus, and at Jackson, Bethel, and other places on the Mississippi Central and Mobile and Ohio railways.

The military features of west Tennessee and northern Mississippi will be readily comprehended by the reader who will examine a map of that region

PROVOST-MARSHAL'S OFFICE, CORINTH. FROM A WAR-TIME PHOTOGRAPH.

and notice: (1) That the Memphis and Charleston railway runs not far from the dividing lines between the States, with a southerly bend from Memphis eastward toward Corinth, whence it extends eastwardly through Iuka, crosses Bear River and follows the Tuscumbia Valley on the south side of that east and west reach of the Tennessee to Decatur. Thence the road crosses to the north side of this river and unites with the Nashville and Chattanooga road at Stevenson *en route* for Chattanooga. (2) That the Mobile and Ohio railway, from Columbus on the Mississippi, runs considerably east of south, passes through Jackson, Tennessee, Bethel, Corinth, Tupelo, and Baldwyn, Mississippi, and thence to Mobile, Alabama. (3) That the Mississippi Central, leaving the Mobile and Ohio at Jackson, Tennessee, runs nearly south, passing by Bolivar and Grand Junction, Tennessee, and Holly Springs, Grenada, etc., to Jackson, Mississippi. All this region of west Tennessee and the adjoining counties of Mississippi, although here and there dotted with clearings, farms, settlements, and little villages, is heavily wooded. Its surface consists of low, rolling, oak ridges of diluvial clays, with intervening crooked drainages traversing narrow, bushy, and sometimes swampy, bottoms. The streams are sluggish and not easily fordable, on account of their miry beds and steep, muddy, clay banks. Water in dry seasons is never abundant, and in many places is only reached by bore-wells of 100 to 300 feet in depth, whence it is hoisted by rope and pulley carrying water-buckets of galvanized iron pipes from 4 to 6 inches in diameter, and 4 to 5 feet long, with valves at the lower end. These matters are of controlling importance in moving and handling troops in that region. Men and animals need hard ground to move on, and must have drinking-water.

The strategic importance of Corinth, where the Mobile and Ohio crosses the Memphis and Charleston, ninety-three miles east of Memphis, results from its control of movements either way over these railways, and the fact that it is not far from Hamburg, Eastport, and Pittsburg Landing on the Tennessee River, to which points good freight steamers can ascend at the lowest stages of water. Corinth is mainly on low, flat ground, along the Mobile and Ohio railway, and flanked by low, rolling ridges, except the cleared patches, covered with oaks and undergrowth for miles in all directions. With few clearings, outside of those made by the Confederate troops in obtaining fuel during their wintering in 1861–2, the country around Corinth, in all directions, was densely wooded.

While General Halleck was advancing on Corinth, the Confederates had extended a line of light defensive works from the Memphis and Charleston road on the west, about two and a half miles from the town, all the way round by the north and east to the same railway east. When the Union forces took possession, General Halleck ordered a defensive line to be constructed about a mile and a half from the town, extending from the Memphis and Charleston railway on the west around southerly to cover the Union front in that direction. After the departure of General Buell's command toward Chattanooga this work was continued, although we had no forces to man it adequately, and it was too far away to afford protection to our stores at Corinth. During August I used to go over from my camp at Clear Creek to General Grant's

CORONA COLLEGE, CORINTH. FROM A WAR-TIME PHOTOGRAPH.

headquarters at Corinth, and after the usual greetings would ask: "How are you getting along with the line?" He would say: "Well, pretty slowly, but they are doing good work." I said to him: "General, the line isn't worth much to us, because it is too long. We cannot occupy it." He answered, "What would you do?" I said, "I would have made the depots outside of the town north of the Memphis and Charleston road between the town and the brick church, and would have inclosed them by field-works, running tracks in. Now, as the depot houses are at the cross-road, the best thing we can do is to run a line of light works around in the neighborhood of the college up on the knoll." So, one day, after dining with General Grant, he proposed that we go up together and take Captain Frederick E. Prime with us, and he gave orders to commence a line of breastworks that would include the college grounds. This was before the battle of Iuka. After Iuka I was ordered to command the district, and General Grant moved his headquarters to Jackson, Tennessee. Pursuant to this order, on the 26th of September I repaired to Corinth, where I found the only defensive works available consisted of the open batteries Robinett, Williams, Phillips, Tannrath, and Lothrop, established by Captain Prime on the College Hill line. I immediately ordered them to be connected by breastworks, and the front to the west and north to be covered by such an abatis as the remaining timber on the ground could furnish. I employed colored engineer troops organized into squads of twenty-five each, headed by a man detailed from the line or the quartermaster's department, and commanded by Captain William B. Gaw, a competent engineer. I also ordered an extension of the line of redoubts to cover the north front of the town, one of which, Battery Powell, was nearly completed before the stirring events of the attack. No rifle-pits were constructed between Powell and the central part covering the northwest front of the town, which was perfectly open north-east and south-east, with nothing but the distant, old Confederate works between it and the country.

To add to these embarrassments in preparing the place to resist a sudden attack, Grant, the general commanding, had retired fifty-eight

BREVET MAJOR-GENERAL THOMAS A. DAVIES.
FROM A PHOTOGRAPH.

miles north to Jackson, on the Mobile and Ohio railway, with all the knowledge of the country acquired during the four months in which his headquarters were at Corinth, and I, the new commander, could not find even the vestige of a map of the country to guide me in these defensive preparations.

During the 27th, 28th, 29th, and 30th of September, the breastworks were completed joining the lunettes from College Hill on the left. A thin abatis made from the scattering trees, which had been left standing along the west and north fronts, covered the line between Robinett and the Mobile and Ohio; thence to Battery Powell the line was mostly open and without rifle-pits.

To meet emergencies, Hamilton's and Stanley's divisions, which had been watching to the south and south-west from near Jacinto to Rienzi, were closed in toward Corinth within short call.

On the 28th I telegraphed to General Grant at Columbus, Kentucky, confirmation of my report of Price's movement to Ripley, adding that I should move Stanley's division to Rienzi, and thence to Kossuth, unless he had other views. Two days later I again telegraphed to General Grant that there were no signs of the enemy at Hatchie Crossing, and that my reason for proposing to put Stanley at or near Kossuth was that he would cover nearly all the Hatchie Crossing, as far as Pocahontas, except against heavy forces, and that Hamilton would then move at least one brigade, from Rienzi. I asked that a sharp lookout be kept in the direction of Bolivar. October 1st, I telegraphed General Grant that we were satisfied there was no enemy for three miles beyond Hatchie; also, that prisoners reported that General John C. Breckinridge, of Van Dorn's command, had gone to Kentucky with three Kentucky regiments, leaving his division under the command of General Albert Rust. The combined forces under Van Dorn and Price were reported to be encamped on the Pocahontas road, and to number forty thousand.↲

Amid the numberless rumors and uncertainties besetting me at Corinth during the five days between September 26th, when I assumed command, and October 1st, how gratifying would have been the knowledge of the following facts, taken from Van Dorn's report, dated Holly Springs, October 20th, 1862:

"Surveying the whole field of operations before me, ... the conclusion forced itself irresistibly upon my mind that the taking of Corinth was a condition precedent to the accomplishment of anything of importance in west Tennessee. To take Memphis would be to destroy an immense amount of property without any adequate military advantage, even admitting that it could be held without heavy guns against the enemy's gun and mortar boats. The line of fortifications around Bolivar is intersected by the Hatchie River, rendering it impossible to take the place by quick assault. . . . It was clear to my mind that if a successful attack could be made upon Corinth from the west and north-west, the forces there driven back on the Ten-

↲ In fact about 22,000, as stated by Van Dorn in the report quoted. And see "With Price East of the Mississippi," by Colonel Thomas L. Snead, p. 726.—EDITORS.

nessee and cut off, Bolivar and Jackson would easily fall, and then, upon the arrival of the exchanged prisoners of war, west Tennessee would soon be in our possession, and communication with General Bragg effected through middle Tennessee. . . .

"I determined to attempt Corinth. I had a reasonable hope of success. Field returns at Ripley showed my strength to be about 22,000 men. Rosecraus at Corinth had about 15,000, with about 8000 additional men at outposts, from 12 to 15 miles distant. I might surprise him and carry the place before these troops could be brought in. . . . It was necessary that this blow should be sudden and decisive. . . .

"The troops were in fine spirits, and the whole Army of West Tennessee seemed eager to emulate the armies of the Potomac and of Kentucky. No army ever marched to battle with prouder steps, more hopeful countenances, or with more courage than marched the Army of West-Tennessee out of Ripley on the morning of September 29th, on its way to Corinth."

But of all this I knew nothing. With only McKean's and Davies's divisions, not ten thousand men, at Corinth on the 26th of September, by October 1st I had gradually drawn in pretty close Stanley's and Hamilton's divisions. They had been kept watching to the south and south-west of Corinth.

Our forces when concentrated would make about 16,000 effective infantry and artillery for defense, with 2500 cavalry for outposts and reconnoitering.

On October 2d, while Van Dorn was at Pocahontas, General Hurlbut telegraphed the information, from an intelligent Union man of Grand Junction, that "Price, Van Dorn, and Villepigue were at Pocahontas, and the talk was that they would attack Bolivar." Evidence arriving thick and fast showed that the enemy was moving, but whether on Corinth or Bolivar, or whether, passing between, they would strike and capture Jackson, was not yet clear to any of us. I knew that the enemy intended a strong movement, and I thought they must have the impression that our defensive works at Corinth would be pretty formidable. I doubted if they would venture to bring their force against our command behind defensive works. I therefore said: The enemy may threaten us and strike across our line entirely, get on the road between us and Jackson and advance upon that place, the capture of which would compel us to get out of our lines; or he may come in by the road from Tupelo so as to interpose his force between us and Danville. But all the time I inclined to the belief that it would not be for his interest to do that. I thought that perhaps he would cross the Memphis and Charleston road and, going over to the Mobile and Ohio road, force us to move out and fight him in the open country.

October 2d, I sent out a cavalry detachment to reconnoiter in the direction of Pocahontas. They found the enemy's infantry coming close in, and that night some of our detachment were surprised, and their horses and a few of the men were captured. Those that escaped reported the enemy there in force. This was still consistent with the theory that the enemy wished to cross the Memphis and Charleston road, go north of us, strike the Mobile and Ohio road and manœuvre us out of our position.

To be prepared for whatever they might do, I sent Oliver's brigade of McKean's division out to Chewalla, ten miles north-west in Tennessee. On the morning of the 3d the enemy's advance came to Chewalla, and Oliver's brigade fell back fighting. I sent orders to the brigade commander to make

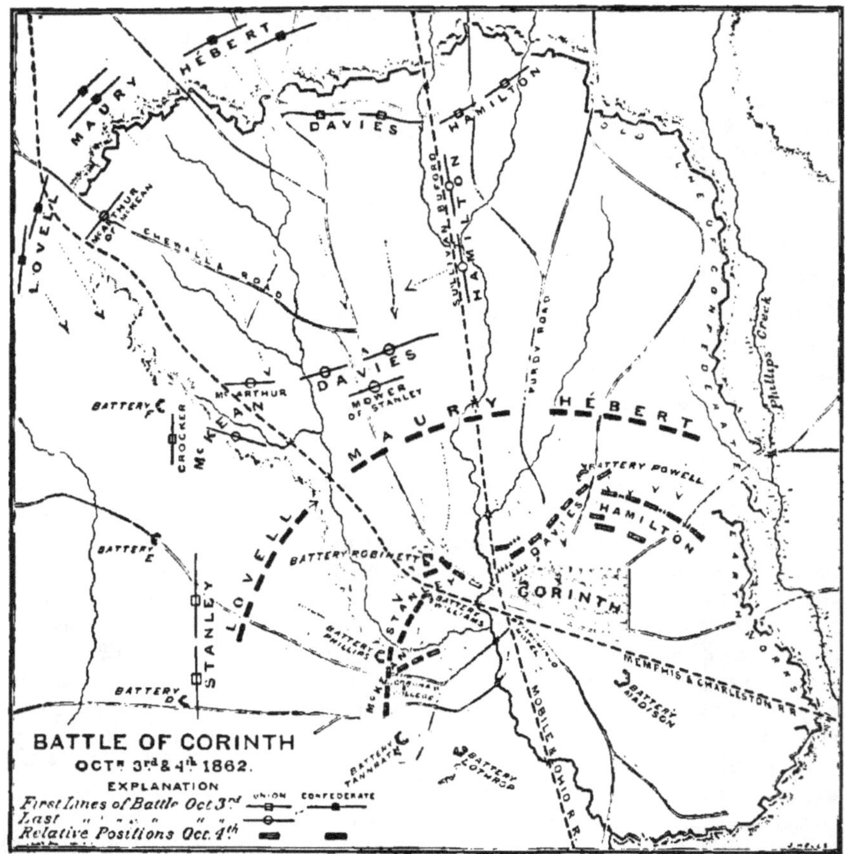

a stiff resistance, and see what effect it would have, still thinking that the attack was probably a mask for their movement for the north. I ordered Stanley to move in close to town near the middle line of works, called the "Halleck line," and to wait for further developments.

An order dated 1:30 A. M., October 3d, had set all the troops in motion. The impression that the enemy *might* find it better to strike a point on our line of communication and compel us to get out of our works to fight him or, if he should attempt Corinth, that he would do it, if possible, by the north and east, where the immediate vicinage was open and the place without defenses of any kind, governed these preliminary dispositions of my troops. The controlling idea was to prevent surprise, to test by adequate resistance any attacking force, and, finding it formidable, to receive it behind the inner line that had been preparing from College Hill around by Robinett.

To meet all probable contingencies, 9 o'clock on the morning of the 3d found my troops disposed as follows: Hamilton's division, about 3700 strong, on the

Purdy road north of the town, to meet any attempt from the north; Davies's division, 3204 strong, between the Memphis and Charleston and Mobile and Ohio railways, north-west of the town; McKean's division, 5315 strong, to the left of Davies's and in rear of the old Halleck line of batteries; and Stanley's division, 3500 strong, mainly in reserve on the extreme left, looking toward the Kossuth road.

Thus in front of those wooded western approaches, the Union troops, on the morning of October 3d, waited for what might happen, wholly ignorant of what Van Dorn was doing at Chewalla, ten miles away through thick forests. Of this General Van Dorn says:

"At daybreak on the 3d, the march was resumed . . . Lovell's division, in front, kept the road on the south side of the Memphis and Charleston railroad. Price, after marching on the same road about five miles, turned to the left, crossing the railroad, and formed line of battle in front of the outer line of intrenchments and about three miles from Corinth."

The intrenchments referred to were old Confederate works, which I had no idea of using except as a cover for a heavy skirmish line, to compel the enemy to develop his force, and to show whether he was making a demonstration to cover a movement of his force around to the north of Corinth. During the morning this skirmish work was well and gallantly accomplished by Davies's division, aided by McArthur with his brigade, and by Crocker, who moved up toward what the Confederate commander deemed the main line of the Union forces for the defense of Corinth. Upon this position moved three brigades of Lovell's division,—Villepigue's, Bowen's, and Rust's,—in line, with reserves in rear of each; Jackson's cavalry was on the right *en échelon*, the left flank on the Charleston railroad; Price's corps of two divisions was on the left of Lovell.

Thus the Confederate general proceeded, until, "at 10 o'clock, all the Union skirmishers were driven into the old intrenchments," and a part of the opposing forces were in line of battle confronting each other. There was a belt of fallen timber about four hundred yards wide between them, which must be crossed by the Confederate forces before they could drive this

VIEW ON THE RAILWAY, LOOKING NORTH-WEST FROM THE CORINTH DEPOT.
FROM A WAR-TIME PHOTOGRAPH.

stubborn force of Davies's, sent to compel the enemy to show his hand. Van Dorn says: "The attack was commenced on the right by Lovell's division and gradually extended to the left, and by 1:30 P. M. the whole line of outer works was carried, several pieces [two] of artillery being taken."

Finding that the resistance made by Oliver's little command on the Chewalla road early in the morning was not stiff enough to demonstrate the enemy's object, I had ordered McArthur's brigade from McKean's division to go to Oliver's assistance. It was done with a will. McArthur's Scotch blood rose, and the enemy being in fighting force, he fought him with the stubborn ferocity of an action on the main line of battle, instead of the resistance of a developing force.

The same remark applies to the fighting of Davies's division, and as they were pushed and called for reünforcements, orders were sent to fall back slowly and stubbornly. The Confederates, elated at securing these old outworks, pushed in toward our main line, in front of which the fighting in the afternoon was so hot that McKean was ordered to send further help over to the fighting troops, and Stanley to send "a brigade through the woods by the shortest cut" to help Davies, whose division covered itself with glory, having Brigadier-General Hackleman killed, Brigadier-General Oglesby desperately wounded, with nearly twenty-five per cent. of its strength put out of the fight. Watching intently every movement which would throw light on the enemy's intentions, soon after midday I decided that it was a main attack of the enemy. Hamilton's division had been sent up the railroad as far as the old Confederate works in the morning, and formed the right of our line. At 1 o'clock his division was still there watching against attack from the north. When the enemy prepared to make the attack on our first real line of battle, word was sent up to Hamilton to advise us if any Confederate force had gotten through, on the Mobile and Ohio road. At 3 o'clock when the fighting began and became very heavy, Stanley was ordered to move up from his position and succor McKean's and Davies's divisions that had been doing heavy fighting. Colonel Ducat, acting chief of staff, was sent to direct General Hamilton to file by fours to the left, and march down until the head of his column was opposite the right of Davies's, then to face his brigades south-westerly, and move down in that direction. The enemy's left did not much overpass the right of Davies, and but few troops were on the line of the old Confederate works. Hence Hamilton's movement, the brigades advancing *en échelon*, would enable the right of Buford's brigade to far out-lap the enemy's left, and pass toward the enemy's rear with little or no opposition, while the other brigade could press back the enemy's left, and by its simple advance drive him in and attack his rear.

Hamilton told Colonel Ducat that he wanted a more positive and definite order before he made the attack. Ducat explained the condition of the battle and urged an immediate movement, but was obliged to return to me for an order fitted to the situation. I sent the following:

"HEADQUARTERS, ARMY OF THE MISSISSIPPI, October 3d, 1862. BRIGADIER-GENERAL HAMILTON, Commanding Third Division: Rest your left on General Davies and swing round your

MEMPHIS AND CHARLESTON RAILROAD, LOOKING TOWARD CORINTH—REMAINS OF FORT WILLIAMS
ON THE RIGHT. FROM A PHOTOGRAPH TAKEN IN 1884.

right and attack the enemy on their left flank, reënforced on your right and center. Be careful not to get under Davies's guns. Keep your troops well in hand. Get well this way. Do not extend to your right too much. It looks as if it would be well to occupy the ridge where your skirmishers were when Colonel Ducat left, by artillery, well supported, but this may be farther to right than would be safe. Use your discretion. Opposite your center might be better now for your artillery. If you see your chance, attack fiercely.—W. S. ROSECRANS, Brigadier-General."

I added a sketch of the line on a bit of paper. The delay thus caused enabled the enemy to overpass the right of Davies so far that while Ducat was returning he was fired on by the enemy's skirmishers, who had reached open ground over the railway between Hamilton and Corinth. Two orderlies sent on the same errand afterward were killed on the way. Upon the receipt of these explanations Hamilton put his division in motion, but by sunset he only reached a point opposite the enemy's left; and after moving down a short distance Sullivan's brigade, facing to the west, crossed the narrow flats flanking the railway, went over into the thickets, and had a fierce fight with the enemy's left, creating a great commotion. Buford's brigade had started in too far to the west and had to rectify its position; so that Hamilton's division thus far had only given the enemy a terrific scare, and a sharp fight with one brigade. Had the movement been executed promptly after 3 o'clock, we should have crushed the enemy's right and rear. Hamilton's excuse that he could not understand the order shows that even in the rush of battle it may be necessary to put orders in writing, or to have subordinate commanders who instinctively know or are anxious to seek the key of the battle and hasten to its roar. ⚓

At nightfall of the 3d it was evident that, unless the enemy should withdraw, he was where I wished him to be—between the two railroad lines

⚓ See General Charles S. Hamilton's statements, p. 758.— EDITORS.

and to the south of them—for the inevitable contest of the morrow. Van Dorn says:

"I had been in hopes that one day's operations would end the contest and decide who should be the victors on this bloody field; but a ten miles' march over a parched country on dusty roads without water, getting into line of battle in forests with undergrowth, and the more than equal activity and determined courage displayed by the enemy, commanded by one of the ablest generals of the United States army, who threw all possible obstacles in our way that an active mind could suggest, prolonged the battle until I saw with regret the sun sink behind the horizon as the last shot of our sharp-shooters followed the retreating foe into their innermost lines. One hour more of daylight and victory would have soothed our grief for the loss of the gallant dead who sleep on that lost but not dishonored field. The army slept on its arms within six hundred yards of Corinth, victorious so far."

Alas, how uncertain are our best conclusions! General Van Dorn, in his subsequent report as above, bewails the lack of one hour of daylight at the close of October 3d, 1862. I bewailed that lack of daylight, which would have brought Hamilton's fresh and gallant division on the Confederate left and rear. That hour of daylight was not to be had; and while the regretful Confederate general lay down in his bivouac, I assembled my four division commanders, McKean, Davies, Stanley, and Hamilton, at my head-quarters and arranged the dispositions for the fight of the next day. Mc-Kean's division was to hold the left, the chief point being College Hill, keeping his troops well under cover. Stanley was to support the line on either side of Battery Robinett, a little three-gun redan with a ditch five feet deep. Davies was to extend from

BRIGADIER-GENERAL PLEASANT A. HACKLEMAN, KILLED AT CORINTH. FROM A STEEL ENGRAVING.

Stanley's right north-easterly across the flat to Battery Powell, a similar redan on the ridge east of the Purdy road. Hamilton was to be on Davies's right with a brigade, and the rest in reserve on the common east of the low ridge and out of sight from the west. Colonel J. K. Mizner with his cavalry was to watch and guard our flanks and rear from the enemy, and well and effectively did his four gallant regiments perform that duty. As the troops had been on the move since the night of October 2d, and had fought all day of the 3d (which was so excessively hot that we were obliged to send water around in wagons), it became my duty to visit their lines and see that the weary troops were surely in position.

I returned to my tent at three o'clock in the morning of October 4th, after having seen everything accomplished and the new line in order. It was about a mile in extent and close to the edge of the north side of the town. About 4 o'clock I lay down. At half-past 4 the enemy opened with a six-gun battery. Our batteries, replying, soon silenced it, but I had no time for breakfast. The troops got very little. They had not been allowed to build fires during the night, and were too tired to intrench.

The morning opened clear and soon grew to be hot. It must have been ninety-four degrees in the shade. The enemy began to extend his infantry line across the north of the town. I visited the lines and gave orders to our skirmishers to fall back the moment it was seen that the enemy was developing a line of battle. About 8 o'clock his left, having crossed the Mobile and Ohio railroad, got into position behind a spur of table land, to reach which they had moved by the flank for about half a mile. When they began to advance in line of battle they were not over three hundred yards distant.

I told McKean on the left to be very watchful of his front lest the enemy should turn his left, and directed General Stanley to hold the reserve of his command ready either to help north of the town or to aid McKean if required. I visited Battery Robinett and directed the chief of artillery, Colonel Lothrop, to see to the reserve artillery, some batteries of which were parked in the public square of the town; then the line of Davies's division, which was in nearly open ground, with a few logs, here and there, for breastworks, and then on his extreme right Sweeny's brigade, which had no cover save a slight ridge, on the south-west slope of which, near the crest, the men were lying down. Riding along this line, I observed the Confederate forces emerging from the woods west of the railroad and crossing the open ground toward the Purdy road. Our troops lying on the ground could see the flags of the enemy and the glint of the sunlight on their bayonets. It was about 9 o'clock in the morning. The air was still and fiercely hot. Van Dorn says the Confederate preparations for the morning were:

"That Hébert, on the left, should mask part of his own division on the left, placing Cabell's brigade *en échelon* on the left — Cabell having been detached from Maury's division for that purpose, move Armstrong's cavalry brigade across the Mobile and Ohio road, and, if possible, to get some of his artillery in position across the road. In this order of battle, Hébert was to attack, swinging his left flank toward Corinth, and advance down the Purdy ridge. On the right, Lovell, with two brigades in line of battle and one in reserve, with Jackson's cavalry to the right, was ordered to await the attack on his left, feeling his way with sharp-shooters until Hébert was heavily engaged with the enemy. Maury was to move at the same time quickly to the front directly at Corinth; Jackson to burn the railroad bridge over the Tuscumbia during the night."

The left of General Van Dorn's attack was to have begun earlier, but the accident of Hébert's sickness prevented. The Confederates, from behind a spur of the Purdy ridge, advanced splendidly to the attack. The unfavorable line occupied by Davies's division made the resistance on that front inadequate. The troops gave way; the enemy pursued; but the cross-fire from the Union batteries on our right soon thinned their ranks. Their front line was broken, and the heads of their columns melted away. Some of the enemy's scattered line got into the edge of the town; a few into the reserve artillery, which led to the impression that they had captured forty pieces of artillery. But they were soon driven out by Stanley's reserve, and fled, taking nothing away.

At this time, while going to order Hamilton's division into action on the enemy's left, I saw the L-shaped porch of a large cottage packed full of

THE DEFENSE OF BATTERY ROBINETT. FROM A WAR-TIME SKETCH.

Captain George A. Williams, 1st U. S. Infantry, who commanded the siege artillery, says in his report:

"About 9:30 or 10 A. M. the enemy were observed in the woods north of the town forming in line, and they soon made their appearance, charging toward the town. As soon as our troops were out of the line of fire of my battery, we opened upon them with two 30-pounder Parrott guns and one 8-inch howitzer, which enfiladed their line aided by Maurice's battery and one gun on the right of Battery Robinett, which bore on that part of the town, and continued our fire until the enemy were repulsed and had regained the wood.

"During the time the enemy were being repulsed from the town my attention was drawn to the left side of the battery by the firing from Battery Robinett, where I saw a column advancing to storm it. After advancing a short distance they were repulsed, but immediately re-formed, and, storming the work, gained the ditch, but were repulsed. During this charge eight of the enemy, having placed a handkerchief on a bayonet and calling to the men in the battery not to shoot them, surrendered, and were allowed to come into the fort.

"They then re-formed, and, re-storming, carried the ditch and the outside of the work, the supports having fallen a short distance to the rear in slight disorder. The men of the 1st U. S. Infantry, after having been driven from their guns (they manned the siege guns), resorted to their muskets, and were firing from the inside of the embrasures at the enemy on the outside, a distance of about ten feet intervening; but the rebels having gained the top of the work, our men fell back into the angle of the fort, as they had been directed to do in such an emergency. Two shells were thrown from Battery Williams into Battery Robinett, one bursting on the top of it and the other near the right edge. In the meanwhile the 11th Missouri Volunteers (in reserve) changed front, and, aided by the 43d and 63d Ohio Volunteers with the 27th Ohio Volunteers on their right, gallantly stormed up to the right and left of the battery, driving the enemy before them."— EDITORS.

Confederates. I ordered Lieutenant Lorenzo D. Immell, with two field-pieces, to give them grape and canister. After one round, only the dead and dying were left on the porch. Reaching Hamilton's division I ordered him to send Sullivan's brigade forward. It moved in line of battle in open ground a little to the left of Battery Powell. Before its splendid advance the scattered enemy, who were endeavoring to form a line of battle, about 1 P. M. gave way and went back into the woods, from which they never again advanced.

Meanwhile there had been terrific fighting at Battery Robinett. The roar of artillery and musketry for two or three hours was incessant. Clouds of smoke filled the air and obscured the sun. I witnessed the first charge of the enemy on this part of the line before I went over to Hamilton. The first repulse I did not see because the contestants were clouded in smoke. It was an assault in column. There were three or four assaulting columns of regiments, probably a hundred yards apart. The enemy's left-hand column had tried to make its way down into the low ground to the right of Robinett, but did not make much progress. The other two assaulting columns fared better, because they were on the ridge where the fallen timber was scarcer. I ordered the 27th Ohio and 11th Missouri to kneel in rear of the right of Robinett, so as to get out of range of the enemy's fire, and the moment he had exhausted himself to charge with the bayonet [see p. 759]. The third assault was made just as I was seeing Sullivan into the fight. I saw the enemy come upon the ridge while Battery Robinett was belching its fire at them. After the charge had failed I saw the 27th Ohio and the 11th Missouri chasing them with bayonets.

The head of the enemy's main column reached within a few feet of Battery Robinett, and Colonel Rogers, who was leading it, colors in hand, dismounted, planted a flag-staff on the bank of the ditch, and fell there, shot by one of our drummer-boys, who, with a pistol, was helping to defend Robinett. I was told that Colonel Rogers was the fifth standard-bearer who had fallen in that last desperate charge. It was about as good fighting on the part of the Confederates as I ever saw. The columns were plowed through and through by our shot, but they steadily closed up and moved forward until they were forced back.

Just after this last assault I heard for the first time the word "ranch." Passing over the field on our left, among the dead and dying, I saw leaning against the root of a tree a wounded lieutenant of an Arkansas regiment who had been shot through the foot. As I offered him some water he said, "Thank you, General; one of your men just gave me some." I said,

THE GROUND IN FRONT OF BATTERY ROBINETT. FROM A PHOTOGRAPH TAKEN AFTER THE BATTLE.

GRAVE OF COLONEL WILLIAM P. ROGERS, LOOKING TOWARD CORINTH FROM THE EMBANKMENT
OF FORT ROBINETT. FROM A PHOTOGRAPH TAKEN IN 1884.

"Whose troops are you?" He replied, "Cabell's." I said, "It was pretty hot fighting here." He answered, "Yes, General, you licked us good, *but we gave you the best we had in the ranch.*"

Before the enemy's first assault on Robinett, I inspected the woods toward our left where I knew Lovell's division to be. I said to Colonel Joseph A. Mower, afterward commander of the Seventeenth Army Corps, and familiarly known as "Fighting Joe Mower": "Colonel, take the men now on the skirmish line, and find out what Lovell is doing." He replied, "Very well, General." As he was turning away I added, "Feel them, but don't get into their fingers." He answered significantly: "*I'll feel them!*" Before I left my position Mower had entered the woods, and soon I heard a tremendous crash of musketry in that direction. His skirmishers fell back into the fallen timber, and the adjutant reported to me: "General, I think the enemy have captured Colonel Mower; I think he is killed." Five hours later when we captured the enemy's field-hospitals, we found that Colonel Mower had been shot in the back of the neck and taken prisoner. Expressing my joy at his safety, he showed that he knew he had been unjustly reported to me the day before as intoxicated, by saying: "Yes, General, but if they had reported me for being 'shot in the neck' to-day instead of yesterday, it would have been correct."

About 2 o'clock we found that the enemy did not intend to make another attack. Faint from exhaustion I sought the shade of a tree, from which point I saw three bursts of smoke and said to my staff, "They have blown up some ammunition wagons, and are going to retreat. We must push them." I was all the more certain of this, because, having failed, a good commander like Van Dorn would use the utmost dispatch in putting the forests between him and his pursuing foe, as well as to escape the dangers to him which might arise from troops coming from Bolivar.

Even at this distant time memory lingers on the numerous incidents of distinguished bravery displayed by officers and men who fought splendidly on the first day, when we did not know what the enemy was going to do. Staff as well as line officers distinguished themselves while in action.

The first day my presence was required on the main line, and the fighting in front of that did not so much come under my eye, but on the second day I was everywhere on the line of battle. Temple Clark of my staff was shot through the breast. My *sabre-tasche* strap was cut by a bullet, and my gloves were stained with the blood of a staff-officer wounded at my side. An alarm spread that I was killed, but it was soon stopped by my appearance on the field.

Satisfied that the enemy was retreating, I ordered Sullivan's command to push him with a heavy skirmish line, and to keep constantly feeling them. I rode along the lines of the commands, told them that, having been moving and fighting for three days and two nights, I knew they required rest, but that they could not rest longer than was absolutely

COLONEL WILLIAM P. ROGERS, C. S. A., KILLED IN LEADING THE ASSAULT UPON FORT ROBINETT. FROM A PHOTOGRAPH.

necessary. I directed them to proceed to their camps, provide five days' rations, take some needed rest, and be ready early next morning for the pursuit.

General McPherson, sent from Jackson with five good regiments to help us, arrived and bivouacked in the public square a little before sunset. Our pursuit of the enemy was immediate and vigorous, but the darkness of the night and the roughness of the country, covered with woods and thickets, made movement impracticable by night and slow and difficult by day. General McPherson's brigade of fresh troops with a battery was ordered to start at daylight and follow the enemy over the Chewalla road, and Stanley's and Davies's divisions to support him. McArthur, with all of McKean's division except Crocker's brigade, and with a good battery and a battalion of cavalry, took the route south of the railroad toward Pocahontas; McKean followed on this route with the rest of his division and Ingersoll's cavalry; Hamilton followed McKean with his entire force.

The enemy took the road to Davis's Bridge on the Hatchie, by way of Pocahontas. Fortunately General Hurlbut, finding that he was not going to be attacked at Bolivar, had been looking in our direction with a view of succoring us, and now met the enemy at that point [Hatchie Bridge]. General Ord, arriving there from Jackson, Tennessee, assumed command and drove back

the head of the enemy's column.   This was a critical time for the Confederate forces; but the reader will note that a retreating force, knowing where it has to go and having to look for nothing except an attack on its rear, always moves with more freedom than a pursuing force.   This is especially so where the country is covered with woods and thickets, and the roads are narrow. Advancing forces always have to feel their way for fear of being ambushed.

The speed made by our forces from Corinth during the 5th was not to my liking, but with such a commander as McPherson in the advance, I could not doubt that it was all that was possible.   On the 6th better progress was made. From Jonesborough, on October 7th, I telegraphed General Grant:

"Do not, I entreat you, call Hurlbut back; let him send away his wounded.   It surely is easier to move the sick and wounded than to remove both.   I propose to push the enemy, so that we need but the most trifling guards behind us.   Our advance is beyond Ruckersville. Hamilton will seize the Hatchie crossing on the Ripley road to-night.   A very intelligent, honest young Irishman, an ambulance driver, deserted from the rebels, says that they wished to go together to railroad near Tupelo, where they will meet the nine thousand exchanged prisoners, but he says they are much scattered and demoralized.   They have much artillery."

From the same place, at midnight, after learning from the front that McPherson was in Ripley, I telegraphed General Grant as follows:

"GENERAL: Yours 8:30 P. M. received.   Our troops occupy Ripley.   I most deeply dissent from your views as to the manner of pursuing.   We have defeated, routed, and demoralized the army which holds the Lower Mississippi Valley.   We have the two railroads leading down toward the Gulf through the most productive parts of the State, into which we can now pursue them with safety.   The effect of our return to old position will be to pen them up in the only corn country they have west of Alabama, including the Tuscumbia Valley, and to permit them to recruit their forces, advance and occupy their old ground, reducing us to the occupation of a defensive position, barren and worthless, with a long front, over which they can harass us until bad weather prevents an effectual advance except on the railroads, when time, fortifications, and rolling stock will again render them superior to us. Our force, including what you have with Hurlbut, will garrison Corinth and Jackson, and enables us to push them. Our advance will cover even Holly Springs, which would be ours when we want it. All that is needful is to continue pursuing and whip them. We have whipped, and should now push them to the wall and capture all the rolling stock of their railroads. Bragg's army alone, west of the Alabama River, and occupying Mobile, could repair the damage we have it in our power to do them. If, after considering these matters, you still consider the order for my return to Corinth expedient, I will obey it and abandon the chief fruits of a victory, but, I beseech you, bend everything to push them while they are broken and hungry, weary and ill-supplied. Draw everything possible from Memphis to help move on Holly Springs, and let us concentrate. Appeal to the governors of the States to rush down some twenty or thirty new regiments to hold our rear, and we can make a triumph of our start."

As it was, Grant telegraphed to Halleck at 9 A. M. the next day, October 8th:

" Rosecrans has followed rebels to Ripley. Troops from Bolivar will

QUARTERS AT CORINTH OCCUPIED BY THE 52D ILLINOIS VOLUNTEERS DURING THE WINTER OF 1862–3.
FROM A WAR-TIME PHOTOGRAPH.

occupy Grand Junction to-morrow, with reënforcements rapidly sent on from the new levies. I can take everything on the Mississippi Central road. I ordered Rosecrans back last night, but he was so averse to returning that I have directed him to remain still until you can be heard from."

Again on the same day, October 8th, Grant telegraphed to Halleck:

" Before telegraphing you this morning for reënforcements to follow up our victories I ordered General Rosecrans to return. He showed such reluctance that I consented to allow him to remain until you could be heard from if further reënforcements could be had. On reflection I deem it idle to pursue further without more preparation, and have for the third time ordered his return."

This was early in October. The weather was cool, and the roads in prime order. The country along the Mississippi Central to Grenada, and especially below that place, was a corn country—a rich farming country—and the corn was ripe. If Grant had not stopped us, we could have gone to Vicksburg. My judgment was to go on, and with the help suggested we could have done so. Under the pressure of a victorious force the enemy were experiencing all the weakening effects of a retreating army, whose means of supplies and munitions are always difficult to keep in order. We had Sherman at Memphis with two divisions, and we had Hurlbut at Bolivar with one division and John A. Logan at Jackson, Tennessee, with six regiments. With these there was nothing to save Mississippi from our grasp. We were about six days' march from Vicksburg, and Grant could have put his force through to it with my column as the center one of pursuit. Confederate officers told me afterward that they never were so scared in their lives as they were after the defeat before Corinth.

I have thus given the facts of the fight at Corinth, the immediate pursuit, the causes of the return, and, as well, the differing views of the Federal commanders in regard to the situation. Let the judgments of the future be formed upon the words of impartial history.

In a general order announcing the results of the battle to my command, I stated that we killed and buried 1423 officers and men of the enemy, including some of their most distinguished officers. Their wounded at the usual rate would exceed 5000. We took 2268 prisoners, among whom were 137 field-officers, captains, and subalterns.⸸ We captured 3300 stand of small-arms, 14 stand of colors, 2 pieces of artillery, and a large quantity of equipments. We pursued his retreating column forty miles with all arms, and with cavalry sixty miles. Our loss was 355 killed, 1841 wounded, 324 captured or missing.

In closing his report General Van Dorn said:

"A hand-to-hand contest was being enacted in the very yard of General Rosecrans's headquarters and in the streets of the town. The heavy guns were silenced, and all seemed to be about ended when a heavy fire from fresh troops from Iuka, Burnsville, and Rienzi, who had succeeded in reaching Corinth, poured into our thinned ranks. Exhausted from loss of sleep, wearied from hard marching and fighting, companies and regiments without officers, our troops — let no one censure them — gave way. The day was lost. . . . The attempt at Corinth has failed, and in consequence I am condemned and have been superseded in my command. In my zeal for my country I may have ventured too far without adequate means, and I bow to the opinion of the people whom I serve. Yet I feel that if the spirits of the gallant dead, who now lie beneath the batteries of Corinth, see and judge the motives of men, they do not rebuke me, for there is no sting in my conscience, nor does retrospection admonish me of error or of a reckless disregard of their valued lives." ⸸

And General Price says in his report:

"The history of this war contains no bloodier page, perhaps, than that which will record this fiercely contested battle. The strongest expressions fall short of my admiration of the gallant conduct of the officers and men under my command. Words cannot add luster to the fame they have acquired through deeds of noble daring which, living through future time, will shed about every man, officer and soldier, who stood to his arms through this struggle, a halo of glory as imperishable as it is brilliant. They have won to their sisters and daughters the dis-

---

⸸ The official Confederate reports make their loss 505 killed, 2150 wounded, 2183 missing. — Editors.

⸸ The charges against General Van Dorn (of neglect of duty and of cruel and improper treatment of his officers and soldiers) were investigated by a Court of Inquiry, which unanimously voted them disproved. — Editors.

tinguished honor, set before them by a general of their love and admiration upon the event of an impending battle upon the same field, of the proud exclamation, 'My brother, father, was at the great battle of Corinth.'"\

\ Reference is doubtless made here to the address of General Albert Sidney Johnston to the soldiers of the Army of the Mississippi on the eve of the battle of Shiloh, April 3d, 1862.— EDITORS.

HAMILTON'S DIVISION AT CORINTH.

BY CHARLES S. HAMILTON, MAJOR-GENERAL, U. S. V.

THE following order, issued about 9 A. M. on the first day of the battle of Corinth, fixed the position of my division:

"CORINTH, Oct. 3d, 1862. BRIGADIER-GENERAL HAMILTON, Commanding Third Division. GENERAL: The general commanding directs that you cover with your division the Purdy road, from the swamp on the railroad to where the road runs through the rebel works. By command of MAJOR-GENERAL ROSECRANS.— GODDARD, A. A. A. General.

"P. S. You may perhaps have to move farther out, as Davies does not find good ground until he gets near the old rebel works, and he proposes to swing his right still farther around. By order of MAJOR-GENERAL ROSECRANS.— GODDARD, A. A. A. General."

Again at 2 P. M. the same day the following circular was sent to both Hamilton and Davies:

"For fear of a misunderstanding in relation to my orders, I wish it distinctly understood that the extreme position is not to be taken until driven to it. By order of MAJOR-GENERAL ROSECRANS.— S. C. LYFORD, Acting Aide-de-Camp."

The extreme position mentioned was not understood by either Davies or myself, but probably meant an advanced position. But how we could be driven to it by an enemy in our front is difficult to understand. Just following the circular, this order was received by me:

"The general commanding desires me to say to you not to be in a hurry to show yourself. Keep well covered and conceal your strength. The enemy will doubtless feel your position, but do not allow this to hasten your movements.— S. C. LYFORD, Acting Aide-de-Camp."

About 3:30 P. M. the following was received:

"GENERAL HAMILTON: Davies, it appears, has fallen behind the works, his left being pressed in. If this movement continues until he gets well drawn in, you will make a flank movement, if your front is not attacked, falling to the left of Davies when the enemy gets sufficiently well in so as to have full sweep, holding a couple of regiments looking well to the Purdy road. Examine and reconnoiter the ground for making this movement. By order of MAJOR-GENERAL ROSECRANS,— H. G. KENNETT, Colonel and Chief of Staff."

On the back of this order I indorsed the following:

"Respectfully returned. I cannot understand it.— C. S. HAMILTON, Brigadier-General."

Rosecrans returned it to me indorsed as follows:

"Ducat has been sent to explain it. W. S. ROSECRANS, Major-General.— S. C. LYFORD, Acting Aide-de-Camp."

Now bearing in mind that Davies's division was to the left and in front of mine, if this order meant anything it was that my division should abandon its position on the right of the army entirely, and pass either to the rear or front of Davies in order to reach the place indicated, and would therefore have destroyed every possible chance of attacking the enemy in the flank, and would also have left the right of Davies's exposed, and the way into Corinth open to the enemy. Now this order, which is the one Rosecrans claims as his order to attack the enemy, was given as follows in his article on this engagement, in "The Century" for October, 1886 [see p. 746]:

"Colonel Ducat, acting chief-of-staff, was sent with an order to General Hamilton, to file by fours to the left and march down until the head of his column was opposite Davies's right. He was ordered then to face his brigade west south-west and to move down in a south-westerly direction."

The order, as I have given it, is an exact copy of the original now in my possession, and General Rosecrans's statement of it in "The Century" was made from a defective memory after twenty-three years had elapsed.

At 5 P. M. I received the following order:

"HEADQUARTERS, ARMY OF THE MISSISSIPPI, October 3d, 1862. GENERAL HAMILTON, Commanding Third Division: Rest your left on General Davies, and swing around your right and attack the enemy on their left, reënforced on your right and center. Be careful not to get under Davies's guns. Keep your troops well in hand. Get well this way. Don't extend your right too much. It looks as if it would be well to occupy the ridge where your skirmishers were when Colonel Ducat left, by artillery well supported, but this may be farther to right than would be safe. Use your discretion. Opposite your center might be better now for your artillery. If you see your chance attack fiercely.— W. S. ROSECRANS, Brigadier-General."

As a simple order to attack the enemy in flank could have reached me by courier from General Rosecrans, any time after 2 P. M., in 15 minutes, the verbosity of the above is apparent. I construed it as an order for attack, and at once proceeded to carry it out. Sullivan's brigade of my division had been ordered some time previously to move toward the enemy's left in preparation for an attack, and Buford's brigade was now ordered down on Sullivan's right to support him.

The brigades were some distance apart, and having been concealed in the woods had not been discovered by the enemy. The moment that Buford began to move a detached force of the enemy was seen some distance in his front. They opened on him with a single piece of artillery, and he, taking it for granted he was beset by the enemy in force, moved to his front to drive them out of the way. In thus moving he went almost in an opposite direction to the one necessary to support Sullivan. I sent an officer with a positive order to change his course. His reply was, "Tell General Hamilton, the enemy is in my front and I am going to fight him." Meantime his brigade had been moving toward what he supposed to be the enemy, and was a half mile from Sullivan. I sent a second order to change his course instantly, and move to Sullivan's support. This order he obeyed, first detaching the 4th Minnesota regiment, under Colonel J. B. Sanborn, to attack the enemy. He then moved down to the position indicated, but, meantime, a precious hour had been lost, the sun had gone down, and the attack having to be made through a forest of dense undergrowth, it was too late to execute the flank movement with any chance of success. The enemy's fire on Davies's division had ceased. Waiting a few moments in expectation of its renewal, night closed down upon us, and the battle for the day was over.

General Rosecrans first intended the troops to pass the night in the position now held, as shown by the following order, received about 7:30 P. M.:

"HEADQUARTERS, ARMY OF THE MISSISSIPPI, October 3d, 1862, 7 P. M. GENERAL HAMILTON: Throw out promptly vedettes, grand guards, scouts, and a line of skirmishers in rear of abatis on your front and flanks. Pick up all the prisoners you can. Get all the information possible, which report promptly and often to these headquarters. Furnish brigade commanders with a copy of this order as soon as possible. During the night and coming daylight, much will depend on the vigilance of outposts and guards. Our cavalry is on the southwest front toward Bridge Creek. By order of MAJOR-GENERAL ROSECRANS.— ARTHUR C. DUCAT, Lieutenant-Colonel, Chief of Grand Guards and Outposts."

Between 8 and 9 P. M. a staff-officer brought me the following order:

"Place your batteries on the Purdy road at 10 P. M. and play them two hours in a north-west direction with shot and shell, where the enemy is massed, and at midnight attack them with your whole division with the bayonet. — W. S. ROSECRANS, Major-General." ☆

I was astounded, and turning to the officer said: "Tell General Rosecrans I cannot execute that order till I see him personally, and explain to him the difficulties in the way and what the result must be if carried out." An hour passed, when the officer who brought the order returned, bringing General Rosecrans with him. General John B. Sanborn, of Minnesota, and others heard the following conversation which then took place:

General ROSECRANS [savagely]: "General Hamilton, what do you mean by disobeying my order to attack the enemy?"

General HAMILTON: "General Rosecrans, I am ready to execute your order, but there is too much at stake here to be risked by a night attack. The ground between us and the enemy is a dense forest, with a thick undergrowth in which the troops cannot move ten minutes without breaking their formation. It is dark in the forest— too dark to distinguish friend from foe. If my division is once disorganized it cannot be re-formed until daylight comes. We are ignorant of the enemy's exact position and must feel around in the darkness of the forest to find him. Let me say that your lines are too long. My division is not in supporting distance of any other division, and when the town is assaulted in the morning your army will be cut in two and destroyed. Davies's division has withdrawn so far that the skirmishers of the enemy occupy his last position in line. Your position is a false one. The troops should be withdrawn and placed within the earth-works of the town. Place them within the fortifications and in support of each other. It is a strong position and insures a victory. But as we are now you cannot make a strong defense, and the battle which is certain for the morning will surely be a defeat for us."

General ROSECRANS [after a few moments of reflection without reply]: "Hamilton, you are right. Place your division as you suggest, and the others shall be placed accordingly."

The change of my division was accomplished by 3 A. M., and the troops sought their rest on the morrow's battle-field, full of hope and sure of victory. Thus closed the operations of the day. And thus was brought about the change that led to victory on the following day, but from that time to this no public writing or utterance on the part of General Rosecrans has ever acknowledged the services so rendered.

☆ The "Official Records" do not contain this order or any allusion to the subject of it.— EDITORS.

BY DAVID S. STANLEY, MAJOR-GENERAL, U. S. V.

AN assertion made by General Rosecrans in "The Century" magazine for October, 1886, is misleading. The statement [see p. 751] is as follows:

"I ordered the 27th Ohio and the 11th Missouri to kneel in rear of the right of Robinett so as to get out of the range of the enemy's fire, and the moment he had exhausted himself to charge with the bayonet."

The lapse of a quarter of a century has certainly made the memory of the worthy general treacherous, for at the time that his memory causes him to say that he gave this order, I saw him a quarter of a mile away trying to rally Davies's troops to resist the advancing forces of the Confederates, and I consider it impossible for the two regiments to have heard any order from him above the rifle's rattle and the cannon's roar at such a distance. I cannot say what General Rosecrans may have said to these regiments about using the bayonet when visiting my lines that morning before the occurrence mentioned, but I do know that I posted them myself, and that Colonel J. W. Fuller, 27th Ohio, commander of the brigade during the heat of the battle, gave the order for his own and the 11th Missouri regiments to charge with the bayonet.

SAN ANTONIO, TEXAS, January 19th, 1884.

THE OPPOSING FORCES AT CORINTH, MISS.

October 3d and 4th, 1862.

The composition, losses, and strength of each army as here stated give the gist of all the data obtainable in the Official Records. K stands for killed; w for wounded; m w for mortally wounded; m for captured or missing; c for captured.

THE UNION FORCES.

ARMY OF THE MISSISSIPPI.—Major-General William S. Rosecrans.

SECOND DIVISION, Brig.-Gen. David S. Stanley. Staff loss: w, 1.

First Brigade, Col. John W. Fuller: 27th Ohio, Maj. Zephaniah S. Spaulding; 39th Ohio, Col. A. W. Gilbert, Lieut.-Col. Edward F. Noyes; 43d Ohio, Col. J. L. Kirby Smith (m w), Lieut.-Col. Wager Swayne; 63d Ohio, Col. John W. Sprague; Jenks's Co., Ill. Cav., Capt. Albert Jenks; 3d Mich. Battery, Lieut. Carl A. Lamberg; 8th Wis. Battery (section), Lieut. John D. McLean; F, 2d U. S. Art'y, Capt. Thomas D. Maurice. Brigade loss: k, 55; w, 255; m, 11 = 321. *Second Brigade*, Col. Joseph A. Mower (w): 26th Ill., Maj. Robert A. Gillmore; 47th Ill., Col. William A. Thrush (k), Capt. Harman Andrews (w), Capt. Samuel R. Baker; 5th Minn., Col. Lucius F. Hubbard; 11th Mo., Maj. Andrew J. Weber; 8th Wis., Lieut.-Col. George W. Robbins (w), Maj. John W. Jefferson (w), Capt. William B. Britton; 2d Iowa Battery, Capt. Nelson T. Spoor. Brigade loss: k, 48; w, 248; m, 26 = 322.

THIRD DIVISION, Brig.-Gen. Charles S. Hamilton.

Escort: C, 5th Mo. Cavalry.

First Brigade, Brig.-Gen. Napoleon B. Buford: 48th Ind., Lieut. Col. De Witt C. Rugg (w), Lieut. James W. Archer; 59th Ind., Col. Jesse I. Alexander; 5th Iowa, Col. Charles L. Matthies; 4th Minn., Col. John B. Sanborn; 26th Mo., Lieut.-Col. John H. Holman (w); M, 1st Mo. Art'y, Lieut. Junius W. MacMurray; 11th Ohio Battery, Lieut. Henry M. Neil. Brigade loss: k, 7; w, 48 = 55. *Second Brigade*, Brig.-Gen. Jeremiah C. Sullivan, Col. Samuel A. Holmes: 56th Ill., Lieut.-Col. Green B. Raum; 10th Iowa, Maj. Nathaniel McCalla; 17th Iowa, Maj. Jabez Banbury; 10th Mo., Col. Samuel A. Holmes, Maj. Leonidas Horney; E, 24th Mo., Capt. Lafayette M. Rice; 80th Ohio, Maj. Richard Lanning (k), Capt. David Skeels; 6th Wis. Battery, Capt. Henry Dillon; 12th Wis. Battery, Lieut. Lorenzo D. Immell. Brigade loss: k, 34; w, 227; m, 15 = 276.

CAVALRY DIVISION, Col. John K. Mizner.

(Division organized into two brigades, Col. Edward Hatch commanding the First and Col. Albert L. Lee the Second.) 7th Ill., Lieut.-Col. Edward Prince; 11th Ill., Col. Robert G. Ingersoll; 2d Iowa, Maj. Datus E. Coon; 7th Kan., Lieut.-Col. T. P. Herrick; 3d Mich., Capt. Lyman G. Willcox; 5th Ohio (4 co's), Capt. Joseph C. Smith. Division loss: k, 5; w, 17; m, 14 = 36.

UNATTACHED: 64th Ill. (Yates's Sharp-shooters), Capt. John Morrill; 1st U. S. (6 co's — siege artillery), Capt. G. A. Williams. Unattached loss: k, 16; w, 53; m, 15 = 84.

ARMY OF WEST TENNESSEE.

SECOND DIVISION, Brig.-Gen. Thomas A. Davies.

First Brigade, Brig.-Gen. Pleasant A. Hackleman (k), Col. Thomas W. Sweeny: 52d Ill., Col. Thomas W. Sweeny, Lieut. Col. John S. Wilcox; 2d Iowa, Col. James Baker (m w), Lieut.-Col. Noah W. Mills (m w), Maj. James B. Weaver; 7th Iowa, Col. Elliott W. Rice; Union Brigade (composed of detachments of 58th Ill., and 8th, 12th, and 14th Iowa), Lieut.-Col. John P. Coulter. Brigade loss: k, 49; w, 318; m, 36 = 403. *Second Brigade*, Brig.-Gen. Richard J. Oglesby (w), Col. August Mersy: 9th Ill., Col. August Mersy; 12th Ill., Col. Augustus L. Chetlain; 22d Ohio, Maj. Oliver Wood; 81st Ohio, Col. Thomas Morton. Brigade loss: k, 38; w, 222; m, 73 = 333. *Third Brigade*, Col. Silas D. Baldwin (w), Col. John V. Du Bois: 7th Ill., Col. Andrew J. Babcock; 50th Ill., Lieut.-Col. William Swarthout; 57th Ill., Lieut.-Col. Frederick J. Hurlbut, Maj. Erie Forsse. Brigade loss: k, 21; w, 115; m, 46 = 182. *Artillery*, Maj. George H. Stone: D, 1st Mo., Capt. Henry Richardson; H, 1st Mo., Capt. Frederick Welker; I, 1st Mo., Lieut. Charles H. Thurber; K, 1st Mo., Lieut. Charles Green. Artillery loss: k, 6; w, 29 = 35. *Unattached:* 14th Mo. (Western Sharp-shooters), Col. Patrick E. Burke. Loss: k, 6; w, 14; m, 3 = 23.

SIXTH DIVISION, Brig.-Gen. Thomas J. McKean.

First Brigade, Col. Benjamin Allen, Brig.-Gen. John McArthur: 21st Mo., Col. David Moore, Maj. Edwin Moore; 16th Wis., Maj. Thomas Reynolds; 17th Wis., Col. John L. Doran. Brigade loss: k, 11; w, 67; m, 23 = 101. *Second Brigade*, Col. John M. Oliver: Indpt. Co., Ill. Cav., Capt. William Ford; 15th Mich., Lieut.-Col. John McDermott; 18th Mo. (4 co's), Capt. Jacob R. Ault; 14th Wis., Col. John Hancock; 18th Wis., Col. Gabriel Bouck. Brigade loss: k, 45; w, 108; m, 38 = 191. *Third Brigade*, Col. Marcellus M. Crocker: 11th Iowa, Lieut.-Col. William Hall; 13th Iowa, Lieut.-Col. John Shane; 15th Iowa, Lieut.-Col. William W. Belknap, Col. Hugh T. Reid; 16th Iowa, Lieut.-Col. Addison H. Sanders (w), Maj. William Purcell. Brigade loss: k, 14; w, 111; m, 24 = 149. *Artillery*, Capt. Andrew Hickenlooper: F, 2d Ill., Lieut. J. W. Mitchell; 1st Minn., Lieut. G. F. Cooke; 3d Ohio (section), Capt. Emil Munch, Sergt. Sylvanus Clark; 5th Ohio, Lieut. D. S.

Matson; 10th Ohio, Capt. H. B. White. Artillery loss: w, 8.

Total Union loss: killed, 355; wounded, 1841; captured or missing, 324 = 2520.

The effective strength of Rosecrans's command is not specifically stated in the "Official Records." According to the return for September 30th, 1862, his "aggregate present for duty" was 23,077 (Vol. XVII., Pt. II., p. 246). Probably not less than twenty thousand participated in the battle. On page 172, Vol. XVII., Pt. I., General Rosecrans estimates the Confederate strength at nearly forty thousand and says that was almost double his own numbers.

THE CONFEDERATE FORCES.

ARMY OF WEST TENNESSEE.— Major-General Earl Van Dorn.

PRICE'S CORPS OR ARMY OF THE WEST.— Major-General Sterling Price.

FIRST DIVISION, Brig.-Gen. Louis Hébert, Brig.-Gen. Martin E. Green.

First Brigade, Col. Elijah Gates: 16th Ark., ——; 2d Mo., Col. Francis M. Cockrell; 3d Mo., Col. James A. Pritchard (w); 5th Mo., ——; 1st Mo. Cav. (dismounted), Lieut.-Col. W. D. Maupin; Mo. Battery, Captain William Wade. Brigade loss: k, 53; w, 332; m, 92 = 477. *Second Brigade*, Col. W. Bruce Colbert: 14th Ark., ——; 17th Ark., Lieut.-Col. John Griffith; 3d La., ——; 40th Miss., ——; 1st Tex. Legion, Lieut.-Col. E. R. Hawkins; 3d Tex. Cav. (dismounted), ——; Clark's (Mo.) Battery, Lieut. J. L. Faris; St. Louis (Mo.) Battery, Capt. William E. Dawson. Brigade loss: k, 11; w, 129; m, 132 = 272. *Third Brigade*, Brig.-Gen. Martin E. Green, Col. W. H. Moore (w): 7th Miss. Battalion, Lieut.-Col. J. S. Terral (w); 43d Miss., Col. W. H. Moore; 4th Mo., Col. A. MacFarlane; 6th Mo., Col. Eugene Erwin (w); 3d Mo. Cav. (dismounted), ——; Mo. Battery, Capt. Henry Guibor; Mo. Battery, Capt. John C. Landis. Brigade loss: k, 77; w, 369; m, 302 = 748. *Fourth Brigade*, Col. John D. Martin (m w), Col. Robert McLain (w): 37th Ala.; 36th Miss., Col. W. W. Witherspoon; 37th Miss., Col. Robert McLain; 38th Miss., Col. F. W. Adams. (Battery attached to this brigade not identified.) Brigade loss: k, 41; w, 203 = 244.

MAURY'S DIVISION, Brig.-Gen. Dabney H. Maury.

Moore's Brigade, Brig.-Gen. John C. Moore: 42d Ala., Col. John W. Portis; 15th Ark., Lieut.-Col. Squire Boone; 23d Ark., Lieut.-Col. A. A. Pennington; 35th Miss., Col. William S. Barry; 2d Tex., Col. W. P. Rogers (k); Mo. Battery, Capt. H. M. Bledsoe. Brigade loss: k, 53; w, 230; m, 1012 = 1295.

Cabell's Brigade, Brig.-Gen. William L. Cabell: 18th Ark., Col. John N. Daly (m w); 19th Ark., Col. T. P. Dockery; 20th Ark., Col. H. P. Johnson (k); 21st Ark., Col. Jordan E. Cravens; Ark. Battalion (Jones's), ——; Ark. Battalion (Rapley's), Capt. James A. Ashford; Ark. (Appeal) Battery, Lieut. William N. Hogg. Brigade loss: k, 98; w, 323; m, 214 = 635. *Phifer's Brigade*, Brig.-Gen. C. W. Phifer: 3d Ark. Cav. (dismounted), ——; 6th Tex. Cav. (dismounted), Col. L. S. Ross; 9th Tex. Cav. (dismounted), ——; Stirman's Sharp-shooters, Col. Ras. Stirman; Ark. Battery (McNally's), Lieut. Frank A. Moore. Brigade loss: k, 94; w, 273; m, 200 = 567. *Cavalry* (composition probably incomplete), Brig.-Gen. Frank C. Armstrong; 2d Ark., Col. W. F. Slemons; Miss. Reg't, Col. Wirt Adams; 2d Mo., Col. Robert McCulloch. Cavalry loss: w, 2; m, 9 = 11. *Reserve Artillery:* Tenn. Battery (Hoxton's), Lieut. Thomas F. Tobin (c); Ala. Battery, Capt. Henry H. Sengstak. Artillery loss: k, 1; w, 4; m, 14 = 19.

DISTRICT OF THE MISSISSIPPI.

FIRST DIVISION, Maj.-Gen. Mansfield Lovell.

First Brigade, Brig.-Gen. Albert Rust: 4th Ala. Battalion, Maj. —— Gibson; 31st Ala., ——; 35th Ala., Capt. A. E. Ashford; 9th Ark., Col. Isaac L. Dunlop; 3d Ky., Col. A. P. Thompson; 7th Ky., Col. Ed. Crossland; Miss. (Hudson) Battery, Lieut. John R. Sweaney. Brigade loss: k, 25; w, 117; m, 83 = 225. *Second Brigade* (composition not fully reported), Brig.-Gen. J. B. Villepigue: 33d Miss., Col. D. W. Hurst; 39th Miss., Col. W. B. Shelby. Brigade loss: k, 21; w, 76; m, 71 = 168. *Third Brigade*, Brig.-Gen. John S. Bowen: 6th Miss., Col. Robert Lowry; 15th Miss., Col. M. Farrell; 22d Miss., Capt. J. D. Lester; Miss. Battalion, Capt. C. K. Caruthers; 1st Mo., Lieut.-Col. A. C. Riley; La. (Watson) Battery, Capt. A. A. Bursley. Brigade loss: k, 28; w, 92; m, 40 = 160. *Cavalry Brigade*, Col. W. H. Jackson: 1st Miss., Lieut.-Col. F. A. Montgomery; 7th Tenn., Lieut.-Col. J. G. Stocks. Brigade loss: k, 1. *Unattached:* La. Zouave Battalion, Maj. St. J. Dupiere. Loss: k, 2; m, 14 = 16. Total Confederate loss (including Hatchie Bridge, Oct. 5th): killed, 505; wounded, 2150; captured or missing, 2183 = 4838. General Van Dorn says ("Official Records," Vol. XVII., Pt. I., p. 378): "Field returns at Ripley showed my strength to be about 22,000 men." It is estimated that at least 20,000 were brought into action at Corinth.

MONUMENT IN THE NATIONAL CEMETERY, CORINTH. FROM A PHOTOGRAPH TAKEN IN 1884.

END OF VOLUME II.

F. N.